CW00763091

VOICES FROM KRYPTON
The Complete, Unauthorized Oral History of Superman

By Edward Gross

Foreword by Brandon Routh
Afterword by Mark Waid

Cover Image by D.C. Stuelpner
Voices from Krypton **Logo by Arlen Schumer**

Copyright 2023, 1st Edition, by NacelleBooks

This book was not prepared, approved, licensed or endorsed by Warner Brothers, DC Comics or any other entity involved in creating or producing Superman comic books, movies or television series. The opinions expressed within solely represent those of the author or those interviewed.

ISBN 978-1-7373801-9-1

To my wife Eileen.
She is to me as Lois Lane is to Superman.

ADDITIONAL DEDICATIONS:

To my sons Teddy, Dennis and Kevin, who have spent years on this Superman journey with me and each of whom believe a man can fly (though models may vary by age and year produced).

My daughters-in-law Lindsay, Yumi and Nicole, who have never once (at least to my knowledge) asked, "What *is* it with Dad and Superman?"

My brother Tommy, sister Donna and mother for tolerating my passion for this stuff over the decades.

Tom Sanders, my friend of 40 years who actually flew from California to New York to attend a press screening of *Superman Returns* with me back in 2006.

Kevin Oldham, my friend of nearly 50 years, who joined me at the Patchogue Theater on December 15, 1978 for not one, but *two* viewings of *Superman: The Movie.*

My dear friends Dexter Frank and Jay Starr... just for being my dear friends and sharing a love for pop culture.

John Garry, childhood best friend who came up with the concept of "Kryptonite Gum" when we used to play superheroes.

Brian Volk Weiss, Leah Morris and the team at Nacelle for their enthusiasm and support for this book.

Brandon Routh and Mark Waid for, respectively, this book's foreword and afterword.

Jerry Siegel and Joe Shuster for starting it all.

And another to my wife Eileen: When we were having massive work done on our home, she gifted me with a "Superman Room," my own little Fortress of Solitude. Now *that's* love!

TABLE OF CONTENTS

FOREWORD

Superman is a teacher.

A messenger. A carrier of the light. Superman brings truth. Through this truth, he brings justice, and fights for all of humanity.

As a child, I was not aware of the character's complexity. He had *superpowers!* He could fly, was invulnerable, had heat-vision! He was amazing! Christopher Reeve added charm, compassion and solitude to humanize him. Chris was, and always will be, *my* Superman.

I didn't know it at that time, but *Superman: The Movie* had embedded deeply into my soul. This was the beginning of my journey with the character.

I have had many incredible and surreal connections to Superman throughout my life. These continued and increased as I made my way out to Los Angeles in 1998 to become an actor; too many connections to put into this foreword! Need-less to say, I came to L.A. with the firm (but naïve) possibility of someday playing Superman rattling around in my brain.

After a seven-month casting process that involved the project starting with one director, then falling away, then being resurrected a month later by another, I was finally, officially cast as Superman.

The energy from my childhood, that I still unconsciously carried, was now ready to be fully known, investigated and embraced. As a 24-year-old, I did my best to accomplish this epic quest. Truth is, I'm still learning from him and about him. And as I do, I learn more about myself; how I can be a better custodian of the character, and a better human; how we can all be better to each other; and how we can all carry the energy of Superman.

In addition, I think that everyone who loves Superman is already connected to this energy. Superman's spirit resides deeply in our hearts in myriad ways we may not be aware of. He says, "I can handle this. I've got your back. I see the good inside you — even when you cannot. I'll watch over you. I'm always around."

I believe this spirit, or view, of humanity is more important than his "super-powers." Sure, super-strength, the ability to fly, indestructibility, heat-vision, cold breath, x-ray vision and sonic hearing are still very much needed to save the world from physical destruction. But the ability to look inward, and courageously look back at our past (and his past), and to investigate and understand the traumas and mistakes each generation unknowingly passed on to the next, leads us to truth — the truth that these burdens of past generations bind us, hold us in place and, if blind to them, prevent us from evolving humanity.

The potential for larger-than-life archetypes to teach us real world lessons is a supernaturally powerful use of the arts. Superman's societal evolution has made him an amazingly resonant conduit of the "teach a man to fish" parable. Teaching us how to embrace, and accept, each other leads us down the path to harmony. To a present and future where we save ourselves. Where Clark and Lois can fly off into the sunset and get a hot dog.

Jor-El's quote to Kal-El marks a significant step in this evolution: "They could be a great people Kal-El, if they wish to be. They only lack the light to show the way, this reason above all, is why I send them you, my only son."

This "light" is not in reference to his well-known superpowers, but to the ability to remain open to even the most fearful, hateful and lonely among us. Allowing for the possibility of change to occur. Never giving up hope.

Another great example is the evolution of the motto we've grown accustomed to — "Truth, Justice and The American Way" — to the more universal, "Truth, Justice and a Better Tomorrow," which is exactly why Jor-El sent Kal-El to Earth. In an effort to save his son, he jettisons him to the next best habitable planet. Jor-El's primary goal is to save Kal, but he also wishes to preserve and grow, if possible, the best aspects of Kryptonian culture in the hopes of creating a better tomorrow for his son, and for human life.

Jor-El knows that the Kryptonians didn't have it all right or they would've been able to save themselves. In turn, it becomes Kal's quest to take all that knowledge and grow it elsewhere. He's here to complete the mission Jor-El couldn't complete on Krypton: help save us from ourselves.

Superman/Clark Kent/Kal-El is more than just a comic book character. For me, the unique and surreal opportunity to portray him, not once, but twice, has been one of the great joys of my life. The second, extraordinary opportunity to channel Superman's energy made an unquestionably beneficial impact on my life that closely rivals the first. The chance to take years of gained wisdom and awareness, and integrate it into my return, was a tremendous joy.

His energy will surround me always. The curiosity to seek and acknowledge the best that is within us. The best that is within all humans. To be truthful, this hasn't always been easy for me. I still have much to learn from him, but doing so is crucial in cultivating more grace and compassion. A trademark of Supes.

There have been many books on the history of Superman. This is a testament to the indelible impact that he — through Siegel & Shuster, DC Comics, all the writers, artists, inkers, film and TV crews and cast, voice actors and live-action actors that have portrayed him — have made on modern society. We can't get enough!

A big thank you to Ed Gross for bestowing me the honor of adding my thoughts to this masterful oral history he's so lovingly crafted. Ed has been a part of my journey as we've had many thoughtful and insightful interviews over the years, each one giving me an opportunity to dig deeper into my understanding of our beloved hero. You, reader, are in good hands. I hope you enjoy learning more, and reveling in all the hope that Superman represents.

With Love,

Brandon Routh
February 2023

INTRODUCTION:
"My Journey with Superman"

I own *a lot* of Superman T-shirts. So many, in fact, that when my wife decided to surprise me and have a blanket made out of 30 of them, I didn't even notice any were missing.

One day, in the aftermath of a snowstorm, I was wearing one of those "S"-emblazoned shirts when my son and I went out on an errand. As we were driving down the street, we saw an elderly man grasping onto a walker with one hand, a snow shovel with the other. He would shuffle, shovel; shuffle, shovel. I told my son that we were going to offer to help, which got one of the usual "Why?" moans so common in the young. "Because it's the right thing to do," I said all fatherly.

So, we pulled over, got out and offered a helping hand. The man was reluctant, but ultimately allowed us to take over for him. As my son and I were shoveling, he was leaning into his walker a bit and commented, "Thanks so much, fellows. My neighbor's sick, so I wanted to shovel his sidewalk."

My son and I shared a look and as we got back into the car, I pointed to the "S" on my shirt and commented, "There's meaning to it. You do what you can."

Second tale of the "S"-shirt: Driving to the gym one morning at about 5 a.m. in the middle of a rainstorm, at the last moment I noticed that a tree had fallen from alongside the train tracks and was partially blocking the road. I barely managed to stop before colliding with it. Worried that someone else might not see it in time, I wanted to try and do *something* and got out, moving in front of the car. There I am, rain falling heavily, headlights illuminating the moment as I pondered what to do. Feeling ridiculous, I reached down to see if I could move it and was shocked to find that I *could*. Apparently, its insides had rotted out, which is how it broke free and fell in the first place. *Soooo*, I started to lift this tree — in the rain, headlights shining — and heard the wood cracking as I did so. I tossed it aside and wondered why nobody had been there to take a picture of me in what was my personal Man of Steel moment.

Third tale, no shirt involved: Back in 2013 I interviewed filmmaker Kevin Smith as part of Gillette's "How does he shave?" *Man of Steel* campaign. During that conversation, we discussed our love for Superman, and I mentioned to him that when I was a kid in Brooklyn, my friends and I would play superheroes. In one scenario, I was Superman while my buddy John Garry was Lex Luthor, who devised "Kryptonite Gum," which he pretended to put in my hair. We laughed over John's inventiveness and I was ready to move on. Kevin was not.

"Oh my God, *that's* good," he commented. "Kryptonite is always represented as a rock. But if you could liquefy it and get on to his person — you're *right*. You *can't* just say, 'Throw it over there and I'll be fine.' It's like, wedged in his hair. He's trying to use peanut butter to get it out and shit like that. Ice it, freeze it to break it. And it's close to his brain as well, which means he's down even quicker. It's *so* weird that we end up thinking like a supervillain at all times. The moment we start analyzing Superman's powers, the first thing we start looking for is a weakness."

The "BobbleEd" Stands at the center of the author's collection of Superman memorabilia (photo © Ed Gross; Superman © and TM DC Comics/Warner Bros. Discovery)

Wow!

Superman has always been a presence in my life. I can't tell you the moment we first met, but I'm pretty sure it started in the mid-1960s with reruns of George Reeves' *Adventures of Superman*, and really took root with the 1966 Saturday morning premiere of Filmation's *The New Adventures of Superman*, later to become *The Superman/Aquaman Hour of Adventure*. Comic collecting followed with my trying to obtain any title that featured the character, including *Superman, Action Comics, Superboy, Adventure Comics* with Superboy and the Legion of Super-Heroes, *World's Finest, Superman's Girlfriend Lois Lane, Superman's Pal Jimmy Olsen, Justice League* — I couldn't get enough. And unlike many childhood passions, this one simply never went away.

I was 13 when *Super Friends* premiered in 1973 and dutifully tuned in before tuning out again (curse you Wendy, Marvin and Wonderdog!). Two years later, I stayed up *really* late one night to watch the TV version of the stage musical *It's a*

Bird… It's a Plane… It's Superman, and was kind of sorry that I did — recognizing, even at 15, how poor the production values were. But I never strayed from the "S" path and my faith was rewarded on December 15, 1978 with the arrival of Christopher Reeve in *Superman: The Movie*. So blown away were my friends and I that when it was over, we stood up, looked at each other and sat back down to watch it again.

It went on from there. In my personal life, gifts for birthdays, Christmas and, later, Father's Day, became a cinch — pretty much anything with the "S" logo, my wife *still* amazing me with the oddities she manages to find. In my professional life as an entertainment journalist over the past 40 years, my path has continued to cross with that of the Man of Steel in his various incarnations, having the opportunity to speak to so many of the people who have brought his adventures to life.

I spoke *Superman and the Mole Men* with director Lee Sholem; sat in the New York apartment of David and Leslie Newman to discuss the scripting of the first three Reeve films; chatted *Superboy* with John Haymes Newton and Stacy Haiduk; *Lois & Clark: The New Adventures of Superman* with Deborah Joy Levine, Bryce Zabel and Robert Butler; went a little tooney with Bruce Timm and Paul Dini on *Superman: The Animated Series;* was one of the very first people to interview Al Gough regarding *Smallville* (foolishly telling him I didn't know how a Superman show without Superman was ever going to work — silly me); got Zack Snyder's take on *Man of Steel* and on it went. And then, of course, there were the Supermen themselves: Tim Daly, Tom Welling, Dean Cain, George Newbern, Tyler Hoechlin, Henry Cavill and, several times, Brandon Routh — who also happens to have been the final interview conducted for this book.

And a special memory comes from director Richard Donner: I was supposed to travel into New York City to interview him regarding the original *Lethal Weapon* in 1987, but was sick as a dog and couldn't make it. That morning my phone rang and that distinctive booming voice began, "Ed Gross? This is Dr. Donner, I wanted to see how you were doing and if you wanted to talk." So, we did, which would lead to in-depth discussions of *Superman: The Movie* and his office sending me Xeroxes of scripts, storyboards and more. Just incredible.

Now, take all of that and mix it with the fact that over the past seven years I've somehow managed to write (often with my friend Mark Altman) a total of nine oral history books on such subjects as *Star Trek* (the two-volume *The Fifty-Year Mission*), James Bond (*Nobody Does It Better*), *Star Wars* (Secrets of the

Force), *John Wick* (*They Shouldn't Have Shot His Dog*) and *Stargate SG-1* (*Chevrons Locked*). Having completely fallen in love with the format — and recognizing that there have been many books written on Superman — I was determined to cover the character's 85-year history in this unique way, piecing the puzzle together quote by quote from some 250 people who basically shared about 300,000 words of reflection.

Voices from Krypton is the end result of a lifetime of passion distilled into this book. The true revelation for me along the way was the breadth of love for this character conveyed to me by so many people, each of us willingly looking up into the sky… and still believing!

Edward Gross
February 2023

VOICES FROM KRYPTON:
Dramatis Personae

What follows is a guide to the nearly 250 people who have offered commentary for this book. The vast majority of interviews were conducted by the author and, when generously provided by others, it is clearly noted below. What's also very true is that this book would not have been complete without their assistance, and to each of them I am forever grateful.

J.J. ABRAMS: Writer, unfilmed *Superman: Flyby* (author's archived interview)

LEE ADAMS: Lyricist, *It's a Bird… It's a Plane… It's Superman* (courtesy Lynne Stephens)

NEAL ADAMS: Artist (courtesy Michael Eury)

BEN AFFLECK: Actor, "Bruce Wayne/Batman," *Batman v. Superman: Dawn of Justice, Justice League*

LAUREN AGOSTINO: Co-author, *Holding Kryptonite*

CASE AIKEN: Host, *Men of Steel* podcast

ERNIE ALTBAKER: Writer, *Injustice* animated film

KIRK ALYN: Actor, "Superman" in *Superman* and *Atom Man vs. Superman* movie serials (courtesy Andy Mangels)

TOM ANDRAE: Comics historian, co-author, *Batman & Me*

COLLEEN ATWOOD: Costume designer, unfilmed *Superman Lives* (courtesy Holly Payne)

ADAM BALDWIN: Voice actor, "Superman," *Superman: Doomsday*

CARY BATES: Writer, *Superman* (courtesy Michael Eury)

JIM BEAVER: Actor, George Reeves' biographer

JERRY BECK: Animation historian and author, *The Animated Movie Guide*

MAT BECK: Visual effects supervisor, *Smallville*

GREG BEEMAN: Director/producer, *Smallville*

BRIAN MICHAEL BENDIS: Writer, *Superman* and *Action Comics*

MELISSA BENOIST: Actor, "Kara Zor-El/Supergirl," *Supergirl*

EDDIE BERGANZA: Former Superman editor

STAN BERKOWITZ: Writer, *Superman: The Animated Series*; story editor, *Superboy*

DANIEL BEST: Editor, *The Trials of Superman Vol. I* and *II*

MATT BOMER: Voice actor, "Superman," *Superman Unbound*

JEFF BOND: Editor, *Film Score Monthly*

KATE BOSWORTH: Actor, "Lois Lane," *Superman Returns* (courtesy Steve Younis)

BENJAMIN BRATT: Voice actor, "Superman," *Justice League: Gods and Monsters*

TIM BURGARD: Art department, unfilmed *Superman Lives* (courtesy Holly Payne)

ROBERT BUTLER: Director, *Lois & Clark: The New Adventures of Superman*

MARLON BRANDO: Actor, "Jor-El," *Superman: The Movie*, *Superman II: The Richard Donner Cut*, *Superman Returns* (*The Making of Superman: The Movie*, press notes)

CLANCY BROWN: Voice actor, "Lex Luthor," *Superman: The Animated Series*

BRIAN BUCCELETTO: Writer, *Injustice* comic

ALAN BURKE: Co-host, *All Star Superfan Podcast*

ALAN BURNETT: Story editor, *SuperFriends: The Legendary Super Powers Show*

TIM BURTON: Director, unfilmed *Superman Lives* (courtesy Holly Payne)

CRAIG BYRNE: Webmaster, kryptonsite.com

JOHN BYRNE: Writer, *The Man of Steel* comic (courtesy Patrick Daniel O'Neill and Jon B. Cooke)

NICOLAS CAGE: Actor, "Clark Kent/Superman," unfilmed *Superman Lives*

DEAN CAIN: Actor, "Clark Kent/Superman," *Lois & Clark: The New Adventures of Superman*

MIKE CARLIN: Former Superman Editor at DC (author's archived interview; courtesy Michael Eury and Peter Sanderson)

HENRY CAVILL: Actor, "Clark Kent/Superman," *Men of Steel, Batman v Superman: Dawn of Justice, Justice League, Black Adam*

GERARD CHRISTOPHER: Actor, "Clark Kent/Superboy," *Superboy*

PHYLLIS COATES: Actress, "Lois Lane," *Superman and the Mole Men* (courtesy Andy Mangels)

NEIL COLE: Webmaster, supermansupersite.com

TONI COLLINS: Friend of Bob Holiday, webmaster supermanbobholiday.com

BUD COLLYER: Voice actor, "Clark Kent/Superman," *The Adventures of Superman*, Fleischer theatrical animated shorts, *New Adventures of Superman* (radio interview)

CHRISTINE COLLYER: Daughter of Bud Collyer

GERRY CONWAY: Writer, *Superman vs. The Amazing Spider-Man*

BILL COTTER: Author, *The 1939-1940 New York World's Fair The World of Tomorrow — Images of America*

DARREN CRISS: Voice actor, "Superman," *Superman: Man of Tomorrow*

CAMERON CUFFE: Actor, "Seg-El," *Krypton*

SAM DALY: Voice actor, "Superman," *Justice League: The Flashpoint Paradox*

TIM DALY: Voice actor, "Clark Kent/Superman," *Superman: The Animated Series*

MICHAEL DAUGHERY: Writer, *Superman Returns*

TIM DEFOREST: Author, *Storytelling in the Pulps, Comics and Radio: How Technology Changed Popular Fiction in America*

BRUCE DETTMAN: Journalist, pop culture historian

MARC GUGGENHEIM: Creative consultant, *DC's Legends of Tomorrow*

TOM DE HAVEN: Author, *It's Superman*

STEVEN S. DEKNIGHT: Writer/director, *Smallville*

DANA DELANY: Voice actor, "Lois Lane," *Superman: The Animated Series*

J.M. DEMATTEIS: Writer, *Superboy*

JAMES DENTON: Voice actor, "Superman," *All-Star Superman*

ANTHONY DESIATO: Host, *Digging for Kryptonite* podcast

LORENZO DI BONAVENTURA: Executive in charge of unfilmed *Superman Lives* (courtesy Holly Payne)

DAN DIDIO: Former co-publisher, DC Comics

PAUL DINI: Producer, *Superman: The Animated Series*

LAUREN SHULER DONNER: Wife of Richard Donner; producer, the *X-Men* films

RICHARD DONNER: Director, *Superman: The Movie, Superman II: The Donner Cut*

SARA DOUGLAS: Actor, "Ursa," *Superman: The Movie* and *Superman II*

ERICA DURANCE: Actor, "Lois Lane," *Smallville*

JANE ELLSWORTH: Widow of Whitney Ellsworth (courtesy Jim Nolt)

PAT ELLSWORTH: Daughter of Whitney and Jane Ellsworth (courtesy Jim Nolt)

MARK EVANIER: Writer, comics historian (trial transcript)

RAY FISHER: Actor, "Cyborg," *Justice League*

RICH FOGEL: Producer, *Superman: The Animated Series*

BRENDAN FRASER: Actor, "Clark Kent/Superman," unfilmed *Superman: Flyby*

SIDNEY J. FURIE: Director, *Superman IV: The Quest for Peace*

JOSE LUIS GARCIA-LOPEZ: Artist, *Superman vs. Wonder Woman* (courtesy Michael Eury)

DAN GILROY: Writer, unfilmed *Superman Lives* (courtesy Holly Payne)

BOB GOODMAN: Writer, *Superman Unbound*

AL GOUGH: Co-creator/executive producer, *Smallville*

DAVID S. GOYER: Writer, *Man of Steel* and *Krypton*

ROBERT GREENBERGER: Writer, DC Comics editor

CHARLES GREENLAW: Warner Brothers executive in charge of production, *Superman: The Movie* (courtesy Ric Meyers)

GARY GROSSMAN: Author, *Superman from Serial to Cereal*

BRIAN GUNN: Co-writer, *Brightburn* (press notes)

MARK GUNN: co-writer, *Brightburn* (press notes)

GENE HACKMAN: Actor, "Lex Luthor," *Superman: The Movie, Superman II,*

Superman IV: The Quest for Peace (press notes)

STACY HAIDUK: Actor, "Lana Lang," *Superboy*

JIM HAMBRICK: Kirk Alyn's manager; owner, Super Museum

MARK HARMON: Voice actor, "Superman," *Justice League: Crisis on Two Earths*

DAVID HAREWOOD: Actor, Martian Manhunter, *Supergirl*

DAN HARRIS: Writer, *Superman Returns*

CHUCK HARTER: Television historian; author, *Superboy & Superpup: The Lost Videos*

JUSTIN HARTLEY: Voice actor, "Superman," *Injustice*

TERI HATCHER: Actor, "Lois Lane," *Lois & Clark: The New Adventures of Superman*

MICHAEL J. HAYDE: Author, *Flights of Fantasy: The Unauthorized but True Story of Radio & TV's Adventures of Superman*

RICK HEINRICHS: Production designer, unfilmed *Superman Lives* (courtesy Holly Payne)

TODD HELBING: Executive producer, *Superman & Lois*

FOSTER HIRSCH: Author, *Harold Prince and the American Musical Theatre*

TYLER HOECHLIN: Actor, "Clark Kent/Superman," *Superman & Lois*

BOB HOLIDAY: Actor, "Superman," *It's a Bird... It's a Plane... It's Superman*

SHERMAN HOWARD: Actor, "Lex Luthor," *Superboy* (courtesy Comic Book Central Podcast)

ED HULSE: Pop culture historian; author, *The Blood 'n' Thunder Guide to Pulp Fiction*

JASON ISAACS: Voice actor, "Superman," *Superman: Red Son*

MICHAEL ANTHONY JACKSON: Art department, unfilmed *Superman Lives* (courtesy Holly Payne)

STEVE JOHNSON: Special effects, unfilmed *Superman Lives* (courtesy Holly Payne)

JEREMY JORDAN: Actor, "Winn Schott," *Supergirl*

DAN JURGENS: Writer, *The Death of Superman*

JOE KELLY: Writer, *Superman vs. The Elite*

MARGOT KIDDER: Actress, "Lois Lane," *Superman I-IV*

DARYN KIRSCHT: Author, *The Snyderverse Saga*

LAWRENCE KONNER: Co-writer, *Superman IV: The Quest for Peace*

LOU KOZA: Editor, *The George Reeves Historical Archives*

ANDREW KREISBERG: Executive producer, *Supergirl*

LEE TOLAND KRIEGER: Director, *Superman & Lois*

KRISTEN KREUK: Actor, "Lana Lang," *Smallville*

JIM KRIEG: Writer, *Reign of the Supermen*

JACK LARSON: Actor, "Jimmy Olsen," *Adventures of Superman* (courtesy Andy

Mangels)

JIM LEE: Co-publisher, DC Comics

JASON J. LEWIS: Voice actor, "Clark Kent/Superman," *Justice League Action*

CHERYL LEIGH: Actor, "Alex Danvers," *Supergirl*

JONATHAN LEMKIN: Writer, unfilmed *Superman Reborn*

RICHARD LESTER: Director, *Superman II* and *Superman III*

DAN LEVINE: Executive story editor, *Lois & Clark: The New Adventures of Superman*

DEBORAH JOY LEVINE: Executive producer, *Lois & Clark: The New Adventures of Superman*

PAUL LEVITZ: Writer, former publisher, DC Comics

JEPH LOEB: Writer, *Smallville*

KYLE MACLACHLAN: Voice actor, "Superman," *Justice League: The New Frontier*

ELLIOT S! MAGGIN: Writer, Superman comics and novels

LEONARD MALTIN: Film historian; author, *Leonard Maltin's 151 Best Movies You've Never Seen*

ANDY MANGELS: Film historian; author, *The Superhero Book: The Ultimate Encyclopedia of Comic Book Icons and Hollywood Heroes*

TOM MANKIEWICZ: Creative consultant, *Superman: The Movie, Superman II: The Richard Donner Cut* (author interview and courtesy Mark A. Altman and Ray Morton)

GEOFFREY MARK: Silver Age Comic Book Historian

JAMES MARSTERS: Actor, "Brainiac," *Smallville*

MARK MCCRAY: Author, *The Best Saturdays of Our Lives*

DWAYNE MCDUFFIE: Producer, *Justice League Unlimited*

DREW MCWEENY: Film critic, author

MEHCAD BROOKS: Actor, "James Olsen," *Supergirl*

DOUGLAS MEYERS: Actor, "Bizarro," *Superboy*

RIC MEYERS: Film historian, author and entertainment journalist

JIM MICHAELS: Producer, *Lois & Clark: The New Adventures of Superman*

RAY MIDDLETON: Actor, "Superman," 1939 New York World's Fair (news sources circa 1940)

LOUISE MIGENBACH: Costume designer, *Superman Returns*

MARK MILLAR: Writer, *Superman: Red Son*

MILES MILLAR: Co-creator/executive producer, *Smallville*

KURT MITCHELL: Author, *American Comic Book Chronicles: 1940-1944*

ZACH MOORE: Host, *Always Hold on to Smallville* podcast

PHIL MORRIS: Actor, "John Jones/Martian Manhunter," *Smallville*

RAY MORTON: Film historian and author, *Close Encounters of the Third Kind:*

The Making of Steven Spielberg's Classic Film

JOHN KENNETH MUIR: Film historian and author, *Horror Films of 2000-2009*

ADAM NEDEFF: Game show historian; author, *Game Shows FAQ: All That's Left to Know About the Pioneers, the Scandals, the Hosts and the Jackpots*

NOEL NEILL: Actress, "Lois Lane," *Adventures of Superman* (courtesy Andy Mangels)

ANDREW NEWBERG: Co-author, *Holding Kryptonite*

GEORGE NEWBERN: Voice actor, "Superman," *Superman vs. The Elite*

DAVID NEWMAN: Writer, *Superman 1-3, It's a Bird… It's a Plane… It's Superman*

LESLIE NEWMAN: Writer, *Superman 1-3*

JOHN HAYMES NEWTON: Actor, "Clark Kent/Superboy," *Superboy*

MARC TYLER NOBLEMAN: Writer, *Boys of Steel: The Creators of Superman*

JIM NOLT: Editor, *The Adventures Continue*

DAVID NUTTER: Director, *Superboy* and *Smallville*

JERRY O'CONNELL: Voice actor, "Superman," *Justice League: Throne of Atlantis*

ROB O'CONNOR: Cohost, *All Star Superfan* podcast

DAVID ODELL: Writer, *Supergirl*

JERRY ORDWAY: Writer/artist, *The Death of Superman*

KARLA OGLE: Metropolis Chamber of Commerce

JACK O'HALLORAN: Actor, Non, *Superman: The Movie* and *Superman II*

DENNY O'NEIL: Writer, *Superman: Kryptonite Nevermore*

ANNETTE O'TOOLE: Actor, "Lana Lang," *Superman III;* Martha Kent, *Smallville* (press notes)

MARTIN PASKO: Writer, *Superman*

HOLLY PAYNE: Producer, *The Death of Superman Lives: What Happened?*

JON PETERS: Superman producer (courtesy Holly Payne)

BRIAN PETERSON: Co-executive producer, *Smallville*

JULIA PISTOR: Producer, *Superboy*

ANDREA ROMANO: Voice director, *Superman: The Animated Series*

CHRISTOPHER REEVE: Actor, "Superman," *Superman: The Movie* (various sources as noted)

GEORGE REEVES: Actor, "Clark Kent/Superman," *Adventures of Superman* (various sources as noted)

BRAD RICCA: Author, *Super Boys: The Amazing Adventures of Jerry Siegel and Joe Shuster — The Creators of Superman*

ALAN RITCHSON: Actor, "Arthur Curry," *Smallville*

SAM RIZZO: Webmaster, superboythelegacy.com

WILL RODGERS: Author, *The Ultimate Super Friends Companion*

R.A. RONDELL: Stunt coordinator, *Superman Returns*
MARK ROSENBAUM: Actor, "Lex Luthor," *Smallville*
MARK ROSENTHAL: Co-writer, *Superman IV: The Quest for Peace*
ALEX ROSS: Co-writer and artist, *Kingdom Come*
BRANDON ROUTH: Actor, "Clark Kent/Superman," *Superman Returns*
CHARLES ROVEN: Producer, *Man of Steel*
JOE RUBY: Executive producer, 1988 animated *Superman*
ILYA SALKIND: Executive producer, *Superman 1-3, Supergirl, Superboy*
PETER SANDERSON: Comic book historian and author, *Obsessed with Marvel*
MICHAEL SANGIACOMO: Journalist; member, The Siegel & Shuster Society; author, *Phantom Jack*
LOU SCHEIMER: Founder, Filmation Associates (courtesy Andy Mangels)
JON SCHNEPP: Writer/director, *The Death of Superman Lives: What Happened?*
ARLEN SCHUMER: Comics historian, author, *The Silver Age of Comic Book Art*
JOHN SCHNEIDER: Actor, "Jonathan Kent," *Smallville*
SARAH SECHTER: Executive producer, *Supergirl*
MICHAEL D. SELLERS: Author, *John Carter and the Gods of Hollywood*
TOM SETO: Animator, *Beauty and the Beast, The Little Mermaid* and *The Lion King* (courtesy Arlen Schumer)
ROBERT SHAYNE: Actor, "Inspector Henderson," *Adventures of Superman* (courtesy Jim Nolt)
JOHN SHEA: Actor, "Lex Luthor," *Lois & Clark: The New Adventures of Superman*
LEE SHOLEM: Director, *Superman and the Mole Men*
FRED SHAY: Film and radio historian (courtesy Steve Younis)
JIM SHOOTER: Writer/creator of "Parasite" (courtesy Michael Eury)
JOE SHUSTER: Co-creator, Superman (courtesy Tom Andrae)
JERRY SIEGEL: Co-creator, *Superman* (courtesy Tom Andrae; court papers, press release)
JOANNE CARTER SIEGEL: Wife of Jerry Siegel, model for Lois Lane (courtesy Tom Andrae)
LOUISE SIMONSON: Writer, *The Death of Superman*
BRYAN SINGER: Director, *Superman Returns*
HELEN SLATER: Actor, "Kara Zor-El/Supergirl," *Supergirl* (courtesy Andy Mangels)
KEVIN SMITH: Writer, unfilmed *Superman Lives* (author interview; courtesy Holly Payne)

LANE SMITH: Actor, "Perry White," *Lois & Clark: The New Adventures of Superman*

DEBORAH SNYDER: Producer, *Man of Steel*

ZACK SNYDER: Director, *Man of Steel, Batman v. Superman: Dawn of Justice, Justice League: The Snyder Cut*

KEVIN SPACEY: Actor, "Lex Luthor," *Superman Returns* (courtesy Steve Younis)

KELLY SOUDERS: Co-executive producer, *Smallville*

KEN SPEARS: Executive producer, 1988 animated *Superman*

PIERRE SPENGLER: Producer, *Superman 1-3* (RetroVision Archives)

TERENCE STAMP: Actor, "General Zod," *Superman: The Movie* and *Superman II*

ROGER STERN: Author, *The Death of Superman*

MARK STETSON: Visual effects supervisor, *Superman Returns*

WESLEY STRICK: Writer, unfilmed *Superman Lives* (courtesy Holly Payne)

DARREN SWIMMER: Co-executive producer, *Smallville*

TOM TAYLOR: Writer, *Injustice* prequel comic

BRUCE TIMM: Producer, *Superman: The Animated Series* and *Justice League Unlimited*

ANTHONY TOLLIN: Comics, pulps and old-time radio historian

JEFF TREXLER: Interim Director Comic Book Legal Defense Fund; legal expert, Superman copyright case

MATTHEW TRUEX: Host, *Lois & Clark'd: The New Podcasts of Superman*

AUSTIN TRUNICK: Author, *The Cannon Film Guide, Vol. I* and *II*

JAMES TUCKER: Producer, *Batman: The Brave and the Bold*

ALAN TUDYK: Voice actor, "Superman," *Justice League: War*

ELIZABETH TULLOCH: Actor, "Lois Lane," *Superman & Lois*

MARK VALLEY: Voice actor, "Superman," *The Dark Knight Returns, Part 2*

LAURA VANDERVOORT: Actor, "Kara Zor-El," *Smallville*

MARK VERHEIDEN: Producer/writer, *Smallville*

JULIAN VILAJ: Writer, *The Joe Shuster Story*

MARK WAID: Comics historian; writer, *Batman/Superman: World's Finest, Kingdom Come* and *Superman: Birthright*

LESLEY ANN WARREN: Actor, "Lois Lane," *It's a Bird... It's a Plane... It's Superman*

BEAU WEAVER: Voice actor, "Clark Kent/Superman," *Superman*

LEN WEIN: Writer, *Superman*

TOM WELLING: Actor, "Clark Kent," *Smallville*

JOHN WELLS: Author, *American Comic Book Chronicles*

SCOTT WELLS: Actor, "Lex Luthor," *Superboy*

NICKY WHEELER-NICHOLSON: Comics historian, granddaughter of

Major Malcolm Wheeler-Nicholson

JERRY WILLIAMS: Friend and neighbor to Ray Middleton

JOHN WILLIAMS: Composer, *Superman: The Movie* (featurette)

TRAVIS WILLINGHAM: Voice actor, "Superman," *Batman and Superman: Battle of the Super Sons*

DAVID WILSON: Actor, "Clark Kent/Superman," *It's a Bird… It's a Plane… It's Superman*

SAM WITWER: Actor, "Davis Bloome/Doomsday," *Smallville*

MARV WOLFMAN: Writer, *Crisis on Infinite Earths*

JEFF WOOLNOUGH: Director, *Smallville*

STEVE YOUNIS: Webmaster, supermanhomepage.com

BRYCE ZABEL: Supervising producer, *Lois & Clark: The New Adventures of Superman*

PROLOGUE
The Challenges of Superman

Back in the summer of 2019 it was virtually impossible — very much by design — to watch the superhero-turned horror movie Brightburn *without thinking of Superman in general and Zack Snyder's* Man of Steel *from six years earlier in particular. That film posits a child landing on Earth from an alien civilization, where he is found and raised by a pair of Kansas farmers.*

Things go well — some might say idyllically — until puberty, when his extraordinary abilities kick in, triggering a transformation. Not into the beacon of hope that Superman goes on to represent, but instead, into a predator who uses his various superpowers to inflict harm on virtually everyone (including his adopted parents) around him. It's a true Man of Steel nightmare and in some ways only a few steps removed from a number of interpretations and variations on the Last Son of Krypton that have embraced darker elements rather than the more noble ones for which the the character has been famous. Cases in point include the character of Homelander on Amazon Prime's The Boys, *Omniman in the same streaming service's animated* Invincible, *or Superman himself in the multi-media creation* Injustice.

STEVE YOUNIS (webmaster, supermanhomepage.com): When I first saw the promo for *Brightburn*, it was obvious to me that the director was intentionally mimicking many of the shots that Zack Snyder created for *Man of Steel*. This movie is obviously a "what if" Superman story… which is interesting, because many fans felt *Man of Steel* was too dark. *Brightburn* takes that to a *much* darker place.

ELLIOT S! MAGGIN (writer, Superman comics and novels): It's quite clearly a reimagining of the Superman character in a more sinister light. It's become fashionable to try to evoke fear among a potential audience of anyone who might be, in any sense, more powerful than anyone else.

BRIAN GUNN (co-writer, *Brightburn*): There's a tradition that goes back to

(Photo @Ed Gross; Superman © and TM DC Comics/Warner Bros. Discovery)

Moses up through contemporary superhero stories about childless parents who take in an infant that they find in the wild. Those figures grow up to be noble and heroic, but we wondered what would happen if it went the other way and this child ends up being something sinister.

ELLIOT S! MAGGIN: It's always been obvious to me that Superman's story is a retelling of the Moses story. *Brightburn*, even on the surface, owes far more to the Superman story than Superman owes to Moses.

MARK GUNN (co-writer, *Brightburn*): We were encouraged to play up the superhero element even more than we had in our original script. To put super-powers in a horror context seemed really fun to us — it was an opportunity to mix together two different genres that hadn't really been mixed together before.

BRIAN GUNN: We realized that there are many superhero abilities that, if you were on the receiving end of them, would be terrifying. Flying could appear very ghostly. Laser eyes can be demonic. Super-strength can be horrifying. Lots of super abilities, if you turn them just a couple of degrees, become grist for horror.

MICHAEL J. HAYDE (author, *Flights of Fantasy: The Unauthorized but True Story of Radio & TV's Adventures of Superman*): There was a time when nobility was central to heroism. We had Sgt. Friday, the ideal cop; Perry Mason, the ideal lawyer; James Kildare, the ideal doctor; Superman, the ideal superhero. They weren't meant to be imperfect, they were meant to *inspire*. Since then, we've been persuaded it's pointless to try and emulate such heroes, so let's make them flawed, like we are. The argument is that it's more "realistic," but it's done more harm than good. Now cynicism has replaced idealism. We've lost respect for politicians, for police, for anyone in authority, because we're constantly looking for frailty and fail-ings among them. When you've been tuned in solely to human misery, to greed, to power that corrupts, how can you believe anyone is capable of selflessness? And if you don't believe it, why would you ever strive for it yourself? I fear looking up to heroes has become passé and we are so much poorer for it.

PAUL LEVITZ (writer, former publisher, DC Comics): I think heroes are still relevant. Superman is a harder character to write as a comic book character than a lot of others, because the characters around him that he cares about have become so enshrined in our mythology. You *don't* believe Lois Lane or Jimmy Olsen are really in danger. I'm not keeping up with the current incarnations of all the complexities that they're adding to it, so maybe that's part of how they're conquering it, by adding characters that he cares about, but are more fragile, mythologically.

STEVE YOUNIS: The complaint for those who don't "get" Superman is that he's *too* good, and therefore "boring" and "uncool." These people are usually fans of the antihero archetype, preferring the darker characters like Batman, Wolverine, Punisher, etc. So to "fix" Superman — like he *needs* fixing — they try to turn his story toward this type of model: "How cool would it be to see Superman turn bad?"

ELLIOT S! MAGGIN: The thing about Superman is you've got to write to the man rather than the super. On first glance, everybody thinks Superman stories are about power, but it's the *opposite* of that. Superman stories are about moral and ethical decisions. They're about choices. The premise of a Superman story is you've got all the power in the world, so what do you do in a given situation? *That's* what the story is about. Superman stories are like a dream. The reason you dream is to deal with issues, either past or future that might come up before they happen. Or in retrospect, but you deal with the issues on a fantasy level so you know what to do with your life.

For Joe Kelly, a writer whose credits include the TV shows Big Hero 6: The Series *and Ben 10, as well as the animated feature* Superman vs. The Elite *(based on his classic comic story "What's So Funny About Truth, Justice and the American Way?"), this path to darkness — or at the very least shades of gray — is one the character has been on for quite some time.*

JOE KELLY (writer, *Superman vs. The Elite*): In the '40s he was a representation of hope born out of frustration. But by the time you get to the '80s this sort of cynicism drops in. In *The Dark Knight Returns*, writer/artist Frank Miller uses him as this kind of tool of fascism, which works for that particular story. He gets a little microdot of being redeemed in that story, but he's pretty much played as a sucker, right? And *that* starts to infiltrate how people think about him. Then you get to today, and over the last decade there's a growing sense of frustration and anger and discontent about things that are happening around the world, and it's not just here and it's not just over the past few years. So you have a character that is *so* idealized, and people have a misconception of Superman that he's perfect, so to tarnish the perfect thing, because we live in an imperfect world, is a natural impulse. I get it as a writer where you want to try and say something new about this character or illustrate a point about him, which is what we did with "What's So Funny," but pulled it out at the last second, my take being that you *need* the beacon of hope. We should never give up hope. But there's a lot of people that are kind of feeling beat up, so they use Superman as the extension of anger or discontent with how the world is, or as a mirror saying the world has become ugly. That's what drives a lot of this, but it really is like low-hanging fruit.

DAN JURGENS (writer, credits including "The Death of Superman"): Superman is really the quintessential American superhero in so many different ways. Some of it is because we look at the origin of the character, which is rooted in Midwest Americana in terms of Superman growing up in Smallville, Kansas, in the middle of the country. I mean, smack dab in the middle of the country, yet he was created by a couple of young Jewish men at a time when we had worldwide Great Depression, when we could feel the weight of fascism overseas. And then we carry into it this idea that, when Superman first started, he was very much a hero of the people kind of thing. Go back and look at those early '38, '39 stories, where Superman might be taking on a wife beater, or ready to dangle an evil landlord off his crummy tenement building's edge or something like that. Consider everything that went along with all of that — *and* the fact that Superman is an immigrant, not born in United States. I just find him to be the quintessential American superhero. He doesn't wear a mask. He is very open with people. He does not tell people what to do, what to be or how to live.

JOHN KENNETH MUIR (author and film historian): The so-called "Man of Tomorrow" is about today and the best ideals of humanity. He's also all about the best ideals of America. To me, Superman's story is truly — as many have stated before — the ultimate immigrant story. Young Superman travels to Middle America from a faraway land, with what sounds like a foreign name (Kal-El). Once here, amidst our corn and wheat fields, he internalizes the American dream of freedom and opportunity for all and comes to be a stalwart defender of American ideals via his career as a reporter, practicing the First Amendment, basically, and speaking truth to power. Superman's outsider perspective or status is revealed to readers, and viewers, when we fail to live up to our stated ideals as a people.

PAUL LEVITZ: He survives from an era where the readers were all kids or not extraordinarily sophisticated adults. Nobody sat there and said, "Well, if he's so fast, why can't he just run around and do that thing before the villain notices it?" Now, in a more sophisticated era and with the wealth of powers that he's got, every reader sits there and analyzes *everything*: "This is the way *I* would have solved that if I had Superman's powers, and I could have done that much faster." And I believe that's part of the problem. I don't think it's morality in and of itself.

Certainly we're more cynical than we were before, but we're still really pleased when someone shows up with a higher morality. Look at Ukranian president Volodymyr Zelenskyy. There are *still* people who put us all to shame.

ALAN BURKE (co-host, *All Star Superfan Podcast*): The stories that stick out to me the most are the personal ones. Stories that examine the psychology of the characters. Stories that ask, "What would it actually be like to be as powerful as Superman and to carry that immense responsibility?" Stories that ask what it would be like growing up in Smallville, knowing you're different, knowing that you're strange, that you're alone. How does a man in that situation grow to be the type of person who is not in any way isolated or corrupted? A kind man who sees the good in *everyone*. I like the personal stories, the small moments which examine that element of the character.

ELLIOT S! MAGGIN: He was my favorite character growing up and it stayed that way. I like that he's so basic; that he's definable, accessible and monstrously powerful. He's the same character as Odysseus, Achilles or Zeus. I think every culture has gotten one just like him and he's ours. It was an enormous privilege to get to write him.

DAN JURGENS: Captain America stands up and often makes that speech of rally to the flag. I don't see Superman that way. I see Superman as leading much more by example, that he is the guy who stands in the room and just because of the few things he does say, when he says it, how he says it, the way he comports himself, absolutely commands total and complete respect. *That's* how I see Superman.

BOB GOODMAN (writer, *Superman Unbound*): It has been challenging at times in the history of Superman to tell interesting stories with him. If you look at the Silver Age Superman comics, you see how challenging it was to come up with stories to tell. Since he was required to be physically infallible, all they were left with was the world's biggest Boy Scout. What do you do with that? And what the writers of that time came up with was to tell little mysteries: Why is Superman doing *that*? Superman is behaving in a way that is different from Superman — *why*? Because he's smarter than all of us, and he knows something that we won't figure out until the end of the mystery. So it's a structure that worked, and the writers were able to churn out some comic books, but it did also get repetitive very quickly. Back in the mid-'90s when we were doing *Superman: The Animated Series*, the *Batman* animated series and, later, *Batman Beyond*, all at around the same time with the same gang of guys — Alan Burnett, Paul Dini and Bruce Timm and that whole crowd — Bruce used to argue that Batman was the better character; that Batman was the character that more interesting stories came from. And I get it. But I would argue that Batman is the *easier* character to find interesting stories to tell about. It's more challenging to find an interesting story to tell about Superman, but I'm hard-pressed to say one is a better character, because I love them both and derive a lot of satisfaction from playing in both sandboxes.

BRUCE TIMM (producer, *Superman The Animated Series* and *Justice League Unlimited*): It's a challenge in that there is something really specific and iconic about Superman as the Super Boy Scout. Okay, how do you make that interesting and how do you make that relevant? There are a lot of different ways to make it interesting and there are a lot of bad ways to go. One thing you can do is to make him un-Superman-like; make him break his own rules where he loses it and becomes a vengeful killer or whatever. That's an *easy* out. We've done that too. It's really a hard thing to describe. The minute you push him too far outside the Superman zone, then he's *not* Superman anymore. You have to be very careful to walk that line. On the other end of the paradigm, some works have totally embraced the idea that Superman is this God-like, Jesus-like, King Arthur-like figure of pure goodness. It *is* difficult to do, and there's no easy answer for it.

MARK MILLAR (writer, *Superman: Red Son*): People who say he's difficult to make relevant to the modern audience have never read Superman comics. Growing up, I never felt it lacked drama. Whether it was Kryptonite or Superman trapped under a red sun, or Superman facing other Kryptonians, there was *always* a challenge. Superman was cooler than Batman to me, because the challenges were so much more immense. Batman may have to stop a crime spree of the Joker and his gang, but Superman maybe has to stop an entire dimension that's coming to invade Earth or something like that. What you do when you're doing Superman is that you up the ante. To me, *that's* what makes it interesting. People say they can't relate, but if you actually read these things, there's nothing better than a good Superman story.

DAN JURGENS: I have never found it burdensome to write Superman. And a lot of it centers around this question of what's Superman's power level? How do you come up with stories? And if it's going to come down to a fight scene, then, yes, you have to give that perhaps a little more thought, because you just can't find bad guys on the street corner to go fight Superman. Like you can, again, with Batman. With Superman, it has to be, I think, more insightful and more clever than that.

JIM KRIEG (writer, *Reign of the Supermen*): It's funny, but I can't relate to people who don't see the "Big Blue Boy Scout" and say that's a real person. It means they don't know anybody that nice, which makes me sad. We absolutely need that guy. He's an ideal and he's been around so long that most of us can picture or hear what he would say or what his point of view would be in almost any given situation. He would always choose the right thing. He would always choose to be kind. He would always choose to self-sacrifice. He would choose to give the other person the benefit of the doubt and defend those being oppressed. He's an absolute necessity and it's why he resonates.

DAN JURGENS: What you do is come up with a story of how does that affect Superman's character? How does that, whether it's the villain or the circumstances, or the blend of the two, create a hurdle for Superman or a series of hurdles that he has to get over? And in some ways, if he is going to keep his character of Clark Kent at a certain level of being pristine, and Clark Kent is so much the basis for who Superman is, then I think that it's a little easier to create stories, because of the weight of responsibility to the world and the people around him that Superman feels.

CHRISTOPHER REEVE (actor, "Superman," *Superman: The Movie*): The key word for me on Superman *is* inspiration. He is a leader by inspiration. He sets an example. It's quite important that people realize that I don't see him as a glad-handing show-off; a one-man vigilante force who rights every wrong. Basically, he's a pacifist, a man who comes along and says, "What can I do to help?" He stands on the sidelines until there is real trouble. He does not want to get involved unless it's absolutely necessary, because he thinks people should learn to make their own decisions.

TOM WELLING (actor, "Clark Kent," *Smallville*): When I was four or five, I *demanded* to be Superman two years in a row for Halloween and I wouldn't have it any other way. I think I had grown so much that I didn't really fit into the costume the second year, but I *still* tried to wear it.

BRANDON ROUTH (actor, "Superman," *Superman Returns*): When I was five or six, the first time I was going to see *Superman: The Movie*, I was dressed up in Superman pajamas that I had, and a cape, which my mom still has. And I was jumping around the house, jumping on furniture, so excited to finally see the movie. I got *so* excited that I gave myself a migraine. Migraines have something to do with Superman, obviously. When I get very excited over something, I do that to myself. And I was so excited that I was basically sick to my stomach for the first half of the movie. I was sitting in a daze on the couch, watching the movie. I think I got better toward the end. But I was a *huge* Superman fan when I was younger.

Joe Kelly's 2001 story "What's So Funny About Truth, Justice and the American Way?" features a team of super-powered vigilantes ("The Elite") who arrive on the scene and become the subject of global popularity through their crime-fighting methods, which include the execution of criminals. Their approach is put in direct contrast with Superman's. In the end, it seems that the Man of Steel has been pushed so far that he's adopted their methods as he takes out the Elite one by one, until it's revealed that it was no more than a ruse to show the people of Earth how pointless and dangerous hatred and vengeance can be. The concept was actually inspired by another ultra-violent comic called The Authority *and its postmodern take on superheroes.*

JOE KELLY: *The Authority* was flat out saying, if you believe in any of the stuff that heroes are traditionally supposed to stand for, you're an idiot. And *that* was what pissed me off, because I actually like dark material. I like mature material and most of my taste runs in that direction in terms of what I like to write and consume. But this attitude just, again, pissed me off. As a result, the script for "What's So Funny" was kind of banged out super fast and was totally written with this righteous indignation of, "I'll show you what it would be like without Superman!" And it came from the gut. I really grew to love the character over the course of time, because of what he represented. Once "What's So Funny" got out there, it really blew up. What was sort of remarkable was that all that stuff that I was feeling, apparently other people felt it too. And the way that it came across was that people didn't realize that was how they felt. When people spoke to me, they were like, "I really was taking Superman for granted, thinking he was silly or whatever. Then when you gave us a Superman that murders people, I didn't want it and I was pissed and scared and nervous." I'm so proud of that, because, again, I have no problem with dark superheroes, it was just the idea that those ideals are stupid. That really gets me upset. And then you get to Zack Snyder's *Man of Steel* in 2013 and he's basically like, "Yeah, of course Superman would snap somebody's neck. What's wrong with that?"

DAVID S. GOYER (writer, *Man of Steel*): On the face of it, a character like Superman is more challenging than a character like Batman, because Superman is known for being somewhat of a Boy Scout. But as Zack Snyder has said, with *Man of Steel* we were attempting to depict him in a slightly more realistic way, and our goal was to make you care about him as a real person and get to know him in a way that we've never known him before.

But it isn't just Man of Steel. *The comics have given us* Red Son, *which imagines a more totalitarian Superman landing and being raised in Russia instead of America, and there are the video games, comics and animated adaptation of* Injustice, *where, after the Joker manipulates Superman into killing Lois Lane and their unborn child, the Man of Steel flips, murders the Joker and declares himself emperor of Earth, eventually deciding to take over the governing of the planet.*

JIM KRIEG: There's some interest in seeing the nicest guy in the world, or someone we're used to thinking of that way, come to a moment when he's pushed too far and he unleashes. There's always something interesting in seeing the characters that we know through a dark mirror. It's a taste of Jekyll and Hyde, which is different than, say, the evil Captain Kirk from *Star Trek.* Now *Jekyll and Hyde* is a story about just splitting a guy into two; a guy we don't really know. But the strength of television or any kind of serialized material in an ongoing story is that we get to know these characters inside and out. We know them the way we're used to seeing them and they definitely act a certain way. And the stronger that character is, the more shocked we are when we flip that on its head. Think about Samantha on *Bewitched.* She was always so sweet and kind, amusing and empathetic, but *then* she was replaced by her lookalike doppelganger Serena, who's wicked and mischievous and up to no good and selfish. Seeing that is fascinating. It's a thrill to watch someone misbehave from the way we're used to, because we're used to seeing ourselves in the characters we watch on television or experience in comics or movies. So part of us wonders what it would be like to have the powers of these characters and unleash them. It's exciting to think about.

STAN BERKOWITZ (writer, *Superman: The Animated Series*): When you're a child and you read about Superman, you do *not* want a dark version of the character. You want him to be a good guy who's always helping people. My Superman — the Superman of my era — was the George Reeves show, and the structure of that is that he was the older brother and the two younger siblings were Lois Lane and Jimmy Olsen. One or the other, or both, would get in trouble and older brother Superman would come in and help them. And that works phenomenally well for children, because you want to live in a world like that where someone's going to come help you. But when you get older and you read comics, that's too simple, too childish a dynamic for you. The older reader starts to think, "There are a lot of gray areas in the world; we're bad and good kind of blended together."

What this means is that you're kind of curious to see this guy lose his temper.

They want to see Superman's darker side to see him access the full range of human emotions. The George Reeves Superman was a helpful guy, right? And it never went beyond that. But, again, older readers or viewers want a wider palette of emotions from any character — spite, rage, jealousy and that sort of thing. The modern reader wants to see how Superman or any character reacts to those emotions and how they handle them. And in the case of Superman, if he goes into a snit, he could destroy half the city. In a nutshell, I think *that* is the appeal of the darker side.

ELLIOT S! MAGGIN: For repeated reinterpretation of the character divergent from the original concept, not only in film but in the comics medium as well, he has taken a secondary position among that shared pantheon. There is a case to make that where Superman was once an iconic figure who personified the fundamental heroic character of a nation, he has become simply a comic book character like any other, subject to the vagaries of artists' and writers', of producers' and publishers' whims.

ALEX ROSS (co-writer and artist, *Kingdom Come*): Superman's overall understanding by the general public is well-known, but he is unfortunately seen as less sophisticated than other currently popular properties. I think the traditional artist approach, as well as Hollywood's, is to depict the most attractive person as this character without the bulk and grit he has often shown in his history. Superman was originally a hero shown with grimacing strain on his face as he did his Herculean feats and had the form of Atlas (Charles Atlas, in fact). I don't think the wider world has seen the version of him that people like Shuster, Jack Burnley, Jack Kirby (unaltered), Steve Rude, Jon Bogdanove, Ed Brubaker and myself have been putting forth forever, it seems. I don't know that it would be universally adored to see him more intense and muscular, but I argue it would definitely make an impact.

JOE KELLY: Superman is so important, especially when you're feeling angry and especially when you feel like the world is a cesspool. And, yes, he's a fictional character. For me, he's not like some Christ analog or anything like that. I really don't think he's a perfect guy, I just think he's a *good* guy and I don't think that good people crumble just because they face trauma. That's a really bleak view of humanity.

BRANDON ROUTH: So much about Superman *is* his humanity. He's only alien because he came from a different planet; I guess it doesn't necessarily mean that he's not human. I don't know the science behind that, but he can still be pretty much like us, except that he has these other powers, of course. But I think, for instance, the love story with Lois Lane is very relatable to everyone. Giving up things. Finding the positive in the negatives. All of these are human things. Even though he exudes this confidence, it doesn't seem too far away as a possibility for all humanity to be like Superman.

SAM DALY (voice actor, "Superman," *Justice League: The Flashpoint Paradox***):** Superman seems to always instinctively do the right thing, and I think that's something his character has always stood for and always will. He's always on the right side of things.

JIM LEE (co-publisher, DC Comics): Trying to deal with a character that is so noble and so powerful is difficult for a writer and an artist to tackle. Purely from an artistic level, you look at his power set — heat-vision, X-ray vision, being able to walk through the molten sun — and it's not like Batman driving around in a car, throwing Batarangs. You have to come up with a different visual vocabulary to express that. It's the same with writing in that he has to be firmly attached to his human roots as Clark Kent, but he should also be this inspirational character who rises above that and has this tremendous humility.

BOB GOODMAN: Superman is a deceptively rich character, and there's a lot more to do with him than people give the character credit for. He's much more relatable in ways than Batman. Batman was kind of a response to, "Oh, you have this superhero with all these powers, not as relatable. Let's create a superhero that is just a regular guy and doesn't have superpowers." I would argue that Superman is, of the two, more a regular guy and a relatable character. You can always find stories to do with Superman/Clark that relate to us; that are, this is what I wish, this is how I hope I would react in this situation, this is a situation we can see ourselves in. Plus, he's very much, in my mind, the right character for the century that he's evolved in.

BRANDON ROUTH: Superman changes with society. With the view we took in *Superman Returns*, he becomes bigger. In the '50s, Superman was America. "Truth, justice and the American Way." It's not about that. I mean, it's Truth, and Justice, but it's not limited to the American way. How can it be? How can we say that it's just about America now? Superman came to save the world, not just America. For me, that's what it is. He's got a bigger message and really wants to change the world, not just by saving things, but by being an influence in the world that other people can see. If Superman just saves things, he just saves things and people feel like he can do everything for them. That's all they get from him. *But* if he can influence and say, "Hey, you can aspire to be better in your life or different in your life," that's a great

12

thing.

JAMES TUCKER (producer, *Batman: The Brave and the Bold*): People love Superman the way they love religion. They don't love him as a character, like people don't love Jesus as a character. They love him as a concept, what he represents, which is an all-powerful, kind, pure, salt-of-the-earth icon. But as a character, as a flesh and blood, living, breathing person with a personality… they don't really get that from him. He's always more of an icon — he represents an ideal rather than an individual. That means people put on him their own aspirations, their own wishes. Much like religion, they twist Superman to be what they want him to be. So if they want him to be all-powerful and able to push planets out of the way — if you *don't* show that, they feel cheated. And if he's not perfect in every way, if you show him vulnerable… We had this problem on *Justice League* where every time something happened to Superman, there was a complaint. But he has to be vulnerable to something or there's no story, there's nothing to overcome. We didn't do as well as we could have, but we got better at it.

JIM LEE: I think Batman is something we can get our heads around: If you work hard and make a billion dollars, you, too, can be a superhero. A crime fighter! It makes a lot of sense; it seems doable. It's hard to be an alien who crash-lands on Earth and gets powers because he's exposed to yellow sun radiation. He is the ultimate superhero for me, so I think there's nothing more impressive — and this brings me back to my childhood — than drawing Superman flying across the skies of Metropolis. That's the kind of joy you want to bring to the comic book, and in my gut, it tells me that Superman is a broader character than Batman — this is a character who can reach the youngest of readers and the oldest of fans.

BRYAN SINGER (director, *Superman Returns*): He's the first superhero. *Ever.* People don't realize that, but before the heroes were The Shadow and things like that. He's very American in the sense that he's the ultimate immigrant and he kind of represents who we all are as American settlers. We're all basically immigrants, the descendants of immigrants, and we all bring with us a certain kind of heritage and a certain kind of value system that dates back to our forefathers and other cultures. And Superman embodies that. By virtue of his idealism and noble point of view, he makes us feel safe. He does it with an eloquence we like to see. He also represents the adolescent dreams of strength, flight — the ultimate fantasy to be able to defy gravity and move mountains. I think these things are quintessentially the fantasy of every child, and there's something about the symbol that's just endured. You can take the "S" and cross into the jungle and you're going to have pretty much 50/50 recognition. It's pretty amazing. Such an iconic figure.

Even little kids who don't know anything about Superman, never grew up with Superman, they see the "S" and they *know*.

BOB GOODMAN: He's existed through this period of time that has seen such mind-blowing changes in technology, in our visions of the future, and change like we've seen in the 20th century and now the 21st century. Change like that brings anxiety. It brings simultaneous wonder and optimism with dread and fear. And Superman stories have always embodied that and they've always been able to change and shift, and embodied anxieties that the culture is feeling at any given time. So we can explore, through Superman, stories our worries are about. What happens when humanity does contact aliens? Will they be our protectors and saviors, or will they show up in a Skull ship like Braniac and want to blow us up? At different times during Superman's history we can explore what the bomb is going to mean to us, what nuclear energy is going to mean to us, what growing corporate power in the form of Lex Luthor is going to mean to us, what nanotechnology is going to mean to us, what cyborg enhancements — combining man to metal — is going to mean to us; what chemical contamination is going to mean to us. So Superman has always been a character who grew with the times in enabling us to exorcise our own demons about our future-phobia — and at the end of the day see our hopes triumph.

One concern is that when people respond to the darker version, there will be more of an impulse that the writers behind these stories will be pushed further away from the more noble version of Superman and what he represents.

STAN BERKOWITZ: Twenty years ago HBO with *The Sopranos* made anti-heroes more and more fascinating. Let's put a commercial veil over this: Who's the bigger star, Superman or Batman? It's traditionally been Batman, the darker guy who's got all the demons. To put some in Superman, there's that element of commerce to make him more like that so people will pay money to see him. I know that sounds cynical, but that's the intersection of the real world in terms of a normal person's emotions and commerce, because if Superman isn't commercial and isn't selling, there won't be a Superman anymore. I think this is DC's way of adjusting with the time and also accepting the fact that their audience is much older than it used to be during the George Reeves era.

STEVE YOUNIS: It may, but it could also have the reverse effect where, upon seeing those darker versions, the reaction is, "Nah, that's not Superman," and they revert to what truly makes Superman great: his brightness, positivity and hopefulness.

JIM KRIEG: You just don't have a character if you go dark. I think Marvel proved it with Captain America. With Captain America. I'm sure there were voices saying, "Oh no, we've got to edge him up and make him a badass," and somebody, probably Kevin Feige, said, "No, that's not who he is. He's got to be squeaky clean or there's nothing left." One of the big jokes people make about Superman is that he rescues kittens out of trees, which is in reference to that Christopher Reeve moment in *Superman: The Movie.* Well, the truth is he *needs* to pull kittens out of trees or we're not going to care about him when he stops missiles.

All of which raises the question of what the Man of Steel's role is in the world of the 21st century, arguably one of the more cynical times that the character has tried to exist in over the course of his 85+ years.

STAN BERKOWITZ: I suggest he be a guy who tries to be a noble beacon of light, but doesn't always succeed. And who runs into situations that are not black and white, but are shades of gray and it always challenges him. Like most people, he *wants* to do good, but then you're faced with a world where the definition of good is not as clear as it used to be. He doesn't have to be a darker version of himself, but simply a more *mature* version; a more realistic version of what someone with enormous powers has to consider on a daily or even an hourly basis.

ELLIOT S! MAGGIN: My perception of Superman's position in our modern world is a rather pessimistic one. I'm not pessimistic about our contemporary social character so much as perplexed at the reasons this character has taken a direction that betrays a lack of understanding – or perhaps an abandonment – of heroism and of its nature and purposes in that world. I trust that there will always be the heroes, and that if the essential nature of this particular iteration of the iconic American hero continues to be abandoned in contemporary popular culture, then the legacy of the stories and ideals on which he was built will remain.

JOHN KENNETH MUIR: I have always appreciated that Superman is not, by and large, motivated by darkness. Kal-El lost his parents and his homeland, and yet he's not out for revenge or "vigilantism." He has not turned inward or psychotic or navel-gazing. Some superheroes are motivated entirely by darker, more selfish impulses, whereas Superman doesn't dwell on his tragic past or let it overwhelm his present. I find this eminently more realistic than the approach taken in comics and movies that focus on angst and broodiness. Everyone lives with tragedy. It's a fact of life. Superman mindfully moves past that tragedy to be a functioning worthwhile member (and guardian) of society. He embraces love (Lois Lane), friendship (Jimmy Olsen), career (*The Daily Planet*) and family (Ma Kent), instead of reliving or obsessing on what he's lost. If a superhero should be, theoretically, a model for the rest of us, then Superman lives up to that title. I think it's a commentary, and a sad one, on our modern society that other superheroes are so dark and brooding and psychologically disturbed, and that we look up to them as heroes.

MARK WAID (writer, *Batman/Superman: World's Finest*): When he was first created, he was a crusader for social justice. He was actually somebody who would walk the walk as well as talk the talk. Not brutal, but certainly efficient at what he did. He just became more mannered over the years and sort of sanitized. We took all of the corners off of the character, and in doing so we also managed to jettison the answer to the question: *Why* does he do this? That was the purpose when I wrote *Birthright*, to give him some sort of context. It should be clear in *Birthright* the reason he puts on the suit, and that the reason he goes out and actually uses his powers to make the world a better place is because it's the only way he knows how to connect with humanity. *That's* his connection. We all need to feel that we're a part of something, and there's no time that we feel more a part of something than when we're doing what we do best and when we're letting our light shine. The problem with keeping your light under a bushel, to milk an old cliché, is that it tends to isolate you.

MARV WOLFMAN (writer, *Crisis on Infinite Earths*): Make him human and with faults, but ultimately believing in doing what's right. You don't need to go dark with Superman; you need to remember he's a human being. He was raised since a baby in Smallville. He's more man than super and if you keep it that way, you'll make him interesting. Once you care more about the super aspect of him, you lose the humanity.

JIM KRIEG: He's going to be in the direct-to-video movies that we do, video games and, of course, comics. And the truth is, there is *always* a course correction. And he's still going to be the character we know. When there's a misstep to make him more "mature" and a darkening up of his character and people *don't* like it, they'll step away from it for a while and then bring it back and it will be like, "Hey, it's *my* Superman. He's back and acting the way I expect him to." I think you have to be a very cynical person to say he's a stupid character and try to make him better by making him a jerk or violent or angry. I understand the issue people have that he's not very realistic, or they don't meet very many people like him, but if you look closely, you'll find those characteristics in a lot of people around you. I believe that the kind of Superman you want to see is very indicative of your worldview. If you can *only* relate to a dark Superman, I feel sorry for you. And I hope you don't live next door to me.

CHAPTER I
Siegel & Shuster

Siegel and Shuster.

Their linked names are to comic books and superheroes as Rodgers and Hammerstein are to musicals, Abbott and Costello to comedy, and Lennon and McCartney to pop music. But unlike the others, by the mid-1970s there was a very real risk that the creators of Superman could have been allowed to slip into obscurity.

From today's perspective that seems improbable, but it's fact.

Some 40 years on from the Man of Steel's 1938 debut in the pages of Action Comics, *his creators, writer Jerry Siegel and artist Joe Shuster, had more or less been forgotten by the general public, their names having been removed from the comic decades earlier and the two of them living separate, destitute lives while their creation went from the comic page to radio star, television icon, Broadway hero and soon to soar on the big screen in the form of Christopher Reeve in 1978's* Superman: The Movie.

It was, in fact, the latter that had pushed them — particularly Siegel — too far.

Three years earlier, Warner Bros., by then the owner of DC Comics and, in turn, Super-man, was paid $3 million by producers Alexander and Ilya Salkind for the rights to make a movie about the Man of Steel, and shortly thereafter announced that a $35-million film ver-sion was in development. Marlon Brando was cast as Superman's father Jor-El, with Gene Hackman as arch enemy Lex Luthor, and Mario Puzo, author of The Godfather, *writing the screenplay. A tremendous amount of media coverage followed, not the least of which was due to Marlon Brando's $3.7-million payday for two weeks' work, $2-million for Hackman and $600,000 for Puzo. But not a word about Siegel or Shuster, and certainly not of any sort of payment coming their way. In response, Siegel, who, as a young man had, along with Shuster, signed over all rights to the character to DC, decided to take their struggle to the public in the form of a nine-page press release titled "A Curse on the Superman Movie."*

TOM ANDRAE (comics historian; co-author, *Batman & Me*): What happened is that at that point they couldn't sue DC for the rights unless they took it to the Supreme Court, so Jerry Siegel decided to go public to try and put some pressure on DC and appeal to people's conscience and that sort of thing.

JERRY SIEGEL (co-creator, Superman): Since his first appearance, our character Superman has been known as a symbol of *justice*, the champion of the

Superman creators Jerry Siegel and Joe Shuster (art © and courtesy D.C. Stuelpner)

helpless and the oppressed, the physical marvel who had sworn to devote his existence to helping those in need. Joe Shuster and I shall not rest in our present position. You hear a great deal about The American Dream. But Superman, who in the comics and films fights for "truth, justice and the American way," has for Joe and me become an American Nightmare.

NEAL ADAMS (artist): They had created Superman, probably the most iconic character in American literature. He's more iconic, he's more well-known by people, than Sherlock Holmes and Tarzan. He is the number-one iconic fantasy literature hero. He is the number-one guy, so of course I was curious, and I also grew up reading comic books just like everybody else. I remember seeing Jerry Siegel. I saw their names, and then they suddenly disappeared and I didn't understand. So when I worked at DC Comics and I made friends with guys in the production room, I would casually ask, "What happened with those guys that created Superman?" And I would get the cold shoulder. And the more I would ask, the more of a cold shoulder I got. I'm like, "Is this some big deal? Are they dead? What the hell's going on?"

TOM ANDRAE: They're responsible for creating an industry. Basically, there wouldn't have been a comic book industry that existed in the popularity that it had at the time if it hadn't been for the superhero and Siegel and Shuster. And Jerry was aware of that. He felt that other superheroes were copies of Superman; that Robin was a copy of Superboy and Captain Marvel was a copy of Superman. And that even Batman was a copy of Superman and on and on. I think it's just because he was there first and he created the modus operandi for superheroes with the way they acted as vigilantes in the beginning. He created a format for them and a look that they all adapted, but certainly they weren't all copies. Batman is *not* Superman.

JERRY SIEGEL: Superman's publishers mercilessly gouged Joe and I for their selfish enrichment, stealing our incomes and careers from us derived from Superman, because of their greedy desire to monopolize the fruits of the Superman creation. I can't flex super-human muscles and rip apart the massive buildings in which these greedy people count the immense profits from the misery they have inflicted on Joe and me and our families. I wish I could. But I *can* ask my fellow Americans to please help us by refusing to buy Superman comic books, refusing to patronize the new Superman movie or watch Superman on TV until this great injustice against Joe and me is remedied by the callous men who pocket the profits from *our* creation. Everyone who has enjoyed our creation Superman and what he stood for, those of you who believe that truth and justice should be the American way, can help us.

Adams, an acclaimed artist and a staunch supporter of the rights of comic creators, later read Siegel's press release and decided to bring it, and them, to the world's press and, therefore, the court of public opinion.

NEAL ADAMS: It was a staggering moment. I mean, I stood in my studio and, after I read it, I was quiet. I got myself a cup of coffee and I walked out to the front of my studio and I kind of announced: "Guys, anybody who wants to read this letter can read this letter. But I'm going to see to it that this gets fixed and I am not going to stop until it does. So if any of you want to help me, I'd appreciate the help. If you don't want to help me, there's no obligation. But we are going to see that this gets taken care of or I will know why. I'm not going to stop until it gets done, so it's going to get taken care of."

Adams, along with comic artist Jerry Robinson and others, was absolutely right. By the time Superman: The Movie *reached theaters on December 15, 1978, Siegel and Shuster were given a yearly dividend and health insurance for the rest of their lives. Depending on your point of view, even more importantly, the opening titles included this credit — missing for decades, but returned and continuing to this day:*

Superman Created by Jerry Siegel & Joe Shuster

It was an achievement that was nothing less than incredible, yet in a sense pales in comparison to the fact that this struggle and triumph was little more than a mere "moment" in Superman's history. Over 40 years preceded it, and nearly 50 have followed during which the Man of Steel, like his creators, suffered through his own series of ebbs and flows, triumphs and failures.

PETER SANDERSON (comic book historian and author): Two generations have grown into adulthood never knowing a world without Superman. But it was two members of a third generation, the one that grew up during the Great Depression of the 1930s, who actually created this worldwide symbol of the heroic ideal. A country beaten down by rampant unemployment, poverty and hunger, about to leave the frying pan of domestic troubles for the fire of war, and was in dire need of a hero to stir their imaginations and their hopes. It was two boys, not yet even adults, Jerry Siegel and Joe Shuster, who gave them that hero. And it was not in one of the media through which most probably first learned about Superman: not the movies, animation, the newspaper strips or radio, and certainly not television, still in its infancy.

BRAD RICCA (author, *Super Boys: The Amazing Adventures of Jerry Siegel and Joe Shuster — The Creators of Superman*): I was born in Cleveland, live in Cleveland and as a kid on any random Saturday my dad would throw my brother and I in the station wagon and we'd go downtown from the suburbs to look at his job sites — he used to sell windows — which was something we absolutely didn't want to do. But along the way he would tell us tales of Cleveland, like this is where they filmed *The Deer Hunter,* and the one that struck me the most was when he said the two guys that created Superman were from Cleveland. I just couldn't wrap my mind around *that.* I thought it was totally fake: There was no way something *that* cool could come from Cleveland.

MICHAEL SANGIACOMO (journalist; member, The Siegel & Shuster Society; author, *Tales of the Starlight Drive-In*): I'm often astounded when people are surprised to know Superman was created here. Cleveland is proud of Superman. The *Cleveland Plain Dealer* and Siegel and Shuster Society have been hammering our heritage for a long time, making people aware. I think previous city administrations were not as enthusiastic about it, but they have learned the value of being the *only* city in the world able to make the claim.

PETER SANDERSON: Superman first appeared in the still-young medium of comic books in 1938, only three years after Siegel and Shuster began publishing new material instead of recycled comic strips. *This* is where Superman and virtually everyone and everything in his fictional universe first took form. And it's in the comics that, decade after decade, editors, writers and artists have revised and reshaped Superman and his world to suit changing times and tastes. Many people may know and love Superman and his supporting cast from different mediums, but all of these varying treatments of the Man of Steel, however different in concept and artistic style, ultimately have a single source: Superman in the comic books.

Going back to the earliest days of the comic book medium, and a time before Superman had even come into existence, does present its own set of challenges.

PAUL LEVITZ (writer; former Publisher, DC Comics): If you're looking at the history of *Star Trek*, at least 75% of the people who were involved are alive. And even if the people aren't alive, there's audio of Gene Roddenberry and most of those early guys you can quote from. When it comes to Superman, you're missing most of it, because they're all gone. I'm about as old, not chronologically, but professionally, as anybody left, and there's only one or two people with any connection to anything earlier than that who can offer anything about the earlier period. And even *that*, in the great scheme of things, is about five minutes before I got there. For most of the important history of Superman, there are no witnesses left.

So what do you have? Historians who are trying to be scholars, like Jeremy Dauber, who wrote *American Comics* for W.W. Norton and is a *real* scholar; over the course of a year he must have read or reread a couple of thousand comics. He read every issue of things like *The Comics Journal* as it evolved and any other news periodical. He was not a journalist looking at history, he was a historical scholar doing the best scholarly thing he could have. It doesn't mean everything in it is right, but there was an exhaustive effort put into it. And at the other end of the spectrum, without demeaning anyone, there are the grandchildren who want to investigate their ancestors' connections to comic history. And they *do* find some things we didn't know before and they work hard at it, but the lens is *such* a focused one that it has enormous distortion to it. The lens on those first 40 or 50 years are so distorted that there may not be a way to solve it.

Yet in putting the historical pieces together as best as one can, there would seem to be three early players in the formation of what would eventually become DC Comics and, in turn, the Man of Steel's birthplace. First, Major Malcolm Wheeler-Nicholson (January 7, 1890 to September 21, 1965), a writer and publisher of pulp fiction, who is generally credited with publishing the first periodical consisting largely of original material rather than reprints of newspaper comic strips. He got his start through the writing and publishing of pulp fiction.

NICKY WHEELER-NICHOLSON (comics historian, granddaughter of Major Malcolm Wheeler-Nicholson): The pulps as they are referred to are not what most people generally think of, which is *Pulp Fiction,* the Quentin Tarantino movie; or 1950s paperbacks that have kind of sleazy, salacious covers on them. Although there were pulps that *were* like that, the majority of them were adventure magazines. And there were hundreds of them: *Adventure, Argosy, Sailing, Sea* — I mean, you name it, there was a pulp magazine for it. And these magazines started in about 1890. They had their heyday until about the early Depression. And then, because of the cost of paper, they started to go down, and also because the comics came in, they started to lose their popularity. But my grandfather wrote for adventure magazines a lot and they were PG-13 adventure stories geared for a general audience. The pulps were huge, like television or mass media today. *Everybody* read them, the newsstands were packed with them.

My grandfather started National Allied Publications in 1934, and the first comic was *New Fun* number one, and that was on the newsstands by January 1935. He was not the first person to come out with *all* original comics and *all* original strips, but he is the person who came out with all original comics that lasted, because he is the founder of DC Comics. When he started the comics, he thought that the pulp stories — adventure stories — would make a good template for comics, because they're pretty generic, they usually have a pretty standard plot form and they're easy to read. *And* people really loved them. They have the classic hero and the classic bad guys so perfect for comics. So a lot of his early comics came out of those pulp stories.

Harry Donenfeld (October 17, 1893 to February 1, 1965) became a partner in his brothers' printing company, Martin Press, in 1921. Business boomed, due largely, according to reports, to the fact that Donenfeld had links with gangster Frank Costello and helped move alcohol — illegal at the time due to prohibition — as well as Canadian pulp paper (which was legitimate) across the border. He also obtained a deal for Martin Press to print six-million subscription leaflets for Hearst magazines, an accomplishment, which, again, is credited to those ties to the underworld. In 1923, in what seemed to be indicative of the man's true nature, he took control of Martin Press and forced two of his three older brothers out of the company. Then the business' name was changed to Donny Press, which Donenfeld used to start publishing girlie and pulp magazines — at least until obscenity charges were made against him. Avoiding jail time, he changed his approach and went more legitimate with what he published. Also, recognizing that the finer details of business was not really his thing, in 1929 he brought in Jack Liebowitz to take on that side of the company. The Independent News Company was created in 1932, serving as both a distributor and printer. In terms of the former, once again the underworld allowed Donenfeld to gain a kind of stranglehold on newsstands "encouraged" to carry their publications.

Jacob S. ("Jack") Liebowitz (October 10, 1900 to December 11, 2000) started his career as an accountant for the International Ladies' Garment Workers' Union, where he proved himself extraordinarily adept. Following the crash of Wall Street in 1929, Donenfeld brought him aboard and he eventually became co-owner of National Allied Publications (the forerunner to DC). He went into business with Wheeler-Nicholson to publish Detective Comics *and together they formed a subsidiary company called Detective Comics Incorporated. But, in the way that these things tended to go, as Wheeler-Nicholson found himself further and further in debt (much of it unknowingly being orchestrated), Liebowitz (encouraged by Donenfeld) in 1938 worked things out where Detective Comics Inc. was forced into bankruptcy. At that point he swooped in and acquired its assets. As part of the bankruptcy action, Liebowitz, who was then sole owner of Detective Comics Inc., bought up Wheeler-Nicholson's National Allied Publications, and Donenfeld and Liebowitz assumed control over the entire growing comic book enterprise.*

In between all of these behind-the-scenes machinations, Jerry Siegel and Joe Shuster entered the picture, Shuster having been born on July 10, 1914 in Toronto, Canada, while Siegel arrived October 17, 1914 in Cleveland, Ohio. Both grew up with financial hardships and both ended up in Glenville, Ohio. Siegel's life took a devastating turn on June 2, 1932 when his father, a tailor, suffered a fatal heart attack while being assaulted by a robber, which would have no small influence on his future creation.

In general, school wasn't easy for either Siegel or Shuster as they were frequently bullied by other students and didn't always fit in. Needless to say, their meeting at Glenville High School was fortuitous.

PETER SANDERSON: Superman was the brainchild of those two teenagers. The son of Lithuanian Jewish immigrants, Siegel was born and grew up in Cleveland, Ohio, where he became one of the first members of science fiction fandom, publishing his own fanzines. It was at Glenville High School that he met and became friends with another student there, Joe Shuster, who had been born in Toronto, Canada, and who had moved to Cleveland with his family.

JOE SHUSTER (co-creator, Superman): I came from Canada when I was about 10 years old and our family settled in Cleveland, Ohio. I attended Alexander Hamilton Junior High School, where I was staff artist on their school paper *The*

Federalist. And I did a comic strip called, of all things, *Jerry the Journalist.* It wasn't influenced by anything in particular; the script was given to me.

JERRY SIEGEL: Strangely enough, it was written by a cousin of mine — he was editor of the paper. I don't know the details, but then Joe moved from that neighborhood down into the neighborhood where I was living. It was shortly before that I was talking to my cousin and told him I was interested in comics, and I was starting to collaborate through the mail with some cartoonists. He told me about Joe. He said that Joe was very good and was moving into my neighborhood and the two of us ought to get together. That's what led to the two of us meeting.

JOE SHUSTER: We were just a few blocks away from each other, matter of fact. We were about 16 at the time.

JERRY SIEGEL: Something like that. We were high school kids.

JOE SHUSTER: It was Glenville High School that I met Jerry Siegel; we were both on the staff of the Glenville High paper *The Glenville Torch.*

JERRY SIEGEL: While we were students there, there were also some students who in later years achieved considerable celebrity, among them Jerome Lawrence, who later was co-writer of *Inherit the Wind* and *Auntie Mame.* And then Seymour Heller, who was also a student there, later became the manager of Liberace. There were some other fellows who did quite well in later years. Some of them worked on the newspaper.

In the January 11, 1935 edition of The Brooklyn Daily Eagle *appeared a report about Wheeler-Nicholson, detailing the arrival of* New Fun *comics. Offers the story, "*New Fun *is the title of a juvenile magazine that appeared for the first time today on the newsstands of the principal cities throughout the United States, according to an announcement made by Malcolm Wheeler-Nicholson, president of National Allied Publication Inc. Major Nicholson has secured the cooperation of* The Eagle *for the publication of this tabloid-size monthly periodical which is designed to please 'boys and girls from 2 to 90' with its predominant pictorial contents of new comic strips and special departments devoted to aircraft, sports, the radio and the movies."*

NICKY WHEELER-NICHOLSON: Two of the first people he hired were Jerry Siegel and Joe Shuster. He also hired Bob Kane and Walt Kelly — a lot of people who went on to very long careers in comics got their start with

him. So he knew from the very
beginning that he couldn't just have
one magazine, because he came out
of pulp publishing doing adventure
pulps. He knew that in order to be
a financial success, he had to have a
number of them. So he started with
New Fun. Then he started *More Fun*
at the end of 1935. Next was the
idea for *Detective Comics* and that he
did not own completely by himself.
For many reasons he had to go
into financial connection with Jack
Liebowitz, and Liebowitz and Harry
Donenfeld eventually ended up with

Superman's co-creator, artist Joe Shuster, draws an original sketch for a fan (courtesy Cleveland Public Library/Photograph Collection).

DC Comics. My grandfather was very instrumental in some of the foundations of
how the comics evolved. When Jack Liebowitz and Harry Donenfeld took over,
neither one of them were creative people; Jack was the financial guy and Harry was
a salesman — an *amazing* salesman. Jack Liebowitz was an incredibly gifted financial
strategist without a doubt. Whatever you want to say about them, you have to say
that, but it was my grandfather who helped lay those creative foundations for the
comics and so many things that we think about when we think of comics. He had
a heroine called Sandra of the Secret Service, who comes out in my grandfather's
classic pulp stories. Very straightforward, very unafraid of anything.

They were printing my grandfather's comics, so somehow they figured out that
this might be a good way to get involved. This was the middle of the Depression
and my grandfather is trying to pay all these artists and writing and starting print
magazines and there just wasn't enough money. He ended up getting money from
them and it went downhill from there, because they were used to organizing themselves to take over companies that they wanted. And they did pretty much the same
practice they'd done all along.

ROBERT GREENBERGER (writer, DC Comics Editor): Liebowitz and
Donenfeld definitely chased Wheeler-Nicholson out and took over the company.
Not the most ethical series of moves, yet they ran a really strong company and built
it into something. But it meant controlling the intellectual property and they did
not want to get creators involved. At the same time, there's Shelley Mayer, who cut
the deal with William Moulton Marston for Wonder Woman — to this day DC is
beholden to some of those terms in the contract.

NICKY WHEELER-NICHOLSON: The way it was, the publisher was the last person to get paid. So the printer got paid, then the distributor got paid, and then maybe three or four months later the publisher got paid without really knowing how many books were sold. So there was a lot of room there for some people to gamble. But initially my grandfather was seeing that the comics were selling well and that there's money coming in, but it's taking four months or more for him to get paid. So he's trying to pay all these people and keep everything afloat. And what Donenfeld and Liebowitz did when they got involved is that they would hold back money that he needed to pay people until he would sign a contract that was, slowly but surely, giving things away. They just pulled the whole thing out from under him. *That* was how he lost the company. There's a 600-page document of the bankruptcy proceedings that they forced him into, and that is full of the machinations and things that they did to get the company from him. It's pretty heartbreaking. But on the other hand, it's a great story. These things happen. Usually the creative people don't end up with the company. I've said this before: I don't think my family would have been able to do what Donenfeld did with DC. I really don't. My family is creative, they're *not* corporate, so everything works out the way it's supposed to.

TIM DEFOREST (author, *Storytelling in the Pulps, Comics and Radio: How Technology Changed Popular Fiction in America*): Early on, there were *tons* of comic book companies and they were all pretty much just throwing story concepts at the wall to see what stuck. The genres that were already popular in comic strips or the pulp magazines, like crime and science fiction and such, obviously appeared in a lot of comic books. The various media cross-pollinated each other, and what would become DC was, I think, one of the bigger companies even before 1938. They had pretty good sales, but would strike gold with Superman, which was completely different from what anyone else had seen before. In a visual media like that, it just took off and created the superhero genre and DC became the leading comic book publisher because of that.

LAUREN AGOSTINO (co-author, *Holding Kryptonite*): I don't think people realize that everybody was small potatoes back then. Jerry and Joe were, Jack Leibowitz was — these *weren't* big companies. These things kind of sprang up. Jack never worked in publishing before he went to National. He worked in the garment district in the labor union. His father got him a job with Donenfeld in publishing, so I don't think any of these men were more powerful than the other, they just kind of stumbled into a small business that happened to grow. Jack was originally the accountant that had to take on a bigger role because

Donenfeld was a drunk and never around. He had been just another worker. And Jack *was* an asshole; he was the boss and was trying to get anything happening that he could, not even knowing if there was something there to get. People want to make him sound like this mastermind evil villain that was in this big company stacking up his money, and that's ridiculous.

Between all of this, Siegel and Shuster collaborated on what is believed to be the first science-fiction fanzine, simply called Science Fiction, *but, interestingly enough, Siegel himself disputes this, noting that several years before he even met Shuster he had put out a self-published fanzine titled* Cosmic Stories.

JERRY SIEGEL: It was strictly a typewritten and hectographed publication. I believe that I wrote most of it or at least a great deal of it. It was sold through the mail. This was the first science-fiction fanzine in the U.S., and, for all I know, in the whole world. This was when I was about 14 years old, back in 1929, about a year or so before I met Joe. It must be quite a collector's item if any copies exist. I do remember that when I showed the material to my English teacher, she gave me a little lecture that it was a pity I was wasting my time writing such trash when there were so many wonderful types of literature I could be writing instead. And I said, "Well, I like this kind of stuff, and that's why I write it."

JOE SHUSTER: We were both great science-fiction fans, reading *Amazing Stories* and *Wonder Stories* in those days.

JERRY SIEGEL: When Joe and I met, it was like the right chemicals coming together. I loved his artwork, the stuff that he showed me — and he showed me stuff that he had drawn even years earlier, when he was a teenager, science-fiction stuff. Though he was a beginner, I thought he had the flair of a Frank R. Paul, who was one of the best science-fiction illustrators in the field. And to our astonishment, we found that both of us were great science-fiction fans, and we were both reading the same type of material. Not only that, but when I first met Joe, to my intense delight he showed me that he was a collector. He was collecting some of the early Tarzan pages by Hal Foster and, later, early Flash Gordon; and I found that we were both absolutely interested in the same type of thing. I was crazy about the artists that he was crazy about, and yet he had this wonderful flair. I didn't know then that someday he would be as famous as those other cartoonists, but I thought, "Gee whiz, I would just love to work with him."

After I met Joe, we immediately began working on a wide variety of different types of comic strips: funny strips and adventure strips. We did a strip about a caveman and showed it around to the syndicates. That was one of our first collaborations, but not the very first. It wasn't too long after that that *Alley Oop* came out, and we did a double-take. And then another strip that I had done before getting together with Joe — I worked with another artist through the mails — was called *The Time Crusaders*. It was about some fellows who travelled around in a time machine and had adventures in the past and future. I presented it, and not too long after that, *Brick Bradford* came out.

JOE SHUSTER: One of the first comic strips we ever did together was called *Interplanetary Police*.

JERRY SIEGEL: It was one of our first strips — perhaps the very first. I really can't give you too much detail, except that, as the title suggests, it was about the adventures of the police in the distant future, with the adventures taking place on various worlds. Something funny in connection with it: I submitted it to United Feature Syndicate. Joe and I waited breathlessly. Then one day we got a letter in the mail, and it said United Feature Syndicate on it, and my heart started pounding, and I opened it. There was a real short letter, and the first line was: "Congratulations!" And I thought, "Boy, we've made it." Then what was the rest of the letter? "This is an interesting strip, but we can't use it" — something like that, which was quite a letdown. But we did various other strips.

JERRY BECK (animation historian and author): Being in comic strips was a big deal in the teens, the '20s, the '30s and the '40s. People not only knew the strips, but looked forward to them, followed them feverishly, they knew who wrote and who drew them and those people were *stars*. And the people who had successful comic strips made *a lot* of money. As a result, most cartoonists were aspiring to have a newspaper comic strip, as did Siegel and Shuster.

JERRY SIEGEL: Another early strip that Joe and I did was called *Snoopy and Smiley*. It was a comedy strip *a la* Laurel and Hardy or Charlie Chaplin or Lord knows what. It didn't sell. Around this time, I contacted J. Allen St. John, who had done all the illustrations for the *Tarzan* books, and I worked up with him in my script something called *Rex Carson of the Ether Patrol*. His drawings were very nice. It was submitted around, nothing happened to it, and eventually it just got lost over the years.

JERRY BECK: So comic books began as reprints of the comic strips, but then they started to do *new*, original comics. The thinking at the beginning was, "Let's get these aspiring cartoonists and their ideas out there." Obviously to our eyes, all these decades later, these originals were pretty poor and they were poorly drawn. They were really nothing but the phenomenon of being able to buy new comics without having to wait until the Sunday newspapers and the color section. The opportunity to buy new, original comics started in 1935, '36, '37.

JERRY SIEGEL: Right around this time, Joe and I started our fanzine *Science Fiction*, where I did the first Superman story I ever wrote, and Joe did the first Superman illustration that he ever did. It was called "The Reign of the Super-Man" and I wrote it under the pseudonym of Herbert S. Fine, which was a combination of the names of one of my cousins and my mother's maiden name. Joe did the illustrations for it. That's where National came in.

PETER SANDERSON: The idea of a "Superman" was not entirely without precedent. The word was popularized in the 19th century by the German philosopher Friedrich Nietzsche, although his concept of superior human beings did not entail actual superhuman powers. From Nietzsche the playwright George Bernard Shaw picked up the term and used it early in the 20th century in the title of his great play *Man and Superman*. But the idea of a superhumanly powerful hero goes back to the dawn of human history. One of the earliest known works of literature, the *Sumerian Epic of Gilgamesh*, concerns just such a "superman." The Old Testament gives us Samson, who was strong enough to pull down an entire temple, killing his enemies. Heroes with extraordinary physical strength can be found throughout the world's legends, perhaps most notably Hercules in Greek and Roman mythology.

MARK WAID: Philip Wiley's *Gladiator* with Hugo Danner was a huge influence; Doc Savage too, but to a lesser degree. In 1933 Siegel and Shuster first pitched Superman, so it had been sitting in Siegel's head for a long time. Siegel did that story in his fanzine *Science Fiction*, and that story was very Hugo Danner if you asked the question, "What if Hugo Danner was a total villain?"

PETER SANDERSON: The title character was Bill Dunn, a homeless man who was endowed with telepathic powers. Dunn sought to use his new powers to take over the world, but was thwarted when they proved to be only temporary. This Super-Man has more in common with the larger-than-life villains to be found in the films of the German director Fritz Lang, such as Dr. Mabuse or Rotwang in the silent movie *Metropolis* — the title of which suggests that Lang influenced Siegel and Shuster.

TOM ANDRAE: Jerry himself said the influences were Hercules and Samson. He said that of the night in 1934 when he created the final version of Superman.

So it was the strong-man figure from ancient times, Douglas Fairbanks, Zorro, Robin Hood — *a lot* of film influences. Newspaper strips like *Flash Gordon*, *Tarzan* and many others. Superman is far different than *Gladiator* and people do confuse the two, but that doesn't mean it wasn't a huge influence. I make that distinction; that you can be a huge influence and still be incredibly different. Superman is *not Gladiator* with a cape and tights. Not by any means.

PETER SANDERSON: Other larger-than-life heroes emerged through pulp novels or radio dramas: Doc Savage, with his amazing athletic abilities and genius-level intelligence; crime fighters like The Shadow, whose true identity remained a mystery. Early science fiction conjured up images of alien civilizations on other planets, or in the case of Philip Wylie's short story "Gladiator," a young man who possessed extraordinary physical strength and speed. Some would say that the first superhero was actually The Phantom, from Lee Falk's comic strip; a crusader based in the jungle who wore the kind of skin-tight costume that we now associate with such characters. But The Phantom had no actual superpowers and seems more like a traditional figure between the pulp heroes and the comic book superheroes still to come.

JERRY SIEGEL: A couple of months after I published this story, it occurred to me that a Superman as a hero rather than a villain might make a great comic strip character in the vein of Tarzan, only more super and sensational than that great character. What led me into conceiving Superman? Listening to President Roosevelt's "fireside chats," being unemployed and worried during the Depression and knowing hopelessness and fear; hearing and reading of the oppression and slaughter of helpless, oppressed Jews in Nazi Germany; seeing movies depicting the horrors of privation suffered by the downtrodden; reading of gallant, crusading heroes in the pulps; seeing equally crusading heroes on the screen in feature films and movie serials (often pitted against malevolent, grasping, ruthless madmen). I had the great urge to help the despairing masses somehow. But how could I help them when I could barely help myself? Superman was the answer.

PETER SANDERSON: In 1933, Siegel and Shuster reused the name "Superman," this time without the hyphen, for a new character; a heroic crime fighter, whom they created for the brand new medium of comic books. This Superman had superpowers and was considerably handsomer than the bald "Super-Man," but still had no real costume. They wrote and drew a whole comics story, "The Superman: A Science Fiction Story in Cartoons," but were unable to find a publisher.

JERRY SIEGEL: Joe and I drew it up as a comic book — this was in early 1933. We interested a publisher in putting it out, but then he changed his mind, and that was the end of that particular version of *Superman* — called *The Superman.* Practically all of it was torn up, by the way. Joe got very upset and tore it up and threw away most of it.

JOE SHUSTER: We saved the cover. The rest of the drawings were a crude version of Superman. It wasn't really Superman: That was before he evolved into a costumed figure. He was simply wearing a T-shirt and pants; he was more like Slam Bradley [another Siegel and Shuster collaboration] than anything else — just a man of action. But we called him *The Superman.* That was the second time we used the name, but the first time it was used for a character of goodwill. I'm a perfectionist, and I think the fact that the drawings had been turned down made me want to tear them up. I simply destroyed them. I said, "If we ever do it again, I'm going to redo it properly." It was a very low period for us.

MARK WAID: Jerry Siegel wrote an unpublished autobiography, which helps to flesh him out in his own words. Here's a guy who, clearly, was looking for a champion on several levels. First off, he's a puny, high school kid who's picked on. He's the Jewish kid in an area that is *not* heavily Jewish. And then his father dying as a result of a robbery — it doesn't take a genius to draw a line between that and a champion of the oppressed and weak. I'm sure he was looking for *something.*

BRAD RICCA: I would eventually come to the realization, which I never suspected or would have guessed, that Superman basically begins as kind of a memoir, kind of a semi-autobiographical comic that they put all their trauma into; they put the death of his father in there and all of a sudden it becomes this really interesting, layered, totally different thing. Rocketed from the planet Krypton, Kal-El becomes Superman — that's all there, and that part's awesome, but this is *art.* They were putting all their personal experiences into this guy with his underwear on the outside. There's just a huge appreciation for what they did and for the character.

That concept of Superman, which would hew much closer to the character that would be introduced to the world four years later, reportedly came to Siegel one night in 1934 when the idea was to present Superman in the form of a syndicated newspaper comic strip.

BRAD RICCA: When I decided to write *Super Boys,* it came from the question of how Siegel and Shuster did it. If you take just one step back from the character, it's so strange and weird-looking. Where's this all coming from? I really wanted to know how they created the first superhero, and I believe he absolutely *is* the first superhero. So it started for me in the beginning that I was in kind of disbelief, and by the end I just wanted to know the "recipe."

JERRY SIEGEL: I was up late one night and more and more ideas kept coming to me, and I kept writing out several weeks of syndicate scripts for the proposed newspaper strip. When morning came, I had written several weeks of material and I dashed over to Joe's place and showed it to him.

JOE SHUSTER: That was one very important day in our lives. We just sat down, and I worked straight through. I think I had brought in some sandwiches to eat, and we worked all day long.

PETER SANDERSON: This time, all the familiar elements fell into place. Siegel made him an alien from another world with superhuman powers. Shuster gave him a colorful costume, complete with the "S" emblem and cape. And when he was not fighting crime, they gave him a secret identity, Clark Kent, who would pretend to be as timid and ineffectual as the Pimpernel and Zorro did in their off hours.

BRAD RICCA: I came to realize that the recipe for Superman was a Frankenstein's Monster. They just took all these pieces from everywhere, including their own lives. Lois is the girl who never looks at him in class, and then the sports and physical fitness issues — all of these different things and they just create this creature that is so weird to look at, but it all kind of makes sense in the end.

JERRY SIEGEL: Of course, Joe had worked on that earlier version of Superman, and when I came to him with this new version of it, he was immediately sold. And when I saw the drawings that were emerging from his pencil, I almost flipped. I knew he had matured a great deal since he had done *The Superman*, and I thought he was doing a great job on the new art.

JOE SHUSTER: I was caught up in Jerry's enthusiasm, and I started drawing as fast as I could use my pencil. My imagination just picked the concept right up from Jerry. We worked very closely. At the beginning, he would sit down next to me at the drawing board. We would sit side by side: It was a real collaboration. He would have his script, and he would describe the scene to me. First he would read the scene to me, and I would absorb it and visualize it. And he'd say, "That's just what I had in mind" or "Let's make a few changes here." He would even describe the positions of Superman he wanted and how the character would act; it was almost like a movie scenario. He did almost everything except draw it — he really visualized everything for me, and I picked it up.

BRAD RICCA: Joe Shuster took a lot of stuff from boxing and physical fitness, the strong men. Other people have pointed out that they have the boots like Superman, and then the boxers and wrestlers would wear their shorts on the outside. And the cape from strong men too. Like Jerry with the writing, he just pulled from a bunch of different places and said, "This looks cool, right?" I mean, that's how kids — okay, they weren't kids at this point — but that's how people starting out in creating something, that's how it works. You pick from the things that you like and kind of put it all together.

JOE SHUSTER: Jerry was one of the first I can remember — at least in the comic books — who really used the style of a screenwriter. He would describe each scene, and the shot used — long shot, medium, close-up, overhead shot. It was marvelous. I guess he evolved the technique for himself, because we were both movie buffs. He would study the techniques of the movie serials, but he never saw a written screenplay.

TOM ANDRAE: When I interviewed Siegel and Shuster, they hadn't talked about Superman for years in any kind of depth. They got *so* excited. I mean, I felt like I was right there with them back when they were creating it. All that excitement came back to them and they were *exuberant*. And it was wonderful to hear that. Jerry is characterized as being angry and all that, but he loved writing. He'd always wanted to be a writer, so there's more to him than just the anger or drama.

JERRY SIEGEL: Clark Kent grew not only out of my private life, but also out of Joe's. As a high-school student, I thought that someday I might become a reporter, and I had crushes on several attractive girls who either didn't know I existed or didn't care I existed. As a matter of fact, some of them looked like they *hoped* I didn't exist. It occurred to me: What if I was real terrific? What if I had something special going for me, like jumping over buildings or throwing cars around or something like that? Then maybe they would notice me.

That night when all the thoughts were coming to me, the concept came to me that Superman could have a dual identity, and that in one of his identities he could be meek and mild, as I was, and wear glasses, the way I do. The heroine, who I figured would be a girl reporter, would think he was some sort of a worm; yet she would be crazy about this Superman character who could do all sorts of fabulous things. In fact, she was real wild about him, and a big inside joke was that the fellow she was crazy about was also the fellow whom she loathed. By coincidence, Joe was a carbon copy of me.

JOE SHUSTER: I was mild-mannered, wore glasses, was very shy with women.

Also occurring around this time was the creation of the Lois Lane character and some additional locking down of Superman himself.

PETER SANDERSON: Lois Lane was there right from the beginning. A feisty, aggressive career woman, Lois has much in common with various female roles in movies of the '30s and '40s, such as the woman reporter in *His Girl Friday*. The very first storyline set up the classic "triangle" between Lois and Superman's two identities: Enthralled by Superman, she disdains Clark Kent, unable to see past his ordinary façade. In the early stories, by the way, Clark was not always so "mild-mannered" — he often acted as a crusading investigative reporter, but it was the more familiar shy and timid Kent persona that eventually stuck. Siegel based the Lois character on Lois Amster, a girl he had once had a crush on, while Shuster used a young woman named Joanne Carter as a visual model for Lois.

JOANNE (CARTER) SIEGEL (wife of Jerry Siegel, model for Lois Lane): When I met them, I was struck by Joe's age. We met during the Great Depression. I was just a teenager, and my father was out of work, so in order to have any spending money, I had to earn my own. I found that no one would hire me, because I had no skills or training, and even grown people were having trouble getting jobs. I had read an article about modeling and I thought maybe I could get away with that. So I practiced various poses in front of a mirror, and I put an ad in the *Cleveland Plain Dealer* in the Situation Wanted column, advertising myself as a model, and Joe happened to see it. We corresponded, and he signed all his letters "Mr. Joseph Shuster," so I thought he was an older man. We set up an appointment at his apartment, where he lived with his parents, brother and sister. I went there on a Saturday afternoon, because I was going to school during the week. I was so nervous, because I thought he was going to say I was too young.

It was a freezing cold day, and I was absolutely frozen by the time I got there, because I lived on the other side of town. I pounded on the door and it opened a little bit, and I saw a young boy on the other side, and I said, "I'm the model that Mr. Shuster is expecting." He said, "Come on in," and we got to talking. I asked if I could leave my coat on, because I was still cold. Right away we got excited, we were talking about not only the weather but movies and everything. Finally, I said, "Does Mr. Shuster know that I'm here?" and he said, "I'm Mr. Shuster." That was the way we met.

We went in the back and I posed for him that day; I posed for him every Saturday after that. When I came out to the living room, Jerry was waiting to meet me, because he knew I was going to be coming. I was absolutely astounded with his energy — talk about super-energy! He was sitting on a chair, his feet were going, he was flipping through magazines, anxiously waiting to meet me. We hit it off just great. Then we found that we had all been on our school papers, so we felt that we had a real common bond there. I was at a different school, but I had been on my school paper, and I had wanted to be a girl reporter, so I was very thrilled that I was posing as a girl reporter. Joe was redrawing the strip, and it was going to be more realistic, rather than cartoony. I used to model for him every Saturday until he had enough drawings. He made so many stock drawings that it got to a point where he didn't need any more.

JOE SHUSTER: To me, she *was* Lois Lane.

JOANNE SIEGEL: We became such good friends by that time that we decided we would always stay friends. I did a lot of travelling but kept in touch with Joe; we corresponded, I did a lot of modeling in Boston after that, but the job with Joe was my first modeling job. I posed for a lot of painters and illustrators in Boston and Provincetown and New York — and some photographers in New York. I never did fashion modeling; I never was tall enough. I wanted to grow more, but this is as high as I got.

JOE SHUSTER: She was a great inspiration for me. She encouraged me, she was very enthusiastic about the strip; it meant a lot to me.

JOANNE SIEGEL: Many times he used to write to me and say that he was about to give up on it, and I'd say, "Keep at it and you'll make it." I had such a feeling about the strip and about them. I told him, "You're going to be very famous someday." But Jerry was the brains behind Lois. People get the word "model" confused: there's the model that's an inspiration and the model that poses. I was the model that posed; he thought of Lois Lane before I came on the scene.

JERRY SIEGEL: So in the artwork, Joe was able to translate it; and he wasn't just drawing it, he was *feeling* it. From there, the shy reporter with glasses came out of our own personal lives. Of course we loved Douglas Fairbanks as Robin Hood, and that influenced both of us: me in the writing and Joe in the art. I'm sure that subliminally we remembered Rudolph Valentino in *The Sheik*, and the tremendous romantic appeal to women of a guy in costume.

JOE SHUSTER: Jerry and I always felt that the character of Superman was enjoying himself. He was having fun; he wasn't taking himself seriously. It was always a lark for him, as you can see in my early drawings. His costume was inspired by the costume pictures that Fairbanks did. They greatly influenced us. He did *The Mark of Zorro* and *Robin Hood* and a marvelous one called *The Black Pirate*. Those are three that I recall that we loved. Fairbanks would swing on ropes very much like Superman flying, or like Tarzan on a vine. Before I ever put anything on paper, Jerry and I would talk back and forth. Jerry would say, "Well, how about this, or how about that, or how about doing him like this?" And I agreed on the feeling of action as he was flying or jumping or leaping — a flowing cape would give it movement. It really helped, and it was very easy to draw. I also had classical heroes and strongmen in mind, and this shows in the footwear. In the third version, Superman wore sandals laced halfway up the calf. You can still see this on the cover of *Action #1*, though they were covered over in red to look like boots when the comic was printed.

Jerry and I discussed the S symbol in detail. We said, "Let's put something on the front." I think initially we wanted to use the first letter of the character's name. We thought S was perfect. After we came up with it, we kiddingly said, "Well, it's the first letter of Siegel and Shuster." Progressively, as the strip evolved, the emblem became larger and larger; you'll notice at the beginning it was quite small.

The notion of Superman coming from another planet resulted from Siegel's idea of reversing the normal concept of a human going to another world, but there were a number of influences on the character's creation and the names given to specific things within the mythos.

JOE SHUSTER: Jerry created all the names. We're great movie fans and were inspired a lot by the actors and actresses we saw.

JERRY SIEGEL: I don't think John Carter of Mars had much influence on me when I wrote *The Reign of the Super-Man*. However, when I did the version in 1934, the *John Carter* stories *did* influence me. Carter was able to leap great distances because the planet Mars was smaller than the planet Earth; and he had great strength. I visualized the planet Krypton as a huge planet, much larger than Earth; so whoever came to Earth from that planet would be able to leap great distances and lift great weights.

TOM ANDRAE: Siegel wanted to be another Edgar Rice Burroughs, so Tarzan and John Carter *were* big influences.

BRAD RICCA: The visual side of Superman is the different thing, but for the idea of the character, it's definitely those pulp stories and definitely John Carter, because he liked that and he read pulp fiction religiously. That's what he wanted to be, a pulp writer, and the first Superman story is a total rip-off of a pulp story. Everyone says, "Oh, Superman is *Gladiator*," but I don't think Jerry even *read Gladiator*, but he definitely read John Carter and you can see in that first page where it explains the lighter gravity — I forget the wording, but there's him leaping and there's John Carter with the exact same kind of power set on a different planet. Except Jerry does the genius thing and he *reverses* it in that instead of the guy going to Mars, the alien comes to Earth. I love John Carter, he's a terrific character, but Jerry takes it and makes it even more interesting.

MICHAEL D. SELLERS (author, *John Carter and the Gods of Hollywood*): I think Siegel and Shuster acknowledged that there was a pretty big influence in that they kind of inverted John Carter. I mean, the concept of John Carter gaining superpowers because of the lower gravity on Mars definitely influenced their thought processes about Superman. And initially Superman couldn't fly; that came later. But beyond that core premise of a guy coming from another planet and gaining superpowers by virtue of things like gravitational pull, the characterizations of Superman and Clark Kent didn't feel very Burroughs.

TIM DEFOREST: Jumping back to the newspaper comic strips, which birthed comic books, you had a few costumed heroes — the Phantom would be the one that jumps to mind — but Superman's costume was unique at the time. I can't think of an earlier example of a costumed hero who looked that overtly unique. A lot of them didn't even have costumes; The Shadow had his cloak and hat, but again, outside of the Phantom, Superman may have been one of the first overtly-costumed ones. And his really was a unique image.

PETER SANDERSON: Siegel and Shuster had worked up several weeks' worth of "Superman" comic strips, but once again, were unable to talk anyone into publishing the strip. Apparently realizing they had perfected the concept, they did not change it further over the four years they tried in vain to sell Superman to newspaper syndication.

JERRY SIEGEL: We prepared one week of daily strips, the art for which was completely inked. These strips, sufficient for a six-day newspaper run, were in all respects ready for reproduction and ultimate publication. We also prepared three additional weeks of Superman newspaper comic strip material. These differed from the first week's material only in that the art work, dialogue and the balloons in which the dialogue appeared had not been inked, a step essential for reproduction. In all other respects, the additional three weeks of strips were ready for publication. In all material, the characters were drawn and the story continuity and dialogue were set. In addition, I prepared a synopsis of the story continuity appearing in the three weeks of penciled daily strips, because we did not want to risk the loss of all the art work we had done, either through the mails or a failure to return it. The synopsis was sent to prospective out-of-town newspaper syndicates and publishers, in the lieu of three weeks of penciled strips, together with the first week of inked strips. All of this had been done more than three years before Joe Shuster and I had any contact with Detective Comics Inc.

TOM ANDRAE: If you look at the strip, it's very well done, but part of the problem they had was they went to the wrong venue with Superman. Comic books were a very new medium at the time, or in 1933 when they created Superman. They worked on the comic strip version in 1934 and tried to get it published as a newspaper comic strip. That was a more sophisticated medium than the comic books, and you had fine draftsmen working there; people like Raymond with *Flash Gordon*, you've got Foster with *Tarzan*, *The Phantom* and others. Newspaper comic strips had a sophisticated readership. Their Superman had a real child-like quality to it and appealed to children particularly. So I think it was the wrong venue.

JERRY SIEGEL: When Joe and I first got together, we did attempt to prepare and sell newspaper strips, but they failed to sell. When I saw this publication *Detective Dan*, it occurred to me that we could get up an even more interesting comic book character than that other strip, which seemed to be a takeoff on *Dick Tracy*.

PETER SANDERSON: They began creating new characters and series for the comic books published by National Periodical Publications. None of these new creations were "superheroes," but in their own way a number of them are charming and memorable. For example, *Detective Comics* featured *Slam Bradley*, a two-fisted detective inspired by comic strip artist Roy Crane's *Captain Easy*; and the series *Spy*, which teamed a male secret agent with a female one who seems to anticipate Lois Lane in her feistiness. Perhaps more significantly, however, was their *Doctor Occult*, a detective resembling Dick Tracy who began investigating the supernatural in the pages of the now-defunct *More Fun Comics* in 1935. In one notable storyline, Occult dons a costume to battle mystical enemies, thus becoming DC's first costumed hero.

JERRY SIEGEL: The Superman material was taken by us to a number of prospective purchasers. It is *not* true that the property was uniformly rejected. In 1935, Malcolm Wheeler-Nicholson, a publisher of comic books, expressed interest in Superman and tried to persuade us that the property would be more successful if published in comic book form where it would be seen in color, than it would be in a black-and-white daily strip. Our experience with him had been such that we did not consider him the publisher to entrust with the property and his proposal was rejected.

NICKY WHEELER-NICHOLSON: A lot of people think of the early comics as being done by young guys, but there was a combination of young guys and older guys. My grandfather was in his '40s when he started the comics. Jerry Siegel knew about my grandfather; I think he saw an ad looking for writers and Jerry was so smart, because he knew even at an early age what was going to appeal to my grandfather. So he sent him a comic that my grandfather said, "Okay, I'll take it," and it was *Doctor Occult, Ghost Detective*. It's some of Jerry and Joe's best work. Joe was in really good form then; he wasn't having the problems with his eyesight that he would have, so his artwork is just absolutely lovely. The stories are fun and great to read. The other one that Jerry sent that my grandfather really loved was about a swashbuckler, because my grandfather had written a number of pulp swashbucklers. So I thought that was very clever of Jerry Siegel; it showed some real savvy, even at an early age.

My feeling is that my grandfather saw the potential that was there for Jerry and Joe, and he nurtured them along. He also knew to be very subtle in the way that he would critique them, because Jerry Siegel had a very big ego. That's not detrimental. Good for him, because that's what pushed him forward. I feel like he encouraged them really well.

In elaborating on her praise for Siegel's intuition, she notes that her grandfather had written a letter in which he offered Siegel the character of Slam Bradley, stating what he looked like, how he should behave and the kind of adventures he should have.

NICKY WHEELER-NICHOLSON: But my grandfather was coming from that old school way of doing business, so he wasn't thinking, "Oh, this is mine." He was thinking, "Oh, this is a great idea and I think Jerry and Joe can do this." So he just gave it to them and they ran with it. They did a great job.

JERRY SIEGEL: When we broke into the field, we both indulged in what we thought was very experimental stuff. In the writing, I tried to incorporate what was so popular in the pulp field into the comics field. I used a great number of captions along with dialogue balloons, visualizing the way a pulp comic should be. I feel now that we were pioneering, and that much of the stuff that followed was influenced by the way we handled our very early work, like *Slam Bradley*, which was a dry run for Superman. Superman had already been created and we didn't want to give away the Superman idea, but we just couldn't resist putting into *Slam Bradley* some of the slam-bang stuff which we knew would be in Superman if and when we got Superman launched.

Cover of Action Comics *#1 from 1938 (© and TM DC Comics/Warner Bros. Discovery)*

NICKY WHEELER-NICHOLSON: Slam is very much the beginning where you start to see some of the characteristics of Superman. He looks very much like Superman, for one thing. His life was very adventuresome.

JOE SHUSTER: Jerry often says that *Slam Bradley* was really the forerunner of Superman, because we turned it out with no restrictions, complete freedom to do what we wanted; the only problem was that we had a deadline. We had to work very fast, so Jerry suggested that we save time by putting less than six panels to a page: four panels or three panels, and sometimes two panels. I think one day we just had one panel to a page. The kids loved it, because it was spectacular: I could do so much more. Later on, the editors stopped us from doing that; they said the kids were not getting their money's worth. But the actual character Slam Bradley was Jerry's idea. They wanted an action strip, and Jerry came up with the idea of a man of action with a sense of humor. The character had a devil-may-care attitude very much like that of Fairbanks Sr.'s Zorro. Still, he couldn't fly and he didn't have a costume.

PETER SANDERSON: Siegel and Shuster finally gained an ally in syndication editor Sheldon Mayer, who would go on to become a legendary editor and cartoonist at DC. Mayer was unable to persuade his superior, M.C. Gaines, to publish Superman as a comic strip, but Gaines sent the samples over to Vin Sullivan, an editor at DC, and it was Sullivan who eventually bought the series.

JERRY SIEGEL: In 1936 and 1937, Joe Shuster was doing the artwork and I was writing the continuity for several comic strips, two of which in 1937 appeared in *Detective Comics*. This arrangement called for the strips upon which we collaborated to be submitted to the publisher of *Detective Comics*, Mr. Wheeler-Nicholson, and we were paid by him. In 1937, Mr. Wheeler-Nicholson had an interest in Detective Comics. Toward the end of 1937, the publisher fell behind in its payments for the strips we supplied. Early in December of 1937, I received a letter from Mr. Liebowitz, who introduced himself as the half-owner and treasurer of Detective Comics. Mr. Liebowitz proposed that Detective Comics assume the publisher's obligation of paying the money due us for the strips we furnished for publication in *Detective Comics*. In return, he wanted us to sign a contract which would assure him of receiving art work and continuity for these specific features for a length of time to be agreed on.

KURT MITCHELL (author, *American Comic Book Chronicles: 1940-1944*): They started out working for Malcolm Wheeler-Nicholson on his books before the hostile takeover by Donenfeld and Liebowitz in '37. They went along for the ride and, of course, they continued to put all their hopes on placing Superman with a newspaper syndication service.

Siegel traveled to New York to sign the agreement for what was Slam Bradley *and* Spy. *From there he was told to return to Cleveland to get Shuster to sign the contracts and mail them back. As far as the duo were concerned, the contract was for those specific titles and not additional ones. That same month, Siegel wrote to MC Gaines and McClure Syndicate regarding a pair of potential comic strips,* Snoopy and Smiley *and* Reggie Van Twerp. *He also made mention of additional features sent to Detective Comics to see if they might be of interest as well.*

JERRY SIEGEL: In early 1938, Mr. Gaines informed me that it might be a good idea to furnish Detective with the *Superman* material I had left with him. To the best of my recollection, this consisted of the one week's supply of inked daily strips and three weeks of penciled strips. Mr. Gaines sought my permission to furnish this Superman material to Detective and I gave that permission. But we had no responsibility to Detective regarding Superman. We could well have ignored its requests and placed the property elsewhere. Indeed, we were under no obligation to submit it to Detective in the first place.

KURT MITCHELL: When it came to Superman, they finally gave in when MC Gaines recommended the Superman series to Ben Solomon, then the editor of DC, to be the lead-off spot for *Action Comics*. So they reluctantly sold that first continuity, because they wanted to do Superman. It was the strip they really wanted to put all their time and energy into, and they took the chance they got.

PETER SANDERSON: Considering Siegel and Shuster's extreme difficulties in finding a publisher for Superman, and that no one could possibly have imagined how popular and profitable the character would become, it should not be surprising that they sold all the rights to DC. This was, after all, standard procedure in those days, and besides, for a long time afterwards DC paid Siegel and Shuster's studio to produce Superman stories for them.

KURT MITCHELL: If you come right down to it, DC was under no obligation to allow them to do all the work on the Superman material. They sort of made that point when they let Jack Burnley, the pseudonym for Hardin J. Burneley, draw a number of stories. He drew the cover for *World's Fair Comics* number two, which was the first cover to feature Superman with Batman and Robin, in 1940; and did uncredited artwork for *Action Comics* until 1947.

JULIAN VILAJ (writer, *The Joe Shuster Story*): Siegel and Shuster definitely didn't negotiate the best contract; they basically just signed the check and that was it. However, shortly after that they were already having doubts. And they tried to renegotiate after the fact, because nobody anticipated this success. Obviously *they* believed in Superman, and they shopped it around, but after so many nos, they were just thankful that somebody said "yes."

KURT MITCHELL: They didn't really see what was going to happen when they sold away all rights to the character. They were thinking strictly in terms of this being guaranteed income for a while. And it didn't make them a lot of money; certainly not as much as it made Donenfeld and Liebowitz, who became millionaires because of Superman. But it did allow Shuster and Siegel to support their families in the manner through which they wanted to accustom themselves: comfortable, middle-class lives. The irony is that if they had succeeded in placing the property with a small syndication service, they probably wouldn't have made it. There wouldn't have been the push or public presence of being out on newsstands instead of tucked away in a newspaper somewhere. That cover of *Action Comics* number one — if I'd been a kid in 1938 and saw that cover, I wouldn't have been able to keep my hands off of it.

Shortly after Superman made his debut in the pages of Action Comics *number one, published in April 1938, but cover-dated to June, the rest of the country, and eventually the rest of the world, would come to recognize the Man of Steel as one of the great pop culture creations of all time.*

JULIAN VILAJ: The success was totally a surprise to everyone. Even the publishers were trying to figure out what sells. You know, "Why is this *Action Comics* selling?" Superman wasn't on the cover for a few of the following issues, because they weren't sure what it was. They even did a survey asking people, "What did you like?" and it was Superman. So even though they were ultimately well-compensated, obviously they saw that the publisher made much more money and looked at this as an American Greed story.

TIM DEFOREST: Bottom line, it was work for hire where you sold the rights to your character for a set amount of money. At the same time, I think it's fair to make an argument that when DC started cleaning up — because it was merchandising, the movie cartoons, a novel in 1942 — and when printing Superman was the same as printing money, you can make an argument that they had a moral responsibility to maybe give bonuses to Siegel and Shuster. But legally, as far as I know, it was all on the up and up. And it *is* fair to criticize DC for not treating their creative people better. The situation was standard throughout the industry, but it's just good business, when you're making money, to treat your vital workers better and give them better pay, bonuses and all that. You can criticize the corporate side of DC legitimately just for being stingy, but it was not an overtly illegal thing to do work for hire as standard and not wrong in and of itself.

MARC TYLER NOBLEMAN (writer, *Boys of Steel: The Creators of Superman*): I've been a Superman fan since I could read, maybe even earlier. When I grew up and became a writer, I knew it was only a matter of time before my childhood passion — which I never gave up — and my job would overlap. I felt like the Siegel and Shuster story was a really important one to tell, not just for comics fans, but for anyone, especially kids, because it's about two guys that really weren't good at anything and were used to failing and used to being ignored. And *then* they succeeded beyond their wildest expectations. But it wasn't a happy ending, unfortunately.

CHAPTER II
Superman Arrives

Superman first appeared on the cover of Action Comics #1, *cover-dated June 1938, the interior story consisting of the sample comic strips from four years earlier, rearranged into comic book format. It was an immediate sensation, though National was slow to recognize that fact, not really a surprise given that they had entered unknown territory. As far as they knew, the issue's success could have been attributed just as much to Chuck Dawson, Zatara Master Magician, South Sea Strategy, Stick-Mitt Stimson, The Adventures of Marco Polo, Pep Morgan, Scoop Scanlan the Five Star Reporter, Tex Thompson or Stardust as to Superman.*

JERRY BECK (author, *Of Mice and Magic: A History of American Animated Cartoons*): National wasn't sure just why *Action* was such a success, and obviously we know that they didn't think much of Superman initially, because the character is not on the cover for several more issues until they get sales results in and Superman proves himself to be a phenomenon. And that success does two things: It really jump-starts the idea of superheroes and even more so, the industry of comic books.

PETER SANDERSON (comic historian, author, *The Marvel Vault: A Visual History*): By the following year, *Action*'s circulation had risen to half-a-million copies, and it soon doubled. Superman shared *Action* with other characters, but his amazing popularity won him his own solo comic book, *Superman*, in the summer of 1939, only a year after his debut. Moreover, imitation was the sincerest form of flattery. Not only DC, but other comics companies quickly tried to duplicate Superman's success, and within the next several years, scores of superheroes emerged in his wake. The year 1939 alone saw the first appearance of Batman at DC, the original Captain Marvel at Fawcett Comics and the original Human Torch and Sub-Mariner in *Marvel Comics* #1. This period from 1938 until around 1951 is known by comic aficionados as The Golden Age of Comics, the first great period of the superhero genre.

MARK EVANIER (writer, comic historian): *Action Comics* #1 was phenomenally well-received. It is still the greatest success story in the history of comics. Some people at DC claim that they knew it from the start. It is said that Mr. Donenfeld, the publisher, was the last one to pick up on this. When he saw the first cover, he thought it was outrageous and that the book wouldn't sell. He had ordered subsequent issues to not feature Superman so prominently; so Superman was on the cover of *Action Comics* number one, but he was not on the cover of

Action numbers 2, 3, 4 or, I think, six. There's a lead time in doing comics. By the time number-one hits the stands — actually, by the time you get some distributor or retailer re-action to a comic — you've already got the next three or four issues well under way or off to the printer. Su-perman was the best-selling comic book of its time, of the earlier 1940s. Superman immediately was featured in other media. They immediately spun off a solo comic book called *Superman*, completely comprised of his adventures. He was the first character really honored that way. That was 1939.

In 1939, Superman became the first comic book character to get his own book (© and TM DC Comics/ Warner Bros. Discovery)

TIM DEFOREST (comic his-torian and author): The success of Superman is interesting to think about, because in a lot of major ways it wasn't doing anything original — he was influenced by pulp characters such as Doc Savage, and the idea of secret identities was there with Zorro as a guy who pretended to be meek and mild, but was actually awesome. But the visual component, the art, made it jump out at people even more so than it had in the pulp magazines; even more than it had in the comic strips, because you've got bigger panels and longer stories and color — which you only got on Sundays. So I think it was the graphic aspect of it that made it jump out; also, Superman's pow-ers, even though he was a lot less powerful then.

BRAD RICCA (author, *Super Boys: The Amazing Adventures of Jerry Siegel and Joe Shuster*): Donenfeld had a license to do *Lone Ranger* stuff and he *loved* it, because it was like printing money. But he was *so* jealous of the the guy who owned the Lone Ranger empire, George Trindle. It was just one guy, so he made money whenever the Lone Ranger was in pulp magazines, radio, anything, and Donenfeld was just totally jealous of that, because he wanted that sort of con-trol. He thought this guy was a genius for having one character in all this type of media, and he lost the Lone Ranger license right before he signed Superman.

Now I don't know if it's true — I have no proof — but I always kind of thought that when he saw Superman and how quickly it took off from comics to newspapers, to radio — it was instant — did they have this in mind? Somebody should study that, because it's an open question. The old story goes that somebody brought it to him and they needed something for *Action Comics*, but the other argument is, why is it on the cover? If you didn't like it, why put it on the cover?

JERRY BECK: Superman and Bugs Bunny emerged right around the same time, not long before we got into World War II. Superman obviously comes out of the fantasies of Depression-era America and comes to represent the American spirit — truth, justice and the American way — and when we get involved in the war, it just happens to work out that way. But you have to remember that he's really a product of the Great Depression and he represents the enemies of the Big Bad Wolf in the same way that the Three Little Pigs did. In 1933, the animated *Who's Afraid of the Big Bad Wolf?* was a phenomenon and was being "held over." I have to explain to my students what that means, because they don't understand the phrase. I tell them there was no television, so cartoons, like comic strips, are things that were there one week and gone the next, replaced by a new one. Something like the Three Little Pigs was a sensation and played in movie theaters for well over a year, with people reading into it as the Wolf representing the Great Depression and the pigs representing them. Well, I think the same thing happened with Popeye. The character of Popeye also represented that every man versus the people against us. And Superman became the ultimate version of that by 1939. So our heroes went from the Three Little Pigs to Popeye to Superman.

MARC TYLER NOBLEMAN (writer, *Boys of Steel: The Creators of Superman*): The arrival of Superman was seismic. Part of it was timing; it was coming right on the cusp of two major crises, the Depression and World War II. It was a simpler time in some sense or a less overstimulated time, so it was much easier then for a single character to become very famous, very quickly, to a large percentage of people. Whereas now it's much more segmented. And Superman did represent hope. That's a rose-colored glasses-type of thing to say, but he did. I tried to write about that in my book without being glib or disrespectful to people who were suffering, or the service people who were overseas. But like I said, he was a hero that we knew would always come home. He was reliable. He's fictional, so of course he's going to come back. It was also that he was so larger than life and the first real modern myth. The comic strip characters that came before him were just slices of him: Zorro, Tarzan, Buck Rogers. They all had something cool, but Superman had *everything* cool. I think it tapped into something that people needed, a balm to the realities of the world. That's a big part of why he took off as quickly as he did.

TIM DEFOREST: I cannot think of another hero from comics who had that level of pure power, and used that power — initially, when he didn't fight super-villains — to fight slumlords, street crime, and there was an emphasis on how corruption and crime hurt poor people in the lower class. As a result, he became their champion. *Those* are the elements that made him jump forward and just become the best-seller that he was.

RAY MORTON (film historian and author): He's pugnacious and enjoys messing with his opponents. This is a Superman with an attitude (and who is the perfect rejoinder to those who complain that the character is too milquetoast, too "goody-goody" and too much of a "Big Blue Boy Scout"). I also love the way the character was drawn in this era. Joe Shuster's initial pencils had a rough simplicity to them that really fit this first version of the character. As the character developed, Shuster's work became more refined, as did that of the staff artists who were help-ing draw the books and comic strips along with him. That rough simplicity of the early issues became more sophisticated and detailed in the manner of *Prince Valiant* and similar early adventure strips and books — it's a style that is more illustrative than cartoonish, as many of the more humorous strips were. I find this style to be incredibly appealing and appropriate for these energetic early adventures.

KURT MITCHELL: Boy, the response was volcanic. It changed the game. Flash forward to the first issue of *Superman*, which sold more copies than *Tiptop Comics, King Comics* and *Comics on Parade*, which were big-selling titles back then, combined. I think *Superman* number one was the first million-selling comic. *Action* was selling in the 500,000 to 700,000 range right from the start. Compare that to today's sales, and it's absolutely mind-boggling.

JERRY BECK: There were things in the air that were influences on Super-man, but you know what? Time and time again, it takes a creator or two to put it all together and compile it into something that became even bigger than those original things. Superman is one of them.

MARK WAID (writer, *Superman: Birthright*): It didn't take long for Su-perman to connect with the public. We've heard over and over again that *Action Comics* number one just sold out everywhere. Donenfeld went to newsstands and was told that it was the comic everybody was asking for, but when he first saw the cover, we are told that he thought it was awful: "I hate this cover, because nobody's ever going to believe this. It's just too wild; too completely out there. Don't put Superman on the cover." But if you look back at 1939 more so than 1938, it probably took six months or so for it to really get kicking into high gear.

BRAD RICCA: Nobody really knows why the character connected the way it did. There's always that anecdote that Harry Donenfeld went down to the newsstand and all the Superman issues were gone and the kids were demanding the comic with Superman. But that seems like *such* a story, but who knows? Sales records of the time are so sketchy. But if you kind of go with anecdotes, it's clear that it was a hit right away. You just look at that first cover and it's hard to kind of strip away the fact that we know who it is and how much it's worth. I always show it to people in comics classes who aren't Superman people, and have maybe never seen the cover before, but it is the image of Superman trashing this new car. And somebody in my class, and I'll never forgive myself because I don't remember who pointed this out, said, "Look at that dude in the corner, this guy who's running away from Superman," because we're talking about why the cover is, "that's your dad." I said, "You've got it; 100%, because this guy is running away from Superman." So every kid is running *towards* that comic, saying, "Here's my money!"

JERRY BECK: Part of it is his costume. For years I was against people calling it a costume; it's a *uniform*. Well, with all the jokes about him wearing his underwear on the outside, we've all seen earlier photos of circus strongmen who wear outfits like that, and that outfit was right out of the circus. But you look at that first cover: The colors are primary and they just attract our eye.

BRAD RICCA: Things were changing all over and it just hit at the right time. And it was big for them right away too. They knew it was big, and the other reason I can say that it was successful is *almost immediately* Jerry and Joe are like, "Can we have the copyright back?" DC, of course, says no, and that's just how it goes.

PETER SANDERSON: Superman's personality in his earliest stories would shock his later fans. *This* Superman is a ruthless vigilante who intentionally killed numerous criminals from 1938 into 1942 and threatened to murder even more. Not until 1943 did Superman adopt his code never to kill a human being under any circumstances. The early Superman stories dealt to a surprising degree in social commentary. It has been observed in the past that Superman had great appeal in the late 1930s as a hero to an America struggling out of the

Great Depression and headed towards World War II. And so the Superman of that time took on the enemies of the common man: not just gangsters and thieves, but also corrupt public officials, a munitions maker, a mine owner who endangered his employees and assorted warmongers.

CASE AIKEN (host, *Men of Steel* podcast): This was where we got the closest to the character having a real creator's viewpoint that wasn't weighed down by the history of the character. I love the current run of the book, but Superman is now more a brand first and then a story being told second. So that was an era where Siegel and Shuster got to really put out something that was *their* viewpoint on how a character with powers should act. It was also very new and a lot of things that we take for granted about comics, like the idea that there would be villains to fight, had to be built up to, including the idea that there could be more than one person with superpowers, period. Or the fact that there could be one person with superpowers. They actually had to sell it. In fact, the first page of *Action Comics* has a breakdown of how superpowers could happen: look at ants; look at grasshoppers.

ROB O'CONNOR (co-host, *All Star Superfan Podcast*): One story that always sticks out in my mind is the Golden Age Siegel/Shuster one in which Superman literally tears down a substandard slum tenement so that the city council is forced to rebuild it to code. I think it's important that we never lose sight of the fact that as fun as it is watching Superman pummel Metallo or Mongul, he was originally designed as a champion of the oppressed, the downtrodden man on the street. For all the whining on the Internet that superhero comics have become too political, Superman has always been the wokest who ever woked and it's baked right into his early DNA.

CASE AIKEN: What's remarkable is that Siegel and Shuster could convey to an audience and have the audience accept, and actually be down for, a superhero in a world that didn't have superheroes. They're like, "So there's a guy who can jump over a building, right?" It actually sounds crazy, doesn't it? So the Golden Age Superman really was defining what you could do with a character like that, because no one had really done that in a modern setting in that way. John Carter and the whole Mars setting is a fantasy. If you look at Samson or Hercules — all the things people point to when they talk about these really powerful figures who are doing these wonders or deeds, they're all in the past. Superman's here today; he's all of those myths *today*.

ROBERT GREENBERGER (writer, DC Comics Editor): Jerry really was looking out for stories that would be cathartic for him so he could work through his grief. But as the strip became more popular, first there was *Action*, then there was *Superman* and then the comic strip, then the *World's Finest* stories — all of a sudden he was just having to write *stories*. He had to come up with a wider variety of subject matter to cover, which is one reason why those early stories of social justice rapidly began to include mad scientists. There was just that demand for material every month.

CASE AIKEN: I think the Golden Age Superman is having a bit of a renaissance now. There's a lot of interest looking at the character as someone who is willing to work outside the system and make things better, even if the powers-that-be would prefer it not be better or would prefer to sweep things under the rug. The idea of the champion of the oppressed is really cool and kind of gets forgotten once we get to the '50s and it becomes more sci-fi and out there and weird. But it's definitely there in the comics and radio show and it's why Superman isn't a government agent. It's why he's not a cop; he's outside the system, because he's seeing it from an alien perspective and trying to make things better as he sees it. He'll stumble sometimes too, because he's super. He's still a man, but he's attempting to make the world a better place, and as he finds more information, he reassesses and reevaluates — which is how structure works, because he thinks one person's wrong and he'll go to save the day and finds out that there's more information that changes the story.

TIM DEFOREST: In part changes to Superman came because of World War II, where the attitude became, "Let's be patriotic!" As a side effect of that, there was going to be less emphasis on internal problems in the U.S., because we wanted everybody to want to beat the Nazis and the Japanese.

ROBERT GREENBERGER: It's when everybody made that patriotic shift; that was the seismic change in most publishing — certainly in comics for kids, where the idea was to get the kids on board to spread the "Gospel." And then you've got Superman, who is this incredibly popular character. Back then, when the phrase was truth and justice, everybody saw him as someone who needed to combat the Nazi menace.

KURT MITCHELL: Most of the stories still had him fighting for the little guy in one sense or another. By bringing down criminals, he's protecting the average person. And he does fight natural disasters, which affects the rich and poor alike. But he becomes very much more of an establishment man; more likely to toe the law-and-order line. He ended up, let's say, domesticated. Part of that has to do with the editorial advisory board DC began using in '42, which really softened the rough edges on all of these characters. That's why you saw things like the Spectre suddenly become the invisible stooge of a weirdo, nerd detective instead of the awesome demigod he had been. And why Dr. Fate suddenly only had half a helmet and started punching out crooks and making wisecracks instead of being this Lovecraftian sorcerer. It was all in the name of public relations. For Superman, it may have ensured the longevity of the character for many years.

TIM DEFOREST: In part, I think it was an inevitable storytelling thing that Superman's power, especially as he gradually became more powerful — he could fly instead of leap, his vision powers started to kick in and all of that — would require opponents that challenged him. So supervillains started to pop up.

KURT MITCHELL: Siegel was really reluctant to give them the kind of stories they wanted, because by the time you get to 1941 or '42, the editors are first Mort Weisinger and then Jack Schiff, both of whom come out of science fiction pulps before they went into comics. They had certain ideas about what was appealing and what wasn't, and they found the crime and civic corruption stories that Siegel wanted to do with Superman lacking. Then when Siegel got drafted, they saw their opportunity and they brought in Don Cameron and Alvin Shorts and Bill Finger, as well as several other writers, and let their imaginations loose. That's when we started seeing things like Toy Man and Mr. Mxyzptlk and science fiction-themed stories; even the occasional imaginary story, although they weren't calling them that back then.

MARK WAID: There was also a point where DC became much more hands-on in terms of what could or couldn't be done. What seems to have triggered that was that Siegel had written a 26-page story that established what was basically Kryptonite years before they did it in the radio show or the comics. In that story, Lois also learns Superman's secret identity permanently and they become partners against crime at that point. It clearly set up that this was the new status quo of the series and not something that's here one minute and forgotten the next. And at that point, as near as I can tell from doing my research, that's when DC editorial really stepped in hard for the first time and said, "Nope, you're not doing this." I understand DC's point of view — they had a good thing going, why change the status quo? But Siegel's attitude was, "This is the way things work in comic strips all the time. The characters age and transform." You could tell early on that Whitney Ellsworth and editorial were leaning pretty hard on Siegel and Shuster, but it was really this story — which was designed for *Superman* number seven — as near as I can tell, that made DC editorial go, "Okay, we need to keep a tighter reign on this."

TOM ANDRAE (comic historian, co–author, *Batman & Me*): Siegel and Shuster were losing control of Superman. I have a letter that Jerry wrote me where he describes some of that. DC turned the character in ways that Siegel and Shuster didn't really like. They wanted to stay with the original character as it was written, dealing with social issues, being a champion of justice and a compassionate figure. DC got afraid of that and said, "No more social issues." And that was that.

KURT MITCHELL: There was the problem that the stories had become very repetitive. Siegel was being shown up by the imagination shown by some of the competitors. Captain Marvel was just a wonderland of whimsy and fantasy. Even the Blue Beetle book — some of those stories are better than anything that was being published in the Superman titles at the time, both in terms of story and art.

GEOFFREY MARK (Silver Age Comic Book Historian): Times had changed. The depression was over. There was Jewish angst of those whose parents or grandparents came as refugees and living in squalor and living in slums and living in ghettos. Then the war happens and people refocus. After the war, things got better for everybody and they began to realize that they were running out of things for Superman to do. As evidenced by the George Reeves television series, it's almost a waste of his magnificent powers to be stopping jewel thieves. They needed bigger stuff. It wasn't long before his powers increased, he could travel into outer space and go to other worlds and break the time barrier. It began in the late '40s, but once Mort Weisinger had full control over the books about a decade later, that's when it *really* blossomed with all sorts of concepts.

PETER SANDERSON: A character with Superman's powers eventually demanded far more formidable and colorful adversaries than ordinary everyday criminals. And therefore, *Action* number thirteen, published in June 1939, introduced the first of Superman's "super villains," the Ultra-Humanite, who was a bald criminal scientist with superhuman intelligence — very much reminiscent of Siegel's original "Super-Man" character from his 1934 fanzine story. The strangest thing about the Ultra-Humanite was that his henchmen, finding him on the point of death in a later story, transplanted his brain into the body of a young actress named Dolores Winters. The Ultra-Humanite made his — or, rather, her — final Golden Age appearance early in 1940; perhaps Siegel felt that he had reached a dead end with the character. Instead, Siegel and Shuster gave Superman a new villain, who has retained the status of the Man of Steel's greatest nemesis ever since: Lex Luthor.

Despite how we perceive him today, in his debut in Action *number 23 from April 1940, Luthor had a full head of red hair, and instead of being a scientist, he was a provocateur doing his best to stir up war between two nations in Europe, his ultimate goal to plunge the entire continent into battle.*

PETER SANDERSON: This was also the same story that introduced the name of *The Daily Planet*. Considering when this story was written, it would appear that Siegel was acknowledging that Europe was on the brink of World War II; perhaps Luthor was originally intended to be an analogue of Hitler. Indeed, Luthor's goal in these early stories is to conquer the world, but Siegel changes him from a political Machiavellian into a criminal scientist. Interestingly, in *Superman* number five (summer 1940), Luthor triggers a second Great Depression, plunging America back into the poverty it was only just beginning to escape. From *Superman* #10 (May-June 1941) onward, Luthor is portrayed as entirely bald, and thus he had clearly taken over the role of the Ultra-Humanite, even visually. From this point onward, Superman's arch-foe would be, in effect his other self: the "Super-Man" renamed Lex Luthor.

Most of Superman's other principal 1940s foes were not super-powered like himself, but were tricksters trying to outsmart him. The Toyman was a middle-aged man who built enormous toys he employed as weapons. The Prankster looked like a roly-poly version of contemporary comedian Jerry Colonna and went in for schemes like trying to copyright the alphabet in order to extort money from everyone. And there was conman J. Wilbur Wolfingham, a W.C. Fields clone thinly disguised by his monocle. A standout, though, was the midget imp from the Fifth Dimension, Mister Mxyzptlk, who plagued Superman by playing pranks with his magical powers starting in *Superman* #30 (September-October 1944). Inexplicably, in 1959 his name changed to Mxyzptlk, and that spelling has stuck right into the present. By the way, for anyone interested, you pronounce that "Mix-Yez-Pitel-Ick." The only way to get rid of Mxyzptlk — and then only for 90 days — was to trick him into saying his name backwards. Luckily, Mxyzptlk has proven to be infinitely gullible.

TIM DEFOREST: As long as he was taking on crime lords and slumlords, he was never going to be challenged on a personal level. Especially in the graphic media, you needed villains who could add a cool factor to things visually. So you needed villains who could be a physical threat to him, but it was, again, also World War II and changing social conditions that altered him.

MARK WAID: Becoming a super-patriot during the war years happened, because it was expected that all pop culture characters would be strongly patriotic. But what happened after '45, after we won World War II, is that America began seeing itself as the world's policeman. That's just a sociological fact, and so, Superman mirrored that. Post-World War II is when Superman really became Super Cop and completely became an authority figure as opposed to a rebel in any way, shape or form. That's what really established Superman as an establishment figure — where he doesn't fight for the common man so much as he fights to keep the status quo alive, because we're Americans and we're perfect. It's very much where the view of him as the big blue Boy Scout started and he's completely your dad at this point. There's no law that Superman will not obey if it's on the books somewhere.

Although the basic concept of Superman was fully formed from Action #1 *onwards, many other familiar aspects of the Superman legend took years to develop. For example,* Action Comics #11 (April 1939) *established that Superman lived in Siegel and Shuster's own base of operations, Cleveland, Ohio. But only three issues later, his city was dubbed Metropolis, surely as an homage to Fritz Lang's movie. Moreover, as the years passed, it became increasingly clear that Metropolis was a fictional double of New York City. Moreover, originally Clark Kent worked for* The Daily Star, *edited by George Taylor. The name of the newspaper finally changed in 1942, strangely enough in the second part of a continuing story. Clark and Lois left* The Daily Star *in* Action #22 *to go to Europe, and when they returned in issue #23 it was* The Daily Planet. *There would also be an expansion of Superman's origin.*

PETER SANDERSON: *Action #1* gave only the briefest account of Superman's origin, stating that a scientist sent his infant son to Earth in a rocket when their native world "was destroyed by old age." Only a year later, though, in *Superman #1*, the planet was named Krypton, and rather than somehow expiring of old age, it met its end in a colossal explosion. The baby was adopted by the Kents, originally known as John and Mary, whose "love and guidance was to become an important factor in the shaping of the boy's future." They taught him to use his powers to assist humanity, but not until they died did he begin his adult career as Superman. In subsequent years, more details were added. Superman's parents were the brilliant scientist Jor-El and his wife Lara (originally called Jor-L and Lora), and Superman's original Kryptonian name was Kal-El. Jor-El was the one man who realized Krypton was about to explode, but was unable to persuade his people of their coming doom. As for the Kents, their names were changed to Jonathan and Martha and they were farmers living in the town of Smallville, which was eventually established as located in Kansas. Oddly, Superman did not discover he was an alien until 1949, when he traveled back through time and saw Jor-El, Lara and the destruction of Krypton.

In Action #1, it was explained that Superman had greater physical power than an Earthman just as "the lowly ant can support weights hundreds of times its own" and "the grasshopper leaps what to man would be the space of several city blocks." This is basically the same reasoning Stan Lee used decades later to explain why Spider-Man had the "proportional" strength and agility of a spider. But this is why Kryptonians had superpowers even on their native world. In the late 1940s, the comics instead began to argue that Kryptonians had no special powers on their own planet, but did on Earth because of its lesser gravity. That hardly explained Superman's powers like X-ray vision or flight, and in 1960 the principal source of the Man of Steel's powers is stated to be the radiation from Earth's yellow sun. Krypton, on the other hand, had a red sun.

PETER SANDERSON: As amazing as Superman's powers were when he first appeared in 1938, they seemed rather puny compared to what they were to become. According to *Action* #1, he could "leap 1/8th of a mile; hurdle a twenty-story building, raise tremendous weights, run faster than an express train and nothing less than a bursting shell could penetrate his skin." He had no X-ray vision or other special vision powers and, incredible as it may seem to today's readers, he couldn't fly. Instead, Superman covered vast distances by leaping, much as Marvel Comics' Hulk now does. It has been said that it was Max Fleischer's animated Superman cartoons that firmly established Superman's ability to fly, since the giant leaps tended to look silly. In the comics, Superman did not clearly begin to fly until late 1943.

On January 16, 1939, Jerry Siegel and Joe Shuster saw one of their fantasies come true when Superman finally made his debut as a newspaper comic strip from the McClure Syndicate, which had set it up in hundreds of newspapers across the country with a readership of over 20 million. Siegel would serve as writer until he was drafted into World War II in 1943, resulting in the strip being ghostwritten by DC editor Whitney Ellsworth, Jack Schiff and, from 1947 to 1958, Alvin Schwartz. The last would be Bill Finger from 1959 to the strip's end in 1966.

Joe Shuster was credited as artist, though, more and more, as a reflection of an ever-increasing workload and his own failing eyesight that slowed him down, he depended on artists from the art shop he'd created, among them Paul Cassidy, Leo Nowark and Wayne Boring, the latter of whom would become the prominent Superman artist in the '40s and '50s. Curt Swan and Stan Kaye would be among the last. The strip itself was enormously popular and would continuously run until 1966, playing no small part in the Man of

Steel's popularity and the wealth of Siegel and Shuster during that early era (for instance, in 1944 from the comics they made $19,272 while from the comic strip they made an additional $32,266).

ANTHONY TOLLIN (comics, pulps and old-time radio historian): DC ploughed a lot of the profits from their investment in the comics into things like Superman Day at the World's Fair and the Superman radio show. I don't know the actual figures, but I remember Paul Levitz being astounded when he found the original contracts for the newspaper strip with Siegel and Shuster. This was back in the '70s, but I remember Paul commenting that Siegel and Shuster were getting most of the income from the newspaper strip. Half the money would go to the syndicate, DC was taking a small percentage for doing the production and corrections and editorial, and the coloring and art corrections, on the strip. I have no way of knowing how that may have changed during World War II when Jerry was in the army, but most of the other 50% went to him and Shuster.

TIM DEFOREST: The newspaper strip ran for 25 years; I think it ended in 1966, so it certainly had a good run. It was an important part of the character's history, because it kept people, especially older people, reading his adventures. People used to age out of comic books. That doesn't happen as much now, because they're aimed more at adults, but they would still read the strip and some great stories were told. Often they were rewritten from the comic books, but they were still good. They were keeping Superman in the perceptions of adults as well as kids, which may have contributed to the longevity of the character.

STEVE YOUNIS (webmaster, supermanhomepage.com): At the time, being the great businessmen that they were behind the scenes — and I don't mean Jerry or Joe themselves — National began looking at all of the merchandising options. They created dolls and all these different things. And I guess the next big step for the character was to branch out into different mediums and, other than newspaper strips — which Jerry and Joe saw as being the pinnacle at that time — there would also be radio and so much more for Superman.

MARK WAID: The newspaper strip launch was a big part of Superman's success. His impact was like Beatlemania and Simpsonsmania rolled into one. He was just *everywhere* in an era where mass media wasn't very mass. Batmania in 1966 pales in comparison. He was a balloon in the Macy's Thanksgiving Day Parade, there was Superman Day at the 1939 New York World's Fair in 1940. Like I said, he was everywhere and, again, the newspaper strip more than the comics made him a household name. So you've got the radio show on your side, the newspaper strip and everybody outside of DC is wanting to make coin off of Superman, so the merchandise started really quickly.

ARLEN SCHUMER (comics historian, author, *The Silver Age of Comic Book Art*): Superman was the first multimedia property; the radio show is almost immediate, and then the Fleischer cartoons were almost as immediate. That's what makes Superman the success that he was, because it was kind of like Beatlemania or Bondmania, but decades earlier. If you look at how fast and all-encompassing Beatlemania was in 1964, and then there was the Elvis Presley explosion in the '50s, Sinatra and the Bobby Soxer — I'm trying to think of whenever there was something considered an "overnight success." From what we know of the public record, Superman was the equivalent, because not only did he jump-start other multimedia versions that nobody had ever really done, but he jump-started a whole industry. Wedding the superhero genre to the comic book medium itself was also pretty unique.

Even though the comic book storytelling form existed before Superman in the form of comic strips, the comic book itself had only recently been created in 1933. That fact also makes Superman unique. When you think about it, The Beatles did not come around when the phonograph was invented, they came way later. Superman debuts pretty much not too much longer after the physical artistic medium of comic books itself is created. So the dominance of the genre "superhero" was initially wedded to the medium itself. The fact that the superhero is still the dominant mainstream genre, the fact that all the movies and TV shows which come out of characters created 50, 60, 70 years ago, is still a testament to the dominance of the superhero. And yet, if you go into a modern bookstore, the few that are left, there are rows and rows of manga that aren't superhero-related at all. So, it's a weird dichotomy. But the bottom line is, I think what makes Superman unique as a pop culture, overnight success, are all those elements in the 20th century.

As part of the continually expanding world of the Man of Steel, and recognizing the popularity of radio dramas for kids and adults, National began exploring the format for Superman. The result was The Adventures of Superman, *which made its debut on February 12, 1940 and ended up running until March 1, 1951, with a total of 2,088 episodes produced. Syndicated around the country not long after its premiere, it usually ran in late afternoons for 15 minutes a day, typically at 5:15 p.m., 5:30 p.m. or 5:45 p.m. Like other radio shows, it presented its stories in serialized fashion rather than standalone tales to get people to tune in the next day. The show featured Bud Collyer in the dual roles of Clark Kent and Superman, with Joan Alexander as Lois Lane, Julian Noa as* Daily Planet *editor*

Perry White, Jackie Kelk and, later Jack Grimes, as Jimmy Olsen; plus Matt Crowley as both Inspector Henderson and frequent guest star Batman, Ronald Liss as Robin, Ned Weaver as Jor-El and Bewitched's *Agnes Moorehead as Lara.*

MICHAEL J. HAYDE (author, *Flights of Fantasy: The Unauthorized but True Story of Radio & TV's Adventures of Superman*): The creation of the radio show was pretty cut-and-dry. Robert Maxwell and Allen Duchovny started writing scripts, and wrote four, because this was absolutely going to be a serial. That's what children's radio was at the time, three or five days a week of a continuing storyline.

TIM DEFOREST: What it comes down to is that DC had a chance to make some money by doing a Superman radio show. It started locally, but was popular enough that it was picked up by the Mutual Broadcasting System and went national right away. The thing is, you could produce a radio show, especially starting at a local level, very inexpensively, so you weren't risking a lot of money. Like a lot of the popular culture of the day, you just threw it against the wall to see if it stuck. Superman, because of the popularity of the character and the skill with which the radio show was done, definitely stuck. *And* it had well over a decade on the radio of just extraordinarily entertaining stories.

ANTHONY TOLLIN: In the case of the radio show and the George Reeves TV series that followed, they both worked *for* DC Comics. It wasn't a case like in the '60s where DC licensed the TV series rights to Batman to 20th Century Fox. DC had the foresight to get Superman on the radio in February of 1940, less than two years after the character debuted.

MARK WAID: The radio show is insanely significant on two levels. One is Superman's permutation into society, into pop culture. People who weren't reading newspapers were still listening to the radio. Radio was still the focal point of many families, so it was essential to keep him alive in pop culture.

JERRY BECK: The fact that Superman was on radio was the equivalent of having a Netflix series and instantly being on television. I mean, it was *such* a phenomenon.

MARK WAID: The radio show itself, like the newspaper strip, had the same character of Superman, but they took their own approach to continuity. They weren't slavish to the newspaper strip and they weren't slavish to the comics. And the comics weren't slavish to the radio show or the serials or whatever. It

Voice actor Bud Collyer, who brought Superman to life on radio, the Fleischer animated shorts of the 1940s and the 1966-70 Saturday morning series The New Adventures of Superman *(courtesy Christine Collyer).*

was allowed its own spin on Superman and so much got introduced into continuity. You get him definitively flying for the first time, Kryptonite for the first time, Jimmy Olsen and Perry White are invented for the radio show and later carried into the comics.

MICHAEL J. HAYDE: The next step was to cast, and they were going to be using a facility to record this called World Broadcasting, where another series that was being done there was *Terry and the Pirates* that was transcribed — as they called the pre-recording of radio shows. Among the cast of *Terry and the Pirates* were the two actors who ended up playing Superman's parents, Jor-El and Lara, Ned Weaver and Agnes Moorehead. Also, the fellow playing Terry's sidekick was Clayton Collyer, known to his associates as Bud Collyer.

ALAN BURKE (co-host, *All Star Superfan Podcast*): The man was ahead of his time in terms of voice work, being the first to use two separate voices for Clark Kent and Superman. He was the Kevin Conroy of his generation.

STEVE YOUNIS: I'd said this for a long time, but for me, Clayton "Bud" Collyer is my favorite Superman. I just think that he embodied the role of both Clark Kent and Superman so well that he kind of set the tone for everybody else. What's interesting is that they were thinking of casting two different people in the lead, one to play Clark Kent and one to play Superman so that they could differentiate between the two roles for people listening. But Collyer, being a trained, professional singer, was able to change his voice so much that you couldn't tell it was the same person, so that you knew when it was Clark Kent and when it was Superman. He just really set the tone for what everybody would do later on.

ADAM NEDEFF (game show historian, author, *Game Shows FAQ: All That's Left to Know About the Pioneers, the Scandals, the Hosts and the Jackpots*): He contributed quite a bit to the Superman mythos, because he would veer away from the script or add his own enhancements to the dialogue. "Up, up and away" was a Bud Collyer ad-lib, as was, "This is a job… for Superman!" And Bud Collyer was the reason that Kryptonite was a thing, because he fell ill one week, and given that he was the voice of Superman, you couldn't just replace him. Bud was sick enough that he just couldn't make it into the studio, so they had to come up with a reason that Superman wasn't there. The writers very quickly came up with a storyline about a lethal substance called Kryptonite, which was the only thing that could hurt Superman. And that plot device went over so well that they kept it in their back pocket so that in the years to come, whenever Bud wanted to take a week off and go on vacation, they'd go, "Okay, Superman's going to get attacked by Kryptonite again." *And* it went so well, that that became a part of the Superman mythos.

MICHAEL J. HAYDE: That's a legend. In the first Kryptonite storyline, Collyer appears all the way through it. The way it was presented was in the same way the movie serial would where a scientist comes across a particle of this strange, seemingly radioactive metal and doesn't know what it is. He does the research and finds out that there was a planet that exploded. And in the radio show, that was the moment when Superman discovered who he was. He always knew he was an alien, but he never knew, because he left when he was a baby, where exactly he came from. He found out that it was Krypton from this scientist, who sees the effect this metal has on Superman and locks it up in a lead safe. And that's the end of it for a few weeks. But then, inevitably, somebody was going to come along and get a hold of that metal and use it against him. That, of course, led to several different stories.

Clayton Johnson Heermance Jr. was born in New York City on June 18 in 1908. While many members of Clayton's family were in show business, early on he wanted to follow his father into law instead. Starting off his professional life as a law clerk while going to Fordham University, he found radio to be a much more lucrative career move. So he continued as a law clerk by day, and moonlit as a radio singer and actor. He would become a jack-of-all-trades in the medium, adding announcer to his resume, taking on that task for shows like Ripley's Believe it or Not! *and* Cavalcade of America. *He was also famous for acting on a radio program that would eventually go to TV,* The Goldbergs.

CHRISTINE COLLYER (daughter of Bud Collyer): As a dad, he was the best and just an all-around great guy. He was nice to everybody and was a real person, and so many people, especially in the entertainment business today, are *not* real people.

ADAM NEDEFF: He was really kind of a born showman in that he had actors in the family. His sister Dorothea was an actress, who went by the name June Collyer. His brother was involved in the business end of the movie industry, and his mother was an actress. But Bud was leaning towards law school and in high school had been part of the drama club. He was in four plays, yet he started attending Fordham Law School. While he was at Fordham, Columbia invited him to join their drama club, so by day he was taking law school classes and by night he would rehearse plays at Columbia.

CHRISTINE COLLYER: While he was in school, he became an announcer on the radio because his sister, my aunt June, was an actor in Hollywood and one of the most beautiful people I've ever seen. So dad started working as an announcer on different days at a time when everyone got dressed up to do radio.

ADAM NEDEFF: By the time he had gotten to his senior year, he had gotten into radio and was on CBS radio every day singing for six days a week and he was doing some acting, as everybody in that era of radio eventually did. So during his senior year, he dropped out of law school, because the radio career was booming. I mean, there was just no turning back; he was making so much money on radio, in fact, that he treated himself to a month in Europe. He was on shows like *Dreams of Long Ago, Capital K of America, The March of Time, Gangbusters* and *The Goldbergs.* At the same time, he would record numerous shows, running from one to the other.

ANTHONY TOLLIN: One of the talents Bud had is that he could take catnaps. If it were five minutes before he had another scene, he'd hop on top of the piano and go to sleep for five minutes. Someone would just tap him on the shoulder and he would wake up instantly and go to the microphone. *And* he was letter perfect. That was something Jackson Beck had deep respect for Bud in that regard.

ADAM NEDEFF: When you're in demand, and Betty White talked about doing this too, and if you were good enough — and certainly not everybody was — because radio was such an instant medium, and a quick medium, where programs were only on the air for 15 minutes, and there were so many radio shows, at the time you could kind of pinball back and forth between different jobs during a given day. On top of that, if you did a live national show, because they didn't have satellite technology yet, you would do a broadcast for the Eastern time zone at 8 p.m. and then you would stick around until 11 p.m. and do the show all over again for the listeners in the Pacific time zone. In one instance for the 11 p.m. show, the cast members looked around and realized that a co-star had forgotten about the second show and had already gone home. And Bud, with one-minute notice, stepped up and did the French accent required for the role and the show carried on.

Collyer proved himself versatile. One of the genres of radio that he would work intensely in was the juvenile drama. He was featured as a supporting actor on such series as The Blue Beetle *and* Terry and the Pirates, *and took on the part of the lead hero on* Renfrew of the Mounted. *But when the opportunity came to play another hero — specifically Superman — he initially refused the part.*

CHRISTINE COLLYER: It was actually Jackson Beck, who was his announcer for years on radio and had a very memorable voice, who convinced him to do it.

MICHAEL J. HAYDE: He was talked into auditioning for the parts of Superman and Clark Kent. And when he did, Allen Duchovny thought that he was the only guy who could do both parts. He had that gentle, flowing, almost tenor type of voice as Kent. And then, he was able to drop it down real low when he says, "a job for Superman." It's as good as when George Reeves would rip off his glasses and duck into a storeroom as far as getting the kids worked up. It's the audio equivalent of that.

BUD COLLYER (actor, "Clark Kent/Superman," *The Adventures of Superman* **radio show):** I thought the character would be nothing but an embarrassment, both personally and professionally. Of course, it grew into a magnificent career-within-a-career. It was great fun and a great way to get out all your inhibitions real fast.

MICHAEL J. HAYDE: In addition to being the daily announcer for different shows, he was also acting and had a pretty full plate, but then he was being asked to do this fantastic character who leaps a quarter of a mile and wears this outlandish costume (not that he had to wear it), and he's just thinking, "No, no, no, no." I'm sure he'd seen the newspaper strip, if nothing else. As he put it, "The whole idea embarrassed me." So Maxwell says to him, "Look, we're just doing a pilot, okay? We'd really like to get this done. Just do the parts and maybe we'll cast you in some other roles if the show sells."

BUD COLLYER: I can remember vaguely walking around saying to myself, "I can't play it. I can't go through this again. You're actually out of your mind," but then you get on the air and you give a fine performance. Yeah, I don't understand it either.

MICHAEL J. HAYDE: So he does the four shows and the thing gets shopped around. And at first the networks all turned it down, because it was too fantastic, just like the comic book people and newspaper syndicates originally turned it down. Plus, two of the episodes had war themes and were taking place in a Navy yard in Virginia, but we were not in the war yet and there was definitely a faction in the United States trying to make sure that we stayed out. We didn't want to make any waves there. So eventually what happens is instead of going through the networks, they say, "Fine, let's go to the ad agencies and see what we can do there."

As it happened, there was an agency for H-O Cereals and they were looking to get into radio strictly on an East Coast basis at this point. So the show gets on in New York under the auspices of Hecker's Oats and goes on the air in February of 1941. It became a sensation and the next thing you know, Bud Collyer is Superman.

ROB O'CONNOR: Bud Collyer is still arguably the best Superman voice actor, making a clear and immediate distinction between ace reporter Clark Kent (a likeable Everyman with an earnest, fast-paced James Stewart pitch in his voice) and Superman (whose booming deep voice sounds like a God from the heavens).

CHRISTINE COLLYER: As he explained it to me, he'd get that deep voice by sort of taking a deep breath and trying not to burp to get from Clark to Superman. People don't really know that, because it was so long ago.

JERRY BECK: There's a way you act on radio that's similar to the way you act in silent movies that you don't do in sound movies, because of the medium. Because radio isn't visual, you have to act with your voice in a certain way to communicate what you're doing. So that was Collyer's way of communicating the change from Clark Kent to Superman, which allowed you to visualize it in your mind. I *love* that. I mean, I love George Reeves, please don't get me wrong, but the problem with him is that if he's talking on the phone as Superman, if he puts his glasses on in the middle of the conversation, suddenly the person thinks they're talking to Clark Kent even though he sounds exactly the same. But Collyer avoided that in the same way that Christopher Reeve would later create two distinct personalities for Superman and Clark Kent.

MARK WAID: He did a great job and the best he could with the material. It wasn't Shakespeare; it was aimed at kids in 15-minute installments every day that included five minutes of recap and two minutes of commercials. So there wasn't much to work with there, but I think he did a fine job. It was a good cast and it still holds up if you just listen to the middle eight minutes.

TIM DEFOREST: Bud Collyer *nailed* the role. Everything happening was the theater of the imagination, so to visually bring across the fact that he's changing from Clark to Superman, his vocal change was a brilliant idea. I don't know if it was his or the writers, but he pulled it off perfectly and it never seemed contrived or silly. He's in the supply closet, he's taking off his suit and now he's Superman. You knew from the way he said those words and it was just one of the best examples of how effective radio was as a storytelling medium.

LEONARD MALTIN (film historian, author, *Leonard Maltin's 151 Best Movies You've Never Seen*): Bud Collyer's sister June Collyer was kind of a starlet in the late '20s or early '30s. She married Stuart Erwin, and I met Stuart Erwin Jr., who later became a TV producer in California. The one thing I wanted to ask him about his uncle Bud was if he ever did *the voice* for him. He said that, yes, Bud lived in New York and the Erwins were in L.A., but once a year he'd come out for a visit or something and he *would* do the voice drop: This looks like a job... *for Superman!*

STEVE YOUNIS: Christopher Reeve embodied that in that one scene in *Superman: The Movie* after he's had the interview with Lois on the penthouse of her apartment where he comes in as Clark and is just about to tell her that Clark Kent and Superman are one and the same. He did the physical embodiment where he pulled back his shoulders, stuck his chest out and his voice changed a little there. So you could see that in the physical aspect with Chris, but with Bud Collyer, he had to convey that with only his voice. To me, it was spectacular. They did one episode of the radio show in a cave with Clark, Jimmy and a kid and their lantern goes out. It's pitch black; they can't see anything, so Superman somehow comes in. They don't know how, but he's in the cave with them. And because Jimmy and the kid can't see anything, there's a conversation between the guys, so it's a conversation between all "four" of them. Then you have to consider that this was in the day and age before editing — they did this *live*, recorded on discs. So Bud Collyer was having a conversation with himself in two different voices.

PETER SANDERSON: Many key elements of the Superman mythos originated on the radio show and DC legally retained rights to its scripts. Besides Perry White and Jimmy Olsen, the radio show gave us Inspector Henderson, a police detective now best remembered from the 1950s TV show. It was on radio that Superman first teamed up with Batman and Robin. The radio series introduced Kryptonite; the explosion that destroyed Krypton was now clearly a nuclear one, and the fact that the one thing that could kill Superman was a form of radiation demonstrates the impact that the news of the invention of the atomic bomb had on the public's imagination.

STEVE YOUNIS: Jerry Siegel had written the "K-Metal" story for the comics that was never published originally, so we don't know whether or not the idea came from something that was in the back of their minds or this unused storyline.

TIM DEFOREST: The show was like *The Lone Ranger* in that it was marketed towards kids, but was done well enough that the adults could enjoy it too. *And* it led directly into the George Reeves TV show. Actually, a lot of early TV shows were done because they had been popular on radio. The Superman TV show, of course, was extraordinarily popular, so one led into the other, and if it hadn't been popular on radio, Superman may not have stayed in the public consciousness.

STEVE YOUNIS: *The Adventures of Superman* followed in the mode of other radio shows, because there was a particular template, if you like, of how radio shows were done at the time. Bud Collyer, Joan Alexander and the other cast members were pretty well-established in the radio world. They weren't new to the scene, and so there was a particular way that things were done. I think Superman just exploded in a way that some of the others hadn't and continued on in a way that others didn't and ran for so long. You have to remember at the time that radio was the television of the mind for a lot of people. People would gather around the radio set, look at that little red light and listen as a family and imagine what they were listening to.

BUD COLLYER: The way we did the show is that we did a quick read-through, sitting around a table, and then we did a dress rehearsal; about an hour-and-a-half overall. What's really been forgotten today were those dress rehearsals. There was something about the "out there" quality of the characters we portrayed and the situations we found ourselves in — we used to camp it up and horse around during those dress rehearsals as much as we could. If we *hadn't* done that to get the laughs out of our system, it could have well broken you up on the air, because it was so far out. But on the air, it all sounded realistic. Playing it that far out, but *realistically*, was the right thing to do. It's like a fantasy where you're not apologizing for it. So many people get embarrassed by fantasy when they're directing or performing it, and it loses all of the great charm it could have. But if played honestly and whole-hog all the way, it's great. And that's almost what this was; it's kind of a fantasy.

STEVE YOUNIS: An extra appeal about *Superman* is that it was so fantastic. You'd listen to the sound effect of Superman flying throughout the air and you're visualizing that. And, of course, there was the whole "up, up and away" coming from Superman so that everybody would get a sense of him taking off. And when he was landing, he'd say, "Down there, down, down." So while "up, up and away" kind of hung on throughout history, people forget he always said he was going down, down to land. The radio show introduced many things that were adapted into the comics and, eventually, *Adventures of Superman* TV series. Even the introduction from the radio series was adapted to the Fleischer cartoons series and became synonymous with the TV series. A lot of people don't realize that the radio series and the Fleischer cartoons are where these ideas originated.

Like the early years of the comics, the radio show dealt with Superman taking on many social injustices including intolerance, such as in the 16-part storyline "Clan of the Fiery

Cross," involving a Ku Klux Klan-like organization, where the KKK took a hit from the less-than-friendly commentary offered by the show.

ALAN BURKE: It's an infamous story in which Superman takes on the equivalent of the KKK both in radio and real life, as it turns out. It came to be after a man named Stetson Kennedy infiltrated the KKK in real life, learning many of their secrets. At a time when the KKK was shrouded by fear and mystique, Stetson Kennedy wanted to lift the veil so he went undercover with the KKK and broadcast what he learned in a story where Clark Kent takes on the Grand Scorpion of the Clan of the Fiery Cross, Matt Riggs, after an attempt is made on the life of an Asian teenager due to a perceived slight inflicted upon Matt Riggs' nephew Chuck Riggs. The story negatively affected the KKK in a massive way and the story was recently reimagined as a graphic novel titled *Superman Smashes the Klan.* Overall, I was extremely impressed with the production, with the voice work of legends like Bud Collyer and the ability of the show to keep my interest some 76 years after it first aired.

STEVE YOUNIS: Obviously these legends grow and take on a life of their own. But there is a lot of truth to that story in that there was a person who had been a member of the Klan, or who was inside the Klan, giving certain phrases or Klan "speak" to the radio series and using that to create a group like the Klan. It's obvious who they're supposed to be representing, but I don't think it was supposed to be that they were revealing actual secrets during the show. Yet they were being represented in this negative light and they were the enemy of Superman. Obviously the Klan saw themselves as being in the right, so the fact that Superman was fighting them wasn't something that they were very appreciative of.

MICHAEL J. HAYDE: Back then, conditions were still not equal for Blacks anywhere, really, but especially in the South. Plus, the Ku Klux Klan was broadening their horizons and not just going after Black people, but also certain religions, nationalities and so forth. They were against the idea of all these people who fought to help save the country that they didn't really like so much. Now they wanted to give veterans the shaft.

ROB O'CONNOR: The legacy of "Clan of the Fiery Cross" is that it is still arguably the most important and impactful Superman story of them all, driving out a very real force of darkness and exposing a hate group for the cowardly band of opportunists that they really are.

MICHAEL J. HAYDE: That's the kind of stuff that was going on and it was dealt with in the radio show. There was a villain who wanted to go against the veterans, and one who wanted to take care of kids who were forming a unity organization. That was the very first one. Then there were two based on Ku Klux Klan-type organizations. The first was the "Clan of the Fiery Cross," which is fairly obvious even though they're not named the Ku Klux Klan. The other one was called "The Knights of the White Carnation."

ALAN BURKE: There's a part where a character attends a meeting in the hills, and instead of calling him the Grand Wizard, it's Grand Scorpion. There were all these things that people probably didn't know of at the time in the general populous. But the show dealing with race back then, and listening to it all these years later, absolutely blew me away with the power of what they had done.

TIM DEFOREST: What's interesting about the radio show is that it never left the social justice elements of Superman behind. In the radio show, Clark Kent was a competent and intelligent investigative reporter and the shows were often mysteries where Clark was doing investigative work. Then he changed into Superman at the end when you needed to catch crooks, stop the enemy submarine or whatever.

ROB O'CONNOR: The stories are still tense and exciting nearly a century later and make a serious case for Superman being more interesting when used sparingly in detective-based investigation stories, as opposed to modern comics and movies where it's scene after scene of pummeling people into buildings.

TIM DEFOREST: I always thought it was interesting that they didn't use fantastic elements more often than they did, because there were no special effects budget limitations on radio; you could write virtually anything. But the mystery elements were done really well, and because of that the social justice aspect of it hung around a little longer than it did in the comic books. So you get a storyline with a Ku Klux Klan-like organization that just really trashed the idea of racial prejudice, which was impressive for a show in the '40s, especially when aimed at kids. They were very, very brave.

CHRISTINE COLLYER: A radio story like the one involving the Ku Klux Klan wasn't something my father talked about. I guess it was *too* real, if you know what I mean. There was a lot of that within that show and that storyline apparently did help.

ALAN BURKE: You know, I was driving home the other night and I can't be a more privileged person: I'm a white Irish cop and I have no experience of racism personally. But I was *so* touched by that series of episodes, and I can only imagine what it meant to Black kids in the '40s in America. It gives me goosebumps even thinking about it. The thing is, these are not silly comic books and they're not children's stories. It's so much more than that.

MICHAEL J. HAYDE: There was a legend that Collyer insisted he not be billed, but during the Klan story *Time* magazine did a story about it three weeks after it went on the air, and they said that Clayton Collyer, a former Sunday school teacher, is playing the lead role. So it was never a secret. And it obviously didn't hurt his career and, eventually, he came to enjoy the work.

ADAM NEDEFF: Bud was teaching Sunday school in Greenwich, Connecticut, at the time, and his students were shocked to discover that their Sunday school teacher was Superman. So Bud had to go to the church the following Sunday and explain the difference between reality and fiction and let them know that, "No, I'm not really Superman."

MARK WAID: The Klan wasn't the only thing the show dealt with socially. I mean, they dealt with abandoned kids and they dealt with a bunch of other social issues later on in the program, though that stuff wasn't as memorable as the Klan. At least the show had an impact that way. And I think that, yes, that's important for Superman's mythos or legacy that even *then* the character was inspiring people.

TIM DEFOREST: Within everything you *still* had stories where Superman and Jimmy went to the moon or Superman would go to another planet to fight a dictator or stop a mad scientist. He fought a giant robot on one episode. Their narrator Jackson Beck may have been the best narrator ever in radio. If he was describing a fight between Superman and an army of atomic airplanes launched by a dictator in the U.S., then he was absolutely riveting, painting a word picture.

MICHAEL J. HAYDE: "Clan of the Fiery Cross" got a lot of play in the newspapers, because that was the start of the new direction for the show. The stories became less fantastic, less about outer space adventures of trying to take Superman down one way or another; or stories about gangsters and so forth. It had a new approach where kids were going to learn about being more tolerant and accepting of other people. And Superman, of course, gives that great speech at the end of the storyline when he addresses the kids and says, "If anyone ever tells you that someone can't be a good American because he's Catholic or a Jew or a

Protestant or whatever color he may be, you can rest assured that *that* person is not a good American and not even a good human being."

The Adventures of Superman *would change format and ultimately come to a close on March 1, 1951. However, a number of significant changes would come before it all ended.*

MICHAEL J. HAYDE: In the last year, the budgets were reduced significantly. It had left Mutual and lost its sponsor. The ABC network took it on, because they were hurting for programming. At first, they tried it as a primetime entry, and under that Bud Collyer still played the role, because it was primetime and there was more money and he was getting what he deserved. After that, though, when it went back to being a twice-a-week half-hour kids show for nearly a year — basically a season from the summer of '50 to the spring of '51 — they couldn't pay him what he felt he deserved. So, he gave the role to another actor, Michael Fitzmaurice, who at that time was narrating news reels. You can't really pass judgment on how he did, because only one episode survives and he's barely Superman in it. When you listen to it, he's Clark Kent with an attitude.

For his part, Collyer, whose credits on radio had included game show host, made the shift from radio to television and shows like Beat the Clock *and* To Tell the Truth.

TIM DEFOREST: When you're listening to recordings now of *The Adventures of Superman* without Bud Collyer, you miss him, because he was Superman the way George Reeves would be a few years later on TV. The other actor had a thankless job in following someone who had been so good at the role. But if you take him on his own, he was quite good. By that time the show had gone to half-hour stories, moving away from the serial format and telling a single story in a half-hour. They did a lot of good stories, but it was never as much fun. The stories were more condensed and felt a little more rushed. So, the poor guy came into the role having to follow the perfect actor into a storytelling format that wasn't quite as good as it had been. But that's just the timing of it.

ADAM NEDEFF: Bud was a born showman; one of those guys who sort of fell into that pigeonhole of game show host, but in the later days of the Golden Age of radio, he was a jack-of- all-trades. He acted, he sang — he was one of those guys who could, forgive the cliché, do it all. But once television really took over the world, I guess the powers-that-be decided that his strong suit was hosting a game show, and he gave an air of class in this era of dignity to shows, which was very important. Particularly with *Beat the Clock*, because that was not the most respected show in its heyday. Even producer Mark Goodman was not that crazy about *Beat the Clock*, which he admitted in later years. That was because it was below the standards of the time, not knowing what would come later with shows like *Fear Factor*. But at the time it was like, "Oh my God, people are doing *that* for money?" You know, it's all these stunts where they're balancing tea cups and spraying whipped cream on each other for different stunts.

On his first day as a game show host, and this may speak to what I was saying about *Beat the Clock*, somebody on the staff pulled Bud aside, pointed to the contestants who were about to go on the air and said, "Remember, you're going to be here tomorrow. They're not. This is their big moment in the sun. This is going to be the only chance they ever have to be on the radio, so let them have the spotlight." He really took that to heart and just always saw his job, on radio or television, as being a guide. He helped the average person become comfortable and just enjoy themselves.

MICHAEL J. HAYDE: I do want to note that *The Adventures of Superman* was one of the very last children's radio shows to leave the air. By the end of the '40s and the very beginning of the '50s, television was making inroads and it was inevitable that the show was going to have to move to television if they were going to continue to use broadcasting as a means of publicizing the character and helping to drive more and more comic book sales — which really was the end result here. I mean, let's face it, it's great to have Superman on the air, but he exists because of a comic book and he exists to sell that comic book.

As noted, throughout the 1940s, the growing presence of Superman was demonstrated again and again. In November 1940 his balloon made its debut at the Macy's Thanksgiving Day Parade, standing at 75-feet tall and 44-feet wide. And before that, on July 3, 1940, the character was part of the 1939 World's Fair. There, National Periodicals sponsored Superman Day, the idea coming from the company's publicist Allen Duchovny, who had brainstormed it as a means of bringing more people to the overall event, but more importantly, to boost the sales of an exclusive 100-page World's Fair Comics *(with Superman, Batman and Robin on the cover). Thousands of kids were there, dressed in white T-shirts adorned with the Superman logo competing in various activities, one winner of the boys and one of the girls to be named "Super-Boy" and "Super-Girl." The true highlight, especially from a historical perspective, was the arrival of the first person to wear the Superman costume, actor Ray Middleton, who rode in on a parade float. In addition to portraying Superman, he played President Abraham Lincoln in* American Jubilee *staged there.*

Drawing of actor Ray Middleton, credited with being the first person to portray Superman, in this case at the 1939 New York World's Fair (art © and courtesy D.C. Stuelpner; Superman © and TM DC Comics/Warner Bros. Discovery).

BILL COTTER (author, *The 1939-1940 New York World's Fair The World of Tomorrow — Images of America***):** They sold tickets at 10-cents a piece instead of 50-cents for kids, and what they had done was they formed committees where kids could do athletic competitions and in the end they named a Super-Girl and a Super-Boy, and they got these really great-looking trophies, which would be worth a fortune today, which were about two-feet high or more and it has Superman standing on the top of the world. The girl was 11 years old and the boy was 15 years old. They got down to 80 finalists and when it was over, they announced the winners at the Superman Day event. DC Comics made a big thing over the fact that they had sold 36,000 tickets at 10-cents each, making it the largest children's event at the World's Fair. It was just proof of how popular Superman had become.

STEVE YOUNIS: Interestingly, the costume Ray Middleton wore had the word *Superman* written over the chest shield emblem and the original lace-style boots were worn. A live Superman radio broadcast was done from the fairgrounds. DC Comics in association with Macy's sponsored the event. Notably, Max Gaines, Harry Donenfeld, Jerry Siegel and Jack Liebowitz were among those who attended.

Now think about that for a second. It's pretty incredible that in such a short time he became such a phenomenal character that he was in a parade like that. Can you think of any other character that, within two or three years, is already such a household name that he's featured in a parade like that? It's *enormous.* Yes, there are characters like Harry Potter who, within a couple of years, became household names in modern times, but back then, when you go from the pulp kind of magazines of the day to comic books, they were kind of second-rate literature of the time. Truly amazing.

Over the years, it should be pointed out, there has been some debate as to whether or not it's actually Middleton in footage of the event that can be found on old 8mm film available for viewing on YouTube. That being said, DC officially credits him, and if they're considered the authority, it's the notion that has stuck.

Born Raymond Earl Middleton on February 8, 1908 in Chicago, Illinois, he attended the University of Illinois and shortly after graduating began singing with the Detroit Civic Opera Company. This was followed by gigs with the St. Louis Opera Company and the Chicago Civic Opera. Gradually he found himself drawn to acting, and in 1933 he was in the Broadway play Roberta. *Five years later he starred in the musical* Knickerbocker Holiday, *making the shift to movies in the early 1940s and appearing in films like* Gangs of Chicago *(1940),* Lady from Louisiana *(1941),* Hurricane Smith *(1941) and* Mercy

Island *(1941). Between 1942's* The Girl from Alaska *and 1972's* 1776, *he would appear in a total of seven films. On television, between 1954 and 1984, he guest-starred on several shows, appeared on anthology series and in TV movies like* Damn Yankees! *(1967),* Helter Skelter *(1976) and* Border Pals *(1981).*

RAY MIDDLETON (actor, "Superman," 1939 New York World's Fair): In 1937, producer Frank Lloyd brought me to Hollywood to play the leading role in Paramount's *Wells Fargo*. The picture got bigger and bigger as they thought about it and pretty soon it was too big for a guy like me. They had to have a big movie name, so Lloyd said for me to wait. I didn't mind. I was getting an excellent salary. I waited for nearly a year. Then they were going to put me into *The Vagabond King*. I was to sing the leading role. Then they decided the time wasn't right for a costumed musical. They made a dramatic picture and Ronald Colman got the job. By then I'd been at Paramount a whole year, without ever having acted in anything, and I was going nuts. I went back to New York. (*news sources circa 1940*)

BILL COTTER: Ray was big enough a name that he got billing in the newspaper and that sort of thing, but he was never going to be the sort of guy that carried the movie on his own. Today, if he was nominated for an Oscar, it would be in the Supporting Actor category; he *wouldn't* be the star. He also did musicals, like *Annie Get Your Gun*.

RAY MIDDLETON: Republic sent a scout to look me over for the leading role in *Man of Conquest*. They spent considerable time and money testing me, but I insist I never asked them to. When they got all through, I said, "Thanks, but I'd rather stay in New York." That made Herbert J. Yates, the head of Republic, sore. He said he'd spent $3,000 on me already. So I didn't say anything. I kept my job in New York until the play closed. When it did, I went west to play in the Republic movie *Gangs of Chicago*. When it was finished, I returned to New York to go into *The American Jubilee*.

BILL COTTER: Now if you look at pictures of him as Superman, he's a guy who was in pretty good shape and a pretty good-sized guy. And I think he did a good job of filling out the costume. The trouble with trying to track down information on how he got the role or something is that they really went out of their way *not* to publicize who he was, because they were so worried about breaking the kids' belief that they had just seen the real Superman. As a result, he didn't get any publicity at the time. So as far as those kids were concerned, they *were* watching Superman, which was great, because nobody had seen him in movies or anything else.

STEVE YOUNIS: After starring as Superman at the New York World's Fair, Middleton went on to originate the role of Frank Butler in *Annie Get Your Gun* opposite Ethel Merman in 1946. When Ray had to hit his high notes, he braced himself against Ethel Merman for support. When he tried the same thing with Nanette Fabray in *Love Life*, Nanette told him to hold on to the scenery. She was *no* Ethel Merman. Most of his films were forgettable save for his starring appearance in *I Dream of Jeannie* (1952), an unusually lavish Republic Studios biopic about the life of Stephen Foster. In 1965, Middleton signed on to play the Innkeeper in the Broadway musical *Man of La Mancha*, a role he originated, and retained through six seasons and several Don Quixotes.

JERRY WILLIAMS (friend and neighbor to Ray Middleton): Ray lived right down the street from me, and how I met him is that he used to come into my upholstery shop to have some work done. Then he started coming around to just sort of hang out. He said he loved to hear the sound of people at that sort of work; he was not really good with his hands to do anything like that. He didn't do any gardening or repairs or anything around the house. He had to have everything done for him. He was a friend, though I wasn't really familiar with him outside of the fact that he did some radio, which was my interest at that particular time. As far as the Superman thing, we touched on that a couple of times when he was doing just about anything that came along. He didn't say much about it, though he didn't treat it like a joke type of thing. Basically, it was a job and he took it.

STEVE YOUNIS: Despite the job security of *Man of La Mancha*, those six years were eventful ones for Middleton. He underwent serious heart surgery during the play's run, only to return to his part stronger and in better voice than ever. And, for the first time in his life, Middleton took a bride, dancer/singer Patricia Dinnell. After *La Mancha*, the Middletons devoted themselves to Unitarian church activity and to Ray's one-man touring concert, *America in Song and Dance*. He was active in TV commercials into the 1970s, he made a welcome return in the 1972 film musical *1776*. He died in Panorama, California on April 10, 1984.

JERRY WILLIAMS: At his house he had a pool with an outdoor shower and I was there as he got out and came about halfway across the patio when he said he needed some help. I grabbed him and as I did, he just kind of… not exactly collapsed, because he was about six-foot three-inches and 300 pounds, and I'm five-eight, probably 140 pounds, but I managed to get him to the patio and sat him down in a chair. The last thing he said to me was, "What do you want me to do?"

and I said, "Well, I'm gonna call 9-1-1." And by the time I got back to him, he was gone.

What followed in Superman history is one of the must renowned interpretations of the character, the theatrical animated shorts of brothers Max and Dave Fleischer, which were produced by them between 1941 and 1942 with Paramount Pictures' Famous Studios taking over from 1942 to 1943. The irony is that these influential shorts would never have existed if not for the fact that a live-action Superman movie serial deal with Republic Pictures had fallen through.

TOM SETO (animator, *Beauty and the Beast, The Little Mermaid* and *The Lion King*): Debuting in the first issue of *Action Comics*, Superman was literally an overnight success and quickly spawned a radio show. Republic Pictures optioned Superman for a live-action serial similar to their Lone Ranger one. They began writing the series, but DC had strict contractual oversight and did not think Republic's scenarios were being faithful to the Super-source material. DC had an option to back out of the deal, so they did (Republic recycled the scripts into another serial in 1940, *The Mysterious Dr. Satan,* and used the Superman dummy rig they had already created for the flying sequences for their '41 *Adventures of Captain Marvel*). Thus, Paramount was able to secure the rights.

JERRY BECK: To give you a sense of how big these animated shorts were, there was an ad from back then that says, "Paramount brings your favorite comic book hero to the screen: Superman, in a breathtaking cartoon in Technicolor." The whole ad is about Superman with an image of Superman, and then at the bottom of the ad it says, "On the same programme, *Law of the Tropics* with Constance Bennett." It's like the cartoon is the main attraction. *That's* how phenomenal Superman is in that period.

The Fleischer Studios, which was founded by the brothers in 1929, would go on to produce classic black-and-white animated shorts featuring characters like Koko the Clown, Betty Boop, Bimbo and Popeye the Sailor. Their approach was definitely darker than its closest competitor, Walt Disney. And it wasn't until the success of Disney's 1937 production of Snow White and the Seven Dwarfs *that the Fleischers decided to switch gears.*

JERRY BECK: Their shorts reflected the harsh realities of their times — particularly the depths of the Depression Era. But they also made us laugh and gave us hope. It was a different point of view from the rosy one Disney and his Hollywood contemporaries were painting in glorious Technicolor. Even the critics of the day noticed that Fleischer was the flipside of Disney... Fleischer's studio simply had no feel for the optimism and blue skies common in other cartoons.

TOM SETO: After Walt's success with *Snow White*, Max created his own feature cartoon, *Gulliver's Travels*, which opened in December '39. While it was well-received both critically and financially, there were extenuating circumstances — by then World War II was raging in most of the world outside America, and *Gulliver* could not get the access to the foreign markets that Disney's *Snow White* got during peacetime; it was hard to go enjoy a movie when you were running from tanks and Stuka bombers. Even though *Gulliver* became the the eighth-highest box office earner of 1939, all its success still paled in comparison to Disney's juggernaut.

Fleischer Studios went back to producing shorts, but even Popeye, their biggest success, seemed to be slowing down in 1940. After Paramount acquired the rights to Superman, they approached the duo about the character, and at first they were terrified of the idea due to the fact that it would have to be far more realistic than anything they'd done before. They asked for an outlandish per-animated short fee and was told that Paramount would pay it. Quite suddenly, they found themselves in the Superman business, which in the early 1940s was a good place to be.

In those shorts, Superman was brought to vivid life, with radio cast members Bud Collyer and Joan Alexander reprising their roles of Superman / Clark Kent and Lois Lane. The initial stories had a pretty heavy sci-fi slant whereas the back end was much more patriotic and filled with American propaganda appropriate for World War II (much of it pretty inappropriate for today). As it turned out, the Fleischers produced the first nine shorts, but due to financing from Paramount that ultimately resulted in it being able to acquire the Fleischer Studios, the remaining eight were produced by Paramount's Famous Studios. In all, 17 shorts were created between September 1941 and July 1943.

One undeniable fact is that the animation quality in these 17 shorts never faltered, and while the storylines may not be innovative, visually they remain stunning to this day, beautifully capturing the style of Joe Shuster's Man of Steel from the comics.

TOM SETO: As luck would have it, creators Siegel and Shuster happened to be visiting Miami [location of the animation studio] that spring and toured the studio. Shuster ended up spending three days drawing for the crew detailed model sheets of the characters from every angle.

ARLEN SCHUMER: I remember seeing them when I was a kid growing up in the early/mid-'60s in black-and-white on a 19-inch television set. They were Superman cartoons, but *this* wasn't the Superman I was used to from either the comic books I had been reading or the old George Reeves live-action TV Superman I watched as reruns every day. They didn't look like any cartoons I had ever seen before either. These Superman cartoons didn't have the herky-jerky movement of the Hanna-Barbera stuff, but the smooth-flowing, higher-quality look and feel of the great Disney cartoons that I later learned were the result of the Fleischers' combination of painstakingly hand-painted cel animation and rotoscoping (animating over live-action film). You could *feel* Superman straining to exercise his super-strength, struggling against bigger opponents, be they man, machine or giant animal; you could *feel* his physical effort as he *literally* leapt tall buildings in a single bound, or pushed off the ground or the side of buildings to fly.

TOM SETO: Although the Fleischers were known for rotoscoping live-action, they didn't use it as much in the Superman series, though they did some filming with muscleman Karol Krauser posed as the live-action model for Superman, and some of a model for Lois. But a lot of the actions, like flying, could not be rotoscoped, so, as Fleischer animator Bob Bemiller recalled, "Steve Muffati [lead animator] got the idea to have people act the stuff out, and we'd sketch as they acted." Then they would work from their sketches.

PETER SANDERSON: It's been said that it was Max Fleischer's animated Superman cartoons that firmly established Superman's ability to fly, since the giant leaps tended to look silly. In the comics, Superman did not clearly begin to fly until late 1943.

TOM SETO: In the first comics, artist Shuster had Superman only jumping amazing distances (much like Marvel Comics' Hulk would do decades later). Dave and Max thought jumping from place to place looked inelegant and clumsy on screen. The action of flying looked much better and it served to link together the visual narratives, as it made it easy to go between locations more quickly.

ARLEN SCHUMER: And he flew like we imagined he flew in our dreams, both gracefully and dynamically. He didn't zoom through outer space pushing planets around — he was grounded in our recognizable reality. He was *relatable*.

JERRY BECK: The first episode is the classic archetype superhero, almost a cliché, but it's just well done. It's really great. They did two things in that one that they never did again, which was they gave the mad scientist a comic bird sidekick, which I now realize they might have been aping Snow White, the Witch and the fact that the witch has a comical raven sidekick. I just recently had watched *Snow White* and could see the influence.

LEONARD MALTIN: The marvel of the Fleischer Superman cartoons is that they did them at all. They'd done the Betty Boop and Popeye cartoons, and they're all wonderful, but there was no effort to create any imitation of reality. They live in a cartoon world. The first time the Fleischers and their staff got to stretch their muscles was when they made *Gulliver's Travels*. For that, they invented the rotoscope to trace human live-action movement. But nothing they did could prepare you for the astonishing results they got when they tackled Superman. They not only replicated the look and feel of the comic books, but the staging and look of those cartoons is exceptional.

JERRY BECK: The Fleischers were the perfect people for this. The best use of the rotoscope was for *Gulliver's Travels* and no one had made a science-fiction cartoon or drama cartoon this way. There are a couple of cartoons I can point to that Disney might have done like *The Goddess of Spring* or *The Little Match Girl* from Columbia Pictures. They were sort of serious, non-humorous cartoons, but this kind of science-fiction adventure cartoon, nobody did that before.

TOM SETO: Fleischer's head of writing, Bill Turner, oversaw the creation of the stories, inspired by the rich atmosphere of science-fiction in the books and pulp magazines of the time, like *Amazing Stories*, just as the Fleischer animators drew inspiration from the Noirish illustrations in graphic pulps like *The Shadow*. Fleischer animator Orestes Calpini drew the Superman storyboards and said he paid much more attention to detail on Superman than in their other cartoons.

BRUCE TIMM (producer, *Superman: The Animated Series*): When we did *Batman: The Animated Series*, we could borrow a lot of those Fleischerisms, because they were a perfect fit for Batman — they were almost a better fit for Batman than Superman, because there was a lot of dark, German Expressionism in the staging in the Fleischer Superman cartoons that was totally applicable to Batman.

JERRY BECK: Not only are the shorts significant in the history of animation, but they're significant in their influence on future animators like Bruce Timm, Paul Dini and even people at Hanna-Barbera who did *Johnny Quest*; very much the Japanese animator Hayao Miyazaki, who did *Spirited Away* and has loudly said he has been influenced by those cartoons. And there's even a "Mechanical

Monster" in one of his films. What else were those guys going to look at? There was no other influence for adventure animation at a certain point. That was it. So those were incredibly influential.

ALAN BURKE: To watch them now is an experience I would recommend to any true Superman fan. What always amazes me is their detail, such as the way in which the animation takes real world physics into account.

JERRY BECK: I believe that the visual look, even though they were using Joe Shuster's drawing style primarily for the character, wasn't going to be good enough for the cartoon, so they turned to the look of the pulp covers from the '30s like *The Spider* or *The Shadow*. That's really where I believe they got some of their visual inspiration for the look, the background artwork and the feel for what these cartoons might look like.

STEVE YOUNIS: Story-wise, they're very simple and there isn't a lot of dialogue, but visually? *Wow*. You compare them to some of the cartoons that we got in the '70s with *Super Friends*… there *is* no comparison.

JERRY BECK: The other thing they did in that first film was the strange physics, which is the *Daily Planet* building bending like butter — which is kind of ridiculous; none of the other films do that. They're all very straight as you can be and factual and logical. But things like mechanical telescopes, electrical earthquakes — those films just have all of these great ideas.

ARLEN SCHUMER: At my very first Comic-Con, the 1973 New York Comic Convention, they had a nighttime cartoon program and there it was: not on a tiny black-and-white TV set, but projected in glorious full-color on a big screen, the very first Superman cartoon, which had the *single* most memorable sequence of them all: our hero fighting a mad scientist's death ray, which brings Superman to his knees in almost-defeat, until, phoenix-like, he magnificently rises, *boxing* the ray beam back in mid-air! Fifteen-year-old mind *blown*.

JERRY BECK: But the interesting thing is that when it comes to Superman, he's hardly got any dialogue at all. Jack Mercer, the voice of Popeye, is the Mad Scientist in the first one and he's got more dialogue. Jackson Beck plays Perry White and *he's* got more dialogue. One of the Famous Studios cartoons that I like is a showdown with a crook who is impersonating Superman. He's dressed in a Superman costume and there's a scene where Superman confronts him and I don't think he says a word. The crooks say things like, "What are you staring at?

Why don't you talk?" — and he just doesn't say *anything*. But that's the point: Superman means action.

ROBERT GREENBERG-ER: I love the Fleischer animation, especially the first half of them. The color, the fluidity — they were not the most interesting stories. It was basically, "Here's Lois in danger, here's Superman saving the day," but I did like seeing Superman struggle to save the day. It really kept him a lot more relatable. Plus, there was good music too.

ROB O'CONNOR: As quaint and faintly misogynistic though it may be, I still get a tangible rush of excitement when Lois reminds Clark that the day is saved "thanks to Superman!" and we get that wink that's more powerful than a locomotive.

Ad for the Fleischer animated shorts (Superman © and TM DC Comics/Warner Bros. Discovery)

JERRY BECK: The animated shorts are significant, largely because the craft of them are so good. The first one was nominated for an Academy Award, which it should have won, but a Disney Pluto cartoon won that, which is ridiculous. It's kind of like *Citizen Kane* not winning the year it was nominated, which I believe was the same year of 1941. World War II begins with the Superman cartoons going into it, and the first group of them are basically science-fiction cartoons. That was how people perceived him then — more of a science-fiction character. It also staked a place for the superhero and adventure cartoons.

TOM SETO: While the first Superman shorts were all about mad scientists and diabolical robot monsters, the later cartoons in the series were more about World War II themes: Superman fighting Nazi agents and Japanese saboteurs. Hence "The Japoteurs," with our hero battling Japanese spies intent on stealing a new Howard Hughes–style gigantic plane; "The Eleventh Hour," when Superman clandestinely sneaks around Yokohama Harbor committing acts of sabotage on Japanese industry, *and* saving Lois from being shot as a spy; "Jungle Drums," where Superman goes to Africa and battles Nazi African natives; and "Secret Agent," in which the Man of Steel goes up against German saboteurs this time, ending with the now-familiar iconography of Superman flying off while saluting the American flag.

RAY MORTON: The stories are fun, although I much prefer the sci-fi tinged narratives of the Fleischer bunch (mad scientists, death rays, dinosaurs, giant robots – more please) to the World War II propaganda yarns of the Famous batch — as relevant and necessary as they probably felt at the time, the pro-Allies, anti-Axis bent of those films now make them feel dated in a way that the more classic, timeless Fleischer shorts never do. And there's not a Superman fan in the world who isn't dying to see the Man of Steel battle giant robots in a live-action film the way he does in the Fleischer shorts. Hopefully someday some smart Superman producer will get around to having him do just that.

JERRY BECK: Superman had something that no cartoon series, not even a Disney cartoon series of shorts, ever had: a trailer! No other cartoon series — meaning seven-minute cartoon series — in history has ever had a trailer. A trailer for a short just wasn't done, but it was because Superman was so big. You've got to credit National and the way they were handling the character. It's like, "If you're going to do Superman, we're going to approve things. We're going to be having Whitney Ellsworth be our producer for you. We're going to protect our mythos with this character," and they did that whether it was in the '40s with the Superman cartoons and serials, or when you go into the '50s when you get the *Adventures of Superman* TV series. After George Reeves died, they tried to do *Superboy*, then they ended up doing the very first real Saturday morning cartoons in the '60s. Yes, there were a few things like *Atom Ant* before the *Batman* craze and before *The New Adventures of Superman* cartoons. Saturday morning cartoons really began in 1966, and that was the year of *Batman* and the Filmation Superman. And that leads us to *Super Friends*. And that leads into the Christopher Reeve movies. It's a clean line and it never ends. But the Fleischer Superman cartoons are the first of that line. So that's how important those were: They had to be good and well done, and as a result they're still revered.

With the backdrop of all that was happening in the 1940s with Superman, acrimony between Jerry Siegel and Joe Shuster and Jack Liebowitz and National Periodicals was growing. Its origins can be traced back to 1938 when Siegel and Shuster sold all rights to the Man of Steel to the company. That fact was made plain on the back of the $130 check they endorsed, and in the contracts that were sent their way. And whatever misgivings they *had — and one can only imagine that there must have been plenty — they also recognized it at the time as being an opportunity to see their creation* finally *in print and a means to further enhance their growing careers.*

The March 1, 1938 contract reads as follows: "I, the undersigned, am an artist or author and have performed work for a strip entitled Superman. *In consideration of $130.00 agreed to be paid me by you, I hereby sell and transfer such work and strip, all good will attached thereto and exclusive right to the use of the characters and story, continuity and title of strip contained therein, to you and your assigns to have and hold forever and to be your exclusive property and I agree not to employ said characters by their names contained therein or under any other names at any time hereafter to any other person, firm or corporation, or permit the use thereof by said other parties without obtaining your written consent therefor. The intent hereof is to give you exclusive right to use and acknowledge that you own said characters or story and the use thereof, exclusive. I have received the above sum of money."*

Seems pretty ironclad and signed by Jerome Siegel and Joseph Shuster.

PAUL LEVITZ (writer, former publisher, DC Comics): The deal for *Action* #1 was very much a standard one, and their page rate was better than most guys were getting in those days. Ten dollars was a good number; there were a lot of people still getting $5 or $6. The thing to keep in mind is that people looking back at those days are looking at it *not* from the perspective of how business was conventionally practiced in that era, in that industry, in similar industries; what economics were like, but looking for heroes and villains. I'm *not* saying that Jack Leibowitz was a generous and lovely human being, but it's really not a hero and villain story. It's a sad story.

ROBERT GREENBERGER: I've spoken to a lot of the people who were at DC through the years and what it boiled down to is that Siegel and Shuster chose to sell, because they were desperate to get their creation in print. They were willing to sign the check for $130, eyes wide open. When I personally interviewed editor Vin Sullivan for the corporate history of DC, Vin told me he told the boys to get a lawyer and recommended his brother. But the boys signed the check anyway, ignoring his suggestion.

TOM DE HAVEN (author, *It's Superman!*): The stamp on the back of all the checks when I started my career noted that it was work for hire, and I had to sign all those damn things. Every time I did that, I thought of Siegel and Shuster, but that's what you did if you wanted to publish and you wanted to work. I am talking about well into the '70s, so that went on for a long time. When I was doing research, I loved reading about the Superman TV series in the '50s. People in the cast were taking the bus to the studio every day and were living in little apartments with black-and-white televisions. John Hamilton, the guy who played Perry White, was getting $25 on a Saturday to go open a supermarket. Even George Reeves wasn't making a lot. It was *such* a different world.

LAUREN AGOSTINO (co-author, *Holding Kryptonite*): People really fight me on this, but everybody keeps saying this big corporation took advantage of them. I don't see the corporation. I see Donenfeld was a hustler; he was a street kid. Jack was a little bit educated, but he came from a fairly poor background. On top of that, they got ghostwriters for Jerry Siegel as far back as 1939 and the artwork was going all over the place because Joe was spread thin, so I believe it was a team that made Superman.

MICHAEL BAILEY (host, *Superman: Crisis to Crisis* podcast): People in general — but Superman fans in particular — want heroes and villains in a story. What you've got here is a company founded by two men, one of ill repute and the other constantly cleaning up the other one's mess, who were coming out of the Great Depression. They — Jack Liebowitz in particular — had a strong defense when it came to Siegel and Shuster: "We own this concept, you signed him over to us, we don't owe you *anything*." And then you have two kids from Cleveland, Ohio who didn't have the sense to get a good lawyer, and so I respect the people that are fervently pro-Siegel and Shuster and the belief they got screwed, because I believe they got screwed, but it's not a black-and-white story. I feel very strongly that DC did have a moral obligation to take care of these people, but there was nothing legally requiring them to do so — which is why it would take Neal Adams, James Robinson and a very smart media campaign to get them what they got in the 1970s.

MARC TYLER NOBLEMAN (writer, *Boys of Steel: The Creators of Superman*): I believe that people should get paid what they're worth, and they certainly were getting paid well at the time. And certainly by the standards of the Depression and the aftermath, they were getting paid *very* well. But it *doesn't* mean it was what it was worth. They would have had every right to negotiate a better royalty from the beginning, which they just didn't do. And if they *had* gotten that, it would have been well-deserved.

PAUL LEVITZ: Look, there's no such thing as a magic, right moral number for sharing profits from something. They were entitled to have wanted more, they just didn't have a very good *legal* claim to more. At the same time, the subsequent deal to produce the body of work they did was a pretty high-end deal for that period. And their deal on the newspaper strip, which is, I think, what probably generated most of the money for them, was a very viable deal. I'm sure there was also stuff you could legitimately argue with as to how the company was accounting for it, but the net effect is the guys were getting a very good stream of income.

JEFF TREXLER (Interim Director Comic Book Legal Defense Fund; legal expert, Superman copyright case): Siegel did push back in his own way. The first five issues of *Action* have Superman fighting criminals and so on, but number six is Siegel's response to the unexpected success of his character. What happens is this hoodlum creates a fake Superman and it's Superman's phony manager who starts licensing him to sell different products. Clark Kent and Lois Lane go to a nightclub and there's a woman singing a Superman song, then in the sky there's a plane with a Superman message trailing behind it. There are all of these Superman products, all put out by this crook licensing Superman stuff. He's explaining to Clark Kent how he's Superman's manager so it's not IP theft. It's a recurring theme in the early comics.

TOM ANDRAE (comics historian, co-author, *Batman & Me*): There was a lot more to this than money. They were dealing with editors that were very onerous, like Mort Weisinger. Jerry got to the point where he just didn't want to do comic books anymore; he just wanted to concentrate on the strip, because he felt so traumatized by the way Weisinger would insult him and his work, and also reject many of his ideas.

BRAD RICCA (author, *Super Boys: The Amazing Adventures of Jerry Siegel and Joe Shuster — The Creators of Superman*): I tried hard not to make Siegel and Shuster overtly the victims. I *don't* think they're victims of DC. The company really wanted to keep them on the first 10 years and they gave them raises and put up with a lot of complaining from Jerry. But it's the system where you create the character, you sell it and you didn't really create the character as work for hire. For so many years their story was just them as the victim. Now, especially among comics people, the story is they actually made a ton of money, which I think is good, because I don't think the victim storyline is completely accurate. At the same time, they had no idea what they were doing when they signed those contracts. This narrative that they ended their lives crying and unhappy is totally wrong. They were really okay with everything at the end.

JEFF TREXLER: If you go back to the original contracts, it's this perfect storm of weird things that get us to this point. Siegel had this agreement, a company changes hands from Major Wheeler-Nicholson to National Periodicals, the new owners after bankruptcy. In the same year, Siegel and Shuster sell Superman and negotiate a contract to give them a cut and enable them to get a cut of newspaper syndication and certain licensing. They didn't have the legal representation, but if they had legal representation, or better legal representation or 21st century legal representation, they would have had a procedure for the accounting of everything. Without the mechanisms that we now have, there's a built-in level of distrust and fear. Publishing in the 1930s is the equivalent of Hollywood accounting where the money's being moved around to the point where you know things are making gazillions of dollars, but they claim they're not making a profit, yet obviously they're getting money out of it.

That's certainly the way that Siegel (especially) and Shuster felt pretty much from right after the moment that Superman appeared on the scene, and it was obvious that all involved realized that they had captured lightning in a bottle. But that kind of success comes with a price, particularly in a situation where you have a writer and artist who are trying to do everything *themselves, ranging from two comic books in the form of* Action *and* Superman*, and the daily and Sunday syndicated newspaper strip. In Shuster's case, he was forced to give up a lot of the work and began to supervise a team of artists due to problems with his eyes and his hand.*

JOE SHUSTER: I did all the work at the beginning up until the point where I couldn't handle the increasingly heavy art production burden alone. I needed, and got, assistance. At that time, the strip was sold to the McClure Syndicate. As time went on, I had quite a production staff, but I was already involved in the drawing — not all of the aspects of it, but I was involved in the initial layouts, the penciling; and I did all the faces of Superman, every one of them — which was very tedious, because Jerry insisted (and I agreed with him) that there was nobody else that could really catch the spirit, the feeling, of Superman. I did all the figures too, as a matter of fact. My staff did mainly the backgrounds and the inking, the polishing up of the penciling — because a lot of my pencils were quite rough. But they were very spontaneous. What I did was get the initial action of the figure, and they would go on from there. The one thing they did not ink was Superman's face. For about an eight- or 10-year period, I did every face of Superman.

DANIEL BEST (editor, *The Trials of Superman Vol. I and II*): As they grew more successful and the money was coming in, Joe couldn't keep up, because he wasn't a fast artist. He had to have a staff, so they started a shop, and out of the money that Siegel and Shuster got, it was split 50/50, but Joe had to pay the other artists out of his 50%. Jerry, of course, was writing and was so fast that he didn't have to pay anyone else. In order to get the strip going, poor old Joe is paying out of his pocket.

TOM DE HAVEN: It seems to have been a strange partnership after a while in terms of how symbiotic it really was. I had the feeling that Joe was dropping more and more out of this fairly quickly in terms of the creative part of it. But it sounds like Jerry was getting crazy advice about suing DC, like, "*This* is what you have to do in the business world, Jerry." It was really the worst advice he could have gotten unless a lot of it came out of his own thinking.

JEFF TREXLER: At one point you've got the *Saturday Evening Post* article about Siegel and Shuster that documents the people working for them at the time, and the two of them are relatively well-off in terms of upper middle classic. They had become symbols of the American Dream and success.

JULIAN VILAJ (writer, *The Joe Shuster Story*): In reading over the letters of Joe Shuster in my research, I realized that certain things were a myth. Number one, they were actually really rich. Or they became rich with Superman. The thing is, they were living big. There were some pictures where Jerry is in his new house with all the knickknacks he'd acquired and so on. Then you had Joe buying a house for his parents. It says a lot about personalities. And don't forget, Joe was losing his eyesight. I don't know what's true or not, but the stories are that Donenfeld paid for some medical bills for him back then. And they still gave him jobs, even if they knew he couldn't work. At one point he was only supervising, and then once he lost everything, he also had to pay his own medical bills. If you look at his letters from then, every second one is him saying that he needs help paying his medical bills and asking to borrow money.

STEVE YOUNIS (webmaster, Superman Homepage): From a creative point of view, Jerry saw that Superman was being taken in a direction that maybe he wasn't happy with. He wanted to regain the creative control and the monetary value. I feel that there was a jealousy factor there, and with 20/20 hindsight, it's like, "We did well, we're still doing well, but there is a *massive* future for this character that we're going to be missing out on."

JULIAN VILAJ: Jerry did make some mistakes. He in particular had burnout, because he wanted to do *everything* and he was angry about anything that was taken away from him, like the original novel written by George Lowther, the radio show and so on. He wanted to do it all. In a way, [Batman creator] Bob Kane was so much smarter. He took the attitude, "I don't care if someone else does it, as long as I get the credit and some money." There are a lot of issues with Bob Kane as a person, but maybe if Jerry had a little bit of *that* attitude, it could have been different. But again, he wanted to do everything.

RAY MORTON: George Lowther, one of the writers and directors of the radio show, wrote the 1942 novel *The Adventures of Superman* as a piece of promotional merchandising for the program. As literature, it's just a fun trifle — a yarn about ghosts and spies and submarines that would have been right at home on the radio show, enhanced by some very cool Joe Shuster illustrations. The novel's key contribution to the Superman mythos is that it canonized the names of Kal-el's Kryptonian parents as Jor-el (previously Jor-L, eventually Jor-El) and Lara (previously Lora). It described the events leading up to Krypton's destruction and Jor-el's decision to save his infant son by rocketing him into space. It then fleshed out Kal-el's boyhood on Earth — his discovery and adoption by Eben and Sarah Kent (they didn't become Jonathan and Martha until the 1950s); their naming him Clark; his growing up on a farm in Kansas; gradually discovering his powers, etc.

ANTHONY TOLLIN (comics, pulps and old-time radio historian): DC recruited a top science-fiction and pulp hero editor named Mort Weisinger, and later Jack Schiff, to give a level of guidance and continuity and planning to Superman and Batman. Reportedly Weisinger was originally hired primarily as a story editor on Batman, because they felt Superman was moving ahead pretty well. Jerry Siegel was drafted into World War II in 1943, and while the four years preceding had tremendous growth and development of Superman and his mythos, when Jerry was away, that was being done by the editors that DC had installed and other writers. Obviously Weisinger was drafted for a while as well, so Jack Schiff took over. But the machine kept running and growing *without* Siegel.

Siegel and Shuster may have had the initial idea, but Superman was tremendously blessed to have some very excellent editorial guidance over the years. And it was pretty much unheard of in any other case. You look at things like Timely licensing Captain America for a movie serial and not having any control over the character, so he becomes Grant Gardner, crusading district attorney instead of Steve Rogers. DC produced the newspaper strip, the radio show and the TV show themselves. On the TV show, Whitney Ellsworth was producer and Mort Weisinger was story editor. The only other company like this with that kind of control was Disney and its protectiveness over Mickey Mouse, overseeing and approving *everything*. Naturally Siegel and Shuster wouldn't have been suing over the ownership of

Superman had the character failed. Their idea was brilliant, but how much of that success was also due to the fact that DC owned their own distributor, Independent News, and could strong-arm news dealers into giving Superman better placement?

In the years prior to his being drafted, Siegel married neighbor Bella Lifshitz on June 10, 1939. Together they had a son, Michael, and lost another in childbirth. The marriage was not a happy one and, after the war, the duo divorced in 1948, with Jerry segueing over to a relationship with Joanne Carter (the original model for Lois Lane), who had re-entered his life at a costume party on April 1, 1948. The two married that November and had a daughter, Joanne. Ultimately, Siegel by all reports pretty much abandoned his first family, Michael Siegel having very little contact with his father throughout his life and growing as bitter towards him as Jerry Siegel was towards DC.

During this period, Siegel achieved his greatest success, but also his greatest loss based on the actions that he and Shuster attempted against DC. But truth be told, given the increasingly acrimonious relationship between he and the publisher, particularly Liebowitz, in many ways what happened seemed inevitable.

In the pages of the book Holding Kryptonite *and in online articles and documents posted by Jeff Trexler and Daniel Best, the relationship between Siegel and Shuster and Liebowitz/DC is laid out pretty bare. Via letter, Siegel, the spokesman for he and Shuster, is constantly pushing for greater page rates and bigger royalties, while Liebowitz, seemingly backed by other editors and even comic strip syndicator McClure, grows increasingly frustrated with what seems to be slip-shod artwork, scripts that need constant work and storylines that aren't provided with enough lead time for editorial comments and suggestions. Advice that he and Shuster move from Cleveland to New York for greater interaction was ignored — all in all, a difficult relationship.*

LAUREN AGOSTINO: *Action Comics* #1 was published on April 18, 1938, and five months later is when the problems started, with Jerry Siegel *haunting* Jack Liebowitz. If you read the letters between them, it's constant antagonism. It's one threat after another, and within five months Siegel wanted more and he was saying that signing the contract was a mistake. Things were taking off in that first five months, so they could see the popularity of the character already. But Liebowitz was like, "Calm down, because you've got to put work into it." There came a constant push for higher quality from both Siegel and Shuster. Now there's no question that when he wrote Jerry back he could be a dick, but you could see things snowballing between them. You'll also see that Liebowitz never fires the first shot. If you read the letters and see his tone, it's always in response. And you can see that some of the letters from Jerry are *so* aggravating, that Liebowitz waits a few days before he writes a response so he can cool down.

ANDREW NEWBERG (co-author, *Holding Kryptonite*): When Lauren brought me this information that makes up *Holding Kryptonite*, she was definitely stacked up on the corporate side; she very much felt that National and those guys didn't get a fair shake in the story of Jerry and Joe's demise. She was more frustrated, because she had proof that they did, in fact, get compensated rather well, and that DC still had to be on them all the time for edits and rewrites. Frankly, I don't know why they kept working with these guys, actually, after the first or second year. I went into this thinking, "Take it easy, Lauren, I'll take care of it," but then as I read it all, I was getting kind of mad as well. I saw at the very beginning that this wasn't their first project; that they had been paid for other gigs and been compensated likewise for those. And when Superman turned out to be the cover of *Action Comics*, they thought it was great. And it is. It's iconic and a great story, but no one knew — or could know — it would take off the way it did.

JEFF TREXLER: In most instances, if someone was being as sharp with them as Siegel, and accused them of all he did through his correspondence, most companies would have just cut him loose — particularly after the comic book exploded in 1938 and they had plenty of people in their teens and early 20s who were willing to write stuff. I tend to believe the Liebowitz side, where they said, "After 1947 or '48, we would have renewed your contract, so just stay the freaking course," and that would have gotten Siegel and Shuster into the TV show. Beyond that, I think they would have been going for one five-year contract after another. They might have even been able to negotiate something more and they could have been part of the whole PR thing. I don't know if this *would* have happened given that Jerry Siegel had a strong sense of the way things should be.

PAUL LEVITZ: From a Marxian point of view, it's the difference between the value created by the worker and the value created by the capitalist. Robert Maxwell created a lot of value; Allen Duchovny created a lot of the value. Jack Leibowitz, Harry Donenfeld and their sidekicks created a lot of value. Should it have been more than $6.7 million for Siegel and Shuster? Maybe. Multiples of that? Maybe. Nobody has the numbers of what DC actually made. Those numbers didn't survive, they didn't exist by the time I had access to anything, so you can't even sit there and say, well, you know, morally, it's in the universe of fair.

And we still have many industries where, if you invent the new antiviral drug that's going to be used to combat COVID, you get your name on the patent, you probably get a bonus that year, and you get a handshake. And if the company is a decent company, you have a laboratory to play in for the rest of your life. But you ain't getting six-million bucks. Is that fair? Well, maybe it is, because the company has had to invest a lot in research and development to create the laboratories and the possibility of what you're doing. But is it *fair*? I'm *really* grateful to that guy or gal, whoever they are, but I'm not going to send them all of my money.

Siegel was drafted into the United States Army on June 28, 1943, where he was trained at Fort George G. Meade to be an airplane engine mechanic, but found himself stationed in Honolulu, where he was assigned to be a writer at the Stars and Stripes *newspaper. He would be discharged on January 21, 1946 with the rank of Technician 4th Grade. He had not been a part of battle during his time in the Army, but was ready for all-out war once he returned home.*

Insofar as he was concerned, there was so much that had been piled on him and Shuster. Every time the duo pushed for more, they were pummeled with reminders that National owned Superman, that outside of their work on that character, nothing else they'd created had gained any sort of traction; there was criticisms of Siegel's writing and Shuster's art. And then, despite the fact that Leibowitz had twice rejected Siegel's pitch for a comic book called Superboy *(about the adventures of a young Superman in Smallville), while he was in the Army, the company published the comic — which Shuster actually drew, feeling he didn't have much of a choice. At that point, a furious Siegel was ready to take back what he felt was rightfully his, encouraged by a lawyer buddy in the Army that Superman could be his and Joe's again. And that certainly National had no right to publish* Superboy *without buying those rights from him.*

Being in a courtroom was certainly nothing new for National Periodicals, as they had gone after virtually anyone who treaded too closely to Superman territory, most notably the characters of Wonderman (which was proven to very specifically have been created to cash in on the Man of Steel) and the original Captain Marvel (better known as Shazam today), but obviously this was different.

Although years in the making, there are many who retrospectively feel that this lawsuit — to capture the rights to Superman and Superboy, and for financial reparations from the fact that the Man of Steel inspired so many costumed heroes in the National stable — was a major misstep.

JEFF TREXLER: I've read a lot from the post-war era where one minute you're out there fighting, you have a sense of cause, but you also have a sense of things slipping away at home, because you're not there taking care of them. And

Superboy for Siegel was clearly a sense of, "I'm losing everything." Many of the soldiers returning felt like men out of time. They felt like power dynamics in the household changed, they weren't cut out for the new postwar business world, so marriages were slipping away, jobs were slipping away or, in this case, "My creation is slipping away."

TOM ANDRAE: When Jerry came back from the war, other people were working on Superman. He used to do pretty much all the Superman scripts; there were few things he *didn't* do, until he went away and he was gone from 1943 to early 1946. DC took over production and Joe did very little at that point, because he was having some of the problems with his eyes, so he wasn't making much money. And again, when Jerry came back, he was not the sole author of Superman anymore. Their situation drastically changed and he wanted to get back to the way things were, but it never did.

JEFF TREXLER: For Jerry Siegel, it was like, "I made a deal for Superman which I thought was going to be worth something, and then you went ahead and made all these other heroes that reduced the value of Superman, because you're just taking powers and costumes and concepts and making all this money over here and I don't have a pot. So I should have a piece of that." But what do you do? Did The Beatles deserve a piece of every member of the British Invasion that came to America? I get where Siegel's coming from *and* I get where the company's coming from. But I think nine out of 10 lawyers at the time would have told Siegel *not* to file that lawsuit.

ANTHONY TOLLIN: When Siegel came in and said they were going to sue, Liebowitz said, "We'd rather spend the money on you than lawyers. Drop the lawsuit and we'll raise your pay to $150,000 right now." This was huge money in the '40s, but they had resentment towards DC and refused.

TOM ANDRAE: Joe was a very shy guy. Jerry handled all the financial transactions and negotiations. And Joe was far more amenable to negotiating, making a settlement, rather than create waves. But he went along with what Jerry wanted to do.

ANDREW NEWBERG: The relationship between Jerry and Joe and DC started like a normal relationship, but then as soon as fame or success hit, it becomes a story of how that can be a real divider of people. It's like Jerry thought, "This is it; I've made it." But the truth was, he *didn't* make it. He was making it and he had won the lottery by getting Superman selected. You wonder why he didn't say, "Thank God this one's more successful than *Slam Bradley* or *Doctor Occult*," some of which he made more than $130 on. So, by my logic, everything that they did they expected to be on a Superman level, which it just couldn't be. With Jerry, it really felt like it was all about the money, but there was so much pride wrapped into it that it choked him.

ROBERT GREENBERGER: Their attorney didn't really know much about intellectual property law, which was still a new concept in legal terms. I think the guys saw dollar signs and they got really bad legal advice.

PAUL LEVITZ: In a perfect world, the thing would have been settled along the line of a reasonable basis and their lives wouldn't have gone to hell for the next batch of years. But Donenfeld and Liebowitz were tough, immigrant-fueled kind of guys used to scrapping their way up on one level, probably uncomfortable setting precedent on another level, just sort of angry at how it had been handled over the years. Whoever the lawyer was that Siegel and Shuster used convinced them that there was simply no middle ground, and to me that's a real shame. And the truth is, it's not unusual for great creative people to have one great idea in their life, and Superman was theirs.

ANTHONY TOLLIN: I'll tell you my opinion: I think if Siegel and Shuster had been successful in taking the character away from DC, that we wouldn't know who Superman was anymore. First of all, they probably would have believed in someone else and had the character stolen from them. DC was just the right company and had the right amount of greed to capitalize on Superman. I don't think Superman would still be here if DC had not gotten him on the radio and then on to television.

MARK WAID: There's also the fact that a contract is a contract. Contracts can be renegotiated, but at the end of the day, there's a world in which no one paid attention to Superman. There's a world in which DC Comics publish *Action Comics* #1 and something else newsworthy happened that week, nobody bought the book and that was the end of it. They took a risk. They took the financial gamble, so it's a really not as cut and dried as to whether the contract was fair. It's also the benefit of hindsight to be able to look at how big Superman was. In 1938, before sales reports starting coming in, he was worth no more than *Spy, Radio Squad* or any of the other Siegel and Shuster features that DC was doing. The compensation was the same: "Here's your 130 bucks." From DC's point of view, it was a complete fluke that Superman took off in a way that *Radio Squad, Spy* and whatever else the boys were doing *didn't*. That's the part that we always overlook; in that moment, before Superman was proven, it was a completely fair deal.

ANTHONY TOLLIN: Batman co-creator Bob Kane used the Siegel and Shuster lawsuit to become a multi-millionaire. Kane worked for the company very well, but when Siegel and Shuster sued, he came to Liebowitz and said, "You know, to avoid this happening with Batman, you should renegotiate my contract." They said, "Why should we do that? We own Batman lock stock and barrel. You sold the rights to us in 1939." And Bob Kane said, "Yes, but I was underage." He was lying through his teeth; I think he was 22 or 23 when he sold Batman, but his father made his birth certificate disappear. He claimed he graduated early from high school when he'd actually been held back. He bluffed them and got a contract that, among other things, allowed that if and when DC Comics was sold, Batman would be sold separately. When Kenny bought DC Comics and became Kenny National, Bob Kane got them to negotiate the sale of Batman. At the time I'd heard he got $1.3 million for seven years and it went on from there.

In the end, on November 21, 1947, Judge J. Addison Young of the Supreme Court of the State of New York, ruled that the rights to Superman belonged to National Periodicals, but that Superboy did not. As things unfolded, National paid Siegel and Shuster a grand total of $94,000 for the unequivocal ownership of both Superman and Superboy. As a result of the lawsuit, Jerry Siegel and Joe Shuster were fired and their names were stripped from all things Superman. Sadly, much of the settlement fee would go to cover the lawyers, and in Siegel's case, towards his divorce from Bella.

And that was it. National would chart the Man of Steel's future unfettered, while the character's creators would, for the first time in a decade, be fending for themselves.

LAUREN AGOSTINO: When *Holding Kryptonite* came out, I *hated* doing interviews or panels, because people wanted to fight with you about what you were saying. I finally got to the point where I told everybody: "Here's Siegel and Shuster's side of the story. Here's DC's side of the story. Here's the gray area. Choose whatever side you'd like."

BRAD RICCA: *Holding Kryptonite* really gives the other side of the argument — DC's side — in a way no one has, making the point that editorial was not just sitting there with a big cigar counting their money. They were hands on, saying things like, "You need to do this, and you're late." And the fact is that Jerry would not stop asking for more. There's this fascinating back and forth with DC saying, "You need to do this," and Jerry saying, "Yeah, but you need to pay us more."

ROBERT GREENBERGER: Siegel and Shuster each made a series of decisions that did not turn out well for them, because they were young men without much of an education beyond high school. They really needed a manager at a time when there were no managers or agents for comic writers and artists. That's compared to guys like Donenfeld and Liebowitz, who were sharp cookies and made the best deals for themselves possible. And any time Siegel would come around with his hand out, saying things like, "Hey, you make a lot of money off of me. What are we going to do?" Liebowitz wanted to cut him a check to get him to go away. They *were* compensated over time and they got the settlement in 1948. After that, they each did their own thing.

BRAD RICCA: Somebody should do a focus on Jerry Siegel and Jack Liebowitz and the relationship between them. I don't know what it would look like, but I think it would be fascinating, because there's always some guy at Comic-Con who claims Liebowitz is the true father of Superman. He says, "Don't let anybody ever tell you anything else," and then there's a huge list of everything he did that made the character "the character." Jack Liebowitz didn't create the character, obviously, but it *is* compelling.

MARK WAID: We always talk about how Warner Bros ripped them off and DC ripped them off, and that's true, and you understand it's a very difficult thing to talk about, because you don't want to be perceived as defending the corporation's behavior, but at the same time you cannot turn a blind eye to the fact that to some minor degree, these guys were the authors of their own downfall.

CHAPTER III
Serial Adventurer

National dusted their corporate selves off following the Siegel and Shuster lawsuit, and continued pushing Superman in new directions, the next of which would be in the form of movie serials. Interestingly, there was a connection between the rise of the motion picture and pulp fiction in the early 20ᵗʰ century, the latter of which was frequently offered in weekly installments in print, which would lead to the idea of movie serials/cliffhangers/chapter plays based on them.

ED HULSE (pop culture historian, author, *The Blood 'n' Thunder Guide to Pulp Fiction*): They appealed to the same basic type of person; someone who was looking for escapist entertainment. If you were working in a factory all day and you either wanted to go to the movies or you wanted to read at night, you were looking for escapism. You didn't want *things*. There was a realistic trend in fiction at that time, but those were for the elite, really. The audience for pulps and for movies in those early days was middle class or even a lower-class audience just wanting relief from their daily lives or the oppressiveness of their household chores or whatever it may have been. Of course, both got more sophisticated as the years went by. The serial was kind of a fusion of both fiction and film mediums, because the initial movie serials were actually promotional gimmicks to build newspaper circulation. At that time, a lot of newspapers and their Sunday supplements still carried fiction and somebody said, "You know, if we're running fiction and want to draw somebody to our newspaper, we should serialize stories in the Sunday supplement and then have film versions of them that people can see and one will promote the other." There would be some people who would go the movies and maybe not be familiar with the newspaper, but they'd come to the newspaper because they'd want to read the next installment of the serial. Conversely, there were people who might only be newspaper readers who would say, "Gee, I'm really enjoying this story. It'd be nice to see how they turn it into a motion picture."

Looking back at the form historically, the general consensus about movie serials is that they were designed solely to get each chapter to the cliffhanger ending with the hope of enticing the viewer to return to their local theater the following week.

ED HULSE: The early serials actually didn't have cliffhanger endings, per se. What they did do, though, was they ended each episode at a point of interest that would make the viewer want to come back the following week, or in the case of the reader make them want to buy the next chapter. There were situational endings as well as what we call the cliffhanger endings. Even something like *The Perils*

Actor Kirk Alyn, who played the Man of Steel in the Superman *and* Atom Man vs. Superman *movie serials in, respectively, 1948 and 1950 (art © and courtesy D.C. Stuelpner; Superman © and TM DC Comics/Warner Bros. Discovery)*

of Pauline, which has become kind of synonymous in the popular culture with this kind of entertainment, only a couple of its 20 chapters had cliffhanger endings. But the serial, when it first started, was a big deal, because feature-length movies had not taken over the motion picture industry. And the serials were one-reelers, running 10 to 15 minutes, or two-reelers, which ran 20 to 25 or even 30 minutes. The serial became a feature attraction by virtue of the fact that it was something that would bring people back to the theater on a given night, every week. They were hugely successful and virtually all of them had newspaper counterparts. Some of them even appeared in pulp magazines.

By the 1930s, and before the explosion of the comic book industry, a large part of the pulps shifted over to so-called "Hero Pulps," and included characters such as The Shadow, Doc Savage and The Spider, with them and others being spun off into radio dramas and movie serials. By the time Superman arrived on the scene in 1938, there were also serials based on Zorro, The Lone Ranger and, most importantly, Flash Gordon.

ED HULSE: The one that kicked everything into high gear was *Flash Gordon* with Buster Crabbe as the star. The newspaper strip at that point was only printed on Sunday, but it was run by the Hearst newspapers, which were very successful and therefore it had an enormous circulation. Science-fiction at that point was not the well-established genre it is today, and there were a lot of people who didn't want to have anything to do with science-fiction and thought it was trash. But it emerged thanks to things like *Flash Gordon* as something that attracted popular attention. And *Flash Gordon* was one of the first serials in many years to kind of break out of that ghetto of Saturday kiddie matinee and actually play first-run downtown movie palaces. And there were quite a few bookings along those lines, which made *Flash Gordon* phenomenally successful.

Well, *that's* when the floodgates opened and at that point Universal said, "Clearly this is the path to success. You start out by licensing a comic character that has a built-in following, and most of it's going to be kids, and we get that, but maybe some of the better ones are going to appeal to adults too." Within just a couple of years, usually three out of every four serials were adapted from a comic strip character.

And those would include such properties as Mandrake the Magician, Dick Tracy, Buck Rogers, The Green Hornet, Captain Marvel, Captain Midnight, Batman, The Phantom, Captain America, Brenda Starr, The Vigilante and the various sequels they spawned. Surprisingly, the Man of Steel wouldn't appear in serial form for a full decade after his comic launch in the form of 1948's Superman, *a 15-part Columbia Pictures serial. In it, Superman's origin is retold as Krypton explodes and he is rocketed to Earth, where he's adopted by the Kents and grows up to be the Man of Steel in Metropolis. The real focus of the storyline is on a villain calling herself The Spider Lady and her criminal machinations.*

Two years later, fans flocked to theaters for Atom Man vs. Superman, *another 15-chapter tale that this time has Luthor (no first name) blackmailing Metropolis — the city must pay or he'll destroy it. Obviously, Superman has to stop him.*

There actually was an attempt to adapt the character into the serial format in 1940 when Republic Pictures negotiated to bring Superman to the live screen, and this was prior to the Fleischer Brothers/Paramount animated shorts that would kick off in 1941. Republic, however, pushed back against National's contractual creative control over the character, even though they would twice announce the project. Republic was ultimately shot down and Columbia landed the rights in 1947.

Hulse has a level of fascination for the unmade Republic Superman serial, which was aborted midstream. In the summer of 1940, Republic prepared what the studios called a campaign book that included the title.

ED HULSE: In those years, the studios were still doing what you call a "block book," where they are trying to convince theaters to buy their entire year or reserve their entire year's output, which they then would get for a discounted price and for which they'd pay off in increments throughout the year. They would send out these books with ads for all the things that they planned on making. Some of them would be made, some of them would never get made or be replaced by other projects. But this was the grift — to try and get theaters to commit to big blocks of product.

In Republic's 1940 campaign book, they announced a Superman serial. They wrote a script and DC, as part of the contract, had script approval. And this had been an issue for Republic before, because they made some changes in *The Lone Ranger*, which the copyright owners were not happy with. But the story of the Superman serial involved the mad scientist who plans on conquering the world and furthering his own criminal empire with an army of robots. And this is why you need Superman, because the robots are going to be more powerful, and you need someone like Superman to fight them effectively.

JERRY BECK (film historian, author, *Pink Panther: The Ultimate Guide to the Coolest Cat in Town!*): They started writing that script, but it just wasn't Superman, and National was wisely so protective of their baby and pulled it back.

We don't know what Republic would have exactly done with the character, but we may get an idea from the fact that they later did *Captain America*, which has absolutely nothing to do with the comic. It was just the costume and the name; they don't even use the Steve Rogers secret identity. At the same time, Republic *did* have an exception, strangely enough, with Captain Marvel, which they did fantastically.

ED HULSE: When DC took back the rights, Republic was *really* pissed off, because they had announced this thing and exhibitors were expecting it. They'd already invested a fair amount of money in it, because they got five writers working on the script, the whole thing was plotted out and they made costume tests. They designed a dummy for the flying scenes, which they ultimately used for *Adventures of Captain Marvel*.

Although there are no records indicating how much Republic was paying DC for the rights to Superman, what is known is that Paramount very much wanted the rights and pursued them aggressively for what would become the Max and Dave Fleischer theatrical animated shorts. Word is that they offered $10,000 for those rights, which most assuredly would have been more than Republic would have paid.

ED HULSE: On top of that, at the time, Paramount, unlike Republic, owned its own theater chain, which meant that those cartoons would get tremendous exposure. Also, the fact is that it was the Fleischers, who had at this point done *Gulliver's Travels* and were doing the other Paramount cartoons. DC knew that these cartoons were going to get top production value, and they were, indeed, the most expensive cartoons ever made up to that point. I have a feeling that DC said, "We're going to do a lot better with Paramount than we are with Republic," which was one step above poverty row, "and Paramount's going to get these cartoons into the big downtown theaters, which is really going to enhance our property." It's my belief that they really fudged all this bullshit about not being happy with the Republic script and pulled the plug.

JERRY BECK: The thinking back then was that, clearly, since this is a comic strip, it's either got to be an animated cartoon or a movie serial a la *Tailspin Tommy, Flash Gordon, Buck Rogers* and many others. I think about a lot of the comic strips that were adapted into animated cartoons in the teens, '20s, '30s and beyond, and the thinking was not to make a major motion picture with this superhero, and in the end the Fleischers were the perfect people to do it.

ED HULSE: What does Republic do in response? Having already invested this much money into it, they said, "Look, we're not going to throw out this script." They changed the character and titled the serial *Mysterious Doctor Satan* after the villain, and the army of robots became one, which he was trying to perfect and turn into an army. They cut the scale way back, and all the scenes that would have involved Clark Kent and Superman now involve a character named Bob Wayne, who is a hero called the Copperhead and is decidedly non-superheroic. They had a girl reporter who instead of being Lois Lane is Lois Scott, and her father is the inventor of an electrical device that Doctor Satan needs to put in his robot so that he can control it from far distances. This was their way of salvaging the Superman script, and the *Mysterious Doctor Satan* was released at the tail end of 1940, just as Superman was planned to be released.

JERRY BECK: If you look at the growing relationship between DC and Columbia, I think Superman was headed for Columbia as soon as the Paramount deal was over, and that deal seemed to be over in something like 1947, having started about 1941. It seems like it was a six-year deal and my theory is they were able to use Superman or the concept in Popeye and Little Lulu cartoons, among others, during the remaining years after the Superman animated shorts. That's just my theory, meaning when that was over, Columbia took over with the serials.

ED HULSE: What a lot of people don't understand is that the marketing of serials and the profit margins were very small, because a lot of theaters did not use serials. In the sound era, you never had more than 35% or 40% of theaters showing serials. A lot of them just didn't bother, especially the big downtown picture palaces that were owned by the major studio chains. And, of course, they were just starting to be broken up by the government and the divestiture came down just around the time that the first Superman serial came out. The other was that, unlike movies, which paid a percentage of the box office take, serial chapters were rented to the exhibitors on a flat fee basis. Usually it was only like five bucks a chapter. So on something like *Superman* or *The Lone Ranger*, or even *Batman*, where the property had a much greater value in visibility, they would charge the exhibitors more in some cases, because they realized they were likely to get more kids in the front due to built-in markets.

After the war, Republic did not license anything; their serials were all original and featured characters created in-house like *Rocket Man, Commando Cody* and that whole deal. The other thing is they did *not* want to spend money. They said, "Whatever money we are going to spend on serials, we are going to put into the production," whereas at Columbia the value was you lay out money to license the property and you just take that out of the budget. And you do whatever you can do for the budget. So once Columbia hired Sam Katzman as a producer and director to do all their serials in 1945, they had the perfect guy. He knew how to cut corners like nobody else.

ANDY MANGELS (film historian; author, *The Superhero Book: The Ultimate Encyclopedia of Comic Book Icons and Hollywood Heroes*): Production began on the first Superman serial in late 1947, with the sometimes too-thrifty Sam Katzman producing. *Superman* was initially directed by Spencer Bennet and Thomas Carr, the latter of which did not like working with Katzman, and who later directed several of the *Adventures of Superman* TV shows. Bennet was a master of trick photography and in-camera special effects while controlling the budget. Both abilities proved beneficial on the low-budget Superman serials.

ED HULSE: Bennet was the director who used to cut the movie in his head. In other words, a lot of directors would shoot a lot of material and they would take the best stuff in the cutting room. Well Bennet, by virtue of his long experience going back to the silent era, knew what angles he would need to get the best effect, so he wouldn't shoot as much film. He saved Sam Katzman enormous amounts of money just by not shooting as much film, and when you are not shooting as much film, you are not spending as many days and you are not spending as much time. Time is money on these movies. At that point, it did not matter that they were paying big money to license things like Superman and Batman and the other DC heroes, because Bennet was saving them money on the production. And that is also why the animated scenes in *Superman* look so piss poor — when Superman flies, he's suddenly animated.

ROBERT GREENBERGER (author, *The Essential Superman Encyclopedia*): Well, they did the animated transformation for Bela Lugosi when he turned into Dracula; it was a tried-and-true trick of the era.

ROB O'CONNOR (co-host, *All Star Superfan Podcast*): The serials pale in comparison to the grounded approach of the legendary George Reeves series, but more importantly, their animated flying scenes look like garbage compared to the vastly superior Captain Marvel serial from Republic Pictures starring Tom Tyler (which contains, and I'm being serious here, the best flying scenes in live-action prior to Christopher Reeve).

STEVE YOUNIS (webmaster, supermanhomepage): The serials are really dated, obviously. You look back and you think, "Wow, these are really cheesy," but what they were for their time were cliffhangers, intended as one of those things they used to put at the beginning before a movie in the cinema. These cliffhangers were big at the time.

ROBERT GREENBERGER: I finally saw the serials at a convention some-where and thought it was really interesting. Kirk Alyn as Superman was certainly a good, square-jawed hero. There was a sense of fun he brought to it.

KIRK ALYN (actor, "Superman," in *Superman* **and** *Atom Man vs. Super-man***):** When I would do conventions around the country, I'd usually get up and do an hour's talk and I used film to show what I meant. I'd say, "How many of you know what a cliffhanger is?" Very few people would raise their hands, so I would say, "Serials are broken up into 12 or 15 chapters and you see one chapter a week. You've got to come back next week to see the next chapter. The reason you've got to come back is because of the cliffhanger. The leading man or the leading lady or somebody gets into such a precarious position that you swear they'll never get out of, so you have to come back next week to see how they do."

ED HULSE: The *Superman* serial had much more impact than many other serials, because it was one of the few serials where the character was *so* popular, not only in the comic books, but the Sunday comic strips, the daily newspaper strips and the radio show. By that time, it had been around for 10 years and had a mas-sive following. As a result, they were able to get some of the first-run houses that normally did not run serials. They would rent *Superman*, which had not really been done to any great extent since the first Flash Gordon and Lone Ranger serials in 1938. Or the first Dick Tracy serial — those were such phenomenally popular properties that you occasionally had some of the big downtown theaters book them. Superman was that kind of thing.

TIM DEFOREST (author, *Storytelling in the Pulps, Comics and Radio: How Technology Changed Popular Fiction in America***):** I'm a fan of both serials with Kirk Alyn; I think he did a great job. He was effective as Clark and had a bit of geekiness. *And* he was a good Superman.

Born John Feggo Jr. on October 8, 1910 in Oxford, New Jersey, Kirk Alyn began his career working as a chorus boy on Broadway, in the 1930s appearing on stage in such shows as Girl Crazy, Of Thee I Sing *and* Hellzapoppin'. *There was also an opportunity to sing and dance as part of vaudeville, though by the early 1940s he decided to relocate to Hollywood with the dream of movie stardom in his eyes. Unfortunately, he scored mostly un-credited roles in about 20 films between 1942's* My Sister Eileen *and 1944's* Storm Over Lisbon. *A few character parts followed, as did the serial* Daughter of Don Q. *Besides the*

Superman productions, there would be a number of other uncredited parts and bigger roles in the serials Federal Agents vs. Underworld Inc.*,* Radar Patrol vs. Spy King *and the starring role in* Blackhawk*, based on the National Periodicals comic of the same name. Eventually he would return to New York for more stage work.*

FRED SHAY (film and radio historian): I didn't meet Kirk Alyn in person until 1989 at a show in New Jersey, but he had called me many times over the years before that. He had first contacted me in 1979. He was working on his second book, which he never finished, and he asked DC Comics for material from the serials. They basically told Kirk to get lost. When DC refused, Kirk contacted me about the serials. I still don't know where he got my name, and at the time I wondered why I had gotten a call from him. He had contacted me about the serial and we stayed in contact with each other over the years. I made a deal with DC for the items Kirk needed plus copies for the National Broadcasters Hall of Fame Museum. DC got what they wanted in return — film of the unaired *Superboy* and *Superpup* pilots in exchange for the serials.

KIRK ALYN: I did six pictures for the same producer, and when they were going to do *Superman*, people from DC came out. They wanted to be in on the interview. They interviewed and interviewed and interviewed. Finally, Sam Katzman, the producer, called me up and says, "Kirk, do you want to do *Superman*?" I said, "What is it? A publicity stunt of some kind? Because how are you going to get Superman on film?" He says, "Well, there's a couple of guys here from DC Comics that want to meet you. Come down right away." I went down and I took the shirt off, showed them the muscles and everything. I heard one of the guys from DC Comics whisper, "Jesus! He looks just like Clark Kent!" And I go, "Oh boy. I'm in!" After a little bit more, they said, "Take off the pants." I made a joke out of it and Sam said, "You're going to wear tights, Kirk. We want to see your legs." So, I did. It was very quick. I think I spent 10 minutes there. Maybe less.

FRED SHAY: Actually, Kirk *was* a lot like Clark Kent. He was a quiet, reserved man. He was just one of the nicest people you'd ever meet.

JIM HAMBRICK (Kirk Alyn's manager; owner, Super Museum in Metropolis, Illinois): He was just always in a good mood. I *never* saw him in a down or bad mood. We got along well. He used to call me his son. He had his own son, but they parted in a bad or difficult way and all that. But he called me every day for 15 years. He'd say, "I just wanted to talk; you're like a son to me and I want to share things with you." So that was nice. I was his manager for a time and he toured with my mobile museum and would meet the public.

KIRK ALYN: I went down to sign the contract. I knew the secretary; I'd signed many contracts with her before. She looked at me and says, "Oh Kirk, you don't know how happy I am that they finally picked you. Do you know how many people we looked at before we called you?" I say, "No, how many?" She says, "About 125, that's all." I didn't know whether I should be hurt, because I wasn't there first, or happy that I got the job. She said half of them couldn't speak English; they were just musclemen and weightlifters.

JIM HAMBRICK: He was a hoofer. He spent a lot of time on Broadway dancing with Ginger Rogers, Fred Astaire, Gene Kelly and all those people. He was a good dancer and it helped him maintain his balance as Superman.

RAY MORTON (film historian and author, *Close Encounters of the Third Kind: The Making of Steven Spielberg's Classic Film*): Kirk Alyn is fine as Clark Kent, but I've never believed him as Superman. He doesn't look the part and he doesn't feel the part. He is just not physically imposing or impressive in the way Superman should be and his face is too non-descript. Alyn always felt that his ballet training was a big asset to his performance, feeling it gave him a lightness and grace appropriate for a man who could fly. Had he actually flown in the serials on wires or some other method that allowed him to employ that grace, it might have been true. But since he could only display it in scenes in which Superman was running around on the ground, it just looked like prancing. And there just wasn't the force of personality in his performance that Superman requires.

Noel Neill, born November 25, 1920 in Minneapolis, Minnesota, was cast in the role of reporter Lois Lane, playing her a bit feistier than she later would on the 1950s television series Adventures of Superman. *As a child, at the age of 4, she was enrolled at a school for aspiring performers, not surprising given the fact that her mother was a stage dancer and, appropriately enough, her father was a news editor at the* Minneapolis Star Journal. *She spent much of her teen years singing, dancing and playing the banjo at different country fairs throughout the Midwest. Upon graduating from high school in 1938, she began working as a writer for* Women's Wear Daily. *Neill pursued acting and modeling and actually found herself one of the top pin-up models for GIs during World War II (reportedly right behind Betty Grable in terms of popularity).*

Eventually she signed with Paramount Pictures and then Monogram Pictures, and worked in a variety of roles, including in Westerns and serials. She started working with producer Sam Katzman in 1945 in a number of teen musical comedies, and he thought of her when the role of Lois Lane came up.

Tommy Bond, best known for playing "Butch" in the Our Gang *comedies, was cast as cub reporter Jimmy Olsen; with character actor Pierre Watkin as* Daily Planet *editor Perry White; Nelson Leigh and Luana Walters as Jor-El and Lara, respectively; Edward Cassidy and Virginia Carroll as Eben and Martha Kent; and Carole Forman as Spider Lady.*

NOEL NEILL (actress, "Lois Lane"): My agent got me the job. I was under contract to Paramount at the time. It was a very simple job to get, because I looked like the Lois Lane of the comic books. I hadn't read any of the comics though. I think that was more of a boy's thing than a girl's thing in those days. I just looked at Lois Lane as a working girl. My dad was in the newspaper business, so even though the serial and the TV show had nothing to do with a newspaper office really, I kind of knew what was to be expected.

RAY MORTON: I do like Noel Neill's performance in the serials as a very spunky Lois Lane. She's also really young – Neill really puts the girl in the girl reporter and she has an intrepid feistiness missing from her TV version of Lois, which I always found to be bland and matronly.

ANDY MANGELS: Tommy Bond played the role of Jimmy Olsen as a gutsy go-getter, with little regard for his safety. He even brought some sense of menace to the role, although that could be more because of his hard-edged facial features than his actions. Bond did continue the trend that Jimmy would continue to follow for over 40 years: acting first, thinking later.

RAY MORTON: Tommy Bond made for an appealing pugnacious Jimmy Olsen, while Pierre Watkin is fine as a stock "Big City Newspaper Editor" Perry White in a conception of the role that cried out for James Gleason.

FRED SHAY: I honestly don't believe that there isn't anybody that isn't a Superman fan in some way, shape or form. And Kirk was such a fantastic actor and tried his best to make every role work for him. Plus, he had a lot of fun playing the part.

KIRK ALYN: The first day in the studio, they asked me if I had ever read the comic book. I did listen to the radio show, but I said no. They said, "You haven't? Jesus, run out and get him a comic book." So they got me a comic book, I opened it and said, "Who? Me?" They had a photographer there. "Hold that pose, Kirk!" And that's the picture in the beginning of my book, *A Job for Superman.*

One of the challenges that Alyn had to face is the fact that he was the first person on film tasked with having to play the distinctions between Clark Kent and Superman.

KIRK ALYN: First of all, our scripts were adapted from the radio shows. For the first serial, that is. They left little things in like, "Up, up and away!" and "This looks like a job... *for Superman!*" I went to the director and said, "This is ridiculous when you can see the character." It's all right on radio when you don't see what he's doing and you say, "Up, up and away," because he's going to take off. Or, "This looks like a job for Superman," because he's going to change. But I can do it with just an expression, a little motion and they'll know I'm going to get into the Superman outfit. He says, "Well, it's in the script all the way through, Kirk. Just do it once and we won't do it the next time." It's in that picture once. As far as changing goes, I said to the director, "Now you *see* this guy is two different fellows. I'm a 'meek and milk' person as the script called me. But I have to be stronger when I do Superman." I showed him how I would do it. We studied it a bit and then came to a mutual decision on how much change to make. I also said that if I'm going to show my muscles, the voice has to match it. And then [*voice goes up half an octave*] I'm just a mild fellow.

FRED SHAY: As I said, he did have fun with the role. Now, he was only billed as Clark Kent, because DC Comics and Columbia Pictures wanted this, but Kirk did a good job as both Kent and Superman.

KIRK ALYN: When playing Superman, I knew that nobody could hurt me. I welcomed five guys attacking me, because I just slapped them around. I never punched a man. I always slapped them and they went flying off to the sides. I noticed in the television show he sometimes acted like a boxer would; he punched fellows. In keeping with the character, I thought if Superman ever punched anybody, his head would fly off. Getting back to being happy, I knew they couldn't hurt me. They could shoot guns at me, and I'd laugh at them. And that irritated the hell out of them, which is what I wanted.

STEVE YOUNIS: Kirk Alyn himself obviously was a dancer, and you can see that in the way he moves around as Superman. He doesn't have the masculinity that you would get from George Reeves' Superman later on, but he really had nothing to go by visually other than the cartoons. As a result, there wasn't a lot to determine who this character is. Other than that, he's this stoic kind of guy who comes in, saves the day and gets out of there. He's not a guy that really hangs around for the praise. But I enjoyed watching the Kirk Alyn serials just for the historic look at what they did back then. I appreciate what he brought to the role, but I don't think he'll go down as anybody's favorite Superman.

JIM HAMBRICK: I used to tease Kirk Alyn, because I became his manager and he knew how I felt about George Reeves, who he called the imposter. He'd say to me, "Is he still your favorite Superman?" And I'd go, "Always has been, Kirk. The serials weren't out when I was born in '54."

KIRK ALYN: Sometimes what we were doing felt silly, but I had to make it look real. And I start laughing. I mean, there was the time I ripped a bumper off a car and tied those guys up in the bumper. I had to do that five or six times, because those guys were making funny faces, whispering to each other. If they know you'll take it, they'll do it to you. I worked with some jokers. I mean, that's awfully silly, picking one guy up and throwing him, hitting the other guy, and I tear the bumper off and tie them with it. Before I got through tying them up, I was laughing like hell. The director would say, "For Christ's sake, Kirk, let's do it again." They'd have to straighten the bumper out and we did it again. It was lead, of course. But you had to get some laughs out of the thing, or you'd go crazy. You made some stuff that was very funny.

FRED SHAY: There were also some rough moments making the serials. One time, Kirk was near an airplane in a scene, and his Superman costume almost caught on fire.

NOEL NEILL: Working on the serial was like working on a Western. Most of the men had the work, what with all of the stunt work and location work. Gals didn't have that much to do. We just had to sit around and be rescued.

ANDY MANGELS: Although Kirk Alyn was Neill's savior on screen, their relationship off-screen was not so chummy.

NOEL NEILL: We didn't get along very well. We became fine friends, but I never really knew him that well.

KIRK ALYN: Every once in a while she'd do a scene over and over. With the short time we had to do the picture, it was important to do it right the first time. As close as you could. With her it sometimes took several takes and the director would say, "Come on, honey, get the lead out of your ass and do it!" He wouldn't say that often, he wasn't a bad guy, but once in a while. And she'd go and pout and think it was my fault, because — well, I don't know why. I never yelled at her. Anytime that I'd do anything, I wanted it to be as right as I know how to make it. With Superman I did that. If anybody gets in the way, I gently tell them, "I'm trying to do this, would you mind doing something that'll match

it?" Maybe this happened. That was the best acting she ever did, what she did in
Superman. But otherwise we got along all right. I didn't pay any attention to her
pouting.

NOEL NEILL: I think he made a wonderful Superman. He was excellent,
because he was very athletic, and with his dance background, it was very easy for
him to look good doing what he had to do as Superman.

KIRK ALYN: They always hire a stunt person for the leading role for fear
that if the lead does anything and gets hurt, he'll hold up production. But this
guy did about two days' work, and when they looked at the film, this guy didn't
even look like me from the back. The director says, "Kirk, kids won't believe him!"
When a guy puts a hat and coat on, you can get away with it. But in tights, his
legs were different and he didn't run like me, he didn't move like me. The director
said, "Kirk, would you mind doing your own stunts?" And I said, "Hell no. There's
nothing to it." I explained to people at conventions that I did all my own stunts.
Somebody will always raise their hand and say, "Did you ever get hurt?" and I say,
"No, I never got hurt, but I damn near got *killed* a couple of times."

FRED SHAY: There was the famous train scene where Superman had to
straighten a piece of the railroad track back while a train with Jimmy Olsen and
Lois Lane barreled through. Kirk was worried, because the train was going 90
miles per hour. The crew deserted the area while the cameras were rolling. He had
his foot braced against the piece of the track and panicked when he felt the tracks
vibrating.

KIRK ALYN: The idea was that these guys were bending the rail out of place,
the train was coming and surely would turn over and destroy everybody in it. I
fly down just in the nick of time, push the track back and held it there while the
train went over. This is all right while we talked about it, but when I went down
on location, they had a fellow from the railroad to oversee what we were doing so
we couldn't hurt ourselves. And no lawsuits. The director says, "How far back from
the track can Kirk be and not get hurt by the train?" And he asks, "You want him
there while the train goes through? If he stays 15 inches back from where those
railroad ties end, he'll be perfectly safe, because the train only comes a little beyond
the ties. If you'll brace his feet on the tracks in back of him and he holds on to
those ties real tight" — the camera on the other side pointed up on me — "that'll
make a good shot with the wheels going between the camera and him and his face
there." I'm standing there looking at this, paying no attention, because I've done a
lot of car chases, and those car chases are never as fast as they seem, because they

shoot them slow speed and on the screen they're fast speed. I thought, "They're going to slow the train down and then when they show it on the screen, it'll look like it's going through there fast." I say, "Okay."

I got down there. They lined up the camera. And I looked back to see where the guy was that told me to stay back 15 inches. Well, he was about 50 *yards* away. I say, "Oh, well, the director and the cameraman will be here." And the director says, "When the train comes, Kirk, give me a nice firm, strong look." So up he got. The cameraman put it on automatic and they both ran like hell about a hundred yards away. Well, I've got butterflies in my stomach. The train was coming. I thought, "Jesus! He's not going to slow down." I almost said nuts to this and was going to run too. But before I could make up my mind to run, the train was on me.

FRED SHAY: The train speeds through and creates its own personal cyclone as each car goes by. The locomotive disappears into the distance as the crew comes back. Director Spencer Gordon Bennet clapped Kirk's shoulder and said, "Great job, Kirk! That was terrific! And we got it all in one take!"

KIRK ALYN: And when he said, "We don't have to come back tomorrow," I said, "The hell with that. We do anymore of those, I quit!"

Beyond the physical stunts, there were the flying sequences which, as noted, ended up taking a rather unique approach in the first serial, Superman, *with Alyn starting the leap into the air and abruptly turning into an animated version of Superman flying away.*

STEVE YOUNIS: Obviously the special effects in these serials represented a situation where they weren't able to have Superman flying, so it is pretty jarring when you see him going from being live-action to a cartoon as he takes flight.

KIRK ALYN: The original idea was that they were going to take piano wires and hang me up on them. They didn't want to put a harness on me, because you can see something is pulling on you. With the breastplate on, you hang in the sky with the piano wires through the uniform in the back. You don't see the pull on it, so it's floating or flying. For one day, I spent eight hours flying. I was hanging up there and the guy says, "Hold your legs up, Kirk." They didn't make any provisions for my legs. You lie on a table, sometimes on the edge of a table, and hold your legs up and see what that does to your stomach muscles. I was up there for eight hours, trying to hold my damn legs up.

Originally the special effects guys actually went to the producer and said to him, "Now if we make a breastplate to hang him up with the piano wires, I think you'll like it, because we'll paint the wires and photograph them in such a manner that you won't see the wires." He believed them. After I worked the whole day — I hurt all over from doing it — they looked at the screen and they could see the wires just as plain as you could see me. You should have heard the producer: "Get them all out of here! You're all fired! Get off the set; you're not working here anymore!" He called them all kinds of names.

TIM DEFOREST: What's surprising is that I have twice watched both serials with kids; once with my nephew, who was a kid, and some other kids. I was babysitting on a weekly basis, and the serials *still* entertain children. I was wondering how they would take when the special effects of him flying turned him into an animated figure. They thought it was *so* cool. It might have even drawn them more into it. Then we started keeping track of who got knocked out more often, Lois Lane or Jimmy Olsen. It became a drinking chocolate milk game. The truth is, both of them would have had serious brain damage in real life — which is why, I guess, they never knew Clark was Superman.

ED HULSE: I have a friend named Sam Sherman who was, himself, a movie producer. He had a company called Independent International Pictures and he was the co-editor of *Screen Thrills Illustrated* magazine in the early '60s. He was born in 1940 and he vividly remembers seeing the first *Superman* serial. When it opened then, it was a really big deal and the house was packed; wall-to-wall kids. But as soon as the first animated flight scene came up, Sam said the kids shrieked, "He's a cartoon!" It didn't fool anyone and the kids were pissed off as the serial went on, but in the end they enjoyed it enough and were willing to suspend their disbelief and they liked Kirk. At the same time, a lot of the filmmakers counted a lot on kids being fooled and forgetting things from week to week, which is one of the reasons they would cheat a lot in the cliffhanger endings, because they figured, "The kids are never going to remember things exactly."

KIRK ALYN: Later, we went to a special effects studio and we did it differently. I stood on the floor and looked straight up. On the ceiling they had a fan blowing down at me with a smoke pot for clouds supposedly coming by me. I'm making motions like I'm turning from side to side and flying, but I'm standing on the floor, looking straight up at the ceiling and I even did some dialogue up there. They then got the camera over on its side and photographed me standing up, so when they projected it on the screen, I was horizontal rather than vertical. That worked fine. In the second serial you'll notice when I'm flying, you don't see my feet. You'll see my legs, my knees, but *not* my feet. But it looks good.

ED HULSE: Look, the kids knew what was what, but they also knew that was the game, because it was part of a ritual. What guys like us are missing is that if we sit down in our living rooms, we are watching these things on DVD on the small screen. We are *not* watching them on a 40-foot screen in a dark theater surrounded by other kids and people. Every kid knew that no matter how dire the cliffhanging ending was, the guys were always going to survive. It just stands to reason given that you've got a 15-chapter serial, they're not going to kill somebody off in Chapter 2.

ANDY MANGELS: Kirk Alyn's portrayal of Superman won over the masses. *Superman* became the most popular — and profitable — serial ever done. A second serial, *Atom Man vs. Superman*, was rushed into filming. This one featured the same heroic cast, but a new villain. The hooded man who menaced Metropolis under the name of Atom Man was none other than Superman's arch nemesis Lex Luthor, played by Lyle Talbot, who wore a bald skull-cap for the role, just as Gene Hackman would do decades later.

NOEL NEILL: I never expected another Superman serial. I never went to the serials, and had never even seen the Superman ones for a long time. *Superman* was just another month's work. I had done some other serials for Sam Katzman, so this was really no different.

ED HULSE: Superman, especially the first one, was kind of the last gasp of what they called the first-run serial. Now serials were just part of the profit picture for the studios, and what finally happened was between costs rising and the theaters using them declining, it finally got to the point in the mid-'50s where they said it's not worth it anymore. The Columbia serials from that time were doing maybe $20,000 to $30,000 in profit, and by this time Columbia was starting its Screen Gems unit and starting to sell their movies to TV. And if they were focusing so much on TV, why make all of those serials? *That's* why the serials kind of died out.

But what's difficult to convey about serials is that when you're talking about them, or even writing about them, you have to be really specific about the fact that there was definitely a ritualistic aspect to these things and the kids were willing participants. It would be too much to say it was an interactive experience, but as soon as the music swelled, they knew they were on the verge of action or just getting into a big fight scene. So again, that was all part of what they expected; it was something they were conditioned for. And overall, they loved it.

RAY MORTON: The tales that the serials tell aren't particularly involving. The Spider Lady plot of *Superman* is pretty standard-issue serial stuff — serviceable but never compelling and completely forgettable. *Atom Man vs. Superman* does better in the villain department because it brings in Superman's all-time arch foe Lex Luthor, which is cool. And the storyline has some sci-fi elements (including a dry run of the Phantom Zone) that brings it in line with the Paramount cartoons and anticipates the comic book tales of the '50s and '60s. But any assets the serials have are undermined by the overall (and very obvious) cheapness of the productions.

ANDY MANGELS: *Atom Man vs. Superman* was not as successful as the first serial, but still brought in huge revenue for Columbia. More gimmicks and outlandish weapons were used, and the flying sequences were live rather than animated. This was destined to be the last Superman serial. Talk had been made of a third serial, but the days of the great movie serial were coming to an end. Kirk Alyn left Hollywood typecast and the other actors resumed their careers none the worse for wear.

Alyn was the first, but certainly not the last, actor to portray Superman who in a sense was made captive by the role, the rest of the world not really imagining him in different parts. It's something that George Reeves, Christopher Reeve and Tom Welling would eventually be forced to deal with as well.

KIRK ALYN: I was very happy I'd made a picture that everybody liked, but when I started to go around to the studios, everybody looked at me and said, "Hi, Superman." I said, "Wait a minute, cut that stuff out, you're doing a picture here. I know there's something in it that I can do." And they'd say, "But we can't use you, Kirk. You're Superman." So I went to Columbia, where I made the serial. Columbia gave me the same thing! I said, "I can't get another job in pictures as a result of this goddamn thing." I said the hell with it. I decide to go back to New York. I'd done 14 years on Broadway. I knew all the agents, the producers, and I'd work all I want back there. I was all set to go and they called me for the second one. I thought to myself, "I can't do myself anymore harm. I'll do the second one, and then I'll have that much more money to spend when I get to New York."

While I was doing the second one, they called me from the Chamber of Commerce; Harry Sugarman, who owned Suggie's Tropics, a famous restaurant out here at one time. He called me and says, "Kirk, what do you think about having your star in the sidewalk with your name on it? After all, you were the first Superman."

I said, "Thank you very much, please don't advertise it anymore. I can't get a job now; I'm back to New York, the hell with it. I don't want any part of it." They make such a big thing out of getting a star in the sidewalk, but I didn't want anybody to call me Superman.

JIM HAMBRICK: Sometimes Kirk was very paranoid talking to reporters and so forth, because he didn't want to stay typecast. But the more I got him out there with the mobile museum and he met different people, the more he liked it. And he was able to kind of fish for answers to his own questions he had about it.

ANDY MANGELS: When I spoke to Kirk, I was surprised at the affection he still had for the role of Superman and the attention he paid to its following. His sometimes unnerving candor and honesty allowed for some surprising revelations about the serial and its cast.

KIRK ALYN: These are things in show business you don't think about. But that's how I felt about it. I felt miserable about not being able to get another job. It's difficult, especially when you're working all the time, from out of one picture into another, to all of a sudden the barn door closes. I knew you could get typed, but I always thought it happened to *other* guys. All I did was a picture. What's so big about it? I went back to New York and I did four plays and about 125 commercials in the two years I was there.

ED HULSE: From the anecdotal evidence from people I've spoken to who had seen the serial during their original release, aside from the thing about it going animated when he flew, they liked Kirk and the way he looked. Nobody complained about his suit being too baggy at the knees. They thought he was very impressive as Superman. And, oddly enough, even though he had done several serials before that, and some other feature pictures, it seems that everybody I spoke to who saw the Superman serials in the theaters, none of them had the slightest idea who he was. They could not remember having seen him in anything else, so a lot of them did not think of him as an actor. They just thought of him as the guy who played Superman.

ROB O'CONNOR: Of every 20th century version of Superman, this is the one I have the least fondness for. I love old movie serials and have quite a lot of nostalgia for the Robert Lowery Batman one (cheerfully flawed as it may be), and while the Superman ones are technically superior, they're just too convoluted and downright boring compared to other serials of the time to really become invested in. Producer Sam Katzman was known for pumping stuff out fast and cheap and it shows. While Alyn looks the part, his performance as Superman is a touch wooden, Tommy Bond is totally miscast as Jim Olsen and Pierre Watkin is ridiculous as Editor White. Noel Neill as Lois and Lyle Talbot as Luthor are quite good though.

ED HULSE: Over the years, Kirk was pretty much forgotten until he started going to comic book, movie and nostalgia conventions in the late '60s and early '70s, and there he was a big celebrity. Those conventions are also what led him to write his book *A Job for Superman.* He would go to those shows and get asked the same questions again and again about Superman, so he wrote the book based on that, because he was pretty much a forgotten guy up to that point. The serials had not played on TV in this country because of the TV series, so people had forgotten about them.

JIM HAMBRICK: There were times when he and I would be sitting next to each other and people would start talking about him, not knowing he was right there. After they left, he started to cry. He looked at me and said, "You said that you were going to make sure that I was not the forgotten Superman. *Now* I believe you."

CHAPTER IV
The TV Adventures of Superman

While Kirk Alyn's time in the costume had come to an end, Superman still had a long and varied future ahead of him in different mediums. And National Periodicals was certainly ready to bring him to the next level, which was, naturally, television, and the series Adventures of Superman, *which would run in syndication for six seasons from 1952 to 1958, producing a total of 104 episodes and turn actor George Reeves into a household name, making him one of the most popular Men of Steel ever.*

JIM NOLT (editor, *The Adventures Continue*): I found the first indication of a Superman TV show through Newspaper.com from a 1950 newspaper blurb that said Bob Maxwell was thinking about ending the radio series and moving to television. And then, that's what happened.

CHUCK HARTER (author, *Superboy & Superpup: The Lost Videos*): In May of 1951, Robert Maxwell, who had acted as producer of the radio series, along with colleague Bernard Luber, formed a production company called Superman Incorporated with the express purpose of producing a new television series featuring Superman. The first project to be lensed was *Superman and the Mole Men*, which was planned to be released to theaters as a feature in late 1951 to introduce a new actor in the role of Superman. This would later be edited into two episodes titled "The Unknown People" Parts 1 and 2. But the *first* task at hand was to cast an actor in the dual role of Superman and Clark Kent.

KIRK ALYN (actor, "Superman" in the *Superman* and *Atom Man vs. Superman* movie serials): While I was doing the second serial, Bob Maxwell from DC came to me and he said, "Kirk, how do you feel about doing the television series? We can't pay a lot of money, because we don't know whether it'll go or not." I looked at him. He doesn't know whether it's going to go or not. He can't pay a lot of money. And I can't get another job if I do it. "No, thank you very much. I'm going back to New York." So everybody thought this guy on television was such a hero. I could have done it before they even thought of him.

GARY GROSSMAN (author, *Superman from Serial to Cereal*): Kirk Alyn wanted to do the TV series, but he was never really considered. I don't want to disparage Kirk at all, because he really had a great look for Superman, but George Reeves was a more dynamic actor. We got to see it in "Panic in the Sky," where he has amnesia and he's got to play a character who doesn't know who he is. But *then* realizes he has these abilities, and whether or not he's really Superman,

George Reeves, who was the Superman of the 1950s on Adventures of Superman
(art © and courtesy DC Stuelpner; Superman © and TM DC Comics/Warner Bros. Discovery).

he's going to go out to save the Earth and fulfill his sense of responsibility and duty.

ED HULSE (film historian, author, *Blood 'n' Thunder's Cliffhanger Classics*): Kirk claims that he was offered the role in the *Superman* TV series and turned it down. I'm not so sure about that. I have seen stories in the trades about [producer] Bob Maxwell conducting auditions for the part and seeing a lot of actors. Now, it seems to me that if he had any real interest in Kirk Alyn, saying, "Oh, this guy's already played him twice. He's got a following. Let's use him," he would *not* have been auditioning all these other people — unless it was a money issue where Kirk asked him for some phenomenal amount that Maxwell was not willing to play.

ANTHONY TOLLIN (radio historian): When the Superman radio show eventually lost a hell of a lot of sponsors, its days were limited. But National saw the value of keeping Superman out there. Maybe you couldn't do a regular movie with him, but a low-budget TV show was sustainable, because at the end of every episode it would say that Superman was based on the copyrighted character appearing in *Action Comics* and *Superman* magazine.

CHUCK HARTER: After several auditions, George Reeves, a film veteran who had appeared in various motion picture productions since his film debut in *Gone with the Wind* in 1939, was cast in the lead role. He proved to be an ideal choice, bringing a strong degree of believability in his portrayal of a stern avenging Man of Steel *and* a crusading newspaperman in the form of Clark Kent.

ED HULSE: By that point, George Reeves is appearing in features. He plays the heavy in the first *Jungle Jim* movie in 1948. And then he's working for Robert L. Lippert, who was known as "The King of the Bs," so to go from Lippert movies into the Superman TV show wasn't a big deal for him. I'm told he didn't actually think much of it in the beginning. His view was probably like Clayton Moore with *The Lone Ranger*: "Great, I'm doing a series of shows for so many weeks and I'll get paid for that. I won't have to worry about looking for another job."

JIM BEAVER (actor, George Reeves' biographer): As I began to dig into his story, it seemed much more interesting than I had realized. And the more people I talked to, the more I felt like there was the subject here of an interesting book. Obviously most people come to George Reeves with one or both of two angles. One is that he played Superman and the other is the controversial circumstances of his death. But what interested *me* is the fact that here was a guy who got pretty famous without ever really getting the trappings of success. Oscar Wilde said there are two tragedies in life. One is *not* getting what you want and the other is getting what you want. In some ways, George Reeves got what he wanted, but it didn't play out the way he'd hoped. I'm an actor myself, I've made my living at it, so I felt a real kinship for him, because this is a success story with very little actual success attached to it. This is *not* an actor who got rich and famous. It's accurate he got famous. Not that riches are the only interesting part.

JIM NOLT: George never fully realized how loved he was. He wanted to be admired for his talent and never knew the recognition he would have received if he had been around just a little while longer.

GARY GROSSMAN: I believe, just as Adam West had been adored and found by new fans in life after *Batman*, especially on *Family Guy* where he was Mayor Adam West, George Reeves, had he lived into the '70s and '80s, would have been the go-to guest star on everything from *Family Guy* to *The Love Boat* and other types of shows. Jack Larson [Jimmy Olsen on *Adventures of Superman*] said that George told him, "If I only knew I had adult fans, I'd feel better. I'd be happy." But he didn't have the opportunity to see all the adult fans grow up and recognize that people of all ages, even in the 1950s, were watching *Adventures of Superman*.

He was born George Keefer Brewer on January 5, 1914 in Woolstock, Iowa to Donald Carl Brewer and Helen Lescher early on in their marriage. Shortly after his birth, they separated with George and his mother moving to Illinois. Eventually mother and son ended up in California where she met and married Frank Joseph Bessolo, who adopted George in 1927. George, in turn, took his new father's last name. As noted by Wikipedia, "The Bessolo marriage lasted 15 years, ending in divorce, with the couple separating while Reeves was away visiting relatives. When he returned, his mother told him his stepfather had committed suicide."

JIM NOLT: George found himself under the sole care of his mother who, it was often said, was slightly doting and over-protective. And it wasn't until he enrolled at Pasadena Junior College that he discovered Bessolo wasn't his actual father.

GEORGE REEVES (actor, "Clark Kent/Superman," *Adventures of Superman*): My mother is a real pixie. It was during spring housecleaning, with everything all torn up, that I came across a picture of a good-looking guy, a big fellow, and idly asked who that was. Mother said, "Oh, that's your father," and then stopped dead when she realized what she'd said. Well, I went right after her. I wanted to know who he was and all about it. Then I learned she was 16 when I was born, that she divorced him before I was a year old and that when she married Bessolo, he adopted me. I've never seen my father or heard of him. Don't know whether he's alive or dead. But Bessolo was a grand fellow, never had said a word about the adoption to me. I thought I was Italian, little Georgie Bessolo, who talked Italian and Spanish with the other Bessolos and ate spaghetti, and all of the rest of it. And then I found out I was Irish. All Irish. (*The New York Sun*, 1943)

MICHAEL J. HAYDE (author, *Flights of Fantasy: The Unauthorized but True Story of Radio & TV's Adventures of Superman*): Growing up in Pasadena, and attending its community college, George was undoubtedly aware of the drama students who moved on to the prestigious Pasadena Playhouse. And once he made his decision to try acting, he enrolled there. Hollywood talent scouts were always in attendance, and after a few years of "seasoning," he got his break.

GARY GROSSMAN: George was a boxer in high school, on a Golden Gloves trajectory. He was doing well, but from what I understand, his mother said, "You have too pretty a face to keep doing this." Instead, he went to the Pasadena Playhouse and began taking classes. He became secretary to the director there and that got him to travel a little bit.

MICHAEL J. HAYDE: Reeves was both gregarious and drawn to physical activity. When boxing didn't work out, acting was a way for him to engage in something physically strenuous and also draw upon his natural charm. Plus, he was blessed with an exceptional memory, making it easy to remember lines.

GEORGE REEVES: I went over to the Community Playhouse in Pasadena just to learn how to get on and off a stage. I wound up staying there for five years and became a Shakespearean actor. We were thinking about stage contracts. The movies seemed too far away. We all had our eyes on Broadway. (*St. Louis Post-Dispatch*)

It's important to mention the one aspect of George Reeves' life that seems to have been lost to time, which is the fact that between 1940 and 1950 he was married to fellow Pasadena Playhouse actress Ellanora Needles.

JIM NOLT: I spoke to Ellanora several times and she had nothing but positive things to say about George — practically to the level of praising him. By all accounts, they had a good marriage for most of the years they were together, but according to Ellanora, she left him when they lost some money on an investment and someone richer came along and "swept me off my feet." She was not proud of that, but those were her words. George was deeply hurt and preferred not to talk about Ellanora after that.

His first on-screen role was in Gone with the Wind *(not a bad way to start), as Stuart Tarleton in a short sequence early on the film. Once he was hired, he had to agree to have his hair dyed, a point that he signed an agreement for on June 20, 1939. That letter read, in part, "In consideration of your paying me $108.34, which payment shall be made at the completion of the services referred to below, I agree to have my hair dyed in such manner as you may deem necessary in connection with my services in the photoplay* Gone with the Wind, *and I hereby release you from any and all liability that may arise by reason of such dying of my hair."*

After Gone with the Wind, *George had returned to the Pasadena Playhouse, where he scored his biggest role to date: the lead in a play called* Poncho, *in which he used a Mexican accent. After the first night, he had offers for tests from Paramount, Warner Bros and 20th Century Fox. Warner tested him first and signed him immediately. For the next two years he played minor roles in some of the bigger pictures at the studio, and leads in a few of the minor pictures. In addition to a few short subjects, he appeared in* State Cop, Ride, Cowboy, Till We Meet Again, The Fighting 69th, Torrid Zone, Calling All Husbands, Always a Bride *and* Strawberry Blonde. *He was also "loaned out" for the Ritz Brothers film* Argentina Nights. *Despite all this, those two years didn't do a lot to advance his career and he remained a relative unknown in the business. His contract with Warner dissolved by mutual consent, and he signed a new one with Fox — which didn't really work out much better. This despite the fact he played the lead in* Man at Large *and* Blue, White and Perfect. *A small part in* Blood and Sand *followed, during which he was borrowed by United Artists for* Lydia. *His contract ended uneventfully, which led him to a particular conclusion about his career.*

GARY GROSSMAN: George had leading-man good looks in a Warner Bros way. I say that because his first contract was with them and he was in a series of shorts, but then put into a bunch of James Cagney movies. With his jaw and his nose — his broken nose from boxing — he kind of fit in with the tough guys from the Warner Bros stock company, whether it was Cagney and Bogey or George Raft and others.

GEORGE REEVES: I decided that I knew about horses even if I didn't know how to get ahead in Hollywood, so I thought I'd get me a job in Westerns. Anyhow, I knew a swell girl, Tedi Sherman, who'd studied at Pasadena. She introduced me to her father Harry. He put me to work in a beard as a villain. I did everything around that lot. And finally, there was an opening in the Hopalong Cassidy leads; I became one of the trio which carries the pictures. It was fine. It was fun. (*Schenectady Gazette*)

This, in turn, led to him co-starring with Claudette Colbert in So Proudly We Hail! *and Paramount deciding to sign him up for two films a year. While* So Proudly We Hail! *seemed to signify a true launch for George's acting career, in early 1943 he decided to put it on hold by enlisting in the U.S. Army.*

GEORGE REEVES: I guess it was the picture; I couldn't get it out of my mind. I didn't bring up the fact that I was an actor. You know how people feel about actors. I didn't ask for special duty, so I went right along with the others. That was fine for a while. Then one of the men saw me in a picture and everyone asked why I hadn't told them I was an actor. That was fine too, except that they began giving me special duty work as an actor. I'd do my regular job in the daytime and often give a show at night. It could have been all right, except that I couldn't do both jobs well, so I asked that I be assigned to either one; wherever I fit best. But it's all strictly G.I. with no one getting any publicity. (*The New York Sun*)

GARY GROSSMAN: George didn't go into the infantry, he went into the entertainment corps and traveled with various shows. What happened, though, is that when he came back three years later, the movie industry had changed. People were not picking up contracts. This is from Jack Larson, but according to George, when he was loaned to Fox for *So Proudly We Hail!* which also starred Claudette Colbert, director/producer Mark Sandrich took a real liking to him. This was before he went into the service, but Mark died and George said that if Mark had stayed alive, he promised he would make George a star. George came back from the war and things had changed. He'd end up in B movies, playing bad guys and good guys, and it was like he had gone back to the beginning in a way.

JIM NOLT: After the war and with each passing year, it seemed the roles that George was offered became less. By 1949 he was cast as Sir Galahad in Sam Katzman's low-budget Columbia serial *The Adventures of Sir Galahad*.

GEORGE REEVES: Things got tough and I started digging cesspools. I'm not one of these four-figures-a-week actors. Don't get me wrong, I'd like to be. I can live on what I make, *if* I work regularly. But when five months go by and no movie job comes up, you begin to worry a little — especially if you have a wife to support and a one-acre estate to pay for. I'm not worrying. More and more people are moving out our way, and they all need cesspools. (*Long Beach Press-Telegram*)

MICHAEL J. HAYDE: In truth, he was struggling. Up to mid-1949, he had been under contract to three major studios, all of which had released him. *And* he had done a lot of freelancing. In late summer of that year, he tried New York City in hopes of being cast in a Broadway show, but his work there consisted of live television dramas and occasional radio programs. When he returned to Hollywood in April 1951, it was specifically to appear as a supporting player in Fritz Lang's *Rancho Notorious*. That was immediately followed by another supporting role in *Bugles in the Afternoon*. It's possible that he could've gone on to become a stock character actor for one or two directors like Lang, but leading roles and stardom were unlikely.

When the decision was made to produce the syndicated series Adventures of Superman, *George auditioned for and was cast as the Man of Steel.*

JIM NOLT: When he took on the role of Superman, and with few exceptions, his movie career came to an end. Ironically, it was during these years portraying this strange visitor from another planet, that the caring, compassionate and human side of George Reeves became most evident.

MICHAEL J. HAYDE: He was a journeyman actor with a pleasant, charming presence, but in all the films he did before Superman, it could hardly be said that he lit up the screen. Like William Shatner in *Star Trek* the following decade, he won a role that would bring out the best of his looks, his ability and especially his personal warmth. More than one newspaper critic pointed out that Reeves looked almost exactly like his comic book counterpart as he was then being drawn. That might've led viewers to their TV sets the first time, but it was Reeves' personality, plus the chemistry of the rest of the cast, that brought them back. Jimmy Fidler, a Hollywood columnist, summed it up best back in 1954. Noting that Reeves had appeared in *Gone with the Wind*, he added, "Nobody noticed George at that time, but as the fabulous Superman on the air waves, he's kicking up a lot of dust."

GEORGE REEVES: When I was offered the part, I said, "Superman, what's that?" I'd heard of the comic strip, but that's all I knew. Then I said, "Why not?" and went to work. It started as a batch of 25 pictures and it got to be fun, but then it became a whole career. You have to get used to being laughed at and have to laugh at yourself a little. At first, I wasn't too sure about doing the show, but any actor likes his own series, though it means identification with one character. I took the job and the show has grown like Topsy. It's sort of a fairy tale. Sort of *St. George and the Dragon* all over again. (*St. Louis Post-Dispatch* and the *Press-Telegram Long Beach*)

RAY MORTON: Reeves makes an impressive debut as the Man of Steel. From the jump he looks terrific and is instantly formidable in a way that Kirk Alyn's version of the character never was. In his first stab at the role, Reeves presents a tough, no-nonsense Superman who is supremely confident and incredibly self-assured. George Reeves' version of Superman is fully aware that he has incredible powers far greater than anyone around him — he knows it and he knows that we know it and therefore he feels no need to flaunt those powers or show them off. He doesn't threaten; he doesn't intimidate — he just *is* and that's enough to get almost any situation under control. And if it isn't, he has no compunction about knocking heads or kicking ass. Reeves' Superman could have used his powers to take over the world and serve only himself, but has instead chosen to use those powers to oppose evil and serve the collective good. And again, he is so confident with this choice that he feels no need to announce it — there's no self-righteousness; no grand statement of mission or principles from this Man of Steel — instead he just *acts*. And it is by those actions that will tell you all you need to know about who this man is. In these early days, Reeves' performance presents a Superman very much in the vein of Siegel and Shuster's original, take-no-shit, tough-guy social-justice crusader.

JIM NOLT: Although it was a role that he seemed born to play, it must have been difficult for him to spend his working days in the dual part of Clark Kent and Superman from 1951 until 1957. He so often climbed into the flying rig, jumped off ladders and out of windows, collared crooks and saved the entire city of Metropolis from a multitude of close calls. The hours were long, the pay was short and undoubtedly it was not satisfying professionally.

GEORGE REEVES: Our idea is to give the children good entertainment without all the guts and blood and gore. We think the series should teach them something too. That's why I decided to do this. In *Superman* we're all concerned with giving kids the right kind of show. We don't go for too much violence. Once, for a big fight scene, we had several of the top wrestlers in town do the big brawl. It was considered too rough by the sponsors and producers, so it was toned down. Our writers and the sponsors have children and they are all very careful about doing things on the show that will have no adverse effect on the young audience. We even try, in our scripts, to give gentle messages of tolerance and to stress that a man's color and race and religious beliefs should be respected. (*TV Radio Life*)

Given the idea that Superman and the Mole Men *would appear as a 1951 film leading into the 26 episodes making up season one of the series, casting for the main group of characters took place. These would be for the parts of Lois Lane (the only regular to appear in the film), who had previously been voiced by Joan Alexander on the radio show and in the Fleischer shorts, and Noel Neill in the pair of Superman serials starring Kirk Alyn. Continuing the characterization as presented on radio and in the early comics, producers locked on actress Phyllis Coates. Jack Larson was signed as cub reporter Jimmy Olsen, John Hamilton as* Daily Planet *editor Perry White and Bob Shayne as new character Inspector Bill Henderson, who would have a recurring part.*

ANDY MANGELS (journalist, co-author, *Lou Scheimer: Creating the Filmation Generation*): They skipped over serial veteran Noel Neill for budding screen actress Phyllis Coates. Phyllis had been in several musicals, screen comedies and a few serials.

BRUCE DETTMAN (journalist; pop culture historian): Phyllis Coates must have made an immediate impression on Bob Maxwell, because in many ways it was as though her Lois Lane had leaped directly from the early depiction of the character in Shuster and Siegel's comics to the radio production featuring Joan Alexander to the Paramount cartoons also with Alexander. Coates was an independent female as glimpsed in any era of TV viewing who suffered no fools and was as inclined to give a piece of her mind and sometimes a stinging slap — to anyone who crossed her.

CHUCK HARTER: Phyllis Coates had appeared in the popular short subject series "Joe McDoakes" of the late 1940s and several low-budget Westerns. Her portrayal of an aggressive, independent reporter was one of the highlights of the film and the excellent 1951 first season.

PHYLLIS COATES (actress, "Lois Lane," *Adventures of Superman*): I was born Gypsy Ann Everts Stell. I always wanted to be Gypsy Ann. Gale Getterman interviewed me one time at Metro-Goldwyn-Mayer. He told me, "You can't use that name. Here's a name: Coates. Phyllis Coates." He took them off two books on his desk. He wrote it down on a piece of paper and from there on that was my name. It stuck. It has nothing to do with me or my family, but I still answer to it. With Lois Lane, Bob Maxwell told me I had the quality and that was that. I had never read the comics or seen the serials. I never was interested in Superman. I only became interested in it after I met my good friend George Reeves.

RAY MORTON: The film's other great debut is Phyllis Coates as an assertive, determined, all-business Lois Lane who is as formidable in her way as Superman is in his. When I was a kid, I preferred Noel Neill's Lois to Coates' because I found Coates' steely toughness to be really scary — Little Me always thought she was kind of mean. It was only when I got older that I realized how smolderingly sexy Coates was in the role — the heat between her and Reeves is palpable. For me, she is the sexiest Lois ever. She's a Lois you have no trouble believing is going to get whatever story — or anything else — she is after.

CHUCK HARTER: Next to be cast was Jack Larson as *Daily Planet* reporter Jimmy Olsen. Larson had appeared in several features during the late 1940s and was a promising character actor who brought sensitivity and earnestness to the part of the cub reporter.

JACK LARSON (actor, "Jimmy Olsen," *Adventures of Superman*)**:** How I got the job is that they wanted me. I had been under contract to Warner Brothers. I wanted to get to New York, but I didn't want a stock movie contract again. After I talked to them, I didn't want to do *Superman* at all. My agents talked me into it though. They told me, "Look, you want to go to New York, but you don't have the money. This is a few months' work, then you can take the money and run. Nobody will ever see it." Nobody really knew what television was or would become at that time. So, I did it, in late 1951. I had read all the Superman comics. My father told me that what they were paying me to do the Superman show was only making back everything I had spent on the comics as a kid. Since I had never seen the serials, and didn't listen to the radio show, I did not know the character of Jimmy very well.

PHYLLIS COATES: Jack Larson was a very cute guy. I've always liked him. I just thought he was cute from the first time I met him. I saw Jack at one point and he was just cute as a button. A little grey — the biological clock has ticked on, but he's still terrific.

JACK LARSON: I loved working with Gypsy. She was completely different in the part of Lois than Noel. Noel is one of the most adorable people in the world. She's beautiful, voluptuous, a darling person, and just great fun to work with, as Gypsy was. Everyone was very good-natured and liked working together.

CHUCK HARTER: Jack Larson became *so* popular, that in 1954 National Comics launched a *Jimmy Olsen* comic book, which quickly became one of its best sellers.

MICHAEL J. HAYDE: The comic books *Superman's Pal, Jimmy Olsen* and *Superman's Girlfriend, Lois Lane* both came about while the series was still in production, and they only came about because the characters had become so popular on television that it was felt they could carry their own books, which they did for many, many years. There's the television series selling comic books — again, that's what it was about.

JACK LARSON: *Superman* finally went on the air in 1953 and became a huge success right off. Within a month, I had people following me down the street and I couldn't even eat in the places I wanted to eat in. It was so popular, and Jimmy became something that kids could easily identify with. I suddenly went from a young actor in New York named Jack Larson to Jimmy Olsen. I never did any press for the show, because I felt that if I did, it would only typecast me further as Jimmy. I never even posed for publicity shots. I hoped that the typecasting would pass away, but by the time the show ended, even though I had done lots of other stuff, I knew I was as typed as George was, so I decided to quit acting.

CHUCK HARTER: John Hamilton, a screen veteran usually cast as judges or politicians, was chosen for the role of *Daily Planet* editor Perry White. His blustery performances and his comic byplay with Jack Larson were positive assets to the series. Robert Shayne, a film veteran with a long series of Broadway theatrical appearances, was cast as a new character that had not appeared in the comic books, Inspector Henderson.

JACK LARSON: Working with John Hamilton was a treasure. The last time I saw him was at George's funeral, where we were both pallbearers.

In Superman and the Mole Men, *reporters Clark Kent and Lois Lane are sent to a small town called Silsby, home to the world's deepest oil well. Things go awry when the drill penetrates the deepest layer of the Earth and a previously-unknown race of small, bald humanoids climb up through that hole to discover a new world that they didn't know existed. It isn't long, however, before they're deemed a threat by the locals. Jeff Corey's Luke Benson stirs up a mob determined to hunt down and kill these strange creatures — which, naturally, requires Superman to step in. It was written by Richard Felding (a pseudonym for National Comics' Robert Maxwell and Whitney Ellsworth) and directed by Lee Sholem.*

LEE SHOLEM (director, *Superman and the Mole Men*): How I got the job was that Robert Maxwell called me one day to have a chat. Apparently he'd heard about me, said they'd like to get going in about three weeks and I said, "Fine." The fact that it was Superman didn't mean anything to me. I just looked at it as another job, though I treated it professionally. You know, it's interesting. This business has its ups and downs and as a director you have your own ups and downs. You're running around like crazy for three or four years, and all of a sudden you have a dry spell. But that was a busy period for me.

JIM NOLT: *Superman and the Mole Men* started shooting on July 10, 1951 and shot for 11 days. That came out in November of that year, and the original plan was to go from *Superman and the Mole Men* directly to the first episode of season one. In terms of production, they had a weekend off after the movie and then came back and started the show. The original idea was to do 24 and then cut *Superman and the Mole Men* into two more episodes so they'd have 26 episodes the first season. But then they found out they couldn't do that. Films produced after 1948 could not be used on television without further compensation to the producers and actors, and Maxwell was loath to pay the extra money. They settled for 24 episodes, and from the '50s until about 1961 the first season was 24 episodes. Then a different contract was negotiated with the Screen Actors Guild when the series began airing five days a week.

MICHAEL J. HAYDE: It was a chance for them to absolutely ensure that they would recoup their investment. When I say "them," I mean the comic book company National Comics, because they fronted the money for this. There was no sponsor in the beginning; it was on spec, as you would say. By having a theatrical release concurrent with the production of the TV series, they had the opportunity to repurpose that movie as two episodes, so they only needed to shoot 24 others. It was entirely money-driven. It was a business decision. *And* it was designed to sell more comics, which is why every episode ends with "Superman is based on the original character appearing in Superman magazines." They said it every week; they didn't want us to forget it.

JIM NOLT: DC Comics produced *Superman and the Mole Men* before the series, hitting upon the idea to make a movie first, distribute it, get a return on it and then look for a sponsor for the television series before finally getting it on the air. But when the first season ended production in October of 1951, nobody was even sure that it *would* get on the air. They hadn't secured a sponsor yet and the only thing they knew was that the movie *Superman and the Mole Men* would be released that fall of 1951, but the 24 episodes, they had no idea what would happen with those. If they hadn't found a sponsor, they may very well have languished forever on the shelf someplace. But that's not the way it turned out, fortunately.

PHYLLIS COATES: We knew it was going to become a series, but we never dreamed it would become what it did. As a matter of fact, when we did it, we considered it the bottom of the barrel. We got together after I was cast, and George Reeves made a pitcher of martinis with his lady friend Toni Mannix, and he toasted me with, "Well, kid, this is it. The bottom of the barrel." We both needed work at the time and that was the way it was.

RAY MORTON: The film is incredibly strange in a marvelous way. In 1951, science-fiction was not yet a significant genre in American cinema, so I can only imagine how weird this tale of little hairy people who glow in the dark and climb up from the center of the Earth was for audiences of the day to encounter. The primitive costuming and creature makeup only added to the disturbing creepiness and oddness of the entire conception. Although the film's production values are clearly rock-bottom low-budget (nowhere better exemplified than in the Mole Men's weapon — an Electro-Lux vacuum with a funnel stuck on the end — how awesome is *that*?), it's actually a thoughtful piece with something interesting to say. The script tells the story of a town that is terrified by the Mole Men, not because of anything they've done, but simply because they are different, and makes an impressive plea for tolerance. The determination of the film's villain Luke Benson (played by actor and acting teacher Jeff Corey) to immediately wipe out anything he finds foreign or unfamiliar must have had particular resonance in a time when reactionary attitudes were running rampant in the country. And Superman taking a stand for the Mole Men in opposition to Benson and his fellow townspeople bent on wiping out the underground visitors makes a pretty strong statement about the need to combat mob mentality and mob violence.

MICHAEL J. HAYDE: *Superman and the Mole Men* is a neat little piece of social commentary wrapped in a sci-fi veneer. Of course, Rod Serling became famous for that with *The Twilight Zone*. This was along the same lines: a morality tale told from a sci-fi standpoint and it worked on that level.

JOHN KENNETH MUIR (film historian, author, *The Encyclopedia of Superheroes on Film and Television*): The film, sensitively written by Richard Fielding and produced at the height of the Red Scare and the McCarthy Hearings in the 1950s, seems to recognize that the real danger in a democracy is not "the other," but rather the hateful, overreaction to that "Other" by the dominant population. America is forever a melting pot, and as a nation we suffer when we forget that fact. "*It's men like you that make it difficult for men to understand one another*" Superman informs Benson (Corey) in a crucial sequence, making a salient point about hate-mongering and the ginning-up of xenophobic anger. Indeed, at one point, Superman stops a mob by reminding the gathered rioters that they are acting like "*Nazi Storm Troopers.*" He name-drops the Nazis not as an exaggeration, not as an insult, but rather as an explicit reminder of true American greatness; our country's ability to broach shared sacrifice for the common good, in the face of extreme difficulties and challenges. During World War II, Americans of all stripes put aside differences to meet and defeat a threat, and that is the "better angle" that Superman seeks to recall here.

LEE SHOLEM: I thought *Superman and the Mole Men* had a continuity to it, it was fun and, let's face it, it was for children. Apparently they enjoyed it and still do. I didn't see it as an allegory to McCarthyism, though other people did.

RAY MORTON: Another impressive aspect of the film is its deadly seriousness. As directed by B-movie maestro Lee Sholem (a.k.a. "Roll 'em" Sholem), the film takes its fantastic narrative, its fantastic hero and its weighty themes straight — there's no spoofing, no camp and no winking at the audience. The result is a film that is quite effective in its way —it has a certain gravitas while always remembering to be entertaining.

MICHAEL J. HAYDE: I actually think it worked on that level better than it worked on a superhero movie level, because Superman really doesn't do anything phenomenal. You don't get to see him fly, and the one time that you do, he's an animated cartoon and a pretty poorly animated cartoon. You see him catch a dummy in midair and it looks for all the world to see like a guy on a wire catching a dummy.

ANDY MANGELS: The story is poignant and moving, with many ties to the feelings of the public at the time. America was in the grip of McCarthyism, with the "Red Scare" showing a Communist under every bush. Unintentional as the threads seem to be linking the two, *Superman and the Mole Men* was still a powerful message for peaceful co-existence with all inhabitants of the Earth, no matter their appearance. It spoke of mankind's unity, and begged the right of each person's freedom.

JIM NOLT: As far as the script goes, I think it was a good, moral message of tolerance. It was written mostly by Whitney Ellsworth, and his daughter provided an article for *The Adventures Continue* magazine back in the '90s about their trip to California, saying he wrote *Superman and the Mole Men* on his way West. Then he and Box Maxwell polished it up when he got there. If you look at the credits, it says written by Richard Felding, which was a pseudonym for Maxwell and Ellsworth.

ANDY MANGELS: *Superman and the Mole Men* finished filming in fall 1951 and was subsequently released to once-again packed theaters. The Kirk Alyn serials were pulled from all theaters and never allowed to be shown again until their video release.

JIM NOLT: The movie was released, usually as a second bill to something or another, a science-fiction film or comedy. It was certainly not a blockbuster, but I think it gave DC Comics some money in return on their investment. I think DC has always looked upon that movie and the television series as a commercial for the comic books. If you look, you will hardly ever see George's image in advertisements for the movie. They used the comic book character, because they would've had to pay George a little extra to use his image. But from DC's point of view, if they put this show on the air, it would sell a lot of comic books — which is why you keep the cost as low as you possibly can, because you're using it as an advertisement. But in the process, George and the other actors got short-changed.

With *Superman and the Mole Men*, I was impressed at how quickly George fell into that role. I mean, he was perfect from the very beginning. If you look at something like *The Andy Griffith Show*, Andy at the start has a very broad Southern accent and he was the comedian in the show. It took him a little while to adjust to the character and find out exactly who he was. But George, if you look at *Superman and the Mole Men* and then the last episode of that first season, they are the same. He knew *exactly* from the very beginning who he was and what he had to do.

JOHN KENNETH MUIR: I've always loved how Superman is portrayed in this early film (later rerun on *Adventures of Superman*). He's an adopted child of America and yet, as an immigrant, also possesses the ability to see matters objectively. Because he has bought in voluntarily and happily to "The American Way," he can see how to apply its ideals in an impartial, idealistic fashion to everyone. He is all about justice for all, especially the weak and the endangered.

CHUCK HARTER: When it came to the series, Robert Maxwell's vision was that it was an extension of the radio program. The show was conceived as an *adult* murder-mystery series and was planning for an evening slot for the *entire* family.

JIM NOLT: The first season was absolutely no nonsense, which was Bob Maxwell's vision. He came from the radio series where the shows were violent and he transferred that over to television. I thought it was very effective, but you look at it and, yes, there are some gruesome things in that first season.

CHUCK HARTER: Many of the episodes were of a dark and mysterious concept, easily falling into the Film Noir attitude of many films of the late 1940s. There were elements of violence, and the odd instances that concerned the death of some characters, usually villains, was not uncommon.

BRUCE DETTMAN (journalist, pop culture historian): Bob Maxwell is generally given most of the credit for steering the first year's episode in the hard-edge direction it took, and certainly his credentials back much of this up. But Maxwell, who had a certain reputation for enjoying the spotlight, was surrounded by a top flight crew of colleagues: producer Bernard Luber, writers Ben Freeman, Eugene Solow and Dick Hamilton and great action directors Lee Sholem and Tommy Carr, all of whom certainly had a hand in the finished product.

MICHAEL J. HAYDE: The plots were about as adult as a show featuring a comic book character who wears a cape and flies around and stops bad guys could be. Its stories shifted away from the science-fiction angle towards gangsters and just nefarious underworld activities within Metropolis. And Clark Kent is pretty much the star of that show. So when television reared its head and children's radio started to go away, Maxwell said, "Look, if we have any chance of selling this, it's going to have to appeal to adults, because parents control what kids watch and don't watch. We need to think in terms of appealing to the entire family. Keep the fantastic elements as fantastic as we can under the money that we have, but at the same time provide plots that are compelling enough that adults are going to want to tune in, even if the children are otherwise occupied." So that was the goal. And, of course, they had Tommy Carr, who had worked on the Kirk Alyn serials, as a director. Tommy Carr also helped to recruit Lee Sholem as the second director for the series that year.

CHUCK HARTER: The series was filmed from July of 1951 through the middle of October of that year. The cast worked five days per week. The budget was $15,000 per episode with four episodes completed every ten days.

JIM NOLT: The production schedule was exhausting. The first season, they would put the episodes in groups of five so they'd do five episodes at a time — they'd basically do all the scenes in Perry White's office and other standing sets first, and then do the others. There were two episodes that featured Ed Cobb, so part of the day he was being the character in one episode and part of the day he was being a different character from another episode. That would happen more than once. They didn't follow that same production schedule in the second season; at that point they pretty much did one episode at a time and it was that way through the rest of the series. I just marvel at what they did that first season when you look at the coordination that was required.

PHYLLIS COATES: In those days we worked six days a week. That was really tough. There was one suit and one hat as far as I was concerned. I never knew which episode I was in. The script girl kept track of such things. We might be shooting scenes from four or five different episodes all the same day. I had about two or three attitudes. In those days, it was not that wonderful thing that Margot Kidder could do, where she can joke around. If I looked at George, or smiled too much, or got too intimate or relaxed, they'd scold me. It was really restrictive. I felt like a horse with a bit in its mouth. I never thought about motivation or characterization. My mind just didn't run that way. I didn't think about Lois being liberated or anything. Maybe I've just always been that way myself.

JACK LARSON: I realized coming onto the show that we had a top crew. George and Bob Shayne were top actors, as were John Hamilton and Gypsy [Phyllis Coates]. The first season crew was the same crew that did *Citizen Kane*. I approached the show as an opportunity to learn. One of the first locations we did was on the Hal Roach lot. It was the first day I met George. I was tied up inside a safe and it's falling. Superman catches it and frees me. Sitting on the lot that day, I felt like a pioneer at the beginning of something — a new medium as well as to experiment with a comic character. I loved the show and I loved playing Jimmy. It was the chance to learn and be inventive. I did a lot of development as an actor. They gave me the leeway to be inventive and do comic bits to create this character. It was the closest I could do to becoming a Mack Sennett comic in the early days, when people just left you alone, and hoped that people liked you. I did the best job I could possibly do. If I'm no good in some of the shows, it's not because I didn't try. I'm grateful I didn't turn it down, because that show will outlive me.

PHYLLIS COATES: We rarely did any scenes with a second take. We almost always shot it on the first take. George had a photographic memory. I didn't. But he sure kept me on my toes with the dialogue. We used to average about twenty pages of dialogue a day! That's a lot of dialogue for just two people.

CHUCK HARTER: The entire first season's output was of a high quality with nearly all of the episodes being among the finest produced during the original series' run. Robert Maxwell's vision had proven to be a sound one, and the combination of a first-rate cast, excellent directors in Sholem and Carr and polished production combined to provide an excellent (for its time) filmed adaptation of the comic book character's exploits.

PHYLLIS COATES: Things didn't always go smoothly. I got knocked out on the set one day. The episode was "A Night of Terror." Truly, it was my fault, not the heavy. I moved about two or three inches too close to him when my placement was critical. When he threw the punch, I missed my mark, he caught my jaw and knocked me out. He felt dreadful and later was almost in tears. But they left it on film, so when I saw it, you could see the impact and you knew it looked too real. Boy, after that I watched my mark. And not only did the scene make it in, but the director asked me to finish the scene before my jaw became too swollen.

LEE SHOLEM: Oftentimes you would get stunt people, because you had risky things to do, but both Phyllis and George got knocked out cold on the same day in two different scenes, one in the morning and one in the afternoon. In a fight, one of the stuntmen actually punched Phyllis and knocked her out. But it wasn't George's fighting that got him knocked out, it was a special effect. He had a door we had rigged so that he could run through it, but the cross members in it were never taken out. It was supposed to be balsa, which was the norm, and he went right into these two-by-fours and got knocked out colder than a mackerel. When he woke up, he was stunned. You know, you can't rehearse these things. Of course, we removed the special effects man after the episode was finished; he was fired. It was really something. George handled himself beautifully in fights when he would land up with a broken nose and the like. But these things happen.

When National Comics viewed the completed season, there was much concern among the executives who were not prepared for Maxwell's adult approach to storytelling. In early 1952, there was some editing done of certain episodes at the comic book firm's insistence.

CHUCK HARTER: After the cutting had been accomplished to eliminate some of the violence, the series was prepared for airing. To make the package more attractive, previews were added to each episode's ending to herald the following week's show. Done in the style of the popular motion picture serials, the previews would feature a montage of the following week's show with this narration: "Don't miss the next thrill-packed episode in the amazing adventures of Superman. Join with the Man of Steel as he wages war against the forces of evil. Thrilling adventure and tense excitement, pounding action and spine-tingling mystery. You'll find them all in the next startling episode of the *Adventures of Superman*."

In mid-1952, Kellogg's Cereals, who had been involved from the beginning, agreed to sponsor the series for broadcasting. National Periodicals Publications then combined with distributor Flaming Films and the Leo Burnett Agency to set up their own in-house syndication. The show was set to debut in early 1953.

CHUCK HARTER: After test runs in Chicago and Davenport, Iowa in late 1952, the series made its official debut in Los Angeles on February 9, 1953 with other premieres around the country from February to April of that year. The show was an immediate hit and dominated the ratings for its respective time slots. In Los Angeles, the series aired at 8:30 p.m. Pleased with the response, the Leo Burnett Agency, with Kellogg's sponsorship, renewed the series with plans for an additional 26 episodes to begin filming in May 1953.

During that month, Robert Maxwell stepped down as head of production, apparently disagreeing with the terms offered to him in the renewal deal. Replacing Maxwell as producer of the series was Whitney Ellsworth, who had been editorial director at National Comics since 1940. He had served in the capacity of advisor on the first season of the show as well as several adaptations of National Comics' characters at Columbia Pictures, including the two Superman and Batman serials.

JANE ELLSWORTH (widow of Whitney Ellsworth): Whit always wanted to be a cartoonist, and one of his first jobs was at King Features Syndicate. At the time he ghosted *Tilly the Toiler* and *Just Kids*. He wasn't much more than a kid himself. Cartoonists are a breed apart. For one thing, they never really grow up and they are funny. That was still part of Whit's personality when, in 1940, he went to work for DC Comics as editorial director. His philosophy in regard to the comic books was that they were for children; that they should be fun, clean, non-violent and that the English should always be correct, though he did allow for some slang. This is pretty much what became the so-called "Comics Code," and it stood DC Comics in good stead when a national investigation into violence in the comic books occurred later on.

JIM NOLT: When Whitney Ellsworth took over in the second season, he saw Superman as more of a comic book character. He was definitely a comic book man, and that's the direction he wanted to take things. At the same time, there were pressures on Superman Inc. from Kellogg's and others to lighten up the series. I don't know what would have happened if Maxwell had stayed on as producer after the first season. Some people lament the fact that he didn't continue and wanted more episodes in the style of the first season, but I'm not sure that would've been there even with him, because he would have been under the same pressures that Ellsworth was under. It's just that Ellsworth — I don't want to say gave in to those pressures, but it was the direction he wanted to go anyway.

PHYLLIS COATES: In the first season we had a lot of special effects done live on the set, such as exploding bombs and so forth. Everyone just pitched in on the set. There was an energy there that was very high. That's why I think the quality went so far downhill later. I don't think it was because of Whit Ellsworth, as some people do, just because he didn't have as much violence. I think Bob Maxwell just had more fun and action in his shows. Some of the later shows got kind of sweet and cute and funny.

CHUCK HARTER: Ellsworth, who had worked in the comic book industry for most of his life, envisioned the show to be one that was geared for children, as were the comic books. This meant that although there still was an occasional degree of violence, the majority of the episodes were of such a high caliber that the previous season's darker approach was not missed. In fact, the new shows were received with tremendous enthusiasm by the viewers with the *Adventures of Superman* series frequently winning top ratings for its respective time slots.

JIM NOLT: Another problem was that Maxwell had a great ego and I believe DC thought that he was getting a little too big for his britches. In a sense he was *becoming* Superman Inc. and DC didn't want to lose control. I don't think remaining as producer was ever offered to him, but it's never been clear whether Maxwell left or DC simply didn't offer the series to him again.

MICHAEL J. HAYDE: As he did in radio, he was also looking for additional projects to work on. It was in between the radio show and the TV show that he acquired the rights to do a series of *Lassie* based on the movies. Obviously he didn't starve when he was cut from *Superman*, but it was, again, all about business. DC wanted the show to more strictly be their creation, and Ellsworth was the man for that. He had done some creative work on the Kirk Alyn serials, he'd done some creative work with the Max Fleischer cartoons; he was a consultant on those back in the early '40s. He lived in Hollywood for a time and married a Hollywood starlet. Apparently, these were all solid qualifications. And, of course, he did have some creative input on the first season as well, just not as much as he would have later on, obviously, as producer.

JIM NOLT: On top of that, and I had talked to Jack Larson about this many times, Maxwell was not particularly liked by the cast and crew and DC didn't like his ego. It was just sort of a mutual parting of the ways there. And Ellsworth was eager to produce; he had been looking for an opportunity like that for a long time. Everything fit together again and fell into place.

JANE ELLSWORTH: Whit thought Bob's work was excellent. That doesn't mean, however, that he approved of the TV Film Noir approach for *Superman*. But this was Bob's domain and not under Whit's control at the time. Bob and Whit were completely different, but good friends.

MICHAEL J. HAYDE: Season two falls somewhere in the middle between the later silliness and the darkness of season one. It's more comic book fantasy, while some of the plots are still adult. The first episode of the second season was "Five Minutes to Doom," which was about a man on death row who had been wrongly convicted and was actually innocent. That happened to be a storyline in *Action Comics* number one. Whitney Ellsworth kept Tommy Carr, so there was still going to be some of that stylistic approach to the second season. Overall, it was still a strong show and the best part is that they had the money to work on the flying effects and make them more exciting, more realistic-looking. It wasn't just the same shot over and over again, like it would become later on.

JIM NOLT: The second season is still serious with a crime-busting reporter, though there are a few lighter moments. And it wasn't filmed the same way. The first season was filmed with many more interiors, but as it went along, it started introducing things like Professor Pepperwinkle — *that* was Ellsworth. That was his take on the character and he was quite happy with that. There were fun things, but the show definitely got lighter. The thing that holds it all together for me is George Reeves, because no matter what the situation, George Reeves was still Superman/Clark Kent. To some extent I think John Hamilton's Perry White was also a glue that kept the whole thing together, because he was *always* in character and his character remained true-to-form. Jimmy Olsen got silly some-times and Lois Lane got silly sometimes, but Clark and Perry White were father and grandfather to us.

RAY MORTON: There will probably never be a greater Perry White — a newspaper editor who in this show never goes to a newsroom — than John Hamilton. Grouchy, perpetually pissed-off and forever shouting orders into a phone he never seems to dial, Hamilton was the quintessential irascible boss. Although he was a veteran character actor, one gets the feeling that Hamilton wasn't acting as Perry, but was a crabby dude in real life and just playing himself. Anyway, he's marvelous in the part — immortalizing the exclamation "Great Caesar's Ghost" in the process and even gave Perry some unexpected colors beyond his gruffness. He's authoritative when dealing with the ruling class, brave when facing down villains, and there are even a few episodes of the show — "Great Caesar's Ghost," Money to Burn" and "Perry White's Scoop" come to mind — in which Perry is knocked off his game and is seen to be in physical and/or emotional distress, and Hamilton delivers Perry's vulnerability as well as he does his bluster.

NOEL NEILL (actress, "Lois Lane," *Adventures of Superman*): John was so funny. He would just sit there with this benign, wonderful face. We would be standing around his desk and he would have his dialogue spread out on the desk. We would come in and we would have to be remembering our lines and he would just look at us with this straight face and just come out with some of the most outrageous remarks and we would forget what we were talking about. But he was a charmer and, of course, a wonderful actor. He and George were quite naughty together. They would just break you up and the producer would be screaming, "The money, the money, you're wasting film." It was a wonderful group to work with.

MICHAEL J. HAYDE: John Hamilton was wonderful in the role of Perry White and was always the authority figure on screen in films that I've seen him in. And it's something he's always very good at. Jack Larson brought that boyish innocence and exuberance to the part of Jimmy Olsen. Of all the people, he must have felt really put out that he had to play such a dim bulb. He was constantly being berated by Perry White, but he knuckled down, did the role really well and became legendary for it. Thankfully he learned to embrace it as he got older. We all want something that's going to keep us alive when we're pushing up daisies, as it were, and that was Jimmy Olsen for him.

CHUCK HARTER: The interplay among the five principal cast members continued to improve to the point where many young viewers believed that the actors really were their comic book counterparts.

MICHAEL J. HAYDE: Somebody did an interview with Bob Shayne — Inspector Henderson — and the guy said, "Aren't you tired of hanging your hat on that role all the time?" And he said, "Heavens, no. I'm happy to hang my hat on anything," because he really didn't think he did anything all that memorable. But people remember the role, despite the fact it could be frustrating for him, because he didn't get paid regularly, he wasn't on every week and he never solved a crime by himself. He worked with his buddy Superman and Superman did all the work. He just swooped in and made the arrests at the end. It wasn't the happiest experience for him, because he started in the theater and in the '30s was one of the founders of the Theater Guild, the unions on the East Coast to improve conditions for actors. And here he is in the '50s playing Superman's policeman pal. But people remembered him and loved him for it, and he learned to love it too. He learned to appreciate it.

GARY GROSSMAN: I got Bob's number from Whitney Ellsworth, the executive producer of Superman, as you know, and he said I could interview him for my book at Du-Par's, a restaurant on Ventura Boulevard. We met and I realized when we first started talking that he wanted to meet me there rather than home, because he was still highly suspicious of people approaching him to talk, because he had been blacklisted in the 1950s. But he always had the best feeling about DC Comics and Whitney, because they kept him on the show. I think it was the "Human Bomb" episode where someone else plays the inspector, because he was taken off the set the day before to be questioned. They had to rewrite that to bring in another actor. But the Superman company and Kellogg's stuck with him, which was above and beyond what almost anybody else did in Hollywood. He was always faithful despite the low income, to the Superman people. And he was grateful.

ROBERT SHAYNE (actor, "Inspector Henderson," *Adventures of Superman***):** I was served a subpoena on the set of *Superman* in connection with the House of UnAmerican Activities Committee. George and Phyllis Coates both asked, "Bob, subpoenaed? Why, he's the squarest guy we know and the straightest guy." That was the same thing the investigator told me years later. He told me that I never should have been subpoenaed; that they had never had anything on me or against me. In my mind, this was a disgraceful period in history. Whitney Ellsworth, the producer at the time, was told by Kellogg's to let me go. I was never guilty of anything anyway, but I almost got blacklisted. If you thought differently from the higher-ups, you were immediately suspect. The whole thing started because I had some difficulties with some of the policies the Screen Actors Guild board espoused at that time. Since I was on the board, I was suspected as UnAmerican.

MICHAEL J. HAYDE: George and Bob Shayne had a strong connection. They would run through lines together in the dressing room, and then they would head out there and just do it. At least that's how Bob Shayne remembered it. And it worked; they did have a chemistry, a rapport, and that's just one of those little things you can't figure on ahead of time. The only thing Bob Maxwell asked him was, "Can you gray your temples so you look a little older than George Reeves?" Which he did. That was the only instruction he got; everything else was what he brought to the role. The fact that they had these two actors who managed to hit it off and actually work well together in the limited time they had on screen, they did manage to create a whole that was greater than the sum of their parts.

BOB SHAYNE: I loved working with George. We became very good friends, although we didn't see much of each other socially. On the set, though, we worked harmoniously together. Very often, he would come onto the set early and ask, "Do you know your lines, Bob?" I'd say yes and he'd say, "Well, I don't, so let's go in my dressing room and learn them." We'd go in there and rehearse our lines, and in a few minutes we'd have them down pat. He was a great guy, a very sweet guy. He was thoughtful and kind to everybody.

CHUCK HARTER: One big change of the cast in season two was the departure of Phyllis Coates, who had been committed to a TV pilot and was unavailable for the new production. Replacing her in the role of Lois Lane was Noel Neill, who had played the part in both of the Columbia serials produced in 1948 and 1950.

PHYLLIS COATES: I wanted to play some comedy. I got tired of that restrictive game they would play. Every chance I got, I would bleach my hair and go off to find another part. Whit Ellsworth called and offered me the moon to return. I think they offered me about five times what my initial salary had been, but I just didn't want to go back. I eventually did do some comedy work, including the DesiLu sitcom *This is Alice*. There was never any satisfaction in doing Lois Lane, If you had the suit and the hat, you were Lois Lane. I never took it seriously or identified with the role.

NOEL NEILL: George was such a wonderful person when I joined the group after the other gal had done the first 26. George one day realized that I was having a problem with the director, who obviously liked whatshername better then myself and she will remain nameless. But anyway, she chose to leave the show and so it's her problem, but George was very nice. He knew that this director was really… whatever, and he said, "Can we take a break?" and he took the gentleman aside and said, "Give the kid a break, she's breaking into a family that's been together for 13 weeks." I really appreciated it so much. He was so wonderful to work with.

PHYLLIS COATES: George tried to introduce me to Noel Neill once. He knocked on the door and she said to come in. She turned and looked me right in the eye — and this is the craziest thing, because I thought we'd have some laughs together — and she said, "I hate you!" George grabbed me by the arm, closed the door and said, "Let's get out of here." I do know that it's hard to replace somebody on a series. I got along great with everybody, and I would imagine some of the directors may have told her, "Oh, do it like Phyllis did." She evidently grew to dislike me. She has said in interviews that she never met me, but we did, just that once. I never took the role that seriously, though. I never said, "Gypsy Ann, you're Lois Lane. This woman's playing your role." It was never that important. Noel always referred to me as "that other lady." I don't know about actors. It's all crazy sometimes, and we all have egos, whether we're big actors or little actors.

JACK LARSON: The fact is that there is something very humorous in the question about the two Lois Lanes. The first 26 shows were produced by Bob Maxwell and I know they're very beloved; I always read they verged on Film Noir. They were very interesting to do. We had some of the same directors and they got into trouble on these shows. They were more serious. When Whitney Ellsworth took over, they could never have made that kind of show again. The scripts had to be more humorous, the villains had to be less… Phyllis Coates, the nameless one, wouldn't have been as good in the shows as we did them and Noel was more of a comic performer. It was wonderful for me working with Noel, because what I was interested in was comedy and Phyllis was more of a straight actor, so I got to do more comedy things than I would with a straight actress. The show changed a great deal and it would have changed anyway, but I don't think that Phyllis was suited for the comedy show in the way that Noel was. Noel was great fun to work with.

MICHAEL J. HAYDE: Noel brought that element where you might think that, yeah, she does maybe have a crush on Clark Kent. She's head over heels about Superman, but she's also attracted to Clark to a certain extent. She brought just enough of that into her personality and interaction with Clark. Even when she was being "nasty," she wasn't being cutthroat nasty, like Phyllis. She was just frustrated, like, "You're such a good guy, but if you would just man up, you'd be somebody worth paying attention to." I think she gets a bum wrap when she's compared unfavorably to Phyllis, because they're two different characters in a lot of ways. Phyllis' Lois was interested in her job, Noel's Lois was interested in marrying Superman.

BRUCE DETTMAN: There was little suggestion or indication that Lois had any sort of private life away from the *Daily Planet,* although she is seen taking a vacation in the episode "Night of Terror." People cite actresses like Mary Tyler Moore and Candice Bergen as forging a path for independent women on TV, but Phyllis was nearly two decades ahead of these ladies in creating a no-nonsense, tough and self-reliant female character. When she left the series, the guts were partly ripped from it. Noel Neill had a softer, more vulnerable and malleable personality and persona that fit in with these more juvenile storylines. It is hard, if not impossible, to imagine Phyllis' Lois in the later episodes.

LOU KOZA (editor, *The George Reeves Historical Archives*): I'm not really sure it matters, because both did a wonderful job with the role. I look forward to every show and never felt bothered by either one not being on screen. On a personal level, Noel was kind to me. She had invited me to her Santa Monica home twice, so I *do* have a steady dearness for her.

TIM DEFOREST (comics historian, author, *Storytelling in the Pulps, Comics and Radio*): I liked them both, including Noel in the movie serials. It was kind of nice when she came back into the TV show, but I think Phyllis has the advantage of having been in the first season where they had the black-and-white photography and almost a Film Noir-kind of lighting, and some of the villains in it were pretty creepy, villainous and murderous. I kind of agree that Phyllis was the best Lois, partly because she was in the best quality stories. But as actresses? I don't know. I would have to watch them both again to pick, because they're both great as Lois.

GARY GROSSMAN: Phyllis Coates was more true to the comic books and radio show, and she was a strong, tough woman. When she was in trouble, she re-alized she got into trouble because she was tough. With Noel Neill, you had the feeling she got into trouble because that's where the plot had her go. They were very, very different. I don't know if they considered other people or just went right to Noel Neill, because she had done the serials and then she, as far as I know, did not act again except for her appearances in the Superman movies. For *Superman: The Movie*, I actually had recommended her to producers Alexander and Ilya Salkind when they were shooting it, and they cast her and Kirk Alyn. And in *Superman Returns*, Jack Larson was in it as well.

JIM NOLT: I'm conflicted when it comes to Lois Lane on the show, because I knew Phyllis and Noel. I had many conversations with Phyllis back in the early 2000s, and I could say I was Noel's friend for 20 or 25 years. I spoke at her memorial service; I loved her dearly. But I also found Phyllis' performance to be extraordinary and she had a great deal of appeal. Because 2021 was the 70th anniversary of the show, I really gave a lot of attention to that first season all through that summer, and I have just fallen in love with Phyllis. Anyone who prefers her won't get any argument from me. If Phyllis had continued, that would've been fine, but I'm also glad that Noel is there for the remainder of the series. I don't consider Noel better or Phyllis better. They're different actors and, to some extent, different characters. I do think it would have been easier for Phyllis to have transferred into the later seasons than it would have been for Noel to do the first season.

MICHAEL J. HAYDE: As I got older, I saw how George Reeves brought the character to life in those early episodes, and if there's any drawback to them, it's that Superman is all fists and fury and a serious demeanor. And later on, Reeves got to bring more of himself into the role and became more of a personality and less the super traffic cop.

JERRY BECK (film and animation historian): In a way, Superman worked better in black-and-white in the serials and the first two seasons of the TV show. It almost helps make it look *more* real back then, because it doesn't look as silly in some ways as it does when it's in color. And you completely buy George Reeves in the costume, whether it's black-and-white or color. You believe he could punch someone out with a single punch, he can fly and have X-ray vision.

GARY GROSSMAN: It definitely became more of a kids' show in the color years. Some of the reason for that was that they had to cut back on the sets and expenses, because the choice to go color was costing them more. The scripts had to be more contained.

JANE ELLSWORTH: One reason Whit felt so warmly toward George is because George understood the economic pressure under which Whit worked. In addition, Whit admired and was grateful to George for his professionalism. He was always on time, completely prepared and never missed a day's work. He seldom complained if things went wrong, and he insisted on doing all his stunts himself — and they weren't all too easy. He had a very sunny disposition and an outstanding personality. He was a great role model, one might say, and was responsible to a large extent for the marvelously cooperative and happy spirit that existed on the set.

GARY GROSSMAN: Some of the directors and writers changed. The early B-movie action directors left and it became more a a studio, on-stage contained show with very few location shoots, which is what had made those first 26 so gritty and so good. They were shooting on the back lot of what was 40 acres at the back of the Selznick Studios, which was the back lot that MGM actually used to have and is where *Gone with the Wind* was shot.

ROBERT GREENBERGER: You think about some of those episodes, like "Panic in the Sky" — that's real drama. There was one where he figures out how to destabilize his molecules to pass through a really thick wall. *Where'd* that power come from?

ANTHONY TOLLIN: When you look at shows like *Gilligan's Island* or *Wild Wild West*, their first seasons in the 1960s were in black-and-white. By 1955, *Superman* was being filmed in color and that was due, I believe, to DC being a company that had a lot of input from people who had been in science-fiction and understood that things were going to change. People realized the show would be more valuable in the future if they were filmed in color — at a time when most TV stations still couldn't broadcast color. As I said before, Superman became the preeminent superhero not because he was the first in comic books, but because he was the first superhero to move *beyond* comic books.

JERRY BECK: A good friend of mine, Mark Trost, is an expert on the Superman radio show. We were watching first and second season episodes of *Adventures of Superman* on the Decades network, and I told him how it slightly bothered me, because although I love George Reeves so much — I grew up watching the show — he didn't play Clark Kent like Kirk Alyn or Christopher Reeve did. They played Clark Kent meek, which is exactly what you're supposed to do. It makes Superman better. And Mark said something I did *not* know, because I'm not the biggest expert. He said that there's a connection between the last season of the radio show and the first season of the TV show. In the last season on radio, they started to change things up, because it was waning. Clark Kent became more of a mystery detective character, more aggressive and he barely turned into Superman at the end of those episodes. He's mainly Clark Kent and punching people and he's like a detective who turns in to Superman. They just carried that Clark Kent into the TV show.

TOM ANDRAE: I like George Reeves' take on Kent. I like the fact that — and this is something most people *don't* like — he didn't differentiate the timid, weak guy enough from the strong, tough and reactionary guy. I actually like the fact that he was a crusading journalist, and that really fits more with the way Jerry Siegel originally conceived of Clark Kent. As a matter of fact, the character was inspired by a play called *The Fighting Journalists* that Jerry wrote about the Clark Kent character. Jerry wanted him to be a crusading journalist, which is partly why he had all that stuff about social issues in there.

ROBERT GREENBERGER (author, former DC editor): George Reeves didn't make a strong effort to differentiate Clark from Superman; none at all, because his Clark had an urgency and immediacy to some of the stories that felt more like it belonged to Superman than the reporter, but it served the story. I know they shot the episodes really hard and fast and I'm sure you didn't have a lot of time to get into the method of it all, but he certainly made an impression, because he was the only live-action version of Superman I knew. It was years before I saw the Kirk Alyn serials, so I had no other frame of reference.

As in the comics, Superman was TV's first flying hero and that certainly presented challenges on a number of levels, ranging from practical matters of achieving flight and the impact those sequences were having on the audience.

JIM NOLT: The evolution of the flying is interesting. When they were doing *Superman and the Mole Men*, there's a moment where he takes off, but you don't see him, you see the crowd right below and the camera tracks along. When he gets to the dam to save one of the Mole Men, he's animated. That's another amazing thing about the series: They started it and weren't really sure *how* they were going to make him fly. But they made it up as they went along, and what amazes me even more is that they kept some of the experimental scenes in. If you watch "Haunted Lighthouse," the first time he flies, Superman looks like a puppet on a popsicle stick. It's really odd-looking and I'm not sure whether it's a real person or a doll, because it's in this odd pose with one arm down, the other arm out. I've looked at it again and again and I still don't know exactly what it is, but that was their first experiment. None of the episodes of the first season were released until all of them were finished, so they could have easily edited in a later flying scene, but they didn't.

LEE SHOLEM: We did the flying several ways and the way that worked out really well was when we made George a body cast. He'd lie on this thing, stick his arms out and, of course, the wind machine was going. You could photograph him against a sky and the thing that was holding him could be masked out. If you get the same color, say white on white, you don't see the white — *if* you light it properly. The wires were done the same way. We had this pan and he could lie in the darn thing and there was no problem at all.

JIM NOLT: Almost everybody is familiar or knows about Si Simonson's body pan that George laid on, with the pole perpendicular to it. But in the first season they had an even more elaborate contraption. There was a bend to the pole, sort of an S shape, with a harness hanging from the front side of it. So George is hanging in a harness from this pole and you can see that. If you take a close look at some of those early flying scenes, Simonson simply improved on that with the body pan. It's a little hard to explain without looking at it.

Wires were used in the first season; if you look at some of the shows, he just stands there and suddenly goes up. I have a great series of pictures showing him as Superman in the moment getting ready for that. He's standing there and you can see the contraption that's used to pull him up. They pull down and he goes up. I think Lee Sholem is the only director who used that and George was dropped. He went to the floor and then he refused to do the takeoff after that. Any standing takeoffs were stuntmen. They changed to the springboard that he would run and jump on. The second season he used the body pan, which was connected to a trolley above so they could move him. But that's different from the wire takeoff, because there's no quick pull on that. He's also locked in place and is not going to fall.

PAT ELLSWORTH (daughter of Whitney and Jane Ellsworth): I remember watching the shooting of some of the scenes and that's when I got to see Phyllis Coates act, and that must be about the time I got to know George. It was on that set, with us watching, that George took off and then fell off the wire. *Everybody* gasped. Frankly, it looked to me as though he'd fallen no more than seven feet. I remember seeing him fall and I remember Mr. Maxwell gasped and said, "Oh, my star!" Somebody said, "Oh, he's worried more about his star than about the person getting hurt." I don't think he meant not to care that a human being might possibly get hurt. I just think he *also* thought of the show. At any rate, George picked himself up and went right on with the scene.

PHYLLIS COATES: I remember that one specific incident, which could have ended in disaster, but didn't. The wires broke on George one day and he fell. I don't know if the rubber muscles helped him bounce or what. Nothing was broken. He maybe got a few bruises, but poor George really got scared.

LEE SHOLEM: George was marvelous at going through windows and things. We had a board which propelled him out the window, and he would land on a bunch of cardboard boxes. He wasn't afraid of anything, although there were things he didn't want to do, because they were too hazardous. If he's out, there goes the show.

CHUCK HARTER: The September 25, 1953 issue of *TV Guide* featured George Reeves on the cover as both Superman and Clark Kent. The article inside, "How They Make Superman Fly," told of the growing popularity of the series and also the growing concern of Reeves and producer Ellsworth about the reports that some youngsters had injured themselves attempting to fly like their video hero. The power of the growing medium of television combined with the increasingly progressive special effects had indeed convinced a nation of children that Superman could actually fly. Reeves and Ellsworth filmed a short subject called "Only Superman Can," in which George Reeves as the Man of Steel tells viewers not to attempt to fly like their hero. The short was shown in several markets during late 1953 along with the second season's premiere broadcasts. Indeed, the flying effects for the second season proved to have the most variety and remained the best of the show's entire run. At times suspending Reeves by wires in front of a back projection screen, and at other times using a molded breastplate worn by Reeves under his uniform and suspended by a counter balance, the results were spectacular and believable.

GARY GROSSMAN: When George Reeves took off and did that leap off a springboard over the camera, none of the movies have ever come close to the excitement of those takeoffs. This slow little glide up and then just lifting off — I've even talked to Ilya Salkind about it. I was at a Superman event and said to the group, and didn't realize he was in the audience, that I love the Chris Reeve movies, love what they'd done. But with George, there's that excitement where he's diving out over the window and that music is there and there's nothing like it.

RAY MORTON: The flying sequences in the show are usually derided for being cheap and subpar, but if you look at them in the context of the times, they're actually fairly impressive. First of all, no live-action Superman has ever had better takeoffs than George Reeves. In some of the early episodes, his takeoffs were accomplished using wires and they look okay, although they were apparently quite dangerous because at one point the wires broke and Reeves crashed to the concrete floor of the studio and was knocked out cold. From then on they used a springboard — Reeves would leap onto the springboard and then vault up and over the camera. And in this he really committed. Reeves' pounding leaps off of the board launched him skyward in a manner that left no doubt in the viewer that this was a man who could truly break free of gravity and soar above the Earth whenever he damn well pleased.

Once Superman was in the air, visual effects took over. In the black-and-white seasons, there are actually a variety of flying shots — most of them showing Reeves matted in over a city or country landscape. While the matting itself is often crude, it's no cruder than similar shots in B-pictures of the time, the design of the shots is usually visually ambitious and impressive. Considering that all of this was designed to be viewed on a small, low-res screen, the results were more than acceptable for the day. And while many of the shots were reused in the interest of economy, new shots were often generated for specific episodes, which must have cost a pretty penny. When the show went to color, the shot designs were simplified to basically just two shots -— a long and a medium — of Reeves positioned horizontally against a process background. The backgrounds were sometimes changed to be episode specific (but usually weren't), and the images of Reeves were flipped or tilted as needed, but it was essentially the same footage reused again and again. Technically, though, the matting was superior to that of the black-and-white episodes. The most familiar flying shot — the long shot of Reeves flying across a cityscape that eventually turns into countryside — is technically just about perfect and completely convincing, with its only flaw being that we saw it too many damn times.

JIM NOLT: Beyond the flying, Whit Ellsworth talked about the fact that George wanted to do his own stunts rather than have a stunt double. Now if you watch the series closely, you'll see that in the first season, he was doubled several times for some of the fight scenes. But after the first season, I haven't spotted any stunt double for him. He did do everything himself. That's the way George wanted it. And Jack Larson told me many times how much George liked to burst through the walls. He also tells a story where George, just before they filmed the scene, would look around the wall and say, "Don't you worry, Junior. Super-Boo's gonna save you." Then they'd yell action and he'd come through the wall. Jack's problem is that he was laughing from the Super-Boo line, and had to get serious when filming started.

JACK LARSON: I was usually laughing or smiling. It was hard not to. George was so good-natured, despite the fact that he knew his career was being eaten up and destroyed by playing Superman. From my point of view, he gave his life for the part.

MICHAEL J. HAYDE: When we get to season three and Ellsworth is fully in charge, the show can be summed up with four words: *Seduction of the Innocent,* the name of the book by Dr. Fredric Wertham that came out between seasons two and three. And it was obviously a bombshell; a lot of newspapers picked up on it and there were editorials against the horror of comic books, quoting Wertham. And, of course, he went on the 1950s equivalent of talk shows, a lot of them on radio.

CHUCK HARTER: A scathing attack on the comic book industry and the effects of comic book violence on impressionable youngsters, the book had an immediate impact on the entire industry. Wertham blamed comics for social ills such as juvenile delinquency, moral decay and contributing to a lowering literacy rate among readers.

MICHAEL J. HAYDE: That was a big deal and Wertham kind of excoriates the Superman TV show. He *really* had it in for Superman. He saw Superman first and foremost as a Nazi, the Ubermensch, the Aryan race and Hitler's dream full bloom and come to life — which is ironic considering the character was created by two Jewish boys. Comic books were under attack, and that included Superman. Even though the radio show won all those awards in the '40s for its views on tolerance, there wasn't enough of that, I guess, in the TV show to deflect criticism. The show became a lot about Superman bending the barrel of guns and bullets bouncing off his chest and him, especially, bursting through walls. The characters did become a little more cartoonish, but that happened in the comic books as well.

CHUCK HARTER: As a result of this published diatribe, the U.S. Government formed a commission to investigate the truth of Wertham's allegations. Entire publishing houses such as E.C. Comics, headed by William Gaines, were forced to close down completely or at least soften their editorial policies. National avoided too much criticism as they had already adopted a policy of self-censorship. However, when the *Adventures of Superman* series began preparation for its third season of filming, Wertham's influence was clearly felt.

MICHAEL J. HAYDE: A lot of tough storylines got watered down in the comics. Batman and Robin just became really good buddies and Superman became America's Boy Scout. So the TV series had to follow suit to a certain extent. And that's really what happened. It did actually become a children's show.

CHUCK HARTER: The majority of the stories were presented in a more lighthearted manner. While there were still new episodes being filmed that could stand along the predominantly excellent showing of the first two seasons, there was an increasing adoption of a formula. The villains were not as evil as before and often appeared as incompetent gangsters without any realistic menace. On the positive side, the interplay among the principals continued to improve in believability. Reeves' Superman became a warmer version of his previously grim avenger.

MICHAEL J. HAYDE: And especially as television became more and more important and primetime became more and more expensive, it was inevitable that a show like *Superman* was going to wind up in the early afternoon hours. The changes didn't hurt the show, because it quieted some of the more distraught voices among parents. And there were still adults watching, if only to monitor what their kids were watching. It's not as if they lost any audience to a significant degree, they just tempered down the controversy. And I don't know if the show would have lasted another year beyond the third season if it *hadn't* changed. It simply had to, and there are still some strong shows among those too.

LOU KOZA: I'm okay with the softer approach. The truth is, 1950s' *Superman* is based on a comic book character and comic books *are* children's products. What type of product is aimed at children? Toys and breakfast cereal and the show would naturally attract a sponsor that sells products for children. When we follow the money, it certainly traces back to the sponsor and the sponsor is not going to want to incorporate the harder-edge stories. Whit helped keep the sponsors satisfied with a compromise where the two brands would be in line with selling their products.

CHUCK HARTER: Another radical change in production, which was producer Ellsworth's concept, was to film the remaining 52 episodes in color. He believed that with the growing number of color TV sets being purchased, that there was a future market for shows that could be broadcast in color once technology was refined so that color sets could fit into most consumers' budgets. This proved to be a most astute plan and a great deal of the series' longevity can be attributed to its eventual broadcast in color. This didn't occur until the fall of 1965, and the final four seasons of *Superman*, although lensed in color, were broadcast in black-and-white during their initial airing.

MICHAEL J. HAYDE: Obviously budgets went up quite a bit when Kellogg's came on board and started paying for seasons in advance. That helped. But when they went to color, they again found themselves in the position where they had to really watch costs, because Kellogg's was only paying for half a season now. They were doing that with *Wild Bill Hickok* too. Also, I found out while I was researching my book, it's not as if *Superman* was a special case when they went to color in cutting their seasons to 13 a year. That's what they did from '54 to '57. Costs were going up astronomically. TV had become so big, so fast, that suddenly you had to spend money if you wanted to get studio space and a crew — and everybody was in the unions by then. Eventually they had to cut production down to five days a week, whereas in the first few seasons it was six days a week. You only got Sunday off and had to run through your lines for the next week.

CHUCK HARTER: When the third season began filming in November 1954, having moved to California Studios, there were several obvious changes from the previous two seasons. The increased budget costs as a result of a significant salary increase for Reeves and the added expense of color lensing caused the demise of most exterior sets. New flying scenes were shot to feature the color uniform now worn by Reeves. These were straight profile angles, and although convincing, were reused for the rest of the series' run.

ANDY MANGELS: National and Kellogg's contracted George Reeves for another 52 episodes, although not initially letting him know the plans behind the filming of those episodes. Production was halved on the show, with only 13 episodes produced each season for the next four years rather than 26 per season for the next two years. Reeves was already unhappy with the role, and now with his contract. He had wanted to hang up his cape, but was talked into fulfilling the contract by a hefty raise. The other actors remained on standby, not quite sure when filming would be for the next episode or season, and as a result unable to properly pursue their own careers. It's no wonder the 1954 shows betray a certain lack of enthusiasm. The new season lacked the charm of its two predecessors. Although Clark Kent got more double entendres and overall humorous banter was included for nearly everyone, the action and adventure sequences were trimmed to a minimum, making it seem as if the show had been retitled "The Adventures of the *Daily Planet* Staff."

NOEL NEILL: Nothing funny ever happened on the set. There wasn't enough time. One morning, though, George got stuck in a wall. The breakaway wall didn't break away and he got one foot and one arm through, and got stuck. Of course, that delayed my rescue a little.

CHUCK HARTER: The show continued to rise in popularity and the new changes seemed to have no detrimental effect on the viewing audience. In fact, when someone today looks at the series as a whole and considers the last four seasons on their own terms, the series holds up quite well and there are many color shows which are entertaining and enjoyable. During the initial run, the warmth of Reeves' lead and the sympathetic support of the rest of the principal cast proved to be so interesting to the viewers that in some cases the plots didn't matter. Just to be in the "presence" of the Superman "family" was enough to keep the audience faithful.

Connecting with children was one of Reeves' primary interests, and during the show he worked with underprivileged kids, sponsoring, along with friends Henrietta and Natividad Vacio, something that was called the Mambo Club.

GEORGE REEVES: When I was in motion pictures, Natividad, who is a close friend of mine, was telling me about the youngsters at the school. He mentioned that no one ever came to see them — no one of any kind of prominence, that is — so he asked if I would come over and talk to them. I said I'd be glad to. I spoke the Spanish language, which is probably unique for an Irishman like myself. Anyway, I brought my guitar along, and Natty and I not only talked to the boys and girls, but we also put on a show for them. From that moment on, I became interested in these young people. I was also supposed to attend a meeting of the club — and there was some interest among the boys and girls in seeing Superman. Since there were about 150 in the club, I was totally unprepared for the mob that greeted me when I went to the school. There were about 3,000 children waiting for me. I managed to get to the recreation hall and I talked to them until the police finally had to come and send the kids home. There was just too much of a mob to handle. (*TV Radio Life*)

Production wrapped on the new 13 episodes in January 1955. Prior to this, Reeves had begun to make a few personal appearances as either Superman or Clark Kent. On one occasion during June of 1954, he appeared as Clark Kent in Memphis, TN along with fellow cast members Larson, Neill and Hamilton. He signed autographs, handed out cards featuring a photo of himself as Superman and gave brief inspirational speeches to the assembled children. This was the only time that the entire cast appeared together at a personal appearance.

CHUCK HARTER: During early- and mid-1955, Reeves began to increase the frequency of his personal appearances. As well as riding in several parades, he visited many children's hospitals and orphanages. When appearing in person, he would hand out the autographed cards featuring his portrait as Superman. The deciding factor that determined whether he would appear as the *Daily Planet* reporter or the Man of Steel did *not* primarily concern his fearing for his safety. Although a report had been published describing a near-escape from death when a young admirer had borrowed his father's pistol and intended to "watch the bullets bounce off Superman," this appears to have been a falsehood.

JIM NOLT: I try putting myself in George's place and I'm not sure why he did those public appearances. I would think it would have been very difficult for him to go out in public and I asked myself, "What if something tragic had happened at one of those appearances?" — not to him, but somebody else that he couldn't prevent. And in front of all those kids who would be wondering why he didn't do something.

MICHAEL J. HAYDE: I think he enjoyed the *money* he made from those appearances. At the time he started doing personal appearances, he realized, "Okay, this is it. Unless I become a director or work behind the scenes, nobody's gonna cast me in anything really important again." That story about his appearance in *From Here to Eternity* and people in the theater whispering, "Look, it's Superman!" when he came on screen, is absolutely true. It was reported in *The Hollywood Reporter* at the time. Kids went to the screening of that film with their families — obviously it's not a children's movie — and one kid was overheard to cry out, "Why doesn't Superman stop those planes? He's right there!" It's like, "Shut up, kid. You're not helping." So I think his view became, "Well, this is my life right now. I should make the most of it while it lasts." And so there were personal appearances for extra money and there he was eventually getting the opportunity to direct three episodes when it looked like production was going to wind down for good. He was doing what he felt he needed to do to eat regularly.

JIM NOLT: Sometimes he would agree to appear in costume, other times he just preferred to be Clark Kent. If he was up on stage, away from the crowd, he didn't mind being Superman, only because they couldn't put as much direct pressure on him to do certain things. There he was more in control of what he was doing. If he was surrounded by kids, he wanted to be Clark, because they wouldn't put that same pressure on him as if he were Superman. So it was more a matter of where he was and the circumstances. Over time he didn't transition from one to the other, it was the circumstances of the appearance. The story about a kid pulling a gun on him was made up by his manager to explain why George didn't want to appear in costume sometimes.

MICHAEL J. HAYDE: When he visited schools, orphanages or hospitals, he went as Clark Kent. He explained, "When I wear the suit, people want me to do things like jump out windows and fly. I can't and I don't want to destroy the myth. I don't want to destroy the illusion."

CHUCK HARTER: In later interviews, Art Weissman, Reeves' manager, explained that if the kids were too young, they would ask and expect Superman to fly, and would be disappointed when he couldn't. He would then appear as Clark Kent. For an older crowd, he would appear as Superman and explain how the flying rig worked

GEORGE REEVES: I told them that the flying is accomplished through an elaborate rig instead of wires. We discarded wires when I fell 30 feet once. As for my jumps, which I'm always taking, I explained that they were done with the help of a springboard from which I took my dives. I didn't say that I usually land in a net. Occasionally I miss the net, but there are always two or three Supermans warming up in case I don't come out of a dive too well. I do all my own stunts, which consists of going through windows and walls and, of course, jumping. The highest jump I ever did was 20 feet. To keep physically fit, I do tumbling and calisthenics, primarily to learn how to fall without being hurt. (*Statesman Journal*)

CHUCK HARTER: Just the same, when he did appear as Superman, he would be situated behind a protective fence or would appear on a stage a considerable distance from his audience with the addition of several security guards. From all reports, he was received rapturously by the kids and was a most believable Superman in the flesh. During the years, Reeves completed a 10- city tour for the City of Hope Hospital to raise funds and give the children lectures on safety. So popular had he become in the part that an appearance in April of 1955, "Superman" appeared at two Los Angeles department stores.

Of those events, the local media reported, "Superman, in the person of George Reeves, visited the Broadway Downtown yesterday morning and the Broadway — Crenshaw in the afternoon, to the delight of thousands of children who have seen his exploits on television. Fifteen-thousand children greeted Superman at the downtown store and 20,000 at the Crenshaw store." Those are pretty astounding figures.

GARY GROSSMAN: George made so many personal appearances in order to make money, because he got so little of it from *Adventures of Superman*. It represented more income for him. Now I never had the chance to see him in person, but I've seen so many pictures and you *do* see the joy on his face *and* joy in the face of people he interacted with.

GEORGE REEVES: The burden of being Superman is not a light one. In fact, it's a frightening responsibility. I can never go in a bar or smoke a cigarette, because Superman doesn't do those things. And I can't get in arguments in public. And like champion prizefighters, I'm always beset by some character who wants to boast that he took a poke at Superman. I had to take up judo in self-defense. There is a certain small segment of the public which apparently delights in trying to prove that I'm a bum. You know the type. They come swaggering up to you, all sneers, and look you right in the eye and say, "So, you think you're Superman, eh? You're not so tough. I can lick you easy." And then, pow!" A trained boxer, he could take on these people, but someone in the public eye, like a Jack Webb or a Roy Rogers or any of the others, just can't do that sort of thing. George Reeves could punch one of those idiots in the nose and and nobody would care, but "Superman" can't. He'd be criticized for taking advantage of his supernatural powers. So, paradoxically, I've been forced to learn a few judo powers, which are even more effective than the things Superman himself is supposed to be able to do. (*Statesman Journal*)

In September 1955, Superman Inc. moved to the Chaplin Studios for the new season's production. The 13 episodes continued in the tradition established during the previous year, containing some shows that were played as outright comedies, a few mysteries, a human interest show and an episode featuring Kryptonite titled "The Deadly Rock."

A year later, production moved yet again to the new facility at ZIV Studios, which was well-respected as a producer of high-quality/low-budget series. Those 13 episodes, which had wrapped production by November 1956, had a few good shows, but the reliance on the stock formula and comic villains gave an indication that perhaps the series had begun to run out of steam.

CHUCK HARTER: A much-needed boost occurred in mid–November of 1956 with the filming of a guest appearance of George Reeves as Superman on the extremely popular comedy series *I Love Lucy*. The episode, "Lucy and Superman," was a complete success and showcased the comedic timing of Reeves while working with one of the great comic actresses of all time. This was Reeves' only TV guest appearance in the role of Superman and the show is not only popular with fans of the *Superman* series, but remains one of the best-loved episodes of *I Love Lucy* as well. The show originally aired on January 14, 1957 and was a ratings success.

MICHAE J. HAYDE: I was thinking about *I Love Lucy* and the question of whether or not George enjoyed being identified as Superman. One of the things I was thinking was that if every encounter with children had been as idealized as it was in the "Lucy and Superman" episode, where he burst in on Little Ricky's birthday party and invites the kids to wrestle with him, that was a big contrast to the guy who was encountering kids who wanted to slug him in the arm or the stomach, just to feel that steel against their hand. Obviously, he's a flesh-and-blood man.

JIM NOLT: Appearing on *I Love Lucy* must have been a real thrill, because it was a network broadcast of one of the most popular shows on television. I think he was more himself on that show than on anything else. I've spoken to Keith Thibodeaux, Little Ricky, and he was just so thrilled to be boosted up on George's shoulders at the time. I didn't expect him to remember details of the show because he was so young, but it was a great thrill for him. And George looked great. The costume he wore was a color one, but it shows up very well in black-and-white. That was actually something that the *Superman* production had trouble with when they went to filming in color in 1954. He wore a color costume, but it didn't photograph well in black-and-white. Initially they didn't make color prints and continued to show it in black-and-white. And the contrast between the blue and the red wasn't distinctive enough, so they had trouble with that. But on the *Lucy* episode, the costume looks great and fits well.

MICHAEL J. HAYDE: It's a very enjoyable episode. One of the things that I think gets missed, and you have to watch for it carefully, but when Superman bursts through and lands in the living room, Desi Arnaz turns away from the children and says, "How about that?" He's *not* looking at the kids when he says it, he's looking at the studio audience. They were just as surprised as the children were that he was actually there. It's kind of tipped off ahead of time, because when Fred says to Ricky, "Isn't Lucy in the kitchen?" he says, "No, but guess who is? Superman!" And the audience goes, "Oh!" They didn't know he was going to be the special guest star. They might have suspected, but weren't sure.

GEOFFREY MARK (author, *The Lucy Book*): The script was so brilliantly written with DC looking over their shoulders to make sure that they didn't do anything to tarnish the character. And because Lucy Ricardo believes he's Superman, *we* believe it. And we see him doing something that isn't quite so cartoony: When they're out on the ledge in the rain, it looks like Curt Swan and George Klein drew the episode. How many times have you seen Curt Swan's Superman with his arms folded and one leg over the other leg? That was Curt Swan and George Klein's Superman standing there.

STEVE YOUNIS (webmaster, supermanhomepage.com): It worked so well, because he had so much fun with it. And there you got to see the thing about George Reeves: He seems *so* genuine. He didn't seem to be acting, he seemed to be genuinely enjoying it — which was contrary to what you'd hear behind the scenes, where he supposedly said he would like to burn the suit because he hated it. He called it the monkey suit and whatever. But at the end, when he makes that comment to Ricky Ricardo about Lucy, "And they call *me* Superman?" it kind of breaks the fourth wall. We know what Ricky has to deal with being married to Lucy, but for Superman to be the one to say it is hilarious. He didn't get to do a lot of comedy on *Adventures of Superman*, so to be in that situation where the rain's pouring down on them and Lucy is looking like a drowned rat, is just hilarious, and George is able to be standing there, just having fun with it.

GARY GROSSMAN: He is just full of this charm and self-effacing joy in the role. You could really see how much he was enjoying it. When Paramount colorized the episode a few years ago, they corrected a wrong. And the wrong was that George Reeves received no credit on the closing credits of the original episode, which is still a fact in the black-and-white version today. It is credited as Superman appears courtesy of DC Comics, but it did *not* credit George Reeves. Credit in the colorized version is wonderful and deserved. I'm sure he was watching it that night and must have been like, "What happened?" No doubt that contributed to his down feelings about the role. It was kind of like Kirk Alyn in the movie serials where he was credited as Clark Kent, but Superman was himself.

I Love Lucy *not withstanding, by 1956 Reeves' frustration with the role and the way he was treated by others, particularly the media, was growing apparent. For instance, in May of that year, he had gotten into a car accident, which generated headlines like, "Superman Sues for Damages After Wreck" and "Superman is Hurt Like Other Mortals." In August 1956 he made an appearance on The Perry Como Show — being hosted by Tony Bennett — to sing accompanied by his guitar. By December of 1957, word reached the media that his contract for* Adventures of Superman *had come to an end and that the show itself was drawing to a close. At the time, his attitude seemed to be a fairly healthy one, telling* The Los Angeles Times *— the reporter for which asked him if he had sold out by accepting the part of Superman — that he hoped to move into directing.*

GEORGE REEVES: How can a starving actor sell himself out? I wasn't doing anything when this chance came along. The way I look at it, a working actor is a good actor, no matter what he's doing. Until I got my cape and badge of courage, I was never the height of success. You know, some people may not be aware of it, but I've done other things besides playing Superman. I wanted to be a singer, but I got my start in Hollywood with Hopalong Cassidy. If you remember those early "'Hoppy' movies," I was the kid who used to look at Cassidy and shout, "Gee, Hoppy, what are we gonna do now?" From that I graduated to roles with Claudette Colbert. When the war came along, I wound up in Moss Hart's Army production of *Winged Victory* and in 1946 I went back to Paramount. Except for the Sgt. Stark role in *From Here to Eternity* and a new part coming up in Walt Disney's *Westward Ho! The Wagons,* I haven't done much else. That's why I was glad to get this spot with Tony Bennett. It gave me an opportunity to prove again that I haven't always been Superman.

After the series, it's like Hopalong Cassidy trying to get an acting job in white tie and tails. Producers wouldn't give me a job. They'd take one look at me and say it was impossible. The idea of directing appeals to me. I took over as director on the last 13 *Superman* segments we made last fall. I did it as sort of a chance, but I was surprised to find out how much I knew. I suppose you ought to absorb some knowledge after being in the business as long as I have. Now I'm enthused about doing more. I'm forming a production company and we plan to make a couple of science-fiction features back to back. The trick stuff should come easy. We've done everything imaginable in the Superman series. (*Los Angeles Times, Akron Beacon Journal*)

That all sounded more promising than it actually was — and Reeves more optimistic than people have generally painted him to be at the time.

CHUCK HARTER: In August of 1957, prior to the filming of the sixth and final season of the *Superman* series, George Reeves organized and toured several state fairs with "The Superman Show." This revue featured Reeves performing musically as Clark Kent. He sang Spanish folk songs and played guitar and string bass with a Mariachi band. He also appeared as Superman in a segment of the show where he would wrestle a costumed villain named "Mr. Kryptonite." Noel Neill appeared as Lois Lane and also sang some songs accompanied by Reeves and the band. There were also various acts on the program and many charitable appearances by Reeves and Neill at various children's hospitals and orphanages.

NOEL NEILL: George was a wonderful singer. He spent a lot of time in Mexico and spoke Mexican. He was like a native and he had this dear friend that worked with us a lot, Natividad Vacio, who is in the movie *The Milagro Beanfield War*, and it was so much fun to see him. But George was literally afraid to go out in the uniform, because of a child getting the family gun and blasting poor Superman. But all of a sudden he said, "I think we will go out and do a little variety show." I had done some singing when I was young, so Nati played his guitar and George played his guitar and we had an accordion player and Nati and I did the little Hirabi Tot Teal and everybody sang. At the end we had Gene LaBelle, who is one of the world champion judo masters, who would come out in the black Mr. Kryptonite uniform as I was dancing or something and he would swoop me up and dash off with me and of course I was screaming, "Superman, Superman, save me!" Then George would come in in his outfit and then the two of them would do the judo wrestling or whatever on the stage and that was always the finale.

JIM NOLT: Unfortunately, many of those were not well-attended, partly because his manager Art Weissman didn't publicize them well. George lost *a lot* of money on that. He put his own money into that tour.

MICHAEL J. HAYDE: At that time, he was thinking about a recording career too. He had recorded a couple of songs as demos and was shopping for a record deal. That was after he appeared on *The Tony Bennett Show* as a guitarist and singer. Of course, he also appeared as Superman, but at least he got to do his singing in a tuxedo and not in a cape and tights. My understanding is that he fronted the money expecting it to do very well, but there was one venue where there were like three people in the audience.

JIM NOLT: Noel said he came back from that feeling very, very depressed. She said he was doing a little bit of drinking along the way, and with each stop he got more and more depressed.

The final 13 episodes of Adventures of Superman *went into production in September of 1957 at ZIV Studios. There was a bump in quality of the scripts, the last three of which — "The Brainy Burro," "The Perils of Superman" and "All That Glitters" — were directed by George Reeves.*

CHUCK HARTER: Realizing that at age 43 he was becoming too old for the part, and feeling a degree of typecasting, Reeves had obtained his Directors Guild card and intended to pursue a directing career when the series concluded, which it did in mid-November. The show for the most part had maintained a high level of quality with the first two seasons being excellent examples of early 1950s television production. George Reeves had performed admirably in the lead and for several succeeding generations he *was* the visual interpretation of the Man of Steel.

JIM NOLT: For the cast, I think the appeal of the show is that it was a good job and steady work for those periods of time when they were doing it. Early on I don't think they felt the show would ever amount to anything. Jack often said he was told to just take the money and run; nobody's ever going to see it anyway. It'll never get on the air. And it *was* a struggle to get it on the air. It didn't really take off until early 1953. That's when they got Kellogg's as a sponsor and then they had to distribute the show. It wasn't a network show, so they had to sell directly to individual stations.

MICHAEL J. HAYDE: I never got an impression one way or the other if the actors enjoyed doing the show. They were all professionals, none of them were prima donnas, none of them were out to use the show as a platform for anything other than just doing their job. It was their day job, it was what they did and they took pride in it. It's not as if any of them felt that they were slumming. Even George Reeves, as frustrated as I'm sure he was at times with having to wear that costume on those hot sound stages, where there was no air conditioning — he had to stand beside a giant fan to keep cool in between takes wearing that heavy wool uniform. I have felt that uniform, and that is a *heavy* piece of clothing. I don't know how he managed to keep his marbles as long as he did, really. And it's no wonder that the martinis came out as soon as he got home, though there was talk of drinking during the day. Phyllis Coates has said that during the last season — she was on the lot for *I Was a Teenage Frankenstein* — George invited her over to his dressing room in the morning before either of them had started work, and he had broken out the booze. Now I'm taking her word for that. Whether it actually happened or not, who knows? I have no reason to doubt her, let's put it that way. He did like his olive, as he put it.

There is one episode, "The Magic Secret," where Perry White does a levitation trick. In the end, Superman does the scene in Perry White's office leading up to Perry performing that trick on Lois. Watch carefully: George is definitely *not* sober. Hey, it's a human moment. That scene must have come at the end of the day. In fact, it almost certainly did, because they had to set up that rig for Noel. Perry gets up indignant like, "I'll show you how commonplace this trick is." He gets up from his desk and George salutes for no reason at all; he's just standing there. That sounds like an olive moment. I promise you that was *not* in the script.

With Adventures of Superman *ending its run in 1958 (filming having wrapped the previous year), Reeves' professional life was more or less running in place. Projects he'd hoped to develop fell through, and he was extremely frustrated with his career and with a personal life that was in turmoil. All of it would end tragically.*

ANDY MANGELS: Each cast member went his/her own way when *Superman* ended. George Reeves suddenly found himself in a world that no longer acknowledged him as George Bessolo or George Reeves. Everywhere he went, he was greeted with reminders of *Superman*. Eventually Reeves decided to direct several upcoming projects.

PHYLLIS COATES: He approached me and told me that he had a property to direct. He wanted me to play the lead in a sci-fi movie. He told me he would be in touch, but within a few months, he was dead.

ANDY MANGELS: The first week of June 1959, Reeves was in a car accident, and suffered a serious brain concussion. He was prescribed several painkillers, but drank heavily besides to ease the pain.

BIOGRAPHY.COM: In addition to his professional problems, Reeves was burdened by his relationship with longtime lover Toni Mannix, the common-law wife of Eddie Mannix, vice president of Metro-Goldwyn-Mayer. In 1958, Reeves began a relationship with young New York socialite Leonore Lemmon. When he broke off his romance with Mannix, she was enraged and began to harass the new couple, causing Reeves to file for a restraining order against his former lover. On June 16, 1959, Reeves was found dead in his bedroom from a gunshot wound to the head. He was 45 years old. The police ruled his death a suicide, but rumors quickly surfaced that Reeves was murdered. Although Lemmon and Mannix were both suspected of killing Reeves, no arrests or convictions were made. His death remains shrouded in mystery.

RIP VAN RONKEL (screenwriter): George Reeves had been unhappy, because everyone thought of him as Superman, not as an actor. George was not a weak man, but he was soft and sensitive and this jungle we live in out here killed him. They couldn't make a buck off of him anymore, so they discarded him. (*Mirror News*)

GARY GROSSMAN: George was going through a lot at the time he died. Whitney Ellsworth said he had been in a traffic accident not too much earlier. He loved to drink, but Whitney said he was on these pain killers and really didn't know what he was doing at the moment. *That* was the story I believed for a long time, and I think Jack Larson tended to follow that story. But then Jack said, "No, no, no, I believe he did *not* take his own life." You also have to remember that in those days, MGM was a very powerful studio with very powerful tentacles into the LAPD and into the gossip columnists and into the legitimate press. Eddie Mannix was powerful enough to keep stories out of the press. His wife Toni Mannix was unhappy. Maybe somebody said something to somebody and somebody did something and that's what I choose to believe. Leonore Lemmon did do interviews for *Entertainment Tonight* and *Inside Edition*, and kept to the story about suicide, but there have been reports that Toni Mannix, on her deathbed, confessed. I don't know if that's true. I will say, though, that George was the first time that I was really aware of somebody dying. I remember the headlines and going to school the next day and we were all shocked, because the headlines were, "Superman Kills Self."

TIM DEFOREST: When I first read about it as a kid, I just remembering being sad, not necessarily shocked. He was *such* a wonderful Superman. Why did he have to end that way? I didn't know any of the details when I heard, just that he had killed himself.

JIM HAMBRICK (owner, the Super Museum in Metropolis, IL): Hearing that George was dead was like when JFK died. It affected me the same way. And it taught me a whole lot about myself; I ran the gamut as far as having balls the size of grapefruits. That's what it took. I felt obligated, like I was the chosen one that could get this figured out, and I did. I was right.

MICHAEL J. HAYDE: I went through what everybody goes through, and here's the progression: You hear that George Reeves shot himself in the head. You go back and scroll through microfilm and through newspapers, which is what I did. Then you start seeing newspaper stories about there being no fingerprints on the gun. Then you see a newspaper story about two addition- al bullet holes are found and you see a news story about how his mother has raised a probe to find out what really happened. And, of course, you think, "Why didn't I hear about this before?" Later, stuff comes out about how he was seeing a married woman and then he broke off with her and hooked up with this New York socialite, and the first woman had mob ties back East. So it really got convoluted and there were so many things that didn't look normal that you start to think something nefarious *must* have happened. The other thing is that in the newspapers was the report that George's alcohol level was just under twice the legal limit at the time.

JIM HAMBRICK: Watch *Hollywoodland* and you'll see my name as the last credit before it fades to black. I'm the one who investigated the case of whether or not it was suicide or murder. I got involved with the L.A. police department and things like that, so I'd have access to the files. I went the whole gamut and was able to extract certain information; driver's license, plate number and things like that. And this is not an opinion, it's cold, hard fact. I have an audio confession of the lady that did it. I have morgue photos and everything that go along with that. I just didn't want to exploit George and that's the direction they wanted to go in. There's a lot that happened during that time period that people don't know, and that's too bad. You know what I mean? I've had my life threatened several times by the mob and there's all kinds of things that went on during that time that would have kept anybody from going any further than I did.

JIM BEAVER: It's human nature that if someone doesn't live out their lifespan, or if something happens to someone where you're left questioning what happened, it's very natural for human beings to look at that and start pulling the threads out to see if we can unravel this. But sometimes a cigar is just a cigar. And sometimes the mystery is something that we as curious people just sort of create. After so many years of research, I don't personally think there's a mystery to what happened to him, but the fact is that people will always disagree about it, and then that sort of perpetuates a sense of mystery.

CHUCK HARTER: Right in the mix there in mid-1959, DC Comics, in co-operation with Whit Ellsworth, began making overtures to George Reeves in the hope of his participation in the filming of 26 additional color episodes. Apparently the 26 shows produced by Robert Maxwell for the 1951 season, after being edited in 1952, contained substandard negatives and were considered "too adult" for the current children's market. The plan was to shoot 26 additional episodes in color to build on the syndicated package.

JIM NOLT: One of the things that Whit Ellsworth and I talked about was whether or not there *was* going to be another season of the show in 1959. Whit said no, there was not, but his daughter Pat told me that when she heard about the news of George's death in New York on her way to work, she immediately called her dad in California and he wasn't aware of it yet. He said, "Oh my God, he just agreed to do another season." Over the years there have been "discussions" on whether there was going to be another season or not.

MICHAEL J. HAYDE: At some point George was told, "It looks like we're going to need to make another batch of 26." Apparently there was still an option available to the company, but George's attitude was, "Hey, if I can direct X number of episodes, I'm interested." Some people have said that he demanded to do half the episodes. I don't know if that's true or not, but it was on the table that he'd direct at least some of the episodes.

CHUCK HARTER: George Reeves, who had not done much work in the year-and-a-half since the show wrapped, was financially strapped and going though a lot of personal issues, was contacted. And it wasn't that he was thrilled to do it again, but they offered him 26 episodes instead of 13, I think $5,000 an episode instead of $5,000 a week, and he had gotten his Director's Guild of America card and directed in the last three seasons of the old show, and would direct a third of the new season. In that case he was, like, "Okay, it'll bail me out financially, I can really get a reel of directing film, and I'm sort of typecast and I want to move behind the camera." But they kept going back and forth in the spring of 1959 and wouldn't make a decision.

JIM NOLT: There's no physical evidence of an additional season. No scripts were ever found. Noel and Bob Shayne both said that they had agreed to another season, but they didn't have contracts. I suspect that there was *talk* of another season, but nothing had been finalized yet. So, yes there was, and no there wasn't.

MICHAEL J. HAYDE: What I ultimately think happened is that Monday morning or afternoon he found out that Kellogg's was putting up the money to do another batch of episodes and they would be going back into production in September. George started "celebrating" fairly early and kept on drinking all day. He and Leonore went out to dinner, words were exchanged apparently, and it got a little uncomfortable. At home, George decided to go to bed and then visitors came over. He drank with them and it just depressed him. He had an alcohol-fueled depression. He had gotten up earlier when he heard that he was going to be working again, but he came down from all the alcohol and it just put him in a state of mind where he made a tragic mistake. I also came to that conclusion after seeing actual autopsy photos of the head wounds. There was no possible way that it could be anything *other* than self-inflicted, because of the way the wound was created around the head.

JIM NOLT: His depression was growing. His relationship with Toni ended and then he started one with Leonore Lemon, and to my thinking he bit off more than he could chew there. She alienated him from many of his former friends, and another thing is that when he was with Toni, he didn't worry too much about money, because she provided money to him. An actor will go out and seek work, because he needs to be making a living, but George didn't necessarily have to make a living after he met Toni. She had money and the Superman series gave him spending money. So I don't think George was as eager to get work as he might have been. I don't want to put the blame on Toni or Leonore, but it was just all these things happening at the same time. And they were not really uplifting for George, so if he did commit suicide that night, I can easily understand it.

JIM BEAVER: I very much did come around to the idea of suicide from the forensic evidence and personal evidence of people who knew him closely at the end of his life. Being drunk and filled with despair may not have been his daily attitude, but he happened to be at that moment when things came together in a way that he felt really bad and he had enough alcohol in his system to do something impulsive. And he had a history of impulsive behavior when he was inebriated. I've heard from reliable sources of a couple of occasions where he made efforts or gestures toward taking his own life. It doesn't mean that that's what happened, but generally the outcome suggests that the simplest answer is usually the correct one.

JIM NOLT: I do believe George committed suicide. There was a lot going on in his life at the time, but his life was not going well. There's arguments back and forth about how could he commit suicide when he was going to do another season of *Superman* perhaps. My answer to that is that very well may have been one of the reasons. He's 45 years old, and this was not what he aspired to do. So at 45, what does he have to look forward to, but another season of jumping off of ladders and that type of thing? While we revere that, it may not have been what George wanted to do. In the end, it was ruled a suicide and there's nothing concrete to counter that. So that's what we're left with.

NOEL NEILL: I don't like to discuss this. I really liked George. As far as anyone knew, it was suicide. It was investigated and the "official" report stated that. It was such a terrible waste. It's one of those things that you don't know what turns people to it.

BOB SHAYNE: It was a greatly tragic event. It was a shock… a terrible blow to all of us. I have no professional opinion on whether or not George committed suicide. I'm not a real-life detective. The one thing I do know is that a friend of mine's father was called in to patch up some holes in the walls of his bedroom. This would indicate that several shots were fired. George would have only had to shoot once to kill himself, so who fired the other shots? I don't know. Again, I have no professional opinions on it.

JACK LARSON: I was the first person to go in the house after it was unsealed by the police. I went in with the woman who had inherited it. Indeed, there were, in the upstairs bedroom — I saw them with my own eyes — three bullet holes. That's all I know.

PHYLLIS COATES: There's been so much rumor. I don't know if we'll ever know the truth. Toni Mannix called me and told me about the death, and she wanted me to go over with her to the house. I wasn't able to, because I was working, but I think Jack Larson did. There were some very strange, odd things surrounding it. There was an officer with the sheriff's department in Monterey named Bill Cassaras, who studied the pictures of the body. From the angle of the bullet's entry, they deduced that George had actually pulled the trigger that killed himself, although there were random bullet holes around the room. The sheets had been used to wipe the gun clean, though. It was very confusing. I didn't socialize with him as much at that time, so I wasn't really close when it happened.

JIM BEAVER: Whenever the topic of George's life or death came up, Jack Larson and Noel Neill would get contacted. And as much as they love George, both of them would admit that they didn't see much of him the last year or two of his life. I was on *Supernatural* for 15 seasons and I don't think any of the series regulars on that show had ever been to my house and I've never been to theirs. We're friends, I love to see them and work with them, but I don't know what they're doing from day to day. Actors largely do their job and go home and see their co-stars at the studio. In George's case, it had been a couple of years since they had worked together. They might have crossed paths here and there, but they were not the people to tell you, "Oh, here's what George was feeling the last six months." And the people who *were* there are not necessarily people that are well-known to the public. For example, George was a silent partner in an electronics store and his partner who ran the store saw him almost every day in the last six or eight months of his life. His picture of George's attitude toward life in the world during that time is very different from Noel Neill's. He saw him for the last time on the last day of George's life and he was not surprised at all when he heard that George had killed himself. But if you're doing a story on *Entertainment Tonight*, it's a lot cooler to get Jimmy Olsen and Lois Lane to talk about it.

In the aftermath of Reeves' death, there were several attempts to keep the Kryptonian goose laying its golden eggs, some worse than others. The first was a bizarre idea of a Jimmy Olsen television series, which would have starred Jack Larson and used stock footage of Reeves and shots of a new actor from the back to "double" him. Then there was the pilot Superpup, *which cast "little people" in dog costumes and had characters like "Bark Bent" perform on the live action show's sets; and, finally, the 1961 pilot for* Superboy, *starring Johnny Rockwell as the Boy of Steel in Smallville. The making of the latter two were chronicled in Chuck Harter's book,* Superboy & Superpup: The Lost Videos.

CHUCK HARTER: *Adventures of Superman* had been a big money-maker and it hadn't gone into five day a week syndication yet, so I guess the big shots at National wondered how they could keep things going. Larson told the story many times that he was contacted for the Jimmy Olsen series, but he refused, because he felt bad about Reeves killing himself. *Superpup* came about at the end of filming the sixth season. The producer had the idea for a children's show, so he approached National, but they weren't really interested. However, because Whit had done a good job with the series and made a lot of money, plus he was a company man, they funded half and he funded the other half — that's how little they cared. The final scenes were shot for the Reeves series, and they had a day or two until the end of the week, so they knocked out *Superpup* really quickly, which is funny now when you see it, because the sets were for the regular-sized actors on the Reeves series and you have little people sitting in big chairs. It didn't go anywhere.

With *Superboy*, they shot the pilot and it looked promising. In fact, Rockwell was told to spend the summer working out to get in shape, but they ended up dropping that one, too. I'm guessing here, but I think now that the Reeves series was going five days a week in syndication, they didn't want another product to complete against it, so *Superboy* died on the vine.

Despite all of that, there's no question that Adventures of Superman *lived on for decades after it wrapped production, and the main reason for that is, of course, George Reeves.*

MICHAEL J. HAYDE: When I was a child, I was just in awe of him. You watched the episodes and you see the moment when he's taking off his glasses and ducking into the store room and I would start to get goosebumps. It's the thrill all children get when they're seeing something that excites them. So in that respect, it's a lot of what has stayed with me. And, of course, as a child I had a fairly vivid imagination and I'd like to pretend that I was Superman. I would get the costume every year and I would wear it throughout the year. I even got cheap toy sunglasses and popped out the lenses so that I could be Clark Kent.

ROB O'CONNOR (host, *All Star Superfan Podcast*): While I didn't grow up with the George Reeves series, I fell in love with them so quickly when I finally discovered them that I might as well have. While the series came out in the height of the Silver Age, it is a Golden Age series through and through as Clark, Lois and Jimmy battle grounded, realistic villains with the power of the printed word, with Superman arriving to provide necessary muscle when words will no longer suffice. Where other actors (including his immediate predecessor) had special effects to aid them, Reeves does so much with just the authority of his voice and his stature. He moves and talks with such a God-like grace that it's easy to see why generations of children were transfixed by him. And the series had some gems — "The Stolen Costume," "The Human Bomb," "Crime Wave," "Panic in the Sky" and many more. An episode named "Around the World with Superman" has Superman restore the sight of a blind (and cynical) little girl and bring her on a sightseeing tour of the world, whereupon she remarks something as close to profound as has been heard in a Superman story: "Oh Superman, I wish people could see just how beautiful the world really is."

TOM ANDRAE: When I was growing up in the '50s, I was not a fan of Superman comics, but I *loved* George Reeves in *Adventures of Superman*. That was a huge influence on me as a little kid; I went around with a cape and I had a dual identity. I just loved George Reeves, because I felt like he was also sort of a father figure-type of guy. He could be very tough, but also very kind and loving. I would say he was a wonderful Superman and I loved his interpretation of the character. Some people talk about him as being flabby, particularly towards the end; that he wasn't muscular and had a padded suit. But when I was a kid, I just heard that music, I heard truth, justice and the American way, and I saw the flag. I'm a patriot and I loved seeing that flag waving. I got shivers every time and I still feel the same way.

ANTHONY DESIATO (host, *Digging for Kryptonite* Podcast): I had only ever watched a tiny bit of the George Reeves show years ago. But then I covered it on the podcast and watched all of the first two seasons and a sampling of episodes from the color years. And boy, did I love it. I enjoyed it so much more than I thought I would. Again, it's been a real joy to come to some of this stuff and discover something new after all this time. I'm a little bit torn between the first and second season; I feel like the second season struck a nice balance where it was getting into the more kid-friendly territory, but it's still got enough of the energy maybe of the first season. Once we get to the color years, it is what it is.

GARY GROSSMAN: For kids, he was the embodiment of a fantasy that when we were in bed falling asleep, no matter what our days were, we could pretend we could do phenomenal things; that we could save our friends or get the bad guys or get a bully that maybe in real life we couldn't deal with in school. And all we needed to do was take off our glasses or jump into an outfit. And, of course, nobody could recognize us and we could do those impossible things. So, growing up I think Superman represented the possible to us in using the impossible. He was the fantasy we wanted to live out.

ALAN BURKE: I was born in 1984, so the George Reeves show was well before my time. But I was impressed by George Reeves himself, who plays Superman like a cross between your dad and a friendly local police officer. The stories are simplistic with most villains being interchangeable mobsters, but I can only imagine the impact that it had on the minds of children watching it live in the 1950s. I especially admire how respectful George was to the role of Superman, refusing to smoke in front of the children, etc., and how he took the material seriously. While most of the characters are very one-dimensional, I think there is a lot of enjoyment to be had with it. I honestly think George, a man with his own demons and ego, would smile today, knowing that this silly job he took to get by, on a medium he thought beneath him at the time, is still so very fondly remembered 70 years later.

JIM BEAVER: He had an innate ability to take seriously something that kids took seriously, and at the same time connected to the audience in a way that let both children and adults feel like they were in on a secret. It was his persona that not only were we privy to his secret identity and all the other secrets that grew out of that dynamic, but that somehow or another we were connected to him and that he knew us. He knew we were out there and he made us feel like we were members of a club that nobody else was privy to. There are a lot of other superheroes and TV heroes who *don't* have what he had. It's a gift that Reeves had that only a few actors are blessed with. And it doesn't even have a great deal to do with talent — not that he didn't have talent. But there are a lot of talented people who can't do what he did in that role, and that is to connect on a personal level with the audience. I think *that* is his legacy.

JIM NOLT: The appeal of the show to me *is* George Reeves. I see something in him that I don't see in many other actors; a sincerity, a connection that just appealed to me from the very first time I saw the show in 1953. And, of course, like many others, I played Superman when I was a kid, I got the Kellogg's shirt for 50 cents and a Corn Flakes box-top. And I always had this desire to connect with the show or with George in some way. But as a kid, I didn't have the least idea how to go about doing that. But it stayed with me. And then in 1976, when Gary Grossman's book came out — *Superman: From Serial to Cereal* — it opened up a lot of windows and doors for me. That's when I realized I could do something and I contacted Jack Larson and Noel Neill and Bob Shayne and Whitney Ellsworth and it just grew from there.

LOU KOZA: While the episodes seem low-key compared to contemporary drama, adventures and rescues, the *Adventures of Superman* still resonates for its charm, magic of wonder and simple message that crime does *not* pay. Yes, it has its various story flaws, its bloopers and its obvious low budget, but we baby-boomers just ate it up and never questioned or judged it. We were then, and still are now, wide-eyed about it all. Best of all, it had George Reeves, who simply had a trustworthy presence about him.

TIM DEFOREST: Some of the scripts on *Adventures of Superman* were undoubtedly kind of silly, but George Reeves, Noel Neill and Jack Larson played their parts straight and with respect. I know that George Reeves had problems with typecasting, but he did a great job as Superman and they brought their characters to life, never putting their tongue in their cheek and that's what appeals to people. It made you willing to accept that, okay, he took his glasses off and became Superman and no one knew he was Clark Kent. Christopher Reeve actually made it seem like two different people, but George didn't even bother trying and it didn't matter. You just accepted it for what it was.

STEVE YOUNIS: I think one of the big strengths was his portrayal of Clark. Clark Kent was obviously the dominant character in that series. Superman would show up to save the day, but Clark was doing the investigating and had the relationship with Lois and Jimmy, and then Perry White. I guess Clark almost played a father figure role, not just in the way the viewers of the show saw him, but the characters of the show too. He was that guy that was looking out for everybody. He was just kind of endearing.

PHYLLIS COATES: George was a love. We socialized a lot together. We'd meet after the shows and talk, or party together on the weekends, so we had a wonderful working relationship on the set. George was the kind of guy that while you were filming, he'd be just off of the set, ready to read your lines to you rather than the script girl. I used to call him Super-Boo. I don't know why, I just called him that and the name stuck.

NOEL NEILL: George was a wonderful person to work with. He was such a wonderful friend, a gentleman and, of course, a fabulous actor. The whole cast was a joy to work with. Everyone considers George to be *the* Superman. No offense to what's-his-name [Christopher Reeve], but everybody grew up with George. It's still on all over the world and everybody just relates to George as Superman. He was such a good actor. That's how we could carry it off, year after year, through the funky scripts and whatever. He was a bright, wonderful person.

BOB SHAYNE: I don't think there has ever been anyone who has equaled

George as Superman. The Superman movies are not anywhere as good as the job George did.

LEE SHOLEM: George Reeves or Christopher Reeve? I'm a little partial.

JIM HAMBRICK: George Reeves was like a surrogate father to a lot of people. When I got my museum out there, I was able to see exactly what that means, not just because of people's reactions, but the fact that they noticed things like the wink of the eye he gave them and the different things that George was able to put across with very little effort. There was a trust there: "You know who I am, we'll keep it our secret." That kind of thing that really drove the show. The flying wires and all of that didn't mean anything. We didn't care about the special effects; we were just into that character.

JIM NOLT: I think I can speak for most of those who love the series and love George Reeves when I say that the reason he stands out from all the others who have worn the cape is his sincerity in the role. He exhibits no bluster, no false bravado. He is supposedly the strongest man in the world, yet he takes time to cure a girl's blindness and to take a girl stricken with polio for an exciting flight above the city. We know it's the writers who created those scenarios, but no one could have carried them off better than George.

MICHAEL J. HAYDE: George Reeves really resonated for a lot of people of my generation, and I wasn't even really the first generation; I was on the tail end of the Baby Boom. But it was just his performance that resonated with us, the warmth, the charisma that he personally brought to the role. He wasn't a great actor, he was a personality. He was no better or worse an actor than William Shatner was in the one role that made him famous.

CHUCK HARTER: In late 1965 the first color broadcasts of the series began and the results were a ratings phenomenon in all domestic and foreign markets that featured "new" color episodes. The *Adventures of Superman* had truly become one of the *world's* most popular television series. It was the second oldest show still in syndication with *I Love Lucy* being in first place. Thanks to the brilliant performances of George Reeves and the rest of the cast, professional production under Robert Maxwell and Whitney Ellsworth, along with the many technicians who worked on the series, the *Adventures of Superman* stands not only as an enduring popular classic of television, but one of the finest filmed interpretations of the Superman character.

CHAPTER V
Welcome to the Silver Age

A little more than midway through the 1950s, comic books as a whole had been the victim of something of a smackdown. Between sliding sales following the end of World War II, most superheroes going out of fashion and the controversy of, and panic triggered by, Frederic Wertham and Seduction of the Innocent, *few seemed to know what direction to go. The answer came from, of all places, superheroes themselves.*

JOHN WELLS (author, *American Comic Book Chronicles*): For many fans, the Golden and Silver Ages were defined strictly by superheroes, ignoring the other popular genres that flourished and overlapped with the early decades of costumed characters. The First Heroic Age — as groundbreaking fan/historian Jerry Bails called it — gradually ended after World War II as various titles dumped their superhero leads from 1945 to 1951 in favor of genres that were becoming more popular: funny animals, Westerns, war and humor. The big bang of the Second Heroic Age was the tentative revival of the Flash in mid-1956's *Showcase* #4. There had been both new superheroes and short-lived comebacks of old ones earlier in the 1950s, but this was the one that demonstrably clicked. Following three more test issues, an ongoing *Flash* comic book premiered in 1959. As DC got to work on creating or reviving other heroes, publishers like Archie and Marvel began developing their own superheroes in the next few years.

Originally, the Flash was a Golden Age character whose identity was that of Jay Garrick, who was credited as the fastest man alive. In the reboot, the helmeted speedster gave way to the masked Barry Allen. After that, readers were given a new version of Green Lantern, with Alan Scott making way for pilot Hal Jordan; and then the Justice Society of America morphed into the Justice League of America. Things didn't slow down from there.

Insofar as Superman was concerned, the character found himself under the aegis of editor Mort Weisinger, who was given full editorial control of the Man of Steel. A story editor on the Adventures of Superman *television series (as well as the proposed* Superboy *followup in 1961), he came from a background in science-fiction pulps and had joined National Periodicals in 1941, frequently banging creative heads with Jerry Siegel in regards to stories for Superman. He became the character's sole editor in 1958 and remained in that position until he retired in 1970. The results were perhaps one of the most unique periods in the Man of Steel's comic book history.*

PETER SANDERSON (comic book historian): Superman was still going strong in the 1950s, as were Batman and Wonder Woman, but virtually every other

Many believe this issue of Action Comics unofficially ushered in the Silver Age
(© and TM DC Comics/Warner Bros. Discovery).

superhero that had been created following Superman's debut was gone. By the end of 1951, the "Golden Age of Comics" was over. Only half a decade later, though, National Periodicals began testing the waters to see if a new generation of readers would respond to superheroes as enthusiastically as their elders had. Beginning in 1956, Julius Schwartz relaunched many of the company's classic heroes in revamped forms with a heavy dose of science-fiction, which was gaining widespread popularity in post-war America through movies and television. This period, stretching from 1956 to at least the end of the 1960s, is now known among comics fans as the Silver Age of Comics, the period when the superheroes were revived and given a creative momentum that carries on right into the present day.

GEOFFREY MARK (Silver Age Comic Book Historian): You could say the Silver Age began with "The Super-Key to Fort Superman" in *Action* No. 241 in 1958. It's the first time we actually look inside Superman's Fortress of Solitude, and the first time it's referred to that way. We see the huge key sitting outside it that Superman needs to open it. But why? He's smaller than the lock; he can just fly through it. Well, that's Wayne Boring's fault, because he drew it that way. That issue is also the first time we see how close he is to Batman. New pieces of the puzzle were being added to the tapestry of what Superman's Silver Age mythos was.

JOHN WELLS: *Superman* #113 (on sale March 1957) feels like the start of the Man of Steel's Silver Age. It was the first cover-to-cover Superman story ever, "a special 3-part novel" that flashed back to Jor-El's adventures on Krypton. Historically, it was also the first comic book to use Superman's given name, Kal-El. That was followed within a few months by two pilot issues of a Lois Lane series that became an ongoing comic book in 1958. In rapid succession, the first half of 1958 also introduced the Legion of Superheroes, the Arctic Fortress of Solitude, Brainiac, Kandor, Elastic Lad and Supergirl and Bizarro prototypes.

PETER SANDERSON: Just to show you how fast Weisinger's writers were coming up with ideas, the same issue in which Supergirl first appeared also showcased new villain, Metallo, a criminal who had been turned into what we would now call a cyborg, half-man and half-machine. And his robotic parts were powered by Kryptonite.

GEOFFREY MARK: What's interesting is that the *Adventures of Superman* show reflected the comics of the late '40s. This is also the thing that affects the Silver Age as long as the show was on in first-run syndication. So through '58 and early '59, the comic books had reflected the screen; it couldn't go too far astray.

JOHN WELLS: The fact that Superman and his Gotham City counterpart Batman mostly fought ordinary crooks seems more like simple complacency to me. Their comic book sales were still fantastic and no one was thinking long-term. Well into the 1970s, many editors still saw fantastic menaces and costumed villains as elements that should be used sparingly in superhero stories, lest readers get sick of them.

GEOFFREY MARK: Once *Adventures of Superman* was finished, Mort was free to just do whatever he wanted after that. So '56 to '58 is when it starts; he plants the seeds. It starts growing slowly, and then when *Adventures of Superman* goes away into syndication forever, he's free to now just let it all hang out.

MARK WAID (writer, *Superman: Birthright*): It was about 1958 when they just handed everything Superman-related over to Mort. That's when you can see, like a shot, editorial suddenly coming in with a *very* heavy hand and Mort really shaping that Superman universe with sort of an internal consistency and continuity that really wasn't there before then.

TIM DEFOREST (author, *Storytelling in the Pulps, Comics and the Radio: How Technology Changed Popular Fiction in America*): Weisinger's idea was that every six months or so you would introduce some new element into Superman's mythology, and that's what I think was the strength of the Silver Age, because they did do wacky things within that, but you also got a lot that became an important part of Superman's mythology.

ARLEN SCHUMER (comics historian; author, *The Silver Age of Comic Book Art*): Think of what a modern showrunner does on television. You pace a story in such a way that each episode has to have a kind of a cliffhanger, but you're also telling a larger story. Weisinger knew enough as a businessman and an "entertainer" who was used to periodical publishing his whole life, that you have to keep it fresh so every now and then you've either got to throw a wrench into the mix or do something to gain attention. I'm going to go off on a tangent, but think about The Beatles. One of the reasons they were so successful in the '60s was that they had a real work ethic from those days of performing in Hamburg. They were proud of the fact that every six weeks or so they had a single or something released and they were diligent about putting out albums. Starting with *Sgt. Pepper,* because they weren't touring anymore, they were able to take their time, but from

'63 to '67 they had this tremendous commercial work ethic, including putting out singles between albums. Nowadays, a "rock star" taking five years between albums is no big deal. But that's the way it was done back then, and Weisinger was part of that commercial generation. But for every great story, you had to wade through 25 forgettable ones. Yet when Weisinger and his team were all being the craftsmen that they were, when Weisinger let them *craft* a great Super-man story, *those* are the ones we remember.

MICHAEL EURY (editor, *The Krypton Companion*): It got to the point where Mort would not let Superman appear in *The Brave and the Bold*. He flat out would not allow it. The one exception to the rule was that Bob Haney, who was writing the title, got to do a Supergirl/Wonder Woman story and Superman appeared in the story. But that was the only time they got to do it. Originally *The Brave and the Bold* started with the odd pairing of Green Arrow and Martian Manhunter, and there were a bunch of different characters that were rotated in and out with Batman popping in occasionally. Batman eventually usurped the book, but Superman would have been a player in that mix if Mort hadn't kept such an iron fist on that character. But he *did* know what he was doing. You might not have liked what seemed to be his regime if you were a writer or artist working for him, but those people did it for a long time.

ARLEN SCHUMER: What's funny is that after DC basically sues Captain Marvel out of existence, they basically hire all of Captain Marvel's creatives like Otto Binder and Kurt Schaffenberger, who start to turn Superman into Captain Marvel with their own version of Mary Marvel — they launched Supergirl in 1958 — and they already had Captain Marvel Jr. in the form of Superboy. It's in-dicative of Weisinger being given the green light by Liebowitz and Donenfeld to use those creatives, "even though we sued them because they were outselling us." So what happens? Superman becomes a knockoff of Captain Marvel and within that knockoff initiative, nobody cares. The original was years ago — back then a couple of years ago, today ancient history. There weren't reprints and nobody cared what happened three or four years earlier. Weisinger knew that. He and fellow editor Julius Schwartz came from the pulps where that's just what you did. They knocked off their own ideas. There's a quote from Weisinger where he says, "If you're gonna knock something off, do it well." Totally upfront about it.

ROBERT GREENBERGER (writer, former DC editor): Mort had a really strong commercial sense; he knew that every couple of months you needed to do *something* to jazz up the line. And you had those 1/3-of-a-page ads promoting the line. It was like, "Oh my God, Jimmy Olsen's turning into a turtle in this month's *Superman's Pal Jimmy Olsen.*"You'd want to go and check out what was going on there. He would introduce these elements largely to goose the sales and it was almost like clockwork; probably every four to six months.

PETER SANDERSON: Reflecting the 1950s trend for science-fiction movies, in the comics Superman began fighting giant monsters from other worlds. And Weisinger worked more science-fiction elements into his series, making the Silver Age probably the most creative period in Superman's history. The primary Superman artist of the 1950s was Shuster's former assistant Wayne Boring, whose Man of Steel may have moved stiffly, but looked grimly determined and massively muscular. Boring also played a large role in setting the 1930s science-fiction look for Krypton. Also, Weisinger, like Jerry Siegel, was a former self-publisher of science-fiction fanzines.

RAY MORTON: I am not overly fond of the 1950s/60s era of Superman. I did not like artist Wayne Boring's version of the character. The proportions of Boring's Superman always seemed off to me — he had a chest that seemed to take up his entire torso, a tiny head with a chin that was way too big for his face and curly hair that never seemed appropriate for a Man of Steel. I much preferred Curt Swan's version of the character, which replaced Boring's in the 1960s. Still, the stories of that era were too fanciful for me — with both the Depression and the war over, the realistic contexts that kept Superman grounded were gone, replaced by mermaids, giant monsters, mad scientists and aliens. Kryptonite in many colors put Superman through many freakish physical changes and transformations, and a fleet of lookalike robots helped him sidestep the many problems caused by having two separate identities who can never be in the same place at the same time. Some of these stories are quite enjoyable on their own terms, but overall for me the era is too light, too fluffy and entirely too inconsequential.

TOM DE HAVEN (writer, *It's Superman!*): I love the '40s stuff and Superman as the activist, but the stuff that *really* pulled me in was the Mort Weisinger era. Part of the appeal to the person who was going to be a writer was the kind of world-building that was quite wonderful.

TIM DEFOREST: As great as so much of that stuff was done, you had some silly stuff in there too. I still remember one where Superman is kidnapped by aliens who don't realize he's intelligent and have him living in a doghouse on their planet with a Kryptonite chain. At the same time, they allowed his mythology to grow into this really vibrant universe within the overall DC universe. As silly as it was with different kinds of Kryptonite and with things like Super Monkey and all all of that, it all fit together into something that I think was just a wonderful modern mythology.

CASE AIKEN (host, *Men of Steel* podcast): The Silver Age Superman had the benefit of having Superboy as part of the story as well, where you could be like, "Okay, this is the learning curve for the character. These are his adventures when he is young and a little more fallible." And *then* in his adventures as an adult, he's supposed to be more infallible and we're supposed to look up at him. In later incarnations, of course, like in the '80s, they got rid of the Superboy stuff and he's reset as being a little bit younger in his career. He's a little bit more prone to mistakes and it's kind of making him more like a Marvel-style character in that regard.

PETER SANDERSON: It's said that when he went to the barber, Weisinger would ask the kids he saw there what they wanted to see in the Superman books to incorporate ideas based on their suggestions. It is certainly true that his stories had tremendous appeal for young readers. But in those days, no one expected people to keep reading comic books much beyond their early teens, and the Weisinger books had a lot of concepts that readers would soon outgrow. Take the Legion of Super-Pets, for example, consisting of Krypto the Superdog, Streaky the Supercat, Comet the Superhorse and Beppo the Supermonkey; or Krypto's other team, the Space Canine Patrol Agents (S.C.P.A.), whose war cry was, "Big Dog, Big Dog, Bow Wow Wow!").

This was just the start of the Weisinger-guided era of Superman. In rapid succession, readers were given the criminal Metallo, a cyborg armed with a Kryptonite heart; Kryptonian villains from the nebulous Phantom Zone, who would escape and cause havoc on Earth; the backwards "clone" of Superman, Bizarro, whose attempts at doing… well, pretty much anything… all went wrong, but who would also inspire a variety of stories on his own to accompany his growing popularity.

PETER SANDERSON: In *Superboy* #68 (October to November 1958), a scientist named Professor Dalton used a faulty "duplicator ray" to create an "imperfect duplicate" of Superboy who became known as Bizarro. This allegedly "unloving" creature had chalk-white skin, a face resembling a cubist painting and — although this was never stated explicitly — a mentally-challenged mind. The Bizarro Superboy quickly perished, but in *Action* #254, published the following year, Luthor rebuilt Dalton's device and created a new, adult Bizarro-Superman. This time, Bizarre was here to stay. Originally Bizarro was portrayed with pathos, a powerful being incapable of fitting into the world of normal humans. But as time went on, Bizarro became a comical character, determined to do everything backwards, as if in defiance of the normal world that rejected him. And so he would say "Goodbye" when he arrived and "Hello" when he left. Bizarro was paired with a Bizarro version of Lois Lane and ended up living on the Bizarro World, a planet sculpted to look like a cube instead of a sphere. He populated the planet with innumerable other Bizarro Supermen and Bizarro Loises as well as Bizarro versions of other characters in the Superman mythos, and even Batman.

Then there was the Legion of Super-Heroes, a group of powered teens in the 30th century who invite Superboy to be a part of them in the future, though he conveniently loses his memory of events and knowledge when he returns to the 20th century; Lois Lane and Jimmy Olsen would get their own comics, the aforementioned Superman's Girlfriend Lois Lane *and* Superman's Pal Jimmy Olsen, *both relatively silly affairs filled with fluffy and campy stories.*

PETER SANDERSON: One of Weisinger's most extraordinary innovations was his "imaginary stories." At this time, before Stan Lee and Jack Kirby's storytelling revolution at Marvel Comics, the status quo of a comic book series was nearly inviolable. Almost nothing would ever change in Superman's world: No one would die, certainly Superman would never marry Lois and landmark events like Supergirl's public debut were exceedingly rare. Imaginary stories, on the other hand, enabled Weisinger's writers' imaginations to run wild. Lying outside the canon of continuity, these were stories that projected possible futures for the Superman cast, or asked what would have happened had certain key events or relationships in past stories been different.

TIM DEFOREST: The imaginary stories were actually a great showcase for stories asking questions like what would have have happened if Superman married Lois, or if he died? Or what would happen if he were found by Thomas and Martha Wayne rather than the Kents? It was just another great element of the Silver Age which would later become *Elseworlds* stories. If we treat Superman as a legend and tell great Superman stories and not worry about where they fit into a continuity, there are advantages to that as well.

PETER SANDERSON: One of the best and most famous of the imaginary stories was "The Death of Superman" in *Superman* #149 [November 1961], in which Luthor convinces both Superman and the world that he has reformed, only it's a set-up to trick and murder Superman with Kryptonite radiation before the horrified eyes of Lois and his closest friends. But the story does not end there: It shows how Superman is honored by the world at his funeral, as if in anticipation of the funeral of John F. Kennedy; and how Supergirl and other fellow Krypto-nians hunt Luthor down. Luthor is taken to Kandor and is put on trial in a booth of unbreakable glass, conjuring the memory of the trial of Nazi war criminal Adolf Eichmann, and exiled to the Phantom Zone.

ARLEN SCHUMER: At the end of "The Death of Superman," Supergirl is flying with Krypto with tears in her eyes, thinking, "I have to take over the mantle of my cousin Superman," and in the final panel she sees him in the clouds, basical-ly giving her his benediction and waving at her. I remember that I was eight years old in my grandmother's apartment, visiting her in the Bronx, I'm reading that story for the first time and getting to the last panel and my eyes were just filled with tears.

PETER SANDERSON: The second is "The Saga of Superman Red and Superman Blue," in which Superman, still haunted by the many world problems he has failed to solve, finds a method to turn himself into two separate beings. Two Supermen are indeed better than one: Together they turn Earth into a utopia, eliminating hunger and crime. This also solves other questions: one Superman marries Lois, the other marries Lana; one stays on Earth while the other moves to New Krypton, site of the enlarged Kandor.

Kandor would actually be introduced through another early innovation, which took place in the pages of Action #242 *(July 1958), where readers first encountered Luthor's greatest rival as the Man of Steel's arch-enemy in the form of Brainiac, a bald, green-skinned alien who traveled through space in a bright-red 1950s-style flying saucer.*

PETER SANDERSON: Originally Brainiac went about shrinking cities from different worlds with an ominous ray from his ship and imprisoning them in bottles, forming a sort of collection. He shrank Metropolis too, but, of course, Superman saved the day and used Brainiac's enlarging ray to return the cities to their true size. But there was not enough of the rare element that powered the ray to enlarge the last city, which ironically proved to be Kandor, the former capital of Krypton. In years past Superman had encountered a few Kryptonian villains who had somehow survived the planet's explosion, but now there was a whole city full of Kryptonian survivors. Superman placed the Bottle City of Kandor in his For-tress of Solitude, and it figured in numerous stories over the years. By temporarily shrinking himself using Brainiac's ray, Superman could visit Kandor and experi-ence life as it had been on Krypton before its end. Although it was never convinc-ingly explained why, Superman had no powers in Kandor. In some of the most memorable Kandor stories, Superman and Jimmy Olsen became masked crime fighters down there with their own secret identities, Nightwing and Flamebird, consciously mimicking Batman and Robin.

TIM DEFOREST: There was a story in the early '60s where Lex and Brainiac teamed up and basically captured Superman, and to get out of the trap, Superman has to *think* his way out, which was great. A lot of that era took place on alien planets with these wonderful, vivid visuals drawn by Curt Swan. It's just timelessly entertaining.

PETER SANDERSON: That issue in which Brainiac and Luthor teamed up [*Superman #167*] gave a startling new slant to Brainiac. He proved to be a highly-advanced robot created to serve as a spy by massive, sentient computers that had taken over a distant planet from their humanoid creators. Luthor rewired Brainiac's computer mind to make a "twelfth-level" computer, far superior to the "sixth-level" intelligence of a typical human being.

Even after the arrival of the Kandorians, Superman remained the lone Kryptonian superhero on Earth, but Weisinger went to work and within a year Superman received unexpected company in the pages of May 1959's Action Comics #252.

PETER SANDERSON: Weisinger gave him a young female counterpart, Supergirl, whom writer Otto Binder suspected might have been inspired by a similar character in the old *Captain Marvel* series, Cap's sister Mary Marvel. Supergirl was really Superman's teenage cousin Kara, the daughter of his uncle Zor-El. Lara was born in Argo City, a Kryptonian Metropolis — which had a Greek name — protected by a vast overhead dome. When Krypton exploded, somehow the entire city was hurtled into space, protected from the vacuum there by the dome. The rock foundation far beneath the city had, like the rest of Krypton, turned to Kryptonite, whose radiation finally seeped through to Argo City itself. By that time, many years after Krypton's explosion, Zor-El knew of Superman's existence on Earth and saved his daughter by dispatching her to Earth in a rocket ship.

Superman gave Kara a secret identity, Linda Lee, disguised by a brown wig with braids, and sent her to live at the Midvale Orphanage while he secretly trained her in the use of her powers. Eventually Linda was adopted by a couple named the Danvers and Superman revealed Supergirl's existence to an astonished, overjoyed world. By then she had a berth as star of the backup feature in *Action Comics*.

ROBERT GREENBERGER: It really started with the Fortress of Solitude, and within 10 months you already had Supergirl; Krypto the superdog had been introduced even before the Fortress, but then he became part of the adult Superman storyline.

PETER SANDERSON: It should be no surprise that if morally upstanding Kryptonians like Supergirl and the good people of Kandor were going to start turning up, a few rotten apples would show up as well. It was in *Adventure Comics* #283 in 1961 that readers first learned about the criminals exiled before the planet's destruction to a dimension called the Phantom Zone. It was Jor-El himself who discovered the Zone and proposed exiling criminals there as an alternative to capital punishment. There Krypton's greatest criminals — Jax-ur, Professor Kakox and Superman's relative Kru-El, among others — existed in ghostly form, drifting in a void, no longer aging. From the Zone they witnessed Krypton's destruction and they could now see Earth. *And* they held Superman, Jor-El's son, responsible for their imprisonment. Every so often, one or more of them would escape to Earth where, of course, they gained superpowers equal to Superman's. Luckily, he had his father's Phantom Zone projector and always managed to send them back.

ROBERT GREENBERGER: Bit by bit, pieces started to cross from one book into the next. The Legion of Super-Heroes from *Adventure* are now adult Legionnaires, Supergirl meets the Legion or Jimmy becomes a reservist. It really tied the line together to give it a distinct look and feel. And every couple of months you would know something was going to happen. And these things showed up again and again and again until they seeped into the consciousness. There's a lot to be said for the fact that Mort did it before Stan Lee did.

PETER SANDERSON: During this time, even the leftover pieces of Krypton, Kryptonite itself, were part of the vast expansion of the Superman legend. Perhaps this has something to do with the fears of nuclear war and radiation during the Cold War of the 1950s and 1960s. Now there was a rainbow of different varieties. There was the original form Green Kryptonite, whose radiation was lethal to Kryptonians — you knew it had killed one when his body turned green. And the most celebrated variant was Red Kryptonite, first appearing in *Adventure Comics* #255, which triggered an often bizarre change in a Kryptonian that would last 24 to 48 hours, ranging from loss of powers or memory to uncontrollable hair growth to even being transformed into a flying sea serpent! Red Kryptonite seems to have reflected Cold War Americans' fears of mutation caused by exposure to radiation. Luckily, once a Kryptonian had been exposed to a specific chunk of Red K, it could never affect him again; it was Superman's version of building up an immunity to chicken pox. And then there was Gold Kryptonite, which permanently wiped out a Kryptonian's superpowers, and Blue Kryptonite, which killed Bizarro Supermen and White Kryptonite, which was lethal to all plants regardless of origin, among others.

MARK WAID: Boy, there are two ways to look at what Mort brought to it. It's good in the sense that it gave the titles fresh blood — not just to one story, but the legend of Superman itself. That went on for six or seven years and got infused with *Legion of Super-Heroes* and many others. So all of that made the books hang together. But the downside to Mort's approach is that, on a psychological level, the entire universe became about Mort, *not* about Superman. Mort himself has said that he looked like a toad, a fat loser that nobody loved. And if you look at the Superman books during that period, the worst things you can be in the Superman universe are fat and bald. How many stories were about, "Lois has found the perfect man, but wait, he's secretly bald!" Or really fat — how many stories had Lois becoming really fat? Or the Kents figuring out the way to punish Superboy is by pretending they don't love him anymore?

Those are all of Mort's vulnerabilities put on paper. His views on women, which are not necessarily endemic just to him, are very much a 1950s, 1960s chauvinistic view that women belong in the kitchen. Lois Lane went from being Hildy Johnson in the '40s and '50s, a reporting dynamo and woman of her own agency, to just this lovesick, sappy idiot, brought to a Lucy Ricardo level, scatter-brained and pining after Superman in every issue. *And* carrying around a pair of scissors in her purse, as one does at all times, so she can try to cut Clark's hair and prove he's Superman. I mean, these things happened before, but it wasn't recurring every month until Mort came along, and his distrust of women is reflected in the way women are distrustful in the stories. So again, the upside of it is that it's a beautiful, coherent continuity and universe, but the downside is you get a lot of Mort's darkness.

NEAL ADAMS (writer/artist, *Superman vs. Muhammad Ali*): I'll tell you a story that will make you understand every horror story you've ever heard about Mort Weisinger and make you realize what was going on. I went into Mort's office one day, because I was perturbed by shit that people said about him. I could see that he was a grumpy fellow in general, but he treated me evenly and I was fine. But it bothered me, so we were talking about it. We went over a cover and whatever. We finished that conversation and I said, "Mort, I'd just like to ask you why you are so grumpy at people. You know, everybody thinks you hate them and you just seem grumpy." And I could see his face change in front of me and he said, "I'll tell you… I don't tell people this. Try to imagine that you get up in the morning and you go into the bathroom to shave, and you look into the mirror and you see *this* face." Now, for everybody out there who thinks he was grumpy, I say to you, the man had a soft side, dealing with his reality as best he could. Underneath, he was a good, sensitive man.

JOHN WELLS: By almost all accounts, Mort Weisinger was a tyrant whose sense of self-worth seemed to come from bullying most of the writers and artists he worked with. He was also reputed to take a heavy hand in editing scripts that writers turned in. Curt Swan recalled being mentally exhausted and wracked with headaches after some of his altercations with Weisinger.

ROBERT GREENBERGER: He wasn't kind to his creators with all that bluster and yelling, and apparently taking a story from one writer, rejecting it and then giving it to another writer and making it look like it was his idea — Mort was terrible about all that stuff and some people write it off that he was insecure or fighting to stay relevant as he was aging or whatever. I believe his son is still defending his memory. But the anecdotal stuff out there makes it sound like working for him was just horrible.

MARK WAID: The other downside of Mort's approach was that it made Superman passé
and it certainly allowed the Marvel Comics ethos to eclipse it month by month. It's not just that the Marvel characters were actually having fights with super-villains while Superman was trying to outwit criminals, it's also that the Marvel characters had problems that you could identify with. Spider-Man has to get medicine to Aunt May across town, but Doctor Octopus is in the way. Superman's biggest problem was, "I don't know, how to enlarge the bottle city of Kandor," which is nothing that I, personally, as a reader can relate to. That's why the Parasite, who was created by Jim Shooter in 1966, was a breakout character, because it's the first time in forever that Superman was given somebody new to fight with. I believe he was the first lasting villain between Metallo in 1959 and Terra-Man much later. Any other Superman villains used in the 1960s were recurring and part of his tepid rogue's gallery. But Jim was heavily influenced by Marvel Comics as a kid and brought that kind of energy to DC.

JIM SHOOTER (writer/creator of "Parasite"): I was in ninth grade at the time, taking Biology I. We were studying parasites and I needed a villain.

JOHN WELLS: I'd argue that Marvel's success came from using exactly the same basic recipe as Mort Weisinger, but more by accident than design, changing enough ingredients to create something new. Each approach employed a growing continuity that enthralled regular readers. In Weisinger's case, the readers he was targeting were young children and the stories were written with them in mind. The strange transformations, silly adversaries, grand spectacle and high drama all played into a child's sense of wonder, playfulness and general perception of adulthood. Despite Stan Lee's retroactive assertion that a more adult approach was always the plan, he actually stumbled into it. Even as he, Jack Kirby and others began molding a shared world, they avoided the most childish aspects of the Weisinger approach. Humor was more character-based than situational and the teenagers who scoffed at fifth-dimensional imps and giant turtle-men stuck around.

As Kirby took an ever-increasing role in the plotting and pacing, he decompressed the Weisinger formula. A tightly-plotted *Superman* "three-part novel" in a single comic book became a four-issue *Fantastic Four* opus at Marvel with fight scenes extended over multiple pages. In this expanded approach, there was also room for more character bits that were often a luxury in a plot-heavy Superman tale. Like Weisinger, Lee, Kirby and company wrote with their target audience in mind. In their case, the Marvel heroes embodied the attributes of their teenage fans, full of angst, cynicism and a heightened sense of melodrama.

ROBERT GREENBERGER: Jim Shooter was this 13-year-old kid and Cary Bates was also a teenager who had such passion for the material that they each reached out to Mort in different ways. Cary would do these cover ideas and then be hired to write stories for them, whereas Shooter had these great story ideas and just wrote them. At 14 he was so busy providing for his family because of their horrible circumstances in Pittsburgh, he was willing to take the berating from Weisinger.

JIM SHOOTER: At first, Mort had just bought stories I'd written on my own, so there wasn't much "working" relationship. His finding out how old I was roughly coincided with his starting to give me assignments. He told me right then that he wasn't going to cut me any slack because I was a kid — that he intended to treat me the same as any other writer. That seemed fine — till I found out that he treated all of his writers like crap. Once we were really working together, discussing plots, covers, characters and all that on a regular basis, I quickly learned that he was nasty, abusive, foul-mouthed, cruel and vicious. Mort would call me anytime he needed to, of course, but we had a regularly scheduled call every Thursday evening at a certain time — right after the *Batman* TV show — to go over the work I'd sent in that week. I came to dread that call. When you're 14 and the big, important man from New York calls to yell at you and tell you you're worthless and stupid, you tend to feel bad. Often those calls would end with him telling me that he'd give me "one more chance" because he knew my family was desperately poor and we needed the money. He used to call me his "charity case."

That sucked, but as time passed, it finally started to occur to me that if I was so bad, they wouldn't keep sending me those checks. Also, several times Mort did things that were inexplicable if I were as lousy as he made me feel. For instance, he got me a gig writing an episode for the *Batman* TV show — an odd thing for your "charity case." The show was canceled while that was still in the early stages, so nothing came of it, but the fact that he apparently thought that I could cut it in that world at age 15 was a boost. He arranged publicity for me. Because of Mort, I was featured in an article in *This Week* magazine, a newspaper insert with a national circulation in the many tens of millions. Years later, I found out from Mort's former assistant that he thought I was his best writer — the go-to guy that he could give any character, any assignment, and I'd come back with good stuff, all usable copy as delivered. The assistant, E. Nelson Bridwell, said Mort used to *brag* about me to the other editors; I was the prodigy that he, in his profound wisdom, had pulled out of the slush pile.

CARY BATES (writer, *Superman*): I know there are a lot of stories out there about the way Mort mistreated his people, and he was definitely not warm and fuzzy, but being a naïve 19-year-old college kid visiting from Ohio, I had no working experiences with other editors to compare him to, so without a frame of reference, he didn't seem all that bad — at the time. Also, I think it helped that he basically liked me, or my work, so maybe he didn't give me as hard a time as he did a lot of the other guys, some of whom apparently loathed working for him.

ROBERT GREENBERGER: Jim Shooter had been reading Marvel, so he knew to bring some of the angst, some of that fresh thinking about what these characters were. The others who were there had been at this for over 20 years, so the ideas were a fresh look at how to be a superhero. When you look at what Shooter did with the Legion and then when it came to writing some of the Superman stuff, it was a very fresh and different look. He gave us the Parasite, the very first Superman foe since Brainiac, and it was nearly 10 years later. He also wrote the first Superman/Flash race.

JIM SHOOTER: The race was my idea, but way before I was a teenager. I think I was about six years old when Julie Schwartz and company revived the Flash. I immediately wondered who was faster. In my first-grade school tablet I used to draw pictures of the two of them racing.

JOHN WELLS: In some ways, the characterization of the Marvel heroes may have been what really made Superman seem passe. The Avengers and company may not have acted like mature adults, but that just made them more attractive to a teenage audience. Superman, on the other hand, was the ultimate authority figure and that was no longer cool going into the 1970s.

PETER SANDERSON: Within less than a decade, Weisinger and his writers, including Siegel and science-fiction writers Otto Binder and Edmund Hamilton, devised an extraordinary mythos for the Superman line of titles. During the height of the Silver Age, Weisinger oversaw seven regular series that starred Superman and related characters: *Superman, Action Comics, Superboy, Adventure Comics, Superman's Girlfriend Lois Lane, Superman's Pal Jimmy Olsen* and *World's Finest*, in which Superman and Batman teamed up.

JOHN WELLS: He did create a vast tapestry that rewarded young readers who returned month after month, eyewitness to the birth of a great mythology. Weisinger also broadened the scope of what a Superman story could be. Short stories involving low-stakes battles of wits and pranks still existed in abundance during his tenure, but they now mingled with longer adventures with an epic sweep, whose characters were visibly affected by the events taking place. And, again, he created concepts and an overall mythology that was so much more than the *Daily Planet* and its core employees. As a result of all of this, Superman became a more serious character during the 1960s, a consequence of the more dramatic extended-length adventures that he now starred in frequently. The increased emphasis on Krypton and its history also played up the personal tragedy that the planet's destruction had on its greatest son. At the same time, Superman somehow seemed less isolated thanks to new confidantes like the Legionnaires and his beloved cousin Supergirl.

Particularly of significance in the above is the mention of the name "Siegel," as in Jerry Siegel who, thanks to the efforts of his wife Joanne, and her guilting of Jack Liebowitz, was brought back on staff at DC, but in a decidedly unheralded way. His page rate was reflective of an earlier time, he didn't get a byline and the indignity of being berated by Weisinger continued. Yet he never seemed to let any of that get to him when it came to the actual process of writing.

JOHN WELLS: As I understand it, the Siegels were in dire financial straights in the late 1950s, and Jerry's wife Joanne got in touch with DC exec Jack

Liebowitz. She essentially begged him to rehire Jerry as a Superman writer, threatening an anti-DC campaign in the press if he didn't agree to the deal.

GEOFFREY MARK: Superman in the comic books did not know where he came from until 1948, and then it just sort of sat there. But Jerry, when he came back to DC, opened it up and gave us what life on Krypton was like. He gave us what life in Kandor was like. Jerry had a hand in really developing *Superman's Girlfriend Lois Lane*, *Superman's Pal Jimmy Olsen*, and fleshing those characters out and making them specific — making them more than just a pretty brunette and a goofy redhead. He wrote *Legion of Super-Heroes* stuff, he wrote a great deal of what happened to Superboy and set up things that eventually happened in the pages of *Superman*. The retro Superboy stories could have been very muddy. Things we read about in Superman, well, it turns out it happened in Smallville first. Jerry handled it seamlessly. He showed us *why* Lex Luthor hates Superman.

JOHN WELLS: At his best, Siegel brought passion to Superman. In the early 1960s, he was a virtual Clark Kent who didn't dare respond to his tyrannical boss. All his years of anger and resentment and pride had no outlet *but* his typewriter. Siegel's epic tragedies like "Superman's Return to Krypton" and "The Death of Superman" were rich with emotion and high-water marks of the era. Much of his later work for other publishers was, frankly, mediocre at best, but Siegel had a deep personal stake in Superman and it showed.

BRAD RICCA (author, *Super Boys: The Amazing Adventures of Jerry Siegel and Joe Shuster — The Creators of Superman*): Siegel did a ton of stuff at DC. He did Supergirl, the return to Krypton, which is a *really* good Superman story. And when you read the stories a little more closely, you can see that so much of them are about what he's going through, just expressing it really subversively. They had no idea he was doing this. So he's back there under horrible conditions, being told his name will never see print, people are changing his scripts and changing his plots. It's all really crazy, but he still puts out amazing work — actually, some of the best work of his career.

JOHN WELLS: Siegel contributed extensively to characters he didn't actually create, like Superman's lost mermaid sweetheart Lori Lemeris. He also took a one-off group called the Legion of Super-Heroes and developed them enough through successive guest-appearances that they became viable headliners in their own series. Although the core Superman status quo could not be changed, Siegel was able to launch a recurring feature that depicted a hypothetical marriage of Clark Kent and Lois Lane. That, in turn, led to dozens of anything-can-happen "imaginary tales" that enlivened the Superman family of books for years.

GEOFFREY MARK: Jerry was good at answering *why* and building a back story for ideas and characters. His love of the character was obvious. And he didn't need to prove anything; he'd already created the character. So he was serving the character, expanding it in the way that a creator would, knowing its fullness and not just have the attitude, "I must put my fingerprints all over this thing." I think it was a shame that it didn't continue out past 1966, because at that time *Superman* didn't run out of ideas and Mort Weisinger didn't just dry up all of a sudden, and Superman didn't just get bad in 1966. Jerry Siegel left. And when he left, all those wondrous new things that he created left with him. There were people there who loved the character, but Nelson Bridwell wasn't Jerry Siegel. Mort was not Jerry Siegel. The other wonderful writers who were there weren't Jerry Siegel.

JOHN WELLS: Most significant was Siegel's retroactive revelation that Superman and Luthor had been boyhood friends who suffered a bitter, life-defining split. Along with giving the villain the first name of "Lex," Siegel used another story to reveal the existence of Luthor's sister Lena Thorul, and his humanizing efforts to shield her from association with his shameful reputation. In the short term, the episodes fueled a more complex, sympathetic characterization of Superman's greatest enemy, long before the *Smallville* TV series decided to mine that territory anew.

PETER SANDERSON: Wayne Boring continued drawing the Man of Steel in this new era, but the premier Superman artist from the 1960s into the early 1980s was the great Curt Swan. His crisply handsome artwork gave the stories a more modern look that proved more appropriate to the new science-fictional elements being introduced.

ARLEN SCHUMER: Weisinger's era was diligently and beautifully illustrated by Curt Swan in his classic phase where everything was a frozen tableau. The DC style was like going to the Museum of Natural History. You walk through looking at those frozen tableaux beautifully rendered; life-like, but frozen. Now there's a beauty to that as well, and Curt Swan was the epitome of the DC style.

JOHN WELLS: Wayne Boring was the last link to the Superman who debuted in 1938; a barrel-chested Goliath whose debt to Joe Shuster was still visible at his core. Twenty years later, those visuals looked dated and stodgy. For all his storytelling skills, Boring's rendition of Superman and his cast were stiff, robotic and rather unattractive. The 1950s Wonder Woman comic book paralleled the situation with its own old-fashioned artwork by H.G. Peter now out of step with the times. Both the Superman and WW books of the era tacitly acknowledged this by assigning more stylish, modern illustrators to draw the covers in advance of new artists being assigned to the interiors.

GEOFFREY MARK: Besides having Jerry Siegel writing many of the scripts, so important to Superman was making Curt Swan his primary artist. Wayne Boring shifted over to the newspaper strip and Curt was brought in with different inkers. Putting him with George Klein was brilliant; he really improved the look of Curt's work. Every book they drew together improved. To me, they made the stories look like a film. The shading he brought to dramatic moments, the expressions that Swan and Klein were able to give all the characters… even on *Legion of Super-Heroes* when they drew it, those were 17 or 23 different personalities; not just a bunch of ciphers in different costumes.

JOHN WELLS: One issue published a full-page Swan model sheet that depicted Superman's face contorted in every possible manner from pure joy to deep sorrow. In an age when narration redundantly described every image on a comic book page, Mort Weisinger trusted Swan enough in one 1965 story to permit a few panels with no words at all. Swan's images of the broken-hearted Lois Lane and Lana Lang said it all. Serendipitously, some of the most emotional, character-based Superman stories were being written just as the artist with the perfect skill-set was becoming the series' principal artist.

PETER SANDERSON: Swan could sensitively capture the character's emotions, which now more frequently became the focus of the stories. The other great Superman artist of the 1960s was actually the Lois Lane specialist Kurt Schaffenberger, who had formerly drawn Superman's rival at another comics company, the original Captain Marvel. Schaffenberger superbly blended superheroic action, humor and romance while endowing his characters with a seemingly three-dimensional reality on the flat printed page.

In the end, the Weisinger era of Superman has its share of supporters and detractors, but there is no question that the era was an important one for both the Man of Steel and the comics medium.

CARY BATES: Mort had a tremendously inventive and ingenious mind, and used it to great advantage to embellish just about every facet of the Superman myth imaginable during the so-called Silver Age. Despite various attempts over the years to chuck a lot of this stuff (Kryptonite, Supergirl, Kandor, the Phantom Zone, etc.), it seems like the powers-that-be at DC always end up going back to his concepts in one form or another. Certainly the best Superman films (*I* and *II*) embraced many of his innovations, as well as *Smallville* and *Superman Returns*.

JIM SHOOTER: Though he was very harsh in his methods, Mort knew his stuff, and when he yelled at me about something, he was almost always right. He taught me a great deal about the creative part of the craft — including writing, penciling, inking, coloring and even production. He also taught me about the comics *business* and all related businesses, including film, TV, licensing, merchandise and more. In retrospect, it seems clear to me that he was grooming me for a career in the entertainment business. Because of Mort, when I got the chance to be editor-in-chief at Marvel, I was prepared. For all he did for me, I am grateful.

PETER SANDERSON: If stories about the misadventures of Superboy amused the younger readers, the best of the Weisinger-era tales reached out towards an older, teenage audience, pointing the way towards a greater sophistication for the superhero genre. But Weisinger's peak was in the late 1950s and early 1960s. Starting at the end of 1961, Marvel's Stan Lee and his collaborators brought about a revolution in comics storytelling that would eventually consign the Weisinger stories to the realm of dated nostalgia, but it is nonetheless important to recognize how innovative the Silver Age Superman stories were in their time.

While the Silver Age continued to play out, Jerry Siegel's return to DC and writer of Superman came to an end in the middle of the decade. Under the Copyright Act of 1909, a copyright lasted 28 years, and towards the end of this time the original owners of the copyright could apply to have the copyright renewed for another 28 years. The result of this would be that the copyright would return to them. Siegel believed that this was the opportunity that he and Joe Shuster had been waiting for, and he convinced his former partner to join him on yet another lawsuit to try and recapture ownership of Superman. In April of 1965, Siegel and Shuster applied to renew the copyright and two months later DC did the same thing, without missing a beat and publishing adventures beyond the 28-year term date of April 18, 1966.

JOHN WELLS: Ever since he returned to Superman, Jerry Siegel had been bullied and verbally abused by Mort Weisinger. His editor sneered at every script and trivialized any idea he conceived. Elsewhere, Joe Shuster's eyesight had deteriorated greatly, and he was working as a messenger in the mid-1960s. Siegel and Shuster placed their bets on successfully reclaiming the rights to Superman through its 28-year copyright renewal, but their optimism was unwarranted. After news of the lawsuit was leaked to a syndicated columnist in January 1966, Siegel was fired from DC immediately.

JEFF TREXLER (Interim Director, Comic Book Legal Defense Fund): From the straight law angle, there was probably no chance that Siegel and Shuster were going to succeed. There had been previous case law that said that when you assigned all the rights to something, that includes the right to renew. This is where Siegel used to get hung up in court — they had sold the rights to Superman and the courts landed on the notion that when they sold the rights back in 1938, that meant you sold *everything*, including the right to renew. When they tried to sue in 1948, the court looked at the contracts from 1938 and said they were valid and not signed under duress. And that contract included all rights to everything that comes after the first story that appeared in *Action #1*. Under *that* basis, they said Siegel doesn't own Superman. At the same time, they said there was a contract violation with Superboy. The individual looking at it said from their perspective that Superboy was a distinct character. That's how you end up with something of a negotiation to get a settlement. Without that, Siegel would have had nothing.

Then in the 1970s, the Second Circuit Appeals Court said that the contracts were valid and binding — they sold *all* rights. My personal take on all of this, as I've said, is that they probably *wouldn't* have been cut out of their creation if they hadn't filed that lawsuit in the 1940s, but they did. Just a very costly mistake. The way I look at Siegel is that he's like something out of a Greek tragedy. He keeps thinking that he is doing these things to escape a certain fate and achieve justice, to do the right thing, and they end up causing the thing he's trying to avoid. It's just tragic. He gets second chances that you don't often get in life, but he keeps thinking that there's this higher principle that he needs to stand for and he blows it up. It's a quintessentially human thing and an American thing to think that you have this ideal and you lose sight of the practicalities.

It is Trexler's view that if one looks at the plight of Siegel and Shuster, there has to be equal attention paid to DC's side of things, notably that the company in essence "tore up" the existing financial contract and provided greater profit participation, which continued to be expanded.

JEFF TREXLER: Each side was looking ahead to the future, but Jerry kept saying, "It's not enough, it's not enough. I have to have the whole thing." And *that's* where he becomes his own nemesis. I was an Ancient Greek major in college, so I had to read the works of Plato in Greek. And one of the things I love is that Socrates is found guilty of corrupting the youth and he's asked what his penalty should be. He jokingly says it should be the same award that's given to the winners of the Olympics games, which is basically you get a pension and a special meeting area; you win this and bring glory to your city. You know, you get eternal praise and the money and perks to go along with it. And I think there's something to be said for the notion that people who do one spectacular thing should be taken care of, because sometimes doing one spectacular thing is more than 99% of humanity. And there's a sense that Siegel is like Walter White in *Breaking Bad*: He came up with this idea and the company goes on to make millions upon millions without him after he sells

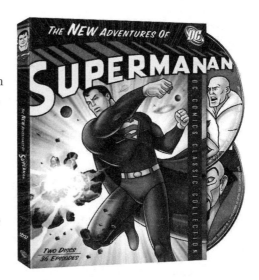

DVD Cover for the animated series that put Filmation on the map and changed Saturday Morning television (© and TM DC Comics/Warner Bros. Discovery).

his stock for $5,000. Jerry Siegel is Walter White without the meth; he's convinced he was screwed over and he is going to do whatever he can to get that money back. And he's *so* blinded by it that the people he hurts are himself and his family.

The case went to trial in the United States District Court for the Southern District of New York in 1969, and in 1973 the court ruled that Siegel and Shuster had lost their ability to obtain the copyright in 1947 when they had settled with National Periodicals and signed an agreement assigning them all rights to Superman and Superboy. As far as DC was concerned, it was over. Again.

Superman's Silver Age would play out in the comics throughout the 1960s, achieving some historic greats, but it was inevitable that the character's popularity would peak and suffer a decline. Yet while things played out in the pages of DC Comics, the Man of Steel was still enjoying great success in other mediums. That was most apparent when he used his Kryptonian abilities to alter Saturday morning television with the arrival of The New Adventures of Superman *from Filmation.*

The show aired on CBS in different forms between 1966 and 1970, for a total of 68 episodes consisting of two animated adventures of Superman and one of Superboy. The series would give us the first non-comics versions of Braniac, Titano (the giant ape), Mister

Mxyzptlk, the Prankster and the Toyman. As to casting, producer Lou Scheimer went back to the radio series cast, which reunited Bud Collyer (Clark Kent/Superman), Joan Alexander (Lois Lane), Jackson Beck (as both the narrator and Perry White) and Jack Grimes (Jimmy Olsen). Naturally, Collyer utilized his voice to differentiate between Clark and Superman and sounded just as fresh as ever doing so.

WILL RODGERS (author, *The Ultimate Super Friends Companion*): Norm Prescott, having been a radio man, had connections to the entertainment industry and was able to hire Bud Collyer, who was to Superman what Kevin Conroy was to Batman in the present day. Unlike the Fleischer cartoons where Superman spoke very few words, in the Filmation cartoons he would speak *a lot* since the scripts were written in the style of illustrated radio. And Lois Lane actually had two different voices. If Lois sounds older in some episodes, it was the voice of the late Joan Alexander, but in other episodes, if Lois sounds younger, she was voiced by the late Julie Bennett, who not only appeared in one episode of the live-action *Adventures of Superman* TV series with George Reeves, but was also the voice of Cindy Bear in the classic Yogi Bear cartoons.

CHRISTINE COLLYER (daughter of Bud Collyer): As it happened, when I was pregnant with my second child, they came out and asked my dad if he would do *The New Adventures of Superman*. And I think he really loved it, because he was reunited with some of the old cast. What was weird is that my one son was about three years old when my dad died, and those cartoons would come on and he'd hear grandpa's voice. That was kind of a weird situation. And for him, who would have thought he'd be back playing that role so many years later?

MARK MCCRAY (author, *The Best Saturdays of Our Lives*): *The New Adventures of Superman*, in my opinion, is never given enough credit, because that show really singlehandedly changed the entire landscape of Saturday morning television forever. Prior to that, Saturday morning was sort of a dumping ground for the networks. If a show like *The Jetsons* or *Top Cat* didn't get renewed beyond the first season, and they had a two-year contract, they would then plant those shows on Saturday morning, because they had space to fill. There wasn't really a huge strategy or marketing behind Saturday morning.

But in 1966, you have this young hotshot programmer Fred Silverman, who is very ambitious. The way it was explained to me by Lou Scheimer, one of my mentors who ran Filmation for years, CBS was doing pretty good all around. Primetime was working for them, daytime television had a lot of soap operas and game shows that were working for them. The only thing Fred Silverman could really tackle or be in charge of was Saturday morning, and the first thing he did was basically get all the black-and-white cartoons off the air, saying, "The entire schedule is going to be in color." They called Fred Silverman the Man with the Golden Gut, and it was appropriate, because he always seemed to know what was coming down the pipeline. And when the *Batman* series with Adam West and Burt Ward premiered in January 1966, that show really blew up ratings-wise. Fred Silverman saw that and said, "We've got to get superheroes on the air and we have to have some type of strategy."

He ordered *Space Ghost*, which was sort of a poor man's Batman cartoon, because he couldn't get Batman as the rights were tied up with ABC. He definitely wanted Superman and he went to Norm Prescott, Lou Scheimer and Hal Sutherland, who created Filmation, then a struggling company. Norm Prescott had a relationship with DC. I used to talk to Lou all the time and one of the things he said was, "All of us had experience in animation, we all knew how to do animation, but I guess for DC, since no one had ever heard of us, they had to come see if we were legit."

WILL RODGERS: The story of how Filmation got the job to animate Superman is the stuff of legend. In their earliest years, Filmation produced animated commercials, but in 1965 they fell upon hard times — until they were contacted by Whitney Ellsworth of DC Comics, known at the time as National Periodicals. DC had been hunting for an animation studio to bring Superman back to the small screen for Saturday morning TV. Lou, Hal and Norm jumped at the opportunity and were more than willing to do it. But there was one problem: DC executives wanted to visit them and check out their studio. Due to their financial problems, their "studio" at that time only consisted of the three of them, a mannequin at the entrance and a room full of empty desks. In a bold but desperate move, Lou Scheimer contacted family, friends and fellow animators he knew at other studios, brought them all together and filled up the empty desks, having them work on fake drawings. One of the connected "friends" Scheimer called in was none other than the late Ted Knight, who is well remembered as Ted Baxter on *The Mary Tyler Moore Show*, Judge Elihu Smails in the comedy film *Caddyshack* and as Henry Rush in *Too Close for Comfort*. Knight put his acting skills to work by pretending to be a floor director.

LOU SCHEIMER (Founder, Filmation Associates): He knew nothing about animation except having done the voice work for us, and he wasn't famous yet, though he had been working in Hollywood since the late '50s. We borrowed a Moviola to make it look like we really had an editorial department, and I told Ted, "If the guy asks you any questions, just tell him there's trouble at the lab and you can't talk to him right now, because you don't know what you're talking about." Ted always had a tendency to overact. He said, "Yeah, don't worry, Lou."

ANDY MANGELS (author, *Lou Scheimer: Creating the Filmation Generation*): Ellsworth arrived for his tour of Filmation and Lou had packed the place. Only one desk was empty — ironically, the person who had been planned to fill it and hadn't shown was a CPA who knew Ellsworth, and who would have blown the whole plan.

LOU SCHEIMER: Don Peters, who did gorgeous backgrounds, was in there pretending to paint backgrounds. Some of the guys were already animators. The studio was humming. We had like 20 people in there, everybody furiously at work, but it was noon and half of these guys had to take off and get back to work. We showed Ellsworth some of the stuff from *Journey Back to Oz* that was sitting in our little office that Hal and I had.

WILL RODGERS: When one of the artists had to return to his "other job," Scheimer gave the okay for him to leave, but afterwards instructed that the person in their employ by "docked" of his pay. The DC executive was really impressed and believed that Lou Scheimer ran a tight ship.

ANDY MANGELS: Scheimer explained to Ellsworth that they normally didn't allow visitors in the office, except for one hour on Wednesdays, and hoped that the executive would be impressed enough by what he saw that day to *not* need to come back again. Ellsworth finally left and called Jack Liebowitz at National Periodical Publications in New York, telling him, "They have a little studio, but they run a tight ship." Liebowitz trusted Ellsworth's opinion and signed a deal with Filmation, without even a completion bond for insurance! Norm Prescott flew to New York to meet with Jack Liebowitz.

LOU SCHEIMER: Norm told me that Liebowitz pulled a gun out of his desk drawer. Norm thought he was threatening to kill him if we did anything wrong, but Liebowitz said, "You know, Norm, if anything happens and you don't deliver on this thing right, I'm going to have to shoot myself." Well, nothing went wrong and we ended up with a relationship that lasted for years.

MARK McCRAY: I can't talk enough about a gentleman named Allen Ducovny. Lou told me Allen was a good friend and represented DC Comics, because at the time that the show was green lit, a lot of the people that worked in the comic book office did not have media experience, but Allen went all the way back to the Superman radio show. He was part of that production pipeline and process. When they were ready to get this series launched, they relied very heavily on Allen to get things moving. And he's the one who picked some of the DC guys who had some background in writing cartoons to work on the series. There were some outside writers who were hired as well, but all of it was a match made in heaven. And *no one* expected *Superman* to do the ratings that it did.

Just a little bit of ratings history here: *The Beatles* cartoon during the 1965 to 1966 season was the number-one-rated cartoon overall. And then *Superman* came and pulled the rug out from under *The Beatles*; ABC had been the top-rated network on Saturday morning, but CBS took over. ABC countered with Marvel shows based on the Fantastic Four and Spider-Man.

WILL RODGERS: *The New Adventures of Superman* and *Adventures of Super-boy* were actually the classic Silver Age versions of these heroes come to life. In the case of *Superboy*, who was accompanied by Krypto the Super Dog, the duo contended with crooks with unusual weapons, mutations, aliens, monsters, etc. Ted Knight voiced Jonathan Kent and all other male characters and villains, while Janet Waldo was the voice of Martha Kent and Clark's high school friend Lana Lang, who was pretty much a carbon copy of Lois Lane. Finally, the voice of Superboy/Clark Kent was none other than the late Bob Hastings, a character actor who's had many live and voice acting credits to his name. In live-action, Hastings was part of the sitcom *McHale's Navy*. Unlike Bud Collyer, who used two different voices as Clark and Superman, Bob Hastings pretty much used one voice for both.

The success of The New Adventures of Superman *in its first season from 1966 to 1967 opened up the floodgates for a variety of superheroes, among them* The Herculoids, Frankenstein Jr. *and* The Impossibles, The Mighty Heroes, Birdman *and the* Galaxy Trio, Moby Dick *and* The Mighty Mightor, Samson *and* Goliath *and* Shazzan!. *Even the Man of Steel himself brought additional heroes in his second season, airing from 1967 to 1968, when the show's title was changed to* The Superman/Aquaman Hour of Adventure, *which, besides Superman, featured segments devoted to Aquaman and Aqualad, individual cartoons starring the Flash, Green Lantern, Hawkman and the Atom, plus the Justice League of America and the Teen Titans — all accompanied by new shorts featuring Superboy. And then for season three, from 1968 to 1969, the show's title was changed yet again, this time to* The Batman/Superman Hour, *featuring 16 new Superman and Superboy segments as well as new adventures of Batman and Robin, which hoped to pick up fans of the Adam West/Burt Ward live-action series.*

MARK MCCRAY: Fred Silverman, being as aggressive as he was, green lit the *Batman/Superman Hour*, which became the last new superhero show to be green lit in the 1960s because of backlash that had started in 1967 with parents concerned about violence on Saturday mornings. That backlash would continue for years, although a lot of '80s cartoons started challenging groups like Action for Children's Television and challenging the censors. In 1969 to 1970, there were no new superhero shows at all, part of the reason for which is the other thing that happened in 1968: *The Archie Show* premiered and got higher ratings than the *Batman/Superman Hour* or anything that had happened prior to that. For Fred Silverman, it kind of gave him and the other networks an out to dump all the superhero shows and go with lighter material. Reruns of *Superman* remained on Saturday mornings from 1969 to 1970 — he was the first and the last super-hero to claim Saturday morning at the time, which I think is very cool.

LOU SCHEIMER: There was nobody even close to our ratings for *Superman*. It made CBS a big winner. As for the impact the show had on us, simply put, it *made* us. And once the other networks saw the ratings, it start-ed a rash of imitations. Superheroes were all over the networks within two or three years. But *Superman* was unique and so potent that some of the imitators really screwed it up. Some of them led to the problem of violence on Saturday morning television. Whereas *Superman* was done, I think, with some degree of sensitivity toward the audience, other programs that were sold later just increased the tempo.

For Bud Collyer, who had voiced the Man of Steel so many times, The New Adven-tures of Superman *pretty much marked one of his final performances. He was asked by producers Mark Goodson and Bill Todman to host a revived syndicated version of* To Tell the Truth, *but he responded that he just didn't feel up to it. He died on September 8, 1969 of a heart ailment. He was only 61.*

CHRISTINE COLLYER: There was a commercial on television around the time that he died; it was one of those telephone company commercials where the little girl with braces and braids is upset about not being popular or something. She sits on her dad's lap and he talks to her. At the end, the narrator says, "When was the last time you had a heart-to-heart talk with your father?" I saw that commercial for the longest time, and it's the kind of thing where you hope that the average person would've had a strong figure in their life at some point that pointed them in the right direction and helped them go down the road in whatever direction you decide to go. My sister and I talk about this, with all the junk going on in the world, we were lucky we had him and we turned

Publicity photo of Bob Holiday as Superman in the Broadway musical It's a Bird ... It's a Plane ... It's Superman (Superman © and TM DC Comics/Warner Bros. Discovery).

out just fine.

ANTHONY TOLLIN (comics, pulps and old-time radio historian): Bud was actually buried in the churchyard at this colonial church in Connecticut. And all the Superman cast members — Manny Kramer, Joan Alexander and Jackson Beck — are sitting together and suddenly they burst into laughter. Jackson had said to the others, "You know, that coffin's not going to hold Bud. Superman is going to be busting out of there any second now."

Every decade since the 1940s has introduced a new actor as the Man of Steel in a live-action version of Superman — Kirk Alyn in that decade and George Reeves in the '50s. In the 1960s, it was Bob Holiday as the star of the Broadway musical It's a Bird… It's a Plane… It's Superman, *directed by Harold Prince with book by David Newman (who with wife Leslie would be among the writers working on the first three Christopher Reeve Superman films in the 1970s/80s) and Robert Benton (the writing duo behind* Bonnie and Clyde*), with music by Charles Strouse and lyrics by Lee Adams.*

The plot deals with Superman's efforts to defeat Dr. Abner Sedgwick (Michael O'Sullivan), a 10-time Nobel Prize-losing scientist who seeks to avenge the scientific world's dismissal of his brilliance by attempting to destroy the world's symbol of good. Additionally, Superman comes into romantic conflict with Max Mencken (Jack Cassidy), a columnist for the Daily Planet *newspaper, who resents Lois Lane's (Patricia Marand) attraction to Superman, and later teams up with Sedgwick to destroy the hero.*

DAVID NEWMAN (writer, *It's a Bird… It's a Plane… It's Superman*): Robert Benton and I were freelancing magazine articles, and two guys, Lee Adams and Charles Strauss, the composers who had written *Bye Bye Birdie* and a lot of great shows, went to lunch with us and they suggested we write a musical. That didn't happen, but we had a wonderful time.

LEE ADAMS (lyricist, *It's a Bird… It's a Plane… It's Superman*): After [*Golden Boy*] opened, Strouse and I wanted something that was lighter. We had both been fans for years of Newman and Benton, who worked for *Esquire*. We met them and we asked them — and they *were* very funny guys — if they had ever thought of writing a musical comedy. They said, "No." We asked them to come up with an idea and they came back to us with the idea of doing Superman, and we thought that sounded pretty good.

DAVID NEWMAN: Our son Nathan was eight years old at the time and he was reading comic books, and Leslie came out of his room and said, "You know what would make a great musical?" And she held up a Superman comic book. And I thought, "Wow, what a *great* idea."

LEE ADAMS: We then went to the people who owned Superman, got the rights to do a musical and we wrote it. That's easy to say, but it took us a year-and-a-half. Then we looked for a producer.

DAVID NEWMAN: Benton liked the idea, and then Adams and Strauss liked it, so we wrote this musical called *Superman*, which Hal Prince produced and directed.

FOSTER HIRSCH (author, *Harold Prince and the American Musical Theatre*): It was the musical that Harold Prince did right before *Cabaret*; he did *Cabaret* that same year, the next season, and it changed his career. *Cabaret* was the first musical that had the Hal Prince imprint, and that led to a series of historic collaborations with Stephen Sondheim. In effect, he changed the face of the American musical theater in terms of staging, in terms of content, and *Superman*, right before that was, in his mind, strictly a commercial project. He *was* proud of it. I saw it and liked it very much. It deserved a better fate than it had, but it was not a Hal Prince musical. It was a commercial entity tailored to the demands of Broadway of that era, the mid-'60s. And it was very much based on the staging of *Bye Bye Birdie*, which got it into trouble critically, because Prince was accused of imitating Gower Champion's staging of that show, which was written by the same composer/lyricist team as *Superman*, Strouse and Adams. I liked it a lot; the score is better than it's credited as being. And Prince was proud of it, but it was nothing that he ever talked about in detail. We talked about *Cabaret, Company, Follies, Pacific Overtures, Sweeney Todd, Evita, Phantom of the Opera* over and over, but this one got lost in the shuffle. *Superman* was just a blip in his career.

One person whose career was heavily impacted by the show was actor Bob Holiday, who was ultimately cast in the dual role of Clark Kent and Superman. Born November 12, 1932 in Brooklyn, New York, he spent his early days of education, according to the New York Daily News, *majoring in "getting out of school." Filled with a desire to be in show business, he performed in amateur shows that were staged at his neighborhood Skouras Theatre, while also taking part in his high school glee club. Upon graduating, he began to sing in nightclubs and gained professional experience — prior to serving time in the Army as part of the infantry at Fort Dix, N.J.; followed by advanced infantry training and some time overseas in Germany, where he reportedly qualified for Special Forces. As part of the Army, he became a radio announcer and was discharged in the mid-1950s. He continued with more performances in nightclubs, summer stock and comedy routines, all of which led to his making his singing debut in the Harold Prince-produced* Fiorello!, *which in turn led to TV commercials. When it came to* Superman, *he auditioned against 33 other hopefuls.*

***THE PHILADELPHIA INQUIRER* (January 9, 1966):** Remembering the final audition of *Superman*, Holiday recalled feeling like a "complete veteran" among 40 or 50 hopefuls who crowded the corridor of the New York studio, waiting to be heard by producer Hal Prince, composers Charles Strouse and Lee Adams, choreographer Ernest Flatt and librettists David Newman and Robert Benton. There were all types: singers and non-singers, experienced and inexperienced actors, sallow-complexioned young men in turtleneck sweaters, sports figures, and a bass-baritone from the New York City Opera Company, who was looking for "money and variety."

Finally, the field was narrowed to Holiday and Charles Rydell, a square-jawed personality who had appeared in off-Broadway productions of *Threepenny Opera* and *The Secret Life of Walter Mitty*. An exhausted Prince ordered the "contestants" across the street to the Imperial Theater. On stage, under glaring white light, Holiday and Rydell took turns singing, reading a scene from the musical, doing an impromptu soft shoe and stripping to their shorts to show off their physiques (Rydell was naturally muscular while Holiday was beginning to fill out his chest, arms and thighs after four weeks of weightlifting). Their auditions completed, Holiday and Rydell retired to the wings while Prince and associates consulted for several minutes and finally made their selection. A disappointed but bravely smiling Rydell thanked them and left the theater. Holiday walked around backstage in a daze of happiness and relief. Left practically speechless by the experience, he was able to come up with few answers to questions about his career. But after five weeks of boning up on his role and regaining his assurance, Holiday was able to remedy his earlier mental lapse.

BOB HOLIDAY (actor, "Superman," *It's a Bird… It's a Plane… It's Superman*): If you can work under those conditions, you can do anything. The old pros in *Fiorello!* taught me a lot of stage techniques. Suddenly I began understanding myself. It was like cleansing the system. Everything bad was coming out. (Press Conference)

LEE ADAMS: Hal Prince said that it was going to be very tough to find our lead character. Shirley Rich, the casting director, began searching for an actor who could match Prince's specifications: 190 pounds, 17" neck, 50" chest, 32" waist, 37 ½" hips, 18 ½" biceps and 26 ½" thighs. So we started auditions and the first guy to walk in was a guy named Bob Holiday. He was 6' 4", handsome, black hair, good singer — he was a perfect Superman. We kept auditioning, saying, you know, he was too good to be true. And finally, we came back to the first guy who walked onto that thing. He was sort of a methodical kind of actor, but it worked for Superman. He was terrific, wonderful. After the show, he would stay in his cape and sign autographs for kids backstage.

TONI COLLINS (friend of Bob Holiday, webmaster supermanbob-holiday.com): *Superman* was my one and only Broadway show — I was 11 — because I'm in California and I don't get back there very much. Bob Holiday was just so gracious to all the children. My mom actually knew a friend of his, so she'd sent a little note and, after the show, he invited all children to come in the back and get autographs. We went back and my mom made sure we were the last ones in line. She introduced herself and he said, "I thought you were going to come back *before* the show." I still remember his big booming voice saying that. Quite frankly, I think it would have spoiled the magic of the play for me if we had met him beforehand, but to meet him afterwards was just incredible.

BOB HOLIDAY: To actually put on the cape just felt right. I enjoyed it. I knew and identified strongly with the character from the time I was seven years old. Playing the part was great fun and I loved it. Becoming Superman was a matter of acting, not of clothes. We rehearsed for a long time in street clothes, so I got used to being Superman without the suit. It was natural to put it on. Once I started to get into the part, I felt, "I *am* Superman." It's a feeling. You just get into the role and it's all summed up in that statement. You can't say anymore, because words just reduce the feeling. But that was my approach as an actor; it was my responsibility to create both parts. I had to capture the spirit of both characters. My goal on stage was to personify both characters, even if I was nothing like either of them in everyday life. (*Mark Editz, sliceofscifi.com*)

TONI COLLINS: He really loved playing Superman, and he felt like he had to work his absolute hardest to even be considered for the part. When you have that kind of longing within you, I think it develops a respect for the role. Playing Superman was a genuinely life-changing experience for him. He said that when he put the Superman suit on, it just changed him. It was like the culmination of everything he'd been working for, for months.

BOB HOLIDAY: I grew up with Superman, and the thrill of actually playing the part on Broadway was one of the most wonderful, greatest feelings I've ever had in my life. And I've never forgotten it. It's tough to remember certain things, but the great moments are in my heart and they will always be in my heart. And I say that very humbly, because so many of the fellows that played the part, I call brothers. I understand Superman very well. I understand the other men that played it very well. You can't know what's in their head unless you are the chosen one to play that part.

LEE ADAMS: Christopher Reeve did that nebbish thing so well as Clark Kent. It is *not* easy to do. Holiday tried to play it like Reeve eventually would. He wore the glasses and he tried to be Clark Kentish, but he couldn't quite do it as well as Reeve would in time do it on film. Still, he was a terrific Superman, and in his cape, he was just great.

TONI COLLINS: The show was magical. It starts with, I believe, a bank robbery, but very soon after, Superman flies in on the scene. A young interviewer once asked me, "You could see the wires, couldn't you?" I was like, "This was the day and age when we had television shows with puppets and you could see *all* the strings." So that is a generational difference. He really couldn't see how a wire could be any kind of a magical experience, but it was. In any case, right after he flies in, Superman is singing "Every Man Has a Job to Do," and his Clark Kent clothes start flying in towards him on wires and he starts changing from Superman into Clark Kent. It was all, of course, perfectly Broadway timed and it was just so exciting to watch that.

Most people will talk about the phone booth following him around the stage. I actually don't remember that, but I *do* remember those clothes coming in and how he, just as a dancer would, changed bit by bit while he was singing. He told me that they didn't know how to get his shoes on, so he came up with the idea of taking some rain shoes and cutting off the backs of them and he just slid the Superman boots into the arranged shoes. You'll also notice that the S on his chest is much larger than, say, George Reeves, Christopher Reeve or Henry Cavill, and that's because it had to show all the way to the back of the theater as opposed to being on camera where they can focus in on it as they choose.

DAVID NEWMAN: It was a wonderful show, which took a year to get on as Broadway shows do. We were in trouble in Philadelphia, we got it whipped into shape and opened in New York in March of 1966, and got the greatest reviews you've ever seen in your life.

LEE ADAMS: The out-of-town tryout took place in Philadelphia in 1966. The show received unenthusiastic notices. Tinkering with the elements, we removed Joan Hotchkis as Lois Lane and replaced her with Patricia Marand. I don't recall specifically why she was replaced, but some people audition great and then somehow, when you get in to work, they don't come up to what you need. Maybe she just didn't hit it off with the other actors, maybe the balance was wrong.

FOSTER HIRSCH: Though it was incredible out of town, I think they saw the issues when it opened, but it got basically good reviews. It got nominations, it didn't close right away. People think it opened and closed, but it ran for 19 previews and 129 performances from, I think, March to July. In a big theater it had 140 performances, and that's not nothing. So it wasn't a hit, but it wasn't an instant failure either.

DAVID NEWMAN: We thought we had a smash hit… there was a line at the Alvin Theater, now the Neil Simon Theater, which went around the block, and we thought, "Here it comes, guys. Get me that house in San Jose." We went off for a week thinking we had made it big,

FOSTER HIRSCH: I understand that die-hard fans of Superman resented the show for a number of reasons, because the characters of classic Superman don't appear in the show. Perry White is just a blip, Lex Luthor is turned into another character altogether with a different name and a different look and the focus of the show is really on the villains and *not* Superman/Clark Kent. So for them, it doesn't tell the story the way they want it told and it doesn't follow the way things were laid out by Joe Shuster and Jerry Siegel in the original. It's very much a free adaptation and it's humorous. It's more like the Batman flavor of that time, and *Batman* on TV stole a lot of the thunder of this show. People who loved *Batman* didn't love this show. There seemed to be only room for one kind of comic book parody and it was *Batman*, it wasn't *Superman*. It just didn't find its audience.

DAVID NEWMAN: We had our own theories as to what happened. Benton called it "Capelash," as opposed to backlash. The *Batman* television show had come out on television at about the same time, and one of the things that happened, I think with some hindsight…

LESLIE NEWMAN (co-writer, *Superman: The Movie, Superman II* and *Superman III*): It was a very different approach to the subject than we later took in the films.

FOSTER HIRSCH: The traditional Broadway audience may not have been that interested in Superman and, like I said, Superman fans didn't find this authentic enough.

DAVID NEWMAN: It was a musical. It was fun, but it wasn't camp. We took the character very seriously, though it was playful. He sang and danced… we're not talking about *The Bible* here anyway, but it was a lot of fun. Jack Cassidy played the villain.

FOSTER HIRSCH: The villain was Max Mencken, played by Jack Cassidy, who has more time and more songs than Superman. He was a big Broadway star of the time and this was a vehicle for him. The problem was that Jack Cassidy wasn't playing Superman, so it was about *his* ego and his romantic affairs. He's a character stuck on himself and an amusing one, but where's Superman? If you listen to the album, which I recently did again, Superman is very well-sung and played by Bob Holiday, who looked the part, but doesn't have that much musical material.

LEE ADAMS: Jack Cassidy's character of Max Mencken was a gossip guy, but he was also very powerful politically. He was also ultra right-wing and he destroyed careers. Of course, we didn't play him like that, we played him for comedy. Jack Cassidy delivered his songs with a sort of clumsy dance, as if he were great. You could see it in his acting. *He* thought he was great, although he was clumsy and very, very funny. Behind the scenes, he was no laughing matter. During rehearsals, he would approach Prince and the others with scenes that he had rewritten in favor of his character. He was a bit of a prima donna, but he was *so* good. And yes, he was a pain in the ass, to use a technical term. Cassidy was a comedy lead and Superman was very, very straight. That's what made it funny, but there was no camp in the show.

TONI COLLINS: Bob made a wonderful Superman. Yes, the play was written as a vehicle for Jack Cassidy, who needed kind of a boost on Broadway, but from what I understand Bob loved him and got along with him great. They were always playing tricks on each other on stage, so they had a camaraderie that was *really* good. In his biography, Bob says that he could tell Jack was working to get himself more lines and change his part of it, but he said that he just focused on what he was doing and didn't worry about any of that. He wanted to be a good Superman, and he looked the part and his voice was powerful.

I bought his other Broadway show cast album, which is *Fiorello!*, and I didn't even recognize his voice; it got so much deeper and richer by the time he played Superman just four years later — whereas in *Fiorello!* he was supposed to play the young law clerk and uses a different voice; he's kind of younger and skinnier, if you will. What's really funny about that song is it's a perfect prelude for him becoming Superman. Lyrics like "battling the evil, fighting till we die" is why Harold Prince, who produced *Fiorello!*, remembered Bob when it came to *Superman* — whereas Bob literally did not know, even into his 70s, that Prince had him in mind from the beginning, because Bob had played that kind of Boy Scout, do-gooder character in *Fiorello!*. Bob had a sincerity that was incredible.

DAVID NEWMAN: One or two things happened. One, I think, was the *Batman* show, just because it was a time for pop-art. A lot of magazine coverage had Batman, Superman and Andy Warhol's Campbell Soup as though it was all part of the same phenomenon, and I think people said, "Why should I pay twelve bucks a ticket when I can watch *Batman* for nothing?" The other thing, de-spite the reviews and everything like that, people kept coming up to the box office and saying, "I want 15 tickets for my son's birthday party on a Saturday matinee."

LESLIE NEWMAN: Nobody wanted tickets at night, because they thought it was a kids' show. It was a very sophisticated kind of humor in which the attempt to destroy Superman was done through psychoanalysis.

DAVID NEWMAN: There was this wonderful sequence we call the brain-washing scene, where the evil scientist asks why he dresses up like that. Is it a need to be noticed?

LESLIE NEWMAN: But this was hardly stuff for five-year-olds. People just had this notion that it was for kids. It really was ahead of its time.

TONI COLLINS: The psychological manipulation of Superman was some-thing that I bought and I was 11, but it was not a kids' show even though it was perceived that way.

DAVID NEWMAN: We were selling out matinees and going empty at night. They changed the advertising and used sexy girls, but *nothing* worked.

TONI COLLINS: Oh, you could see posters where Bob's posing with the dancers in the show and they have little college cheerleader outfits on. It definitely didn't work.

LEE ADAMS: Every hit musical is a fluke — a fluke of the right combination of creators, writers, directors, actors and designers. The whole thing has to gel to-gether, which means that everybody is doing the same show. That's really so tricky, because of all of the egos and different talents involved. It's all such a crap game.

DAVID NEWMAN: After three months, one day in July it just closed and that was the end of that. Then I forgot about superheroes and many years later the Salkinds came to us, and they had no idea that I had done this show. I began to think that there was something in fate that this red-caped creature would fly into my life every ten years and save my ass.

Insofar as Holiday was concerned, he would also appear as Superman in an ad for UniRoyal Carpet, and made personal appearances on I've Got a Secret, The Tonight Show Starring Johnny Carson *and at the Sixth International Fashion Show in New*

York City's Macy's in 1971 and, finally, there was a TV commercial for Aqua Velva.

Following the end of the run of Superman, *Holiday moved to California where he appeared in the musical* Promises, Promises, *and was initially cast as Mike Brady by producer Sherwood Schwartz for* The Brady Bunch, *but that was vetoed by the studio, with Robert Reed being hired instead. After that, he left acting and spent the next 30 years as a very successful home builder in the Pocono Mountains. He would die at the age of 84, after suffering from Alzheimer's disease, on January 27, 2017.*

CHUCK HARTER (author, *Superman on Broadway*): When I approached Bob with the idea of writing his biography, he was a little wary at first. I went to his house and stayed with him for a week or so in New York, and the more I interviewed him, the more he started remembering and the more he got into it. When he went to the Metropolis Superman Celebration, he signed pictures and actually sang. For the rest of his life, he was happy to be recognized as one of the Supermen. He even attrended some rather minor theatrical revivals of the play and posed with whoever the kid was playing Superman. And he enjoyed it. As someone who kind of rejected it for so many years, to go, in the last 10 years of his life or so, to embracing it so fully, was great to see.

TONI COLLINS: Towards the end of his life, Bob was becoming more and more homebound and I felt like I was his link to the outside world, because I would call him every week. His daughter Kelly and her husband moved into his house to take care of him. He had had open heart surgery in 2007 and he told me the doctor had said it would fix him up for another 15 years. What Bob said to me was, "The only thing I care about is that my brain lasts," but the surgery really robbed him of that. The dementia — it was Alzheimer's — started right afterwards. I recently read a study they've done that says any kind of general anesthesia after the age of 65 has a risk factor of dementia, and certainly he was deprived of oxygen a couple of times.

But it's important to remember that Bob was the Superman of the 1960s, and one thing I'd like to point out that most people don't realize is that even though he had this short stint as Superman, he actually played the character or appeared in costume as Superman more than any other actor before or since. He appeared in the Philadelphia tryouts, the New York tryouts and then the actual performances. Most people may not know this, but in 1967 two different light opera companies restaged the show in two cities in Missouri. Bob was the only cast member who came to do those two shows and, in total, he was Superman about 200 times. That's not so bad a legacy.

CHAPTER VI
Bronze Champion

While 1967 was deemed the Summer of Love, for DC it was a time of change and an indication of tumult to come. In the aftermath of the debut of the Adam West/Burt Ward series Batman *a year earlier, a trend toward lightness spread across the line, which did nothing to help stave off Marvel Comics' ascension on newsstands. At the same time, National Periodical Publications was actually purchased by conglomerate Kinney National, which in turn purchased Warner Bros-Seven Arts in 1969 and would eventually sell off its non-entertainment assets in 1972 and change its name to Warner Communications Inc. (which succinctly sums up how WB ended up owning DC as well as the start of a growing corporate influence).*

ROBERT GREENBERGER (writer and former DC editor): What you've got in 1967 is Jack Liebowitz sells the company to Kinney and gets his package. And Irwin Donenfeld, Harry's son, gets his, so it's suddenly a different dynamic. The veterans like Sol Harrison and Jack Adler are doing production and Carmine Infantino is art director. Jack Liebowitz calls Carmine and tells him that he sold the company and Carmine asks who's in charge. Jack's like, "I'm gonna be on the board. I guess you are. Don't forget to turn the lights out." It was that sort of thing. There was no planning; he sells this company he created and then just walks away from it with no real plan in place for who's to run it. Carmine is an artist become art director turned into the president and publisher. And he has no training to be president *or* publisher.

The comic that was supposed to usher in a new era for Superman — but it wasn't long-lasting (© and TM DC Comics/Warner Bros. Discovery).

PETER SANDERSON (comic book historian and author, *The Marvel Vault: A Visual History*): Mort Weisinger's time had passed; the creativity of the late '50s and early 1960s was soon replaced by weak repetition of the same motifs and storylines. Readers grew weary of startling changes in continuity that turned out to be "a dream, a hoax or an imaginary story." Moreover, whereas Weisinger basically aimed for an audience of children, even if he challenged them with his material, the comics readership was changing. Weisinger's friend and fellow editor Julius Schwartz was appealing to an older, teenage audience by incorporating pulp science-fiction elements into superhero comics. Schwartz had been a science-fiction fan in his youth; now he was doing comics that would attract the same kind of intelligent, imaginative young people that he had been.

JOHN WELLS (author, *American Comic Book Chronicles*): In the late 1960s, the Superman books were tangibly tired, not merely in terms of scripts, but poor inking choices for Curt Swan that drained the vitality out of his pencils. Mort Weisinger's retirement left opportunities to refresh the series through editors like Murray Boltinoff and Julius Schwartz.

PETER SANDERSON: Over at Marvel, Stan Lee and Jack Kirby added new sophistication to characterization and plot and a dynamic energy to the art that gripped the imaginations not only of teenagers, but of adults. While the Fantastic Four or the Hulk engaged in spectacular battle royals and Spider-Man coped with his own inner demons and a society that distrusted him, Superman seemed to be spending most of his time outwitting Lois' schemes or bailing Jimmy out of trouble or coping with the latest Red Kryptonite-induced transformation. In other words, Superman was out of step with the times. At the beginning of the 1970s, Weisinger retired and his Superman empire was divided among other editors. Julius Schwartz inherited the flagship title *Superman*, and set about modernizing it as he had *Batman* in 1964. Schwartz remained in charge for a decade-and-a-half until the mid-1980s.

PAUL LEVITZ (writer, former DC Publisher): Superman's sales and distribution were going down, month by month, quarter by quarter. Some of that may have been that the execution in Mort's last couple of years was slipping creatively. As a longtime reader, it felt like his heart was not in it in the same way or he hadn't assembled a strong team around him. Maybe it was getting out of phase with the times. And some of it obviously was that Marvel was gaining strength and momentum thanks to the style that Stan Lee, Jack Kirby and Steve Ditko had created there. *And* because comics in those years were an impulse purchase, where you went to the newsstand and made a pick that day based on what was on the cover… you know, does that look exciting? And Stan was doing covers the world cared about — maybe more than DC was, and that was hurting disproportionately.

JOHN WELLS: Purely in terms of sales, *Superman* was still far and away the best-selling superhero comic book in the industry in the late 1960s. Even critical darlings, like several Marvel titles, weren't coming close. Objectively speaking though, the books were simply going through the motions, rehashing old plot elements and hooks with nothing new brought to the table. Signature penciler Curt Swan was saddled with deadly dull inkers who only made things worse. That being said, pairing his pencils with Murphy Anderson's lush inks immediately gave *Superman* and *Action Comics* the contemporary sheen that they'd been missing.

MICHAEL EURY (editor, *The Krypton Companion*): Marvel had come up with a totally new way of doing comics, but that doesn't necessarily mean that has to be the formula for everybody else. Look at *The Dark Knight Returns* and *Watchmen* from the 1980s. They were brilliant pieces of work that came out back-to-back and great kudos were given to DC for publishing them at the time, but they were not meant to be the shape of things to come. They seemed to be a fractured lens through which they were looking at the world and through comic books and through superheroes, and not necessarily meant to be the Bible for how we're going to do it from now on. They were not meant to become a formula after that, and it was the same thing here. DC still proudly plastered "The #1 Bestselling Comic Magazine" above the Superman logo for many years of the '60s. And it *was* still a top-selling title for the longest time, though in the late '60s it started to show its age.

CARY BATES (writer, *Superman*): Mort Weisinger and Julius Schwartz were both geniuses in their own right, and although they were always cordial to each other, by the time I met them it was impossible to imagine them as teenagers who were once putting out fanzines together. Each man had very definite ideas about what made a good comic and both would take an active role in co-plotting every story with their writers. Of the two, Mort was a bit more rigid and dogmatic. Julie had very specific likes and dislikes as well… though as time went on, he was more flexible and open to new ideas. After 1971 he was working primarily with writers under 30 who had replaced the so-called "old guard" (John Broome, Gardner Fox, Bob Kanigher, etc). Mort on the other hand retired in 1970, just before the major influx of younger writers began. Although he was obviously more comfortable with seasoned pros, to his credit Mort bucked the status quo when he brought both myself and Jim Shooter into the business. And Shooter was even younger than I was.

JOHN WELLS: By 1970, Schwartz had a well-earned reputation as DC's rainmaker, having modernized virtually the entire superhero template through his revivals of the Flash, Green Lantern, the Justice League, et al. Those successes resulted in his assignment to retool Batman in 1964, and he used the same basic strategy on Superman at the outset. The perceived sillier characters from the feature were dropped without comment and a nod towards modern technology saw Clark Kent shifted from newspapers to television journalism.

PAUL LEVITZ: Superman paid the rent for the company probably from the time that the George Reeves show premiered through the next 20 years. As late as the end of Weisinger's tenure, Superman's print run was still hovering around a million copies, which at that point was vastly more than the print run of any unrelated title. And anything that had the red S on it still was outselling anything else. Now, both in terms of Marvel, certainly at that time, but even when you looked at DC, my favorite comic *Legion of Super-Heroes* outsold *Batman*. And it wasn't because the Legion was so popular, it's because Superboy was out there, front and center. Even *Jimmy Olsen* outsold *Batman*, and *Batman* was not a bad selling title by the standards of the industry. Superman was just the dominant franchise, at least out of the action-adventure stuff. I don't really remember the numbers on the Disney stuff or the Looney Tunes stuff that Western had been very powerful with in the 1950s. It had slipped by that time, but still was a significant business.

PETER SANDERSON: The new age for the Man of Steel began with *Superman* #233 (January 1971), which boasted the cover copy "Kryptonite Nevermore." And there on the cover was the familiar image of Superman bursting through chains simply by expanding his chest — but this time the chains were made of glowing Kryptonite. Through this single image, Schwartz served notice to comic readers that he was making radical changes in the Superman mythos. This issue's story, "Superman Breaks Loose," showed how a nuclear accident transformed all the Kryptonite on Earth to lead. Confronted by a criminal bearing Kryptonite in this first issue, Superman nonchalantly took it from his hand, chewed and swallowed it!

The idea was that Superman had become too powerful for the reader ever to believe he could be in serious danger from anything other than his Achilles' heel, Kryptonite. Weisinger's writers even had Superman dive into the sun without harm and move entire planets. As a result, Kryptonite, the supposedly rare metal, turned up in seemingly every story, since there were few other ways to put Superman in peril. Getting rid of Kryptonite was getting rid of a story device that had worn out its welcome through overuse. It was also only the first step. By the end of the first Schwartz issue — the storyline was written by Denny O'Neil — readers also learned that the explosion that transmuted Kryptonite had created a strange doppelganger of Superman composed of sand. Over the next year, this "Sand Superman" would drain off half of Superman's powers. The idea was that from now on, Superman was no longer invincible, and the writers would come up with superpowered adversaries or high-tech devices that could believably pose a threat to him in combat.

MICHAEL EURY: If I had the chance, I would ask Julie if he ever considered the idea of really just going all out with Superman in sci-fi stories. You know, let Clark Kent take a sabbatical from the *Daily Planet*, bring Superman into space and team him up with Adam Strange, see what's going on with Hawkman, who was not in print that much at that time in the early '70s. It would seem to have been a whole missed opportunity that could have been a whole different early '70s Superman world, but I also don't think DC wanted to mess with it. Everybody who I talked with for *The Krypton Companion* said that Denny O'Neil wanted something new, but not *too* new. It's like they brought in Jack Kirby from Marvel, but they wouldn't let Jack Kirby be Jack Kirby.

JOHN WELLS: Weisinger had cultivated a younger demographic with occasionally silly characters, over-the-top scenarios and plot devices that caused older readers to scoff at the feature. Murray Boltinoff stripped the excesses away when he took over *Action Comics* in 1970, but he still placed great importance on plot-driven stories with strong cover hooks. In *Superman*, Julius Schwartz needed to come out of the gate with a clear message that challenged perceptions of what a story about the Man of Steel was expected to be.

DENNY O'NEIL (writer, *Superman: Kryptonite Nevermore*): The Kryptonite stuff — Kryptonite was a real inspiration for the guys who scripted the radio show, but it had become such a cliché and such a crutch. I mean, how much Kryptonite was orbiting the Earth? And again, we recognize we're doing fantasy melodrama, but even within that, if you have a world that generally obeys recognizable laws of physics, then those things couldn't have happened. For me, as an audience, it's always too big a suspension of disbelief unless the creative people set it up somehow.

ROBERT GREENBERGER: The cliché for Denny was always, "Superman can solve the problem by listening hard," so for him there was not a lot of challenge. When Julie asked him to come in and revamp the character, they both agreed they had to bring the level of powers down. They *did* do big changes. Clark Kent goes to work at WGBS and puts on clothes that are blue.

LEN WEIN (writer, *Superman*): The TV job made *some* sense, but it was really never what Clark Kent was about. Trying to update the character — that happens with every character, even now. Everybody's constantly being revamped. But I'm a traditionalist. There were elements of the character that could have moved forward with the times, but there are certain aspects that make him who he is. I think Clark Kent ought to be a reporter. Newscasters aren't reporters — newscasters sit there and read off of a monitor. As a reporter, Clark could go anywhere and do anything. As a newscaster, he had obligations — what if a volcano was about to erupt just as he was about to deliver the six o'clock news? In one story, it's a fun bit trying to find a way to get off camera and save the world, then get back on camera — but that works only *once*. It was a problem. Also, frankly, Christopher Reeve has arguably my all-time favorite superhero moment on film, in the first *Superman* film, where he demonstrates that Clark Kent and Superman look nothing alike. If you're on TV every day, for *thirty minutes* a day, eventually people are going to go, "You know, that guy *does* kind of look like Superman."

ROBERT GREENBERGER: Clark Kent is a TV reporter, Superman's powers get diminished a little bit, Kryptonite is no longer the crutch… they genuinely thought this would sell, but it didn't.

DENNY O'NEIL: Julie asked me if I'd like to take a shot at Superman and there was no reason for me *not* to write it. If I had any hesitation, it would have come from an earlier experience of writing *Justice League*. It was difficult, at least for me, to work with gods. But I agreed to do it, and I thought if I was going to write stories with conflict — after all, that is the essence of drama — and stay logical within the parameters of the story, I can't have this guy who can do anything; who can search every room in Metropolis in a 10th of a second, making it hard for anyone to hide from him. I noticed that sometimes on television they would just ignore problems like that, but if you're writing good fiction, you *can't* ignore problems like that. Things have to be consistent. Within the universe, when you've set up something, it nags at the reader and maybe they don't know what it is, but it's there. I just agreed that I'd do the book, but I had to be allowed to make those changes and Julie had no problem with that.

JOHN WELLS: O'Neil delivered on the challenge presented to him. Characterization was sober and serious. Threats were, more often than not, grounded rather than fantastic. And a subplot, as opposed to the full-on multi-parters of the Silver Age, progressively cranked up suspense. It read like nothing that came before and, significantly, it also looked different. Boltinoff's inspired pairing of inker Murphy Anderson with Curt Swan in *Action* was transformative, instantly making the feature look lusher and more modern without losing the underlying recognition factor that the veteran penciler brought to the feature. Coached by DC editorial director Carmine Infantino, Swan also stepped up the dynamism of his layouts and the "Swanderson" art on Schwartz's *Superman* was golden.

RAY MORTON (film historian, author, *Close Encounters of the Third Kind: The Making of Steven Spielberg's Classic Film*): Although he had been drawing the character since the '40s and had been the principal artist on the series since the '60s, it was in the '70s that Swan began drawing Superman in the realistic style that for me will always be the definitive (and most visually impressive) version of the character. Although the Superman of earlier decades was always well-drawn, he always looked like a cartoon. Swan's '70s Superman looked like a real person, which paradoxically made the fantasy more believable._

TOM DE HAVEN (author, *Our Hero Superman on Earth*): When I wrote *It's Superman*, it was way more fun to not have a world-pushing Superman, but one who could get a little cut once in a while or get knocked down. Otherwise, I couldn't even imagine how you would write a character like that. My admiration for the comic writers went up enormously when I had to figure out how to write that and make it interesting compared to a man who had all those superpowers. I was glad I used the Siegel and Shuster version rather than the far more powerful one. That guy could build a replica of a city in a fraction of a second to confuse somebody. He could read through the Metropolis telephone book in half a second. That's great, but *why* would you want to do that?

JOHN WELLS: The through line of O'Neil's first eight months was the progressive reduction in Superman's powers, an inadvertent consequence of the eradication of Kryptonite that created a parasitic doppelganger called the "Sand Superman." Threats that would have been an appetizer under Weisinger — volcanoes, Central American bandits — became the main course during this run and the Man of Steel got beat up a lot more. It's not a bad story, but conceding that many love it, not one I'd ever count as one of my favorites.

DENNY O'NEIL: I had a job to do and the idea of the Sandman Superman was to solve a problem. That problem was, how do we get this guy down to a manageable level of power? I didn't want to take him all the way back to what Joe and Jerry started with. For example, the original Superman couldn't fly, but we left that part intact. Faster than a speeding bullet and more powerful than a locomotive, that should be enough. I think we left X-ray vision intact, but not the ability to see into the past or another world. I mean, there was just no limit to what he could do. And that's because in Superman's developmental years, the conventional wisdom was that nobody really pays much attention to this stuff and your audience has a complete turnover every three years. I don't think they ever worried about things like consistency and damn little about characterizations. Stories were plot-driven. That's where those guys were often refugees from the pulps and I think their accomplishment is sometimes underestimated. Trying to do what Cary Bates did and think of a new use for super-speed 12 times a year was not something I could do. And the characterizations were kind of cookie cutter, generally, and existed merely to serve the plot.

JOHN WELLS: O'Neil by his own admission was never comfortable writing Superman, and one can get a sense of that in reading his stories. His solution was to "permanently" reduce the hero's power level in the hope that it would create more dramatic tension. It was an idea that was narratively untenable, lest Superman be reduced to stopping threats like bank robbers and tornadoes that could be found on low-budget TV shows. It was a fundamental misunderstanding of what made Superman great and an early example of trying to introduce a bit too much realism into a feature that was all about wish-fulfillment. A character who could fly to the stars under his own power was infinitely cooler than someone a couple of steps up from a circus strongman. There was so much story potential in exploring the challenges of superpowers, the reaction of others to such a being in their midst and, as Elliot S! Maggin, observed, the ethical and moral dilemmas created when human and superhuman collided.

MARK WAID (writer, *Batman/Superman: World's Finest*): The changes could have been very strong, but boy, there were hurdles, because he's part of a bigger universe. If Superman were just published in his own little bubble, that's the kind of thing that could have sustained, but I don't think you can sustain that with Superman in a broader DC universe. Wonder Woman can't be the strongest person in the Justice League; that's gotta be Superman — not because he's a man, but just because that's his role. He can't be half Supergirl's strength. Once you get into that, you're kind of boxed into a corner with Superman.

MICHAEL BAILEY (comics historian; host, *Superman: From Crisis to*

Crisis **podcast):** What was so strange was that when reading *Superman* and reading *Action* from that era, it doesn't even seem to be the same character.

DENNY O'NEIL: I guess now I would find it an interesting assignment, but back then I was realizing it was taking me three days to write a Batman story and I was having fun. Or at least there was nothing terribly hard about it. But it was taking a lot longer to do a Superman story. So after about a year, I decided that this is *not* my assignment. So I left, and like I said, it reverted with no explanation.

ARLEN SCHUMER (comic book historian, author, *The Silver Age of Comic Book Art*): The episodic storytelling along with the overall arc that Denny O'Neil was telling was pretty great. And the nemesis in the form of the Sandman Superman is one of the great Superman villains, but it's actually the Silver Age idea of Bizarro and Superman duplicates. How many stories were about that? It's almost like O'Neil paying homage to one of the Superman duplicates by coming up with his Sandman Superman.

PAUL LEVITZ: I loved the art; I think Curt Swan and Murphy Anderson were a terrific combination.

ARLEN SCHUMER: When you talk about the art, in some of the layouts it's like Swan got a B12 shot of energy and Anderson inking him became what we look back at as Swanderson. You had those scripts and that art — you have all of these levels which is what makes any work of art great. When you talk about *Citizen Kane* being considered, according to a recent poll, the greatest movie of all time, it's because when you parse the movie from a creative standpoint on every creative level, Bernard Herrmann did the music, Robert Wise was the editor... On *every* creative level, it was operating at 110% and you end up with a great creative work. Well, in a sense, the Sandman Superman story worked on every creative level and it shined.

DENNY O'NEIL: Deeper characterization was one of Stan Lee's contributions to comics. When I first started looking at comics again, back in the early '60s, DC's Hawkman was a guy who flew and *maybe* characterization went as deeply as Barry Allen, the Flash, was always late. Isn't that funny? In that era what Stan did was bring vivid language back, bring in an attitude that we're not taking this so seriously, we're having fun. That's one of the things I recommended. His characters never became anti-heroes. At the end of the day, they were good guys who served and protected, but they would squabble. They used questionable grammar. They didn't always get along. They were not perfect by any means. It was just a lot more fun reading those stories than a story about a virtually perfect character. His perfection might be defined by a Boy Scout leader. When I and other people moved from Stan's shop to other places, it's one of the things we brought with us. My thesis has always been that Stan and Julie, between them, reinvented comic books and superheroes. Without those people, I don't know what direction it would have taken. I *don't* think we'd have a comic book convention that draws 100,000 people or $200 million movies.

PAUL LEVITZ: I don't think Denny was ever cast well writing Superman. It was a well-written story, but Denny didn't enjoy writing cosmically-powered characters. He enjoyed writing human-level characters. He's better at Green Arrow than he is Green Lantern. He's better at the Question and Batman. Those are the series that you really feel he made a lasting and unique mark with.

ARLEN SCHUMER: O'Neil in bringing Superman "a little down to Earth" is laying the foundation for what they've been trying to do ever since. After the Sandman Superman story, O'Neil basically said, "Hey, this is my Magnum Opus; it's my Superman story. I can't really do anymore." And you have to respect that. Whereas somebody else would say, "I have a lot of Superman stories to tell." Listen, Cary Bates wrote Superman for like a decade-and-a-half. I wasn't reading Superman at the time, but he was a regular writer. And there was Elliot Maggin. How did these guys come up with stories? I don't know, but it seems like O'Neil laid out his modern take on Superman, which is exactly what he did with Deadman and Green Lantern/Green Arrow.

MICHAEL EURY: When we were coming of age, you'd start getting these "a whole new kind of Superman is coming" kind of house ads that were flirting with a dynamic new Superman for the hippie generation and now generation — the generation that grew up with civil rights, war protests and more reality-based storytelling like Marvel was giving us, and that worked from time to time with Superman. There had been some wonderful stories along that line, but was that what the character is all about? I mean, Clark Kent was a reporter, so there were a lot of stories that press the right buttons, but there were also some horrible misfires. The black Lois Lane story? It's just misaligned. Some years back I was doing an historical presentation on the evolution of African-American superheroes and, of course, I had to bring up that story. The contemporary audience would kind of laugh and moan at the same time when they saw the cover. It was well-intentioned but a misfire, and it was still a kids' comic at the time that was offering a variation of a soft-core porn movie.

This is the problem that DC was having. Editorially, it was this house of stodgy, professional guys in jackets with elbow patches and pipes, and while it was okay to have one or two of those guys around, when you had Stan Lee being really cool and speaking at college campuses, and these young guys with big hair like Neal Adams, Denny O'Neil, Walt Simonson, Len Wein, Marv Wolfman, and they were all taking chances — DC got left behind, yet were trying to do triage and fix it when not everything had the same formula. You look at something like *Green Lantern/Green Arrow*, that's perfect, but to try to do that with, say, *Jimmy Olsen*, that wouldn't have worked. Things were all over the place, and while some of it was really kind of cool, it went from one extreme to another. And then, over time, it all started to fall under Schwartz's purview again, and by the time it was all firmly under his control, maybe he was getting a little tired — so there it goes again.

ROBERT GREENBERGER: My impression is that the reaction from licensees to this new take on Superman and the fan mail and early returns gave them doubt. It took as many as nine months to get the final sales report, but I do know the key cities would be able to report within two or three months. If *Superman* 233 came out in October of 1971, it would be early the following year when they got the sense that the first numbers were not doing as well.

ELLIOT S! MAGGIN (author, *Superman: Miracle Monday*): Nobody wanted to write or draw Superman. That's why Cary and I got in on the wire. The character was losing popularity; it was measurable in sales and in the attitudes of artists and writers for them. When Denny didn't want to write Superman, I feel like we figured out what to do with him. Cary and I both — we concentrated on the extension of that "what can one man do story" and not one man who must be a Superman.

DENNY O'NEIL: It was my idea to walk off the assignment, and when I asked Julie why there was that sudden reversion to the previous version of the character, he said that what we had done wasn't selling. Now in those days, editors didn't see sales figures. You got books canceled all the time and the excuse was always sales. In some instances, I knew it was not possible for them to have anything like accurate sales figures yet. But yeah, I don't know who wrote that next one, but Superman was God again for a while. Eventually very good writers figured out ways to work with him, and he was depowered, ultimately. I mean, he doesn't go around blowing out stars anymore.

ELLIOT S! MAGGIN: The idea of "Must There Be a Superman" was the fountainhead, the pivot point, on which I stood to determine what Superman's place in the universe really was. The premise I set out in that one story pretty much defined the fundamentals of everything I ever wrote about the character afterward. Julie and Denny's approach to Superman at the time was to "depower" him; to make him less powerful than he'd grown to be in order to bring him down to a more human scale. I disagreed with that approach. I disagreed with it and still do. Every time since that anyone's gotten the chance to redefine Superman — and there have been more than just a few of these chances since 1970 — the first thing they've thought to do was "depower" him. Julie said at the time that he can't juggle planets anymore, but he can juggle buildings. I didn't and don't see the point. It's been my point of view that Superman stories are not about power. They're about moral and ethical choices. Each one asks the question: *What does a good person do in a given situation if he's got all the power in the world?* Writers and artists and editors — and producers and directors and actors, for that matter — don't get to limit Superman's powers. Once you do that, it's not the character you think you're dealing with anymore. Every "superman" in every culture — Zeus and Odin; John Henry and Paul Bunyan; Beowulf and Arthur — gets to decide the answer, in his own context, to that question. The success or failure of a storyteller's attempt to convey that is based on the degree to which the character gets to illustrate that for himself. If you start by "depowering" such a character, then your mythology is flawed. You don't know which archetype it is you're dealing with.

PETER SANDERSON: Schwartz at first ignored many of the characters and elements Weisinger had created, although eventually most of them crept back in. He held the line on most of the super-pets, but Krypto came back, as did Green and Red Kryptonite, Mxyzptlk, Kandor, Bizarro and the Phantom Zone criminals. Luthor, however, exchanged his gray prison uniform for purple tights, making him look more like a super-villain. Brainiac underwent a physical transformation into a clearly mechanical creature. The main villain created in this period was Terra-Man, a native of the 19th century American West who had been taken into space by aliens and returned in the 20th century as an outlaw on a winged horse. Imagine Clint Eastwood's Man with No Name equipped with high-tech weaponry. It seemed to be Schwartz's idea to pit Superman, a 20th century mythic hero, against another brand of mythic hero from the Western.

CARY BATES: It was the result of just another plotting session with Julie. Either he or I had hit on the idea of a space-cowboy character as a new villain. I remember him being particularly keen on the Old West origin, the idea of combining the SF genre with a Western; taking this Western character and amping him up to make a worthy adversary for Superman. It was my idea to give Curt

Swan some of Clint Eastwood's Man with No Name imagery as reference.

TIM DEFOREST (author, *Storytelling in the Pulps, Comics and Radio: How Technology Changed Popular Fiction in America*): Elliot Maggin asked the question: If Superman existed in real life, would he be hindering our social development and our growth as humans? It's an interesting thing to think about. It was dealt with there quite effectively. Of course, he went back to rescuing people, because he's Superman. It's not like he's going to stand there and not stop the earthquake or whatever it might be, but it's an interesting aspect of the character to talk about.

ELLIOT S! MAGGIN: When I went to see Julie with ten or so sketchy ideas scribbled on a legal pad, this sociology treatise that turned into *Superman* #247 was the idea that Julie latched onto. We worked it all out, with the Guardians of the Universe planting an idea in Supe's head and making him have second thoughts about solving the problems of a bunch of Mexican farm workers in California. When I gave Julie the story, he said, "Okay, I want to know what happens next." I said, "Well, can I write more stories?" "Yeah, but this is a complete left turn on everything that's come before." I said, "I didn't realize that," but it turned out to have been the premise for all the stories I wrote after that. I didn't know that was going to happen, but he did. Superman's best power is to explain to people, "Here's what I'm *not* going to do. I'll fix your earthly problem, because that doesn't come up every day, but I'm not going to kill your boss for you. Sorry."

JIM SHOOTER (creator, The Parasite): When I did some Superman writing for Julie Schwartz in the 1970s, I think that in essential ways, Superman himself was about the same. Details had changed. Clark Kent was a TV newsman and there were new supporting cast members. But Julie Schwartz had a more formulaic approach than Mort did. Every story *had* to have a [*Daily Planet* sports reporter] Steve Lombard prank, and a surreptitious Clark/Superman revenge; every story *had* to have a secret-identity-threatening situation and a clever escape, etc. Lots of rules.

Writers like Bates and Maggin continued to push the Man of Steel forward throughout the 1970s and early 1980s, penning stories in Superman *and* Action Comics, *their ranks eventually joined by people like Len Wein, Gerry Conway, Bob Rozakis, Marv Wolfman, Keith Giffen (both a writer and artist) and Paul Kupperberg. There were also such artists as Neal Adams (largely for covers, as he had been doing since the late '60s), the ever-present Curt Swan, Nick Cardy, Jose Luis Garcia-Lopez, Rich Buckler and Gil Kane.*

RAY MORTON: Under editor Julius Schwartz the writing of the character came up a notch. As earlier versions of the character had been, the '70s Superman was dedicated to truth, justice and serving mankind, but he was never the one-dimensional goody-goody detractors often slagged him as being. The '70s version of Superman was mature, smart and compassionate. As expected, he was noble, idealistic and had a certain gravitas, but he also had a rather wry outlook and a decent sense of humor about himself and the world around him. He struggled with moral and ethical issues and he also had a bit of an ego (one of my favorite aspects of '70s Superman was the way that every time he did something amazing, his thought bubbles would show how impressed he was by how amazing he thought whatever he was doing was). This was the most three-dimensional and adult the character had ever been. Comics were also becoming more adult during this period as they began to address topical issues and social trends, which allowed Superman to use his powers and abilities to deal with the real world in a way he hadn't done since the early days. This made the character feel a bit more relevant than he had in the previous decade.

JOHN WELLS: Cary Bates was the last holdover from the Weisinger school, a reliable scripter of plot-driven stories, while Elliot S! Maggin brought an outstanding character-based quality to his scripts when he joined the Schwartz stable in 1972. Bates and Maggin's interaction, to my mind, made each of them better writers as their respective strengths mingled. Both men embraced the Man of Steel's dual existence, playing off Superman's adventures with Clark Kent's workplace environment to great effect. In their hands, the archetypal bullied Clark Kent of old was neatly updated for the 1970s with a bad boss and arrogant co-workers. Bates and Maggin paved the way for Martin Pasko, whose criminally underrated 1977 to 1978 *Superman* tenure deepened the characterization of all the principal cast members and reconceived written-off villains as credible, sometimes sympathetic threats. Pasko's depiction of the decades-old Superman/Lois Lane romance, in particular, was arguably the most adult portrayal of the couple to that date.

RAY MORTON: Although the subject matter of the Superman comics was getting a little more realistic, things hadn't yet gotten hopelessly glum and serious, the way they later would. The Superman books of the '70s didn't forget to have fun. There was still plenty of sci-fi, fantasy, comedy and pure adventure, although the approach was a little smarter, a little less fluffy. One of my favorite bits of fun in this era were the "imaginary stories" — Superman stories set in alternate realities set outside the series' primary continuity. These tales gave the writers and artists a chance to try out new ideas without derailing the canon.

MARTIN PASKO (writer, *Superman*): From the beginning of Julie's editorial tenure on *Superman* to my arrival, a rogues' gallery was, with a few exceptions, conspicuously absent. Luthor appeared a handful of times; Cary "retconned" the Toyman and created Terra-Man, and Superman would get a worthy opponent whenever Len Wein did a fill-in. But there was little beyond that.

LEN WEIN: A character like the Galactic Golem came about because I needed somebody Superman could hit! The problem with Superman's rogues' gallery was that they were all *thinkers* — they were scientists or guys who built toys. With the Golem, he could hit Superman, and Superman could hit him back. Same thing with Mongul; he provided direct contact in a Superman villain. Most of the stories with Superman villains, Luthor especially, involved him making something to deal with Superman. Superman would stop it, swoop down and grab Luthor by the collar and take him off to prison. If you remember the old Superman stuff, especially Mort's, they always dealt with *puzzle* problems. I always wanted to see Superman duke it out with the aliens, but because Superman was so powerful, there was this approach: "I've become an old man. How do I deal with this?" Or, "I weigh a thousand pounds. How do I get around like this?" Here's a circumstance, a situation for Superman — how does he solve that problem? — as opposed to, here's a threat that he can just hit with all his might, and have a great time doing it. That's why I liked the Galactic Golem, because he gave Superman somebody he could deck and vice versa. My thinking was, "Superman is powered by a yellow sun. Well, here's a character who's powered by every star in the sky."

MARTIN PASKO: Somehow Julie had become convinced that there weren't any viable villains, and so Cary and Elliot Maggin did story after story pitting Supes against balding guys in jackets and ties. Gerry Conway and I came to *Superman* determined to change all that. But, unlike Gerry, I believed that the only problem with most of the existing villains was that they needed to be made "bigger" — more powerful, more grandiose, more desperate — to give Supes a real challenge. The only exception to that was the Prankster, who could only be played for comedy in my judgment, so I relegated him to 8-pagers and one sequence in the *World's Greatest Super-Heroes* syndicated strip, where I gave him a civilian name, Oswald Loomis. In any event, my goal was to take the old villains that Julie disdained and give them an edge, in hopes of attracting new, older readers. I seem to have succeeded in doing that since the numbers on *Superman* went up while *Action*'s sales plateaued, and the only difference in the creative teams on the two books was the writer. I also continually pressured Julie to let me make *Superman* as different from *Action* as humanly possible, and do it by giving the book more of a serial structure, with multi-issue story arcs, "B"-stories and runners that would continue for half-a-year or more. In short, a structure more familiar to readers of Marvel, who at that time had finally eclipsed DC in sales after a decade of nipping at its heels. This was necessary to give us enough space to cut loose with the action.

GERRY CONWAY (writer, *Superman vs. The Amazing Spider-Man*): One of the things that anybody who looks at my stuff over a period of time will probably pick up on is that I'm really not that compelled by the super heroics or the superpowers. Somebody like John Byrne can sit down and figure out how all this stuff works and make it consistent and interesting, but I don't really care. My favorite character is Green Lantern, because all he has to do is wish for something and it happens. The part I care about is the characters themselves — Clark Kent, Lois Lane… you know, the people behind the scenes — so the *real* story in any comic I've written is the *subplot*, to the point where there was practically no story! To the extent I added some emphasis to the secondary characters, *that* was my contribution.

MARTIN PASKO: Both Gerry and I were into going for more extreme action — Superman and the villain knocking each other through buildings and planets, and that sort of thing. Gerry's results were generally more effective, because most of his scripts were assigned to guys like J.L. Garcia-Lopez and Ross Andru, who had a much better sense than Curt Swan of how to use extreme angles, detailed backgrounds, forced perspective and movement into and away from camera to make the action look as dynamic as possible.

In terms of comics there would continue to be big events as the '70s played out, most notably in the form of tabloid-sized specials, including 1976's Superman vs. The Amazing Spider-Man, *the first time these iconic heroes were brought together, with Conway providing the script and art by Ross Andru and Dick Giordano; and the 1978 trifecta of* Superman vs. Wonder Woman, *from Conway with art by Jose Luis Garcia-Lopez;* Superman vs. Shazam! *scripted by Conway and drawn by Rich Buckler; and the one that works amazingly well, despite the fact that it probably shouldn't,* Superman vs. Muhammad Ali, *with a story by Denny O'Neill and script and art by Neal Adams.*

JOHN WELLS: The fondly remembered 1970s tabloids were an effort to get DC's comics into other venues than the traditional spinner racks. With cardboard covers and larger dimensions, they had greater durability and suggested something special that one might hold on to as a keepsake. The format was an immediate hit, spilling over into locations like chain stores in special cardboard displays. Marvel quickly followed suit with their own tabloid line and momentarily made a deal with DC to co-publish a groundbreaking edition titled *Superman vs. The Amazing Spider-Man* in early 1976.

GERRY CONWAY: *Superman vs. Spider-Man* was a huge deal and one of the things where, before it happened, you could never have imagined that it would, because Marvel and DC were so antagonistic to each other just as corporations and publishing entities. The creators for the most part were perfectly willing to go back and forth between the two, but the corporate mindsets of both companies were so dismissive of each other's creative directions. So how do you put these two things together? One guy who wanted to be Stan Lee's agent, got everyone to agree. Now, creatively, the notion of bringing those two together simply didn't give you any way to rationalize it, other than getting so nerdy and weird that it would've interfered with the fun of it. You just have to try and be a fanboy and go with what you'd like to see.

And what I wanted to see was a level playing field that acknowledged the strengths of each character's particular universe and storytelling. You want to see a story that has the fun of a Marvel comic in the interplay of characters and the way those characters confront each other, and at the same time an overarching DC-type plot where a villain has an agenda that involves lots of pseudoscience and tech, and has to be outsmarted in the end. Those are the elements I perceived as essential to a combination of those books. It's sort of meta where you're trying to do something that operates on two different levels and observes both. I don't know that I was necessarily fully conscious of that, but that was ultimately the approach that both Ross Andru and I took, to do a Marvel version of Superman and a DC version of Spider-Man and be true to the inherent qualities of both at the same time.

JOHN WELLS: Unlike the bulk of the tabloids that reprinted old content, this story was all-new, meticulously giving equal time to its two stars. Gerry Conway wrote the script with a great sense of fun and humor, but it was the artwork that truly sang. Brilliant, idiosyncratic penciler Ross Andru drew with the extra-large pages in mind and the book was filled with huge, dynamic figures and imagery. Unsurprisingly, sales were terrific and, after Jenette Kahn came aboard as DC's publisher, two logical follow-up bouts for Superman were commissioned: Wonder Woman, a household name thanks to the Lynda Carter TV series, and Captain Marvel, recently featured on Saturday morning TV's *Shazam!*, starred in tabloids in 1977 and 1978 that once again made good use of the larger canvas.

GERRY CONWAY: It was actually my interest in doing Wonder Woman as she had been done in the '40s. The Wonder Woman of 1960 on was pretty lame, in my view. But the Wonder Woman of the '40s had dynamism, and I was more interested in that version of the character. And the original *Wonder Woman* TV series certainly reminded us that the '40s was a good period for her, although the TV series took the '40s era and did the '60s character. I also like doing stories in the past.

JOSE LUIS GARCIA-LOPEZ (artist, *Superman vs. Wonder Woman*): I was more interested in the politics of war than in the war itself, and besides, it's a genre I don't feel comfortable doing. But I did the required homework to get it right, even if it was a "superhero war style."

JOHN WELLS: *Superman vs. Wonder Woman* artist Jose Luis Carcia-Lopez actively studied Andru's previous tabloid, successfully bringing that sort of spectacle to his own work.

When it came to Superman vs. Muhammad Ali — *which essentially has the two of them doing what they can to prevent an alien invasion — Neal Adams had agreed to do the project so long as there was no specific deadline, yet he continually heard that it was taking him too long to turn in pages.*

NEAL ADAMS: Oh, it didn't take me that long to draw it. "No deadline" to me means "no deadline." I don't know what it means to anybody else, but to me, it means *no deadline*. After a while, they start hocking me and they were really worried, because in the middle of the thing, Ali lost the championship, which was going to hurt it. And I'm going, "Guys, he lost it twice before and got it back. What are you worried about? He's going to get it back, right?" And he *did* just before we came out.

JOHN WELLS: False! The comic went on sale in February 1978, the same month that Ali was defeated. He didn't regain the title until September 1978. Actually, the comic went on sale January 31, 1978, so Ali *was* still heavyweight champion — for the first two weeks that the issue was on the stands. But this was the most highly-publicized of the volumes. It was a match-up initiated by Kahn and produced by Adams. Already renowned for his realistic, dynamic visuals, Adams pulled out all the stops to deliver one of the most impressive works of his career. Chain stores like Target and K-Mart bought copies in bulk and the project was deemed a success.

Naturally Superman was only one part of the different challenges facing DC Comics in the 1970s, although a solution arrived in the form of children's magazine publisher Jenette Kahn, who had previously launched Kids, written by children, *and* Dynamite *for Scholastic Inc. and* Smash *for Xerox Education Publications. When she joined DC on February 2, 1976 at age 28, she was named publisher (much to the chagrin of Sol Harrison) and five years later became president. To her credit, one of the first things that she accomplished was convincing Warner Publishing not to cancel the comic division to focus exclusively on licenses.*

ROBERT GREENBERGER: Paul Levitz tells all these horror stories about Carmine Infantino throwing stuff against the wall to see what sticks, because he didn't know how to read the sales figures and figure out what the trends were. In the meantime, Marvel's eating their lunch at the newsstand. This is where Sol Harrison starts moving up from production director to being president with Carmine, and the two of them are doing it without any training whatsoever — it was a real mess. Finally, Warner looked under the appropriate rocks and said, "Something's wrong here," and decided that they needed to make a change. So, they bring in this 28-year-old female publisher to an all-boys network, basically. It was a seismic change, but *exactly what* was needed to shake them out of their doldrums. Jenette, to her credit, sat there and read *everything*, talked to *everybody* and made herself available to the creative community. And it took her and Paul Levitz a couple of years to figure out what to do in the meantime. Everybody would be like hamsters on the treadmill, just keeping the lights on until they could get a plan in place to grow the company the way they felt it needed to be.

JOHN WELLS: Jenette Kahn's arrival at DC didn't really affect the approach to Superman, but she did see the character as someone who appealed to a younger demographic, and one of her first decisions was the launch of a comic book based on the Saturday morning cartoon *Super Friends*. Kahn also saw Superman as a character who could be used to get DC into new venues, whether through her Dollar Comics initiative (including the expanded *Superman Family* title) or the retooled tabloid line. Kahn's mid-1978 "DC Explosion" was designed to promote DC's other properties while increasing the page count on regular titles with an attendant price increase. Warner Communications shut the expansion down at the last minute and all comics selling below a certain threshold were canceled. Still, among DC's best-sellers, the Superman-related books were unaffected.

PAUL LEVITZ: Jenette brought a sincere desire to see creativity prosper and creators prosper with it; a modern outlook on what we'd now term representation and diversity, courage and open mindedness… and fresh thought as the first outsider in a position of power, and the first young person in that role in decades.

And yet there were still serious issues with the Man of Steel that needed to be addressed, though no one seemed to have a handle on exactly what to do. Significant changes wouldn't be initiated until 1986 when Julius Schwartz retired with 42 years of his life having been spent at DC.

ELLIOT S! MAGGIN: I think Julie's most significant contribution to Superman was saving the character from oblivion. I don't think anyone knew what to do with Superman when he got dropped on Julie's desk and there wasn't the wealth of licensing opportunities there is now to fall back on. Superman might have been canceled or — more likely — bought by another company. In fact, there's someone I was trying to convince to buy him around 1974, who could have done it if I'd been more convincing and he'd been more of a visionary. But the deal would have been to bring Julie with him. I never told Julie about that.

MARTIN PASKO: Perhaps against his better judgment, Julie allowed Superman to be done by writers and artists who didn't think of superhero comics as the exclusive province of small children. By doing so, he provided the bridge between the high-concept silliness or campiness, if you will, of the Weisinger years and what would be produced in the '90s and later. Without Julie paving the way, subsequent developments like John Byrne's relaunch and the burst of creativity that followed it under editor Mike Carlin's guidance, would not have been possible. Julie is probably just as responsible as anyone for the fact that the character is still viable today.

MARK WAID: The state of Superman at this point was status quo, and I mean that in the worst possible way. The comic adventures were unremarkable. There were some great writers during that time — Elliot Maggin and Cary Bates were the people handling Superman and were doing their best — but Julie Schwartz liked a very specific kind of story. He liked puzzle stories that didn't really involve emotion. He liked science-fiction and wasn't as keen on social activism and things like that. While some of the stories were pretty good, they're very repetitive. And Curt Swan, who we both agree was an amazing artist, was not served well in the mid-'70s by his inkers. Murray Boltinoff was the editor who put Murphy Anderson on him, which was a great call. Then, when Murphy left about a year-and-a-half in, it seems like Julie replaced him by grabbing whoever was walking the halls and it just drained the life out of Curt's pencils. The comic was just on a treadmill of mediocrity.

ROBERT GREENBERGER: I think Julie was floundering for a formula that would work if the one he wanted didn't work, and he didn't have a regular writer, so it was a variety of people. It's Bates and Maggin and then, later on, Pasko and Len Wein. It became a free for all. They didn't add to the mythos; we didn't learn a lot. Elliot tried questioning if the world needed Superman; he did the most thoughtful stuff. Cary came out of the Weisinger school and Len was just a fan of the character, so he was writing these standalone adventures. The Bronze Age for Superman was hit or miss, but then the entire DC line was meandering through most of the '70s until Jenette Kahn was brought in to replace Carmine Infantino to fix it.

MARK WAID: Julie Schwartz didn't love Superman. Julie liked Batman, Julie liked Green Lantern — Julie was very attached to the stuff he helped resuscitate. Superman was a job to Julie and he took it mostly because Mort was such a close friend and he was known as DC's go-to editor for revitalizing characters. For a brief while, the Superman books were split between several editors, but Julie took on the flagship book because of his relationship with Mort, and my conversations with him verify that he took it on reluctantly. Julie always looked at it as, "Man, I've got to do *something* with this character." Even though he was the shepherd of the character for like 15 years, I don't think he had a vision for Superman.

PAUL LEVITZ: When we went through the implosion and Jenette Kahn made the decision to consolidate the primary characters' titles under an editor, Julie was the senior guy, so he had the first pick and he picked Superman and gave me the Batman titles and I always felt Julie made a mistake, because he had much more affinity for Batman and would eventually do a better job editing Batman than he did editing Superman. I don't know that I could have done any better on Superman, but I at least had more affinity for him as a character than I had for Batman, and I'd like to believe maybe I would have done something interesting.

There would also be a market shift that would ultimately have a positive impact on both Superman and DC Comics as a whole. After decades of kids (of all ages) purchasing comic books from their local newsstands, a growing phenomenon was the rise of comic book shops around the country, which would really change the game.

ROBERT GREENBERGER: As time went on, the direct sales, non-returnable comics market proved to be a lifeline as the dynamics changed and newsstand became more atrophied. The comic shops started to rise, so it became a big change. And as Jenette was starting to put the pieces in place and bringing fresh creators and fresh editors and fresh approaches, they were poised to take advantage of the direct sales market. Marvel beat them to it with a direct sales manager, but DC quickly followed and grew their direct sales force. And they brought in people with marketing experience who knew what they were doing. That helped change the culture and change the business.

Jenette's impact really starts being felt in 1980 and she benefits from Jim Shooter and Marvel imploding, chasing away all these creators who are now coming to DC, and she now has a larger roster of available really good talent to put on the key books. Jenette relaunches *Teen Titans* with George Perez as the artist. Marv Wolfman is writing, the thing comes out in the summer of '80 and everyone goes, "Holy shit!" And Jenette tried all of these different incremental things here and there and all of a sudden, readers are going, "Wait, this feels different. This reads differently."

The surprising thing is that while Superman struggled for direction — and a reading audience — throughout the 1970s, and even into the '80s, as far as the public was concerned, he was as much a pop culture phenomenon as he ever had been. There was merchandise, product placement, TV commercials and so much more. And on top of that, the decade saw additional television-filmed adventures, and even the christening of Metropolis, IL as the city of Superman, an official commemoration for which took place in 1972.

The city of Metropolis, located along the Ohio River in Massac County, Illinois, was founded in 1839, a century before the publication of Action Comics #1. *Although it has its place in history — particularly during the American Revolutionary War and Civil War — as far as Superman fans are concerned, the most important date in its history is June 9, 1972, when the Illinois State Legislature passed Resolution 572, declaring the city (with the permission of DC) the official "Hometown of Superman." Early plans to help revitalize the area called for a Superman theme park, but that notion went the way of Krypton when the oil crisis of the '70s hit. There is, however, a 15-foot painted bronze statue of Superman that stands in front of the county courthouse, a bronze statue of Noel Neill's Lois Lane a few blocks away and, as of 1993, the Super Museum, hosted and owned by collector Jim Hambrick, located between the two.*

In 1979, the city launched Superman Celebration, held annually during the second weekend of June. However, anyone expecting a Comic-Con-type experience, even on a smaller scale, will be disappointed. A better description would likely be that if the people of Mayberry from The Andy Griffith Show *threw a convention, it would be Superman Celebration.*

KARLA OGLE (Metropolis Chamber of Commerce): The Superman Celebration originally started as a small hometown event. A small crowd of local citizens enjoyed a weekend of music and activities, which included a tug-of-war

Superman statue greeting visitors to Metropolis, IL (photo ©Ed Gross; Superman © and TM DC Comics/Warner Bros. Discovery).

and a chug-a-lug contest. The event was popular and grew slowly over the years, adding more events and eventually adding in celebrity guests. Social media has played a big part of the event expanding. People who have attended have returned with other friends and family in tow for the next year. Many attendees have attended for as many as 15 to 20 years and keep returning.

JIM HAMBRICK (owner and operator, Super Museum): When I first got here in 1993, the Superman Celebration was like a company picnic with about a hundred people showing up. The idea was let's try and get some celebrities in here and open it up, and that's what we did. But before that, they just kind of left it alone for years; the locals didn't show up except for a corn dog or something. Then I was asked to be on television shows and it kind of mushroomed into something that was different than the conventions — kind of like with a Mayberry twist.

NEIL COLE (webmaster, supermansupersite.com): We attend every year and for us it's more like a family reunion. The first couple of years we came, we were new to the whole thing, so it was all new experiences. And there's enough stuff that they switch up each year — the celebrity guests are always different — and there's just something wonderful about meeting up with people year after year.

STACY HAIDUK (actor, "Lana Lang," *Superboy*): The Superman Celebration is pretty amazing, just because everybody's there for that one thing. It's not like when you go to the Comic-Con conventions where there are all sorts of things being celebrated. It's amazing to see the love the fans who attend have for all things Superman.

BRANDON ROUTH (actor, "Clark Kent/Superman," *Superman Returns*): *Superman Returns* made a big impact on many, many people, and that's all that matters. They still love it, and for them it's their Superman movie. And if it's not, it's a transitionary movie and people appreciate it. That's why they keep coming back to places where I am, I guess, and they like my version of Superman. And in the people that I meet — like at Superman Celebration — it has a ripple effect. You throw a stone into the pond, the ripple effect continues and creates other ripple effects. Everyone who has an experience to share about *Superman Returns* is part of that story and it affects me in some way.

KARLA OGLE: Superman Celebration has become a must-see event for not only Superman fans, but fans of the comic book/superhero genre as well. Our 15-foot bronze Superman statue is a frequent stop for people of all ages. Many will see an article or mention on social media and decide to come to Metropolis to see it in person while others see the sign on I-24 as they are traveling through and make a quick detour to pose next to Superman. Both the Superman statue and the curiosity of a city named Metropolis get a lot of attention from visitors yearly. The statue is a busy place pretty much all day and night with visitors stopping by to see it. Most citizens of Metropolis appreciate the attention that the Superman connection brings, but don't give it much thought throughout the rest of the year. Unless you are seeing the carloads of people stopping at the Welcome to Metropolis sign, the Superman statue or Super Museum, you don't think about it unless the subject comes up in conversation. It is a very cool thing having the Superman connection and being the only Metropolis.

JIM HAMBRICK: I had a mobile Superman museum 15 years before I got to Metropolis, so in total I've got 45 years in the Superman Museum business. It's done well and I didn't expect the town to be as receptive to it as they are, but it's worked out. After 25 years they started figuring out that I wasn't taking the money and running. I'm part of the community. I even ran for mayor.

STEVE YOUNIS (webmaster, supermanhomepage.com): The Super Museum has got to be seen to be believed. The collection of Superman memorabilia, props, costumes, toys, etc. is amazing! Jim has some fantastic items in his collection; breathtaking stuff. I wandered through many times during my stay in Metropolis, taking photos, reading the plaques, staring in amazement. It truly is something every Superman fan should see. And the Superman Celebration in Metropolis, Illinois is fantastic! I went there looking forward to seeing the Superman Statue and the Super Museum, and came away really cherishing the wonderful people I met and the friendships I made. If I had to rate my time in Metropolis on a scale from 1 to 10, I'd give it 11.

KARLA OGLE: It's a great addition to Metropolis. Any Superman fan would be thrilled to see the collection of all things "Super" housed inside the Super Museum. Having items from film, television and comics representing every year since the first appearance of Superman in 1938 is an interesting look at how popular the Man of Steel is and how his look has changed over the years.

As she explains it, a full year of planning goes into the following year's Superman Celebration, and the payoff at that time is fairly instant.

KARLA OGLE: We're always amazed about how early the fans start arriving into Metropolis. Many will arrive mid-week and take time to walk through the Museum and soak up the Superman vibe before the crowds arrive. Crowds have been difficult to accurately guess, but an average year is 20,000 to 30,000+ over the weekend. 2022 will be noted as our largest crowd to date. Without a main gate for fans to enter, we rely on hotel numbers and visual crowds to estimate our attendance. Personally, I've been involved with the Superman Celebration as a committee member, chairman or co-chair since 2000. The thing I enjoy most is to talk to visitors. I love hearing the reasons that Superman the character is important to them. He really is a hero to many — all ages, all genders. And I love the enthusiasm that visitors have when they've attended for the first time.

On television, it seemed that the Man of Steel's adventures had come to an end with the conclusion of The Batman/Superman Hour *from Filmation, but that wasn't the case, with the animation studio — Filmation — giving fans just a little bit more in 1970 and then again in 1972.*

WILL RODGERS (author, *The Ultimate Super Friends Companion*): In

1970, they animated a series of one-minute PSA segments that aired on *Sesame Street*. After Bud Collyer's passing, the late Lennie Weinrib took over the voice of Superman in those PSAs. And finally, in 1972, Superman/Clark Kent and Lois Lane guest-appeared in Filmation's *The Brady Kids*. The episode was called "Cindy's Super Friend." Weinrib reprised the voice role of Superman and the late Jane Webb, who was already part of the voice cast, would voice over Lois Lane.

MARK MCCRAY (author, *The Best Saturdays of Our Lives*): Even though *The New Adventures of Superman* had come to an end, Filmation still had certain rights, so both Superman and Wonder Woman — in what was her first appearance — were separately guest stars on *The Brady Kids*. What was great about the Wonder Woman appearance is that in one fell swoop they demonstrated her super-speed *and* her super-strength, which is not something you'd see a lot of in *Super Friends*. The crazy part is that *The Brady Kids* featuring Superman and Wonder Woman, when they premiered, were the highest-rated episodes of the series, and when they repeated they also generated high ratings. So that gave ABC the idea that maybe kids wanted to see superheroes on Saturday mornings again. I think Filmation probably would've done a new Superman series based on the ratings information, but Hanna-Barbera had already swooped in and gotten the rights for what would become *Super Friends*.

The interesting thing about the Superman episode is that Clark Kent had changed jobs and was on WGBS, and *The Brady Kids* captured him being an on-air reporter on television — that was the only television episode to do that. I want to say that in the '80s, maybe after *Crisis on Infinite Earths*, he became a newspaper reporter again, but I thought it was really cool that we saw that on *The Brady Kids*.

Next up was the Hanna-Barbera series Super Friends, *which debuted on ABC in 1973 and ran in different permutations until 1985. Usually at the core of the show were Superman, Batman and Robin, Wonder Woman and Aquaman. Besides interchanging additional heroes, there would be the goofy sidekicks and animals that were so a part of kids' TV of the time, among them Wendy and Marvin along with Wonder Dog as well as Wonder Twins Zan and Jayna and their space monkey Gleek. The show aired in America as* Super Friends *from 1973 to 1974,* The All-New Super Friends Hour *from 1977 to 1978,* Challenge of the Super Friends *from 1978 to 1979,* The World's Greatest Super Friends *from 1979 to 1980,* Super Friends *from 1980 to 1983,* Super Friends: The Legendary Super Powers Show *from 1984 to 1985 and* The Super Powers Team: Galactic Guardians *from 1985 to 1986. Through it all, Superman was brought to vocal life by voiceover artist Danny Dark.*

In some ways, the production of the show was fairly surprising given the backlash against "violence" on Saturday mornings.

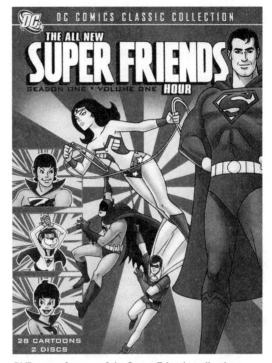

DVD cover for one of the **Super Friends** *collections* *(© and TM DC Comics/Warner Bros. Discovery).*

WILL RODGERS: One of the groups that got the superhero cartoon format pulled from Saturday mornings was a woman named Peggy Charren and her group Action for Children's Television. They were on a mission to remove anything violent, from actions to dialogue. They also wanted to bring more education to Saturday mornings, hence the health and safety tips from various characters and Saturday morning programs such as *Schoolhouse Rock* on ABC and *In the News* on CBS. Charren and her group were also determined to keep toy lines and cartoons separate, starting with Hot Wheels in 1969. This is why we never had an official *Super Friends* toy line in the '70s. Luckily that got overturned in the '80s, and the Super Powers toy line by Kenner was the closest we got to having the Super Friends in action-figure form.

ALAN BURNETT (story editor, *Super Friends: The Legendary Super Powers Shows*): When you're talking about '80s Saturday morning TV and before, Superman could not make a fist. He literally could not shake his fist. Nobody could. If he had heat vision, it came out in a fan as opposed to a piercing beam. Any sort of impactful action — I call it violence, but we use the word action a lot — you just couldn't do.

WILL RODGERS: In 1972 — I'm wildly guessing — bringing superheroes back to Saturday mornings was experimented with in the form of a couple of trial runs. Batman and Robin appeared on a couple of episodes of *The New Scooby-Doo Movies* along with the Joker and the Penguin. And then there was Superman and Wonder Woman (and the Lone Ranger and Tonto) each guest-appearing on episodes of *The Brady Kids*. In 1973, Hanna-Barbera acquired the DC license to animate the Justice League of America, but the series and the episodes had to be approved by child psychologists to make sure they were safe to air on Saturday mornings. Supposedly the name Justice League sounded too violent to the higher-ups approving the storylines, hence the team would be officially called the Super Friends.

As noted, there were various incarnations of Super Friends *between 1973 and 1985, history seemingly forgetting that the show had that sort of run. But in 1973, it was a brand-new entity.*

MARK MCCRAY: Because *Super Friends* was going to be the first real superhero show since 1968 to show up on Saturday mornings, I think the network was maybe a little gun shy and didn't want to take much in the way of chances.

WILL RODGERS: The original *Super Friends* was the one under the heaviest of restrictions to appease the parent watchdog groups and broadcast Standards and Practices. While I liked the original Junior Super Friends — Wendy, Marvin and Wonderdog — as a kid, they get on my nerves now. On the downside, the episodes' plots moved very slowly and there were no DC villains in this series, just some misguided scientists and inventors and the occasional alien in need of help, plus moral lessons, and, especially, ecological messages were drilled into our brains.

ALAN BURNETT: When I started on *Super Friends*, I had dreams of it being great. *That* got shattered as I started to go through the process with broadcast standards. They said to me that the show had to be safe enough for a two-year-old to watch. They were aiming for between two years and 11 years old because of the advertising. And the earlier in the morning that the show was on, the younger the age the show had to be geared for, because that's when the little ones were really watching. The older kids wouldn't be watching until the latter half of the Saturday morning schedule. As a result, in that first year they came down *hard*. I had an episode where the juvenile members of the *Super Friends* — Robin and the horrid Wonder Twins — were shrunk down in size. At one point, Robin had to knock a spider off a table, which he did, so that they wouldn't get eaten by it. The note I got was that we have to show that the spider is okay. I'll never forget it; we put in a shot of the spider walking away on the floor, and I'm thinking, "Oh my gosh, I'm doomed."

MARK MCCRAY: There was *nothing* going on; they were talking about the environment. I felt like in order for Hanna-Barbera to sell the series to the network, they had to take an environmental slant. I had been excited that the superheroes were back on Saturday mornings and that they would actually all be together. When you look at the *Superman/Aquaman Hour of Adventure* or *The Batman/Superman Hour* that Filmation had done previously, Superman and Aquaman or Superman and Batman didn't appear together. We were getting all these heroes together and it sounded so great, but I was like, "Where are the super-villains? Where's the action? Where's the fighting?" I even talk about this in my book, but I really despise Wendy, Marvin and Wonderdog. The show could have been a little more tolerable if maybe those three sidekicks *weren't* there.

WILL RODGERS: Because of the lack of action in this first season, it is highly recommended when introducing kids to the Super Friends, start them off on *any* of the other seasons and come back to this season down the road. On the plus side, the fun part of this series are the portrayals of the original five voice actors, Danny Dark, Olan Soule, Casey Kasem, Shannon Farnon and Norman Alden; plus, having Ted Knight from the Filmation DC cartoons narrating this series. The first season does have a few gems: the one-time-only cameo of Plastic Man, the first guest appearance of the Flash, the one-time-only guest appearance of Green Arrow, and the origin of Superman being told.

MARK MCRAY: I *will* say that one of the cool things about season one is that is showcased the first appearance of Plastic Man. In my opinion, Plastic Man up until that point was always a bridesmaid, never a bride. The studios were constantly trying to do animation with him, but no one was interested. The only other thing I can offer on season one is that it didn't really do that great in the ratings and was canceled. In prime time, if you have three of the lowest-rated shows sharing a time slot, one of those series would survive. But on Saturday mornings, it just seemed like all three got canceled. *Super Friends* was going up against the animated *Star Trek* on NBC and *The Hudson Brothers Razzle Dazzle Hour* was on CBS, and all three bit the dust — though *Super Friends* came back.

THE ALL-NEW SUPER FRIENDS HOUR (1977 to 1978)

WILL RODGERS: I will always have a special place in my heart for *The All-New Super Friends Hour*. While this is the second season, this was the very season that introduced me to the Super Friends. Because of this series, I have always considered Superman, Batman and Robin, Wonder Woman and Aquaman as the five mainstays of the *Super Friends*, while any and all other DC superheroes to be guest heroes. This was also my introduction to the Wonder Twins and Gleek. I always loved Zan and Jayna, because they have always reminded me of Donny and Marie Osmond. I loved the format of this series — three short-length episodes sandwiching a half-hour episode: two of the mainstays battling a sinister scientist or inventor or the occasional costumed villain; a weekly adventure with the Wonder Twins and Gleek coming to the rescue of America's youth; the Super Friends' big half-hour adventure starring the core group; the five mainstays and the Wonder Twins battling some major threat; and the last short featuring one of the mainstays and a guest superhero teamed together in a rescue mission. And in between each episode were the PSA segments (health and safety tips, craft and magic tricks and the DeCoder segments that were tied in with the half-hour episode). *The All-New Super Friends Hour* is definitely the Super Friends' answer to variety shows, which were big in the '70s.

ALAN BURNETT: The second year, ABC was willing to take more chances with the show. They went to half-hour stories, which helped, and they went on the air later in the schedule, which was a *big* help. They changed the name for the toy line and that season was more successful, but I never got to where I wanted to go with it.

SUPER FRIENDS 78 & CHALLENGE OF THE SUPER FRIENDS (1978 to 1979)

MARK MCCRAY: Back in 2005 I was in touch with one of Hanna-Barbera's longtime productions designers and animators. He told me that DC Comics sent Hanna-Barbera hate mail over the first season of *Super Friends*. He said, "They wanted our heads. They said, 'We'll get you guys for this.'" I'm sure the writers were maybe looking to submit story ideas or scripts, so they were pretty annoyed that the show got canceled.

WILL RODGERS: This was the year that I felt the Super Friends reached their peak of popularity and it couldn't have happened in a better year. Wonder Woman had a live-action TV series on CBS, *Superman: The Movie* was released in theaters in December of 1978 and the Super Friends finally got to battle DC super-villains from the comic books. And in this case, there were two separate Super Friends series sharing the same hour. While *Challenge of the Super Friends* was the only one that got promoted on the ABC Network, the other series, *Super Friends 78,* aired first in the hour and was the warm-up. This 16 half-hour episode season is for fans who wanted to see the Wonder Twins and Gleek since they were not part of the other series. This season featured battles with Count Dracula, a trio of Kryptonian villains from the Phantom Zone and the first appearance of Mr. Mxyzptlk. Meanwhile, *Challenge of the Super Friends* gave the comic book fans what they were longing to see: 13 DC super-villains formed a team called the Legion of Doom, and the Super Friends now added Green

Lantern, the Flash, Hawkman and three Hanna Barbera-created heroes: Black Vulcan, Samurai and Apache Chief. All three were guest stars on *The All-New Super Friends Hour*, joining the five mainstays in this series. Many fans consider *Challenge of the Super Friends* to be *the* best Super Friends series of all, and I strongly agree. The biggest change occurred this season with Bill Callaway replacing Norman Alden as the voice of Aquaman in both.

MARK MCCRAY: *Challenge of the Super Friends* is my favorite of the *Super Friends* series, mainly because you finally get to see Lex Luthor, Solomon Grundy and Giganta. What's also cool is that it's the first series that actually explores the origins of the Super Friends.

THE WORLD'S GREATEST SUPER FRIENDS (1979 to 1980)

WILL RODGERS: This was the last season that featured the core group of five and the Wonder Twins and Gleek in half-hour episodes. This was also the shortest season of the Super Friends ever produced, with only eight new half-hour episodes, but they aired around reruns to fill out and make a full hour. These episodes were inspired off of stories from great literature, most notably Aladdin, King Arthur and the Knights of the Round Table, Tolkien, *20,000 Leagues Under the Sea*, *Frankenstein* and *The Wizard of Oz*. Plus, there were the returns of Lex Luthor and Mr. Mxyzpltk and the ever-popular Universe of Evil episode featuring the Super Friends' evil counterparts.

MARK MCCRAY: This was the season that introduced the Multiverse: a universe where all of the Super Friends — including Gleek the Monkey — are evil. And Aquaman is wearing a patch over his eye like a pirate, and it was a nice surprise to see that.

SUPER FRIENDS THE SHORTS: *THE SUPER FRIENDS HOUR* 1980/ *SUPER FRIENDS* 1981/ *SUPER FRIENDS THE LOST EPISODES* 1983

WILL RODGERS: I consider the '80s shorts of the Super Friends to be the low rent period of the show. Hanna-Barbera began animating seven-minute shorts with various team-ups. The 1980 and 1981 shorts followed the same format. Superman, Batman and Robin and Wonder Woman were guaranteed to be seen each week. There would always be a team-up with any of them along with Black Vulcan, Samurai and Apache Chief, while the abbreviated 1981 season first introduced El Dorado. The Wonder Twins were usually in the middle short and were teamed up with either Superman, Batman and Robin or Wonder Woman or all four of them. Aquaman would be featured in water-based episodes, and we would see the return of Bizarro, Mr. Mxyzpltk and one episode with the Riddler in 1980.

The seventh season is known today as the "Lost Season" or the "Lost Episodes." Hanna-Barbera produced these shorts, which changed things up, but they were only seen by fans on Saturday mornings in Europe and Australia, but *not* in the U.S. until years later in syndication packages. This particular season finally saw the Wonder Twins teaming up with Aquaman, the Atom, the Flash, Green Lantern and Hawkman and Hawkgirl. We would also see the return of the Legion of Doom as well as a pair of Superman and Batman team-ups, and one episode with Superman, Batman and Wonder Woman.

SUPER FRIENDS: THE LEGENDARY SUPER POWERS SHOW (1984 to 1985)

WILL RODGERS: The Super Friends' return to Saturday mornings in the U.S. was a partial tie-in to the Kenner Super Powers toy line, and I do mean partial. This season had two 15-minute episodes each week and the newest elements to this series were the introduction and inclusion of Firestorm the Nuclear Man, and turning him into a superstar overnight. (Firestorm also replaced Aquaman, whose only presence in this season was in the series intro). Wonder Woman had a slightly new look and a new voice, and Adam West joined the cast and took over as the voice of Batman in this season and the last one as well. The presence of the original Hanna-Barbera-created characters Black Vulcan, Samurai, Apache Chief, El Dorado and the Wonder Twins were very strong that season. Lex Luthor in his new green power suit, and the new design of Brainiac, were featured in this season, and we also saw the return of Mr. Mxyzptlk and the one-time appearance of the Mirror Master. This season also introduced Darkseid, and two of his minions, Kalibak and Desaad from Jack Kirby's Fourth World comics. Plus, the Kenner Super Powers toy line added Firestorm, Darkseid, Kalibak and Desaad to their action-figure lineup.

ALAN BURNETT: Cyborg would soon become our minority character on the show, and we dealt with some others too. But the minority characters from Hanna-Barbera were just token manufactured things who had no background, no life, no history, no nothing. Even in 1983 they were embarrassing to me.

SUPER POWERS TEAM: GALACTIC GUARDIANS (1985 to 1986)

WILL RODGERS: For the Super Friends' final season, this was the graduation series. In addition to the change of title from *Super Friends* to *Super Powers Team*, Hanna-Barbera changed the animation style and character designs, which puts this series much closer to the Super Powers toy line. While Superman, Batman and Robin, Wonder Woman and Firestorm were there, another new star would join them: Cyborg, of the *New Teen Titans*, became the last new superhero to join their ranks, and was frequently teamed up with Firestorm. In addition to Darkseid and his minions, Lex Luthor, Brainiac and Mr. Mxyzptlk, this season also featured appearances by the Joker, Penguin, Scarecrow and the Royal Flush Gang. With the exception of Samurai, most of the Hanna-Barbera-created Super Friends characters were eliminated, but this series saw the return of Aquaman, Hawkman, Green Lantern and the Flash, who were primarily seen in the background. This final season has two memorable episodes: the first telling of the origin of Batman in "The Fear," and "The Death of Superman," which was the only episode to feature the entire Super Powers Team.

ALAN BURNETT: "The Death of Superman" came straight from a 1961 comic book written by Jerry Siegel and drawn by Curt Swan. In that issue, Luthor was as mean as he's ever been, pretending to have reformed and then killing Superman. I went back and read that as an adult, and was kind of startled. It's pretty powerful stuff for a kid, because there was no recovery from that story. He was dead. When it came to *Super Friends*, we did that story delicately. In the original story, Superman turns green from Kryptonite poisoning, and one of the notes was, "Do we have to have him turn green?" I said, "*Yes*, you have to have him turn green." We got away with that story and it's one of my favorites.

MARK MCCRAY: "The Death of Superman," where Superman seems to die from Kryptonite poisoning, was a pretty progressive episode, with Firestorm blaming himself somehow for the death. They really went for it there.

ALAN BURNETT: Obviously Superman lives at the end of the episode. Firestorm blames himself for not coming to Superman's aid quickly enough, and Superman was poisoned by Darkseid. In the course of going to the Fortress of Solitude and putting tags on everything, the Super Friends discovered that Superman was working on this method where he could slow down his metabolism to keep himself from fully dying from Kryptonite. But for the cure they have to throw him into the sun to recharge him. Firestorm ended up being an important part of the Super Friends, getting Superman's body into the sun. After that he was revived and life went on.

ANTHONY DESIATO (host, *Digging for Kryptonite* podcast): Despite some hokeyness, I found myself pulled right into *Super Friends*. Yes, the Friends will always win, but you never know *exactly* how. And one of the final episodes, "The Death of Superman," really had some teeth as it showed — however briefly — the world mourning the Man of Steel. It's extremely easy to see why this show captured the imagination of an entire generation, and I was further struck by how long the series ran. In terms of presenting these characters outside of comics, it carried the torch admirably for more than a decade.

Born December 19, 1938 (the same year as Superman's debut) in Oklahoma City, Oklahoma, Danny Dark voiced the Man of Steel through the entire run of Super Friends *in all its incarnations. Beyond that, though, he is more popularly known for his commercial voiceover work, proclaiming "This Bud's for You" (for Budweiser), "Sorry, Charlie" (StarKist tuna) and "Raid Kills Bugs Dead" (Raid). In the late 1950s he was a radio DJ, working as one for Los Angeles' KLAC between 1963 and 1966. If you re-member CBS network promos in the '70s and NBC's in the '80s, that was Dark's voice you were hearing. He died on June 13, 2004, at age 65, of a pulmonary hemorrhage.*

DANNY DARK (voice actor, "Clark Kent/Superman," *Super Friends*): The Superman I voiced was very broad and big. Everybody who has played him since has toned him down, which is cool. I liked my Superman, because he was both good-natured and bigger than life, and I loved that there was never any violence. I never hit one person on that show. I may have pushed them back with super-breath, but I never punched anyone. (*Pat Jankiewicz*, Star-log *magazine*)

WILL RODGERS: Most comic book and Superman fans who are older than me got their start with Bud Collyer as the voice of Superman, whether it be the Superman radio series, the Fleischer animated shorts or the Filmation cartoons of the '60s. But for me, it was the late, great Danny Dark who would be my first animated Superman. I remember reading an interview that when his daughter was in grade school, Danny called one of her school friends, who was a big fan, and spoke to him as Superman. In my adult years, I could tell that Danny Dark was a radio man, just by his speaking sound. Whenever I would hear any commercial or network promo that Danny Dark did, I would always think of Superman. And whenever I read any DC Comics from the '70s to early-to-mid-'80s that Superman is in, whether it be *Superman, Action Comics, World's Finest, Justice League of America* or *DC Presents*, I would always hear the voice of Danny Dark.

MARK MCCRAY: I liked Danny Dark, but I thought his characterization was a little too literal. It took me a while, but I finally got used to him in the episode "History of Doom," which has three aliens arriving on Earth after a huge disaster. They go through the files of the origins of the Hall of Justice and the Legion of Doom to find out what happened. Danny Dark is actually great in that episode, because he sounds scared, he sounds concerned and he sounds like he can't believe that this has actually happened to the planet. He freaking delivers the emotion that was needed for that episode.

MARK WAID: *Super Friends* was a very childish show and there were no true villains, just misguided scientists, and you always learned a corny lesson at the end of the episodes. But boy, did that show do so much to keep Superman in the public eye during the early '70s. That was a big accomplishment. It also made Aquaman a household name. There *is* a cool episode in the first season where they have Clark telling the origin of Superman to the Wonder Twins, Marvin and Wendy. That's fun to watch; it's a long sequence in the middle of the episode. There are no new details in the origin, but it's always fun to see it in different media. Even though they made only 13 episodes, they managed to keep them rerunning on the air for four or five years before they did any sort of refresh to it. It was clearly popular.

WILL RODGERS: I honestly and firmly believe that the *Super Friends* series helped pave the way for future media like the *Justice League Unlimited* animated series as well as *Justice League Action*, the various Justice League animated movies, and even the live-action Justice League movie (both versions). The Super Friends is, to this day, *the* longest-running animated series of a DC Comics property.

ANTHONY DESIATO: After watching almost all of the Superman-centric *Super Friends* installments, it quickly became clear why it resonated with me: A colorful team of do-gooders, with largely interchangeable personalities and a cool base of operations, relying on each other to beat the bad guy — it's essentially an earlier version of *Mighty Morphin Power Rangers*, which I did grow up with and remember fondly.

The Broadway musical It's a Bird… It's a Plane… It's Superman *may have had a Broadway run, but more people likely caught it in the ABC late-night version that aired on February 21, 1975. It was shot on video over a total of three days and was changed from its progenitor in a number of ways. For starters, its runtime was much shorter and Mafia-like gangsters replaced the Chinese acrobats of the play (the belief possibly being that this would somehow be perceived as less racist — though that point is arguable). Songs "Doing Good,"*

"It's Super Nice," "So Long, Big Guy" and "We Don't Matter at All" were excised, while the song "It's a Great Country" was added.

Producing was Norman Twain, with Jack Regas serving as director and Romeo Muller adapting the book by David Newman and Robert Benton. The cast featured Kenneth Mars (the original The Producers, Young Frankenstein) as Max Mencken, Loretta Swit (Hot Lips Houlihan on the TV version of M★A★S★H) as Sydney, David Wayne (The Andromeda Strain and the 1974 version of The Front Page) as Dr. Segwick, Lesley Ann Warren as Lois Lane and David Wilson in the dual roles of Clark Kent and Superman.

David Wilson as Superman in the 1975 version of It's a Bird ... It's a Plane ... It's Superman (photo courtesy David Wilson; Superman © and TM DC Comics/Warner Bros. Discovery).

Warren was born August 16, 1946 in New York City. At age 17 she made her debut on Broadway in 110 in the Shade. Two years later, in 1965, she received acclaim for her portrayal of the title role in Cinderella for television. Appearing in a wide variety of films, she was a Golden Globe nominee for her role as Dana Lambert in the 1970 to 1971 season of Mission: Impossible, winning in 1978 in the category of Best Actress in a Drama Series for the NBC miniseries Harold Robbins' 79 Park Avenue. An Academy Award nomination came her way for 1983's Victor/Victoria, with two additional Golden Globe nominations for 1984's Songwriter and 1990's Family of Spies. Her most recent film roles have been 2019's The Bay House and 3 Days with Dad and 2020's Echo Boomers. On television, she was seen in the TV movies Twinkle All the Way (2019) and Blind Psychosis (2020) as well as a 2020 episode of Broke and a 2021 episode of All Rise.

Wilson was born David Patrick Wilson on February 26, 1949 in Jamaica, New York. Pursuing sports in high school, in his senior year he decided to star in Northport High School's production of South Pacific, opposite future star Patti LuPone. Stage roles in New York and Chicago followed, though in 1971 he made the move to Los Angeles. There *he appeared in films like 1973's* The Seven-Ups, *1977's* Audrey Rose, *1978's* Gray Lady Down *(which also featured Christopher Reeve), 1983's* Eddie and the Cruisers, *1991's* Flight of the Intruder *and 2015's* Collar. *His TV debut was in 1975 as the Man of Steel in* It's a Bird… It's a Plane… It's Superman. *Guest appearances on episode television and roles in miniseries followed.*

DAVID WILSON (actor, "Clark Kent/Superman," *It's a Bird… It's a Plane… It's Superman*): I grew up with George Reeves; I watched *Adventures of Superman* religiously when I was a kid. Norman Twain, the producer, came to me and I thought, "Okay, this could be kind of fun." I'd never seen the musical, so I was kind of surprised that they were even making the thing. But it seemed like it was going to be fun and they'd already assembled a pretty good cast. They already had Lesley Ann committed to it as well as David Wayne and Allen Ludden. There were a bunch of people there who were pretty significant. But he must have been operating on a fairly small budget — they didn't pay me anything. When they came to me, they were in a bind looking for somebody and I happened to fill the bill.

LESLEY ANN WARREN (actor, "Lois Lane," *It's a Bird… It's a Plane… It's Superman*): I don't know if I actually saw the Broadway show, because by that time I was living in L.A. But I certainly knew about it, and I knew Norman Twain from Broadway and my theatrical ventures. So I felt excited about the project and looked forward to doing it. It was definitely a big deal. It was, and is, an iconic comic book and I felt honored to do it. Just a great opportunity to play Lois Lane in any form.

DAVID WILSON: This was shot in only a few days. It was just like, bam! bam! Like a live production. There was just no time for thought processes about anything. Norman hired Jack Regus as director, who directed Las Vegas revues, and that's how we did it, because he was used to that kind of thing. It was amazing that we got what we got out of it, but it was because of the professionalism of the other people involved.

LESLEY ANN WARREN: We probably rehearsed for maybe a week before we started taping, but having come up through the ranks of summer stock where you have to rehearse an entire show and learn it in five days, I felt up to the challenge. And I *loved* working with David. We got along famously and we had a lot of fun. We laughed a lot through the whole thing, so it was really great to work with him.

DAVID WILSON: Lesley Ann just likes to have fun and she is fun. She was always fun to work with and I really liked her. She's one of my favorites, and it was just kind of wacky. She comes from a musical theater background, so for her it wasn't a big deal to play Lois Lane. The problem she had is that she wanted to be considered for more powerful, lofty roles, like in *Superman: The Movie*, but she ran into the same thing that I did: They were basically having us come in to audition, because I think Dick Donner was on a fishing trip, and that would kind of shorthand his job. We got caught in their whirlwind where they were seeing everybody even though we were kind of ruled out right away because of *It's a Bird*.

In approaching the roles of Clark Kent and Superman, Wilson was particularly struck by the idea that there were two ways to look at the fact that he was an alien.

DAVID WILSON: First, that he was so revered and valued by his parents, they put him in a rocket and shot him off of Krypton. The other side, though, was the vulnerability or frailty in that. At the moment they shot him off the planet, he's this infant who's essentially being abandoned by his parents. They're throwing their child into the unknown, casting him out into the universe. He's got all of this information that's coming to him that's supposed to let him fit in, but when I was playing it, what was going through my mind was, "Why didn't they love me enough to keep me there? Why would they throw me away?" Which went into a whole thing in there when Lois shows up when I fail to do something. I *failed* in my job as Superman. I couldn't save something. So, there I am, she shows up, and I'm just falling apart. She's trying to soothe me, but it's very comical this big superhero guy having that kind of vulnerability. But in that moment, that failure tapped into the idea of being cast out in the universe.

The audience wouldn't know that, but that's just part of the process that, as an actor, you look at. It's not just technique, it's all about your imagination and creating imaginative events based on things that are not really true. You're always working in imaginary circumstances and a lot of acting techniques deal with real things in a person's life where they're constantly going back and digging up these events and trying to replicate the emotions that they went through — or that they went through at that time. Well, there's nothing honest or truthful about that, because that's through a glass darkly at something that may or may not have happened. That's an interpretation that's made by a child… or somebody that's no longer there. The technique that I was taught, and that I really loved, was really healthy, because you had to use your imagination based on things that were in your life; things that were real and current to create the right kind of emotions. What you want to do is take things that are present in your life now and use them to create imaginary circumstances as they happen, because that would evoke the real emotion. That would evoke the real behavior without having to be attached to some event that you might not be able to bury.

There was a challenge during production of creating the flying sequences and It's a Bird *was apparently the first to use green screen rather than blue screen, due to the fact that David Wilson has* really *blue eyes and, as a result, on tape it looked like he had holes where his eyes should have been.*

DAVID WILSON: The way they had me flying around — to tell you how hokey this was — they took a rolling table and I had to stretch myself out on the table and arch my back so that you couldn't see any fat on my stomach. My stomach would have to be in one position for hours as they rolled me back and forth across the stage in front of the blue screen. Well, they went to dailies the next morning and the problem was that the blue screen was the same color as my eyes, so it looked like I had holes in my head. They're flying me back and forth and you're looking right through my skull. That's when they said they had to go with a different color, which is when they chose green, figuring nobody's eyes would be green. All of the CG stuff happened afterwards, but the flying stuff with green screen was the first time that was used.

Unfortunately, It's a Bird… It's a Plane… It's Superman *did not fare well either in the eyes of the critics or the ratings, but both Warren and Wilson appreciate the fact that they have been, and forever will be, part of the lore of the Man of Steel.*

LESLEY ANN WARREN: Because it was a takeoff or comedic fantasy take on Superman, I knew that in my interpretation of Lois Lane there needed to be some quirkiness and an unusual quality that the actual Lois Lane in the comic book version or the television version *didn't* bring. Beyond the professional young woman, there had to be other aspects to work in the genre that they were present-ing. And even though it didn't do well, to be part of the the Superman legend is a wonderful gift.

DAVID WILSON: Having played the part of Superman, I don't think it ever leaves you. That's a real effect of the character on the artist. It's like people that play Jesus Christ, they have a tough time afterwards in the choices they make. I think any of the superhero roles affect you in that way. All of a sudden, you're taking a look at the choices you're making. There's got to be something in there that calls to doing those characters, number one. And one of the things I think is building the strength of character to make positive choices, rather than the negative.

RAY MORTON: I've never seen this musical performed on stage in either of its versions, although I have read the script for the original production. I did see the 1975 ABC-TV version, which I know was greatly altered from the stage production, and it was *terrible*. It is my understanding that the Broadway version received good reviews and is well thought of, but I found the text to have the same problem as Newman and Benton's drafts of *Superman: The Movie* — it's clear that they have trouble taking Superman and his mythos seriously, and so end up treating the whole thing a little too lightly; not quite mocking it, but definitely letting us know they are smarter than the material. The result is neither satire nor camp, but just a bit silly and therefore utterly inconsequential.

There's no question that 1975 was a bumpy year for the Man of Steel, notably from the critical drubbing that It's a Bird… It's a Plane… It's Superman *took (check the musical out on YouTube to form your own opinion), but also the fact that it was the same time period when Jerry Siegel and Joe Shuster returned following the very public announcement of* Superman: The Movie *being in development — not with what would have been their third lawsuit to recapture the rights to the character, but rather Siegel's extended "press release" that he sent out to the media that would, in the end, change everything for them and conclude decades of struggle between the duo and DC.*

DANIEL BEST (editor, *The Trials of Superman*): In 1975, Jerry Siegel, annoyed and frustrated over decades of living in poverty, decided to take the bull by the horns and prepared a press release that he sent to the media. Naturally the mainstream media were never going to print it as is — it's far too long — but it had the desired effect. News outlets sat up and took notice and began to sense that this was a story that had a lot of legs: The creators of Superman were poor and in ill health; DC Comics was making millions and they were getting nothing. Even better, or worse — depending on how you saw it — DC was standing to make even more money with the multi-million-dollar-budgeted *Superman* movie, and its trickle-down-effect in the form of increased sales of merchandise, comics and the like, and not a cent of that would be going to the two people whose vision had made it all possible.

MICHAEL SANGIACOMO (journalist; member, The Siegel & Shuster Society): The worst blow came when Jerry and Joe learned that they were not going to be credited with Superman's creation in the upcoming 1978 movie. Jerry publicly asked for support to force the issue, and got it.

DANIEL BEST: Siegel's essay (really, it was an essay, not a press release per se) documented all of the issues that both he and Joe Shuster had faced — the legal battles, the broken promises and, most importantly, by singling out Jack Liebowitz, Siegel was able to give the whole sordid saga a human face. People finally had a name to chase, as opposed to a company which could hide behind corporate structures. And the media lapped it up in spades.

JERRY SIEGEL (co-creator, Superman): For about 12 years Joe and I had sought the renewal rights to Superman under the copyright renewal terms. In April of 1975, Joe and I agreed not to take our case to the Supreme Court, because we were informed by our attorney that if we did not do so, he had been informed, National would then consider making a financial arrangement which would benefit Joe and me. Again, we placed our trust and faith in the good intentions, fairness and generosity of National. Six months since then… there had been nothing offered. We hoped that we had not been victimized into giving up our rights to appeal to the Supreme Court without receiving anything in return.

NEAL ADAMS: They had been silent for 15 years on the advice of their lawyers who told them that, when they got to be 60, they will go, if they have to, to the Supreme Court and get the rights to Superman back into their hands. And then, when the time rolled around, the lawyers didn't answer their mail or phone. They essentially deserted the boys, these 60-year-old boys, and so Jerry, in frustration, wrote this very, very powerful letter. And it got to *The Washington Post* and it got to *The New York Times* and it got to various people, and when *The Washington Post* wrote an article about it, it was carried on the news wires and it was carried in other newspapers. I read it and then I saw the article in *The Post* and I sat back and I thought about it. I thought, "Well, you know what? This will slowly go away. And that's not going to fix things. What has to happen is somebody has to stand up and say, 'Okay, starting today, we're going to decide that this is going to end; that those guys are going to get some kind of pension from DC Comics, the people that are making all of this money, and we are not going to stop working on it until it happens.'"

JEFF TREXLER (Interim Director, Comic Book Legal Defense Fund Inc.): The thing that keeps ringing out for me in Jerry Siegel's press release in the early 1970s is that he talked about his American Dream turning into the American nightmare. If you read *The Epic of America*, James Trunzo Adams' work where the term "American Dream" is coined, it's not that everybody's equal and it's not even about owning a house. The original American Dream idea is that everybody has the opportunity to exercise their talents, to benefit from their talents. Everybody has things they're good at, and the American Dream removes all the obstacles to doing that. The book is amazing, because it's against consumerism, it's against acquisition and it's against who has the most toys wins.

America is about a whole lot of people coming together with a lot of different talents and abilities, and they exercise their abilities and something happens. Everybody who is successful is able to benefit from their success, and this is equally important as it shines through what Jerry Siegel writes: They have a responsibility to help others, so once you get successful, then you have a *responsibility* to make sure that everybody else out there with their own talents or their own interests have the same opportunity that you have to exercise those talents and to benefit from those talents. When Stan Lee does the whole "great power, great responsibility" thing, that's going back decades. You're talking about people who grew up in the Depression era. *That's* what people were talking about. It was about if everybody should have this opportunity, everybody should get these benefits. And if you succeed, you have an obligation to help other people out.

MICHAEL EURY: You should never judge history through the lens of today! There is always a perspective that is connected to the era that defines the rational of participants. Back in 1938, did DC or National feel they were taking a gamble? They probably felt they were. Did they say, "Boy, we've got these two hayseeds from Cleveland and boy, did we pull one over on them?" Who knows? Siegel and Shuster, by signing their rights away, they might have felt that was a generous offer at the time. I don't know; I've not gotten in on that battle.

JEFF TREXLER: When you read Jerry Siegel's open letter in the 1970s, which is essentially sort of a 1930s Depression America document, he has a sense of betrayal. It's that there's a way that things are *supposed* to work in this country, but it didn't. And he sees it as a sign that everybody is broken. What really works for Siegel is that if he had written the letter five years earlier or five years later, it wouldn't have connected. But he's writing in the period of time that not only is Watergate happening, but we were approaching the Bicentennial, while there's a sense looming over the country at this time that our national contract is broken; that we're about to celebrate 200 years and we've come through the death of the American Promise. That's part of what made Siegel's letter so powerful; that he could be the symbol of everything that was wrong and that this character he created was a symbol of everything that's right with America, but also a symbol of where we were at in the American Story. It also gave the people an opportunity to very easily make things right. And, in the end, they did.

MICHAEL EURY: It's the same thing with Stan Lee versus Jack Kirby and Jack Kirby versus Marvel. People do their work-for-hire stuff. I've worked for Marvel and worked for DC. I've signed work-for-hire agreements and I understand that going in to it. Is it fair in the long run? No. Did DC ultimately try to make some restitution? Yes, they did. Did they do it voluntarily? No, not really. I just got reminded of this in very great clarity, because in my book *The Krypton Companion*, one of the interviews I did was with Neal Adams, and Neal Adams was sort of the cattle prod to Warner Bros to get them to do right by Siegel and Shuster. Adams kind of primed the wheel to get all this going, more or less. I guess he did for 1977 to 1978 what would be akin to a social media shaming today. He just kind of got the players into place to do right by the creators of Superman and finally got a good deal for them. They *did* get handsomely compensated during the day for the material they were doing, so while I think they were victimized to some degree, I don't think that they were victims. I know that sounds wishy-washy.

ELLIOT S! MAGGIN: I had written a story called "The Man Who Created Superman," and the premise is that it's about a guy who's stranded on a desert island. His name is Joey Jerome and he's like 73. He's got nobody to talk to except the wildlife on this island, so he sits there telling them stories. He's got lions lying down with lambs, because he's such a good storyteller, writing up these vivid stories about this superhero character who comes to Earth and flies around wearing a cape. Everything's the same about him as Superman, except that he doesn't have this big "S" on his chest. As he's creating stories, or thinks he's creating them, they're actually happening in the world with which he's out of touch. It's a pretty good story, and I wrote that I would like to dedicate this story to Jerry Siegel and Joe Shuster, who created Superman. But Julie Schwartz said, "We can't do that." I asked, "Why not?" and he says, "We're not allowed to publish their names." Well, I said, "That's pretty vile," and he published the story but took the dedication out. I told everybody about it and I think it only got Neal Adams more pissed. Then we got this letter from Jerry about a year later.

ARLEN SCHUMER: Neal Adams obviously did not do it "alone" — Jerry Robinson was significant when you look at it — but the converse way to say it is that without Neal, it never would have happened because, and this is part of the Neal Adams story, of the fact that the clout that he had at that point in comic book history was significant. When Neal died, there was such an outpouring of sentiment with people talking about Neal like he was a father to them; so many artists making livings today in various media, various forums, art directors, illustrators, comic book people… you name it. They all come out to say how significant Neal was in their lives. So, when Neal spoke out for Siegel and Shuster, people

252

listened.

DANIEL BEST: At the time, Adams was potentially the most important artist working both in and out of the comic book industry. Highly lauded for his realistic approach and dynamic line work, Adams made an impact upon comic books and artists in the same way that Jack Kirby did before him. Whereas Adams' generation will say that Kirby was the primary influence, those who followed will often point towards Neal. Jerry Robinson was no slouch either. Recognized as the co-creator of Robin and the Joker (or sole creator, if you like — debate that with DC and Bob Kane's family), Robinson had turned his back on the comic book industry, but retained an incredible amount of insider knowledge and, more importantly, both men were far more articulate than Siegel and Shuster. And both had influence and used it. Once they got involved, they drew in others and got the story both in print and the electronic media, appearing on *The Tom Snyder Show*, a nationally-syndicated television show of the time. DC was never going to win this and, to their credit, they approached the duo and worked out a pension plan complete with medical and health benefits and hoped it'd all go away. It *did* go away, for a while, but it eventually resurfaced.

TOM ANDRAE (co-author, *Batman & Me*): After Jerry came out with that blast for the media, I offered to support their cause. I was teaching at the time and I did what I could, which is little, but I was another voice. I was part of fandom and he started opening up more. And yes, he was very bitter and, more than bitter, he was traumatized by the whole thing of losing the rights and all the money that he lost. He grew up with a fairly poor, modest income, and Joe was even poorer than he was.

ANTHONY TOLLIN (author, *The Shadow: The Making of a Legend*): I think there was a lot of sympathy for Joe Shuster, but mixed feelings for Siegel. As a young professional, I didn't want to see Siegel and Shuster starving; they'd created one of the most iconic figures or characters of the 20th century. By the same token, they had also been compensated far better than Walter Gibson had on the Shadow or Frances Striker on the Lone Ranger. A lot of the younger editors — Paul Levitz, Bob Rozakis and Jack Herridge among them — and people in my generation in the business certain had a lot of sympathy for them. The resentment came from people who actually worked with Jerry Siegel.

ARLEN SCHUMER: My take on the Siegel and Shuster issue is that it's the greatest ripoff to take place since the sale of Manhattan Island. Peter Minuit bought the island for $24 from the Indians. Siegel and Shuster sold Superman for $130, and if you consider how much has been made over the years, it's pretty comparable. Now if I were directing a docudrama, the film I see in my mind is a rainy scene in 1966 as celebrities file into a theater for the opening of the Broadway musical *It's a Bird… It's a Plane… It's Superman*. Camera pans to Siegel and Shuster as broken men living on the poverty line, too poor to afford tickets, and they weren't invited because they were blackballed by DC Comics; black-balled from their own creation. How's that for an opening scene? Superman is the ultimate American success and tragedy story. Yes, thanks to Neal Adams and Jerry Robinson, we have a somewhat "happy ending" in which they get their stipends — which was a drop in the bucket. But this was literally a grassroots campaign, started by Jerry Siegel who was mad as hell and wasn't going to take it anymore.

PAUL LEVITZ: You can't go back and say, "What do we owe somebody for the deal that happened 35 years ago?" In part, you don't honestly know. And in many cases there was no real economic issue involved. I remember a lovely conversation with [Wildcat co-creator] Irwin Hasen, who was a good friend and a guy I enjoyed thoroughly. One day he turned around to me looking at some-thing and he said, "We never talked about you paying me for Wildcat." I said, "I'll take you to lunch; it'll cover everything we ever made out of Wildcat." Part of that is a smart-ass response, but it's not that far from the truth. Wildcat has shown up as a fifth banana in the books, and maybe somewhere in the ensuing 20 or 30 years after that conversation, he might get a little more exposure, so I would have ordered him dinner as well as lunch.

TOM DE HAVEN: With Siegel as a civil service worker, Shuster a delivery man — it's such a grim story. And DC in a sense knew they were creating the story and couldn't stop it. And they really ought to have, because it besmirched the company's reputation for 70 years and they could have stopped it anywhere along the line, because they knew what was going on. And they didn't. It's an incredible story of a company and a character's creators.

ARLEN SCHUMER: The minute you say there are two sides to this story, you're endorsing the corporate point of view. Whenever you say, "Hey, they were paid pretty well; look at the money they were making back then, nobody was making that kind of money," you are taking the corporate point of view. And what is the corporate point of view? When you slave in the work-for-hire system, no matter how much you're being paid, you're still not being paid enough. You're still owned and bought. They might have been well paid for the time, but who gives a damn in the scheme of things? This is like saying before free agency, a ball player was paid a lot of money back then adjusted for inflation. They were still cattle;

their lives were still not their own. When somebody said to Mickey Mantle, "Hey, Yankees Dynasty! You were a part of that," he goes, "Let me tell you something, if we had free agency back when I was playing, there would be no such thing as the Yankees Dynasty" — meaning the players were owned. When you begin to examine the Siegel and Shuster case microscopically, there were a lot of wrong turns or maybe they had the wrong lawyer. No matter what it was, who cares? They basically were individuals who went up against the corporate monolith in the 1940s, in the pre-enlightened age that we live in now, and they lost. They lost everything. They lost their lives, basically.

You have to look at the Siegel and Shuster case a little bit more macro than micro. And the macro view is that two kids created Superman, sold it to a corporation and lost everything. Now does the "docudrama" I mentioned have a happy ending? Thanks to Neal Adams and Jerry Robinson, it does. The docudrama of their lives does not end on a totally tragic note, thanks to the efforts of Siegel himself in writing that article; and then Neal Adams reading it and using his clout as an industry giant. It's hard to imagine in today's fractured world of creators around the globe. It's hard to believe that a single artist in New York City, in the comic book world, could have that much "clout" during the pre-Internet, print journalism, television age of the 1970s. But those are the facts about Neal Adams at the time. And the whole point of this grassroots campaign was to shame a corporation, which technically did not have to give a dime to Siegel and Shuster based on what was upheld in court decades before.

PAUL LEVITZ: You know what? You don't have a time machine and you don't have the information of the era. We tried to do what we could for the first generation of creators based on what we were doing with their work on our watch. If we were taking Wildcat and making a Wildcat statue out of it and selling that, well okay, there should be a fair share of that we should send to Irwin as a thank you. What you do is try to play as fair with what you're doing with the understanding of what you're managing. And the parent company was benignly supportive of that. If you want to look at it as trying to be fair, that's part of it. If you want to look at it as trying to build a good relationship with a creative community, if you want to say you're paying for labor peace, there's a part of that too. But we did what we could for folks here and there; we were able to find an excuse to do it in a way that really made a difference in somebody's life.

ROBERT GREENBERGER: When Siegel re-entered the picture, he was bitter. I think he regretted not holding out for a bigger licensing deal in the beginning, which is what prompted those raging letters in the 1970s. And that wouldn't have gone anywhere if not for Neal Adams, who picked up the cause. But Siegel and Shuster, as far as I can tell — especially Siegel — just seemed bitter with a lot of axes to grind. And frankly, after Superman, where he wrote these great stories, he just didn't seem to have a feel for other characters. Stan Lee hired him as a proofreader in the '60s, but that didn't work out terribly well. And then there was Joe with his eyesight problems, which was just horrible, because he was a great cartoonist.

The efforts of Adams and others eventually reached the president of the International Press Corps, who offered a press conference on the subject any time he wanted. Needless to say, Adams accepted the offer.

NEAL ADAMS: The guy was *great*. He set up a press conference; we had many artists, creators of comic strips, that were in the New York area come up. Irwin Hasen came up, he did a drawing of Dondi with a tear in his eye, and we got letters from Milton Caniff and all these other guys getting behind Jerry Siegel and Joe Shuster. It was so impressive that after I made my personal statement, I got the hell out of there. But enter all the cartoonists, and it just totally torpedoed Warner Brothers. They were like, "Whoa, step back! We gotta do something about settling this. This can't go on."

What happened in the end, we sealed it up before the Christmas holidays [1975]. And so when the reporters called and we're finally able to accomplish just a couple of more little things, I said to the reporters, "You know, Warners was never involved in this to begin with. Now they've solved the problem and we have a Jerry Siegel and Joe Shuster that can go to see their character in the movies. Everybody's happy, they're happy, Warners is happy — Merry Christmas, guys." Hurray, great story. Warners came out looking good. In the end, they look like the rescuers.

It's exactly what I told them when I was talking to them. I said, "Look, you guys can end up easily being the good guys here. Question what it would cost you to hire a couple of secretaries and you're the good guys. You're the heroes. Why *wouldn't* you do that? You're gonna, you know, save this and it'll never show up again. You're good." And that's exactly the way it turned out. It's good for Warners, it's good for Jerry and Joe, it's good for the comic book business to get this stupid shit settled — everybody benefits. It worked out great.

Siegel and Shuster were reportedly paid a dividend of $20,000 a year (which would consistently go up in the years to come) as well as full medical insurance. Most importantly,

Creators Jerry Siegel and Joe Shuster in the days after Warner Bros. agreed to pay them annual fees and restored their credit to all things Superman. (courtesy Cleveland Public Library).

depending on who you ask, is the fact that their credit — Created by Jerry Siegel & Joe Shuster — was restored, first in the comics and then on screen as Superman: The Movie *unspooled. It would remain that way forever after. It should be noted that between 2001 and 2013, there were additional lawsuits filed by the Siegel and Shuster estates, but in the end DC retained ownership of Superman.*

PAUL LEVITZ: I wasn't in the executive offices and, frankly, the office of DC had no real control over any of that. The settlement was not made by DC Comics. Our life was on the sixth floor, the accounting department was on the eighth floor. Everything that was relevant to that settlement took place on the 30th and 31st floors where the Warner Communications senior executives were, *and* the legal department. DC was not a big company; it didn't have its own lawyers. The lawyers were provided by "mom and dad." And in the executive offices was Jack Liebowitz's nephew, and we still had Jack Liebowitz in those years. He hadn't gone emeritus yet. This was all transpiring over the heads of the little kids who made the comic books.

ROBERT GREENBERGER: By this time, Jenette Kahn was involved. Being younger with a different worldview than DC's management previous to her, she recognized the value of talent and she recognized that DC *did* owe Siegel and Shuster a debt. At the time, she and Neal Adams were an on-again/

off-again couple, and I think Neal would be whispering in her ear. Jenette made good and she went up the corporate ladder and cut the deal because A, on a moral standpoint something should be done, and B, there was the movie that was in pre-production at that point and they didn't want the bad publicity.

JEFF TREXLER: I think one of the reasons that you had more and more money going to Siegel and Shuster over the years was that you had fans who then got in positions of power in the comic industry, both as creators but also as executives. Paul Levitz ends up writing for DC, editing for DC and eventually becomes DC's publisher. You get to a point where you have people in the company at all levels who do what they do, in part because they love comics *and* they know the history *and* they get a bit of leeway to raise the money paid out here, raise it there and it goes on.

TOM ANDRAE: One of the times I talked to him after they got the settlement, I said, "Jerry, you did something like nobody else. You created Superman. I mean, talk about something to be proud of." In the end, he finally became aware of that. Before he died, he really came more to grips with it, and I think he really loved being in touch with the fans, because he'd been so much in the closet for so many years and worked at a succession of jobs, especially a typist clerk. It was the only job he could get, he said, because he knew how to type. He had such a long history of pain; he couldn't even pay for his child's milk when they were so poor and he even contemplated suicide. It was really a rough thing for him and he was really destitute.

Jerry still had trouble talking about Superman even after the settlement. The settlement was very important to them and, of course, he never felt that it was enough. He did mellow some when people told him how much Superman meant to them, but he never really got over it. For example, they wanted him to come to the opening of the Metropolis, Illinois Superman Museum, but he refused. He was still sort of reluctant to go into any kind of depth about the Superman stuff.

PAUL LEVITZ: Again, the younger generation was terrifically sympathetic to what had happened to Jerry and Joe. Without any sophisticated knowledge of what the legal issues were, access to that kind of information didn't exist and we weren't dealing in a transparency of an information era comparative to where we live now. Everybody was emotionally in favor of justice for Siegel and Shuster, but nobody was going to walk off their job to do it.

ELLIOT S! MAGGIN: Everybody thought they were good guys and the company was the bad guy until the company became the good guy, because we insisted on it. Not that we pushed them, but we just kept honoring Siegel and Shuster, referring to them in public. While I was in college reading Superman stories, I didn't know who Jerry Siegel and Joe Shuster were. Nobody knew, because DC wouldn't publish their names.

DAN JURGENS (co-writer and artist, *The Death of Superman*): The only thing I can say is that in 1993, we were out in California and the creative team on Superman went to L.A. We had dinner with Jerry and Joanne Siegel, hosted by Jenette Kahn and Paul Levitz. And it was a real treat to get to sit down with those two, interact with them and apologize for killing Superman. But one of the nice things about it was, it appeared in that moment that the Siegels had a very warm relationship with DC and with Paul and Jenette, who I think would have moved mountains for them in any possible way. And I enjoyed seeing that. It made me feel much better about things overall. I only can see what I observed and, in that moment, that night, the relationship between Paul and Jenette — representing DC Comics — and the Siegels appeared to be very warm. And it was so nice to see, because it gave us all a little bit of hope for our own future. And it was wonderful to be able to spend time with them. I went up to him and I said, "Yeah, I'm the guy who killed Superman, I'm sorry." "Oh yeah, he'll be back. It's all gonna work out."

And he just kind of laughed and said he enjoyed it and something about getting a kick out of the fact that I both wrote and drew it. I assured him, "We want to treat you right. Everybody here, we want to treat you right."

BRAD RICCA: I look at the story of Jerry Siegel and Joe Shuster romantically, like it's a tragedy. They create this icon and then they lost it, but that's oversimplifying the situation, because they don't *really* lose it. He's still there. And what they got at the end is their name attached to it again. I would argue — and I don't know if they would agree — that that's more important and ultimately has more impact than getting a check. Nowadays, if you see a Marvel movie, at the end the producers thank, like, 30 creators, but if you blink, you miss it. With Superman, you see their names. Every single time. That has the impact that you can create something on your own and it can go on to become something big. *And* you can still have some ownership of that. So I don't think their story is a tragedy at all. I mean, they created *Superman*. And *everybody* knows it. *That's* immortality.

CHAPTER VII
Christopher Reeve is Superman!

"Versimilitude."

It's a word that not too many people bandied about prior to 1978 and one that hasn't exactly become a part of the popular vernacular since. Yet it was the governing force during the making of Superman: The Movie *nearly 50 years ago and a primary reason that the film remains the one by which most other comic book-based movies are compared.*

RICHARD DONNER (director, *Superman: The Movie*): It's a word that refers to reality. I had it printed on big signs which were sent to every creative department — wardrobe, casting, special effects, you–name-it. It was a constant reminder that if we gave in to temptation, and parodied Superman, we would only be fooling ourselves. The story is bigger than life and it has humor, but there is reality in the characters. It's a comedy, a love story, an adventure and its own thing. But it's always true to the Superman legend and to the actors. It had to be total reality and they had to play it dead straight.

JEPH LOEB (writer, *Smallville*): The film's success was simple, really. They made a promise — "You'll believe a man can fly" — and then they delivered. It wasn't just that Superman took off and it didn't look absurd, even by 1978 standards. It was that the *story* flew. Superman as a concept is a bit of a Cinderella story. Clark Kent as the awkward teenager goes to the big city, meets the girl of his dreams and becomes a hero. That requires magic, and Dick Donner and Tom Mankiewicz made something that had it in spades. The real find was, of course, Christopher Reeve, who played both parts with such charm and wit, it defined Superman for generations.

MARK WAID (writer, *Superman: Birthright*): *Superman: The Movie* cemented my fandom for that character. I'd been reading comics since 1966 and had read my share of Superman stories, but he wasn't any more meaningful to me than Green Lantern or Flash. I really saw that movie and Christopher Reeve as an outgrowth of what I knew in the comics: the values, the character and the spirit of the character came through with him.

MICHAEL EURY (editor, *The Krypton Companion*): I can't remember a life without Superman. I'm 65, and so by the time I was watching television as a child, the George Reeves show was in syndication on TV. Then I'm eight when *Batman* with Adam West debuts and then following it, of course, is the superhero

*Christopher Reeve, considered by many to be the quintessential Man of Steel
(art © and courtesy D.C. Stuelpner; Superman © and TM DC Comics/Warner Bros. Discovery).*

mania including the Filmation Superman cartoon, which has Bud Collyer's voice — so I get introduced to a Superman of another generation with a new permutation for my generation. And it just continued on from there. But *then*, Christopher Reeve as Superman really just kind of epitomizes the character for me. He's wonderfully brought to life by him and he elevated an art form for all of us. If it weren't for Reeve taking it seriously in the verisimilitude that Donner insisted upon when they were filming the movie, it never would have worked. But he *was* Superman in the story and just sold it.

ROB O'CONNOR (co-host, *All Star Superfan Podcast*): "Don't thank me, Warden! We're all part of the same team!" Better people than I will write about the power, the indestructible legacy and impact of these films, how they changed the course of comic book films forever and how they'll likely never be bettered. All I'll say is that when I was 14, awkward and miserable, I would cheer myself up by scene-selecting the helicopter rescue scene and it left me smiling every single time. I love this film like it's a person that lives and breathes.

LAUREN SHULER DONNER (wife of Richard Donner; producer, the *X-Men* films): *Superman: The Movie* had an influence on me, an influence on Bryan Singer and so many other people. Bryan Singer just idolized Dick and looked up to *Superman: The Movie* as his template. When I approached Bryan with *X-Men*, I said to him, "We need to base these characters to be based in reality. If you feel that Logan is a real man or Aurora is a real woman, when she creates weather, you'll believe it. And Logan, with his healing power, you'll buy it. You have to do what Dick did when he shot the Kansas part of *Superman* with Glenn Ford and Phyllis Thaxter as Pa and Ma Kent. They were living, breathing characters, and when you met Superman as a young man, he was a *real man* even when you realized he wasn't from Earth." So *that's* how the movie influenced us: to make these things as grounded as possible so the audience could accept that they had superpowers.

JOHN KENNETH MUIR (author, *The Encyclopedia of Superheroes on Film and Television*): *Superman: The Movie* speaks trenchantly to the post-Watergate age of the mid-1970s. Specifically, Donner's film offers Superman up to audiences as a positive role model, a kind of wish-fulfillment alternative for a country that appeared mired in partisanship, bickering and corruption. Superman's promise that he would "never lie" to Lois (and to us) reflects this deep, burning national desire during the mid-1970s for a restoration of belief and trust in our elected leaders.

PAUL LEVITZ (writer, former DC Publisher): *Superman: The Movie* helped keep DC a viable company. It came right after the implosion and a time when comic sales were in horrible shape and it reminded the parent company that these things really have value. It doesn't mean we should publish a lot more of them or we should pay everybody a lot more, but we should definitely keep this stuff around and maybe something else good will happen with them. It was extraordinarily profitable for the company. At the time, I think it was the most profitable movie Warner Bros. had ever made. *And* we had solid merchandising around it and there was solid publishing. It was a good demonstration of the power of the character and the power of the category of comics profitability.

ROBERT GREENBERGER (writer, former DC Editor): The movie wasn't perfect, but it had such heart and such winning performances. It has film technology of Superman flying you never had seen before, and you had the John Williams score. All together you had this wonderful film. Richard Donner has a powerful vision that got muddied by the Salkinds and others, but you nonetheless had this amazing icon brought to life.

ALAN BURKE (co-host, *All Star Superfan Podcast*): Richard Donner set the bar by saying, "Hey, we know this is silly, but let's take two hours and imagine what it would be like if this really were to happen." He treated the material, the characters and the fans with respect, and that had simply never been done before when it came to superheroes on the big screen. Donner was the lighthouse, safely guiding the ship home.

CHRISTINE COLLYER (Bud Collyer's daughter): My two sons, who are grown now, were little kids when *Superman: The Movie* came out. It was so strange, because they didn't listen to radio and my father had died in 1969 and his work as Superman was sort of a missed period for them. Yet there was this movie and you could revert back to pictures that I have. It's just funny how it does turn around and the idea of Superman just keeps going and going.

DAVID WILSON (actor, "Clark Kent/Superman," *It's a Bird... It's a Plane... It's Superman*): *Superman: The Movie* wasn't even in the works when I picked up *It's a Bird*. It wasn't even on the horizon, so I guess somebody took a look at the fact that that was being done and said, "Okay, this is a good idea. Let's do Superman," and it started this whole donut rolling.

As originally conceived, Superman began his cinematic life in the form of two movies that were being shot simultaneously. While this may not sound so impressive in the 21st century and the aftermath of the Matrix *sequels and the* Lord of the Rings *trilogy, back in the 1970s it was fairly unprecedented. In fact, it had only been preceded by* The Three Musketeers *and* The Four Musketeers, *which were produced by the father-and-son team of Alexander and Ilya Salkind, who were the people who conceived of the idea of bringing the Man of Steel to the big screen.*

ILYA SALKIND (executive producer, *Superman:The Movie*): I was about five or six years old when I started reading the comic books, and it's the time when I really discovered Superman. I got hooked on the comic books. And then we — my father and I — had done *The Three* and *Four Musketeers,* which were a big hit. We were having dinner in Paris and we were wondering what we would do next. I said, "Why don't we do Superman?" He was very European, so he didn't know what it was, so I told him. Then he said, "Oh yeah, that sounds good." He went to his backers and came back and said, "They're excited." And that's how it all started.

RICHARD DONNER: You never realize how big and impossible a job it is to tackle a picture, because if you did, you'd probably never do it. I knew I had a major picture with major problems, but you surround yourself with very talented people, you have an approach and you're going to correlate all of those suggestions and thoughts — hopefully — into some sense of objectivity, and you go out and make it. We had the task of making that film out of my office. I had *a* secretary, *an* assistant and a wonderful editor. Things were a mess throughout the making of the entire film. Every time we wanted to do something, their production department would cancel it, bills weren't paid, people wouldn't deliver products and we had to hustle, rob, beg, borrow and steal.

JACK O'HALLORAN (actor, "Non," *Superman:The Movie* and *Superman II*): We were working for like eight weeks and I did something you're not supposed to do as an actor on a film: I took off and went across the continent without permission. I flew to America from England, because we had four days off. I flew back to Beverly Hills, got off the plane and went right to a payphone, because there were no cellphones, and called my accountant and asked how much money we had in the bank. He said, "Jack, we have a lot of checks that haven't cleared. They have to go physically back to Switzerland, and blah, blah blah." This was after eight weeks! I hung the phone up, called collect to Pinewood and said to Pierre Spengler the producer, "We have a problem." He said, "Where the hell are you?" I said, "Doctor tells me that I have this spasm in my back and I may have to lay on the beach for a few weeks until it subsides." He's like, "What? What? What? You've got to be at work on Monday." I said, "Well, if I don't have any money in my bank account, this pain may not go away." I hung up the phone and an hour or two later my accountant called and said, "I don't know what you did, but the money's in the bank."

RICHARD DONNER: *Superman* is a tribute to a lot of dedicated film-makers, I'll tell you that. On top of that, after working seven days a week, fifteen hours a day, I'd sometimes go home at night and dream about doing a two-character love story, set in one room. The challenges were enormous — they had to be — and many of them were of our own making. That's what you thrive on in this business. If there were two ways to film a scene — an easy way that would *look* easy on the screen, and a way that we all agreed was impossible — the answer was never in doubt. We'd shoot for the impossible.

Having decided they wanted to film Superman, *the Salkinds turned to Warner Bros./ DC on the subject, eventually announcing that there would be a $20-million budget for* Superman *and* Superman II, *which would be shot simultaneously.*

MARK WAID: The Salkinds approached National Periodicals and signed the contract with them on November 25, 1974 in what was a 25-year deal. When it came to Warner Bros.' involvement, the head of Warners' film production, a guy named Dick Shepherd, turned down any involvement on the studio's part. He chose to simply take the deal money, because he had no faith in the project.

RICHARD DONNER: The Salkinds made one picture called *The Three Musketeers* but, according to [director] Richard Lester, they found they had a long film and Richard said, "Hey, we can chop it in two and, adding a couple of days, we get a second finished film." So they made *The Four Musketeers* out of the footage and didn't want to pay the actors for the second picture. There is now a requirement in actors' contracts called "The Salkind Clause," that says you have to declare how many pictures you're doing when you're shooting. When *Superman* was packaged, I insisted that every contract for every actor had to be drawn on the basis of two films. From the beginning we had the intention of making two films. I used to get a hernia from carrying the script.

No surprise there, considering that the Salkinds had gone after Mario Puzo — at the height of The Godfather's *popularity — to write the screenplay for a reported fee of $350,000. They had first gone after Academy Award winner William Goldman, who turned them down flat. It wouldn't be long before screenwriters Robert Benton and the married team of David and Leslie Newman (Benton and David Newman had previously written* It's a Bird... It's a Plane... It's Superman) *joined up.*

ILYA SALKIND: The biggest question for us was how to give the impression that this was a serious project. That's when I had the idea to hire Mario Puzo. He had done *The Godfather*, so we got Puzo and soon after we got Marlon Brando. And everything started rolling.

ALEXANDER SALKIND (executive producer, *Superman: The Movie*): The problem with Superman is that he is unrealistic. He flies around in the air and he's immortal. Puzo found a way to make him vulnerable so that people can relate to him. When Puzo came to the very first meeting, he said, "My God, I think I want to handle this as a Greek tragedy." His first draft was very "heavy." (*Press Notes*)

RAY MORTON (film historian and author): Unfortunately, Puzo's script wasn't very good. He was a terrific novelist, but not a good screenwriter — he didn't have a great sense of dramatic or cinematic structure (he won Oscars for his scripts for *Godfathers I* and *II*, but those were co-written by Francis Coppola. Given that Puzo's only other screenplay — for 1974's *Earthquake* — was completely discarded, one can surmise that the success of the Coreleone scripts were due mostly to Coppola). Not helping matters, Puzo was also saddled with adapting the early '70s version of the comic book, so in his script Clark was a newscaster and Lois was a weather girl. Puzo's two overlong drafts were a mess of ideas, but buried in that mess was the basic building blocks of what eventually became *Superman* and *Superman II*: Jor-El and Lara send baby Kal-El to Earth just before Krypton explodes. Clark is raised in Kansas by the Kents and when he comes of age creates the Fortress of Solitude, through which he can communicate with the spirits of his dead parents; he then travels to Metropolis, where he gets a job as a reporter and begins his career as Superman; he battles master criminal Lex Luthor and foils his plan to blow up a nuclear bomb in Metropolis; Superman and Lois fall in love and Superman gives up his powers to be with her just as three Kryptonian villains arrive on Earth; Superman gives up Lois, regains his powers and battles the three villains. In the end, Superman wipes Lois' memory and the adventures of Superman continue.

DAVID NEWMAN (screenwriter, *Superman: The Movie*): Puzo's script was well-written, but it was a *ridiculous* script. For one thing, here was this producer, a guy named Pierre Spengler, who was going to supervise making this film for the Salkinds and he had a 550-page screenplay. Well, number one, I said, "You can't shoot this screenplay, because you'll be shooting for five years." And he said, "Oh no, it's fine." I said, "That's totally asinine," but that was literally a shooting script and they planned to shoot all 550 pages. You know, 110 pages is plenty for a script, so even for two features that was too much. It was a parody to start with, in an odd sort of way, but they parodied a parody and kept compounding that felony all the way through until it became much like the *Batman* television series. Obviously, we didn't want to lose the framework of the comic book, but I didn't want to make a joke out of it. There were things like Superman is looking for Lex Luthor, he flies down and taps a bald man on the shoulder. He turns around and it's Telly Savalas, who says, "Who loves ya, baby?" I couldn't see going that way with it.

Neither could the first director they approached, Richard Lester, who would ultimately go on to direct Superman II *and* III.

RICHARD LESTER (director, *Superman II*): I was asked because the Salkinds and I had worked together on the *Musketeers* films. I said, "I really don't think I know how to do this," because most of the work that I try to do has a fairly firm grounding in some form of social reality from which I can take off and go in the other direction. I remember saying, "I don't know how much Lois Lane would pay for her apartment. Or how much a pair of shoes costs in Metropolis." That's where I normally write my gags and do my little bits, and I felt I was wrong for it. I've never had a feeling for comic books or comic strips at all. So I declined but added, "The one thing that I think is really important is that you make sure you do it in period." They thanked me very much for my advice and ignored all of it. I wanted to do it in the '40s, but what do I know?

RAY MORTON: The Salkinds hired David Newman and Robert Benton, the playwrights of *It's a Bird... It's a Plane It's Superman* to rewrite Puzo's drafts. They were later joined by Newman's wife Leslie. It was during these rewrites that the decision was made to transform the project from one film into a two-part, two-movie saga. The Newmans and Benton built a narrative around Puzo's basic concepts and added in many more of their own. During this process, the basic plots of the two films took shape, many scenes and lines of dialogue that ended up in the finished film were created and Luthor's scheme to detonate the San Andreas Fault was introduced. But the Newmans and Benton weren't much better at structure than Puzo. Their scenes and characters are much more fleshed out than Puzo's, but their scripts are still more of a collection of bits than they are a dynamic dramatic narrative. And they still had a hard time taking Superman seriously. The scripts have a light, comedic tone and there is often the feeling they are mocking Superman under the guise of ostensibly celebrating him.

DAVID NEWMAN: The original idea was that Robert Benton and I were going to write *Superman* and Leslie and I were going to write *Superman II* simultaneously. But since we were going to write these two movies with all the same characters, we all had to begin making up the stories and the characters together, so we went to Europe where the producers were based. We wrote the first draft of the first film, and Bob got his next picture, which was *Kramer vs. Kramer*, so after the first draft he couldn't be involved on *Superman*. At that point Leslie shifted over to *Superman I*, then the two of us did both the first and second film.

While all of this was at work, the Salkinds were finding it impossible to raise the financing for the film. As Time *magazine reported, "In May 1974, at 5:30 in the afternoon, cocktail time at the Cannes Film Festival, an airplane flew over the strip of beach trailing a long banner announcing a new movie called* Superman. *In May 1975, three planes flew along the beach, and the announcement was repeated. In 1976, same time, same place, same message — but now there were five planes, two helicopters and one blimp."*

RICHARD DONNER: They had a tough time convincing the powers-that-be to give them the money, because no one was sure if they were going to deliver.

DAVID NEWMAN: They went to all these different guys who controlled distributorships around the world and said, "Would you be interested in Superman?" And all of these people said, "Yes, that character is well-known in my country. We would love to have a movie about Superman, provided it has that character and three major international stars." Those three stars could have been anybody playing anything.

LESLIE NEWMAN (co-writer, *Superman: The Movie*): Charles Bronson could have played an ashtray. They didn't care.

ILYA SALKIND: I had a horrible time with the financing group. They wanted a star in the leading role. We were talking at least a $15-million budget. You have two angles: one is getting the money, the other is selling the movie. My father's sales people felt that if we had a star to play the lead, it would help. I fought like a dog, because I felt that the actor playing Superman himself had to be unknown. I lost the fight then, and had to give the script to a couple of stars. I gave it to Robert Redford. We made him a big offer; nothing crazy, but big. He turned it down. He's a great actor and I think he was absolutely wise. He felt, as I knew, that to see Robert Redford flying through the air is almost impossible to accept. He had an intelligent reaction. I was able to go back and say, "Why don't we drop the idea of Superman as a star and put two big stars around him? One to play the villain and one to play his father from the planet Krypton?" That's how Brando got involved.

DAVID NEWMAN: People ask, "Why did Brando [who played Jor-El] get $3-million for 10 minutes of film?" Because, thanks to Brando they got the financing to make the movie, and thanks to Brando, Gene Hackman came in [as Lex Luthor, a role originally designed for Dustin Hoffman], and so on. Instead of being a Saturday morning kiddie movie, it became a big movie because the world's most famous actor was in it. It lent class to the production and made it a serious film.

ALEXANDER SALKIND: Brando would only work for 12 days and he would get the entire amount before he showed up on the set. I am convinced that he is the only actor to play Superman's father. I didn't flinch when we finally agreed on his price. His role is relatively a minor one, but I still felt it absolutely necessary to have him. I believe Superman is part of the American heritage and everybody will go to see the movie. It is a calculated risk on my part, but I'm betting to make it all back — and more. (*The Evening Standard*)

PIERRE SPENGLER (producer, *Superman: The Movie*): Even though people knew what Superman was, they didn't see how it could be a film. We needed to give credibility to the project. We needed names that were recognizable and intrigued the distributors. We then engaged James Bond director Guy Hamilton to direct *Superman*. Again, people said, "Ah, James Bond. Superman." The final coup was signing Gene Hackman and Marlon Brando. People saw that it was a real movie. (*Retro Vision Archives*)

ILYA SALKIND: The moment we got Marlon, it was very quick to get Hackman. His agent at the time called and she said Hackman would like to be in the movie with Brando, and that was it. They made it happen. The whole point was to make it a serious, big movie and not to make it a comic book movie or to make it a cartoon.

MARLON BRANDO (actor, "Jor-El," *Superman: The Movie*): Superman is an heroic symbol to children. All children — because they're small and because they feel uncomfortable and inferior to adults — have fantasies. They enjoy themes which they can be a part of, where they can be big. They enjoy seeing themselves as Superman. It will be a big release for them to go and see this film. And most of their parents will go too, because so many of the parents feel helpless in the face of taxes, laws, chaos, crime — the "distress of life." They feel helpless to do anything, so it's good for them. And, naturally, it's enjoyable. There are times you just want some kind of popcorn and happiness. We all have to find a way to unwind. All this getting and spending — it gets to us. (*The Making of Superman: The Movie*)

GENE HACKMAN (actor, "Lex Luthor," *Superman: The Movie***):** I don't know why they thought of me; I'm not sure *I* would have thought of me. But Brando had already committed to the film and I felt that his name gave a certain credibility to the project. And I had always wanted to be involved in a film with Marlon Brando. My main concern, however, was whether or not I could make the part work for me. But Lex Luthor was the best time I've had in years. Someone once said that the villains have all the fun, and Luthor is the ultimate villain. (*Press Notes*)

RAY MORTON: Many Superman fans complain about the comic nature of Hackman's Luthor scenes, feeling they are too broad and cartoonish and silly and '66 *Batman* for a film that is otherwise striving for verisimilitude. I understand this complaint and agree with it to some extent. But the two things that cause me not to object too strenuously is that, while one can argue that the villains in this film shouldn't be funny, if you accept that they are, at least they actually *are* funny. In too many larger-than-life and comic book-inspired films that followed in the wake of *Superman* and especially in the wake of *Batman* (1989), too many of the villain performances were hammy, over-the-top and campy without ever actually being entertaining. When Hackman and Ned Beatty go for the funny bone, they actually hit it, because they're giving finely-honed comic performances, not just mugging it up to show they're superior to the material.

The other thing that saves the Luthor scenes for me is that when the time comes for Lex to be a bad guy, Hackman injects a slight cold-bloodedness into his performance that lets you know that beneath the comic exterior lies the heart of a true sociopath. The two best examples of this are in the moment when Lex incapacitates Superman with Kryptonite and gives his "old, diseased maniac" speech. Even better is the moment in which Miss Tesmacher, upon learning that one of the nuclear missiles is headed for Hackensack, New Jersey, reminds Lex that her mother lives there. Luthor's response, which is to look at his watch and then shake his head no, is wonderfully and chillingly evil.

RICHARD DONNER: Following the casting of Brando and Hackman, the Salkinds ran a sign at Cannes that said, "The Salkinds Bring You Superman... Written by Mario Puzo... Starring Marlon Brando and Gene Hackman." Overnight they were accepted, so when I came on the picture these two guys were going to do it. I was thrilled, because neither part could have been played better by anybody. We were also married to the dates that were promised to Brando and Hackman, and that was an awesome responsibility.

Before that even became an issue for Donner, the intent was for Guy Hamilton, who had directed several James Bond films, including Goldfinger *and* Diamonds Are Forever, *to direct the film in Rome, but that became an impossibility because of Brando's standing there.*

DAVID NEWMAN: Guy Hamilton was an Englishman with a tax problem, which a lot of English people have. A lot of guys have their residency outside of England but they maintain their England citizenship, because if they're in England for more than so many days consecutively, they jump into a terrible tax bracket and lose like three quarters of their salary. Guy was one of these tax exiles, so he couldn't shoot in England because of his tax problem.

ILYA SALKIND: Hamilton would have had to spend a week in Rome, then a week in London and back to Rome and back to London again. It was just an impossible situation.

DAVID NEWMAN: When we got Brando, the idea was that we were going to shoot in Italy and they were building sets. We worked the entire summer in Rome. Then Marlon Brando was cast, and Brando, they found out, because of *Last Tango in Paris*, had an obscenity charge hanging over him, and the charge was that if he set foot in Italy, they'd throw him in the slammer because he was in a supposedly obscene movie. So, Brando couldn't shoot in Italy and Guy Hamilton couldn't shoot in England. At that point, to the producers, it seemed that having Marlon Brando was much more important than Guy Hamilton. Hamilton said goodbye and Brando said hello and Richard Donner became the director.

ILYA SALKIND: We lost a small fortune when we shifted in the midst of pre-production. Hundreds of thousands of dollars' worth of sets had already been constructed. As I said, we also lost our director, who's a tax exile from his native Britain. But unquestionably we gained in the long run by moving the production to England. We were at work way before anyone had heard of *Star Wars* or *Close Encounters*. We were the first kids on the block to foresee this renewed fascination with science-fiction, space and fantasy. It just took us a little longer to get it on the screen.

RICHARD DONNER: When they contacted me about directing, it was a complete surprise. As was their [the Salkinds'] custom, whoever was hot was who they used. *The Omen* had just come out in 1975.

RAY MORTON: Why they thought the director of a dark horror film about the Anti-Christ would be suitable to helm their big-budget comic book fantasy is anyone's guess. Fortunately, Donner turned out to be the ideal choice.

RICHARD DONNER: I got a telephone call one morning and some guy said, "This is Alexander Salkind." I said, "Yes...?" "You don't know who I am?" "No." "Have you ever been to Cannes?" "No." I thought it was someone trying to sell me a story or something. He said, "I'm a film producer." I said, "Oh really?" Who *was* this guy? He said, "Did you see *The Three* and *Four Musketeers?*" I said, "Yes," and he said, "We're doing *Superman* and we want you to do it. We'll pay you a lot of money." I said, "Terrific, I like a lot of money, but I don't know anything about the film." He said he would send me a script and literally 30 minutes later a messenger delivered a 500-page Mario Puzo screenplay. I read it and turned it down. Right or wrong, the way they were going was not the way *I* would've gone with a Superman project. They offered me a lot of money, but I still turned it down, because *The Omen* had been very successful for me, and I really wanted to pick carefully. Besides, the script needed a major rewrite. They called back and insisted, and suggested they fly me out to Europe to talk to him. My agent and I flew over on the agreement that if I did the film, I could bring in a new writer. They resisted that idea, but ultimately agreed to it. I wanted to use Tom Mankiewicz, who had been a friend for 20 years, but we'd never worked together. He also knew Benton and the Newmans.

TOM MANKIEWICZ (creative consultant, *Superman: The Movie*): I knew Dick Donner very well. We'd never worked together, but we'd known each other since the '60s. And he has a voice that's like the all-clear on a submarine; it's just unbelievable. So, this is absolutely, literally true. I had just rewritten *The Deep* for Peter Yates and I rewrote *The Spy Who Loved Me* for Cubby Broccoli. I'm laying in bed, it's five in the morning, phone rings, it's Dick Donner: "Get up, Mankiewicz. I'm in Paris. I'm gonna direct *Superman.* It needs a lot of work and you're gonna write it." I said, "No, I'm not," and he said, "Yes, you are. And there's a woman coming to your house right now with your scripts; I know you're too nice a guy to go back to sleep. You're gonna answer the door." I said, "Aw, Jesus, Dick," I hang up. The doorbell rings five minutes later. Here's this woman at five in the morning. The scripts were, I think, between 500 and 600 pages long — the two of them. I put them down and went back upstairs to go to bed.

The phone rings. It's Donner. "Are you reading?" "No, Dick, they're too heavy to get upstairs. They're on the table." He said, "I'll be back tomorrow. We're gonna do this. We'll have a meeting. Read 'em." So, I read them. They were five- or six-hundred pages long and very campy. And here's a piece of advice to writers: Sometimes when you're writing something… like *Superman*… for whatever reason — whether it's the money or you think it's good or whatever — you want to show the audience that you're smarter than the material. You camp it up to show them, "We're not *really* taking this seriously. This is all tongue-in-cheek." And it was very campy. Some of it was very funny, but it just went on and on and on.

Dick arrived back. I called him, I said, "Donner, listen, I'm not gonna do this. I've just been rewriting stuff, I want to do something of my own and I just…" He said, "Come over here, we'll have a meeting." I said, "No, Dick, really… " "Come on over." So I drive over there and I ring the doorbell, there's no answer. I go around the back of the house… and there he is standing on his lawn in the Superman suit. They'd given him the Superman suit, he's *dressed* in the Superman suit. And he turned to me and he said, "Just try it on and you'll do it." And he started running at me and the cape was billowing and I started to laugh. And then he looked at me and he said, "If we can get the love story right between Clark and Lois and Superman — if we can get that right; if it can be two kids out on a date — this whole movie's going to work." And I stared at him and literally cursed him out. And off we went.

Before doing so, Mankiewicz, who was very close friends with Robert Benton ("He's like my brother"), called him up to be sure that there wasn't an emotional attachment on Benton's part to the script.

TOM MANKIEWICZ: He said he was thrilled that I was going to get involved. So Dick Donner and I took over. Our approach was to basically say that this was really happening. As to the nature of my work on the script, let's say the Puzo and Newman scripts had a scene where Superman landed on Lois' balcony at night, a two-page scene. I made it a five- or six-page scene and had him take her flying at the end. It was mostly building around what was there. I think most of these pictures work when you don't make fun of what's going on. The ones that are best are the ones that are done balls-out as though it's really happening. *Raiders of the Lost Ark* is a great adventure because everybody plays it like they mean it and they don't wink at the audience. When Superman lands on her balcony, it's a guy asking a girl out on a date.

RICHARD DONNER: Tom Mankiewicz is solely responsible for my *Superman* script, as far as I'm concerned. He took a great outline by Mario Puzo and a good script by Robert Benton and David and Leslie Newman and then created a different aura. Writing-wise, he interpreted it totally different and made it better. That's not to knock the other writers, but Guy Hamilton had a different approach than I did. The original was a different form of reality.

CHRISTOPHER REEVE (actor, "Clark Kent/Superman," *Superman: The Movie*): In the original script, that was the kind of style that had to go. Puzo had done a beautiful job, but Mankiewicz cleaned everything up. We used his stuff as a guideline, then all of us improvised the new dialogue on the set. The writers squirmed; that's what we had to do (*Press Notes*).

RAY MORTON: Following Donner's instruction to focus the scripts on the love story between Superman/Clark Kent and Lois Lane, Mank reworked the narrative of the first film into what was essentially a romantic comedy featuring a love triangle in which the two men vying for Lois' affections are the same man and then bracketed that concept with Superman's origin story on one end and a Bond-like conflict with Lex Luthor on the other. The script for the second film became the story of a man who defies his father and gives up everything for love, only to learn that he has made a dreadful mistake and then must redeem himself. In the process, he transformed the Newmans and Benton's loose collection of ideas into a solid dramatic narrative with thematic coherence, lots of forward build and momentum and a twin set of spectacular climaxes. Mank also replaced the goofy comedy that permeated the previous drafts with witty humor that invited the audience to laugh along with Superman rather than at him.

TOM MANKIEWICZ: The separate "Creative Consultant" credit was Dick's idea. There was unbelievable acrimony between Dick and the Salkinds — Dick and I used to call that movie *Close Encounters of the Salkind*. I became his de facto producer, helping with locations, casting — we didn't have a Superman or a Lois or a Perry White or a Jimmy Olsen or a General Zod — and stayed on through the editing, scoring, etc. Dick insisted that I have a separate card in the main title which accurately reflected my contribution. I almost certainly would have received first credit as a writer — more than half the sequences and about 80% of the dialogue is mine — but I couldn't have gotten both credits. Dick also insisted that my credit appear in all paid advertising.

RICHARD DONNER: The picture had been prepared for a year in Rome. When I came on, we had to throw out the entire preparation, because we couldn't use it. It was originally going to be directed by an Englishman and produced by two Russian-Frenchman, and yet they were doing a classic American fable without an American eye looking at it. When I agreed to do the film, I was concerned that

Superman shouldn't get screwed up. I never realized what a challenge I was taking on. When I arrived at Shepperton Studios and saw the preparation, I asked them to show me the flying material. I watched it and was stunned to see a man walking along who's jerked off the ground by two wires, and then landing out of control. So that was the first thing we had to correct. Then we had to cast the role, and they wanted to use Robert Redford or something.

Finding an actor to play the Man of Steel was one of the biggest challenges of the film. Every major Hollywood actor was considered for the role, but the vast majority of them just couldn't get beyond the idea of wearing the famous Superman costume.

ILYA SALKIND: I started with all kinds of stars, including Paul Newman. I offered him the parts of either Lex Luthor or Superman and he turned it down. Then when he found out what Brando got — points and all — he was absolutely sick, because I think I offered him $2-million and he turned it down.

RICHARD DONNER: We had seen just about every actor imaginable from television to motion pictures to everything else. Nobody fit the costume. Nobody could fly. If you saw Bob Redford flying, it would be Bob Redford flying. There was no sense of reality. That was the key to it, the flying. You had to believe that a man could fly. I tested quite a few of the actors, but nothing worked. The producers even sent over their dentist. I swear to God that's true.

DAVID NEWMAN: When Leslie and I were writing the script, we had Burt Reynolds in mind for the title role. We did not want to be camp. We had to present this character who was truth, justice and the American way, but not someone who was going to be a Boy Scout. We needed someone who you would see seriously as an action figure, but there had to be a little bit of playfulness, a wink. The take we had was Burt Reynolds; the Burt Reynolds then, who was at the peak of his career. He had this thing where he would wink at you and say, "I'm having fun here, folks," but then you'd like it anyway when he punched somebody out. We're talking about the Burt Reynolds of *The Longest Yard*.

Although Reynolds was indeed considered for the role, certainly the most bizarre possibility was then heavyweight champion of the world Muhammad Ali! As David Newman explains it, when the production team was pursuing Dustin Hoffman for the role of Lex Luthor, they dealt with his European agent Sir Jarvis Astaire, who was reportedly knighted due to his success with "enormous betting shops."

DAVID NEWMAN: He was also one of the guys who started

close-circuiting boxing matches in movie theaters in the U.K. and all over Europe. In 1975, Muhammad Ali, when he was making his comeback, fought a professional wrestler, a Japanese wrestler, and it was a ridiculous fight. But it was a big deal, a big publicity stunt. Sir Jarvis Astaire had the close-circuit rights, showed it all over Europe and made a fortune. When we wanted Hoffman, the producers said, "Let's go see Sir Jarvis Astaire," and we all flew down to Cannes. We're sitting in the bar and Sir Jarvis comes in. Ilya is the dreamer and the one who thought of the idea of Superman and Santa Claus [which became another Salkind feature film]. Alex, who is Ilya's father, doesn't know anything about any of these characters. He always calls them "Mr. Superman" and "Mrs. Lois Lane." Santa Claus he called "Mr. Christmas Man." He's wonderfully brilliant in some ways, but he doesn't keep up with things in other ways. So Ilya has to keep him filled in.

We're sitting in this bar and before we get down to business, we're having small talk and someone says, "What's new, Sir Jarvis?" And he said, "Well, I made a bloody fortune with this Ali/Wrestler fight. We made millions and millions of pounds." Alex hears this and says, "Who is this Mr. Ali?" And Ilya says, "He's the heavyweight champion of the world. He's on the cover of every magazine in the world." Alex says, "Why couldn't he play Superman?" And there was just silence. Nobody dared speak. Part of the deal was that DC had general approval over the image of Superman. DC never really interfered, but they had some approval rights, so their character wouldn't be screwed up. So there was this long silence. Sir Jarvis doesn't give a shit, because it's another opportunity to make some money. He said, "I'll get Muhammad on the phone. It's a great idea." And finally — finally — Jarvis is halfway to the phone to call Muhammad Ali, who I'm sure would have loved to play Superman, and all of a sudden Ilya says, "Maybe it's not such a good idea, Dad. Before he was Muhammad Ali, he used to be Cassius Clay." And Alex says, "Oh" — the light bulb goes off — "that's a person of color. Okay, not such a good idea." I swear to you, there was five minutes there where we saw this whole project blowing up sky high with Muhammad Ali as Superman.

ILYA SALKIND: It's true. Absolutely. I had made a list for National Periodical Publications, who own Superman, of all the actors who could play the part, and they approved people like Muhammad Ali, Steve McQueen, Al Pacino, Dustin Hoffman — they absolutely approved all kinds of people that were wrong.

TOM MANKIEWICZ: We didn't know who could possibly play Superman. We had Jon Voight in the wings for a lot of money and we were trying to find *somebody*.

ILYA SALKIND: The first temptation was to go with the biggest star name we could find, but if we had cast a well-known star, as he soared over the city of Metropolis, you would never have been able to forget his star personality. It would always have been the star up there, *not* Superman.

RICHARD DONNER: Things were looking hopeless until Christopher Reeve walked in. I met Christopher Reeve in New York. I had gotten a call from someone who said, "There's a kid who's terrific, would you like to see him?"

ILYA SALKIND: We — Donner and myself — had a meeting with him in New York at the Sherry-Netherland. He came in and looked *very* skinny. He auditioned for both Superman and Clark Kent and was very good but, again, we both said, "Too skinny; impossible."

RICHARD DONNER: He was about 20 or 30 pounds lighter, his hair was a sandy color and he had dressed in the burliest clothes he could find to make him look good. He just had this great look and I gave him my glasses to wear, and he looked so much like the part it was unbelievable.

ILYA SALKIND: And then we kept going through all kinds of other actors, including, as I said, Newman, Jon Voight, Perry King — we even offered it to Travolta — and were turned down. Finally, I was looking at the *Motion Picture Almanac*, then in London, where you had all the pictures of different actors. I had made a note on the face of Chris Reeve and was looking at his face every day, saying, "My God, he looks great." I mean, he's got the neck, and if he works out he could do it. Then I convinced Donner to retest him — full camera test — and he was great.

RICHARD DONNER: *Nobody* wanted to go with him, because he was an unknown, but the idea to me was that we *should* go with an unknown so that you could make it believable. It ended up just that.

There was a time when Christopher Reeve gave an interview in which a reporter asked, "How do you define a hero?" Chris considered the question a moment before responding. Finally, he noted, "For me, personally, a hero is somebody who will make sacrifices for others without expecting a reward."

"Superman is all that," mused the interviewer, to which he replied, "That's what I try to play." But then came the biggie: "How about Christopher Reeve? Is he a hero?" The

answer was an honest one: "I don't know. I can't start leaping to those conclusions."

Thankfully, the rest of the world can — and did — given the global response to the actor's passing on October 10, 2004, nearly a decade after the horseback riding accident that paralyzed him from the neck down. Many people might have given up, but Reeve — following the initial realization that he would likely never walk again — began an effort that he carried through on until his final days. Together with his wife Dana Reeve, who would subsequently pass away from breast cancer in 2006, he began The Christopher and Dana Reeve Paralysis Resource Center, a New Jersey facility dedicated to teaching independence to paralyzed people. Additionally, they created the Christopher Reeve Paralysis Foundation, which funds research on a cure for paralysis and for which the actor tirelessly lobbied Congress for additional funds for research. The Foundation ultimately received $55-million in research grants and $7.5-million in quality-of-life grants.

So, Christopher Reeve a hero? Many would say that he genuinely embodied the word.

HELEN SLATER (actor, title role of *Supergirl*): I had the opportunity to meet Christopher Reeve at Pinewood Studios and then we became friends. Just one of the kindest, sweetest men. One time we were in New York City and it was 1 in the morning. Chris and I had dinner and we were hanging out on a park bench on Central Park West or Central Park South, and these three fire trucks come zooming by. Chris turns to me and he says, "Here's Superman and Supergirl and there's nothing we can do." Just an example of what he went through with his injury and then how he just devoted his life to giving back and to be of service. I think in terms of the definition of what a real superhero is, his life was a *spectacular* example of that. And we should *all* take a page from his playbook.

Born on September 25, 1952, at the age of nine he discovered a love for acting when he found himself cast in an amateur version of the operetta The Yeoman of the Guard, which was just the first of a number of student productions. When he was 15, he spent a summer as an apprentice at the Williamstown Theatre Festival in Williamstown, Massachusetts. Upon graduating from Princeton Day School in June of 1970, he acted in plays in Boothbay, Maine, where he caught the attention of critics almost immediately. By the following year, the audience was noticing him too.

PORTLAND PRESS-HERALD (July 16, 1970): Despite its jerky pace, the play *Another Language* has moments of fragile beauty, all of them created in superb performances by Harryetta Peterka and newcomer Christopher Reeve, a young man of great promise.

EVENING EXPRESS (July 29, 1971): Christopher Reeve, the 22-year-old fiancé of the heroine of some 40 years, is known around these parts having spent a summer at the Boothbay Playhouse. This handsome young man was besieged by the gals, including Allyn Warner, this year's Miss Maine, who looked long and lean in a printed long dress. Chris was full of praise for the experience and training he'd received at Franklyn Lenthall's playhouse.

CHRISTOPHER REEVE: I started acting at 11, and by the time I was 14 I was coming into New York looking for summer stock work. I'd walk through the theater district, looking at the marquees and say, "I'll be there someday." (*The Herald Statesman*)

He attended Cornell University as a member of the class of 1974, though he transferred over to Juilliard Drama School and studied under the late John Houseman. In 1975, he co-starred with screen legend Katharine Hepburn in the Broadway play A Matter of Gravity, *a show that he remained with for its full one-year run while simultaneously appearing on the soap opera* Love of Life *as the character Ben Harper. His first feature film role was a small one on* Gray Lady Down *(1977), though naturally it was being cast as the Man of Steel that would transform both his career and his life.*

CHRISTOPHER REEVE: I remember sitting in my dressing room on *Gravity's* opening night, surrounded by champagne and telegrams, remembering all those summers of walking around Broadway. Opening night was one of the scariest moments of my life. The moment before I was supposed to walk on stage as a character full of zip, I'd rather have been pushed out of a very high tree. It was a shock treatment you chalk up to experience. I don't think I'll ever be so frightened again. Every time you do something like that, it prepares you for the next experience. (*The Herald Statesman*)

DAVID WILSON: My first Hollywood film was with Charlton Heston *and* Christopher Reeve in *Gray Lady Down*. I played the submarine's cook; it's a submarine film based on the Thresher Incident. In any event, I knew Chris and he was just a tall, lanky drink of water man. We'd heard about Dick Donner casting for *Superman: The Movie*. Donner didn't want to hire me, because I had done the musical. He didn't want anybody that had been attached to another Superman thing. He wanted it to be about *his* vision and didn't want any predisposition to somebody saying, "Oh yeah, this is the guy that did that hokey TV musical."

CHRISTOPHER REEVE: When I tested for the part, I was fairly skeptical about it. It seemed such an unlikely subject for a film, but then I read the script and was converted. But my skepticism *was* justified. Until I came along, they'd been testing athletes and dentists for the role. The producers' view seemed to be that they didn't need an actor for Superman, they just had to find someone who looked physically right for the part and the other stars would carry him through the picture. (*San Francisco Examiner*)

RICHARD DONNER: I still have photos from Chris' screentest. He was this string bag, this skinny, skinny kid in blue leotards with an "S" cut into the front of it, sweat pouring out from his arms and black shoe polish on his hair to give it a black look.

CHRISTOPHER REEVE: When I put on the glasses, Ilya Salkind looked kind of excited and swapped a couple of quick glances with Dick Donner. Two weeks later it was confirmed that I had the part, which is when I started to get excited — and also nervous. At the testing stage, you've nothing to lose: You haven't got a part. But once I was in, everybody expected me to *be* Superman. I believe that it's better to gamble, to go for high risk than to stand around testing the water. The acting rewards of this part are such that it is worth doing. Anybody in my position would have done it. (*The News and Observer*)

RICHARD DONNER: As skinny as he was, Chris swore to me that he was an athlete and that he could put on weight and build up, so we hired him. We gave him a given amount of time, set him up with this Olympics body trainer and poured all kinds of protein into him, and one day he flew in to our office and was perfect.

DAVID WILSON: Chris went out and gained 50 pounds and worked out incessantly to build himself up to do that role. He was 175 pounds when we did *Gray Lady Down,* but he transformed himself. That's not an easy thing to do. I talked to him later on about that, God rest his soul, and he said he was eating like 20,000 calories a day. It was *constant.*

CHRISTOPHER REEVE: I think it was basically because they had to have someone who could look like the public's idea of the comic-magazine character. And that is a very precise image which has existed for forty years. So, the producers had the responsibility of taking the image the public had known for all that time, and then they had to "modernize" it, bring it up to date with the seventies, because the public conception of the character has, of course, been influenced by the George Reeves television series of the fifties. I think that I was a pretty good compromise, that I do — once the makeup and stuff is complete — look like the guy in the comics. And yet, I also look like a man of the seventies, rather than a fifties person. The reason I was selected was that I answered a very specific physical description… well, of course, they needed a good actor too. But the public reaction on that score, I think, is fairly low. People are assuming that the actor who plays Superman really doesn't matter as long as you have somebody who looks the part… and I think the producers would have settled for that. What I'm trying to do is give them more than they expected. (*Press Notes*)

Nobody is Superman, so I had to bring the character down to my own level — which was to do my best and play it with some understatement. I felt that Superman doesn't always have it covered, and if he doesn't know everything, his achievements are that much more impressive. To a lot of people, it's just a huge joke. I understand that. When they see me coming, they say, "Where's your phone booth?" It's funny the first 200 times. But what I'm trying to do is humanize the legend. Otherwise, Superman's just an uptight, brick-built figure and nobody will care. I decided he had to be a real person. (*Sunday Telegraph*)

His transformation was under the tutelage of actor David Prowse, who had physically portrayed Darth Vader in the original Star Wars *trilogy, only the first chapter of which had been filmed at that point.*

CHRISTOPHER REEVE: I thought I was in good shape, but by the time we went before the cameras, I was ready to challenge Muhammad Ali. I was also trying to develop my take on both Superman and Clark Kent. The caped hero is only one aspect of him; there is more to him than that. In a sense, he is a stranger in a strange land; a solitary man with extraterrestrial powers, trying hard to fit into his adopted planet. He has warmth and a fine sense of humor, even about his own super-human strength. (*Press Notes*)

ANTHONY TOLLIN (comics, pulps and old–time radio historian): I was working at DC at the time of the movie and got to spend some time with Christopher Reeve. He was somebody who wanted to learn, who wanted to talk, and it was my job to bring him around and introduce him to the writers and editors. He really wanted their take on the character, which he had tremendous respect for. You have to realize that Chris was a person of the theater.

ALAN BURKE: This 26-year-old, underweight, Julliard-trained and ego-filled actor with no feature film credits to his name stepped from a stage balcony one day wearing a makeshift Superman costume with heavy sweat patches under each arm and loudly said, "Good evening, Ms. Lane." And with those four words, an actor vanished before our very eyes and a Man of Steel was born. Christopher Reeve simply was Superman. It was as if he had stepped straight from the pages of the books themselves and, like Donner, he treated the material with the respect and dignity which it so rightly deserved.

MARK WAID: I remember sitting in the theater, we're on Krypton and my brain immediately goes, "That's not Krypton. This is *not* going to be faithful to continuity," and it bothered me until Krypton exploded and I was like, "That's *not* what the rocket ship looks like." I was one of *those* guys. But then I was won over. The spirit of Superman, the earnestness in the way Donner and Reeve represented the character and the faithfulness of who Superman is and who Clark Kent is and who Lois Lane is, all of those things felt very much like the comic. There is a kindness and a sincerity that exudes from Christopher Reeve that I haven't seen to that degree in a lot of the other adaptations. And that carried through all the films, even *Superman IV*. That's a terrible movie, and he's got a terrible wig and he didn't bulk up, but he still inhabits the role and brings that same sense. When he addresses the UN and tells them he's going to rid the world of all nuclear weapons and all the delegates cheer — it's such a great speech, and as long as you're willing to buy into comic book logic, then it's a great moment. It's the people who are cynical that will go, "Ah, that's not the way the UN would work." I didn't care. It's not a documentary. If you can't buy into that, you don't believe a man can fly.

TOM MANKIEWICZ: When he was confirmed for the part, I remember Chris' reaction was, "Wow, this is terrific." Then he said, "Is this the end of my career? Will I always be Superman?" I arranged a meeting between him and Sean Connery, who had broken free of the Bond image. Sean gave Chris three pieces of advice: 1) Just worry about making the first film, because if it's a flop, he'd be out of a job anyway; 2) After this, find something different he'd like to do; and 3) Get the best lawyer in the world and get all you can out of it.

Nearly as pivotal a role to the film was that of Lois Lane, because her relationship with Superman would be the one that locked the film firmly into reality. In other words, if you believed that this was a real man and a real woman falling in love, you'd accept everything else as well. As was the case with Superman, every Hollywood contender was considered for the role of the Daily Planet's *ace reporter. According to Tom Mankiewicz, the choice was narrowed down to two. Among the others who auditioned, however, was Lesley Ann Warren of the 1975 ABC broadcast of* It's a Bird… It's a Plane… It's Superman, *as viewed in the 2006 documentary* Look, Up in the Sky: The Amazing Story of Superman.

LESLEY ANN WARREN (actor, "Lois Lane," *It's a Bird… It's a Plane…*

It's Superman): I was very happy to be a part of that release of the actors that tested for Lois Lane. It was really great and fun to see everybody's interpretation. I was in Chicago doing *Vanities* with Elizabeth Ashley and I simply got a call from my manager at the time, telling me to fly to London to do this screentest. I prepared on the plane and that was it; I didn't really know anything about the project until I got that call. It was actually a big, big meeting for a big-budgeted movie at the time. For me, any time I'm testing or auditioning for anything, it's a big deal. I get really nervous and anxious, so it requires a lot of preparation on my part. I do remember that Christopher Reeve was so wonderful and so generous, and I got to know him a little bit after. I think we presented at the Golden Globes together after that and I took some wonderful pictures of the two of us. He was just such a loving, generous, totally professional man

TOM MANKIEWICZ: The two finalists for the part were Margot Kidder and Stockard Channing, and the reason for that was that they were both so charming. We had hired Chris first and he was so young. The way I'd written the part of Lois was that there was a goofy quality about her, and it just worked out that the best tests were by Margot and Stockard. The real truth is that if Chris had been five years older, Stockard Channing would have gotten the part. She looked a little older than Chris. Margot, on the other hand, had this total kind of naiveté about her, a goofiness, and they worked better together.

MARGOT KIDDER (actress, "Lois Lane," *Superman I – IV*): I didn't know anything about Superman. I was in a bad marriage and it was one of those obsessive ones where you can't leave and you can't stay, and it was a big mess. I knew I had to get the part, because that was the only way I was going to be able to get out of my marriage, because the husband was chauvinistic and didn't think women should work. So I didn't have a clue this was going to be iconic. I flew there knowing my main job and the screentest were to look like I was in love with this guy, and if I did, I would probably get the part. So I had that figured out, but when I got on the set, here's the skinniest, the geekiest guy you've ever seen in your life. That was Christopher before he got his muscles. His pant leg was six inches above the ankle and I was like, "*This* is Superman?" But I just went, "Look like you love him, just love him, love him, love him." And it worked.

But I still didn't think anything at all about it. When we were making it, I thought, "What is this?" I mean, I'm hanging from wires for 14 hours a day and I just didn't get it. So it was a big surprise for me. When I first saw it, I cried at the flying scene. I felt like such an idiot, because it was me, but I thought it was such a great scene. The movie was great.

Additional casting took place, including Ned Beatty and Valerie Perrine as Luthor cohorts Otis and Miss Teschmacher, Jackie Cooper as Daily Planet *editor Perry White, Marc McClure as Jimmy Olsen and Terence Stamp, Sarah Douglas and Jack O'Halloran as Kryptonian villains Zod, Ursa and Non.*

SARAH DOUGLAS (actress, "Ursa," *Superman: The Movie* **and** *Superman II***):** Do you know what it's like being on set with Terence Stamp? What a joy and a delight every morning. It was an absolute pleasure. And I have to just quickly say, because people say they know I'm a fidget, they know I mess around and I'm all over the place, but the stillness of the super-villains is all down to Terence. He was so wonderfully still and so calming. I remember you once said to me, "We need to be different, because we are aliens." I was fascinated, because you drank mint tea and you made "mmmmm" noises and stuff. I'd never known anything like it. I want to thank you for us, because I honestly would never have got there without you.

TERENCE STAMP (actor, "Zod," *Superman: The Movie* **and** *Superman II***):** Listen, I'm looking for a lover that won't blow my cover. With Jack [O'Halloran, Non], he's a genuinely ferocious guy; he was a heavyweight boxer. There were these rumors about him getting up to all kinds of stuff with the Mafia, but on the set, he was what I call a heavy rapper. He would intimidate people into listening to him, and he would tell these amazing stories. He was really keen to be a straight actor. He saw this as a big start for him. After I'd sussed him out the first couple of days, I said to him, "Now listen, I'm the General, okay? And just between you and me, I only want you to think that that's all I want from you. I just want this one thing is that whenever you see me, remember, I am the General."

And I'm a real wicked bastard, you know? So he said, "Yeah. That's the way we'll do it. We'll practice, it's like method acting, and we'll practice it off set. But when we get on the set, it will come over. We're doing this together." He said, "Right." So then, that afternoon, I was called to the set, and it was in a big sound-stage that was empty, but the set was quite small. And I think it was the interior of the White House. And we just come in through the roof. And so they call me, I arrive, and everybody's there. And nobody's doing anything. And I ask what the problem is, and I hear, right on the other side of the set, Jack rapping to somebody. And it's a long story. So I said, "Jack, you bastard. I'm ready. And I'm waiting." All the crew went like, "Shit." Talking stopped immediately and there was this kind of silence. And then there were these huge footfalls all the way across the stage, and he came in, he came very close and said, "Sorry, General!"

JACK O'HALLORAN: You know, when I read the script, I really liked what I saw. When I met Richard Donner, I *truly* liked what I saw. And after I met the cast — Sarah and Marlon and Terence — I said, "This is gonna be one hell of a movie." You could just feel it. You feel when something gels, and to do it for three-and-a-half years all total, it was an amazing experience.

At the same time, the script was being tightened up by Tom Mankiewicz, flying sequences perfected and sets constructed at England's Pinewood Studios. Production was ready to begin with everyone determined to update Superman for modern audiences, while never losing sight of his origins.

LESLIE NEWMAN: Superman is one of the basic American legends. David's always said that it was our King Arthur. People asked why we were doing a movie about a comic book hero, but nobody thinks it's odd to do a movie or musical about King Arthur or Robin Hood. Superman isn't just a comic, it's a myth and it contains elements of so many of the basic myths: the god who walks among men.

DAVID NEWMAN: The notion of a god who walks among men disguised as a man occurs in every mythology, and there are biblical connotations in this legend as well: a father who says, "I will send my only son to Earth to save mankind!" We all know where we've heard that story before. It has such resonance

LESLIE NEWMAN: The loneliness of the god-like figure.

CHRISTOPHER REEVE: The key word for me on him is "inspiration." He is a leader by inspiration. He sets an example. It's quite important that people realize that I don't see him as a glad-handing showoff; a one-man vigilante force who rights every wrong. Basically, he's a pacifist, a man who comes along and says, "What can I do to help?" He stands on the sidelines until there is real trouble. He does not want to get involved unless it's absolutely necessary, because he thinks people should learn to make their own decisions. (*Press Notes*)

RICHARD DONNER: People often asked me, "Where did you find Christopher Reeve?" I say, "I didn't find him. God gave him to me."

DAVID NEWMAN: What was so interesting about Chris is that he was *so* protective of that character, because he really knew the character better than anyone, because he *lived* it. When we were making *Superman II*, we were in Niagara Falls doing that scene where the kid falls in. As you know, a lot of it was done on blue screen in London, but certain things were done on location that was worked in. There was a shot of Chris — in the story it's right after he saves that little boy — where you see him descend, carrying the little boy and giving him to his mother. The little boy says, "I want to do it again," he pats him on the head and says, "One ride to a customer," and he flies off. That's when Lois realizes that Clark is never around when Superman is around. In order to do that shot, which was done live, they had Chris hanging up in this harness on a crane. He's there looking like a guy hanging from a crane and then they drop him into the shot. Because we were shooting in a real location at a famous place, there were a thousand tourists behind a rope with their little cameras, watching not only a movie being made, but a Superman movie. Chris suddenly realized that he had to go up on this crane, looking like an idiot, basically.

LESLIE NEWMAN: He went over to the crowd, which was excited, because he was in full costume. He said, "I'll make a deal with you. If you don't take my picture while I'm up on that crane, when we finish the shot, I'll come and sign autographs until everyone's got what they want." And they all put away their cameras. That's when I realized that Chris had a real connection with the character. He didn't like to send that character up, and what's really very funny is that Chris also, on the days when he was shooting as Superman and he's in character, he kind of carried himself a certain way. On the days when he was Clark Kent, he sits there completely relaxed.

RICHARD DONNER: The idea was to bring a purist view to the film, keying in to the original Superman mythos and avoiding the treatment given the legend via the 1950s television series. I knew the Superman legend and grew up on it. I knew I didn't want to do what television had done to it. Every kid remembers the TV show. My biggest responsibility to the project, I felt, was somehow having to find some sort of objectivity in visualizing Superman, because everybody has seen him in their own way — either in the reality of a drawing or in the fantasy of their own mind. So I had this tremendous responsibility of trying to find some sort of middle road. Also of jumping the time lap from 1938 to 1978 — that was the most difficult flight of them all: not just making him fly, but making him fly through that time warp to be accepted then.

As we got into it, I saw it as three separate films. It was a trilogy in our eyes. One was Krypton, where we broke away from tradition, because when I came on to the project, their preparation for Krypton was exactly the way it looked in 1939 and I just knew that was wrong. Then a very wondrous man John Barry, who had also done *Star Wars* and died shortly after making this film, came up with a "modern" Krypton, which we felt was crystalline, like the inside of a stone. Then came the second part of the trilogy, which was Smallville. We didn't research the comic book all that much, but we did spend a lot of time in Norman Rockwell. We just wanted to make it Kansas-Americana. When we got to Metropolis, we wanted to go back to the comic book.

JOHN KENNETH MUIR: By featuring the three-movement structure that focuses, respectively, on Clark Kent's origin, upbringing and adult life, *Superman: The Movie* also provides a perfect allegory for the American immigrant experience. That experience, in short, is about coming to a land of opportunity, assimilating its cherished values, and then living those values at the highest level possible.

One of Superman's *greatest strengths was also one of its most intimidating elements: Marlon Brando, portraying Superman's Kryptonian father Jor-El, whose sequences were the first to be shot under a very tight schedule.*

RICHARD DONNER: Two days into the role, Marlon came to me late in the afternoon and said he was tired and had a cold and was still a bit jet-lagged; would I mind if he finished early that day? That floored me. Knowing how little time we had with him, I'd even been figuring out what it cost us every time he went to the bathroom. Now this. But I said the only thing I could say: "You're Marlon Brando. How can I stop you?" Then he said, "Tell you what, I'll give you an extra day. How about that?" Well, at his salary, that extra day was worth a fortune. And it meant we could get everything we needed. So I sent him home happily.

ILYA SALKIND: I think one of the worst things about making the movies was meeting with Brando. He was already hired when he said he wanted to play Jor-El as a *green bagel*. And he was being being very serious.

RICHARD DONNER: I had to go meet with Brando. I called Jay Kanter, who was a very powerful agent and studio executive, and I said, "Can you give me any hints?" And he said, "He's going to want to play it like a green suitcase." I said, "What does that mean?" He said, "It means he hates to work and he loves money, so if he can talk you into the fact that people on Krypton look like green suitcases, and you only photograph green suitcases, he'll get paid just to do the voiceover. That's the way his mind works." Instead, he suggested that he play the part as a bagel.

MARGOT KIDDER: Marlon said, "Nobody knows what people from outer space look like, so I think I can play it like a bagel." And Donner knew enough to know that he was just testing him and he said, "They don't have bagels on Krypton," so he gave up that idea.

ILYA SALKIND: He drove directors crazy. When he shot the movie with Jack Nicholson, *The Missouri Breaks*, he drove director Arthur Penn crazy. It was totally nuts.

TERENCE STAMP: I was in India when I had this telegram arrive asking if I would come back to London to meet Dick Donner about this movie and that Marlon Brando was going to be in it. That was just irresistible, to be in a film with Marlon. The experience wasn't a letdown, but he was very different to anything I'd imagined. He's hysterically funny, for one thing, and he really doesn't learn the lines. He has them kind of written up behind the lights, so you can't really see his reading. And in the scene that I did with him, I saw he had a little bit of paper and he was trying to learn the first line so that as he turned towards me, he could be speaking before he had it written down. Do you see what I mean? He was trying to learn this one line so it looked natural. I just couldn't believe it. I went up to him and asked him about it and he said he was trying to learn the line. I asked how you could play *Macbeth* if you can't learn a line and he said, "I've learned *that* already," without a moment's pause.

MARGOT KIDDER: Marlon is one of the most heavenly men on the planet. I met him before, because my husband had read in a movie called *The Missouri Breaks* and I was filming the documentary on the making of it. And the first time we went to see him, he comes to the door and he's like 360 pounds with egg all down the front of his sweats. I thought, "Oh my God, *this* is Marlon Brando?" And within 20 minutes you're eating out of that man's hand. I mean, he's so wonderful and amazing. I had a big public nervous breakdown. I flipped out, and he was the first person to call and see if he could help me. I mean, he was really, really special.

CHRISTOPHER REEVE: I don't say this to be vicious, but I don't worship at the altar of Marlon Brando, because I feel he's copped out in a certain way. He's no longer in a leadership position that he could be. He could really be inspiring a whole generation of actors by continuing to work. But what happened is the press loved him whether he was good, bad or indifferent; where people thought he was this institution no matter what he did. So he doesn't care anymore. It's too bad that the man has been forced into that hostility. On [*Superman*] I had a wonderful time, but the man didn't care. I'm sorry, but he just took the $2-million and ran. (*Late Show with David Letterman*, 1982)

Throughout its production, Superman: The Movie was plagued with budget overruns, much of it attributed to the fact that the filmmakers were treading new ground from a special effects point of view. The other part of it, which made it particularly challenging, is the fact that Donner had no notion of the budget that he was working with, though Ilya Salkind saw the budget issues a different way.

RICHARD DONNER: Whatever the budget was, I wasn't privy to it. That's the way these producers worked, apparently. It didn't make my life any easier, I can tell you. I had now way of knowing whether I was going over-budget or not.

MARK WAID: The Salkinds were always one step ahead of the creditors at every stage. And they didn't make any money on *Superman*. It was only on *Superman II* that they actually recouped some of their expenses and actually made some money. Warner Bros. kept funding them little by little and acquiring more rights, like foreign television rights. Things were so bad that the father, Alexander Salkind, was at a German hotel and got a knock on the door and it was the cops looking for him. In Germany apparently you can be arrested for credit debt and for dodging that credit debt. He managed to get out and then snuck out of the country, taking advantage of the fact that he apparently is an informal dignitary of some sort or another in another nation and was able to fly out, but he had to take certain routes so he didn't land in certain countries. It was nuts.

ILYA SALKIND: The problem we had, mainly, was that Donner could not make up his mind. He would reshoot scenes endlessly. I mean, we were just shooting and shooting and shooting and shooting — which is why we started going *way* over-budget. So that was the main problem, though he was obviously a good director.

MARK WAID: The Salkinds were trying to go as cheap as possible and this is where they ran into trouble with Donner. From their perspective, Donner was throwing money around like nobody's business, but the disconnect, according to Pierre Spengler, was that Donner was not allowed to know the budget or how much they were spending or not spending on things, because every time it came up, it was just a contentious battle. Eventually he was cut out of the process of that end of the information chain, and in doing so just kept spending money.

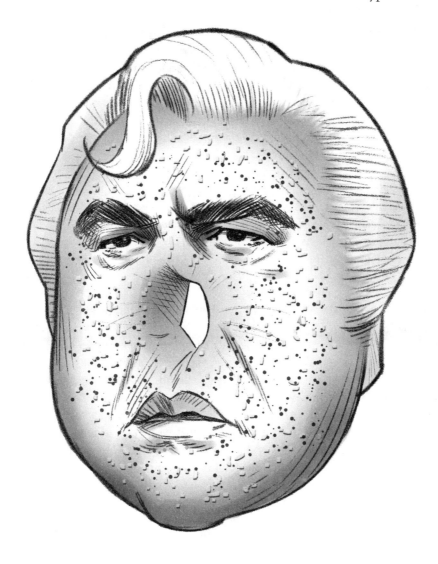

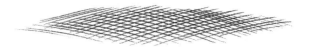

*Marlon Brando wanted to play Jor-El as a bagel, which this image nicely captures
(art © and courtesy D.C. Stuelpner).*

Everything was financial with these guys. The first day, Donner had asked for a driver, so they allocated money for a driver and, instead, he spent that money renting some sort of fancy convertible, and that felt very "Hollywood" to them. It's a European mindset, as I've learned from working with European publishers and European creative, that they see that sort of thing as tacky and showy. So Donner made a bad impression in terms of, "I'm just gonna be spending money like the coffers are bottomless." And once the Salkinds got that impression, true or false, it locked into their brains.

Things got so bad financially that everyone was forced to jettison the idea of shooting the two films back-to-back. Not only did this force production of Superman II to be temporarily halted, but it nearly shut the entire operation down. Lost in the chaos was a cliffhanger that would have connected Superman: The Movie with its sequel, and as a result the conclusion of Superman II — the Man of Steel turning time backwards to avoid a tragedy — was rewritten for the first film.

DAVID NEWMAN: As you know, the Salkinds got in trouble once because they made *The Three Musketeers,* but it was so long that they cut it in half and made two movies out of it. But they didn't pay the actors for two movies, so a lot of people collectively hit the fan and there was a tremendous lawsuit and contracts were renegotiated. As a result, the Salkinds got a reputation for being naughty guys for a while. Well, when we did *I* and *II,* the original ideas were that they would be shot back-to-back for financial reasons; having actors on call and keeping them there and having massive sets that were built to remain standing rather than having them struck and rebuilt for a sequel. In other words, you do all the scenes in the Fortress of Solitude for both movies, you do all the scenes in the *Daily Planet* set. It was very clear that it was going to be two movies, but there was a brief moment where we said we weren't going to get caught in the middle of of this. When the script was going to go out to Dustin Hoffman or Gene Hackman, they said, "Instead of writing 'The End' at the end of part one, just write a sort of transitional scene so it will look like one movie." We said, "Look, these are professional actors and they're going to know that something is up when they get a 400-page script. Plus, they know that you guys have done this before." But at that time, there was a cliffhanger, because at one point, for some silly reason, we thought part one would close and a week later part two would open.

RICHARD DONNER: I did steal certain script areas from the second picture that I felt all of a sudden worked better in the first. When the picture was finished, I had to cut an hour out of it because we had an excess amount of material. It's the kind of picture, thank God, that I had an hour to cut out. If this had come in on time, we would've been in a lot of trouble, because it's got to be kept as fast and alive as a comic book. It has that bigger-than-life attitude. I also decided that if the first film wasn't a success, a cliffhanger ending wouldn't bring them in to see *Superman II*. We'd done what we set out to do, and there was no real way of capping it. And I felt it wouldn't hurt the love scene between Lois and Superman in the end if I went on and did that, so I just said the hell with it. The way the film originally ended in terms of the cliffhanger is that Superman was going to leave Hackman and Beatty in prison, fly up past the camera — just as he does —and then I was going to pan up into the sky and pick up the rocket that he had left tumbling. You see it shut off and you see the Zone of Silence with the three villains in it; then, all of a sudden, the rocket goes past them and there's an atomic explosion, and it blows up the Zone of Silence, freeing Terence Stamp, Jack O'Halloran and Sarah Douglas. Then you see them going to the Moon, where they destroy a Moon mission. Then they go to Earth and start breaking up the White House and such. But I figured it was just too much like television — you know, "Tune in next week." So, we chopped it.

DAVID NEWMAN: The original idea was that Superman would throw one of those nuclear rockets into space and release the villains. I loved that too, because in order to save one thing, Superman inadvertently created another problem for Earth.

LESLIE NEWMAN: It was a great idea, but unfortunately you had the time lapse of two years between movies. And Richard Lester said, "Nobody's going to remember how part one ended."

DAVID NEWMAN: So that's when we came up with the Eiffel Tower scene and the terrorists in *II*. The cliffhanger, which I now remember quite vividly, had the villains being freed, with us not knowing if Superman was alive or dead because of the nuclear explosion. The villains yelled, "Free! Free!" That later became the beginning of *Superman II*.

During all of this, Donner's relationship with the producers disintegrated completely, much of the blame for which he puts on producer Pierre Spengler.

RICHARD DONNER: Spengler was the liaison to Alexander Salkind, and he supposedly had this knowledge of production. My God, I've been in this business long enough to know what a producer is, and it was ridiculous for him to have taken this job. As far as I was concerned, he didn't have any knowledge at all about producing a film like that. If he'd been smart, he'd have just laid back and let us do it, but instead he tried to impose himself. So not only did we end up producing it, but we also had to counter-produce what he was doing. It was very difficult. At the same time, though, I will admit my naiveté. Because if I were producer of a film like that, the first thing I would have done was put "X" number of dollars into proving I could make a man fly, and then go from there. Probably the stupidity on Spengler's part made the film possible, because if anybody had tried it for the money *I* suggested — $100,000,000 — they would never have made the picture. Nobody knew how to go about it. It was just the blind leading the blind, all experimentation. But I was very fortunate. I was surrounded by a terribly talented group of dedicated filmmakers, and somehow or other, we pulled it off.

This was the hardest thing I've ever done. For a start, you don't fool around with Superman. We're dealing with American literature here. The British have their Shakespeare, we have our Superman. So it had to be good. But flying human beings around and making it look *real*? That wasn't easy. But what kills me is that monies were just flushed away — totally wasted. And that was heartbreaking to me. I hate to see money thrown away when it should've been up there on the screen. None of it was wasted flamboyantly, you know. Nobody lived big or did ridiculous things with it. It was just a total lack of knowledge, that's all. If I were arranging a picture like this, instead of hiring people that were more stupid than I was so I'd look bright, I'd have hired the brightest people in the whole goddamned world — if for no other reason than just to save me. And he did just the opposite.

Additionally, as problems mounted, rumors arose and then dissipated regarding the possibility of Donner being replaced as director. This didn't happen primarily due to the fact that Warner Bros. had taken over distribution and had directorial approval. The studio wanted Donner.

DAVID NEWMAN: Warner Bros. Wasn't actually involved with the film for quite a long time. The original idea was that the Salkinds were going to own this movie lock, stock and barrel. They would make separate deals country by country and it would be released in different places by different people and, theoretically, would make much more money. What finally happened with *Superman* is that it cost so much money that the Salkinds didn't have it. They gave more and more of it to Warner Bros. until it came to the point where it was a Warner Bros. picture everywhere around the world except for four or five countries.

CHARLES GREENLAW (WB executive in charge of production):
Let me put it this way. *Superman: The Movie* was a Salkind production and it was supposed to have been delivered on a certain date and it became obvious that that date would not be met. The president of Warners finally said to me, "Would you go over to England for a couple of months?" So I came over basically without portfolio or planning or power or responsibility to see if I could help. I discovered that while Donner had brought a tremendous amount of inventiveness to the picture, he had been thrust into it blind and the crew was ill-prepared and under-financed. Let me give you an example. When I first came to England in December of 1977, there was the climactic desert road sequence set up on Pinewood's back lot. It consisted of two mounds of dirt piled up and a winding sort of road. The opening in the ground required to let Lois' car drop in needed pumps to keep the water out of it. It looked about as much like New Mexico as the room I'm in does.

The Salkinds were still putting up their own money at that time and they kept insisting that the scene be done at Pinewood. But it was gray and overcast, you could see your breath and the actors shivered no matter how much clothing they had on. Finally I said, "There's no way you can make this look like a desert. Let's talk." Then, after a series of negotiations, Warner Bros. made a deal. We'd give extra money for a say in the production. At that point I was given the responsibility of the head of production.

RICHARD DONNER: *Then* they brought Richard Lester in to serve as a kind of a liaison between me and them.

RICHARD LESTER: Shortly after production began, it was obvious that there was trouble between Donner and the producers. I was then asked to come in to try and, I suppose, listen to both sides and smile at everyone. I had to serve as a liaison and tried to smooth away some of the problems, and it involved a little bit of rewriting the ending. I helped form another model unit, miniatures, just to try and help it get through. I certainly did no directing on the first one at all. I would go back at night with my face in a perpetual grin. I became Nancy Reagan before Nancy Reagan was invented. The problem had to be on both sides.

RICHARD DONNER: I knew Dick, so it was just wonderful. The deal stipulated that he wasn't allowed to attend dailies or be on the set unless he was invited, and he turned out to be a charming, delightful guy, and they would go through him and the same thing back from me. That was his function on the film and we became good friends. But that turned into him taking over *Superman II* without picking up a phone and calling me.

RICHARD LESTER: They must have had some elements on which they agreed in the beginning, but by the time it was into shooting they certainly didn't have any common ground and there was a great danger that the whole project, which was employing a lot of people, was going to collapse… maybe even because of a fist fight, which Donner would have undoubtedly won. It became necessary for somebody to try and help them carry on. I wasn't able to raise more money so Dick Donner could do things the way he wanted to, and by the same token I just tried to find a means by which they could operate. But you could see the difficulties. Nowadays you can do the effects digitally. Of course, none of that existed then. We had to use these bloody wires and paint them out frame by frame. Even the most basic of traveling matte was not really well-developed at that time. And the double zoom front projection system hadn't been invented until then. There were problems, but we overcame them as best we could.

I remember somebody had come up with the idea of having a clockwork motor and some whale bone in the cape on *Superman I* to try and get the cape to flutter in the right way in some of the long shots for flying. The cape moved moderately convincingly, but it looked like Superman was also going to appear in *The Hunchback of Notre Dame*. All sorts of ridiculous ideas were tried out. Dick Donner was very good in that if anybody had an idea, he would listen to them and indeed tried them out. That's why he was good for the project and why the producers were going crazy. Money was being spent and they were getting months — indeed, years — over schedule.

RICHARD DONNER: The cape situation *was* a bitch, but frankly there was no way to anticipate everything. We spent months getting our first flying shot, and then we looked at it and something wasn't right. It was the cape; it didn't move right. So we had to build all kinds of gimmicks and little things to go under the cape. We tried electronic movements, bottled air, *everything*. And finally we came up with the idea of wiring the cape inside like an umbrella, which we could fit with little gears to give a feeling of flight. But even that was good only from certain angles. Other times we had to add air and stuff. We had about fifty capes in different weights and sizes for different lenses and perspective changes. It was endless. I'd like to throw out half the things I see on the screen now because I hate the costumes. It was a major pre-production decision, before I came on, and so we didn't change it. Sheer stupidity. There were so many things I wanted to do right, but I couldn't do right then. They had absolutely wasted a year's worth of pre-production work, as far as I was concerned. Boots! I threw out the boots and redesigned boots, but then finally I had to go with what I had. They were awful. I had to keep changing them. Sometimes I had the zipper on the side, sometimes on the back, sometimes on the front, depending on how he was standing. Those sorts of things were so easily anticipated, but nobody did.

CHRISTOPHER REEVE: I never had a stop date. I never knew when I'd be free. They'd say, "We'll spring you by March." Then it would be June. Then July. I could never make plans for the future or tell my agent when I'd be available. I used to come on to the set really angry and snap at Donner, "When are you going to get me out of here?" Then, in the same breath, I'd say, "Listen, that shot where I come in backwards. Maybe…" I really cared about what I was doing, you see. But I got $250,000 for this film and the sequel, which wasn't bad when they were both supposed to be wrapped up inside 10 months. But when you remember I've been working for a year-and-a-half and there's still a lot to do on the second, it isn't so much. I'd have made more money doing a TV soap opera. I did get overtime after a year and they offered me merchandising and profit participation, but even so, it's no fortune. (*The San Francisco Examiner*)

Entertainment journalist Ric Meyers, who was on set during filming for Starlog *maga-zine, observed one particular situation that, as he would come to understand much later on, was indicative of the sort of fatigue that had begun to settle on the production.*

RIC MEYERS (film historian, author and entertainment journalist): The cast and crew were ready to film the Lex Luthor lair sequences. The set was huge. We could play rugby without the camera seeing anything. There was the open expanse of Grand Central, the giant stairway, the swimming pool between the banisters, Luthor's office to the left at the top of the stairs and his lab, including the glass map of America covering its floor, to the right. Watching the filming was an absolute pleasure, especially since I discovered his hulking monosyllabic assistant was being played by Peter Boyle. I was especially excited since this would be their reunion after the excellent scene they did together in *Young Frankenstein* three years before.

Later, through the grapevine, I heard the disappointing news that Peter Boyle had been replaced in the film by Ned Beatty because the production was so over-schedule that Boyle had to contractually move on to another project. On opening day, I went to the film and things were going great for me… until Otis showed up, complete with an incongruous "dum de dum dum" theme song at odds with the rest of John Williams' extraordinary score. I might have managed to live with him/it, except that I had been on the set, I had seen Boyle and I had seen how his character's relationship with Luthor had supported and strengthened the film that Donner said he wanted to make. Hackman's Lex was the brains; Boyle's hulking henchman was the muscle. He fit with Luthor's psychology and needs. But Otis? Otis' presence not only nudged the film dangerously close to "campy," but established the unfortunate precedent that Luthor was not a cunning genius, but an emotionally weak bully who needed someone unfathomably stupid, not strong, around him at all times.

Some time later I visited Donner's California home while researching my books *The Great Science Fiction Films* and *TV Detectives*, and he explained the reasons for what I considered weaknesses in *Superman*. It had been a pitched battle with the producers pretty much all along, so when Boyle had to leave the production, they had no time to faithfully and realistically create the character of Otis. Further, Donner was exhausted and Hackman had lost almost all of his patience. So when everyone collaborated to reshoot the henchman scenes, they understandably took the easy road, and either consciously or subconscious, reflected and refracted the production's worsening, pressurized atmosphere and their feelings toward it. Why keep slaving to get the tone right? Let's just take the simple way out and get this thing over with. The producers wanted stupid silly camp? We'll give them stupid silly camp.

RICHARD DONNER: The fact is that I had a major problem on this picture, because I was as naive as anyone else — even more so. I read a script and rewrote it but the project was approached like Indians attacking a fort in a Western. The script would indicate that Superman flies here, he flies there, he does this, he does that — without anyone ever really figuring out how he was going to do all that. They simply turned a script over to us which we would change, and there were all these incredible effects to be created.

RAY MORTON: The flying sequences are marvelous. Many SFX techniques were employed to create them — wires, front projection, blue screen, miniatures, etc. But there were two key factors that really make the flying sequences work. The first is Stuart Baird's editing. In almost all of the action-oriented flying sequences, Baird cuts rapidly on the action from shot to shot. Each individual shot usually employs a different SFX technique to create the appearance of flight, but Baird mixes them together so rapidly that you never have the chance to dwell on how each shot was done and instead just accept an overall illusion of flight that is remarkably effective. None of the sequels employed this editorial technique, and thus hold on the individual shots so long that the seams begin to show and so the illusion is never quite as persuasive.

RICHARD DONNER: A film like *Superman* can work only if the audience accepts the fact that a man is flying. They will react with gasps, sighs and screaming — but in an odd sort of way, our feats in this film would be totally taken for granted by the audience. They applauded them and they were excited by the things the character does as Superman, but they wouldn't be impressed by "special effects," as they had been in other recent films that had been made. It's the takeoff, the landing, the attitudes in flight. To put Superman up in the air as a one-dimensional angle and keep him like that would have been an easy answer to the problem, but not an adequate answer for me, because it wasn't the ultimate. It was what I had seen before, or what had been done before, in certain motion pictures, but I wanted a more convincing illusion of reality. *Star Wars* and *Close Encounters* enjoyed a tremendous advantage over *Superman* at the time. They had the advantage of dealing with inanimate objects — space machines — that they could fly from place to place. When these spaceships came into the picture, they came in with a great deal of noise and light and, being inanimate, they could be computerized for multiple exposures on the film. In other words, their movements could be repeated precisely in order to add piece after piece of foreground and background detail. Since they were all inanimate objects, this was relatively easy to do, although still tremendously complicated.

RAY MORTON: The second key factor is the flying sequences is Christopher Reeve. The way he subtly adjusts his body and uses his arms to steer himself through the imagined currents of wind and air gives the flying shots a marvelous reality that, along with the remarkable visual effects, really allows us to believe that a man can… well, you know.

RICHARD DONNER: In *Superman* we were dealing with a man who is flying. You could never repeat his movements precisely — even with the best computer in the world, because he was a human being. If a finger moved in the wrong direction or his cape fluttered slightly differently, you could never reproduce that exactly. So we faced an incredible problem, because we couldn't computerize the operation. We could computerize movements of the background or camera, but we could never repeat the human movements precisely. Secondly, as I mentioned before, the spaceships came on to the screen with a great deal of noise and light. Sitting in the theater, you were shaken right out of your seat. It was magnificent! But Superman didn't make any noise or emit any light when he flies. This meant that there was a danger that his flying could seem uninteresting — especially if we simply had him going left to right, right to left, up or down.

CHRISTOPHER REEVE: The actual flying is completed in one's own mind. They used to ask, "How come the stuntman doesn't look real?" And I said, "Because the flying happens in the eyes." The flying comes in the conviction that you know where you are, what the altitude is, what speed you're going and you know what you're looking at. If that's not supplied by the actor, it doesn't happen. Subsequently, I'm not doubled anywhere in the picture — I did all my own flying on rigs where one stuntman broke his collarbone and another had to be put in traction.

RICHARD DONNER: As we actually filmed him, however, he twirls, he loops, he spirals — he flies! A great deal of the credit for this goes to Christopher Reeve. He knows what it is to fly, he feels it — the flying is as beautiful as it is because Christopher brought it to life. Anybody could have done it physically after we mastered the technique, but it is only real when he does.

CHRISTOPHER REEVE: The flying is done with me maybe 30 feet off the floor, looking at an English crew reading the racing forms and drinking tea. I'm just looking at a vast sea of blackness, 45 bored technicians and a few very funny-looking camera machines. I enjoyed the physicality of Superman's flying, but a year of the same thing day after day was not easy. There was a time, six or seven months, when I didn't speak a line. It was just interior mental work on the "A Stage Airline." Fly us.

And while Donner may view the "delivery" of Reeve as some sort of miracle, for her part Margot Kidder had a very different view of him.

MARGOT KIDDER: The thing about doing four movies with someone, and one of them went a year over schedule, is that you get to know someone really well and they become family. You know their bad side, you know their good side, you know what makes them laugh and what doesn't. There were times that Chris and I would be incredibly annoyed with each other, often while stuck to the ceiling, flying and bickering away until they said "Action!" and we had to go. There was a lot of that and then, you know, we hung out a lot together. I remember once we went ice skating and we both loved talking. We're speeding around this rink and the English people were clutching the side. It's like, "Ooh, wonder who these two people are speed-skating around." But he was *very* serious about his work, and *terrible* at improvising. If something happened that hadn't been rehearsed, he just wasn't an actor who adjusted very well to that. I love it when accidents happen and you do something totally unexpected. He used to cut takes on me and we'd have a little bicker and the crew would say,

"There they go again." He was very meticulous in his work, and I tend to like to have spaces for the unexpected to happen.

Even bigger was the fact that somehow — despite everything that they had gone wrong throughout production — it all came together in post-production, helped immeasurably by the addition of composer John Williams into the mix. By this point, Williams had already begun a string of movie themes that would prove iconic for decades to come, including Jaws, Star Wars *and* Close Encounters of the Third Kind, *with* Raiders of the Lost Ark/ Indiana Jones *only a few years away.*

RAY MORTON: John Williams' score for *Superman* is my favorite of his work and my favorite film score of all time. As always with Williams, the marches and themes are brilliant, but it is his furious intermixing of them in infinite combinations throughout the picture to weave a complex musical tapestry to accompany and support the visual narrative that takes my breath away every time I listen to it, which is very, very often.

JOHN WILLIAMS (composer, *Superman: The Movie*): One of the essential things about the film to me was the fact that it was fun and didn't take itself too seriously. And the way Richard had directed it, and particularly the way Chris and Margot had played the parts, it had almost a kind of theatrical camp, if you like, that didn't take itself too seriously. If one could strike a level of theater and sleight of hand and tongue-in-cheek in the creation of the themes, that might be the right idea. (featurette)

JEFF BOND (editor, *Film Score Monthly*): John Williams arguably wrote his most cohesive and powerful large scale symphonic theme for Richard Donner's *Superman*. It's unified by a pulsing ostinato that propels the piece rhythmically, and the bright opening trumpet line is celebratory, encapsulating the character's heroism, goodness and optimism, while a secondary theme for horns amply suggests Superman's superpowers — it's this theme that reportedly had Donner ecstatic at the scoring sessions as he pointed out that the theme's last three notes musically exclaim "Superman!" Add what is probably Williams' most soaring and lyrical love theme (ingeniously built into the title music as a bridge) and you have something uniquely American and iconic even by Williams' standards.

RICHARD DONNER: The day we went into the recording studio and we ran the opening credits, and as Superman came on screen, I swear to God, if you listen carefully, the music speaks the word. I screwed up his take, because I just ran out on the floor hailing, "Genius, fantastic!" The orchestra applauded him and everything, but again, if you listen, you can actually hear the music say the word "Superman."

LAUREN SHULER DONNER: I met Dick after *Superman,* so this is all second or third hand, but he did tell me that John Williams promised him that the theme would "sing" and that he'd hear the word Superman in it, and he certainly delivered.

JOHN WILLIAMS: The hero theme, which is Superman himself, is made up of several parts and is kind of a fanfare. Each time he opens up his shirt, you get this sort of three-note Superman musical motif; we established a kind of modus operandi that each time he revealed his shirt, there was this musical balletic preparation. I tried to have the music constructed in such a way that it would be heroic and big and operatic, but not take itself seriously.

As the decades passed from 1978 until his death in 2021, Donner remained justifiably proud of what was achieved with Superman, *holding the legend of the Man of Steel, and his contribution to it, in great regard, as do many others who continue to recognize its significance.*

RICHARD DONNER: The thing that got to me on the film and I wanted to do much more of, and I guess if I didn't have so much story I would have, is the idea of Superman appealing to our daydreams. How many of us have had a great desire to *be* Superman? To be impervious to pain and accomplish anything that you set out to do? Also, the idea that Superman is here to help us, and wouldn't we all like to be him for one goddamned minute? It's a mythology that reaches what is real today. Most mythology, as you know, is period in its being. He just seems to have gone along with time so very well.

RAY MORTON: If one is allowed to be pretentious and differentiate between movies (popular mass entertainments) and films (personal works by auteur directors), then *Superman* truly is a Richard Donner film. Prior to *Superman,* Donner had mostly been a journeyman television director (albeit an excellent one). He had made a few low-budget features in the '60s, but none made much of an impression. *The Omen* is a marvelous piece of cinematic craftsmanship and was an incredibly popular success, but doesn't have a particularly personal feel to it. *Superman* was something different. While Donner didn't generate the core material or conceive the idea for the film as one would expect an auteur to do, and while the movie was always intended to be a big commercial mass-audience entertainment rather than a personal art film, Richard Donner's personal vision is stamped into every frame of that film.

It was Donner who brought the underlying affection and respect for Superman and what he represents to the project — neither was present in either the Puzo or Benton/Newman drafts. It was Donner who made the decision to focus the entire narrative around the love story, thus giving the movie an emotional center it hitherto lacked. Donner's love of actors comes through in all of the film's carefully shaped and calibrated performances. His big energy, sentimental heart and sometimes raucous sense of humor are all over the picture, as is his expert craftsmanship and ability to use celluloid to generate a true sense of cinematic wonder.

TIM DEFOREST: It was *wonderful.* The moment where Christopher Reeve is in Lois' apartment as Clark and she's in another room, and he almost decides to tell her; he takes off his glasses, straightens up and smiles a Superman smile, before he gets nervous and reverts to Clark Kent. I still remember in 1978 thinking that people can actually believe they're two separate people. He's the actor who pulled that off more than anybody else.

ANTHONY TOLLIN: George Reeves always played Superman and Clark like they were the same person, but Chris Reeve — the body language, the height, the posture and just the whole manner he played it with was a phenomenal acting job. One of my problems with the current Superman in the films, Henry Cavill, is that he has not been given much to do with Clark Kent. He also has this bull neck from pumping iron that you never accept him as a wimpy Clark Kent. While I would say Bud Collyer pulled it off on the radio and the Fleischer cartoons, Chris was the only person I've seen on screen as Superman who made me believe that people could actually know Clark Kent and Superman and not instantly realize they were the same person. It's just the purest example of superhero dual identity acting ever on screen.

RAY MORTON: Christopher Reeve gives one of the all-time great performances as Superman/Kent. An actor who could often be awkward or self-conscious in other roles, Reeve's two-roles-in-one performance in *Superman* is perfect. His decision to underplay Superman by "letting the suit do most of the work" allows him to create a Man of Steel who is warm, relatable and human — "a friend." Reeve's Superman is not as instantly intimidating as George Reeves' interpretation, but in his own unique way he is no less formidable.

Reeve's Cary Grant in *Bringing Up Baby*-inspired concept for Clark is equally good. Awkward, clumsy and slightly goofy, Reeve's Kent comes across as a brilliant disguise — a costume that this already costumed hero dons to hide his true self from others… and an extremely effective one. Thanks to Reeve's marvelous use of body language — his Clark is stooped, slope-shouldered and a few inches shorter than his Superman; his adoption of an entirely different set of mannerisms and way of speaking, as well as a set of oversized glasses to obscure the similarity of features — it is entirely believable in context that no one in the film ever thinks that Clark Kent and Superman are one in the same. I must admit that when I first saw Superman, I didn't care for Reeve's Kent. I found him much too nerdy. Only later did I realize that this was because I was used to George Reeves' tough guy Clark Kent, which was my introduction to the character. Only when I realized that Reeve's Kent was more Superman than Clark did I recognize what a great job Reeve did in capturing the original essence of the character.

ALAN BURKE: As far back as I can remember, Christopher Reeve's Superman has been a part of my life. He has been everything to me, from a comfort blanket to a surrogate father figure, an inspiration and a friend. Those films have shaped my life in ways that I will never fully comprehend myself.

MARK MILLAR (writer, *Superman: Red Son*): I saw *Superman: The Movie* in the ABC cinema in Glasgow. I was nine years old when it was released and actually threw up with excitement whilst waiting in the queue. One of my four older brothers took me and, as I've said to him countless times, it changed my life forever. I'm writing comics thanks to that movie. It's still my all-time favorite.

J.J. ABRAMS (writer, unfilmed *Superman: Flyby*): I will never forget the first Superman film. It was opening week in Westwood, and back then movie openings were like events. It was remarkable. From the first frames — the images of the comic book panels — and the opening titles literally flying through space, leaving those awesome silver trails… it was inspiring. The charm, the characterizations, the comedy, the jeopardy, the visual effects, the music — it was all just an incredible journey. Dick Donner just totally captured it. For me, it was a seminal experience. That film is what great movies should be: intelligent, good-natured, good-humored, heart-lifting, and most of all, empowering.

TIM DEFOREST: It was unapologetically a superhero movie; it wasn't embarrassed by it and didn't tone things down. It treated the characters with the same kind of respect the George Reeves TV series had. I can still watch it today with just as much enjoyment.

TOM MANKIEWICZ: The weird thing was, when *Superman* came out it was a big hit, but everybody was lying in wait for it. And you get that with movies, where critics are gonna write a bad review even if they like it. And we got some wonderful reviews, but we got some where people had already written the review. And then *Superman II* came out, it got slightly better reviews, but now the first one is so far more memorable than the second. One of my favorite critics ever — Joe Morgenstern, who writes for the *The Wall Street Journal* — wrote a column selecting five big-budget films to treasure and one was the original *Superman*. He said, "Go back and look at this again." The picture touched a lot of people.

JOHN WELLS: I saw Christopher Reeve fly into action in early 1979 when I was 14 and he is still the perfect Superman for me. The screenplay had great fun with placing a sincere, trustworthy fantasy hero in cynical, corrupt situations and mining comedy from the contrast. The reason this worked so well was Reeve's ability to sell his role flawlessly. His Superman is earnest, but leavened with charm, humor and heart that never treats the character as a campy laughing stock. Reeve's depiction of Clark Kent also can't be praised enough, using body language and vocal techniques in a way that silenced the critics who laughed that no one recognized Superman when he put on a pair of glasses.

ELLIOT S! MAGGIN: I think the movie was important, not only for Superman as a cultural figure, but to all the comic book characters who have movies out now. And the only reason they're successful is because *Superman* was successful. Okay, not the *only* reason, but they were able to gather the budgets and expertise and talent that they did.

JACK O'HALLORAN: Donner and Mankiewicz ate, drank and slept Superman. Donner was an amazing director and having a backup like Mankiewicz was terrific; they worked together so well. He was the real deal, everybody loved him because he was real about what he did. And he brought the best out of people. He had that ability.

RAY MORTON: What Donner brought most to the movie was joy — pure, uncynical, optimistic joy. *Superman* is an incredibly positive picture. It is unabashedly about a hero and celebrates that hero and all he stands for without snark or irony or sarcasm. It's a movie that loves all its characters, even the evil ones. It's a film that knows all of the things popular movies do so well — action, spectacle, thrills, humor, technical magic and heart — and it gives them all of these things in great, big, generous helpings; particularly in the film's most spectacular set-piece — the helicopter rescue which delivers all of these elements in a breathtaking five minutes. It's a movie that pulls its audience in and embraces it to the extent that, at the end, it literally smiles at them. All of this is due to Richard Donner.

PAUL LEVITZ: Donner really wrote the superhero movie bible. If you dissect what he did there, most of the Marvel Cinematic Universe maps to it. That's partly due to the fact that Kevin Feigi worked for Donner at the beginning of his career and that was where he learned some of his trade, some of his craft, partly because Donner got it right. I mean, it was an incredibly difficult thing for Donner to do. The scripts came from four or five different sources and it was stitched together with spit and baling wire. There were all kinds of incredibly difficult people to be working for, but he pulled it off. I only spoke to Donner a couple of times later in his life; I don't know whether the success was his love for the character or whether it was his skill as a director.

LAUREN SHULER DONNER: Dick was a very grounded guy. He had an ego, but he didn't have an ego that got in the way. He was a giant television director, and he had done the movies *X-15* and *Salt and Pepper*, which didn't do much for his career. Then he did *The Omen*, which was a giant hit. When he did *Superman*, because it was such a huge undertaking and he was so demanding on it, it put him into the stratosphere of directors — where he wanted to be — and he could pick and choose. But it's success never changed him.

RICHARD DONNER: As for my personal feelings? I obviously have a tremendous affection for Superman and what he stands for in my life. I owe him *everything*.

BRAD RICCA: Jerry Siegel and Joe Shuster loved that their credit was restored. I don't think this is over-romanticizing it, because certainly it was about money, but to them it was — especially for Jerry — more than money, it was just DC completely abandoning them and leaving them nothing in terms of acknowledgement that they created it. But at that point they had it from then on, which was really cool.

ANTHONY TOLLIN: The second time Chris came up to DC, when he was doing a drawing to win Superman's cape, somehow *every* secretary in the building managed to be on our floor. And I can say, in a totally heterosexual sense, he's the handsomest man I've ever met — just incredibly handsome, but a very good actor whose dual performance in those two roles was so amazing that people don't even realize what an acting challenge it was.

CHRISTOPHER REEVE: Right after *Superman* opened, it was difficult for me to accept the hero worship that came at me. And I immediately made choices of material that, in a way, gave everybody the finger. My actions were meant to tell the public, "Don't look up to me. Don't think of me as a hero." For example, one of my immediate choices was to play a screwed-up homosexual playwright in *Deathtrap*. As an acting chance, it offered Michael Caine, [director] Sidney Lumet, screenplay by Jay Allen — a really nice pedigree. And yet, the character I played was one the audience couldn't possibly like or identify with… It was almost necessary for me at the time to play characters who were gay, crippled, psychotic, neurotic, killers, whatever. It was almost a pompous, self-important way of telling the public, "Screw you, I'll tell you who I am, so you don't tell me." That is what was going on in my head at the time. I have to admit that I was a particularly ungraceful and unsympathetic person at the time. (*Interview*)

One of the perks of Superman: The Movie *actually came to Elliot S! Maggin, who was able to take his love for the Man of Steel and his talent to craft a pair of original Superman novels,* Superman: Last Son of Krypton *(1978) and* Superman: Miracle Monday *(1981).*

TIM DEFOREST: Elliot Maggin wrote a couple of original Superman novels which were concurrent with the first two movies. Apparently there was some sort of legal issue with getting the movies novelized, so they just got Maggin to write originals. Legally, Mario Puzo had to novelize the script, but he didn't want to. I think he wanted his son to write it, but that never happened. Again, that was actually to the benefit, because Maggin's novels are two of the best Superman stories out there. He catches the character well, the humanity of the characters and his desire to right a wrong in the universe.

ELLIOT S! MAGGIN: Nobody really decided it, but Mario Puzo made it necessary. I had written a film treatment for a *Superman* movie in 1974 and made a case to Carmine about how the time of heroes was returning and it was getting to be time for a Superman feature film. He seemed to agree, but rather than think about my treatment he must have made the same case to the guys at Warner Bros. A year or so later, sci-fi writer Alfred Bester showed up at the office and wanted to talk to me about a Superman movie that he was negotiating to write. That fell through, and not long afterward I came in one day and there's Mario Puzo wanting to have the same conversation that Bester had been interested in. Cary Bates and I spent two days in a conference room with Mario explaining how Superman was basically a Greek tragedy (those were Mario's words, actually) and then he went off to write his movie. So I dusted off my film treatment and went upstairs to Warner Books and asked them to consider my story for a novel. That was *Last Son of Krypton*. It was never supposed to be a movie tie-in. It was supposed to be released midway between the first two films to keep the franchise afloat in the interim.

Mario had the rights to do a novel adaptation of his film, but he got all tripped up in Hollywood politics and wasn't able to do it. He sat on the rights, though, so no one else could do it, and they put my book out the same day the movie was released. There were nine publishing products that came out with that movie and mine was apparently the only one that sold worth a damn. Neal Adams had done a comic booky cover for the book; beautiful stuff. But they substituted a movie still, and the next time I saw Neal's cover it was in around 1989 in an Andy Warhol swipe at the Museum of Modern Art. Warhol claimed it was "adapted" from a Superman drawing circa 1955 or so, but it was clearly Neal's Superman novel cover from 1978. I don't know whether Neal ever saw that Warhol exhibit — he used to go to the Museum a lot — but I doubt he ever tripped over Warhol's swipe of him. I should tell him about it.

Superman was released in the United States on December 15, 1978, and while the film's budget grew to a then-enormous $55 million, it would ultimately gross over $300 million at the global box office and laid to rest the question of whether or not production on Superman II *would pick up again. What wasn't so certain was whether or not Richard Donner would be returning given the growing war of words between him, the Salkinds and producer Pierre Spengler. In the end, the decision was made that the first film's liaison, Richard Lester, would step in as director.*

RICHARD DONNER: My original contract was to deliver two films and everybody who signed was told that they were doing two films. We started both and shot everything with Marlon Brando, Gene Hackman, Ned Beatty and Valerie Perrine for both pictures, and then we realized that if we were going to deliver the first one by Christmas 1978, we had to stop and put all our efforts into that. Having completed everything with those actors, we put *Superman II* on the side burner and all our efforts into the first film. *Superman* was a success and the Salkinds, for whatever reason, chose not to bring me back after I waited to hear for six or eight weeks. I got a telegram one day that said, "Your services are no longer needed." That's the Dick Lester story.

LAUREN SHULER DONNER: By the time I'd met Dick, he'd resolved the situation internally. He had the response that any man or woman would have had: anger, hurt; but he had the good sense to move forward.

ILYA SALKIND: In those days, there was a guy, very famous, named Army Archerd, who would write for *Variety*. And he would say that Donner had said he would not do *Superman II* unless it was on his terms. Then I said to my father, "Look, we can't work with this guy." I mean, he often insulted us, he said we were assholes and all kinds of shit. So we decided not to use him for the remainder of *Superman II*. Then we hired Lester, who had directed *The Three* and *Four Musketeers* for us, which were fantastic. He reshot a lot of the stuff so that he would get his credit. I think we offered Donner a credit, but he refused it.

MARK WAID: Pierre actually swears he was at a Christmas party and heard from film critic Army Archerd, who said he was on the phone with Donner just a few days earlier, that Donner had resigned from the movie. Pierre says that was news to him. According to him, Donner just gave up and quit.

RICHARD LESTER: Dick shot a small portion of *Superman II*. We did a count, finally, of how much Dick had done of the second film and I think it was something like 12%, and there were a few other second unit directors who had done some other material, but his work was that much. There is a sheet somewhere the producers have which lists every single shot, how long it lasts and how much it is. That doesn't tell you anything emotionally, but technically that tells you how much was preshot by Donner himself.

JACK O'HALLORAN: They used the excuse that Donner was spending too much money, but that was because we were doing *Superman I* and *II* and it only cost $50-million for both pictures. They had to spend a lot more money to go back and reshoot material to make Lester the legitimate director.

TOM MANKIEWICZ: Dick Donner shot most of *Superman II*. The major thing that Lester shot was Niagara Falls where Lois falls in. Lester shot the actual aerial fight between Superman and the three villains, and also the thing where they land and destroy the town. Everything inside, for instance the scene with Gene Hackman inside the Daily Planet leading up to the aerial fight, was shot by Dick. But Dick didn't want the credit for *Superman II*. He said something that was absolutely right. He said, "If the first one had been a flop, they would have *made* me finish the second one. But because the first one was a big hit and I kept calling them assholes, they fired me." And that's absolutely true.

TERENCE STAMP: The tragedy of it was that we were all crazy in love with Richard Donner. I just can't tell you what a great guy he is. He's kind of big in every sense of the word and he's funny. And he's a wonderful director. Replacing him with Richard Lester was terrible for him and it was terrible for us, because we loved him. And there was no way we could not go back.

SARAH DOUGLAS: And I cannot tell you how different the two directors were. And I have to say, as a young actress, we reshot a lot of the scenes with somebody that was so different, so experience-wise, that was amazing. But we went from having this wonderful, larger-than-life, loving gregarious man to Dick Lester, who was much quieter and didn't have the same sort of humor. And everybody was pissed off. The cast, particularly Chris and Margot, were deeply upset and felt much betrayed. It was difficult.

JACK O'HALLORAN: Working with Donner was extremely wonderful. Lester was an amateur compared to Donner and the Salkinds were fools. The person who really made it fall apart was Christopher Reeve, because he should have stood up and said, "No Donner, no me," because Donner gave him every-thing that he needed. He made the magic happen, so when they said they were going to bring Lester on, he should have turned around and said no. The whole franchise would've been better and *Superman III* would have been a better movie too. But this kid's head was up his ass for some reason and I don't know why, because before Donner he had no notoriety at all. That's why Hackman didn't come back. Hackman wouldn't work with Lester. They had to use the footage that Donner had already shot. And then how do you cut Marlon Brando out of a movie? Because they didn't want to pay him. And *The Donner Cut* is so much better — Marlon's right where he's supposed to be, tying things together. So the foolishness is that by stealing the money, they cheated themselves.

TERENCE STAMP: This is something I feel I should explain: One of the magic moments of making movies is that from time to time, you get a crew that becomes a troupe. And you really feel like you're in one of Shakespeare's compa-nies, with Shakespeare writing and touring around England doing stuff. In other words, two and two make seven, and that happens rarely. But when it happens, it's so wonderful, because you can't wait to get to work, and that was really down to Richard Donner. I'm a romantic, but I just felt he had this aura that just enclosed all of us. And the fact is, when he was let go, we just didn't want to go back. You know what I mean? It wasn't the fact that we didn't think Richard Lester was a great director, but it was Richard Donner's project. And as the only really successful film I've ever been in, it's nice. We can rarely get through the day without somebody coming up to me and saying, "Kneel before Zod."

ILYA SALKIND: As I said, we reshot a lot of stuff with Lester and then used some of the scenes Donner had shot. But overall, I would say we shot three quarters of the movie.

RICHARD LESTER: By the time *Superman II* was supposed to happen, there was already litigation between Donner and the producers, so there was no way they were going to work together. For one thing, he was suing the Salkinds for money owed. He also had set a list of demands like they would have to leave the picture if he was going to carry on. They then came to me and said, "Would you do it?" Having been involved that little bit on the first one, I was astonished at the technical possibilities that were available to which I was totally and woefully ignorant in terms of miniatures and traveling mattes, which I had never been involved with. I came on more like an open university course, viewing it as a chance to learn what I felt I should know.

TOM MANKIEWICZ: When *Superman II* was gonna be finished, Terry Semel came down to my office before they started up again and said, "Would you go back? Dick Lester wants you to finish up the picture with him." I said, "I can't do that Terry. Dick [Donner] is my friend, he brought me on, he's right across the street here. I can't do that." And he said, "Well, could you go to London and accidentally bump into Dick Lester and have dinner with him and give him…?" I said, "No, I can't do that." And then the Salkinds did the unkindest thing of all: They cut Brando out of the second one because he had a piece of the gross.

ILYA SALKIND: The decision was totally financial, because he would have had 11¼ percent of the gross of *Superman II*. *That* was the reason. It was unbelievable: He would have made another $18 million in those days, which was about $50 million today.

TOM MANKIEWICZ: They read in his contract that if he didn't appear in the film, he didn't get it. And they cut him out. And the whole arc (and I hate to use pretentious words like that), where Marlon is sending the kid to earth — it is God sending Christ to earth, it may be Allah sending Mohammed to Earth — and then he defies him by turning the world backwards in the first and bringing Lois back to life, and then in the second film when he loses his powers, Brando comes and commits suicide through reaching out for him to give him new life. So this was all one story and these pricks cut him out. They didn't want to pay a piece of the gross even though they knew the picture was going to be a big hit, there was going to be plenty of money for everybody. And they put out this lame story: It cost too much to get him back – he'd already shot all the scenes. They were there! He'd done it all.

MARK WAID: There were two things going on. First off, I don't think they fought to get Donner back, because it was such a contentious relationship. The other was that the reason Richard Lester signed on at all was because they still owed him money on *The Three Musketeers*, so he figured, "Maybe this is a way to get some of my money back." So that worked to the Salkinds' financial advantage; they could write part of his salary off against money already owed him.

RICHARD LESTER: Now the problems I felt were there on the first film were still there in that there wasn't any reality. I think you can see by the third one, where I had some input on the storyline — or at least more input — that I was playing around with the toys of reality by getting an actor like Richard Pryor and starting the whole film off in an unemployment office. In essence, it's really examining how far you can go towards a reality. That being the case, *II* was more of a technical exercise, which was very interesting. I also found that I'd enjoyed the experience on *I* and had a very good time on *II*. There's something remarkably easy about working on a film with four units. If anybody has a problem, if you find you're up against some problem on that unit, you just say, "I'm terribly sorry, lads, but the flying unit needs me desperately," and you can walk away from that problem and whistle along in the studio. Nobody knows where you are and they all assume you're hard at work on one of the other units, so when you come back they've solved that problem and you go on day after day.

He did feel that there was a very human core at the heart of the film in terms of the Lois/Clark/Superman relationship.

RICHARD LESTER: I think you have to work hard at that. My theory is that in a film that's very technical, it is important to always have a sequence, especially after a very special effects-heavy scene, where two actors could work easily together; where they didn't have to stand on a particular spot and have a cable up their backside, so you could have a naturalistic character/actor in to do a scene before you go zooming off into another technical, and therefore slightly stiff, sequence. We tried to make sure that we wrote, with the Newmans, sequences where the actors could get their teeth into something that had a little bit of reality about it.

As far as actors are concerned, Superman II *got off to a rough start. Although Terence Stamp, Sarah Douglas and Jack O'Halloran had been signed to reprise their Kryptonian villain roles of, respectively, Zod, Ursa and Non (who come to Earth and plan to take over the planet), there were actually some difficulties with stars Margot Kidder and Christopher Reeve. Kidder made it clear to anyone who would listen that she was not pleased with the* *shoddy treatment given to Richard Donner by the Salkinds and, if not for the sheer necessity of her participation, the odds are fairly strong that she would have been dismissed. Reeve, for his part, had grown upset over the fact that he had been paid a reported $250,000 for both films, while* Superman: The Movie *went on to gross nearly $300 million. Things got so bad, in fact, that he actually walked off the film. The Salkinds attempted some posturing, claiming that if James Bond could be replaced so could Superman, but a settlement was worked out and Reeve donned his tights.*

MARGOT KIDDER: On the first film, Chris and I were the most inexperienced, so we got the lowest salaries of anyone. For the second one, we renegotiated our contracts, because I found out they had ads with Chris in Japan holding Pepsi cans in his hand. He then found out they had Taco Bell glasses with my picture on it and we weren't getting part of the proceeds, so we were able to sue the producers. Chris was too nervous about it all, so he turned up to work every day, but I said through my lawyers that I wasn't going to turn up until we renegotiate my contract for it to include part of the merchandising... so they upped both of our salaries.

Having renewed his flying license, Reeve was more than happy to discuss his feelings about both Superman and Clark Kent.

CHRISTOPHER REEVE: Both identities are more sharply defined in *Superman II.* In the first picture, we had to establish who Superman was and why he disguised himself as Clark Kent. This time, we come out swinging. Like most people of my age, I was brought up on Superman. I knew the classic stance — hands on hips, cape blowing in the breeze, bullets bouncing off his chest. That's the way the six-and-a-half billion people have loved Superman, and I wouldn't dream of changing it. But I wanted to find other dimensions as well. In a sense, Superman is a stranger in a strange land, a solitary man with incredible powers, trying to fit into his adopted planet. He has warmth and a great sense of humor. And while he has sworn to uphold "truth, justice and the American way," there's nothing self-conscious about him. That's simply because it's what he believes in, in a world filled with arch-criminals and evil geniuses. However, Clark Kent is more fun to play. There's more scope to the role because he is such an awful mess.

When you approach the Superman character, you must remember that when a man, superhuman or not, is capable of heroic deeds, he becomes a bore, a very pompous bore, if he doesn't have a sense of humor about himself. Because of all the amazing things Superman can do, he must temper his achievements with a certain kind of human modesty in order to make himself acceptable to others.

He must be secure enough about himself to make jokes and to be vulnerable in that sense. If he didn't, he would be impossible to relate to and no one would like him. The vision of Superman we have tried to portray is that of a superhero in every sense of the word. Besides being a super-strong athlete, he is also a gentleman and a scholar. He is someone who sincerely tries not to take unfair advantage of other people, even though he has superhuman powers. The whole idea of a musclebound vigilante crusading around the skies, knocking people's heads together, has never really appealed to me. Above all, I wanted to portray Superman as a hero for the '80s, a gentleman who is liberated and intelligent, and who has a definite sense of humor and fair play. (*Press Notes*)

RICHARD LESTER: I think that Donner was emphasizing a kind of grandiose myth. There was a kind of David Lean-ish attempt in certain sequences, and enormous scale. There was an epic quality which isn't in my nature, so my work really didn't embrace that. We didn't want to destroy the myth until we deliberately did in *III*. I don't think I could have done that sort of work, the early Kansas/Smallville scenes. That's not me; that was *his* vision of it. I'm more quirky and I play around with slightly more unexpected silliness. I've never really worked with storyboards before these films. I've never really prepared sequences in that way. I've been inclined to look at the day and see what's there and wing it.

DAVID NEWMAN: Our favorite is *Superman II*. The problem with the first film is that there was so much back story to get out of the way. I think *Superman* is three different movies. There's the Krypton part, which you had to tell because that's the legend, although there's something which seems pretentious about it to me.

LESLIE NEWMAN: On the other hand, you really don't have the time to get to know the individual characters on Krypton as characters, so you can't make Krypton have any reality.

DAVID NEWMAN: Then there's the Smallville stuff and that's a kind of John Ford-looking film, with all those landscapes, Glenn Ford, farmers and all that stuff, which is another movie. And once you get to Metropolis, that's another movie. To me, there was an unavoidable clash of styles in *Superman I*, although the film works wonderfully. *Superman II*, to us, was just a dream to do because you didn't have to go into all that stuff. We were actually able to recap the original under the credits. And I love those three villains. To me, *Superman II* was a fairy tale. First of all, it was a fairy tale about love, second of all it had the greatest threat because it was three against one with a slam-bang finish.

LESLIE NEWMAN: And the thing we love most is the intercutting; the pacing of the stories. We also love the Lois/Superman/Clark triangle.

DAVID NEWMAN: There's that great aspect of the mythos, which is Lois Lane. She loves Superman but doesn't like Clark. Clark loves her and is jealous of Superman, so he doesn't like Superman.

LESLIE NEWMAN: And in the love scene, which is our favorite, she says, "But if it wasn't for him, I wouldn't have met you" and it's all so confusing, because she's just found out the truth. I was fascinated by Lois and her relationship to both Clark and Superman, and the very nature of Lois. She reflects changing attitudes towards women. I couldn't bear the Lois of the '50s, but then it was pretty unbearable being a woman in the '50s. When you write film, it helps to have somebody to write for. It doesn't matter if they're alive or dead. It's just a notion in your mind, although it's not likely to be that person in all probability, but it's who gives you the germ. So in this case, she didn't want to give it all up and settle down. She was spunky.

DAVID NEWMAN: Whereas the Lois Lane of the '50s thought, "If he'd only marry me, I could settle down."

LESLIE NEWMAN: And she always got herself into dumb scrapes, not because of ambition but because of stupidity.
One of the most talked about aspects of Superman II *was the aerial battle between Superman and the three villains from Krypton. Surprisingly, Lester doesn't feel that achieving that sequence was as daunting as one would think.*

RICHARD LESTER: It was only insane in the fact that you sit down in a room with people, many of whom have quite reasonable brains and have gone to universities and taken degrees and are good with their children and wash their cars, tend their garden, who say, "Okay, he's going to pick up the bus and throw it at Superman. How do we do that?" And these grown men sit around for a while and find the answers. Once you accept a certain set of ground rules, you realize this is the scale that looks real and we can do, and these are things we can't do, and get the balance right. I've always felt about all films of this type that unless you explain to the audience precisely what the powers are, they are happy with them. They are pre-set in their minds. Then you just go crazy. I think in the film *Supergirl*, someone's powers seemed to alter arbitrarily, and it wasn't set up. It just seemed clumsy to me, and I think audiences feel that if suddenly you switch the rules in the middle of the film, you don't know where you are. You want to know that this power is equal to that power so they cancel each other out, and you can't just invent a new power.

To be fair, Superman II *actually did include a sequence where the villains levitated someone with a beam from their fingers and blasted Superman with a similar beam — neither of which existed in the comics prior to that moment.*

RICHARD LESTER: I don't see that that's any worse than super-breath in terms of scale. Certainly all of the scripts and changes were always sent to DC Comics to make sure they're in the canon. And, in fact, there was a representative from DC Comics who saw the dailies every day. Certainly nobody said, "Well, that's something that wouldn't happen." Mind you, I think if you did something absolutely insane but looked terrific, they'd say, "Okay, we'll go and write that into the next comic and have it out before the film comes out." I have my own feeling about that. I think the myth and the tricks within the original idea, whether they be conscious or unconscious, were treated with respect, sometimes more than others. In general, we were all careful to respect that basic idea and that will always work. Today a *Superman* film would be a little easier to make, because other people have already done it, but it was bloody hard work at the time.

Upon its release, Superman II *(which premiered around the world in 1980 and made it to the States a year later) was greeted with near unanimous praise, with a great many critics claiming it was actually better than its predecessor, achieving the perfect mix of romance and comic book action. Some of that enthusiasm would diminish over the years, largely because of the way that certain elements of the film seemed tacked together given the fact that some elements were directed by Donner and the rest by Lester. Fans would get a greater sense of what the former had intended in 2006 when* Superman II: The Richard Donner Cut *was released on DVD.*

RICHARD DONNER: Let me put it to you this way: All the good parts of *Superman II* are mine. Everything with Hackman, Brando — well, they cut him out, but that footage was released later — Beatty and Perrine was shot by me.

RAY MORTON: Even without knowing the production back story, the sequel has a patchwork quality to it. It also looks cheap and in some places is remarkably sloppy. The first example of this is Margot Kidder's appearance. The actress had lost considerable weight between *I* and *II* and looks gaunt and unhealthy. Also, no attempt was made to match her hairstyle to the way it appeared in *I*. Instead, she was given a dreadful wig that doesn't look anything like real hair, much less the hair she had in *I*. Had these changes been consistent throughout the picture it might not have been so bad, but shots of Kidder's new appearance were freely intercut with shots of her filmed during the original production, and as a result she frequently looks noticeably and at times shockingly different from shot to shot in the same scene. It's mind-boggling that professional filmmakers allowed this to happen.

RICHARD DONNER: My version was going to be more in the tradition of the first one. The villains were going to be much more believable. I *hated* that stuff they did with the villains in the small town. It looked like an Englishman's point of view of what America would be like, with the army, the jeeps, the people — there was no sense of size to it. It lost its sense of importance.

TOM MANKIEWICZ: Then we had the scene — which is in *The Donner Cut* — where Jor-El basically commits suicide. It's God touching the hand of Adam as Jor-El touches his son and rejuvenates him, and "kills" himself by expelling the last of his energy. That scene's as chilling as anything you've ever seen on the screen. It was shot with Brando and was wonderful, but because the Salkinds would have had to pay him money, Superman says, "Mother, mother," instead of "Father, father," which is what he should have done and did do in the script. Brando appeared and said, "Even though this will extinguish what is left of my life — I warned you, I told you…" And he reaches out through the void. Clark is unconscious and it's, again, God touching the hand of Adam.

RAY MORTON: That was the second most egregious example of the patchwork feeling — the same shocking cheap and shoddy production design colludes with the British production team's apparent complete ignorance of small-town American life to create a town with unpaved streets supposedly located in the Midwest, but populated by Southern hicks, including at least one kid who wears farmer's overalls and doesn't wear shoes, but for some reason has a British accent and, when the bad guys come, is defended by U.K. special forces. The town not only doesn't look like a small American town, it doesn't look like a town at all, just some random assemblages on a backlot somewhere. Once again, it's shocking that professional filmmakers perpetrated such an abomination.

TOM MANKIEWICZ: *New York* magazine's David Denby, upon viewing *Superman II*, wrote, "Well, you can tell the difference between Dick Donner and Richard Lester in terms of sophistication, because in this picture, *Superman II*, Gene Hackman really had something to do, he's really wonderful, arch and so on as opposed to his performance in the first one." Well, I wrote a letter to David Denby and said, "Just for your information, and this is not to denigrate Richard Lester, who's a very nice man and a good director, every foot of film of Gene Hackman was directed by Dick Donner and written by me. So much for your being able to tell the difference between Richard Lester and Richard Donner." They never printed the letter.

JACK O'HALLORAN: Lester's version had too much comedy in it... oh my God!

The Richard Donner Cut, *an attempt to as closely as possible resemble Donner's original take for* Superman II, *featuring footage, filling out sequences with audition scenes and adding a bit of digital effects, has its own critics.*

ALAN BURKE: While I appreciate having a much better and more rounded understanding of Donner's overall vision for the franchise, a vision which I believe to be truly superior to that of Richard Lester and the Salkinds, I don't think the film works overall. Although I thoroughly enjoyed seeing so many new scenes featuring Christopher Reeve's iconic performance and though it cannot be denied that the sacrifice of Jor-El carries much more weight and significance than its equivalent in the theatrical cut, I simply much prefer many of the theatrical scenes over those included in Donner's finished film.

I also take issue with the removal of one of the most iconic lines in the entire franchise for no reason whatsoever. "General, would you care to step outside?" is, for lack of a better descriptive, *badass!* It's even more badass when it comes after the scene which immediately preceded it in which all hope seems lost in Metropolis until... we hear the familiar hint of the John Williams theme and see the rustling of newspapers as the people of Metropolis look up into the night sky knowing that their hero has finally arrived to take out the trash. *The Donner Cut* removes the theme music, has Superman arrive with no fanfare whatsoever to flatly declare, "General, haven't you ever heard of freedom of the press?" I take issue with changing things for the worse simply for the sake of changing things. My final issue with the film is the ending. I understand that no other ending was shot so they simply reused the ending of the first film, and while far from ideal, I accept that there was only so much material to work with. The issue I have is the insertion of footage from what is clearly contemporary 2006 in the montage of time reversal. I find it lazy, inexcusable and again, it only serves to take me out of the overall experience.

There are positives too, however. The removal of all slapstick comedy makes for a much more sinister threat and significantly raises the stakes resulting in the overall tone of *The Donner Cut* being far superior to that of the theatrical cut. The Jor-El scenes are formidable and bring the father/son story arc from *Superman: The Movie* to a satisfying conclusion in a way not nearly achieved by Lester's version. Overall, I am more than grateful that *The Donner Cut* exists and that Richard was afforded the opportunity to heal some old wounds and show fans a glimpse of what could have been going forward, if not for the shortsightedness of the Salkinds at the time.

MICHAEL BAILEY: I think *The Donner Cut* is an interesting artifact. It's weird because, ultimately, it's not the film we would have gotten. The ending would have been changed and I'm sure other parts of the movie would have gone differently. Seeing the Brando footage was cool. I do find it odd that WB pushes this as an official version of the film in box sets. To me this is a big-budget special feature, not an actual, factual film. It's incomplete and the CGI on the scenes to fill in the blanks is distracting. Ultimately, I am a fan of the Lester cut, which is somewhat controversial, but I think having Lara play a larger role was neat and the line, "General, would you care to step outside?" is so much better than the one about the freedom of the press. And it does show how much they reshot. I do agree with the idea that it puts those claims to rest.

LAUREN SHULER DONNER: When he had the opportunity to do his cut of *Superman II*, it wasn't like, "Oh, now I get to tell *my* story." That just wasn't him. I do think there was some satisfaction in it, but he just tackled it like any other movie he did. It didn't mean any more or any less. He was a pretty balanced guy. My philosophy as a producer when I needed a potential director for my movie is that I know that 99% of the time the director's personality gets on the screen. Dick Donner's personality was big, larger-than-life, fun, warm, emotional, sort of strong, a little bit macho, but kind, kinetic, fun energy — all that got up on the screen no matter what the film was. *That* was a Dick Donner film.

MARK WAID: As per directors' guild regulations, in order to call it *The Donner Cut* and remove Richard Lester's name, Michael Thau, the editor who worked with Donner to restore his footage, was required to include a specific percentage of Donner's footage no matter what. It's evident that hard choices had to be made in certain scenes; no one on Earth could *possibly* think it was any sort of improvement to, for instance, drop the Lester line, "General, would you care to step outside?" In the end, it's more of a curiosity than an actual standalone film. In my opinion, compared to Lester's version, it's a better story but a worse movie.

Straight continuity.

That's the way director Richard Lester describes the genesis of Superman III, *a sequel that* had *to be produced given the worldwide success of the first two entries in the series. The question, though, was where to take the Man of Steel next.*

RICHARD LESTER: When you're in the third of a series and a man has a certain amount of power and you have to find a way to destroy his invincibility in order to create a story, you begin to think, "Oh dear, we've done that before." These are the powers on a certain scale we can work with and, yes, you do begin to run out of ideas. Aside from that, I don't think the script for *Superman III* was that difficult to develop. We deliberately tried to make it as unlike the other two as possible.

JOHN KENNETH MUIR: With director Richard Donner completely out of the picture, it's clear that a fundamental and vital respect for the Man of Steel is missing in action in this under-cooked sequel. The series' overarching symbolism (comparing the Kryptonian messiah to Jesus Christ) is gone, as is any sense of scope or majesty. Instead, *Superman III* lurches straight into comedy with lame physical gags and a dithering Richard Pryor in a starring role. The film's humor — *while problematic* — isn't the only significant hurdle for this sequel. A much more rudimentary problem involves the nature of the screenplay. It flat-out doesn't make sense in terms of Superman's relationships. Basically, Margot Kidder's Lois is written out, leaving him to romance Lana Lang, and the switchover never rings true. Late in the movie, there is a legitimately great scene with Superman getting split apart and having to battle a dissolute version of himself, but it's about the only thing in the whole film that works.

MICHAEL EURY: In *Superman III* they create a robot, right? Why not do Brainiac? A few years back at Superman Celebration I interviewed Ilya Salkind and he said they did want to do Brainiac, but they never got a chance. Even today, every time they roll out another bald-headed bad guy, I'm thinking, "Come on, can't we just do a Brainiac movie with the special effects that are available?"

The Superman/Lois romance of the first two films was to be jettisoned for a variety of reasons, not the least of which was that actress Margot Kidder had absolutely no intention of appearing in Superman III — *a fact which suited the Salkinds fine. However, Richard Lester felt that her presence, in one form or another, was absolutely necessary for the sake of continuity. Kidder reportedly received a substantial payment for her role in the film, which amounted to little more than a cameo at the beginning and end of the story as Lois Lane departs to and returns from vacation.*

That fact suggested a plotline in which Clark Kent returns to Smallville for his high school reunion. There he comes together with his first love (though she probably never knew it), Lana Lang (Annette O'Toole). In direct contrast to his life in Metropolis, Clark finds that he doesn't have to be a complete nebbish and that Lana is falling for him — *not Superman.*

RICHARD LESTER: Margot certainly didn't want to be involved and I tried to find a fairly elegant compromise whereby she wouldn't simply disappear, but where she didn't have to be involved with the producers or the film in any major way. Considering her feelings, I think she was very nice to do it. I admired her, because she was really doing it for Chris and me.

DAVID NEWMAN: During the shooting of the Niagara Falls sequences of *Superman II,* Leslie and I were sitting in a restaurant in this hotel, and there was something about Niagara Falls being spoken about in terms of a place for young couples to go. I had been to my own class reunion two years before, and we started talking about the fact that there was nowhere else to go with the Superman/Lois love story; we didn't want to do the same thing again. Then we were talking about Frank Capra movies, and about going back home again and the notion that you can't go home again. Then the whole Lana Lang/Superman idea of going back to Smallville began.

ANNETTE O'TOOLE (actress, "Lana Lang," *Superman III***):** Lana sees the real person with whom she grew up. As a teenager, Lana was more impressed with football heroes. Now, she realizes that Clark was the guy she enjoyed talking to and being with the most. Everybody in Metropolis knows him from the act he puts on for them. Lana knew him as a boy. She has all this other background on him that no one else knows. To her, he's just a normal man.

CHRISTOPHER REEVE: That was an opportunity for Clark to become a more fully-rounded character whose behavior is not limited to bumping into walls. He realizes when he gets back to Kansas that the clumsiness he uses in the city is merely a disguise. If Lana Lang is attracted to him, he should have something more to offer than awkwardness… I think the audience enjoyed seeing a new side to him. (*Press Notes*)

ANNETTE O'TOOLE: Chris and I got together and talked. His ideas were very similar to mine — to not make this story a cartoon, but to play it as people who have real problems. We discussed what kind of relationship Lana and Clark would have and so it was very, very pleasant. We were playing people who had an early relationship, so we sort of had to fill that area in. We would just sit, talk — we didn't even have to talk that much — and watch what was happening. I found Chris to be a very calming person; he handled all the super-pressure of being Superman very well. From those first days, he made me feel at home, this newcomer added to something which had been going on for five years.

I saw Lana as the young working mother. I looked at everyone in the film and who they represented in America. I always thought of Lois as *the* career woman. Lana was the symbol of all the girls who got married right out of high school, had a baby and were left behind. She's making it on her own and doing *very* well until Clark Kent re-enters her life. Now, she realizes there's this big hole; she wants something for herself again. That was the basic idea. We took it from there. I tried to keep it simple. And there's something very sweet about the lost love between Clark and Lana… and their finding it again.

DAVID NEWMAN: About eight months after Leslie and I were talking in that restaurant, Richard Lester brought us the next element for the script. Richard said, "I want to do something about computers. I don't know what, but I think that's what's happening in the world today and *Superman III* ought to reflect that." We thought about computers and what we came up with is that they're running our lives, we don't know how, and that we're somehow threatened by them.

Gene Hackman had made it clear that he wouldn't be reprising the role of Lex Luthor, so the search began for a new villain. Reflecting Lester's desire for a "computer-oriented" story, the Newmans created industrialist Ross Webster, who is determined to use computer technology to enhance his fortune — no matter what the cost to others. Enabling him to do this is Gus Gorman, a good-natured though misguided schnook who is somehow a wiz at computers and unwittingly creates the ultimate example of one: a machine powerful enough to kill Superman. To play the role of Webster, the production locked its sights on Robert Vaughn, probably still best remembered primarily for his role as Napoleon Solo in television's The Man from U.N.C.L.E.

For the writers, there was also additional Kryptonian fodder in the "relationship" between Clark Kent and Superman, an idea brought home when Gus Gorman exposes the Man of Steel to a piece of artificial Kryptonite, which psychologically splits him into two separate beings: Clark and Superman, and this Superman ain't a happy camper!

DAVID NEWMAN: One of our favorite things about the character is, and always has been, the classic split personality. There's Jekyll and Hyde and Clark and Superman. The thing that never occurred to anyone as much as it occurred to us when we wrote the film, was that it always seems that they didn't like each other. The Id and the Superego battled each other all the time. I was very pleased with the way the film came out, and I think some of the best work Christopher Reeve has done as an actor is in *Superman III* with the evil Superman character.

RICHARD LESTER: The splitting of Clark and Superman was fun to do. The actual fight between them was wonderful and cutting it together was great fun.

DAVID NEWMAN: It's wonderful the way that happens in degrees. There's that little scene with Lana Lang where he starts to come on to her instead of going to stop the bridge from collapsing. And with the big fight between Clark and Superman in the auto graveyard, I think he's just great. It was the first thing shot in that movie too. They started with the hardest part.

RICHARD LESTER: Once we had all that, it was my idea to get Richard Pryor as Gus Gorman, because I wanted to play around with the idea of this very realistic element to go along with the splitting of Superman's personality. Richard works in a very realistic style and the game was to see whether or not it could work.

CHRISTOPHER REEVE: In the other movies, we started big… with the explosion of Krypton in outer space and the arrival on Earth of three super-villains. Here, we begin with something as simple as a matchbook cover and move outwards to epic situations. Richard represents the audience. It's as if someone was plucked out of his seat in a movie house and dropped into the movie. His comedy grows out of the hopes and pains of everyday people. And when the everyday man comes up against Superman, it's interesting to see what happens. Without losing any of the fantasy, and with more humor, this story comes closer to contemporary life than we have before. (*Press Notes*)

Despite Lester's desire to use Pryor to bring more realism to the film, most people — particularly the critics — thought that his appearance made the film too light and threw off the balance. So bad a taste did it ultimately leave, that several years later when it was mentioned that Eddie Murphy might co-star in 1986's Star Trek IV, *everyone said that it was a misstep akin to Pryor being cast in* Superman III.

DAVID NEWMAN: The way Richard Pryor got involved is that Leslie and I were watching Johnny Carson's *Tonight Show*. Carson asked him what he was doing next and Richard replied, "I'm waiting to see the next Superman movie. Boy, do I love Superman, and I'd do anything if I could be in one of those pictures." At that point, light bulbs went off, so we created the character for him. Once you get Richard Pryor, obviously you're getting lighter. I think Christopher feels that what happened on *III* was not that Richard Pryor was in it, but that the balance was tipped in Pryor's favor, or too much towards the Gus Gorman part of the story.

RICHARD LESTER: Actually, I wanted more of a balance between the two stories and had cut some of Richard Pryor's scenes out. But Warner Bros. insisted that they be put back in. That might have hurt the film.

DAVID NEWMAN: Again, it's the Gus Gorman part of it which Christopher felt didn't belong. His own character he loved. That part we all felt was as mythic and deep as anything could be, the fact that Superman splits. Where it got lighter, obviously, was with Gorman.

LESLIE NEWMAN: But let's be realistic, when you have someone like Richard Pryor, the studio wants more than you might necessarily want to do. It's a fine line in how you approach it. When we did the first film, you could not have somebody saying, "Up, up and away," or "Look, it's a bird, it's a plane…" Or change in a phone booth. It would have been horrendous; it's a funny kind of balance you have to pull off.

DAVID NEWMAN: If you look at Richard Lester's films, he loves slapstick and gags, and we wrote for the director. We had a great time doing the opening scene in *Superman III* where one disaster leads into another one. We wrote the traffic light business, where the two signals fight each other, and it still makes me giggle. It is comical and maybe some people feel it's too much. Some people have a certain kind of rigidity. Janet Maslin's review in *The New York Times* said, in essence, "Why don't they leave well enough alone? Why do they try new things with that character?" What she's saying is that each movie should go on doing the same exact thing.

LESLIE NEWMAN: Then they write a review saying, "They do the same old thing. Why don't they do something different?"

DAVID NEWMAN: Then you get those *Rocky IV* reviews at the time saying, "I think I've seen this movie four times."

LESLIE NEWMAN: Plus, we were hitting a problem with the Lois character. It was silly to do the same thing. The Lana Lang romance is not on the scale of a Lois romance, it's on a lighter scale as well.

DAVID NEWMAN: The trickiest thing about these kinds of movies is you walk a very thin line concerning tone. One false move and you're into camp or you're into Saturday morning cartoons. It's very tricky, and I suppose we haven't always been right, but it's much harder than people think. It's not the Penguin going around saying, "Ha, ha, Batman. I'll get you and your little friend." It's a lot easier writing *Ghostbusters* than a superhero movie.

CARY BATES: Halfway through production of *Superman III*, DC sent me to Pinewood Studios in 1983 as their official representative in meetings with Ilya, Pierre Spengler, Richard Lester and Leslie and David Newman. There were concerns over the tone of the film leaning too much toward Richard Pryor at Superman's expense, but we were stymied by Lester and our efforts proved to be too little too late. But it was the beginning of my long-running association and friendship with Ilya.

DAVID NEWMAN: One thing about that movie that *is* structurally strange is that we never brought those two stories together until very close to the end of the movie. In *Superman II* the three stories combined in the middle. In this one they combined, but the Gus Gorman character didn't really come into contact with Superman until the end of the movie, so a lot of what Richard did was without Chris, and a lot of what Chris did was without Richard. If you talk to Chris, he'll tell you that the scene which distresses him is when Gus Gorman skis off the building with the table cloth around his neck. I still think it's funny. It's not epic, and it *is* lighter and it *is* comedy. I don't want to apologize for it, but it did go more in that direction.

ILYA SALKIND: I think the problem with *Superman III* was that it got a little bit out of control; there was a little too much of Lester's "Lesterisms." The humor went too far, like the green and red traffic signals fighting each other. Things like that were just over the top. But it was his cast, and he could do what he wanted. That was the agreement, that he would have his cast and film whatever he wanted to. He actually put in a scene where Pryor falls from the terrace on skis. That was from one of his rushes, and he put it in. I *did* like the scene where Superman is fighting himself — just fantastic and one of the best scenes in the whole series.

LESLIE NEWMAN: The reviews weren't as positive as they had been for the first two films, but the best reviews we got on *III* were the best reviews we've gotten. One doesn't mind negative reviews, if they're the type that you can learn something from, if they're constructive.

DAVID NEWMAN: Sure, mixed reviews bothered me, but I've had a lot of movies open and close with all kinds of reviews, so I think I know how to live with that. It performed well and that's really the bottom line. People are entitled to their opinions and I'm not going to pass the buck. That is our movie, and that's the way we wanted it to come out. Maybe we were wrong.

LESLIE NEWMAN: What interested us may not have been what interested other people as much. To us, the notion of somebody loving Clark Kent and just thinking of Superman as a nice person was interesting, but other people might want to see somebody in love with Superman.

CHRISTOPHER REEVE: Dick Lester, who was responsible for the direction and who had the script written according to his specifications, as an American expatriate he does not share the romantic, nostalgic view of America and Americans of Dick Donner. Dick Donner envisioned *Superman* as a valentine to the country and to a time we dimly remember and sort of fantasize about. Dick Lester wants his comic book to be no more than a comic and deliberately places tongue firmly in cheek and aims for fast, slick entertainment. I've found that people tend to line up right down the middle. Some people might miss the romance and the weight and fleshiness of the characters. Other people say, "Thank God all that pompousness is over and we can get on to playing fastball." I don't take sides. I'm just saying, for me, what the sides are. The critics and public decide for themselves. (*The Windsor Star*)

Even before the release of Superman III, *it was pretty much decided that it would probably be the final entry in the series, even though the Salkinds' contract gave them a total of 25 years to produce sequels.*

RICHARD LESTER: During the film's premiere, Chris Reeve and I went to the head of Warner Bros. and told him that this was it for us. It was over, even though I had enjoyed the whole seven-year period of the *Superman* films. I had a good time. Of course, they were the least personal films I've worked on, but they were very relaxing and technically fascinating. But I didn't want to carry on after that; it was enough for me. I certainly was running out of ideas and I thought it needed a fresh eye and idea.

CHRISTOPHER REEVE: Dick Lester was the first one to ask, "How much further can you go without becoming a TV series in quality?" We proved a man can fly, we've shown Superman in love, we've stopped time, turned the world backwards, and I don't know what you can do for an encore. If I look at the Bond movies, I think, for me, the three *real* Bond movies are *Dr. No, From Russia with Love* and *Goldfinger*. Full stop. The rest are basically a ripoff. Yes, they make money and, yes, you could probably continue, but I don't see the reward in it. (*The Windsor Star*)

TOM MANKIEWICZ: After *Superman III* was made, Terry Semel came down to my office. He said, "What's wrong with *Superman III*?" And I said, "What's wrong with it — and it's not Richard's fault — but it's a Richard Pryor movie. I mean he's wildly talented and he's very funny, but it's a Richard Pryor movie and Superman movies have to be Superman movies." And he said, "Would you and Dick go back — would you go back and do the next one? And really price is no object — I mean we want to get this back on track." And Dick and I had a long dinner and talked about it and we thought, "No." We'd done everything — we'd brought him from Krypton, he'd grown up, he'd turned the world backwards, he'd faced Kryptonite, he'd become a human being, and slept with Lois.

LESLIE NEWMAN: I still remember the film's premiere. There really was a moment of a lot of hugging after the premiere, with tears in the eyes and a lot of "God, it's been wonderful." But we really feel that we did what we wanted to do. We've always believed that the only reason to do a sequel is if you have something more to say, or something more to delve in to.

DAVID NEWMAN: When we finished *Superman III*, every one of us, starting with Chris, said, "No more *Superman*." It turns out we meant it, but Christopher didn't.

CHRISTOPHER REEVE: It's like if you eat too many chocolates, it puts you off it for a while; if you have too much Italian food, you need to have sushi — it's just a change of diet, really. There's also the feeling that *Superman III* had diverted from the original intentions of making these movies. It had gone into parody. I felt, well, maybe it's just better not to do this anymore. But a couple of years go by and everybody agrees that we should get back to the tone and style of the first one. We should go back to the basics. What people want to see is Clark and Lois and the legend of Krypton and Smallville and a real convincing villain. You can change your opinion and get re-motivated again, and that's what happened to me. (*Dayton Daily News*)

The disappointing results of Superman III *(despite the fact that it turned a profit) was not assuaged by the arrival of 1984's* Supergirl, *directed by* Jaws 2's *Jeannot Szwarc, written by David Odell, produced by Ilya Salkind and starring Helen Slater in the title role. The film was budgeted at $35-million and pulled in a global gross of a little over $14-million.*

DAVID ODELL (screenwriter, *Supergirl*): The original script started out with Chris Reeve as Superman going to do battle in outer space with a creature from Krypton. To do so, he assembled all of the atomic and nuclear warheads on Earth in one pile and shoved them into space in order to avert some disaster that's going to attack or hit the planet. There's

Christopher Reeve
En Español

TRIBUTE

(© and courtesy Tidalwave Productions)

also a big meteorite with purple Kryptonite or something and he is seriously injured by the threat in this pre-credit fight ordeal. As a result, he has to go to the Planet of the Healers and recuperate, and he sends for his cousin Kara to take over on Earth while he's gone.

But they couldn't get Reeve. We were basically about three months before shooting and Reeve, who had been doing *Superman III* at the time and had been sort of stringing the Salkinds along, finally said he didn't want to do it. It left *Supergirl* with a huge hole in the middle, but it was actually what Reeve had wanted in the sense that to make him happy, they told him that on the next one he would only have to work four weeks or something. The idea was that he would be in it for about four weeks and would get paid almost the salary he'd get for a full picture. And in the meantime, Supergirl would be introduced and then she would carry the picture and a new franchise. But he would have appeared at the beginning and the end. Like I said, though, his departure left a hole in the picture that was never quite filled. On top of that, Jeannot Szwarc, who had worked with him on *Somewhere in Time*, was brought on as director because they had a relationship and he was convinced he could get Reeve to do it. There was a lot of stringing along going on.

ILYA SALKIND: I think Jeannot may have been too easy to work with. With Dick Donner, we had fantastic fights. With Richard Lester, we had fantastic fights. With Jeannot, not so many and that was a problem. He was a little too sweet.

DAVID ODELL: There was one solution. Reeve wouldn't have done a complete picture; he kept saying he was tired and *Superman III* had been an ordeal. I told them that all they had to do was tell him that he could direct it, and he would have done it. But they didn't want to let him direct.

ILYA SALKIND: I'll tell you the truth — I saw *Supergirl* again recently and I really thought that it didn't work at all. I was very disappointed. It's a very bad one that just didn't come together as a movie. There *was* a better script at the beginning and then there were problems with Warners. They left and we went with TriStar. Just a lot of problems with it. I did think that Helen Slater did very well.

ANDY MANGELS (journalist and author): For a variety of reasons, *Supergirl* did not work. The silly script, bad editing and Faye Dunaway's overacting did nothing for box office receipts. Neither did spotty U.S. distribution or releasing the Japanese videotape (with the better, unedited version) while the movie was still in theaters.

HELEN SLATER: I think the director had the film's best interests in mind, and had his reasons for doing things the way he did. Ultimately, it is the film that he wanted. I don't know why it was not as successful. I think it was because the story was not strong enough. Personally, I had great fun doing it.

Flash forward a few years to the point where Cannon Films offered Sidney J. Furie the opportunity to direct what would become 1987's Superman IV: The Quest for Peace, *which he considered a no-lose situation.*

SIDNEY J. FURIE (director, *Superman IV: The Quest for Peace*): Without being catty, *Superman III* screwed up, and it screwed up because a brilliant director had full reign and he didn't take Superman seriously. They were trying to make it something else with Richard Pryor. The feeling I have with *Superman IV* is that the series already went off track once, so what did I have to lose? If the third one had been as brilliant as the first two, maybe I wouldn't have done *Superman IV*.

But you just jump in. Courage is part of all creative people. When I got hired, I mentioned to Warner Bros. how bad *Superman III* was, and their response was, "Oh yeah, boy was it bad. Fifty million dollars in film rentals. Give us half of that and we'll be happy."

If that was the case, then one would tend to believe that Warner Bros. was ultimately not happy.

The genesis of Superman IV *began in June of 1985, when the rights to the film franchise were licensed from the Salkinds by Menahem Golan and Yoram Globus' Cannon Films. At the time, Cannon was well-known in the industry as the producer of low-budget actioners such as the Charles Bronson* Death Wish *series and just about all of Chuck Norris' films. Even such big-budget ($40-million) efforts as* Invaders from Mars *had a small, cheesy feel to them. For this reason, hopes weren't very high for the newest entry in the Superman series. Apparently to assuage these fears, Cannon made a concentrated effort to make this an "A" effort, first off by pursuing Christopher Reeve to reprise his dual role of Clark Kent and Superman. Additionally, they hired writers Lawrence Konner and Mark Rosenthal, the team involved in such efforts as* Jewel of the Nile *and the subsequent* Star Trek VI: The Undiscovered Country *and Tim Burton's remake of* Planet of the Apes.

ILYA SALKIND: Warner Bros. and DC became more difficult to work with as time went on, because they became more and more angry that they didn't have the rights; that they had sold the rights. Approvals became very difficult. But Cannon paid a lot of money — I think $5-million, which was a lot of money in those days, for the rights to do one movie. That was the reason to do it.

PAUL LEVITZ: I was not in the position through *Superman III* to even be aware of any of the discussions. With *Superman IV,* I got to sit in a couple of meetings with Chris as he was pitching his original idea, which had some solidity to it. And I was involved peripherally enough to be aware of Cannon taking control of the production of it and the ramifications of that. On any of them, even the films where I had a measure of creative involvement and a measure of creative control, you can't control it from the back. The director makes the movie. You can give advice, you can warn, but it's kind of like Queen Victoria's right rules. I'm going to mess the phrase slightly, but she said, "I have the right to be informed. I have the right to warn," and I believe the third part was along the lines of her having the right to be ignored. And if you're the intellectual property rights owner, you're really in Queen Victoria's position. You're not running the country.

LAWRENCE KONNER (co-writer, *Superman IV: The Quest for Peace*):
For a while, Chris wasn't interested in *Superman IV* and Cannon was talking about recasting. Meanwhile, Mark and I were saying that we weren't interested for two reasons. One, we think Chris Reeve is the perfect Superman; and two, it seemed to us that Cannon wasn't committed to making a great movie if they weren't willing to pay his price and give Chris what he wanted. His "price" was not an excessive monetary payment, but the promise of creative control.

CHRISTOPHER REEVE: Cannon didn't have any kind of deal with me. Cannon's thinking was, "If he doesn't want to play Superman, there's somebody else out there who'll play him… no problem." They certainly used that against me in negotiations. They tell you they love you and don't need you practically in the same breath. It was all very amicable. They're good negotiators. I was willing — money was never an issue in my getting re-involved. (*Dayton Daily News*)

AUSTIN TRUNICK (author, *The Cannon Film Guide, Vol. I and II*):
News broke of Cannon buying the Superman rights in 1985 right after they acquired the rights for Captain America and Spider-Man movies from Marvel — perhaps the Salkinds knew that Cannon was now in the superhero-buying business and made a phone call? I would also believe just as easily that it might have happened the other way around. Menaham Golan was known to be a fan of the first two Superman movies, and the company certainly had a long history of producing sequels to others' films (see *Death Wish II-4, Exterminator 2, Texas Chainsaw Massacre 2* and *Penitentiary 3*).

MARK ROSENTHAL (co-writer, *Superman IV: The Quest for Peace*):
Larry and I viewed the first three films in one day, and quickly realized that the original is one of the great American movies. We believe that Chris Reeve wanted to make sure that the budget and the studio commitment from both Warner Bros. and Cannon Films was there to do it properly. Once he was convinced, *we* were convinced.

LAWRENCE KONNER: Everybody agrees that the three Superman films grow progressively worse. *Superman* was a great movie, *Superman II* was okay and *III* was terrible. Chris felt that it wasn't worth doing a *Superman IV* which was more like the third one than the original. I don't think Chris' holdout was about money at all — he was making sure that everyone involved wanted to make a good movie, not just another sequel.

AUSTIN TRUNICK: It was no secret that Reeve had grown tired of being typecast, and that he was trying to distance himself from only being seen as the Man of Steel. Reeve would actually share some funny stories about this with reporters and talk show hosts. One of my favorites is a story he recounted to Johnny Carson about chasing down a thief who snatched his bike in Central Park; when he caught the guy and the thief recognized who he was, his first response was, "I'm sorry, Superman!" When he shared a kiss with Michael Caine in 1982's *Deathtrap*, multiple newspaper critics in different cities commented on audience members shouting things like, "Don't do it, Superman!" at the screen. In the public eye, Reeve *was* Superman, and I think he feared a little bit that might be all he'd ever be.

Before he became Superman, Reeve was a Juilliard-trained classical actor. Most of his non-Kryptonian roles over those years came in mediocre movies, or films that relatively few people saw. Even when he was promoting these movies, interviewers would constantly switch subjects to bring up Superman, and you can tell that drove him a little nuts. You can sense that he was feeling pigeon-holed as an actor. There's an interview around this time where he points at Harrison Ford's recent turn in *Witness*, where he was able to shed his image as Han Solo and Indiana Jones and earn some respect as a serious actor. You can detect a hint of jealousy in there. He wanted to be taken seriously when he wasn't wearing a cape and tights, and he thought all it would take was one big, *Witness*-like hit and people would look at him differently.

CHRISTOPHER REEVE: I wanted to get the old enthusiasm and Superman spirit back, and to do that I needed some control. What I wanted to see was Superman brought a little closer to the real world while staying in the framework of a fantasy film. I wanted him to confront some contemporary issues as a "naturalized citizen" rather than as a visitor from another planet. (*press notes*)

AUSTIN TRUNICK: Cannon grabbed the *Superman* sequel rights before approaching Reeve about returning. When they first asked him to reprise the role, he continued to stand his ground and said, "No, thanks." However, David Freeman's *Street Smart* screenplay had been filed on a bookshelf at Reeve's home for several years, and he stumbled across it again while Cannon was trying to court him back into his cape. He'd never given it a full read before, but flipping through it this time, he began to see a lot of potential in the lead role it offered. Its main character was a dishonest, unscrupulous journalist, who was practically a bizarro version of Clark Kent. It's a juicy role, and one that certainly stands in contrast to the Big Blue Boy Scout. Reeve brought *Street Smart* to Cannon, who had a history of taking on pet projects as a means of securing talent whom they otherwise wouldn't have been able to afford, or been able to convince to work for them. Their willingness to produce *Street Smart* was probably the biggest piece of the deal that brought Reeve out of superhero retirement. They also promised him he could direct some second unit, and come up with the storyline that *Superman IV* would follow. (There were also reports that he was paid up to $6-million for his Cannon contract, which I have to imagine helped.)

MARK ROSENTHAL: Superman is a fascinating character and not just for the obvious story and plot reasons, but for who he is and why. If you look at every culture since the beginning of time, you'll find that each one has some kind of a superhero in its mythology. Superman fits in with what America is and why we are what we are. Our approach was to deal with big issues in a way that will transfer the movie into mythology. The story deals with the question, "Can Superman become involved in human destiny?" What's great about Superman, as well as all the equivalent myths, is the issue of why doesn't the "god" step in and make everything right? That has always been one of the real core fascinations with the character.

LAWRENCE KONNER: The question, simply put, is why doesn't Superman just destroy all the nuclear missiles?

CHRISTOPHER REEVE: I had narrated a documentary called *A Message to Our Parents*. These kids had traveled to Washington and Moscow, asking officials in the State Department and Politburo about their future in the nuclear age. The idea of nuclear disarmament linked with Superman gradually came to me. For me, it's the most personal *Superman* of the entire series. It directly reflects what Superman should be, and what he should be doing.

AUSTIN TRUNICK: Christopher Reeve was recording voiceover narration for a documentary in August 1985, when he heard the news that thirteen-year-old Samantha Smith had died in a plane crash. Smith was a little girl from Maine who had become a Cold War-era celebrity on both sides of the Iron Curtain when, at the age of 10, she wrote a heartfelt letter to new Soviet leader Yuri Andropov asking whether he intended to start a nuclear war with the United States and pleading with him to prevent one. Her letter was republished in the biggest Soviet newspapers, and she became the center of a media flurry in both countries, appearing on talk shows and acting as a sort of peace ambassador. Tragically, she and her father were killed when a small plane they were on hit some trees while attempting to land. Her death was big news, and her surviving family received condolences from both Mikhail Gorbachev and Ronald Reagan. When asked how he came up with the idea of a young boy writing to Superman to ask him to bring an end to nuclear war, Reeve cited Samantha Smith as his inspiration. It's easy to spot a few parallels between the character and its real-life inspiration.

LAWRENCE KONNER: Part of the anti-nuke theme was suggested by the Museum of Natural History's IMAX film *The Dream is Alive*, which featured footage of Earth taken from outer space and project on 60-foot screens. Mark, a Warner Bros. executive, and Chris had met outside the museum when a rainstorm struck. We went inside and decided to see the film.

MARK ROSENTHAL: We were cynically wondering how good it could be. We had seen footage of the planets and the stars, but never anything like this. The film shows the Earth in daylight, and you can not only actually see the boot of Italy's exact location, but you can also pick out the towns. *The Dream is Alive* is proof that reality is more moving than science-fiction. That same week, the lead story in *The New Yorker* just happened to be about a writer who wandered into the theater the same way, and he wrote about how you're brought to tears with the sense that the entire *planet* is your home as opposed to the nationalistic way we're brought up. You begin to see Earth as this small, vulnerable but tender place with no boundaries.

LAWRENCE KONNER: We wanted to investigate the Superman mythology as the story of an orphan and his new home, and to endow it with certain humanistic concepts which are part of SF movie tradition. In *The Day the Earth Stood Still*, the visitor helps us understand who we are and how we should live. That's the same kind of feeling we wanted to achieve in *Superman IV*.

The trio came up with the idea that Superman would use his powers to save humanity from possible nuclear horror and destroy all nuclear weapons. Great concept, but what element do you add to provide some danger to the Man of Steel? Why, Lex Luthor of course.

MARK ROSENTHAL: If you look at the comic books, which we both did, no other villain captures the true adversarial depth that Lex does. The Lex Luthor stories were the special issues, and Gene's performance is special too. He can make Luthor humorous without being silly.

LAWRENCE KONNER: Both Lex and Gene have the size to give Superman a strong adversary. In number three, Robert Vaughn was playing a James Bond kind of villain, a silly, evil mastermind you didn't quite believe posed a very serious problem for Superman. But Lex Luthor brings with him the resonance that he can *really* harm Superman.

MARK ROSENTHAL: *Superman* had the advantage and necessity of restating the essential story for everyone and we figured that the fun of elaborating the origin is seeing how Superman's life continues. We really haven't seen how Lex has grown. *Superman II* made him a secondary character, but we brought him back because the relationship between Superman and Luthor in the original comic book stories is just wonderful. And having Gene return gives it the proper scope and scale. Besides Lex, there is a truly terrifying and exhilarating physical adversary for Superman; Luthor creates something that does combat with Superman on a worldly scale.

That "something" is Nuclear Man, cloned from a strand of Superman's hair and baked within the sun before returning to Earth, full-grown, as Luthor's slave. So besides trying to stop Lex, who is attempting to sell nuclear arms on the black market, Superman must battle his creation as well.

While all of this was developed, Cannon began their search for a director to take command of the film. Richard Lester was, in his words, approached "indirectly" but he wasn't interested, while Richard Donner declined, wishing Cannon the best of luck.

RICHARD DONNER: I had already done it, and it's hard to go back. There were so many challenges in the first one and, hopefully, we accomplished what we set out to do. But it's like trying to flow blood into paper. After that, there was no more challenge in that area.

AUSTIN TRUNICK: Reeve's first choice was reportedly Ron Howard, who wasn't available either. The producers even set up a meeting with Wes Craven, but he failed to hit it off with Reeve. (Although, it's fun to imagine what *Wes Craven's Superman IV* could have looked like.) Both Reeve and Warner Bros. had approval over the director, which was a good thing —otherwise, we may have ultimately seen it wind up in the hands of one of Cannon's go-to guys like J. Lee Thompson or, heaven forbid, Michael Winner. Cannon liked to work with veteran filmmakers, and Sidney J. Furie had decades' worth of experience under his belt.

SIDNEY J. FURIE: They were looking for a director and I had never done anything like it. I was like someone who doesn't know computers, but wants to learn computers. Having been a director for 29 years, I said, "I've got to learn all this because it's something I don't know. It won't be boring." Not that a movie is ever boring, but usually you know how to make it. This was an opportunity to learn about effects and to run a very big picture. It's like being a general and having a little army or squad behind you. My preparation began by doing detailed storyboarding. From the storyboards, everyone can determine how a particular effect will be achieved. It's different questions and different answers, but it's the same process. It's still a scene in a movie that must be achieved and it's exciting. Working on *Superman IV* was the most exciting year of my life.

To aid in capturing the Superman spirit, Furie wanted to ensure that the necessary ingredients be included in the mix, including Gene Hackman as Lex Luthor and Margot Kidder as Lois Lane.

SIDNEY J. FURIE: I wouldn't have done this film if Gene Hackman wasn't in it. The selling point for me was Gene Hackman with Christopher Reeve. That was very important, because that's the Yin and Yang, and what a wonderful Yang because Lex Luthor is a comedic villain. He has a humor about him, and it's just the right soufflé for this piece. And if Margot hadn't joined, I don't know if I would have. I fought for Margot Kidder. Margot asked for a large amount of money, and it wasn't her fault. A man would have gotten that money, but because she wasn't a man, they wouldn't pay that much. It took five months to get her. It was a huge negotiation and, finally, she realized they were going to go without her. She still made a very good deal, and she's very happy with it, but I would like to think that I was the influence, saying, "Gentlemen, without Margot there ain't no picture, because she's the shorthand to the romanticism of *Superman* and *Superman II.*"

Even if we couldn't feature the romanticism because our script went in other directions, having Margot would give the opportunity for those few wonderful moments. I am a romantic and the thing that I loved about the first two films was the Lois/Superman romance. If you're going to make a sequel to two of the best films ever made — and I consider the first two *Superman* movies the best in their genre — you at least want to have the same foundation to hold up your house. The whole idea of a sequel is to relive the best things of the movie again in a fresh way, but not too fresh. If you really want those same thrills, kicks and things, we had to have those characters.

Superman IV, like its predecessors, ran into budget problems, but this time the results were disastrous. There simply was not any additional money to pump into the production, and the results were up on the screen for all to see — and some which no one saw. As is fairly obvious, the matte work is sloppy, the miniatures obvious and the flying sequences, which should have been perfected in the intervening years between the first film and the fourth, were among the weakest. Worse was an entire subplot lost from the film due to subpar effects. Before confronting Nuclear Man, Superman went up against a brainless, Franken-stein's Monster-like predecessor of the creature, who terrorizes patrons of a nightclub.

AUSTIN TRUNICK: I think Cannon set out to make a proper Superman movie, one that would be a box-office hit and hopefully lead to further sequels. Judging by their ability to bring back so much talent both in front of and behind the camera — at least at the project's onset — I feel like there were some people even outside of Cannon who thought they might actually be able to pull it off. We need to keep in mind that there was a very big difference between the Cannon of 1985, when the *Superman IV* deals came together, and the Cannon of late 1986 and early 1987, when the movie was in production. In 1985, Cannon was coming off its two biggest hits of the Golan-Globus era, *Missing in Action* and *Breakin'*. That same year they had three films open at number one at the box office — *Invasion U.S.A.*, *Death Wish 3* and *King Solomon's Mines* — and earned their first Oscar nominations for *Runaway Train*. During this same period, they were publiciz-ing deals with big-name stars such as Sylvester Stallone, Dustin Hoffman and Al Pacino. People were really beginning to take them seriously within the industry. All of these are reasons why in 1985, when Cannon said they were going to spend $30-million on a new Superman movie, it wasn't necessarily a notion to scoff at, or a reason for someone like Reeve to flee for the hills.

Of course, Cannon's house of cards fell apart rapidly and in spectacular fashion. The timing was particularly hard on *Superman IV*. Thanks to new lines of credit and stock sales, the company went into 1986 with somewhere around $300-mil-lion to finance their production slate. Instead, they spent most of that buying up theater chains, Thorn EMI and Elstree Studios. By the end of the summer of '86, they were $100-million in debt and urgently seeking bailouts. They suddenly had to cut back their number of productions quite drastically and slash budgets on all of their more expensive features just so that they could stay above water from week to week. That's why the initial $30-million *Superman IV* budget wound up being cut in half before the movie even began.

MARK ROSENTHAL: The big problem with the film is that it was literally a month before production when Cannon slashed the budget in half, because they were going into bankruptcy. They fired the entire crew that had done all of the *Superman* movies and replaced them with a much cheaper effects crew. From there it was a downhill ride. *Superman IV* went from a $36-million budget down to $17-million. Menahem Golan was essentially saying, "If I put something out with the Superman name on it, who cares what it looks like?" And Warner Bros., for various reasons, made a huge mistake and didn't pick up the slack. From then on in, everyone knew that the effects were going into the toilet and everything was done with a "What the hell, let's try it attitude." It's not like they shot it and said, "Oh God, this didn't turn out right." It was like everybody knew. This disaster happened before the ship left the port.

AUSTIN TRUNICK: Christopher Reeve started to worry about Cannon's ability to finance *Superman IV* before filming even began. Production on *Street Smart* had to be moved from New York City to Montreal after just three weeks of shooting, so that Cannon could save some money and get around paying union workers. Reeve wondered aloud to reporters how Cannon would be able to shoot *Superman IV* in New York, considering that they couldn't afford to shoot the relatively low-budget *Street Smart* there. (He was very right to be concerned.)

The movie's budget shrank more and more the closer it got to production. This led to some of the special effects and technical talents dropping out early on. By the time production was moved from the U.S. to Cannon's recently-acquired Elstree Studios and nearby Milton Keynes, it's hard to imagine that alarm bells weren't going off for everyone involved. But this all happened relatively fast — Cannon had spent two years promising a summer 1987 release date, and I doubt they'd have missed that mark even if it meant filming in front of cardboard backdrops. By the time everybody knew the movie was going to be a disaster, it was probably too late to turn back.

In the end, audiences stayed away from Superman IV *in droves. In offering up an explanation, Furie muses over the possibility that some people may have been turned off to the disarmament theme.*

SIDNEY J. FURIE: To me, the thrill of it all is that *Superman IV* is a family picture — a family can sit there, have a good time and be moved a little bit. Maybe it was too real for an audience. Maybe they can buy whales having to make a sound to save the 23rd century [as in *Star Trek IV*] because it's not real, but they can't accept a disarmament theme. I don't know. The only thing that makes it work for me is Superman trying to disarm the world and Lex Luthor trying to sell the other side missiles. Every time you have a *message* scene, in comes Lex who just beats up on it. It's that quality that keeps it a comedy. *Superman IV* doesn't get that serious, but it's interesting to see if mixed in with the shredded wheat the audience wants some fresh fruit. If the picture didn't work, it's because the audience didn't buy it. But I never felt the theme was a problem.

CHRISTOPHER REEVE: It was not our intention to be politically significant. This is really a very naïve 90-minute fantasy from the point of view of a 12-year-old about what if Superman were really around and could take away nuclear weapons. The whole issue of whether or not that should be done is *not* what we're talking about. But I think one of the messages we'll put over that I think is a good message for kids and is summed up in a line that Superman says: "I just wish you could all see the Earth the way that I see it, because when you look at it, it's all just one world." He doesn't mean that in a political sense, he means when you view it from outer space, you see that the world is just this beautiful marble. It's very fragile and if we all realized that we might treat each other better. The primary function here is to have a good, fun summer movie. At the same time, Superman has got to do something more than just put out fires and catch helicopters, otherwise you'd get really tired of us. (*Dayton Daily News*)

TOM MANKIEWICZ: But Chris Reeve — who was a very nice guy — when he'd wanted to do *Superman IV: The Quest for Peace*, they gave me the script and they said, "Would you meet with Chris and talk to him?" And I just said, "Chris, there are certain rules of writing. And you are now exceeding those rules. Superman can do anything. You don't go to the United Nations about disarmament — you could disarm the whole world in twenty minutes if you wanted to. You can find every Russian silo and American silo and get them down. You don't talk about famine, because Superman could feed the world. No tsunami will ever hit Thailand, let's say, because with your super-breath you'd blow it back and no one would die. That's why you have to get involved in these plots. Superman cannot go to the UN and say, 'You must disarm,' because if I'm the head of the Soviet Union or the United States, I'm saying, 'Well, why don't you go do it?' And if I'm the audience, I say, 'Why don't you go do it?' What happens? I mean, are you willing to see a country blown up because they won't do it?" So these are writing rules about fantasy characters — you've got to figure out where your lines are. When you're dealing with normal human beings, there are no fantasy rules — a guy that loves potted plants can suddenly turn around and kill nine children, if you can do it correctly. But superheroes have their own rules.

SIDNEY J. FURIE: Having courage and guts is part of the insanity of this business. The truth is that whether your film is about the great mythological character you have to do right by, or it's a little movie that nobody has heard of, you still approach it like it's the most important thing in the world. And failing is still the worst thing in the world. But you fail, you go on, you succeed once in a while and you don't think about it too often. It goes with the territory. We're gunslingers, and you don't win every duel.

JOHN KENNETH MUIR: It was a sad end to the tenure of the great Christopher Reeve. Made on the cheap, *Superman IV: The Quest for Peace* just never leaps over the crucial threshold of believability; not in a single bound, not ever. The visual effects look so cheap and unconvincing that it is difficult to pay attention to the plot. There are moments in the sequel, for instance, when we see wires lifting Superman up off the ground, and then horrifyingly inept moments when he focuses his eyes to shoot heat beams… and nothing comes out. It's *inept on a level almost unimaginable*, especially for what had been an A-level franchise just a few years earlier.

ANTHONY DESIATO: I take *IV* over *III*, because I feel *IV* at least had better intentions. It aspires to something greater. It did not have the means to achieve it, but it wanted to be something more than it was, at least.

JOHN KENNETH MUIR: One of the film's most cringe-inducing moments occurs at the Great Wall of China. Nuclear Man blows up huge chunks of the wall, and bricks fly everywhere. Then Superman shows up and instead of using super-speed to reassemble the wall, uses some kind of lame "brick-o-vision" to put it back together. It's just awful. It's not just the special effects that are terrible in *Superman IV* either. Crucially, it's the film's editing. One horrible moment set on the Moon also reveals that the outer space backdrop is actually a black curtain. The drapes are visible for long stretches of time, and thus totally destroy the illusion that this scene is set anywhere but a studio stage. Again, the level of sheer technical incompetence is breathtaking. How about a fan edit?

Despite the failure of Superman IV, *Cannon actually attempted to put a* Superman V *into development, though one could only imagine what that could have been like given what had been happening with the company. And there were even rumblings that Christopher Reeve was willing to give a script for the potential film a read. There was, however, a bit of confusion of who owned what in terms of the film rights to Superman.*

CARY BATES: A Superman film treatment I had previously done on spec in the '80s (and gotten nowhere with Warners) was the catalyst. During *Superboy's* second season I showed it to Ilya, and he decided there was enough good material there to serve as a "jumping off point" for a new Superman movie. This prompted him and his father to reactivate the franchise (which they had leased to the Cannon group for the ill-fated *Superman IV*); subsequently I signed a deal to develop a full screenplay with Mark Jones as co-writer.

AUSTIN TRUNICK: Cannon was already advertising *Superman V* at film markets before *Superman IV* was even released, and before anyone who wasn't involved in the making of the film knew how bad it would be. These official trade advertisements were little more than a logo and the phrase "In Pre-Production." This sort of thing was par for the course with Cannon, which would regularly try to sell a movie before they had any stars, talent, a title, or even a premise attached to it. Another Cannon *Superman* was still a possibility as late as 1988, at least, when filmmaker Albert Pyun was attached to the project. He promised his version would be "getting away from the silliness" of what went on in the later sequels, and a movie that was "much a more realistic, much richer-looking vision of Superman" that audiences could invest in, and wouldn't just rely on special effects and callbacks to prior movies. This was the same time Pyun was attached to Cannon's *Masters of the Universe 2* and *Spider-Man*. Pre-production on those two movies was consolidated and repurposed into 1989's *Cyborg*, with Jean-Claude Van Damme. None of the three were ever made.

CARY BATES: We were in the initial stages of pre-production. The film had been budgeted and they had hired a production designer who came up with some great stuff; I can still recall his kick-ass designs for Brainiac's ship. Unfortunately, other forces were at work that we weren't aware of at the time. Final script approval never came down from Warners because they had their own plans for the character — the newly commissioned *Lois & Clark* series. It wasn't long after that when the Salkinds began negotiations to sell all their Superman rights back to the studio. Given the success of the Superman films and the more recent Batman franchise, by the early '90s Warners had realized in hindsight that they were remiss in letting go of the rights to their flagship comic book character.

AUSTIN TRUNICK: Before its release, *Superman IV* had been cut down from over two hours to under 90 minutes. A great deal of that trimmed footage came from completely removing comic scenes involving Lex Luthor's first attempt at Nuclear Man, played by Clive Mantle. For a while, Cannon entertained the thought of using these deleted scenes as a starting point for *Superman V*, and shooting new scenes around them — *without* Christopher Reeve. To be honest, it frightens me to think about what this movie might have looked like. Considering that Albert Pyun had repurposed footage shot for an abandoned *Journey to the Center of the Earth* movie to make an entirely different version of the tale for Cannon, it wouldn't surprise me in the least if this was part of the plan when he was briefly working on his *Superman V*.

For what it's worth, actor Michael Dudikoff mentioned to me that Menahem Golan had told him that he wanted him to play Superman if they couldn't get

Reeve back — although I'm not sure if this was for *Superman IV* before Reeve signed on to return, or to replace him in a potential *Superman V.*

As things would turn out, Superman IV: The Quest for Peace *would represent Reeve's final turn as the Man of Steel, and even in 1988, a full decade since he made his debut as Superman and only seven years before his devastating horseback riding accident, he was still wrestling with the character's place in his life.*

CHRISTOPHER REEVE: For a long time, it bothered me. I was, and I am, a serious actor and getting dressed up in that suit didn't exactly fit my image of myself. But I finally learned that I could be both a pop hero and a serious actor. Look at Harrison Ford. He's in *Witness* and *The Mosquito Coast* and he's also ready to do another Indiana Jones. He's always been a serious actor, but no one took him seriously until *Witness.* I need one big, non-Superman commercial hit. That's what it takes. I sometimes feel that there's one strike against me every time I get up to the plate. There is a kind of show-me skepticism, because of my role as Superman. The remedy is that I stick to my guns. I need to continue to work for people who will allow me to grow. (*Times-Advocate*)

CHAPTER VIII
Byrned to "Death"

Over the past several decades there have been two seminal events in the comic book history of Superman that have stood far above anything else that has been done with the character during that time. The first was his 1986 full-blown reboot from writer/artist John Byrne, many of those changes influencing outside adaptations for decades as well. The other was the 1992 storyline The Death of Superman, *which just recently celebrated its 30th anniversary and continues to have resonance over three decades later.*

While there's no denying that the success of Superman: The Movie *in 1978 had returned the Man of Steel back into the pop culture zeitgeist, as it would turn out, that was nothing but a proverbial shot in the arm, and by the mid-1980s the character had once again lost its footing with modern audiences. As time went on, it was becoming more apparent to DC publisher Jenette Kahn and those working with her that something drastic would have to be done to re-establish the character's relevancy.*

MICHAEL BAILEY (host, ***Superman: From Crisis to Crisis*** **podcast):** As you get into the '80s, DC was not updating Superman in the way they needed to. This is not me trying to insult the people that were writing those stories, and I think Cary Bates did the best he could to kind of write more current Superman stories. And Marv Wolfman had a *great* pre-*Crisis* run where he's really Marvelizing Superman. He breaks up Superman and Lois, he has Clark starting to date Lana Lang, and that's when they created the new versions of Brainiac and Lex Luthor for *Action* #544.

For whatever reason, all of these changes in Superman weren't connecting with the audience the way that *New Teen Titans, X-Men, Legion of Superheroes* and other hot books

(© and TM DC Comics/Warner Bros. Discovery)

from that era had. Superman just wasn't doing it, and I think part of that had to do with the fact that they didn't update the art. I love Curt Swan. I think Curt Swan is a consummate draftsman, but by the 1980s his stuff was looking kind of creaky compared to everything else on the stands. You had Gil Kane doing a run that was really visually exciting, but he didn't stick around. Jose Louise Garcia Lopez did a couple of issues, but he could never maintain a monthly schedule — that's just not who he was as an artist. So really, you needed John Byrne coming in to kind of make a huge splash and redefine the character for a new era. But that also started the schism within Superman fandom of the pre-*Crisis* and the post-*Crisis* people. And that's because Superman's like religion. Specifically, Superman's like Christianity in that there's a whole bunch of different sects and none of them agree on anything *and* they all think they're right.

PETER SANDERSON (comic book historian and author): The DC Comics' hierarchy had decided that Superman's nearly 50 years of continuity was outdated and that the entire Superman saga had to be started over from scratch. For one thing, it was decided that there were too many Kryptonian survivors around. Hence, as a prelude to the planned overhaul, Supergirl was killed off in the high-profile limited series *Crisis on Infinite Earths*.

In the comics, over the decades DC writers had postulated a multitude of parallel Earths with characters similar to but different in some ways from "ours" on Earth-1. It had all gotten a little out of control, so the idea was to manufacture a "crisis" that would bring those Earths together, with heroes — and whole worlds — being lost along the way. Published between April 1985 and March 1986, Crisis *was the brainchild of writer Marv Wolfman and artist George Perez (the team behind the enormously popular* New Teen Titans*), both clearly aware of the wide-ranging impact it would have on DC as a whole, the intent in the first place.*

MARV WOLFMAN (writer, *Crisis on Infinite Earths*): These days, DC and Marvel are continually trading places as to which company has the most readers. One month it's DC, next month it's Marvel and so on, back and forth. But back in the 1980s, DC's sales lagged *far* behind Marvel. Many Marvel fans wouldn't even bother looking at a DC comic. In fact, they *really* called themselves "Marvel Zombies." They were certain the DC universe couldn't ever be good, and something was needed to show those readers that DC had great characters and great books. So we proposed a 12-part maxi-series that would use every hero DC had to prove to the "Zombies" that, at the very least, they should give DC a try. Something like this, featuring over 400 characters in a universe-altering story, had never been tried before. It was a major risk and it could have failed, but DC approved my idea and, working with George Perez, we created a story that showed the Marvel Zombies how good DC could be.

And it was a daunting task. If we had failed, it was very possible that fans might never check out another DC comic again. But we took several years to carefully work out the story and to make sure it all worked. Fortunately, George and I were totally committed to this series and we built a story even the Marvel fans loved. Our slogan was, "Worlds will live. Worlds will die. And the DC Universe will never be the same." And because we honored that pledge, readers still care for it. *Crisis* made such a big impact that companies are *still* publishing wide-ranging crossovers, hoping to catch that elusive lightning in a bottle.

ROBERT GREENBERGER (writer, former DC editor): By the time I got to DC in 1984, Superman was feeling tired. Then we planned *Crisis on Infinite Earths* and it became clear that we were going to revamp the top three characters of Superman, Batman and Wonder Woman. Everyone recognized that all three of the major characters needed top to bottom revamps, so *Crisis* would give them the excuse to do. Unfortunately, to get the right talent, it couldn't fall the month after *Crisis* ended, which is why you had months of vamping before the John Byrne Superman arrived in '86. But creatively, *Crisis* helped reset the table. It helped DC feel fresher, more revitalized and have an honored legacy. After Barry Allen died in issue 12, Wally West becomes the new Flash. It honored the past and set a fresh beginning commercially, which was wildly successful.

CARY BATES (writer, *Superman*): And though *Crisis* made for some difficult times for quite a few of us, from a marketing perspective the clean sweep in creative teams made business sense. I could see the reasoning behind this, especially in the aftermath of the first *Superman* movie, which certainly demonstrated how effective the dramatic impact of introducing Superman to the world as an adult could be. But Byrne's change of heart — he left DC after two years — points up how ideas that can seem intriguing in the short term sometimes do not always hold up well in the long run. I'm sure some people might place the controversial Clark/Lois marriage in this category as well.

ELLIOT S! MAGGIN (writer, *Superman*): I think every 15 years or so you see a major punctuation in the equilibrium to which we foolishly refer as "comic book continuity." This latest one shows a lot more promise and wonder, I think, than did the one that immediately followed my tenure. I think it's always a mistake to cast away a still rich source of speculation and intellectual stimulation.

MARV WOLFMAN: With *Crisis*, George and I were trying to show the DC heroes in the best light possible and I think, considering how big the story was, that we succeeded. Proof of that is that the 12 issues of *Crisis* were originally published in the '80s, yet the book has not gone out of print for 36 years. Fans still think of *Crisis* as the best company-wide crossover ever done, which makes us feel great, because we worked so hard on it.

PETER SANDERSON: Knowing that DC was bringing the saga of the Man of Steel as generations of readers had known it to an end, Julius Schwartz commissioned Alan Moore, the British writer who was revolutionizing mainstream comics on DC's *Swamp Thing* and *Watchmen* series, to write a grand finale to Superman's first five decades. Moore's "Whatever Happened to the Man of Tomorrow?" drawn by classic Superman artist Curt Swan and appearing in both *Action* #583 and *Superman* #423 in 1986, was an astonishingly powerful tale, which brought together all the major characters in the Superman cast for one last great adventure, in which most of them met their final fates. Amazingly, Moore took concepts that most readers now regard as juvenile, outdated clichés from the Weisinger era — like Krypto the superdog and Jimmy Olsen with his "Elastic Lad" superpowers — and rediscovered their dramatic power. Reading Moore's story, one could feel that perhaps DC was making a mistake in discarding so much of Superman's history: He had proven that a talented writer could still make all of it work, even for older and more sophisticated readers.

But there was no preventing the inevitable, and probably necessary, revision of Superman's history. With Moore's final storyline for the "old" continuity, Schwartz had perhaps the greatest artistic success of his long and admirable stewardship of the Man of Steel's titles.

RAY MORTON (film historian and author): Part of DC's massive overhaul of its entire line and its streamlining of its overall continuity, the story was meant to be the final adventure of the original Superman character and bring to an end the timeline that had been running since the character's 1938 debut. It's a terrific tale — smart, logical and incredibly dramatic as Superman's world is torn asunder and he is forced to violate his most sacred principle in order to save the world one last time. It's a story filled with loss — of old friends, old enemies, and finally of Superman himself, and as such it is terribly poignant. And yet it ends on a note of hope and the reassurance that even when he's gone, Superman will always be with us. As such, it really couldn't be more perfect — a fitting end and a fitting tribute to a classic and beloved character. The conclusion of "Whatever Happened to the Man of Tomorrow?" paved the way for John Byrne's 1986 revamp of the character.

MARK WAID (writer, *Superman: Birthright*): There couldn't have been a better, more fitting capstone to the Weisinger/Schwartz run shepherding the Superman character. Back then, Alan Moore absolutely loved comics, especially Silver Age treasures, and might even have been able to throw down with me on Weisinger-era trivia. *Might.* There was more genuine, heartfelt emotion in those 46 pages than had been in the previous 50 years of Superman combined. The only disappointment for me, and it's a minor point, is that it's a shame that George Perez couldn't have inked the second half of the story as he did the first; I love Kurt Schaffenberger's work, I truly do, but after his cataract surgery, his inks just weren't as tight and crisp as they had been. Still, what a finish. Moore even remembered to end the story with Superman winking at the reader, which is way too often an underrated and misunderstood thing. It was always a way of saying to the kids reading the comic, "Hey pal, you and I now share a secret that no one else knows but you and me." That's just cool.

PETER SANDERSON: When it came to revamping Superman, DC Comics had been contemplating a revision of the mythos for years.

MARV WOLFMAN: Before I left Marvel, Jenette Kahn used to have poker parties at her house, and I'd go there and talk to her, and almost always we'd be talking about Superman. That's always been my pet project, and I'd talk about all the changes I'd like to see and why the book wasn't working for the market that was coming up. I think it worked for the market that had been, but it wasn't anticipating anything. Jenette always liked my ideas on Superman. When I first came to DC, one of the first assignments I was given was Superman, but because I was only one writer among several on the character, and I was not asked to make the changes I wanted; I tried to write it as closely to the style the book was written in as I could, while putting in my own little nuances. But I really didn't change much.

PETER SANDERSON: Later, Jenette Kahn asked for concepts for a revised version of Superman. Regular *Superman* writer Cary Bates came up with one concept for a revision that would work into the ongoing continuity.

CARY BATES: Ironically, it combined two of the themes DC would later incorporate in separate storylines years apart: de-powering (the Byrne reboot) and death (the Doomsday arc). My scenario called for a five- or six-part miniseries in which Superman "died" first and was reborn later, inside a yellow sun. I believe I proposed introducing some never-before-revealed wrinkles in Kryptonian physiology that made this possible, but at a steep cost. The regeneration process permanently consumed a lot of Superman's inherent energy, in effect "de-powering" him. I recall using the analogy of what happened to the Michael Rennie Klaatu character in the classic SF film *The Day the Earth Stood Still*. When Gort brought him back to life, Klaatu explained that he wasn't the same being he used to be and his life-extension could end at any moment. I didn't propose going this far with Superman, but I did think the concept of a Superman who finds he can't do all the stuff he used to take for granted (moving planets, unassailable invulnerability, etc.) could have been an interesting avenue to pursue. Of course, my reboot wouldn't have addressed the issue of all the Silver Age Weisinger baggage that Byrne chose to dispense with.

The comic in which writer/artist John Byrne brought major changes to the Superman mythos (© and TM DC Comics/Warner Bros. Discovery)

PETER SANDERSON: Wolfman wanted to start Superman continuity over from the beginning, as did writers Frank Miller and Steve Gerber.

MARV WOLFMAN: Frank Miller and Steve Gerber suggested one concept and I suggested another one that was not too dissimilar in intent, although it was dissimilar in plot. Frank, Steve and I all wanted to get rid of Superboy, cut down on Superman's powers, make changes in Luthor and make Superman the last survivor of Krypton. They did it different than I did.

PETER SANDERSON: Time passed without any concept for a revised *Superman* series being given a go-ahead. But DC still wanted to revamp Superman, and in May of 1985, editor Andrew Helfer was assigned to find the creative personnel to do it. Helfer began talking to various people in the business about working on a revised *Superman*.

MARV WOLFMAN: Then I discovered that John Byrne was no longer under contract to Marvel. I essentially said to John, "This may cut my own throat, but DC is interested in a new version of Superman. If you're interested, now that you're freelance, why don't you get in touch with them?" I didn't think that he would, but I was hoping. I honestly felt that John's version of Superman and mine would be fairly similar, because we were both fans of the same material: the Jerry Siegel and Jerome Shuster stories and the Paramount cartoons. I felt John would present the Superman I'd like to read. Plus, he would make it sell, and that's more important than anything else, as far as I'm concerned. At the same time, maybe I'd get the other Superman book, which I did.

JOHN BYRNE (writer, *The Man of Steel* comic): It came about basically from me shooting off my mouth for 10 years. After the first *Superman* movie with Christopher Reeve, I just went around saying, "See? They knew how to do it right. DC doesn't know how to do it right." I was under exclusive contract to Marvel and I went off contract… I don't know why. I think I maybe sensed that I was going to have to jump. And almost the instant I decided to go off contract, the phone rang. It was Dick Giordano from DC and he said, "Okay, wiseguy. Put your money where your mouth is. We are, in fact, going to reboot Superman. Tell us what you want to do." So I put together what I called my "List of Unreasonable Demands," which was like 20 things as I recall. I turned it in and they liked 19 of them. Nineteen of them were *not* unreasonable.

MARV WOLFMAN: Once they settled on John, they got back to me and asked me if I'd handle the other book, *Adventures of Superman*. And I said, "Yeah, I'm interested, but hold on." I called John and essentially told him the concept I had for changing Lex Luthor and said, "What do you think?" He liked it. Part of the reason I think he liked it was because my reason why Luthor hates Superman was identical to what he was thinking. I didn't tell John at the time that his decision on Luthor determined whether or not I'd take the book. If he didn't like my Luthor, I wouldn't have taken the book. The fact that he did like the Luthor idea meant that our views were so similar, as I had hoped, that we could easily work together. I then called DC back and accepted the other book.

JOHN BYRNE: I took my standard "Back to Basics" approach. All of the debris that accumulated over the years was the result of people trying to do something different. I took Superman back to basics, and that becomes different because it hadn't been done in so long. My take on Superman was basically Siegel and

Shuster meet the Fleischer Superman. My Superman pays homage to Christopher Reeve. I liked the slightly self-deprecating humor he gave Superman. This guy is *so* good at what he does that if he didn't have a sense of humor about it, he'd be intolerable. I gave him that kind of sense of humor.

To prepare, I went back to the very beginning of the character's history. I read mostly the really old stuff, the first 10 years. I was very aware that, whatever happened in 1938, it was so successful that there was a Superman Day at the 1939 World's Fair. That's how fast it clicked. There must have been something way back then that was magic, and *that* formed the core of what I was trying to do. I asked, "What came after 1938?" And all the additional "Supers" and the emphasis on Krypton came after — much after — 1938. So when I was doing my research, that was the direction I was pointed: strip it down.

MIKE CARLIN (former Superman Editor at DC): In John's editorial that he wrote when he took over the book, he said that everything we knew about Superman before hasn't happened — *yet*. What he did was let a whole lot of people in on the ground floor. They saw Mister Mxyzptlk's *first* adventure. They didn't have to hunt down a 40-year-old comic book or a reprint to understand it. Even if somebody missed that episode and is curious when Mxyzptlk comes back, the original is still available in the comics stores. We passed on the stuff we liked as kids to a new generation. A big part of our audience was people who didn't know the entire Superman history; people who didn't know that there used to be an entire city of Kryptonians living in a jar.

JOHN BYRNE: I tried to take the best parts of all the different versions of Superman — movies, television, the cartoons and all the published versions. My concentration on the TV series turns up mostly in the personification of Clark Kent. I always liked George Reeves' Clark Kent — he was gutsy and no-nonsense. On the TV series, they never apologized for the fact that this guy doesn't turn into another person when he puts the glasses on. They weren't as worried about establishing a wildly different personality for him, or setting up all the traditional comic book cover-ups for why nobody spots him as Superman. If anything came from the show, it's that — the stronger Clark Kent character.

PETER SANDERSON: The Superman revamp was introduced in the six-issue *The Man of Steel* series in 1986, written and drawn by Byrne. From the very first page, readers were put on notice that things were now different, even more so than when Julie Schwartz had destroyed Kryptonite. Instead of Krypton as 1950s sci-fi paradise, it was now depicted as a harsh, barren world, perhaps somewhat reminiscent of the icy planet Donner had depicted. Instead of showing Jor-El and Lara as the traditional loving parents, Byrne dressed them in asexual costumes and set them into a society where human emotions and sexuality had been almost wholly repressed. Kal-El was not the familiar cute toddler, but a mere fetus, growing within a "gestation matrix." This was, as Byrne put it, a Krypton that deserved to die. He subsequently wrote the limited series *World of Krypton*, which depicted the lush, beautiful Krypton of centuries before, showed how it was driven by war and chronicled the emergence of the sterile society of Jor-El's time. Krypton was no longer doomed by a natural accident, but by the long-delayed effect of a doomsday weapon created by terrorists during past wars that was slowly turning the planet's core into unstable Kryptonite.

In Byrne's version, Kal-El was born on Earth when his rocket landed there. He was found by Jonathan and Martha Kent outside Smallville, which was now specifically located in Kansas, where the scenes of Superman's childhood in Richard Donner's movie had been set. The newborn Kal-El had no superpowers whatsoever. There would be no Weisinger-style stories about a flying Superbaby forever narrowly avoiding discovery by the outside world. In the new continuity, Clark would develop his powers slowly over the years as his body absorbed increasing amounts of radiation from Earth's yellow sun. And so there was no Superboy either, nor was Clark a bespectacled bookworm in high school, taunted by Lana Lang the way that Lois would do later. Instead, Clark became a high school football player and Lana was his closest friend, who was secretly in love with him, although he regarded her as a sister.

Eventually the Kents showed Clark the rocket and revealed how they found him, although none of them yet realized he was an alien. Moreover, the maturing Clark had by now discovered that his abilities were ranging beyond conceivable human levels, and that he could even fly. He confided in Lana, but broke her heart by leaving Smallville to pursue his destiny.

PETER SANDERSON: *Man of Steel* then jumped ahead seven years to Metropolis, during which time Clark had been employing his powers to save endangered people and prevent disasters while remaining undetected by the world. Finally though, the existence of a super-powered hero was exposed when he rescued a plummeting experimental spacecraft in full view of a huge crowd of witnesses — not least among them was a reporter riding aboard the "space-plane," Lois Lane. Disembarking, she came face-to-face with her rescuer, who she dubbed "Superman" in the *Daily Planet* stories she subsequently wrote. But the crowd closed in on the two of them and the "Superman" flew off. In a very contemporary comment on celebrity culture, Byrne had Clark become horrified by the acclamation of the crowd. "They were all over me! Like wild animals," Clark told his foster parents. "And it was all demands! Everyone had something they wanted me to do, to say, to sell."

Right from the very first Superman origin story and even in the Donner movie, Pa Kent had died before Clark began his adult career as Superman; other past stories had both Jonathan and Martha Kent die from a mysterious, incurable ailment. But in yet another revision of the legend, Byrne kept both foster parents alive, hence the Kents were there to offer the solution to Clark's problems with his new fame: the creation of his dual identity. Thus, Superman would use his powers in public while wearing the familiar costume. But the Kents create Clark's familiar bespectacled look as a disguise, a "fortress of solitude," as Byrne puts it, into which he could hide from the public and lead a reasonably normal life.

John Byrne and writer Marv Wolfman made significant changes in Lex Luthor that are still felt to this day (© and TM DC Comics/Warner Bros. Discovery).

The changes kept coming: Lois Lane was brought back to her roots as a driven, risk-taking, sophisticated reporter rather than the dopey, "How come Clark isn't here whenever Superman is?" damsel-in-distress who was more concerned about whether Supes would marry her than any story she should have been working on. Byrne also recreated the first meeting between Superman and Batman; instead of them being best friends, they're suspicious of the other and Superman is shocked by Batman's more violent methods. They nonetheless become allies, but their differences are so strong that they'll never be friends. Different villains were also updated and revised, including Lex Luthor, who had gone from mad scientist to corrupt businessman.

JOHN BYRNE: Superman goes to Gotham City, because he's learned there is a vigilante there who breaks people's legs. Whether or not Batman would actually break a criminal's legs, people in Gotham think he would. So Superman says, "This Batman guy, I think I'll go take care of him before he screws it up for the rest of us." Batman scoffs at Superman because, as far as he's concerned, Superman is just a big red and blue buffoon. In the course of the story, they come to realize that each of them is doing a very important job in his own way. And Batman has the line at the end, "In a different reality, we might have been friends."

MARV WOLFMAN: I had first proposed the idea several years before we revamped Luthor and Brainiac. Julie Schwartz wanted me to only handle one of the revamps, and for Cary Bates — the writer of the other Superman title then — to handle the other, so I did Brainiac and I used my corporate honcho idea for Vandal Savage instead. When we revamped Superman in 1986, I re-proposed the idea — confident that no one would remember what I had done with Vandal, and this time it was accepted. I never believed the original Luthor. Every story would begin with him breaking out of prison, finding some giant robot in an old lab he hid somewhere, and then he'd be defeated. My view was that if he could afford all those labs and giant robots, he wouldn't need to rob banks. I also thought later that Luthor should not have superpowers. Every other villain had superpowers. Luthor's power was his mind. He needed to be smarter than Superman. Superman's powers had to be useless against him because they couldn't physically fight each other, and Superman was simply not as smart as Luthor. I thought he should be as legal as possible, and his crimes brilliantly conceived so Superman could not pin them on him, and the best way to achieve that was turn him into a businessman/scientist. He was the toast of Metropolis until Superman came to town. He wanted Lois, until she met Superman. All his problems came from his ego and personality, not because he was bald. He was rich. Successful. Admired. But people instantly knew Superman was his better. *That* made him interesting.

PETER SANDERSON: Interestingly, this new vision of Luthor changes the essence of the conflict between him and Superman. At heart it seemed to be a battle of brain (Luthor, bald, cerebral and, in the 1950s, fat) against brawn (the super-strong and virile Superman). We see the same thing in the opposition between Superman's Golden Age competitor Captain Marvel, and his own archenemy, the bald, grotesque, aged scientist Dr. Sivana. There is a clear anti-intellectual theme at work here. Byrne would now play down Luthor as a scientific genius, preferring to show him employing scientists who came up with war machines and other inventions. Later writers would reemphasize Luthor as a scientific genius; that was too essential an element of Luthor, it seemed, to be long suppressed.

JOHN BYRNE: You can think of him as like Walt Disney. Disney was an artist and an animator, but once he had a studio, he became more of an idea man, and he didn't feel the need to sit down and draw anymore. Luthor hires people to do things. If he wants a super-robot to fight Superman, he hires the best super-robot builder around. He doesn't worry about doing it himself.

MARV WOLFMAN: Luthor spends much of his time seeking pleasure. He is someone who'll bring the entire Metropolis Philharmonic into his mansion. He'll have these lavish parties. He's into the arts. He's into everything. He's not a recluse. In fact, the more people around him — when he wants people around him, they know it.

PETER SANDERSON: The new emphasis, though, was on the power Luthor's wealth gave him and upon how he misused it to dominate the people of Metropolis. The Superman-Luthor stories were no longer suggesting that brains are bad. Instead, there is now something of a class opposition between Superman and Luthor. Despite his powers, Superman is, after all, a middle-class reporter, whereas Luthor is a corrupt member of the super-rich, who exerts undue and unjustified influence over the lives of those around him. Though Wolfman had come up with the idea for the new Luthor, it was Byrne who fleshed it out, making Luthor the head of Lexcorp, an immense corporation that controlled virtually every major business in Metropolis. In his first appearance in *Man of Steel*, Luthor permits a terrorist attack on his yacht during a party in order to witness Superman in action with his own eyes. Superman shows up and stops the hijacking, all right, but he also takes Luthor to jail for endangering his guests. When Luthor points out, "I'm the most powerful man in Metropolis," the major retorts, "No, you're not, Lex. Not anymore." And there it is: From then on Luthor is driven to destroy Superman, not merely to avenge the humiliation of his stay in prison (only two hours before his lawyers sprung him), but because Superman had displaced him from his throne as master of Metropolis.

MIKE CARLIN: John was on the book before I was. I respect John's knowledge of what the readers want. He reached a hell of a lot more people than I ever have with my writing in comics; he's been at it longer than I have and he's really got a knack for getting people to talk about his stuff, whether it's the artwork or the fact that he's messing with their favorite characters. Sometimes John would call with ideas that I just don't think will work, but if he says "Trust me," then I do — and he's generally right. Fans weren't ashamed of admitting they read Superman, whether they liked it or not. People were considering *Superman* as the "beginners' book," where the youngest comics readers would begin. I like to think that the series under Byrne worked on several levels.

PETER SANDERSON: With the conclusion of the *Man of Steel* limited series, DC relaunched its principal Superman series. Byrne wrote and drew a brand-new *Superman* comic book beginning with issue one; the previous Superman series, which had run since the 1940s, was retitled *The Adventures of Superman,* written by Marv Wolfman and drawn by rising artist Jerry Ordway. Byrne likewise wrote and drew *Action Comics*, the first title in which Superman had ever appeared, which was re-conceived as a book in which Superman teamed with a different DC hero or team in each issue. Eventually, creative differences on the Superman teams led to changes in assignments. Byrne took over writing *Adventures* from Wolfman and Andrew Helfer ceded his role as editor to Mike Carlin, a longtime friend of Byrne's who had recently left Marvel.

For nearly two years Byrne wrote three Superman books per month and drew two of them before, due to behind-the-scenes disagreements with DC, he went back to Marvel. During this period, however, he had turned out an astonishing amount of work on DC's flagship character and had managed to reintroduce and rework many of the Superman mythos' leading characters for the 1980s and 1990s.

JOHN BYRNE: I got to do most of what I wanted, but it was mostly a negative experience, largely because DC flipped out at the first whisper of negative press… which, of course, started six months *before* the book came out, and nobody had seen a line of it. But it got out that I was going to do it; that, "They changed Superman!" The fans went ballistic. And DC backed off. I realized I was in trouble when Dick Giordano said to me, "Well, you have to realize that there are now two Supermen, the one you're doing and the one we license." And I sort of went, "Okay, what the hell does *that* mean?" They gave Marv a total free hand too, and I remember a writer from *The Boston Globe* was doing a story and he asked me, "Well, they're doing two Supermen now, right? The one you're doing in your two books and the one in the third book?" And I said, "Well no, actually, it's supposed to be the same guy." Marv only lasted about a year.

But I was constantly being sniped at by the fans and DC was not defending me. They'd say they were supporting everything I was doing, everything was approved, everything was green lit. Not a single thing was done that didn't pass through tight editorial scrutiny that comes with Superman. After about a year-and-a-half, 21 issues, I'd had enough. And I think the straw that broke the camel's back was *Time*, a Time/Warner publication. They did a 50th anniversary story — that was an issue I did the cover for — and the article referred to the reboot as something like "superfluous" or "unnecessary" or something like this. And I said, "Gee guys, thank you for your support." I took it as the death of a thousand cuts, and that was the last cut.

It's this weird thing where fans were clearly of the impression that I had walked in one day and said, "Give me Superman." What still comes around is, "John Byrne destroyed Curt Swan's career." They say, "DC came to John Byrne and said, 'You can have anything you want,' and Byrne said, 'I'll take Superman'" — which, of course, is not what happened. They came and said, "Would you like to do Superman?" I asked them, "What about Curt?" and they said Curt would be taken care of, and I took their word for it.

And with that, John Byrne who, in truth, had done quite a bit to turn around the Man of Steel's fortunes and standing in the comic book world, was gone, though much of his impact would actually live on.

PAUL LEVITZ: The John Byrne relaunch was very significant. I mean, it was the first conscious reboot of Superman, and I guess you can argue that it's the first conscious reboot of a character who's still succeeding. The Flash, Green Lantern, Captain America, Human Torch — those were relaunches for characters who had faded off the scene. Actually, that's not true. You had the Wonder Woman/Diana Prince relaunch in the '60s as the first one, but Superman was the first one that worked. And John modernized a lot of stuff and brought a style that worked for a good stretch.

ROBERT GREENBERGER: John brought a lot of fresh thinking that readers in 1986 responded to. He took the best elements from Siegel and all the writers had brought to it, and gave us a Superman that felt like he fit in the 1980s. Ma and Pa Kent are alive, which was a big change, because now he had his parents to talk to and to continue to get guidance from. The relationship with Lois was a lot more mature. Lex Luthor was now an evil corporate guy, which played well, and John played off that really nicely. He came up with new villains, which I think the character needed. It was a fresh take, the art certainly was more dynamic. I mean, no matter how many people tried to work with Curt Swan, including Joe Kubert, to freshen it and make his work more dynamic for readers who were now a generation raised on Marvel storytelling, it didn't work. Curt's stuff was beautiful, easy to read and he was a great visual storyteller, but it just wasn't dynamic. Superman needed to be dynamic in a new era.

ALAN BURKE (co-host, *All Star Superfan Podcast*): One of the greatest ideas when it came to reinventing something to do with Superman over the past 80 years is what John Byrne did with Lex Luthor, turning him from this kind of buffoonish cartoon mad scientist from the earlier books, into the manipulative businessman. There was one story done early on where Luthor goes to a diner outside of Metropolis and there's a married waitress there. He offers her like a million dollars to leave her life, her husband, her job and sleep with him. She doesn't know what to do and goes to talk to her waitress friends about it, and when she returns, Luthor is gone. In the limo the driver asked him why he did that, and he basically says that he just likes screwing with people's lives, while the waitress is going to wonder what her decision would have been.

ARLEN SCHUMER (comic book historian): If you go back to the Silver Age, DC had its own style and Marvel was the Stan Lee house style. Then this new batch of writers came in, like Marv Wolfman, Len Wein, Roy Thomas and all those guys at Marvel in the early '70s. And Marvel triumphed over DC finally, in sales, because other than Neal Adams, all the creative in the late '60s went to Marvel, so Marvel benefited in the early '70s. Even with Kirby gone, they benefited from the injection of new talent and the results were pure sales that have never relented; Marvel is still number one. But then what happened in the '80s? All those Marvel creatives left Marvel and went to DC, and they went to DC to "Marvelize" it. And guess what? They succeeded, for better or worse. Wolfman and Byrne turned Luthor into a businessman — he's the same bald-headed guy as the Kingpin. Personally, I liked the Curt Swan bald-headed Luthor with the gray janitor outfit coming up with insane plots to take down Superman. If I want the Kingpin, I'll read Marvel Comics.

ROBERT GREENBERGER: In a lot of ways, bringing John in worked, because it forced everyone to rethink what is Superman and what it means to be the last son of this doomed planet. What does it mean to be the most powerful guy on the street? What are his responsibilities? What kind of threats should he be dealing with? What's his galactic reputation? It made people rethink it entirely. In the end, I think it was a good thing for the company. Absolutely.

DAN JURGENS (writer, *Superman*): When I came on, it was just shortly after John had Superman execute the three Kryptonian criminals, General Zod and company, which I thought was out of step for Superman. I don't think I would have done that story. But it gave us something to build on, because I came in during the "Superman in Exile" storyline, where Superman basically was off in space, doing penance for what he had done. And so, we were able to re-balance the character a little bit there, bring him back and sort of start anew, but it was all done with the foundation that John Byrne had already established. In fact, we went out of our way not to power Superman up to where he used to be. At that time, when

Superman went into space, he had to bring oxygen with him. Now it doesn't mean that he had to breathe heavy doses of it, because I think we established that Superman could still take a breath and hold it a really long time. But we did get Superman to the point where he had to work at it a little harder to try and succeed and get the job done. That was good for the character.

One of the other things that John did that we tried to play out for the most part was Superman himself being the last son of Krypton. You can have a slight tweak or two to that — Supergirl probably being a good tweak — but there are probably just too many characters with "S" shields, which waters down the uniqueness of Superman. And if he has this tragic background of Krypton blowing up, and him being put in a rocket ship and sent to Earth, you can't have 50 other Kryptonians running around. I don't care if they're from other universes or wherever. It filters away from the pure essence that is Superman. It's interesting, because the first chunk of years that I did on Superman, we played that up very much. And then when I came back and was doing it as part of *Rebirth* and writing it for a few years around 2016, 2017 or 2018, where I did a General Zod storyline, I felt strangely uncomfortable during that entire period — whereas on one hand, it was interesting to have Zod, on the other hand, it felt like a bit of a cheat.

ROBERT GREENBERGER: I wasn't there when John left, but from what I understand, John just did not feel he was in charge and respected for his vision, because the needs of the company were that Superman needed to be in different places and John lost control of the narrative. He was drawing and writing *Action Comics* as the team-up book, and working with Marv Wolfman on *Adventures of Superman* with Jerry Ordway. But then Superman needed to be in other comics as well, because Superman was cool again. But John wanted more control over that stuff.

DAN DIDIO (former co-publisher, DC Comics): That's a lot of what goes on behind-the-scenes, but the reality is that was probably the most full-handed attempt to really reinvent the wheel from top to bottom. And it succeeded for a while — a lot of these things succeed for a while, but they all default to the original setting, to that core of the character and what people remember best and, in some ways, what worked the best.

RAY MORTON (film historian and author): At the time I really loved what Byrne had done — it seemed fresh and clever and quite logical. However, as time has gone on, I have become less enamored with it, because I feel it made two key changes to Superman that have lessened the core of the Superman character. The first is that he made Clark Kent a cool character in his own right. Previous to Byrne, Kent was always depicted as being unimpressive — shy, restrained, sometimes fearful, clumsy, unromantic, wholly unglamorous and even a bit dull. The original Clark Kent was meant to be unremarkable in every way (the one exception to this was the brief period in the early-'70s when Kent was made a TV reporter, which gave the character a bit of glamour that never quite fit and was eventually abandoned). But Byrne's Clark Kent was a dynamic personality in his own right — a successful, high-profile, yuppie reporter who had style and charm and who engaged in witty, flirty banter with a Lois Lane who saw him as a viable romantic partner. This significantly watered down one of the character's core concepts and the source of much of his appeal — that beneath our unexceptional exteriors (the person we all fear we are) lies something spectacular (the person we wish we were). When Clark is less ordinary, Superman is less extraordinary.

Byrne altered the Superman concept in another way. Among the many comic book heroes who surfaced in his wake, Superman was unique in that the super-hero was the real person and the human persona was the disguise. For most of the other superheroes (e.g. Batman), the human is the real person and the superhero is the disguise. But in Byrne's reconception, Clark is the real person and Superman is the disguise he puts on. And that took a lot of juice out of the character. While many of Byrne's innovations were good ones (especially his reinvention of Luthor as a Trump-like businessman, a concept that gained an unexpected relevance three decades later when the model became a real-life supervillain), these two innovations significantly diminished the character. And while many of Byrne's innovations failed to stick, these two mostly did and I think the character has been a lot less interesting ever since.

DAN JURGENS: I'm a great admirer of the work John Byrne did on Superman. He brought in several things that were very important to who Superman was as a character, and one of them was he gave us back the Kents. It goes back to my feeling that a Superman story is somewhat easy, because of the responsibilities he feels to the world around him and the people around him as co-workers and his friends and relatives. Him having that contact with his human parents, I think helps explain to the reader who Superman was; what we saw was a Clark Kent that was raised by a very tight nuclear family, where they all loved each other. There was a balance of respect across all three parties in that household, that kind of thing. And that gave us an understanding of Clark, which meant we could see how Clark developed as Superman, once he became an adult. So I think what John did there was great. I would also say he got the character back to the point where he had to work a little harder to do the things from a heroic perspective. I think that was quite good. He had just given the franchise a bit of a shot in the arm overall.

PETER SANDERSON: The proof of how well DC's revision of the mythos worked is that the new version was largely adopted by adaptations of Superman into other media. True, the 1980s did bring a new Superboy TV series, even though the revised Superman had never had a Superboy career. But the initial episode of *Lois & Clark: The New Adventures of Superman* borrowed heavily (and without credit) from Byrne's *Man of Steel* series, including the rescue of the space-plane and the sequence in which Ma Kent creates the Superman costume. Like Byrne, it kept Ma and Pa Kent alive and made them major ongoing characters. *Smallville* would later do the same. *Lois & Clark* likewise used the wealthy businessman version of Luthor, although it gave him a full head of hair in contrast to the traditional bald look. It was no surprise that a short-lived 1980s animated Superman series incorporated the new changes, since Wolfman served as story editor. But so did the more successful 1990s' *Superman: The Animated Series* from Warners animation, although it also revised the mythos still further.

MICHAEL BAILEY: John Byrne leaves in 1988 after growing frustrated. He said in an interview that Dick Giordiano told him there were two Supermen: There's the Superman for marketing and the Superman Byrne was writing in the comics. So he was like, "I'm out." And when you really look at it, he did five years' worth of stories in two years, because he was writing and drawing both *Superman* and *Action*. And then he was writing *Adventures of Superman* after Marv Wolfman left. And then, after Byrne leaves, you enter another era that probably goes until around 1995, and that is really like the high watermark of that era of Superman post-*Crisis*.

PETER SANDERSON: Following Byrne's departure, editor Mike Carlin coordinated a large number of writers and artists to collaborate on the Superman titles. By the late 1980s, Batman, Superman and Marvel's Spider-Man were all appearing in a different series each week of the month. Unlike the Weisinger days, now stories would often flow from one title to the next, in effect offering a new chapter of a continuing saga every week.

MICHAEL BAILEY: The creators that came on the book after Byrne: Jerry Ordway, who had been drawing *Adventures of Superman* stayed on after Wolfman left and after Byrne left. He was then writing and drawing *Adventures* and they brought on Roger Stern with artist Carrie Gamel to do *Superman*. *Action* was no longer a monthly book at that point; after issue #600, it became a weekly for 42 issues. It was an anthology book, so you had a Superman Sunday strip written by Roger Stern and drawn by Curt Swan, but you also had The Demon, Nightwing, Blackhawk, Deadman and all these other characters. That experiment lasted until 1989, when the book came back to a monthly schedule right at the end of a storyline called "Exile." And by that point, they had brought in Dan Jurgens to be an artist on *Adventures of Superman*, and eventually he became a writer and George Perez came on to *Action* with Roger Stern. Then after Perez left, it settled into Ordway writing and drawing *Superman*, Dan Jurgens writing and drawing *Adventures of Superman*, and you had Roger Stern and several artists — Bob McLeord, Jackson Geist — doing *Action*, and eventually they decide towards the end of 1990 for the cover date 1991 books that they're going to make these all connected and they start the "triangle era."

The issue of Superman that stunned the world, with many believing the character was truly dead (© and TM DC Comics/Warner Bros. Discovery).

MARK WAID: I was still a little bit stung as a reader because of the Byrne stuff that happened so recently at that point, but I thought the triangle idea was a smart move and really well-run. If you didn't have that creative team in place and that editorial team in place knowing how to run that room, it could have been disastrous. But it worked very well; all the writers worked well together and it felt like there was a flow to it. I felt bad for Mike Carlin at one point over the fact that they didn't want to do a triangle, they wanted to do the "S" pentagon, but some high sheriff claimed there were trademark problems. It's *their* trademark.

PETER SANDERSON: After a period of transition, there were four regular monthly Superman titles: *Superman, Action, The Adventures of Superman* and *Superman: The Man of Steel*, named after Byrne's landmark miniseries. Still later, these would be joined by a fifth, quarterly title, *Superman: The Man of Tomorrow*. But despite all the creative energy at work, Superman's sales went into decline once again. Byrne was gone and the revamping of Superman had already become old news, displaced by such phenomena as the sudden and spectacularly successful rise of new comics companies like Image. To recapture the attention of the comics audience, Carlin and DC decided to stage their own "event," the now celebrated *Death of Superman* saga.

BRAD RICCA: I've always loved comics, but I did not like Superman. He was no X-Men in the '80s, which was excellent all the time. I got into Superman, ironically, when they killed him. That set off this visceral thing in me that it did in so many, which is why it was such a brilliant move because it's like, "You *can't* do that!" That got me really into Superman.

ANTHONY DESIATO: I was five years old with my parents at the Galleria Mall in White Plains, New York at holiday time, and we were walking through the mall and there was a Heroes World store back then. And in their window display they advertised *The Death of Superman*. They had a Superman action figure and a toy coffin. I wish I had a photo of it or something like that... or that I remembered it more vividly. It was either a toy coffin, maybe to go with some kind of horror set or something like that, or just a little box that they repurposed. I'm not sure. But it was the action figure in a box meant to be a coffin. And I had enough of a sense of who Superman was just from having an action figure or seeing something on TV. So there was that connection point. And it just drew me in. And they bought me *The Death of Superman* trade paperback that DC put out instantly. My dad read it to me and that was it. Superman has been my favorite character ever since.

TOM DE HAVEN: I *loved* the *Death of Superman*. I was so invested in that when it was coming out like once a week and then he was going to come back. I was fortysomething years old at the time, but I felt like I was 12 years old again. Just brilliant. The guy who edited the Superman books in those days, Mike Carlin... I loved him. I love what he did; he did a really good job with the character in those days. I felt emotionally invested in it and was surprised at *how* emotionally invested I was.

ANTHONY DESIATO: One of the big things I was trying to answer for myself is what impact does it have when your introduction to a character is that character's death? And the fact that he's then off the board for much of the next year. The impact of that specifically was, you get to learn a lot about who he was through the way he's remembered by the remaining characters, and everything is so heightened because of that grief. That just sort of mythologized him even more in my head based on the way everyone was remembering him in the pages of the comic. So I think there was a little bit of that. And even in the pages of the *Death of Superman* itself, and in fairness, we weren't dealing with the All-Star lineup of the JLA that we would get later. This was sort of the "B" list, but the fact that everyone else fell, he was the last one standing, he was the only one who could hold the line and stop Doomsday, the only one who could go the distance and was *willing* to go the distance, and make that ultimate sacrifice that even as a little kid that had an impact.

ALAN BURKE: I don't think there is a single Superman reader of my generation who does not remember where they were as that saga unfolded in 1993. And while yes, it's a toe-to-toe brawl between Superman and Doomsday, all of those personal moments I love are there too. Many people consider Doomsday to be a dull character — the word character perhaps even being too strong. He is a behemoth, a mindless beast with one thing on his mind: destruction. I disagree. It's what Doomsday represents that fascinates me. He is, for lack of a better analogy, Superman's Kobayashi Maru. He is Clark's unwinnable situation. It's easy to be perpetually courageous when one is invulnerable. It's easy to stand up and do the right thing when no matter what happens, you know you're going home at the end of the day. But what does a person do when the right thing means *not* coming home?

ANTHONY DESIATO: Certainly as I've gotten older, as I've thought about it, and I've gone back to it, that ability and willingness really sets him apart. And then, the fact that he has the power of a God yet chooses to use his powers in the way he does. And I know that's not necessarily anything groundbreaking. I think for a lot of fans, that's probably what it comes down to, but for me, it's certainly the choice to use his powers the way he does.

ALAN BURKE: As a police officer, now blessed with a young family, the question of not coming home often crosses my mind. What would I do in that situation? What would I have done if I had been one of the officers present at scene on 9/11? Would I have walked up those stairs knowing that I probably would not walk back down? Would I do the right thing in the face of almost certain death? Would Superman? *That's* the question that makes the *Death of Superman* so personal to me, and it's why it's one of my favorite storylines.

ROB O'CONNOR: *World Without a Superman* was the first graphic novel I owned, and while Superman is barely in it (death will do that to you) and the storyline is long and meandering, it does a really interesting job of showing how important Superman is to the world of Metropolis and the world at large. The image of Martha and Jonathan burying keepsakes on the farm, because they can't attend the star-studded Metropolis funeral, is a powerful one.

MICHAEL BAILEY: People were genuinely interested to see how and why he died, but the death wasn't the big part of that, because the next chapter was *Funeral for a Friend*, which was collected as *World Without a Superman*, and that was looking at his friends and loved ones dealing with his death. And then it moves into *Reign of the Supermen*, where you had four different characters that all represented parts of Superman, but showed ultimately why Clark is the only one that can be Superman. So I think it's the epicness of it that keeps people coming back to it or keep people wanting to discover it. That era of creators did such a great job of making you care, not just about Clark and Superman, but about everybody in that book that has a storyline. So it's not just Superman died and six months later he came back. Superman died and the world mourned, and then all of these people stepped in to try to be him. Ultimately one of them was a villain in disguise, but that's beside the point. In the end, the one true Superman is back and suddenly you realize he's important. For the general comic book audience, it literally took him dying and coming back for them to go, "Oh, he *is* necessary."

MIKE CARLIN: People still seem to like what happened and that makes it really fun. It was also fun while we were doing it most of the time. Sometimes it was work, but it was mostly fun. When it became work was when we actually got more and more successful once the title started selling more and expanding. More and more things kind of leeched onto what was going on in our books. There was a point where there were three Superman books; John Byrne was writing two of them and drawing two of them, and Jerry was doing the third book. Then John Byrne decided he was done with his Superman ideas for the moment and we were suddenly down to two books. And we put Roger Stern on one of the titles, and Jerry Ordway stayed on his. When it was two guys, it really was our bright idea to kind of link these comics a little closer together. And it was really easy with two guys who were doing it by themselves, and one of them happened to be drawing his comic too, so that was even better. As that got more successful, the third title came back and Dan Jurgens joined our group. Then for a couple of years, Paul Levitz kept bothering me about where his fourth Superman book was going to be. And I was like, we do everything tied together. That's like a weekly comic book. And there hadn't been a weekly comic.

DAN JURGENS: We thought, even leading up to that, that we were doing a damn fine story. And that we were doing something unique, which was the concept of a weekly comic book, for the most part, and that we could tell people were loving it. I had an editor from DC come up to me and said, "You know, with what you guys are doing, it's awesome. You are the best-kept secret in comics." And I just said, "Well, what the hell? Why don't you tell people about it?" And I think in that world, where everything was moving in comics very fast at that point because, when we first came up with the story, whether it was Todd McFarlane doing *Spider-Man*, or Jim Lee and Rob Liefeld, and those guys doing the *X* stuff, obviously all that stuff justifiably sold. And then, we came up with our story around the same time they were going off to set up Image. We didn't know what they were going to do or how it was going to work or anything. And I just think that we were getting to the point where we wanted to do our "Oh yeah? We'll show you!" kind of attitude. "We can do something like that too." And when I say something like that, I mean do a story that gets attention. And by attention, again, we meant just within the comic world. You know, we'll goose sales 25 to 50% or something like that — not 600%!

PAUL LEVITZ: We were doing good work, but the books were selling kind of middle of the road. What can we do? And then they came in with that storyline. *Nobody* expected it to be a phenomenon; we'd killed Superman before — a couple of times. But we got lucky and the news leaked on a slow news day — the world picked it up and decided we were serious and took it very seriously. And everybody got excited. *And* it's a good story.

DAN JURGENS: We knew it wasn't just another story. We knew we had come up with something that was going to be special, and hopefully powerful for readers. But when I say that, while we knew we had probably done something that would get us a bump in sales, we *never* could have seen it becoming the event that it did. The book *Superman* 75 came out, I think November 17, 1992. We planned the story in the first week of November 1991. That's when we laid out each individual issue. We came up with Doomsday and the whole story; everything else up through *Superman* 77. At that time, we didn't know how we would come back, when for sure we would come back. But we knew, just looking at our charts that we had put up on the board, we all felt very confident we had come up with a very special story. That's how we always saw it. It wasn't until later when the press found out, and marketing got involved, that it turned into what it did, which was a much bigger, more expansive event that just lit the fire everywhere and got everybody interested. There's no way we ever could have guessed at that or foreseen it.

MIKE CARLIN: We just were doing our next story when we got to the *Death of Superman*. And if you've read comics for any length of time, you know that the death of the hero story comes around every now and then. And in fact, that already happened to Superman in previous generations, so we were not asked to do it. We were not scared to do it. We had an out, we knew the ending. The miracle to me is that after this happened, and the big success that it was, that they didn't come to us and ask us to top it. They realized that it was an unusual thing. The marketing guys did not come up with this idea. This was just some people in a room who wanted to tell a story. And we thought it was just the next adventure that Superman would hopefully survive, and he didn't for a part of it. But then he did, ultimately. So he got better. And it kind of reminded people why they shouldn't take Superman for granted, which was our personal frustration in the writing room — that people were liking the Punisher- and Wolverine-type murderer characters more than Superman, who we thought was a better role model. So we said, what would they think if he wasn't there? And that was the motivation.

While that motivation feels strong, it's not the reason that all involved decided to tell that story. It actually had completely to do with the fact that in 1993, ABC would be debuting the weekly series Lois & Clark: The New Adventures of Superman, *starring Teri Hatcher and Dean Cain in the title roles.*

PETER SANDERSON: The *Death of Superman* arc was a replacement for a much more positive event that the Superman creative staff had planned for the character: his wedding, after over 50 years of publishing history, to Lois Lane. The creative team had gone so far as to mark the 50th issue of the new *Superman* series (December 1990) by having Lane and Kent finally get engaged. And then they had to put the wedding plans on hold. Warner Bros. now had the *Lois & Clark: The New Adventures of Superman* series in the works, which would begin with Kent and Lane's first meeting and, for the first few seasons, treat the Clark-Lois-Superman triangle in basically the traditional manner. So DC decided to postpone the wedding in the comics until such time as the characters were married on *Lois & Clark*. But what to do in the meantime, since it was now 1993 and *Lois & Clark* would not even debut until the fall of 1993? Carlin and his writers and artists had a running gag when they were trying to come up with major new storylines for Superman: Why not kill him? How could you possibly get more attention for them than *that*? So they decided to do it — after a fashion.

DAN JURGENS: This time when Jerry Ordway said, "Well, let's kill him,"

Louise Simonson, who had been the editor of the *X* books over at Marvel and had presided over the death of many a hero and returned some of them, said, "You know what you get from killing your hero? You get a chance to show what he meant to everybody else in his universe. You get to show the reaction of the friends and the family and the enemies and the world at large — what this character meant," and I think that appealed to a lot of us.

MIKE CARLIN: I just want everybody to understand that the TV series came and pushed our story out. Basically we had planned to do Lois and Clark's wedding for *Adventures of Superman* #500. And we were doing such a great job on the comics with the soap opera side of Lois and Clark's life that Hollywood got interested.

ROGER STERN (Superman writer): Jerry Ordway should get the credit for that. The original plan for *Superman* #50 had been that Lois would turn down Clark's proposal. But when Jerry was plotting that issue, it just didn't feel right to him. As I recall, he was discussing it with Mike and it occurred to him to ask, "What if she says 'yes'?" The two of them mulled it over for a while, and then Mike called me and repeated that question, "What if she says 'yes'?"

DAN JURGENS: We had been on the book and they announced they were going to have a TV series. So even as they started production on it, we got to go out to California. We sat down with the production team for a bit and just talked concepts and ideas. Now we had already gotten to the point where Clark had proposed to Lois and told her that he was Superman, and we knew someday we might get to the wedding. But then, as they said, "No, we're not going to have them get married yet; we want to push that off." So we couldn't use the wedding in our books at that time. That's why we had to shift gears and what we came up with instead was *Death of Superman*. So yeah, we played ball with them, and then when they finally did decide to go ahead and do a wedding, we did a wedding in the book as well *and* did the *Superman Wedding Album* and had a nice wedding between Clark and Lois.

MIKE CARLIN: Jenette Kahn, president of DC, and myself, we thought that if they do a show, it would be better to get to the wedding down the road. So that if they do a wedding on the show, if it's that big of a hit and they get to the wedding, we can do it together and actually mooch off of each other. *That's* a marketing idea, but it wasn't from marketing people. The reality was, if the show bombed, we could just get to the wedding next year. Superman comes back from the dead. It's like, "Oh my God, I died. Maybe I should get married, because I might not be alive next time so that I can get married." We really thought all that stuff through.

So we got to do the *Death of Superman*. The reality is when you say let's kill Superman, the next question to me was always okay, *then* what happens? *Death of Superman* is a fight scene, it's not a story.

LOUISE SIMONSON (Superman writer): You write the best story and you try to keep the emotions and the characters to the point of view of the characters and what it means to the characters who were left behind, keeping it as real as you possibly can. I think that's the way you get any kind of emotional resonance with the readers. And honestly, I as a writer, I can write brilliant stuff, but if I don't get an arc that shows the emotion that I'm trying to put into words, you've got something that's really flat. I was particularly lucky to have Jon Bogdanove be my artist on the book, but with all the art, everybody was just working at 150%, 200%, so it was really good.

MIKE CARLIN: We needed a new villain that was bigger than Superman. We all agreed that for Superman to die and it turns out to be Lex Luthor with a piece of Kryptonite would have been about the worst thing we could have done. There is no Kryptonite involved in the *Death of Superman* story, which is a surprise to people. Everyone's like, "Oh, nothing can kill Superman except Kryptonite." Well, we made up something else.

DAN JURGENS: The first week of November 1991, I walked into a meeting and I had a yellow legal pad with two ideas written on it. One was *Death of Superman* and the other one was monster crashes in Metropolis. I had that written down, because at that point we had so many Superman villains that were guys in suits; I mean, business suits — most notably, Lex Luthor. We had the new Brainiac, who had been a circus performer and normal human being; we had Mr. Z, guy in a suit; The Prankster; Toy Man. And I just said, "I want to draw Superman in a knockdown, drag-out, kick-ass fight with somebody." That was artist Dan talking. We had touched on the idea of doing *Death of Superman* as a storyline at an earlier meeting, but we just never really spent any time talking it out. And as I walked in with those ideas, they were very separate things. And only through a lot of conversation did they eventually become connected. We talked about who could kill him and somebody said, "What if it was Dan's monster and it was the complete opposite of Superman?"

MIKE CARLIN: A lot of people want what they think is an obvious idea, but if you gave it to them, they would reject it. Maybe not vocally, but they just might say, "Oh no, that's what I *thought* would happen." We were also really lucky that the internet wasn't quite as big a thing back then, so we just went with our guts. We didn't react to any outrage or whatever, and we managed to be able to tell our whole story, which was really great. Dan is the guy who wanted to make up a monster. One of the great, I think, democratic things we did was during the conversation when we had the *Death of Superman* meeting, all four of the pencil artists designed their version of Doomsday. Everybody voted and Dan's got picked.

DAN JURGENS: Superman is this creature of thought and reason. He is one of the few heroes who would go to the bad guy and say, "Instead of pulling that trigger and just shooting me in the chest — which is not gonna work — you might want to think about that. Let's just talk this out." The complete opposite of Superman is somebody who's almost incapable of speech, someone who is a force of nature there is no reasoning with. We all became intrigued by doing something new with a new villain. I sat there and I doodled up a sketch of Doomsday.   I didn't have the name for him yet, but he had a little bit of an exoskeleton in terms of protruding bones that are both defensive and offensive in nature. Like I said, we really got into the idea of a villain that was the opposite of Superman and new to readers that would just look so completely different. And then after the meeting, I tightened up the design for it. That's where we had something that would allow me to get to draw my fight and plough through Metropolis.

JON BOGDANOVE (Artist, *Death of Superman*): In addition to having nothing but villains with suits, all of Superman's villains were really long-winded guys. We had all these pages and pages of dialogue as Superman and his villains talk. It's like, "Oh my God, does anyone know Superman can fly? He flies somewhere to go talk to a villain?" I just wanted to have a *fight*.

DAN JURGENS: Once I got into it, it was exciting. The idea for that final issue — *Superman* 75 — was to tell the story in nothing but splash pages. That means 27 pages is 27 panels, and the inclination of the artist is each page is going to be Superman fighting Doomsday, and it's going to be lovely, and big and bold and expressive. But no, from time to time you have to show a shot of people seeing this on TV, or you have to show us a shot of Lois and Jimmy and a helicopter observing the event. *And* you still have to tell a bit of a story. So once it got into that whole area of having to properly tell the story, picking out the final 27 or whatever it is, that was really difficult from a storyteller's perspective. It's fun to draw, but difficult to really set it up as a story that communicates. We ended with a double-page spread that became the three-page fold out of Lois cradling Superman's body. That really brought the story to a close and so, by the time I got that done, it was tremendously gratifying.

MIKE CARLIN: I don't think I've ever even talked about this, but one of the great things was Jenette Kahn coming to these meetings. She watched everybody make up this *Death of Superman* and monster story. Then I went into her office with her and was like, "This could be something." She said, "This villain has to have a personality, and he has to have a motivation. He has to have all this stuff." And I was like, "I think he *shouldn't*. I really think that is the point of this, and it will make him a little different. We can always add stuff on to him later," which is what did happen when he was a popular character. Jenette let us do it. She trusted that the original idea was something that they would actually imbue with heart and they worked it out.

DAN JURGENS: I'm glad Mike stuck to his guns on that one. Because the thing that, for me, makes Doomsday *such* an effective device for killing off someone as iconic as Superman is that he's *not* explicit. He's just elemental.

MIKE CARLIN: If Luther had killed Superman, everybody would have said, "Oh, he's got to get out of this, because he always gets out of it." But nobody had ever seen Doomsday meet Superman before, so it could be *anything*. And I will say if the marketing guys did anything on this project, it was once the sales orders were coming in and they saw how huge this was getting, everybody got scared that our return to life in *Adventures of Superman* #500 was not going to be big enough… and they were totally right.

JERRY ORDWAY (writer/artist, *Death of Superman*): So we had another meeting for *that*.

MIKE CARLIN: But the first thing they did was they said, "Because of the way comic books are ordered these days, if we are soliciting *Adventures* 501 or whatever, everyone will know that Superman is coming back, but maybe they didn't even buy the issue where he died." So we stopped publishing Superman for three months, and that actually convinced everybody that maybe we were crazy; that we were going to leave Superman dead. I thought that was such a great idea. And I was sitting there saying, "Oh thank God. Three months off!" Then I was told, "No three months off. You have to do new *Time* magazine specials, miniseries and all this."

JERRY ORDWAY: As a quick anecdote, I was around when Byrne had

done the relaunch of Superman and I was getting photocopies and things from
Andy Helfer of what Byrne was doing in pencil. One of the things that stuck with
me was the fact that at that point, it was the only time in recent history where a
reader didn't know what Superman was going to be. As a result of a bad Xerox
that Helfer had made, it indicated the Superman costume or something might have
been different. The *Death of Superman* was another opportunity we shouldn't lose,
because no one knows what, if he comes back, he's going to look like or any of
that. It's time to play up all the secrecy and all the mystery of it. In a way, that was
done beautifully with having multiple guys claiming to be Superman.

PETER SANDERSON: Writer/artist Dan Jurgens unveiled the Man of Tomorrow, alias the Cyborg Superman, who resembled him, but half-converted into
a robot-like machine. Writer Roger Stern and artist Jackson Guice introduced the
Eradicator, a ruthless superhuman vigilante. Surprisingly, writer Karl Kesel and penciler Tom Grummett came up with a new version of Superboy for the 1990s, complete with leather jacket and earring who turned out to be a Luthor-devised clone
consisting of his DNA and Superman's. Finally, writer Louise Simonson and artist
Jon Bogdanove created Steel, an African-American who wielded a mallet and was
garbed in an armored battle suit that magnified his strength to superhuman levels.

MIKE CARLIN: That was something where Jerry, as a writer, had an idea of
what he wanted to do. Louise had an idea of what she wanted to do. Karl Kesel,
who was coming in on *Adventures*, had his idea of what he wanted to do. Stern had
an idea, Dan had an idea and everybody had a different idea. And Louise said, "Why
don't we do all of them?"

MIKE CARLIN: It was such a relaxing, freeing idea, because everybody in their
own titles would get to do their own thing that fit a story, but it was at least something unique to their title.

JERRY ORDWAY: It felt competitive between the four teams as to which
one's going to really be Superman before it was decided that they would use
them all. I felt like it fostered a competition between each team to do their best to
convince the reader that this is the one who's going to be Superman. And purely
as a reader, I enjoyed that aspect of the story, because everybody was at their most
competitive and I think you got a really good result.

MIKE CARLIN: And I think we came up with a great way to make each
character unique. The fact that they ran for almost 100 issues on their own, and are
still players in the DC Universe, is a real testament to how cool they each would

have been. But it would have been a sucky world if we had to actually pick one and only do that one, because I think that it was a better idea to go big. We convened this sudden secret meeting that was the most surreal thing that ever happened to me. When it was over, I went back to my hotel room. I put on the news where they were saying, "DC Comics is having a secret meeting to bring back Superman." And their angle was, "See, they're listening to us." We *always* were going to bring him back. We all had jobs and he was never going to go away. But that was bizarre to actually be on the news when all we were doing was working on comics. It was very strange. I don't know if we can pull off the *Reign of the Supermen* nowadays with the internet as good as it is. Even when we showed the silhouettes of the four Superman characters, that was the first time playing up the secret. And today that would be a leak or something.

JERRY ORDWAY: You'd have people tell *you* how they were created before they even saw it. Or one of the artists would go on Facebook and say, "This is one of the images I just did."

MIKE CARLIN: You know, back then people used to still write letters to comic books, and we got a lot of nasty letters, that's for sure. I got death threats over Clark and Lois getting engaged, so you can imagine what was happening with this. We killed it. People were mad: "You're taking away my childhood" and all the stuff that the internet now has taken. We don't want to cause anybody any grief, but at the same time, the fact that you're reacting to that, to some level at all, is a testament to the work that has gone on to make you love these characters. And there's a point where you kind of have to trust that comics is a long-term game. It's like, "Supergirl's back! Superman's back! Everybody's back!" Is there anybody who has stayed dead, really?

TOM DE HAVEN: Superman used to sell a million copies a month, and by the time of *Death of Superman*, he was selling 77,000 copies. The papers were saying, "Well, maybe it's over," so for a time I *did* believe he would stay dead. After a while though, I realized that they were milking this and the storyline was going to be something that was going to be very long. And that once the profits started to wane, Superman would be back. But for a while I thought maybe he wouldn't; the whole thing was brilliant.

MIKE CARLIN: I did a billion TV interviews. I was on all kinds of news shows and *Entertainment Tonight*, which doesn't cover comics anymore now that the Kardashians are out there — the super-villains of our universe. But people really bought into this and we were really just surprised that people honestly believed it — and I admit we did a couple of moves to kind of make it look like we meant it. At the same time, these are serialized stories. At the end of the movie serials you'd see in the '40s, it would look like the characters died at the end of every episode. But then they come back and show you some fake way they got out of whatever trap they were in. In this case, if I think we did anything at all right, it was that we didn't drop the ball once everybody was looking at us. The spotlight was on us and we managed to surprise people, and that just doesn't happen in our business anymore.

PAUL LEVITZ: Since then, they've killed and brought back thousands of characters. At that point you'd had a couple of things like *Dallas* on TV where Bobby Ewing comes back from the dead, but it was a pretty rare trick at that point. And the comic book industry was not perceived to be long for this world. You were in the era of the death of the newsstands, so people weren't seeing comics around them anymore. Comic shops were doing okay, but most people didn't know where a comic shop was, or have any sense of them. The outside world, they hadn't seen a Superman comic for years. I remember for many years being asked by people, when I explained what I did for a living, if comic books were still being published. Of course, the thing that's really made the difference is the graphic novel format and some of the creative work that's being done in that field.

In many ways, the creation of Doomsday was like the creation on Star Trek: The Next Generation *of the Borg — this incredible, unstoppable threat. What do you do to get away from that? In the case of* Death of Superman, *the Man of Steel has to die to defeat Doomsday. But how much does it defuse the power of Doomsday when he comes back again and again, as he did?*

DAN JURGENS: There's always this weird balance, because by the same token, ideally Galactus probably would have shown up on Earth just once, maybe twice, and we wouldn't have seen him again. But then new readers get cheated out of seeing Galactus. And even the old readers were like, "Oh, that Galactus story was so cool. I like seeing him again." And pretty soon he's here to the point where he's now got a favorite restaurant and bar that he goes and hangs out at. I don't disagree with it. But I also see the need to use Doomsday again from time to time and I'm guilty of it. I have done it when I did *Superman Rebirth*. It's funny, because I was in the DC offices and we were talking about whether or not we should use Doomsday and I said, "I'm just not sure if I should go down that road again. I don't know." Geoff Johns was there and Geoff said, "Dan, there's a movie coming out. He's in the movie because that's what people will want to see." And I think like all things, it requires a reasonable sense of balance.

CHAPTER IX
The Many Further Television Adventures of Superman

While Crisis on Infinite Earths, *the arrival and departure of John Byrne and the death and resurrection of Superman in the pages of DC Comics played out, television embraced the Man of Steel in a major way that would carry the character almost continuously from 1988 through 2010 in the form of no less than five live-action and animated series.*

It started with the 1988 Superman *Saturday morning series, which came from executive producers Joe Ruby and Ken Spears (of Ruby-Spears Enterprises). Writer Marv Wolfman served as story editor with character designs by artist Gil Kane. The voice cast features Beau Weaver as Superman/Clark Kent, Ginny McSwain as Lois Lane, Michael Bell as Lex Luthor (a hybrid of the Byrne/Wolfman revamped version of the character and Gene Hackman's portrayal in* Superman: The Movie*), Tress MacNeille as Martha Kent, Alan Oppenheimer as Jonathan Kent, Stanley Ralph Ross as Perry White and Mark Taylor as Jimmy Olsen.*

BEAU WEAVER (voice actor, "Clark Kent/Superman," *Superman***):** I was never primarily an animation voice talent. I started in radio and most of my work was in television promos, and it remains that way to this day. In the '80s I did do some auditioning for voice roles, and when the audition came around for *Superman*, I was *thrilled*, because I was a Superman fanatic when I was a little kid. My grandfather owned a drug store in a small town in Oklahoma and they had a big section of periodicals, including three racks of comic books — I think they were mostly there for me. In the summers I would sit there and read every single comic book I could. But I was a Superman guy from the very beginning.

I was brought in to audition because I was told the quality of my voice was similar to other actors who had done Superman in the past, mainly Bud Collyer, who was from the radio show, and Danny Dark from *Super Friends*, who was also from radio and had a kind of anchorman gravitas to his voice. For some reason, it just feels like Superman has to have that sort of sound. But I prefer the gentleness of Christopher Reeve's Superman, so I had to go with the gravitas of my voice, but keep thinking Christopher Reeve. Apparently that's what got me the role.

The format of each half-hour show consisted of a main adventure as well as the "Superman Family Album," a four-minute segment that chronicled Clark's young days in Smallville. The show's title track incorporates a variation of the John Williams movie theme.

Tom Welling, who enjoyed a 10-year run as Clark Kent on Smallville *(art © and courtesy D.C.*
Stuelpner; Clark Kent/Superman © and TM DC Comics/Warner Bros. Discovery)

WILL RODGERS (author, *The Ultimate Super Friends Companion*): When it comes to the classic animated DC cartoons from the Saturday morning era, this period started with *The New Adventures of Superman* in 1966 and it concluded with *Superman* in 1988. The year 1988 was a pivotal moment for Superman since that was the year of his 50th anniversary in the comics. Following the Christopher Reeve Superman movie "quadrilogy," this new series aired on CBS Saturday mornings from the fall of 1988 to the fall of 1989 with a total of 13 episodes being produced. Ruby-Spears was the animation studio founded by the late Joe Ruby and the late Ken Spears, two former Hanna-Barbera animators who are credited as the co-creators of Scooby-Doo and his mystery-solving teenage friends known as Mystery Inc. Ruby-Spears got their start in 1978 with a Scooby-Doo imitation series called *Fangface*.

Ruby-Spears, with their animation style similar to Hanna-Barbera's, produced many memorable cartoons for Saturday mornings throughout most of the '80s, including *Mighty Man and Yukk, Thundarr the Barbarian, Goldie Gold and Action Jack, Saturday Supercade* (consisting of Donkey Kong, Donkey Kong Jr., Frogger, Q Bert & Pitfall), *Turbo Teen, Mister T*, and *Chuck Norris Karate Kommandos*, just to name a few. From 1979 to 1980, they were the studio that animated the comically stretchy DC Super Hero, Plastic Man (*The Plastic Man Comedy Adventure Show* 1979 and *The Plastic Man & Baby Plas Super Comedy Show* 1980).

ROB O'CONNOR (co-host, *All Star Superfan Podcast*): The Ruby-Spears cartoon from 1988 is a really interesting, lesser-known version of Superman. Combining the secret identity antics from the Christopher Reeve films with the high-flying action of the John Byrne era of comics, it is a really charming Saturday morning cartoon. No, it isn't as polished or well-animated as the subsequent (and more well-known) animated show of the '90s, but it arguably has the charm and the Superman magic that that comparably cold series lacked.

MARK MCCRAY (author, *The Best Saturdays of Our Lives*): The opening of that show is spectacular as Superman is flying through Metropolis and you feel like you're not watching a Saturday morning series, you feel like you're watching a Superman theatrical movie — *and* you've got the John Williams theme, which doesn't hurt. It was also the first Superman series to feature Superboy again, which you hadn't seen since the Filmation series. Those "scrapbook" sequences showcased Superman's early years as a child and teenager, which was a nice touch because they could have just had a straight-up Superman series. Another nice touch was when Wonder Woman appeared on an episode and she could fly on her own *without* the invisible jet, which made quite the impression.

MARV WOLFMAN (story editor, *Superman*): CBS was interested in doing a Superman show, although Judy Price, the head of CBS Kids at the time, was not; she didn't care for superhero shows, but since her bosses wanted it, she did it. I was called in by CBS and hired by them to write the pilot. Once they approved the story I did, it was assigned to Ruby-Spears to do. By the way, despite not liking superheroes, Judy came up with the idea of the Superman Album stories at the end, which I think were some of the best stories we had.

JOE RUBY (executive producer, *Superman*): We went through a lot of different directions in development as to what kind of Superman we wanted. We had several different models — the crying/feeling Superman, the lecturing/do-gooder/save-the-day Superman, then there was the hip Superman and even the long-haired Superman. And, of course, there was the old straight-as-an-arrow Superman. Ultimately, we settled on the Christopher Reeve model — he had personality and a sense of humor, and yet he was still Superman. We figured that it worked for the films, so it would work well for us.

KEN SPEARS (executive producer, *Superman*): I think we were true to Superman to begin with — we produced a show where the audience expected Superman to be the tried and true Superman. That's who they wanted to see, which is the feedback that we continued to get.

JOE RUBY: We basically had Superman tackling anything and everything, with the marching orders to have bigger-than-life fights.

MARV WOLFMAN: We had a lot of problems with Standards & Practices, but still managed to get away with some stuff. I would like to think the slight edge we gave the material was interesting enough for them to okay it. I would have liked to go further, but they were pretty strict. For example, I ended my pilot episode story with a big fight between Superman and the robots, which they forced me to change. Superman couldn't crash through the robots because, and I quote, "Even robots have souls." I had to come up with something non-violent, so I had Superman reprogram the robots to collapse. I would have liked the show to go more into the kind of material done in the old Fleischer cartoons, but there was no way to do that then. Also, they liked lots of dialogue and I would have liked to eliminate most of it during the action. If you look at the pilot, there's less dialogue in that one than later shows, but even that had more than I would have preferred.

Despite the fact that the show only lasted 13 episodes (which Ruby and Spears chalk up to an 8:30 a.m. time slot), the producers have nothing but praise for the series' creative team that brought it to life.

KEN SPEARS: We had the best talent in the business at the time — that was our strength. They were excellent. When you first create a show, you hope your talent will be able to plus it — and they *really* plussed it. There are so many shots in the show that weren't written into the script — those kind of great additions come straight from the artists and the storyboarders.

JOE RUBY: We had a pretty amazing crew — and an especially great crew of artists, including some of the best comic book guys in the business, and that made for good filmmaking. Guys like John Dorman and Gil Kane; we had an army of great talent on that show. Give credit to supervising producer John Dorman — he's a filmmaker and that's the difference. He made sure the show had all the creative shots, the movement, some of that great left-to-right or down-angle camera moves. The show was well-paced, well-boarded, and I think John really put these things together well.

The short-lived Ruby-Spears animated series from 1987 (© and TM DC Comics/Warner Bros. Discovery)

MARV WOLFMAN: And Joe Ruby and Ken Spears were great people to work with. I loved my time at the studio. They asked me to stay on, but there were no shows for me to work on, so I moved on to other things. But I very much enjoyed my time there, and especially working with Joe, who was the creative head of the studio while Ken handled most of the business, at least while I was there.

The other major appeal for many of those involved was dealing with iconic characters like Superman and Lex Luthor.

MARV WOLFMAN: Creatively, I got to do Superman stories I had not seen in kids' cartoons before. I got to blend the Lex Luthor I recreated in the comics with the movie version. He acted like the businessman Luthor I came up with, but talked like the Gene Hackman version, which was a lot of fun to do.

JOE RUBY: As a kid, we all grew up with Superman. He's the favorite, always. Your heroes stick with you, so we wanted to make the best Superman show we could, to really set it apart. I think everyone that worked on it felt that way. He's *Superman*.

KEN SPEARS: It was an honor to do something that classy and classic as Superman. He's the number-one guy. We wanted to do it justice.

BEAU WEAVER: I've had a long career in television promos and commercials, but man, it was just such a thrill to turn on a television in 1988 and see me as Superman. And strange to have almost no one I knew in the business, or civilians, being aware that this was not *Super Friends* or the Filmation series. It was just called *Superman*, so if you looked at the listings back then, you'd never even know it was a new show. This series came and went *really* fast.

MARV WOLFMAN: I saw my first Superman TV show when I was between five and seven, but I always felt Superman was the epitome of what a superhero should be. He represents the right in people; the goodness. I just like that completely optimistic viewpoint he has. He does what's right, because it's the right thing to do, not for any ulterior motive.

WILL RODGERS: Most DC and Marvel Super Heroes who have had numerous animated cartoon series will always have at least one show that's rarer than the others due to not being broadcast again or lack of availability on any form of home media. With Batman, it was *The New Adventures of Batman* by Filmation from 1977. For Superman, sadly, it was this series by Ruby-Spears. It wasn't until 2009 that the series finally got released on a two-disc DVD set that includes all 13 episodes.

BEAU WEAVER: I remember they undertook a new animated show ostensibly to coincide with the 50th anniversary of the creation of the Superman character. So they made plans to do this series, but then they did almost no promotion around it.

JOE RUBY: I think the problem for us — and the reason there were only 13 episodes — was our time slot. It turned out 8:30 in the morning was a killer for *Superman*. Only the little kids were up, and they don't understand Superman as well as the older kids. It wasn't for 4-to-5-year-olds.

BEAU WEAVER: The way CBS used to program the early shows were to do series like *Muppet Babies*. We were in the wrong time slot to find an audience. Typically you'd get promos for shows airing later in the morning, and *Superman* didn't benefit from that at all. As a result, it got no on-air promotion and no outside promotion, so it just kind of died on the vine.

John Haymes Newton, who starred in the first season of Superboy (© and TM DC Comics/Warner Bros. Discovery)

*Given what had happened with the Superman franchise, and particularly the obvious diminishing returns of Su-*perman III, Supergirl *and Cannon's* Superman IV: The Quest for Peace, *it was safe to assume that Alexander and Ilya Salkind were out of the Man of Steel business. That notion got turned on its head in 1988 when it was suggested to Alexander Salkind that while Cannon had licensed the theatrical rights to Superman, the Salkinds could nonetheless produce a Superboy TV show for first-run syndication through Viacom. At that point, syndication was exploding, not just because of the success of* Jeopardy! *and* Wheel of Fortune *(which both continue to run to this day and aren't going anywhere), but especially the 1987 arrival of* Star Trek: The Next Generation, *which had opened the floodgates for original syndicated fare.*

One initial challenge came from the fact that there had been a falling out between the Salkinds during the making of 1985's Santa Claus: The Movie, *and given Viacom's requirement that a member of the family be involved, that was perceived as a potential problem.*

ILYA SALKIND (executive producer, *Superboy*): He had to make a deal with me and make me an offer I couldn't refuse, which was nice. I agreed to produce the show for a lot of money — *up front!*

JOHN HAYMES NEWTON (actor, "Clark Kent/Superboy, *Superboy* Season 1): The thing that bothered me about the show was its name. They wanted to call it *The Adventures of Young Superman*, but the Salkinds had licensed

Superman out to Cannon, so they had to use Superboy. Obviously I always wanted it to be *The Adventures of Young Superman*, which sounded a lot cooler than *Superboy*, but it was what it was.

MIKE CARLIN (DC Editor): My understanding is that the Salkinds had the rights to do it, they just had an obligation to run stuff past us. I had just started at DC about a year before the *Superboy* show got the green light. I'd come on to the Superman comics that John Byrne was doing, with Andy Helfer, who was the editor before I got there. So I guess we were the logical guys for Jenette Kahn to work on this TV show with. At the same time, there was a Superman cartoon starting — the Ruby-Spears cartoon. Paul Levitz and some of the other guys on staff were the ones who took on that project. Ours just lasted longer; doesn't mean it was better, because I actually like that *Superman* series. I thought it was fun, but it just didn't click. So Jenette and Paul split up the duties on that year's TV projects. And since syndication was an unknown arena, people didn't really know what it was going to turn out to be. Instead of having everybody at the company get a vote on it, they boiled it down to Jenette, Andy Helfer and me.

The initial plan was for Superboy *(1988 to 1992) to be produced in Texas, but then the decision was made for the show to move to Orlando, Florida, where Disney had just started the Disney/MGM Studios. As things turned out,* Superboy *was the first series to be shot there, though starting with season two there was yet another move to the larger Universal Studios Florida, which was located in Orlando as well. Behind the scenes, Salkind admits that, early on, he should have been more involved with the series than he had been. As it turned out, he was oblivious to the fact that many of the early scripts lacked a superheroic element to them. The showrunner was Fred Freiberger, who guided* Star Trek, Space: 1999 *and* The Six Million Dollar Man *in their final seasons.*

ILYA SALKIND: At the beginning, I was really laid back and delegated completely to Bob Simmonds, who was the line producer, except when it came to casting. Frankly I was a little lazy. Simmonds and writer Fred Freiberger, who was also a producer, crafted some relatively down-to-Earth adventures with few special effects.

ROB O'CONNOR (co-host, *All Star Superfan Podcast*): *Superboy* is best approached as the "B-movie" Superman show, but that"s not always a bad thing — what was accomplished on such a low budget is very admirable. The Salkinds did what they could to bring the majesty of those early movies to the TV screen and in some ways they really did — the wire work alone is above and beyond anything we saw on television before (and arguably even after) the advent of CGI. You will believe a 31-year-old boy can fly.

MIKE CARLIN: The show could have been great if they had, in my opinion, focused on half of the first *Superman* movie that really worked and is flawless: The Smallville side of things could have been the tone, and that's ultimately what the show *Smallville* got right compared to this show. This show ended up being more of a kids' show than they really wanted it to be. At some point it's all right to embrace that and say, "Okay, we're doing a *good* kids show." But I don't think that was what we had hoped for at the beginning. Before there was a WB, this could have been like *The O.C.*; something that taps into a teenage soap opera — not so adult and not so humorless, but something that just treated the material seriously and wasn't about villain of the week or any that kind of stuff. I always go back to the fact that nowadays they can afford to do the effects a lot cheaper and a lot better; just because computers have come along a lot further, and the artists who work in there are really talented now. I just don't think they had the resources to really do it right. That was a limitation on *Lois & Clark* too, that they might not have wanted to admit.

STAN BERKOWITZ (story editor, *Superboy*): What happened in the beginning is that it was anarchic down there, because they had no culture of film-making. Just take an empty field, you bring in a bunch of people, many of whom had never worked on a crew before, and you start filming. Those days must have been horrendous. Even in seasons three and four there were very long days where people forgot things and this or that wasn't done. And even when it was, it was a non-union crew, which was the other thing. They're cheaper of course, but they tend to work slower. I would think, especially in that first season, there was probably a lot of disorganization and just trying to get everybody to be professional, because there was no culture of professionalism. What if your camera assistant gets sick, what are you going to do there? There's not 20 of 'em on the unemployment line. Of course after doing it for two years, it became easier to do. You learned *how* to do it, you adjust or evolve.

ILYA SALKIND: The show opened with strong ratings; we were huge in syndication when it opened with the bad shows. I was happy with the ratings and assumed everything was fine. Then I started getting these letters that Viacom sent me from the stations saying, "This is a piece of shit show; this is not up to the standards of the Salkinds. What the hell is Salkind doing?" I then spoke to a Viacom executive and I said, "We have a 6.5 rating, what do you want?" It was number 11 or 12 in the syndicated ratings. That was terrific. But I took all of that as a wake-up call. I looked at the first few episodes and wondered, "Where are the bigger-than-life challenges?" That Superboy was going after a guy doing a little tax evasion or whatever was ridiculous.

MIKE CARLIN: The early scripts weren't great. The thing is, they were too small for what his powers were. That was a problem even on *Adventures of Superman*. When you look back at the original TV shows — I just recently watched the first season — there are a lot of threats that the police should be handling, *not* Superman. And the thing is, once in a while you can do the offbeat episode where that happens for Superboy or Flash or *Smallville*, but it's not going to work all the time. You don't need Superman to stop the guy from breaking out of prison. I think for them that was a limitation of their budget and abilities at the time. And they were wise to steer clear of it in kind of the same way they did the Hulk on TV. You'd get 15 minutes of people walking around in street clothes, and then you'd get your two minutes of Hulk. But we were all happy to have it when it got there.

SAM RIZZO (webmaster, superboythelegacy.com): Season one is a training ground; it's like the show with training wheels. Stacy Haiduk has said all along that there is an innocence to those first 13 episodes to try and get your legs under you and figure things out, because you had Ilya and his team and they had no idea how to build towards the commercial break. It was kind of like, "Okay, *how* do we do this?" They were learning on the fly. But you get to seasons two and three and it's amazing. I sit there and go, "I wish we had another 22 minutes per episode."

MIKE CARLIN: The original order, I believe, was for 13 episodes, and then it got expanded. At the last minute they decided to finally do a science-fiction story, but they didn't have scripts lying around and they actually asked Andy and I to do one over a weekend. We introduced an alien character and wrote it pretty fast. They seemed to like it, so then they gave us another one to do, which was the introduction of Kryptonite. It really was last-minute stuff that seemed like an attempt to up the ante. Suddenly it wasn't Superboy fighting homeless people, like it had been at the beginning of the series. That one, with the homeless guy, was actually the first one shot; we went down there while Abe Vigoda was shooting that one and it was a lot of fun. I got to sit next to him at dinner one night and I stupidly noted that he was having *fish*. He laughed.

JOHN HAYMES NEWTON: It was really fun working with interesting guest stars and they would get what they could afford — people who hadn't worked in a while, but had a history like Abe Vigoda, for instance.

STACY HAIDUK (actor, "Lana Lang," *Superboy*): I remember seeing him from *Barney Miller* and *The Godfather*, and he and his wife were so sweet and would tell me stories while we ate. That was part of what Ilya would always do every Friday in the first year, where he would do a dinner to say goodbye to the old director and meet the new director. All the cast members would be there and we would just eat. It was really very cool. It was a really beautiful family group as we grew together.

ILYA SALKIND: I eventually took a more hands-on role and we started changing things, and then the show got better and better. The last three episodes of the first 13, we started to make stronger shows. Then Cary Bates came on as a writer and it really took off. We started bringing in Bizarro and all kinds of things from the comics. The rating went up to 7.2, which was pretty much the same rating, but the show was better reviewed. It was a huge hit for that kind of series.

MIKE CARLIN: Fred Frieberger was on the first season and I have to say, I loved Fred and hanging out with him and his wife. We had a lot of fun with them on the show, but I don't think he thought big enough. That might have been the limitations he was handed as well. The reality of why he was on the show was his science-fiction TV — including *Star Trek* — and movie background. On paper, he certainly was the right guy to do this and, honestly, he was a really sweet guy and fun to argue with, because he was really good about not letting it be a personal thing. That was an advantage and that's why he did keep landing on his feet throughout his career. He was ready to get in there and do the work.

I do believe that when the *Superboy* show started, there was a Writers Guild strike going on. And because the Salkinds hadn't done TV yet, they were allowed an exemption by the Writers Guild to start working while the rest of the world was on strike. I *think* Fred was connected in the Guild and they kind of recommended him, so the Salkinds went with him as showrunner because of that — a great way to get the show done at all when everything else was halted.

SAM RIZZO: The writers' strike of 1988 was the best thing that could have happened with Superboy. That's how they were able to get Cary Bates, Mark Jones, Mike Carlin and Andy Helfer — these guys who knew the heartbeat of Superman. What they put on screen for 22 minutes an episode just screams Superman out of every pore, despite the fact it could be a little campy.

JOHN HAYMES NEWTON: He doesn't remember it or acknowledge it, but I'm the person that literally went to the producer regarding Cary Bates about getting him on the show. I said, "He's smart and he knows the character inside out, backwards and forwards. You need to get him on staff." And they did. Years later I ran into Cary and brought it up, but he says he had no knowledge of that. Whatever. The point is, it was important having those kinds of people that were more cutting edge, but it took a while for them to get those writers.

MIKE CARLIN: Cary Bates did not have a good experience on the show, but less with Salkind than with us. We actually argued to get him on the show with Fred Frieberger, because it was good to have a DC voice down there. The Salkinds seemed to assume that since this was somebody we liked and approved of, they didn't have to deal with us anymore. Ultimately, we *still* had to go over the scripts. I think Cary's situation put him in the middle and that was a little unfortunate for him. I don't know what his story is. He did go on to work on the *Christopher Columbus* movie that the Salkinds made, so he definitely had a good relationship with Ilya.

CARY BATES (writer, *Superboy*): Though it was originally intended to only be a 13-episode sabbatical from comics, I ended up in Florida for five years, staying on for another season of *Superboy*, followed by screenwriting stints on the Salkinds' *Christopher Columbus* movie and the unfilmed *Superman Reborn*, which would have marked the Salkinds' return to the Superman film franchise. Mike Carlin and Andy Helfer were already attached as writers to the show via DC. I brought Denny O'Neil in, but J.M. DeMatteis didn't come on board until the third season, after I left.

MIKE CARLIN: Following Cary Bates, for the second season they hired a guy named Mark Jones, and he was from animation. And then for the third season they got Stan Berkowitz. He was great on *Batman: The Animated Series* and *Superman: The Animated Series*, and he's a super guy. And he came in really armed with a desire to have a point of view on the show, which was great. And he was a hard-working guy. He was another one where if he disagreed with something, it was never a personality argument; it was always logical from his point of view. And you could always at least understand that, which was great. We're still friendly with him too. He was great for me and Andy; he really kind of took us under his wing about Writers Guild rules and stuff like that.

STAN BERKOWITZ: I worked on the second half of the series, so about 50 episodes, as story editor. As it went on, the show looked vastly different when we hired a new cinematographer, and in season three Mike and Andy became much more active in it. I would say that a third of the episodes I wasn't terribly happy with, another third were okay and a final third were great, because it became more comic bookey, but not in a stupid sense. And of the first two seasons, the first one was really earthbound. As we went on, we also made the characters a little more adult.

STACY HAIDUK: With people like Mike Carlin and Cary Bates, I just felt like I was taken care of. I knew it was going to be an adventure, because they would always give me comic books to read and I *wasn't* really a comic book fan. But I did enjoy what they gave me.

SAM RIZZO: As it went on, the show became *so* Silver Age. The scripts were written by the comic book writers and they just hit it out of the park. It shows that they were doing something right.

JOHN HAYMES NEWTON: You could see the changes in the scripts midway through the first season; there was more to sink your teeth into. I feel like it really shifted with the "Revenge of the Alien" two-parter. The show felt like it had legs from then on, whereas before that it was like, "Okay, we're treading water here."

MIKE CARLIN: Writing comics helped, mostly because we understood the material and weren't ashamed of it. I do find a lot of times that with people who work on action-adventure superhero shows — or even cartoons — there's a point where they seem embarrassed about the subject. And then they have to do the wink-wink jokes about it all, which undermines the material. The best stuff on *Superboy* or any of the shows is the stuff that's played straight, maybe with some humor, but definitely not at the expense of the concept. Things like *Hercules* and *Xena* were giant hits, because they were serious about it, and I think that came from Sam Raimi.

STAN BERKOWITZ: When I worked with Mike Carlin and Andy Helfer on *Superboy*, I got the impression that DC kept a *very* close eye on their product, because they didn't want it tainted or destroyed, which they'd come very close to have happen over and over again with different projects, going back to the first Batman serial in 1943.

GERARD CHRISTOPHER (actor, "Clark Kent/Superboy," *Superboy* Seasons 2-4): There were *very* strict restrictions, because Warner Bros. owns

DC Comics, and DC Comics made us all adhere to very strict constraints about what the comic is, what the character looks like, how his hair looks, how his suit looks, how we can't see him sweat, how I folded my arms — just really strict that the character look a certain way. When you put it all together, it makes for very restricted acting. You're constantly thinking, "You can't do this, you can't do that," and you have to kind of work around it.

DAVID NUTTER (director, *Superboy*): DC Comics always had an idea of how the show should be. It's a situation in which you have to go back and forth and get a lot of DC notes; you know, "He wouldn't do that, or she wouldn't do that." They would really tell you how they wanted the show to be done.

JOHN HAYMES NEWTON: David Nutter came in as director, and he really cared. He had a vision. I can't remember how old he was — I would say definitely mid-20s — but he was just young, bright-eyed and bushy-tailed. There was zero taint of Hollywood about him. He was one of those guys that you wanted to work with, because he listens too; zero ego.

DAVID NUTTER: *Superboy* was one of the first jobs I ever got; I finally had a chance to work and I did 21 episodes of that. *That* was my real film school, which is fun. We got to do that in Florida; I had gone to high school in Clearwater, went to the University of Miami and came back and did those episodes. After a few ups and downs, *The X-Files* came along in 1993 and things went on from there. *Superboy* was fun, and I really enjoyed a lot of the stories.

SAM RIZZO: There are some great episodes of *Superboy* like "Body Swap," which shows up on *Smallville* in the form of "Tranference." You had "Roads Not Taken," one of the first parallel universe multiverse stories, and that's everywhere now, including movies and television. Marvel's doing it, *The Flash* is doing it and I think *Superboy*'s Sovereign, a dictator on a parallel world, predated Mark Millar's *Red Son*.

MIKE CARLIN: In season two of *Adventures of Superman*, they'd do an episode like "Panic in the Sky," and they'd shoot their wad, so to speak. I think that *Superboy* ultimately did that in later seasons, and then they'd be saddled by doing their small-budget episodes. But even there, if the writers came in with some cleverness and really thought about it, you could still make those really powerful too. And I do think they spent their money on something like "Road Not Taken," but then J.M. DeMatteis gave us a couple of really good ones.

They actually shot the third and fourth seasons basically back-to-back. I guess it would be cheaper to just do it all at the same time, because they knew they were coming back for the two seasons and that kept their crew together and the actors sewn up, which definitely helped. The third and fourth seasons were mostly line produced by a woman named Julia Pistor who had been the Viacom liaison on the second season, and then she became the day-to-day producer of the show. And Ilya stepped back to start working on his Columbus movie and also a fifth Superman movie he was going to try — and which didn't happen. But she was good too, because she really came in with a lot of energy. She didn't have the history yet with the character, but she was really good about having an opinion about what was working or what wasn't working, without it being, "Well, they would never do that in the comics" or "That happened 10 times in the comics." Sometimes if it's a good idea, it's a good idea, so she was pretty good. Julia had a point of view about the effects and knew what they could and couldn't afford to pull off. And I think, again, she and Stan were a big part of why the third and fourth seasons came together.

JULIA PISTOR (producer, *Superboy*): Viacom thought I was diplomatic, so they sent me down to Orlando to be a production executive on the show. On something like *Superboy*, you had the Salkinds, who were very powerful producers; you have DC Comics, whose baby this was; and you've got Viacom doing this syndicated show, so it really matters to them. After I arrived, Ilya decided to step back and they gave me the show to produce. I still can't believe they did that, but they did. I built relationships with those people and I had a real understanding of the brand, which is not something that was talked about much in those days — "the brand." And I had an idea of the importance of the story and very specific ideas on how to make it better, because I didn't think it delivered on Superman at all.

My analysis of the situation was that they were not relying enough on DC Comics. They were thinking of DC more as an approver versus DC as the creator and keeper of the flame. Mike Carlin was an advisor in the beginning, but I relied on him more; in many ways, it was his baby. Then I worked with Stan Berkowitz, and brought in directors like David Nutter and David Grossman. I hired new production designers, a new director of photography. We hired a lot of directors that were amazing directors and I didn't mind working with filmmaker directors rather than television directors. I wanted it to feel more like film and I wanted to go back to the Fleischer cartoons with the look.

GERARD CHRISTOPHER: The show was low-budget and when you were there, everybody complained a little bit like, "They don't do this, they don't spend on that," but you know what? That's the same with any budget, where if you're President of the United States or a corporation or a small business or household, everybody's got a budget. And quite frankly, nobody ever spends as much money as they'd want. Our show was still done in top-shelf manner, and a lot of what was done I have to attribute to Julia Pistor, who was the producer for two years and was wonderful. She added a lot to it and *always* listened to what we said… and acted upon it. We discussed things and when things she thought I said were right, we did them. She was a good addition to the show.

JULIA PISTOR: The challenge is that the show was shot outside Orlando with harsh, flat lighting on flat green grass. No offense to the Salkinds, but they would just put their Superboy in the middle of that field and shoot it without any kind of texture or anything, and it just looked silly. It was almost like, "Well, if it's Superman and he stands for hope and he stands for good, then he needs to be in a really brightly-lit, calm sort of environment." I saw the opposite from the original roots of Superman, which was created around the time of World War II. There was some real darkness around Superman and he represents the idea that there can be light in the dark. And if there's going to be light in the dark, then you can have some edge to it. So I went back to the Fleischer cartoons and brought things inside and I just tried to mine the existing stories. And that's where you get a parallel Earth story where Superboy is a fascist — just do stories that are really fanboy stories as opposed to feeling like we need to chase typical syndicated television to crank through a hundred episodes. Really lean on the fact that it was 35mm film and shoot it *film* style, *not* sitcom style. Encourage everyone to think that they're making movies and hiring the best directors.

I'm a fantasy literature major. I've read *Lord of the Rings* a trillion times. I love *Star Wars*, I love meaty mythic stories. Even though the Salkinds did *Superman*, Ilya was not of that mindset. They were making it more an American TV show, and when I came in, it was like, "No, let's go back to the roots." It *is* mythic, so let's tell bigger stories with Mike Carlin and the others.

SAM RIZZO: What really got me was just the show's love of doing things that were a lot of firsts — they had the first live-action Bizarro, they had the first Metallo, they had the first live-action Mxyzptlk in the form of Michael J. Pollard. They could not use Toy Man, but they brought in Gilbert Gottfried as Nick Knack, who was just hamming it up left and right. You had such great actors coming in, even in the first two seasons. Ilya found guest stars that were not being used and made them interesting characters. So you had Stuart Whitman, who was famous for his cowboy films of yesteryear, as Jonathan Kent. You had Salome Jens who is famous for *Star Trek: Deep Space Nine*. He had really great actors elevating what was a kids' show.

MIKE CARLIN: Andy Helfer, Jenette Kahn and I were DC liaisons with the show, and we were hoping to get some more of that comic book stuff. And if you went back to the old *Superboy* comics, they really didn't have a lot of personality. Those comics were like going to school; if you read a Superboy comic, he was going back in time to meet Lincoln or having something to do with the Roman Empire or something. The villains that were created for *Superboy* were few and far between, and Kryptonite Kid was one of the good ones, so we used him. We did a Metallo episode, and I love the guy who played him, Michael Callan. But the problems turned up as the lawyer side of DC Comics came around and said that we shouldn't have even done Metallo, because he was a *Superman* villain and we should stick with Superboy villains. But Bizarro and Kryptonite Kid *were* in *Superboy* comics. Outside of that, his rogues gallery didn't have a lot to pick from, so they made up a lot of new things, like Young Dracula. There was a real limitation to which villains we could use. At that time, we only had the rights to do the Superboy stuff on TV, whereas Warner Bros. wanted to get a Superman movie going and they tried for 15 years.

The initial set-up of Superboy *was to focus on Shuster University students Clark Kent, Lana Lang and T.J. White, who find themselves involved in a variety of adventures that (naturally) lead to Clark having to turn into the Boy of Steel in order to save the day. In the third of the show's four seasons, its title became* The Adventures of Superboy *and the setting changed to the Bureau for Extra-Normal Matters in Capitol City, Florida. Clark and Lana would find themselves working there, which would lead to stories that were darker in some ways but certainly captured the flavor of the comics as well. Initially cast in the lead roles were John Haymes Newton as Clark Kent/Superboy and Stacy Haiduk as Clark's childhood friend from Smallville, Lana Lang. Jim Calvert portrayed T.J.*

Newton was born December 29, 1965 in Chapel Hill, North Carolina. He enjoyed an acting career totaling about 20 years, and then stepped away from the business to provide what has been called "energy healing" to others.

JOHN HAYMES NEWTON: I never felt that acting was my calling. I've done this other kind of thing on the side for free for 20 whatever years, and that's what I'm doing full-time now. I'm way more successful and I'm helping thousands of people. I've got almost 20,000 clients all over the world, and I frickin' love it. I just help people with chronic pain, stress and addiction. I work in hospitals, I train doctors and therapists in outside-the-box support for patients. I don't call myself a healer, because that seems very "woo-woo," but it's basically just helping people reset the past and clear burdens that they carry, limiting beliefs and helping them get a good quality of life going. A lot of it involves them connecting to a higher power of their understanding. It's not religious at all, but sometimes when people connect with that, it gives life meaning and helps them move forward.

As to acting, about 15 years ago I started thinking, "Why am I still chasing the acting bone and this business?" You've got to have the stomach for it or do drugs. I couldn't do the drugs and I don't know if I had the stomach. The thing is, to be an actor, you've got to have a certain amount of narcissism and a shitty childhood that makes you want attention. Whether actors will admit it or not, I'd say 80% to 90% of them fall into that category. You constantly read stories about people not doing well in Hollywood. Some do, but I'd say most don't. I seriously love what I'm doing. I can't even imagine a better calling.

Which wasn't the case when he was younger, having been touched by Christopher Reeve's portrayal of Superman in Superman: The Movie, *and his childhood obsession with the classic* Superboy *comic book.*

JOHN HAYMES NEWTON: When I was really little, my grandmother had copies of *Superboy* comics in this basket. They were all tattered from the grandkids and everybody fingering through them, and I found myself really fascinated. There was one cover where Superboy was jumping into a boxing ring to take on this boxer who did an illegal punch or something. I never forgot that comic; it kind of stayed with me. I don't know if it was a kind of foreshadowing or something, because I wasn't a comic person so much, I just remembered that standing out.

Superboy the TV show came into my life while I was on vacation after completing a two-year acting program in North Carolina. I went over to the studios in Wilmington, which they were casting everything out of at the time. I went in and got to audition for *Weekend at Bernie's*, which went pretty well — which wasn't always the case with me auditioning; I did pretty shitty a lot of times — but Lynn Stalmaster was doing the casting and he said, "Would you be interested in a TV series?" I said yes and he made a phone call to, I think, Bob Simmonds, while I was sitting in his office and he says, "Hey, I found this guy. Maybe you guys could meet him." So they put me on camera for that, and I remember being flown to Orlando for a screentest. There, I put on the Chris Reeve costume from *Superman II*, which was pretty crazy. That suit is like a badge of history and what Superman ideally stands for, not so much in the Nietzsche sense, but just in the sense of the history of it. And the whole doing good and making the world a better place. You put the costume on, it changes you *immediately*. That being said, I don't remember doing great at the test. I was probably nervous, but I ended up getting it. Maybe less than a week later I was off from New York City to Orlando, Florida. It was work, which I was grateful for, and I'll be honest, rather than thinking about taking on that iconic role, it was always overshadowed by the feeling that this could be my *last* job, because you're going to get typecast on a low-budget TV show.

There was some conflict early on in that the producers envisioned the show's Clark Kent being modeled after the version of the character introduced by Christopher Reeve back in 1978's Superman: The Movie. *For his part, Newton didn't see it that way.*

JOHN HAYMES NEWTON: I wanted to make Clark more insecure as opposed to bumbling. I love what Chris Reeve did; I thought it was brilliant, but I didn't want to copy that so much. Maybe in hindsight I could have done a little more of that so that there was more of a difference between the two characters. I think I was young and immature in many ways and, in retrospect, I would have probably thrown that out the window as far as being concerned about being pigeonholed with, "Oh, he's just copying Chris Reeve." I only saw a little bit of the *Lois & Clark* show, but I don't remember Dean Cain doing that so much either.

With Superboy, I thought he was someone finding his way in life, just like any teenager or young person would be, but of course he has the added elements of living a secret life and also having a higher purpose, while not being sure what that is. He kind of finds his way through friends and the character development, being attracted to Lana and all that. I wanted him to be relatable, because that's where you get to see his vulnerabilities. What did hit me about the middle of the first 13 episodes, which weren't that great, was the fact that Superman doesn't get his power or perceived power from how he acts as much as how other people react *to* him. In other words, I'd fly into a scene at the campus and no one would even respond. It's like a guy just flew in, in a red cape, and landed in front of you, and the extras weren't told to react. They would just walk by normally and no one would even look. And I'm going, "People need to respond. It's going to give him some weight and lend itself to the reality of the scene." That was kind of an obvious thing that I brought up, among others things. They eventually started to change that, which I felt helped the show.

Born April 24, 1968 in Grand Rapids, Michigan, Stacy Haiduk first achieved fame as Lana Lang. Though scoring the role on Superboy *seemed to take forever, ironically she would be the one cast member who would last all 100 episodes of the show. Of all the regular cast, she would have the most fruitful post-*Superboy *career, including starring roles on the series* SeaQuest DSV *(1993-1994) and* Kindred: The Embraced *(1996), as well as recurring parts on* Melrose Place, Brimstone, Heroes, Prison Break, Twisted, Chosen *and the daytime soap operas* All My Children, The Young and the Restless *and* Days of Our Lives, *on which she is now a regular.*

STACY HAIDUK: For me, this was a huge thing. I remember being in New York when the audition came up and Ilya held it in, I think, the Park Lane Hotel, located somewhere on the Upper West Side. Tons of actors were there; I think he and Lynn Stalmaster the casting director were there. You had Jennifer Aniston there before she was *Jennifer Aniston*. My future husband was there, which I never even knew. I remember that we were all just sitting downstairs, waiting for our call to go up to the room and audition. And that was only the *first* round. Then Lynn held me there for maybe two hours. He said, "Could you go downstairs and just wait?" I said, "Okay… I *think* that's a good thing?"

I waited and waited and then he brought me back up where he had a few Superboys. He was kind of trying to figure out if they were what they wanted and I ended up auditioning with three actors. And that was it: "Thank you," and I went home. I didn't hear anything for another week. And then I got a call asking if I would do a test with this Superboy guy. He said, "We have two actors we chose; would you come audition with them?" I said okay, even though I didn't know what the heck was going on. Again, it was like, "What about me?"

During the auditions, Haiduk thought that she was merely being used so that the actors would have someone to read off of, but as it turned out, the producers were actually doing chemistry reads. The session ended and she… went home. And waited. Again.

STACY HAIDUK: And I was struggling in my life. I wasn't making money and there I was, waiting for a job. I started wondering if I should get a bartending job, a hostess or waitress job. And I didn't hear anything for a week. I finally called my manager and she called me back at the end of the day and says, "They're trying to find a Superboy. They love *you*." And I was like, "Well, it would've been nice to know that from the very beginning; I wouldn't have stressed so much." They didn't want to hire me before they had a Superboy, but then they finally just hired me. Before they got John, they were looking all over and they got him not too long before they started shooting. So it was all nerve-wracking, but also exciting because I'd done a lot of little things, but never anything this big where someone like Ilia Salkind is producing.

At first working with John was really wonderful, but now I tell everybody do *not* get hooked up with your co-star. *Ever.*

JOHN HAYMES NEWTON: We had an off-screen romance and that was interesting, fiery and great. I met her when she had to dye her hair from lighter brown to red, and I just remember like, "Wow, *this* is interesting." She came in and introduced herself. Into the series we became friends, then we hung out and became more than that. You know, you're young, you're on location — what are you going to do? So that was an interesting dynamic for better or worse with those kinds of things.

STACY HAIDUK: We had a ball and it was great, but it was really, really hard at times because when another cute girl would come on the set, they would flirt and I would get jealous. I enjoyed my time on that first season, but I was not happy when we broke up. There was a lot of chaos in the end.

JOHN HAYMES NEWTON: We went to some wedding in Michigan where she's from and it was *just* drama and I was being reactive, because the whole breakup thing was hard for me. I was immature emotionally in every other way. It fell apart quickly.

STACY HAIDUK: He met somebody else right before we were about to come back for season two, and I was crushed. But you know what? I was a baby. I was young and I guess *that* was the learning curve of this whole thing. But working with him was a treat.

Undoubtedly making things easier was the fact that at the end of the season, certain changes were made, among them the departure of Jim Calvert, replaced in the second season by Ilan Mitchell-Smith as Andy McCalister. More dramatically, Newton was let go from the series, though there are conflicting explanations as to exactly what happened.

JOHN HAYMES NEWTON: I was playing two characters, obviously doing almost all of my own stunts and there was a danger aspect that felt like, "Okay, I'm only making 2,500 bucks a week." Now here's the thing: The reality is that I signed a contract and I was a little shit. After the first two sets of 13, they *did* say we were going to work it out; that they would get me some more money. But when it came down to it, no one wanted to pay. I had an executive call me during the interim and say, "They say that you're not going to come back to work." That will be a nameless executive, by the way. And I said, "Well, yes; so and so promised this; so and so said this." Then he was like, "Well, they're not coming up with the money and *we're* certainly not paying an extra dollar. If you don't come back to work, you probably won't work again." And I was a little scared. I'm 23 years old, in New York auditioning for whatever in between, but I just felt I had to stick to my guns. That was out of integrity — I *should* have gone back and signed the contract — and they said, "Well, we're going to recast." I'm like, "Well, do what you've got to do." So I didn't go back. Something that they tried to use in support of not giving me more money was a moving violation I got from some cop who was kind of a jerk.

ILYA SALKIND: We found out that John Haymes Newton had been DUI, so we couldn't hire him back for season two. That was the reason. I don't think it was a money situation; I think he *wanted* more money, but I said there is no reason to get it, because it's not like the ratings were going up. I don't think he was happy with that, and then he got into some kind of DUI.

JOHN HAYMES NEWTON: It was a moving violation on public property. So my dumb ass, instead of just going to court and getting out of the ticket, I wrote a letter to the sheriff's department and said, "Look, this ticket was illegally issued. I was on private property." Whatever I was doing, I lost completely, but it wasn't like anyone was in danger. And I definitely was *not* drinking, by the way. I've never gotten a DUI in my entire life. The point is: I *did* get the moving violation, I *did* write a letter, and at the end of the letter I said, "If you guys are involved with helping the community and I can be of service, let me know." Technically I shouldn't have put that in the same letter as the other one saying, "Hey, could you drop the ticket?" I was 23 years old and what an idiot! So basically a woman in the sheriff's department took a copy of that letter and gave it to the newspaper. Then the production said, "You're representing this character and you shouldn't behave that way." Technically they were right. What am I going to say? They tried to use that as their final reason of why they weren't coming up with more money. I actually didn't believe that they would recast, but they did. And they didn't change their mind. The hardest part of not going back, it wasn't not being in the show. I was bummed because Stacy and I were still dating. *That* was the hard part for me, because she was going to be in Florida with some new guy, and I'd actually moved to L.A. right after that.

On top of that, one of the production people called me and said, "They're making you look like a jerk," and public humiliation was one of my biggest fears. So I was like, "This is horrible," but I made my own bed. In retrospect, I wish I'd had more integrity. My life now, it's only about integrity, that's my work, but at the time, I was *mad*.

Hired to replace Newton in the title role was Gerard Christopher, born May 11, 1959 in New York City. Prior to Superboy, *he was cast in the feature films* Tomboy *(1985) and* Dangerously Close *(1986), and made television guest appearances in* Welcome to Paradise *(1984) and* Murphy's Law *(1988). Following his time as the Boy of Steel, there were roles on* Silk Stalkings, Melrose Place, Women of the House, Days of Our Lives, The Agency *and* General Hospital, *as well as a starring role in the 1997 to 1999 show* Sunset Beach. *His last film role was* The First of May *(1999).*

GERARD CHRISTOPHER: I didn't even know that the show was on the first year. No idea. When my agent called me and said, "We have an audition for this," I thought it was a brand-new show; I didn't know they were firing the actor. But I just went in for the audition, which was a lot of fun. They flew me down to Florida, and although I didn't know it, the producer met me and kind of wanted to hire me right away. He wouldn't let on, because if he did, then the fear was I would ask for more money. So I did a screentest that was bogus, because the other guy he cast was so skinny and unbelievably wrong for the part. At least if they were trying to make it look like I had competition, but they really didn't try that. I was too stupid to know what was going on.

So I was hired and Ilya Salkind brought me into his office. I was standing there in my costume — I think it was right before we were shooting — and he looked me in the eye and he says, "I don't want to make you feel too nervous, but the show before was really tanking and unless the ratings go up really good, you're out of a job. Oh, and I don't want you to feel pressured or anything, the other 120 people on the show will be out of work too." I was like, "Oh, no problem, don't worry about it." He was a character.

SAM RIZZO: John's portrayals of Superboy and Clark were *very* similar. He jokes around once in a while, but he plays it very straight. I think I gravitate toward Gerard's performance, although he was kind of doing Christopher Reeve at first with the bumbling Clark, which a lot of people did *not* like, because they thought he was just copying Chris. In one episode, where Gerard is talking to Lana and she is possessed by this creature from the sea and walking down the hallway, he says, "Lana…," and he stands straight up and takes his glasses off. And it was *awesome*. I mean, yeah, he really took from what Chris Reeve was doing and that seemed to be the most popular way to go with it. At the same time, he really brought it home with seasons three and four and got to make it his own.

GERARD CHRISTOPHER:
My approach was to do it the way
my producers wanted me to. I don't
know what more to say. It's not
something where you're doing a
character and you're bringing so
much of yourself to it. There is a set
character and you're not reinventing
the wheel. I tried to give my personality to a character that was done
before and one that had to be done
the same way more or less. *That's* the
way I approached it. There was a lot
of consistency in the character for
about 50 years, so to try to reinvent
him I think would be really foolish.

STAN BERKOWITZ: It's
hard to be Superman or Superboy, because you're such a perfect
character, but what you have to see
is Gerry playing villains, because we
just squeezed that sponge so much.
Is there any way we can have a thug
who looks like Gerry, and Gerry can
play *that*? Is there any way we can
do another Red Kryptonite story and have him be mean or crazy over and over
again? We did that, because it gave him a chance to show that he actually could act.
But unfortunately, Superman is essentially a bland character without that kind of
internal anger that Batman has. And the stories don't really have that sense of awe
and wonder that the Green Lantern comic books had either.

Gerard Christopher assumed the role of Superboy
in seasons two through four of the series (© and TM
DC Comics/Warner Bros. Discovery).

STACY HAIDUK: I had a ball working with Gerard, and when you keep
it that way, it's good, because we could screw with each other on the set and we
could be whatever we needed and it was good. Each person brings in what they
do and it's my job as an actress to just work off of them and see what they offer.

*When it came to wearing the costume, Christopher points out that the key thing was to
never feel foolish putting it on, because if the actor doing so feels that way, then he can't be
Superman or, in this case, Superboy.*

GERARD CHRISTOPHER: I knew I had to take it very seriously, and it was a job. That character meant a lot to a lot of people when I was a kid growing up. I used to love it, so I just couldn't let it make me ever feel foolish. And I never did. I don't know how I always pulled that off, but no matter where I was on location, or who I was talking to or who was staring at me, I never did feel foolish, because I knew that for me that would be the kiss of death. It was something that you really had to have a lot of respect for. I remember the first time I put it on, it was pretty exciting. There was a little bit of a rush of history for me. I said, "This isn't doing *Melrose Place* or something, it's a piece of American history." That added a lot more to it for me.

Over the course of its four seasons, Superboy *introduced a number of interesting opponents for the Boy of Steel to take on. Most notable among them were Lex Luthor and Bizarro. In the case of the former, originally hired for the part was Scott James Wells, who was born July 4, 1961 in Dayton, Ohio. Prior to* Superboy, *he appeared in episodes of* Emergency!, The Bionic Woman, The Misadventures of Sheriff Lobo *and* Cheers, *followed afterwards by* Beauty and the Beast. *Additionally, he was credited as "party guest" in the 1991 film* The Taking of Beverly Hills. *Sadly, Wells would die in 2015 of a drug overdose, his views below presented from an archived conversation with the author.*

SCOTT WELLS (actor, "Lex Luthor," *Superboy* **Season 1):** This just came out of the blue from an interview, like any other interview. You go on it and hope that you do well and I was overwhelmed, because this is not the sort of thing I would have seen myself picked for. People started making the Gene Hackman comments and what have you. Of course I'm not Gene Hackman, but hopefully someday I'll be as brilliant an actor as him. I definitely have sat down and watched what he did with the part and I'm going to continue doing that. I'm not imitating him, but I'm trying to get the same point across in less time, of course, given that it's a half-hour show. This whole process is quicker; there's not as much time to get involved with the characters, hit the mark and get your dialogue out. But the feeling I'm trying to get is that Lex is the greatest criminal mind of all time, and of course this version is younger and a little bit more obnoxious. I'm trying to bring across the fact that I'm rich and elegant without, of course, being feminine; trying to get some more elegant hand and wrist movements, *and* that he's so full of himself that he wouldn't have any idea if something else was going on around him; very self-indulgent… these are some of the things I'm trying to bring out.

Obviously I don't know what's going to happen. They could call me tomorrow and say, "Scott, we're going to go in a different way with this character." We both know it happens so frequently in this business.

And it's exactly what did happen as part of the "housecleaning" at the end of season one that saw the departure of not only Wells, but Newton and Calvert as well. Wells was replaced with Sherman Howard, who was considerably older at 40 and whose difference in appearance as Luthor was explained as being a result of plastic surgery and acid applied to his vocal cords. It's undeniable that in the 17 episodes in which he appeared, he brought a whole new level of energy to the show.

Born June 11, 1949 in Chicago, Illinois, Howard's background includes dozens of stage roles, beginning in 1971 as part of the American Conservatory Theater in San Francisco. He demonstrated a passion for concert hall music that has seen him perform with several orchestras. On top of that, there have been numerous television guest appearances between 1973 (with a recurring role on the soap General Hospital*) and a 2021 episode of* Blue Bloods. *His movie career has spanned from 1984's* Grace Quigley *to 2018's* Beyond the Night.

SHERMAN HOWARD (actor, "Lex Luthor," *Superboy***):** At the end of the first season, they hired Julia Pistor as a new producer. At that point they spent a lot of money on the show, but they'd already lost their audience and never really got them back. That first season was just *horrible*. Everything about it was awful. I remember my first day on the set; they gave me a video to look at as sort of a reference of a previous episode, and it was a bunch of fat guys in a fist fight with Superboy. That's the big summation of it. And it was like, "What the *hell*?" That's Superman, you can't … *fist fighting*?" My understanding was that they were going to put a whole lot more money into it and really up the quality of the show. Again, they weren't quite successful in bringing the lost audience back.

JULIA PISTOR: I remember after we shot Sherman's first episode, Viacom saw the final cut when we had a new Lex Luthor with real lighting and a real story, and they gave us a standing ovation. They were *so* excited and so was I.

STACY HAIDUK: I loved the changes that they made, like with Lex Luthor and bringing in Sherman Howard. He was just a delight. I always loved working with him and he loved to play. That was definitely a good transitional change.

ROB O'CONNOR: The inclusion of Sherman Howard as a more Joker-like Lex Luthor gave the series a welcome sheen of menace, resulting in episodes such as "Roads Not Taken" and "Know Thine Enemy."

J.M. DEMATTEIS (writer, *Superboy*): In "Know Thine Enemy," Luthor's about to do one of his crazy Luthor things and destroy the world, and Superboy comes across these psycho-discs on which Luthor has put all of his memories. Superboy realizes that the only way he's going to be able to understand this man and stop him is to go into these memories. So Superboy actually lives out Luthor's traumatic childhood. Now *that's* my kind of story, where you're really peeling back the tops of these characters' heads and diving right into their skulls. That story turned out so well; I think Sherman Howard was one of the best Lex Luthors ever. He never gets enough credit for it. And in that two-parter, Gerard Christopher got to play a darker color and gave one of *his* best performances. It was basically a bottle show in Lex's memories. It's all just sort of German expressionist lighting, very minimal sets as they're walking around in these memories.

ROB O'CONNOR: One of my all-time favorite Superman/Luthor showdowns is "Mine Games," where Lex and Superboy are trapped in a mine covered in Kryptonite and forced to work together — and more importantly, talk about their feelings! — to escape.

MIKE CARLIN: Just a great emotional story about Luthor's father and his upbringing. And because Sherman Howard was a good actor, he really was able to command attention for half an hour.

SAM RIZZO: At one point, Superboy asks Lex, "What would make you happy?" He says, "To be king for a day. What about you?" and Superboy says, "The freedom to compromise; being able to live a normal life and basically hang up the cape." It was a *great* line that has stuck with me. And when I met Sherman — who wrote the episode — I brought up that script. That was one of the pages that I showed him. And he was, like, "Sam, how do you remember all this?" "Because, this was *my* Superman." It's like we all have a depiction of what God is in our mind. With Superman, there are so many portrayals that add to the tapestry of this character.

SHERMAN HOWARD: I was always one of those actors who wanted to write. I'd have bright ideas for all kinds of things and tell my friends about them, and they would always say, "That's a great idea, you should write it," and I somehow just never was able to face the empty page. It was a source of great frustration through the decades, so I show up for those first two episodes and my dialogue was so bad — it was just unspeakable — and I rewrote it in such a way that it didn't change the other characters' dialogue, which was kind of a trick: to change all of your own dialogue and still have the scene come out to mean what the scene is supposed to do without forcing anybody else to learn different lines. And it worked. After that, I approached my agent and said I would like to write some episodes, and they negotiated a thing where I was supposed to write two of them. And that's how the writing thing happened. I suppose my rewriting my own dialogue was sort of an audition, and throughout my work on the series they were very generous with me about letting me adjust my own dialogue.

STAN BERKOWITZ: Sherman's a flamboyant actor, and they're always fun to watch. He does, however, have a tendency to change dialogue without asking permission. On one of our alternate world stories, he added a whole stuttering bit which I only found out about while watching dailies — when it was too late to do anything about it. He wanted that world's version of Luthor to go from being weak and intimidated (hence the hesitating stutter) to becoming more like the Luthor we all knew (goodbye speech impediment!). Why didn't he mention it to me beforehand? Maybe he thought I'd tell him not to do it, or maybe he didn't care what I thought. Interestingly enough, when he wrote his own scripts for the show, he'd get upset if even a word had to be changed. Did he not understand the give and take of the creative process? Given his own sensitivity, did he not realize that his colleagues might have had their own sensitivities? Or did he simply feel like he was a giant among dwarves? This is where I point out that his only writing credits to date are the two scripts he wrote for *Superboy* 30 years ago.

MIKE CARLIN: Writing the two-part "Bride of Bizarro" was a lot of fun, because honestly I think Sherman Howard was the best thing that happened to that show. It was just a hoot to write for him, because we knew he'd get it right every single time. I don't understand why he hasn't just been bigger. He's a great comedy performer with just the right over-the-top quality, while also being really menacing. When he was in somebody's face, it was *scary*. I honestly think that 1989's *Batman* and what Jack Nicholson pulled off as the Joker forced them to rethink Luthor completely. And when they found Sherman, it really was perfect.

And then there was Bizarro himself, the imperfect duplicate of Superman and Superboy in the comics, who could have been played either for scares or humor, but on this series the writers went for pathos. The actor bringing him to life was Douglas Meyers, who only appeared in seven episodes, and yet whenever the series is discussed in any sort of depth or there is a visual retrospective, invariably the character shows up.

For his part, Meyers had always enjoyed acting and was able to get his SAG card thanks to appearing on the show. Prior to donning Bizarro's makeup, he was a robotic performer named Mr. Silver, offering up a 15-minute show consisting of music, magic, laser lights and more. Known for that in South Florida, it led the show's casting director to his agent regarding a possible appearance.

DOUGLAS MEYERS (actor, "Bizarro," *Superboy*): When I walked into the casting room, the first thing they said was, "Here, put this bag over your head. Here's the thing, we are looking for the movements. There's going to be prosthetics, so we don't care what you look like." I'm thinking, "I'm going to get my SAG card, so okay." Anyway, Mr. Silver was almost the same thing.

MIKE CARLIN: It was such smart casting, because he was able to do things with his body and was used to being covered up in makeup. I thought that was kind of brilliant of the casting directors; if the guy's face is going to be totally covered, you don't have to get a flat-out actor, really, although mimes *are* acting.

STACY HAIDUK: His performance was so heartfelt and so beautiful. I even told him, "Oh my God, I'm falling in love with you," just because of the oddness of his face in the mask and what he brought to it. I enjoyed those shows a lot. He was just a really good person and a really good actor. I don't know how he could have sat through tons of makeup, getting those blocks put on his face. He had done this body thing where he called himself Mr. Silver, and you can just see it in his movements. He really took it to heart, and I say any actor who puts in that much energy when you put a mask on is someone special.

SAM RIZZO: He is the definitive Bizarro in my opinion. He played Bizarro very much with a heart. In the two-part episode "To Be Human," Superboy tries to talk him into giving up his powers and to be human as his brother. And the scenes with him out of makeup were just as good as him in. And then there are the scenes with him, Clark and Lana at the Bureau and he doesn't betray Clark or expose his secret when he could — such a great moment and a great character moment too, because Clark always wanted to have a brother.

J.M. DEMATTEIS: Stan Berkowitz came to me and said, "Let's so *Flowers for Algernon* with Bizarro," and that's exactly what it was.

DOUGLAS MEYERS: I used to have to sit through two-and-a-half hours of doing the makeup, so when you go to lunch you don't take anything off. I mean, that makeup stayed on *all* day. A lot of times after lunch I might have a break until the next shoot, so I would go back to the trailer where there was a big black carpet on the floor so I could take a nap. There was one time that I actually started dreaming of Bizarro and I woke up on the floor, looked over at the mirror and there was Bizarro. For a nanosecond it was like my dream or nightmare just care true. It took a few seconds for me to settle down.

STAN BERKOWITZ: Douglas was the first on-screen incarnation of Bizarro, and when it came time to do an episode where Bizarro briefly becomes a normal human, the question that came up was who should play normal Bizarro. The obvious choice should have been Gerry, since Bizarro was an imperfect copy of Superboy, but it was brought up that Douglas would be crushed if he weren't allowed to play the part. And then too there might be a desire on the part of our audience to see what the man under all that makeup looked like. I have no regrets about the way it worked out.

DOUGLAS MEYERS: I've been asked if Boris Karloff's portrayal of Frankenstein's Monster was an influence, and I would think so. Somewhere in the back of my head I'm sure it was, because I had to make the voice and even the walk not be quite human. But again, I would also do that as Mr. Silver. Our director David Grossman may have suggested I keep Frankenstein in mind as well. As an actor, when you're trying to find the voice and actions for something that's never been done before, you draw from all kinds of things. I was just happy that *they* were happy with what I came up with.

When it comes to Superman — or Superboy in this instance — one of the major elements that has to be accomplished is making it look as though the character flies naturally and for the audience to believe he's doing so. While the series was fairly low-budget, Ilya Salkind did bring in the flying team from the Christopher Reeve films to handle flight issues.

SAM RIZZO: They had the same guys that flew Helen Slater and Christopher Reeve, including Bob Harmon. His entire flying unit was flying John Newton and Gerard Christopher, and the wire work they did on that series just kept improving. Each season got better and better. Take a look at some of John's takeoffs in the first season — they were freaking amazing; some of the landings too. And with Gerard, he kept going up on the wires better and better. In one of the later episodes, they had Gerard flying on an angle, towards the camera, and it was so awesome to see.

GERARD CHRISTOPHER: The flying was one of the hardest things to do and one of the most fun things to do. Whenever you see me flying and you see a background, it's moving. They do green screen and they project that behind me and that's how they make that work. But that was also a very uncomfortable experience, because the way they did it was they had this huge screen in a soundstage and in front of that they had an apparatus with guys in it above me. I had a flying suit with little holes on the side. They had me wear a harness with little tiny wires coming out of the side that they would take out electronically so you couldn't see them. But that was very uncomfortable because you had to stay flat for maybe half-an-hour at a time. I don't know if you've ever laid on your stomach and tried to keep your arms and legs up, but I did that for 30 minutes to 40 minutes at a time, so it was very uncomfortable.

STACY HAIDUK: The first time I flew I thought, "Oh, let me do gymnastics and flip and have fun." But after a while, you get up there and there are the harnesses that are really painful. I know John had a hell of a time, but it was fun for a while. After that though, you're like, "Do I have to do that again?" The problem is you've got this big diaper on, which is the harness belt with these bolts sticking out on the side of your hip. You look really cute in your little outfits and then you're like, "This is ridiculous." You always had to wear these big oversized things so that they could hook the wires. and you prayed to God that your wire didn't get tangled up in your shirt and you'd end up hanging upside down half the time.

GERARD CHRISTOPHER: The other flying I did was really fun. They would set up a crane, a construction crane, and if I had to do a scene where I'm on the grass and I'm punching somebody out and then have to fly away, they'd hook me up, I do my punch-out scene, they'd cut it, then they'd add me there again with the other costume on, and when I got my cue I would just bend myself at the knees and that was their cue to pull me up and I would just go. They'd bring me to the roof of a building or something. So this stuff was fun, but if you were afraid of heights, you were really doing the wrong thing.

JOHN HAYMES NEWTON: One time I was over an actual alligator pit. We went to Gatorland and filmed the "Birdwoman of the Swamps" episode, and I remember hanging above actual alligators in the swamp and, like Chris Reeve said, "If the wires break and you're more than 10 feet above the ground, it doesn't matter if you're 100 feet or 10 feet, you land on your head, you're not going to make it." And that was a good point. I remember being over these alligators realizing that the wires were only 1.2 millimeters. They weren't thick wires so it was scary. And there *were* accidents. One time the wire guys were back in England for a funeral and they let somebody else handle the rigging who wasn't trained, and I literally almost died. They let go of the ropes, which you're not supposed to do, because what happens is when you shoot straight up really fast, when you reach the top, you go past where you're being lifted and then you're free in the air in a trajectory. *Then* you're coming back down and at that speed you're putting a lot of force on those wires. I exceeded the wire ratings, but the wire didn't break for some reason. I was like, "Oh my God, that was scary!" *Then*, on the same day, they flew me into some telephone wires that happened not to be electrical. This wasn't Bob Harmon or the wire guys who were trained; it was one of the grips, I think, and somebody else who didn't know what they were doing. Luckily I didn't get killed.

STACY HAIDUK: They dropped the weights and he just went shooting up. I'm sorry, it was awful, but in retrospect it was funny to watch. He's standing there and suddenly he's just gone. And I just hear swearing and him yelling, "Shit!!!!"

GERARD CHRISTOPHER: One time in Florida, I'll never forget this, it was a cloudy day and in Florida you have a lot of thunderstorms in the summer. They had me on this crane that's maybe a hundred feet tall and I'm attached to it with steel wires, thunder all over the place. So the crane is on top of a bridge. Florida doesn't have a lot of rivers, but it was something like a river or big lake. In any case, I'm up like a hundred feet over the bridge. Then they swing me out and I'm hanging over the bridge a couple of hundred feet above whatever's under there. And then, because my safety officer, who is my stunt guy and who's supposed to be in charge of your safety, had some girlfriend on his lap or something, he basically wasn't looking out for my safety at the time. And then they swung me and I almost hit power lines. I was going, "Uh, guys, thunder… lightning… power lines, get me down!" It really wasn't the flying that scared me that time, it was that these guys just didn't do the job well. But most of the time it was really fun.

Superboy *concluded its run in 1992 after four seasons and a total of 100 episodes were produced. The idea was that those 100 episodes would be able to be run daily on independent stations which, theoretically, would have given it an afterlife like the one that had grown around George Reeves'* Adventures of Superman, *but that didn't actually happen. The show was seldom seen and Warner Bros./DC shifted its attention to the ABC show* Lois & Clark: The New Adventures of Superman, *which would debut a year later. As a result,* Superboy *was allowed to slip into relative obscurity — although, of course, the fans did find it and it has managed to live on, due largely to the passion of those fans, especially Sam Rizzo and the* Superboy Legacy.

MIKE CARLIN: They wanted 100 episodes for syndication. They wanted enough to run it forever — which is ironic considering how hard it is to find now. They said, "If we can make it past two seasons, we have to do four, and then we'll have enough."

SAM RIZZO: The story has been going around that *Lois & Clark* killed *Superboy*, but that's not the case. Or that DC stopped approving scripts. No. Viacom/Paramount just had the rights for 100 episodes. And once the 100 episodes were done, that was it.

ROB O'CONNOR: The unjustly forgotten chapter in Superman's storied TV career, my fondest memories of the *Superboy* show are of reading about it on primitive websites like DMWC's Superboy site, The Superboy Homepage by Sam Rizzo and Superboy Theater by Rennie Cowan, having never seen a frame of the series. Long forgotten by the time I even found out about its existence, its memory has not only been kept alive, but restored and enhanced by the efforts of its stalwart fans. Many fans will know of Jim Nolt or Jim Bowers, whose love of the George Reeves series and Christopher Reeve movies have kept those eras of Superman alive in the hearts of fans — they should know the name Sam Rizzo as well, as he has put blood, sweat, tears and thousands of dollars into reminding people of how special *Superboy* was.

ALAN BURKE (co-host, *All Star Superfan Podcast*): Though some diehard fans remain, it is definitely the forgotten cousin of the Superman television family. I was encouraged to check out some episodes so that we could review them on *All Star Superfan Podcast*. Unfortunately I made the rookie mistake of starting with the pilot, an obvious choice I assumed at the time. I was wrong. It was *awful*. It was dated, cheap, clumsy and filled with poor special effects and terrible acting. It was the equivalent, in my view, to a bad fan film. I watched in horror as I witnessed this show's version of Lex Luthor, played by actor Scott Wells, deliver what I can only describe as the worst delivery of a line ever put to screen. But then something strange happened. After a few weeks, I gained the courage to watch another episode and then another and then another

ROB O'CONNOR: I've seen the whole series a couple of times now and I think they mostly accomplished something very charming despite a very meager budget. The acting and the writing often leaves a lot to the imagination, but I think nearly every season has a new and interesting quality to it, as though the cast and crew were learning how to make a TV series as they went along. John Newton really grew into the role in that fledgling first season, and while some episodes are so cheerfully crap as to be laughable, his likeable everyday charm as Clark recalls a similar energy from George Reeves (and foreshadows Dean Cain). I am one of the rare few who thinks Newton was better than Gerard Christopher, who was far too old to be playing a 19-year-old and was miscast regardless — his thick Noo Yawk accent, deep features, bouffant hairstyle and overacting made him come across as something more akin to the chorus line of *Grease* than a last son of Krypton. Still, as he learned to tone it down, so did the show, and as it reached its third season, its ambition rose with its ratings, resulting in some surprisingly excellent stories accomplished on (as ever) a pretty low budget.

ALAN BURKE: Yes, it was camp and silly. Yes, they had no budget and it looked cheap. Yes, some of the acting was wooden. Yes, the stories and characters were one-dimensional due to their 22-minute run time, but I started noticing something as I went on: The show had… heart. It cared. It cared about the material. It cared about the characters. It cared about the fans. Each season significantly improved on that which had come before.

GERARD CHRISTOPHER: If we continued beyond the fourth season, I would've graduated to being Superman, because the last show that aired was "Rites of Passage," and in that one I became Superman. But Warner Bros. pulled the plug on the show because they wanted to do *Lois & Clark*.

MIKE CARLIN: Yes, "Rites of Passage" was him supposedly transitioning towards becoming Superman. At least that's what we thought in our little pea brains. When we pitched that idea, it was about using a lot of the crystal-type stuff and things like that from the Superman movie mythos and kind of hinting that that's what was coming next, I guess. There was movie talk going on right at that time, so it might have worked, although from what I remember of the actual story that they were talking about doing, I don't think it would have connected at all.

And yet, many of those involved — particularly the actors — have found themselves connected, even all these years later, to the Superman mythology that has become a part of pop culture history.

JOHN HAYMES NEWTON: I don't consider myself really in the big picture of the character. I consider myself less than 1% of anything truly historical, but yeah, there's a tiny chapter in there. I'm above *Superpup* and you can't negate that. My whole thing is, I feel everybody relates to that character, and getting to play it is maybe one step above just being able to watch it or relate to it in other ways. And I feel grateful for that opportunity. I really do. It changed me in a lot of ways and helped me to see that we all have our own superpower. That seems a little cliché or silly, but we all relate to that. I think it's our life and why we're here to discover what that is and let it grow until it becomes something that you can be proud of at the end of your life and you don't look back with regrets. If nothing else, the character symbolizes that. I feel like that character was a stepping stone in helping me see something that is more than just human.

DOUGLAS MEYERS: It's not a huge thing, I'm not Superman, but I have a small slice in that I am a part of the history of the franchise now. When people hear Bizarro, they think of my character, not *Smallville* or some CGI version. People have asked me if I had seen what was done with the other Bizarros, but I point out, "They didn't really do Bizarro, they just altered Superman's face with CGI," and they didn't really act like Bizarro. The episodes of *Superman & Lois* came the closest.

GERARD CHRISTOPHER: It was amazingly enjoyable, it really was. For a show that was not a network show and didn't have a tremendous audience in terms of viewers, the following when we were on location, the letters I used to get, it felt like it was a huge network show and that was amazing. I attribute that to the genre. I attribute that to the history of the character and the comics and the whole thing. That's what was so exciting about it: It was something more than just a TV show. It was something bigger than all of us together and it's something that's going to live on.

STACY HAIDUK: For a while it was kind of strange to me that people even saw the show. I was like, "*Really?*" But through the years, and doing things like Comic-Con, I realized there are people who the show had a big impact on. Part of it is nostalgia, because there's nothing like it nowadays. We had something very different back then that I kind of feel has been lost. It's like the innocence of it is gone.

And as far as Haiduk and Newton are concerned, the person who had a huge impact on their lives and careers was actually executive producer Ilya Salkind, for whom they both have tremendous respect.

STACY HAIDUK: He gave me my big shot, and that's a big thing. He definitely was a character back then. Like I've said, I'd done a lot of little things, but never something this big where, you know, it's *Ilya Salkind*! It was just this amazing experience. Going into it, I had only been taking acting classes for a couple of years, but it's so different when you're actually on a set. I think the reason I got the part was because I was the same age Lana would have been at the time, and her journey in life somehow mirrored what I was going through on the set. I grew with her at times, sometimes she grew because I grew from my experiences in the real world. I really liked her a lot and the way the writing got better and better with each season. And I remain thankful that Ilya cast me.

JOHN HAYMES NEWTON: Ilya is like a big kid in a lot of ways. I think he always wanted his dad to be proud of him and to take him seriously. This may sound strange, but I feel like he related to the hero in every project he ever worked on. He saw himself as that character; it was almost like he wanted them to be an extension of him. And his alter ego was that of a movie star. I'm not saying he wanted to be an actor, but I feel he's a man about town, very European. At the same time, it gave him a passion for what he was working on. He really *did* care. This guy's doing syndicated TV after doing feature films, and it's probably hard for him on one level, but at the same time he would always stay passionate about every detail and he would micro-manage things that probably helped the show get better and better.

For Salkind's part, even as Superboy *was ending its run, he was already starting to develop — with Cary Bates and the hope that Christopher Reeve would reprise his role yet again — a film that was alternately referred to as* Superman V, Superman: The New Movie *or* Superman Reborn, *dealing with the death and resurrection of Superman before the Death of Superman in the comics. This would ultimately be his last attempt to be involved in the creative process of a property featuring the Man of Steel.*

GLEN OLIVER (pop culture historian): By its third draft, the Bates/Jones/Salkind iteration of *Superman Reborn* was lean, clean, defined and refined — and tremendously ambitious and costly for its era. It would be seen as such even by today's more technologically flexible and forgiving standards, which automatically raises some questions; for example: Was there truly any expectation among Team Salkind that a film of this magnitude would actually be produced, or could even be produced at all, back then? Even if only in some stripped-down semblance? Or was this merely a product of 'swing for the fences,' 'in a perfect world…' wish listing? It's a fascinating, compelling 'What if…' scenario which, had the picture made it to screens in any kind of respectable fashion, might've substantially altered Superman's cinematic trajectory.

It's a tremendously enjoyable script, very often leaning into the kind of earnest gravitas one could frequently find in the previous Salkind Era Superman movies. Predictably it also evoked some of their clunkier elements: significant character exploration, weight and intriguing social-political examination are often counterbalanced by comic-y expostulations and dopey smack talk which seem deployed in an effort to not let proceedings get too serious — even though the prevalent vibe and subject matters of the story are actually pretty serious this time around. As such, Reborn sometimes feels like it has a split personality and is afraid to commit — or completely 'grow up' — like it was so clearly straining to do. Fortunately, solidity generally outweighs the cheese factor here, and the result is a screenplay which, at the very least, would've been quite interesting to see on screen.

This iteration of Superman Reborn finds Clark and Lois in the final days of their relationship. Matters are tortured for both of them — neither wants to leave the other, yet both are committed to fulfilling their own place in the Way of Things… and their places (don't appear to be) compatible. Superman realizes that he simply must be Superman; he belongs to the world, and can't meet Lois' hopes for more attention being focused on their own relationship. It's the ultimate impasse, and something's gotta give. So it does.

Before Lois can manage to leave Metropolis, Brainiac shows up — drawn by media reports monitored from space, fulfilling a purpose we'll later come to understand. He gets into an epic fight with Superman, apparently killing him. We later learn the flash of energy we understood to be the death of Superman was actually, unbeknownst to Brainiac, Kal-El being secretly beamed to Kandor — one city in a menagerie of many cities aboard Brainiac's 'Space Ark,' which also happens to be the last known surviving city of Krypton. The people of Kandor — which on paper feels like a cross between Coruscant in the Star Wars prequels and the Kelvin Era iteration of Vulcan in the Star Trek movies — are aware of the captivity. But bewilderingly to Superman, they do not generally resent this. Instead, Brainiac is, to them, something of a savior, a deity, one to be worshiped, one who afforded them a new lease on life shortly before Krypton's destruction. They're content to be alive and are dismissive of their relatively subservient status.

GLEN OLIVER: Essentially fulfilling the role of his father Jor-El, as evidenced in Donner's first Superman movie — down to wearing white Kryptonian garb similar to Brando's outfit in that film — Kal-El attempts to convince the rulers of Kandor that their deity is dangerous, full of shit and needs to be brought down. He even employs the tremendous opening line from the first film "This is no fantasy" — in the process. He's quickly and summarily ignored and dismissed — in a sequence very similar to the Kryptonian council's admonishment of Jor-El in the first film — leaving Kal-El powerless in the red-sunned environment of Kandor to figure out how to bring down the god-level Brainiac without a wide base of support.

Intercut with all of this, we learn that Brainiac is a rogue extraterrestrial A.I. that, due to a miniscule snafu in its initial programming, took its mission to study as much as possible about life forms too seriously. It overran and/or subjugated its creators, and is now driven by a divine purpose of learning and knowing it doesn't fully comprehend. Brainiac, in this iteration, is basically V'ger from *Star Trek: The Motion Picture* — on a single-minded mission to learn about life and existence and comprehend their meaning, regardless of the havoc it creates when doing so. In this case, it has come to Earth to confront Superman, to understand the 'hows' and 'whys' of Kal-El doing what he does — pulled here by media reports of this specimen who was clearly different from other humans. There's a subplot that members of Brainiac's beleaguered crew actually funneled these reports to him, hoping to force a confrontation with Superman, whom they hope will destroy him.

Along the way, Brainiac captures Lois, attempts to fall in love with her and understand what love is in the process, and shrinks Metropolis down to become a part of his Ark's menagerie deliberately, sadistically draining the oxygen out of Metropolis' protective sphere in the process. This sets the stage for multiple efforts to bring down Brainiac once and for all: Lois and beleaguered denizens from Brainiac's crew, and Kal-El in Kandor, trying to regain his powers and escape the confines of the city to take on Brainiac — an adventure involving invisibility fields, speeder car chases and the like.

When all is said and done, Superman and Lois find their way toward understanding and unity. In the film's final sequence, Clark slowly reveals his Superman identity to Lois, removing wardrobe bit by bit. When she reconciles that the two most important men in her life are actually the same person, collectively embodying every quality she could ever dream of wanting, the couple connects once more. They agree to get married and fly off together toward adventures unknown, with the requisite wink toward the camera as they leave the final frame.

GLEN OLIVER: *Superman Reborn* is a strong script, a very "Salkind-y script," illustrating many of the strengths the Salkind ethos frequently brought to bear in their previous filmmaking, as well as a few of their lesser agreeable qualities. Wit, charm, scale and even profundity is very much evidenced here, but there's a constant proclivity to backpedal and not let proceedings become too heavy. Was this a strategic choice, or merely the writers being non-committal?

Even though it sometimes felt like it was soft-shoeing around a few substantive concepts, its narrative still hinges on a thought-provoking material which might've surprised many viewers, would easily have connected with audiences and would've nicely argued the need to continue the Salkind iteration of Superman. Its driving thematic — the efforts of Superman, Lois and even Brainiac to understand the nature of their existences, their place in the Way of Things and the general meanings of who they, themselves, are — could've played quite effectively on screen if guided by a proper director. The examination of religious zealotry and how spiritual absolutism is ultimately a self-destructive path might even have raised a few eyebrows and prompted a few unexpected conversations publicly. The script's pointed revisit of 'the son becomes the father and the father becomes the son' concept driving *Superman: The Movie* and *The Donner Cut* of *Superman II* would've felt like a warm embrace, and nicely re-connected the franchise to its roots, while also suggesting compelling paths for how it might move forward.

The proposed scale of the picture is suspect, and I can't imagine this script — no matter how cool and fun it may have seemed at the time — was taken too seriously by the powers-that-be given the costs that would've been required to make it happen (if it could even be made effectively at all in its era); especially given the downward creative and box office trajectory of the franchise as illustrated by *Superman III* and *IV* before it. Epic battle sequences involve Superman "bowling" the fallen Daily Planet globe down the streets of Metropolis in an effort to smush Brainiac, multiple alien species, robots and drones of various ilk, Brainiac in both robotic and human forms, Coruscant-like speeder-car chases through towering alien cities, menageries of shrunken cities contained in individualized ecosystems, a knock-down, drag-out in the ruins of a fallen alien civilization and more. This would be a challenge to produce today — but back in 1992? It's hard not to imagine the project being regarded as anything other than summarily untenable. Nonetheless it's a hugely entertaining and noble effort, and a highly compelling glimpse at 'what might've been...'

Whether you loved or hated Ilya Salkind based on first-hand or media-reported knowledge, he deserves the credit for having the original vision that Superman could work on the big screen in the form of a blockbuster film. In terms of the character's history, there's a lot he gets credit for, no matter what went on behind the scenes. Yet the big question that remains in the situation is how, considering that the Salkinds had acquired the Superman rights from DC in 1975 for a 25-year period, ABC was able to air Lois & Clark *(1993 to 1997) less than 20 years later.*

CARY BATES: We were in the initial stages of pre-production on *Superman Reborn*. The film had been budgeted and they had hired a production designer who came up with some great stuff (I can still recall his kick-ass designs for Brainiac's ship). Unfortunately other forces were at work that we weren't aware of at the time. Final script approval never came down from Warners, because they had their own plans for the character — the newly commissioned *Lois & Clark* series. By the early '90s Warners had realized in hindsight that they were remiss in letting go of the rights to their flagship comic book character.

ILYA SALKIND: What happened is quite a story. I had a big fight with my father Alexander Salkind when he took $11-million from my third ex-wife Jane Chaplin, the daughter of Charlie Chaplin, which he said he was going to use for the production of *Columbus*. But he didn't. He *stole* the money and I sued him. And I won at the Supreme Court, but I couldn't get anything because he claimed to the court that he was poor. And when it came to Superman — he sold *everything* back to Warner Bros. without telling me. We were fighting at the time, so I didn't even know what he was doing. That was painful to me. I remember the character from when I was a kid. What it really comes down to is that I love Superman.

CARY BATES: What the naysayers seem to overlook is that without Ilya's vision and ambition, *Superman I* — which provided the template for most of the superhero movies that have come since — might not have happened at all. Ilya was the first to see the potential Superman had as a big-budget film with A-level talent at a time when the rest of the business considered comic book properties Saturday morning material at best. Even the '60s *Batman* TV show only attained its brief surge in the ratings by trashing and ridiculing the source material. With respect to *Superman III*, most fans are not aware that the most interesting (and praised) elements of the film — the schizophrenic split and fight between the evil Superman and the heroic Clark — were Ilya's concepts. The hokey super-computer and emphasis on Richard Pryor scenes were coming from the Lester camp, no pun intended. If *Superman Reborn* — which contained many more of Ilya's concepts — had reached the screen, it would have gone a long way toward erasing the so-called "bad rap."

ILYA SALKIND: I did finally make my peace with my father before he died, which was a good thing. But it was *very* difficult.

Before the critics weighed in, months ahead of its television premiere and prior to ratings talk being in the air at all, there was a key moment that writer/producer Deborah Joy Levine, who had developed Lois & Clark: The New Adventures of Superman, *had been nervously anticipating: The ABC network's 1993 upfront presentation of that season's new shows to advertisers.*

DEBORAH JOY LEVINE (executive producer, *Lois & Clark: The New Adventures of Superman*): I was actually sitting in Carnegie Hall when they showed the presentation for the show and the audience's reaction was so fabulous. But my best phone call came from DC Comics; they called me from a room in a hotel in Minneapolis, where they had all convened — all the Superman writers and artists; there were like 17 people sitting in the room. They put me on the speakerphone after seeing the presentation and they were just *ecstatic*. What's funny is that I said to them, "I was most afraid of you guys, because I know you *are* Superman and you've created the past couple of years of stories and I just really wanted to live up to what you've been doing and to your expectations." It meant a lot to me because it was about a year earlier that I first met with them and just sat down and talked about the concept, and I think they were a little wary about a product for television and that I had a lot of ideas that were sort of new and innovative, *and* that I wanted to do it my way. So the fact that they called me and were so happy, and Jenette Kahn and Michael Carlin and these people that have really devoted their lives to this… the fact that *they* loved it meant more to me than anything.

Lois & Clark *was the first Superman live-action television show since George Reeves'* Adventures of Superman *in the 1950s, and was decidedly geared toward adults, unlike the 1988 to 1992 syndicated* Superboy *show. That focus arose from the fact that it was, at least initially, more inspired by classic romcoms and screwball comedies of Hollywood's Golden Age than standard superheroics. With Teri Hatcher and Dean Cain in the lead roles, it was pretty much unlike any other filmed version of the characters that had preceded it.*

JOHN KENNETH MUIR (film historian, author, *The Encyclopedia of Superheroes on Film and Television*): The *Superman* films of Christopher Reeve were a product of the late 1970s and the 1980s, starting in the immediate post-Watergate Age. The legend was reborn in the "peace and prosperity boom" of the Clinton era/Internet age with *Lois and Clark: The New Adventures of Superman*, a romantic/comedy/adventure that updated the general tone of the story but in a manner that was largely pleasing to mass audiences (if not always to the longtime Superman aficionado). *Lois & Clark* often felt like *Moonlighting* meets *Ally McBeal*.

CRAIG BYRNE (webmaster, kryptonsite.com): *Lois & Clark* played an important role in the Superman mythos, because it not only put Lois front and center of the story, but it was also the first live-action production to really tackle the "post-*Crisis*" part of the characters. Jonathan and Martha Kent were alive, Kal-El truly seemed like the last son of Krypton (until he was not) and Lex Luthor was a ruthless businessman. On top of that, we've all heard the stories about how the TV show delayed the comic book wedding of the characters, which led to the *Death of Superman*, so that was certainly an impact. I would not be surprised if Superman's longer hair after he came back to life was inspired by Dean Cain's longer hairstyle in the *Lois & Clark* pilot. I remember reading the

Dean Cain co-starred with Teri Hatcher in four seasons of Lois & Clark: The New Adventures of Superman *(art © and courtesy D.C. Stuelpner; Superman © and TM DC Comics/Warner Bros. Discovery).*

comic around 1996 and it seemed the show's delay and later sudden reversal with the wedding itself really messed up the packing of the comic book storylines for that year.

ROBERT BUTLER (pilot director and executive consultant, *Lois & Clark: The New Adventures of Superman*): The concept for this show always had good legs. Of course, it really kind of springboarded off Lois, because she's so independent, slightly feministic for the '90s, and it all kind of swirled around her. That's the way the show worked. The civilians just appreciated that Dean is Superman and he's a handsome guy and there was this good-looking gal along for the ride, and that's okay. That's the way the show reached the audience. But the way the show *really* worked is that Teri's independence and ambition and drive against Clark/Superman's modesty was a lot of fun. Superman didn't have anything to be driven about, because he *is* a god. He doesn't have to play god. That's the fun of it. Teri is the frail, ambitious human and Dean is the god-like visitor from another planet who wants to be like us.

TERI HATCHER (actor, "Lois Lane," *Lois & Clark: The New Adventures of Superman*): I have my own little theory that some people were threatened by a woman that has those qualities. It's still not a popular quality that women in the workplace have. While I didn't see her getting less strong as a career woman, I did see her as maturing into being able to express her vulnerabilities better. This is a woman who was a big jellyfish on the inside and had to put up walls, as many women I think really do, to make it through the struggles of being a woman in a workplace and growing up.

DEAN CAIN (actor, "Clark Kent/Superman," *Lois & Clark: The New Adventures of Superman*): I think the show was a decent reflection of its time. It didn't take anyone to extremes. I think Lois was the sort of contemporary ''90s woman who has certain needs. She wanted a man to love and be with. If certain feminist people would say she doesn't need a man to love, my opinion is a man needs a woman, a woman needs a man. People need each other.

ROB O'CONNOR: I remember the exact moment I discovered the character in 1993 when the promo for *The New Adventures of Superman* (as it was known in the U.K. and Ireland) aired on BBC and my mum showing it to me. I was already a Batman fan at that point and somehow, paradoxically, I must have already known who Superman was, because the visual of the man in the red cape didn't feel unfamiliar. I knew that this was something that was going to be with me for a long time, and sure enough it was. Superman has had an enormous impact on my life from stumbling into a degree in journalism to always striving to be a do-gooder (with varying degrees of success or integrity) to my belief that there *usually* is a right and a wrong in the universe for which that distinction *usually* isn't hard to make. As a firmly-lapsed Irish Catholic with no time for the hard doctrines and intolerance of the Church, I find the guy in the red cape (with his ever-changing mythology and evolving belief system) easier to look to for guidance.

TERI HATCHER: I don't really recall where we were collectively as a society with the women's movement in the mid-'90s, but I do know that just the fact that Warner Bros. and ABC decided to put a show on the air that was called *Lois & Clark* instead of *Clark & Lois* was probably a pretty big deal. I personally enjoyed that it was the version of the Superman story that sort of led with the romance of Lois and Clark as opposed to the adventures of Superman as a hero as the dominating storyteller. In many ways, Lois moved the stories. It was her strengths and also her vulnerabilities, her hesitations to fall in love — all of that, which was very human. And those were the parts of it that I personally fell in love with.

DEBORAH JOY LEVINE: *Lois & Clark* was my concept, but I was actually "put on" the project. I was under contract to Lorimar Television and they bought the rights, I guess, in conjunction with Warner Bros., and then brought it to ABC and had already sold it by the time they all came back to me and asked if I wanted to do it. It was actually a shock to me when they came to me, because initially they came to me with Superman, which I wasn't really interested in. They knew they had gotten the rights and they wanted to do it a different way, but they weren't really sure how to do it. I think they came to me because I was someone who historically never wrote action/adventure stuff. I am more of a character writer. I also spent a couple of years on *Equal Justice* and I also used to be queen of the socially relevant movies of the week, so I was really not your typical person you are going to come to write Superman.

My response was, "Why me? There are a lot of other writers better suited for this." They said, "Because we really want to concentrate on the relationships and we know you are a 'relationship writer' as opposed to just an action writer." That was because when I went to the network, I basically said, "You know what? I don't really want to do Superman, but I'll tell you what I *do* want to do…" And I started talking to them and evolved this idea of Lois and Clark. What's funny is when I came up with the title, the show followed. It was more about Lois and Clark than it was about Superman, and then the whole thing seemed very clear to me in that I was doing this show about these two people at the *Daily Planet* who had this love/hate relationship; these two reporters with a little twist that one comes from Krypton. That approach just seemed to fall into place.

BRYCE ZABEL (supervising producer, *Lois & Clark: The New Adventures of Superman*): We had a little mobile home trailer on the lot where Deborah, Dan and I spent a few months kicking things back and forth, and while the thing we kept coming back to was that the relationship of Lois and Clark had to be primary, when we were breaking the stories, at the end of the day you needed a dramatic story engine driver and it was always the superhero stuff. It was always the Superman mythology and the relationship was folded into it.

DAN LEVINE (executive story editor, *Lois & Clark: The New Adventures of Superman*): Upgrading Superman's sensibilities was not difficult at all. In my opinion, it just provided a chance to give him a little bit more depth. The old George Reeves version had very little depth as a character. We never really knew him as a human being. Christopher Reeve was someone who, as Clark Kent, was playing a bumbling shy reporter role. We wanted to create a character that had depth and emotion and the sensibilities of someone growing up in America in this day and age. That part was not difficult. The difficulty was in bringing that to life in a package that would be attractive to a mass audience.

DEBORAH JOY LEVINE: With Clark Kent we weren't interested in doing nebbishness. We had a whole different Clark Kent. He is a guy, when we first meet him, who has come back from studying Aboriginal Methodology with the natives in Australia and he is someone who is more interested in sociology and learned ballroom dancing from a Nigerian princess. *And* he's actually quite charming. He started out innocent in many ways in the city and he did say he had never been there before, but we created a much more worldly Clark Kent who does not bump into things and who is not a nebbish. We tried to attack the situation of people not recognizing him straight on in the pilot when he puts on the uniform and the big punchline when his mother stares at him in the tights is, "Well, no one is going to be looking at your face." And his father says, "What if somebody *does* recognize you?" Clark replies, "Dad, I'm going to be flying around in this red, blue and yellow thing with a cape. I mean, who is going to even put together the fact that I could be Clark Kent?" Again, it was about trying to attack it head on. At the moment when Lois Lane falls in love with Clark Kent and someone says to her, "You know, he does look a lot like Superman," I think someone else comments, "Every woman in love thinks her man looks like Superman."

DAN LEVINE: We knew in approaching this show that we couldn't invent a new super-villain with superpowers every week, because there was no way to film that and make it look good given our budget and time constraints. On the other hand, we couldn't develop stories wherein Lois and Clark are doing something that Jessica Fletcher could do on *Murder, She Wrote.* We had to find our own middle ground where we exercised some imagination and stepped one second into the future, but still kept the series rooted in reality.

DEBORAH JOY LEVINE: An important thing we did early on is to let people know, through the promotions and advertising, that they were going to see something that they hadn't seen before. From the onset, if I was just going to copy the movies and the previous TV show, I really didn't want to do it. The strange thing is that people who were Superman maniacs really took to this for a number of reasons. First of all, DC Comics was constantly reinventing the myth themselves. As you know, when Superman started, he couldn't even fly until the Fleischer brothers decided he could. And then Ma and Pa Kent were dead until they were reinstated by John Byrne and were no longer dead. Clark Kent became a Pulitzer Prize-winning writer, and he wasn't before. So they were always reinventing the myth. When *I* decided to reinvent the myth to a certain extent, I believed that people were open to that, because there is a certain law and a certain myth about Superman that you *don't* want to change; that will always be there.

BRYCE ZABEL: The movies made Clark Kent the secret identity, and I think that's the wrong choice. If a guy's cool enough to be Superman, if he acts like a bumbler as Clark, that means he's putting on a disguise as Clark. It seems to me that this guy grew up all his life as Clark. The idea that he would put on a costume and would attempt to do good — that's clearly the disguise. Once you make that kind of mind frame shift, it's a paradigm shift in the whole Superman legend. I'm not crediting us exclusively with this. Certainly the comics shifted when John Byrne revised the whole myth. In the world of media, no one had, at that point, looked at it that way — although the original TV series, which I recall running home at 3:30 to watch every day, featured Clark as the real guy too. He was not a bumbler. He also wasn't a very dimensionalized person. I think that's the thing that's so great about *Lois & Clark* is that it was so real; it was absolutely real to us that Clark Kent is a strange visitor from another planet.

DEBORAH JOY LEVINE: The constants about Superman are, A, that he comes from Krypton; B, he can fly; C, he has X-ray vision and he could do this and he would do that and those are inviolate and I wouldn't want to change them. For example, the main twist that I did that people seemed to respond to was — because I wanted a more human Clark — basically instead of, as in the old shows, that it's Superman who came to be and had a disguise for himself as a mild-mannered reporter, what I had was Clark Kent is someone who really wants more than anything else to be human and to have a family and to be a good writer and to be a reporter. He comes to Metropolis, gets a job and finds that because he has these things that he has to use to save people, he's got to invent a costume for himself. So it's basically Clark Kent inventing Superman instead of Superman inventing Clark Kent. As a result of that, we have a much more human side to Clark and to Superman because he is not there to fight for truth, justice and the American way. And when a reporter asks Superman if he is, he says, "Sure," and that becomes the newspaper headline. I was trying to use things that existed and put different takes on them.

ROBERT BUTLER: Updating and changing Superman is an ongoing difficulty, because in one conception you need production, big size and scale. In another permutation, like with *Lois & Clark*, it's totally '90s and you have to be a bit more modest as you focus between the two of them, ergo the title. Ultimately it was our belief that the title defined what we were doing and people would understand, like it and appreciate what we had done, because size isn't what television does best.

DEAN CAIN: If it was a feature, I would say I prefer the huge things, but because it's television, it was tough to do them realistically. So in this medium, at that time, I preferred the closer, more intimate shows, because we could do them more realistically. If we had money to spend on the effects to do things right, I would have loved do the huge things, but it was a tough line to walk and those guys were doing a good job doing it.

DAN LEVINE: One of the things that we did deal with, which is something the comics have dealt with, is because he's so powerful, what the heck do you come up with to make you, as the reader, feel like he could really be in trouble here? According to what they told us, there were attempts to scale him back from being too god-like where they were hard-pressed to come up with challenges for him. Our perception was that if I were to punch Superman, he wouldn't feel it. If the heavyweight champion of the world were to hit him, he'd feel it somewhat. And if he were to get hit by someone with a jackhammer, it would knock him back. Our boxer was equipped with bionics, and when he hit him Superman went flying back. He then shakes it off and readjusts himself so he can take the next punch. Our Superman can't fly through the Sun, he can't breathe without air and he can bleed.

DEBORAH JOY LEVINE: We were also concerned that there had been *a lot* of Supermen around that time. That's why, when we started, we decided that we would do something very different. All of us involved in the project decided that we would do something that people hadn't seen before.

BRYCE ZABEL: I wrote the first episode of the series following the pilot, which was "Strange Visitor (from Another Planet)," and to me it felt more like the show's premise than even the pilot did. Clark realizes how alienated he is. He may look like and pass among humans, but he's not human. And that was a cool thing to be writing about in the same way that light-skinned African-Americans in the past have tried to pass in white culture. It's like what Superman's doing. It was interesting to see him through the eyes of an alien who had been raised my humans.

DEAN CAIN: I know that people are married to their idea of the story and that's okay. But we didn't approach it concerned about them. It was a very '90s version. So what we were trying to do was contemporize a lot of the stories and a lot of the ideas as such and make them basically so that the kids and people could relate a little bit more clearly to some of the things than in the past. If you look at some of the old shows, they're extremely outdated and... I don't want to say sexist, but some of the things, if you look back in the '50s or whenever, it was just a whole different time. We were taking and addressing issues that happened then.

BRYCE ZABEL: I also got to do the first episode about "Kryptonite, "The Green, Green Glow of Home," which was wonderful. I got to put UFOlogy directly into the show by creating a group called Bureau 39.

ROB O'CONNOR: *Lois & Clark* crucially knew from the outset that Superman has always been most interesting as a love story and nowhere else has the relationship between Lane and Kent felt more well-constructed. Teri Hatcher is undoubtedly the best Lois Lane ever — as brilliant as she is flawed, racked by imperfections and neuroses, unwilling to be sidelined in a man's world almost as much as she is unwilling to allow herself to fall for mild-mannered Clark Kent when she could stay fantasizing about the Man of Steel. Every version of Lois Lane falls victim to dated, sexist tropes and awkward writing and this character-driven version is particularly egregious at times, but even in these moments Hatcher's performance (and her chemistry with Dean Cain) shines through.

TERI HATCHER: Before I had read it, I thought this was just not something I could do because of the stereotype attached to it. But as soon as I read it... You read so few scripts for women where the character is so broad and full, *and* can be smart and funny and vulnerable and sexy and goofy, and to have all of that happen in one character rather than just sexy or just smart, is wonderful. And I love comedy so much and that romantic bent and all of that was apparent in Deborah's writing that it just felt like I had to do this… right from when I read it the first time. It ended up being extremely challenging for me because I got to go *everywhere*. I got to go from being mad to exposing every vulnerability that you have on a dime. *That's* why I wanted to do it.

Helping to bring Lois & Clark *to life was the pilot's director Robert Butler, who had deservedly earned the reputation at the time of being known as the "King of the TV" pilots. Look at the man's track record in terms of pilots that would ultimately lead to series:* Happy *(1960), the first* Star Trek *pilot, "The Cage" (1964),* Run for Your Life *(1965),* Shane *(1966),* Batman *(1966),* Doc Elliot *(1973),* The Blue Knight *(1975),* Hill Street Blues *(1981),* Moonlighting *(1985),* Our Family Honor *(1985),* Remington Steele *(which he co-created, 1982),* Midnight Caller *(1988),* Sirens *(1993) and, after* Lois & Clark, Sisters *(1991) and* The Division *(2001).*

ROBERT BUTLER: I had a "housekeeping" deal at Lorimar, which is to say Warner Bros. television, and the guys shot me the script, which I adored. It was in a similar tone to *Moonlighting* and *Batman*, which I did years ago, so I'm kind of tuned to that spoofy sort of material. I liked it and thought, "Why not?" I think I talked to somebody in mid-December and by mid-January casting was underway and away we went.

DEBORAH JOY LEVINE: Bob Butler is this huge, big, imposing Irish guy. When I first met him I was like, "Oh crap, this guy's scaring the hell out of me." It was my first show and I thought, "Oh my God, is he going to bark at me?" But we became so close during that show and every morning we'd meet before we'd shoot and we'd sit in his little Mercedes and say, "All right, what are we gonna shoot today?" And the great thing is Bob Butler became really attached to me and was basically telling the studio, "Deborah and I are gonna do what we want." And when they would send someone down from the studio, Bob would call "Cut" and walk over to them, towering over them and saying, "Can I help you?" So Bob and I were a force to be reckoned with.

DEAN CAIN: When I saw Robert Butler — who's just a legend — was there, I was like, "Wow, it's Robert Butler!" I knew about *Hill Street Blues* and all the other things, and that was like, "Here's the guy!" But I walked in and he was such a regular, affable guy. I said, "I think I have an interesting take on this or a different take or a unique take," and he said, "All right, let's see it. No bullshit." And I did it and I read and he goes, "Okay, thanks." That was it and I said, "Thank you all. Bye." I didn't see or hear anything. Normally after an audition you hear *something*: "Hey, they really loved you today" or whatever. Or within the next day; you usually hear within a few hours. Two days and done. Just pack it away in the things that could've been, and I didn't hear anything for weeks.

Born Dean George Tanaka on July 31, 1966 in Mount Clemens, Michigan, Cain is the son of Roger Tanaka and actress Sharon Thomas. In 1969, she would marry director Christopher Cain (Young Guns, The Next Karate Kid), who in turn would adopt Dean and his brother Roger. Eventually they would move to Malibu, CA where Christopher and Sharon had a daughter Krisinda. Dean attended Santa Monica High School, growing up with a number of celebrities and playing sports with many of them. From high school, he attended Princeton University, where he played football and won the Poe Trophy, a top award, and graduated in 1988 with a Bachelor of Arts in history.

DEAN CAIN: I grew up around Chris Penn, Sean Penn, Rob Lowe, Charlie Sheen, Emilio Estevez — my dad directed them in *Young Guns*. I grew up playing football with Chris, baseball with Charlie, watching Sean surf. I was the top athlete in high school and won what's called the Lauren D. Switchenburg Award. All these other kids were becoming very famous actors, and I had the ability to watch them go out there and become the Sexiest Man on Earth and all that sort of thing, and then watch them make horrendously dumb mistakes as young people would do — and as I may have done at that age as well if I hadn't had the upbringing and the education that I had, getting in college, in flag football and playing in the NFL. You realize there's a humility that comes with that while these guys were out there getting told how wonderful, how sexy, how amazing they are. And sometimes you believe it.

Right after graduation, Cain was signed as a free agent with the Buffalo Bills — a dream come true — but during training camp he suffered a knee injury so severe that it ended a potential career in football.

DEAN CAIN: My NFL career was over *really* quickly. I started thinking about acting, and my father — who adopted me when I was four — said three words to me: "Don't do it." I need to say, he's been such a strong guiding force in my life, it's unbelievable. That's why the greatest respect I could pay him was to name my son after him. But he said, "Don't be an actor. Don't go into this industry, because it's mean. They're going to say you're too tall, you're too short, you're too fat, your hair is too dark, your skin is the wrong complexion, you're Japanese, you're this, you're that. Even if you do a great job, you go out there and win an Academy Award, there are going to be people saying, 'I thought that performance sucked; he's wooden as an actor.' You're opening yourself to such ridicule. Why would you want to do that?" I, of course, didn't listen to him and decided to do it anyway.

He also decided to give screenwriting a shot during his years on Lois & Clark, and at one point his father said to him, "Dean, I don't care how long you're going to be an actor, and I don't mean any disrespect by this, but you're never going to be as good an actor as you are a writer right now."

DEAN CAIN: I know it was a compliment, but it felt like I'd been slapped in the face. I'd written for him and behind him on 30 projects. I've written seven or eight screenplays; some novel adaptations, some just from the concept, some completely on spec. He said, "It doesn't matter how pretty you are, or if you bust your knee, when you're writing, nobody cares. When you're an actor, all that stuff matters." Maybe that's part of the reason I've been so diversified from the very get-go. I mean, I like doing a lot of different things, but if I go back in my life and look at when I was an athlete in high school, I didn't just hang out with the athletes. I've always just made my own way, and I think that becomes a strength in life.

Early on, he scored small roles in several films, and guest starred on such shows as A Different World, Grapevine and four episodes of the original Beverly Hills 90210. Then came the opportunity to play the Man of Steel.

ROBERT BUTLER: At first we were thinking of a more mature man — you know, a guy that had sort of kicked around the world and so on, as Clark Kent seemed to have been in all the other permutations.

DEBORAH JOY LEVINE: The funny story about Dean is that DC Comics had really ingrained in me that Clark Kent was supposed to be the typical 30-year-old man. Dean Cain was the first guy to read for me and my friend Lorna Johnson, who was one of the casting directors at the time; and Barbara Miller, a real legend who's deceased now, brought him in and afterwards I turned to Lorna and I said, "What are you doing? I'm casting *Superman*, not *Superboy*." At the time he came in, I swear to you, he looked like he was 17 years old. I just thought Superman had to be older.

ROBERT BUTLER: There *was* discussion about his youth, but he was certainly ingenuous and kind of sincere and all of that. We had barely known about him from *Beverly Hills 90210*. He comported himself really well and, like I said, we discussed his age for a bit and then saw a number of other actors before going back to him.

DEAN CAIN: Listen, I was just trying to get a job to pay the bills. I didn't know what it was going to be. I was a young kid trying to figure out how to work in this acting world. I've watched all these other guys do it, and then I started to get into the real business of it and would go out there and do it on my own. My dad wasn't out there helping me out. He put me in a couple of films early on just to get my feet wet, but that was it. I was out there running around and dealing with so much rejection. It was then that Superman came up, though it wasn't so much Superman as it was the character of Clark Kent. I read the script and thought, "Wow, this is great. I can completely understand this guy."

And then a friend who worked in casting at Warner Bros. told me that I had made a positive impression and the studio was interested. Then he said, "They really like you and they're going to start bringing in actors to do all the pairing ups," which was to see which Clarks worked best with which Loises. I came in and there were still dozens of men — Supermen, if you will — including actors I recognized. We started going through the process and eventually I started thinking, "Wow, I've got a shot at this." And I remember exactly what it was. After we'd been doing this and they were pairing us up, I knew I was in the mix. I didn't know if I was the front runner by any stretch of the imagination, but they wrote a scene that was never actually in a script. Clark Kent is at home at night and Lois Lane bursts in, she's intoxicated, and she wants to get it on. Clark, of course, won't do it, because he's so moral and she's intoxicated. Were she *not*, you'd better believe he probably would have. But the fact that she was not in her right mind, he doesn't. And *that* was the character. When I saw that scene, it was no work at all for me.

DEBORAH JOY LEVINE: I had never seen Dean before we were casting, and the strange story about that is that Dean was the *first* person to read for the show. Period. For any part. So he was the first victim, so to speak. We looked at over 100 people. Not a lot of them came in personally. We saw tapes, other things. I knew we were in good shape with Dean when he came back, maybe for the third time, and when I was walking down to the casting department, there were all these young women hanging around and I thought they were there trying out. But the casting associate said, "Oh no, they heard Dean Cain was here." Apparently he'd been on *90210* or something else, and they were already in love with him. So I had him read again and this time I thought, "*Wow.*" I'm not sure what changed. Partly it was my perception and the other thing is that he had this look about him — he's one-quarter Japanese — that was a little bit otherworldly; just this thing that was a little more than human.

DEAN CAIN: Auditioning was the easy part. What I thought was more challenging was that I was going for the lead of a show. I was just hoping as a young actor that I was likeable. I had no idea if I could carry a series. I had no clue. I didn't know what that would feel like or what it would look like or how it would be perceived. So there *was* a bit of nerves, plus all that talk about chemistry. Choosing two people to have chemistry on film is a very difficult thing, and if I knew how to do it, then I would be the casting guru of Hollywood.

TERI HATCHER: We were so lucky because Dean and I had on-screen chemistry from the first day we started working together. From what I understood from talking to the producers, it's something you either luck in to or you don't. It has nothing to do with being good actors or bad actors. It just sort of happens and that happened with us.

DEBORAH JOY LEVINE: I guess the most surprising thing for me, because I grew up in a household where we didn't read comic books — we were reading Shakespeare — when I *did* start to read the comic books, was how sophisticated they'd become, and this definitely came into play with the casting, the artwork and the dialogue. And when I went to New York to meet with all the comic book writers, I suppose they thought, "Here's this Hollywood writer, this snobby woman coming to look down on us." And, in fact, what happened is that I got there and said, "You guys are fantastic." The writing was really terrific and the stories were complex. There were beginnings, middles and ends, and sometimes in Hollywood we didn't even have stories that good. So I was very surprised and happy to see the sophistication of the comic book. I did see all the *Superman* movies, but had never seen the *Superboy* series.

DEAN CAIN: My background with Superman at the time is that I saw the films of course, but I had never seen the old George Reeves series. I did see the *Super Friends* cartoons, and I think that's where I got most of my Superman background. I wasn't an avid comic book reader at all, but I did watch cartoons. And I started when I was a kid, and that was something that I sort of grew up with. I found it strange because I'd run into a lot of people who *really* were well-versed in Superman's background. There was a guy one day who listed all the different kinds of Kryptonite for me. I had *no* idea. I had a little homework to do, but we were creating a little bit of a different background and different things. I thought it was almost to my benefit that I didn't know, especially for the way the character on this show was. He didn't know everything and it was a lot of self-discovery, and that was very interesting for me because in the beginning I didn't know where he was headed and what was going to happen.

CRAIG BYRNE: The best part of Dean's Clark is that he was a good guy before he was even Superman. The opening hour of the pilot sees him saving people from a careening bus, or he would take the moment to speak to an old actress and ask why she is so upset about a theater being demolished. Even once he's Superman, he'd rescue kittens from trees and do those things Superman is expected to do. If a tornado came speeding toward his father, he'd save his dad. I liked that Dean's Clark allowed himself to have fun with his abilities — and especially in those early seasons, the chemistry between Dean Cain and Teri Hatcher.

DEAN CAIN: I *did* feel a deep connection with Clark Kent and Superman. As a character, Superman was always my favorite superhero because he could do everything. He was amazing. When I was cast, there were people from my junior high school, high school and even college days that weren't that shocked. They joked, "Dude, you've been Superman for 15 years already." I would never say my morality was as good as Clark Kent's or Superman's, but the things that I'd done, and I worked hard and was a positive, straight-forward guy, and didn't have any ill will toward anybody — and still don't. That's part of the whole thing with Superman: There's a kindness that's really important for the character that you have to have.

When it came to Lois Lane, the choice ultimately came down to Teri Lynn Hatcher, born December 8, 1964 in Palo Alto, California. Growing up in Sunnyvale, California, she took ballet lessons and attended De Anza College, where she studied mathematics and engineering. She made the shift to the American Conservatory Theater, where she studied acting. In 1984 she became an NFL cheerleader for the San Francisco 49ers, and a year later became one of the "Mermaid" showgirls on ABC's The Love Boat. *Roles followed on shows like* MacGyver, Karen's Song, Night Court, Star Trek: The Next Generation, Quantum Leap *and* L.A. Law.

ROBERT BUTLER: Teri Hatcher we had all known about for a long time. I had worked with her on another pilot and subsequently she'd done the sitcom *Sunday Dinner*, among many other things, so it was good to see her again. We did some talking about how she could land the job, and she did.

DEBORAH JOY LEVINE: Let me tell you about Teri Hatcher. She came in to read and her hair was down to her waist and it was a *mess*. She had no makeup on, she was dressed like a slob, but when she started to read that scene I thought, "I'm not going to see anybody else." She was brilliant; not a Dean Cain kind of thing where I needed to see another 150 people. That was it for me. She was just *right*. And it's funny, because I had a conversation with her afterwards about cutting her hair. She said to me, "But my hair is sort of my calling card. That's who I am, my hair." I remember very clearly saying to her, "Lois Lane would not have your hair. Lois Lane needs to get up in the morning, run a brush through it and go out and get the story." And that next day she came back with a Bob.

DEAN CAIN: I found myself paired off with Paula Marshall, who I thought was amazing, and one other actress, but *not* Teri Hatcher, who was there, but we hadn't actually met. At the same time another studio was interested in me, so it forced Warner Bros. and ABC's collective hand to make a decision, and they went with me. That happened on a Thursday, and to celebrate a friend and I took a skiing trip, which had to be cut short when they asked me to come back to the studio on Monday so I could read with potential Lois Lanes.

They brought 10 girls in and I read with nine of them in that same scene where she bursts in the door, is intoxicated and wants to sleep with Clark. But I'm in front of the network and I'm mortified now, because as comfortable as I had been — and happy to have the job — I was also very green and concerned that they were going to watch me with all these different Loises and realize, "Maybe he isn't our guy." But *they* didn't seem nervous about it. It took me a few takes, but the first thing that happened is she bursts in, smacks a big old kiss on my lips, and then the scene progresses from there. It was very funny; you know, kissing 10 different girls in a row was fantastic. And the final person was Teri Hatcher. She was the last person I was going to read with, and they said, "Teri, would you like to run lines before we do it?" So I went in to run lines with her. I said, "Hi," and she said — I kid you not — "You don't like me, do you?"

Which, it should be pointed out, was not Lois Lane talking to Clark Kent, but Teri Hatcher talking directly to Dean Cain.

DEAN CAIN: She says, "We've been on these things and you haven't said a word to me or anything." And I was like, "I've been scratching for my life trying to get a job here. I wasn't going to go up and talk to *anybody*. I don't have anything against you; I have no feelings one way or the other." Then we did the scene, and it was clear that she was the best actress *and* the best kisser of the bunch. It was sweet and fun and it worked from there. The relationship on and off camera was great. You know, things get strained here and there over time by a number of different factors, one of them being the fact that you're there 18 hours a day. She'd gotten married after the first season and I don't know how well that was working out by the end; they'd ended up getting a divorce. I had a couple of different girlfriends during that period of time, but the show just takes over your life.

TERI HATCHER: The script was so great and even though I had apprehension about getting involved with the Superman story, I felt strongly about doing it. I was already having some success in doing movies and I didn't want to get stereotyped. But I decided to do it once I read it and saw that it was so well-written and so much like those classic screwball and romantic comedies like *His Girl Friday*.

CRAIG BYRNE: You could absolutely see why Dean Cain's Clark would fall in love with this Lois Lane. She was bold, she was brilliant, she was fun. She had a hard exterior but Clark saw through that, and that banter was well-performed by both actors. Personally, Teri Hatcher is my favorite Lois Lane, just because she was able to juggle so many different aspects of the character.

DEBORAH JOY LEVINE: Let me say off the bat that I was a huge fan of *Superman: The Movie*. And I did love the relationship between Superman and Lois; there's some classic stuff in there. When he catches her and says, "I've got you," and she says, "You've got me? Who's got you?" — just fabulous and unforgettable. I still think she was a little mooney-eyed and a little too weak, but here we had a different Lois who is stronger and, I think, more capable. For its time, this was much more like *Moonlighting* if Bruce Willis could fly.

Margot Kidder's Lois Lane was kind of ditzy. She was somebody who also needed to be saved — a *lot*. I think in the comics you see a Lois Lane who works out, and if somebody mugs her she chases him across the street and gives him a karate kick. The Lois Lane of this show is more of a woman of the '90s and she doesn't really need Clark to save her all the time — or someone to save her all the time. She is really a dedicated reporter and very capable of taking care of herself, except for the fact that sometimes her zealousness in wanting to get a story does lead her into some problems. Although the problem we explored that nobody else really explored is the fact that she is a true typical professional woman of the '90s in that she has no social life and she does go home and watch soap operas and cries and thinks about the fact that she has no romance in her life — although she would never admit it to anybody else.

TERI HATCHER: I think this brings you to that "woman in Hollywood" discussion that you're always hearing about. The continuance of the lack of well-written roles for women in films or in television was also a draw for me. I felt at its best it could be a vehicle for getting me that extra inch ahead in the feature industry. But that would never be the sole reason for doing anything. I think episodic hour drama television is the hardest thing you can do. You work an average of 14 hours a day and you can't really imagine what that is until you do it. I knew that going in and I would never want to come somewhere that many hours a day that I didn't really enjoy. We would kid around on the set a lot and the work was challenging enough for me personally. There was a lot of physical comedy and the writers really gave me a chance to stretch my abilities, so that made it challenging and rewarding and worth putting all that energy in for.

DEBORAH JOY LEVINE: I wanted Lois as important as Clark Kent, and that was also a bone of contention because people were thinking viewers were going to tune in to see this show because of Superman, and because he can see through walls and he can fly and whatever, but I also wanted to get to the meat of what I wanted to do, which was this burgeoning romance between them.

BRYCE ZABEL: When it comes to Lois and Clark, one of the things I feel I contributed, that made the biggest possible difference in the series, is that when the series began with the pilot, Lois and Clark were competitors at the *Daily Planet.* So you had to find a story that they could compete on, but then you'd see what Clark was doing about it and then you'd see what Lois was doing about it, and then you had to find ways to bring them together. For the first six episodes we did that at great cost. It was always like, "Okay, how are Clark and Lois going to get to work? How's this going to work?" It wasn't my show, but I was the supervising producer, so I felt like it was my job to try and make things work if, in my perception, they're not working. So I came in one day and said, "I have a solution to our problem." And my solution was that you have to do the inevitable: Lois and Clark have to be a team. Period. So, in fact, it wasn't about the love relationship, it was the professional thing. We were working so hard to get them together over the course of the episodes, but if they were a team, they could be competitors *within* the team. *And* they could fall in love within the team. Superman can keep secrets from Lois in a team, but at least they're in the same scenes more often than not. And that really unlocked everything for the rest of the series.

DEBORAH JOY LEVINE: There was a huge difference between working with Dean Cain and working with Teri Hatcher, because Dean was somewhat of a novice. He had been a guest in a couple of shows, he'd never actually been a star. Teri had been in a couple of features at that point and was bent for stardom. So it was a little different. The thing about Teri was that she could always find the comedy in a line, and she could always do the line better than I ever imagined. I remember we were at a cast read-through once, and I'm a big parenthetical writer — what that means is that if I want the character to say sadly, I'll say, "Lois (sadly), I'm in love with you," or whatever. We're sitting at this big read read-through, it must have been 25 people at the table, and Teri Hatcher starts to read her part, stops, looks at me way across the table and says, "Cut the parentheticals; I know how you want me to say it." And while it was a little embarrassing to have her say that to me in front of everybody, boy, she was right. She didn't need parentheticals. She knew *exactly* how to say these lines. I can't tell you what a brilliant actress she is.

BRYCE ZABEL: I thought Teri was fantastic. She was a bit of a diva, but she was terrific. I do remember one time I was out on the Warner Bros. lot and I saw one of the assistant directors with one of those little wheels that the insurance guys use at a crash site to measure distances. Now, of course, you don't have to do that; I think now you could just fire a laser from your phone and measure distance, but back then you were rolling around. So this guy, who I know, is rolling down the street and I ask, "What are you doing?" And he says, "This is a little weird, man, but Teri thinks that Dean's trailer is closer to the set." So he measured it and Dean's was, I believe, four feet closer. So they moved Teri's to the same distance. Usually that's the behavior you *don't* get in a first season from somebody. I'm not quite sure what was going through her head. I know she was under a lot of pressure and I also have to say, to me, personally, she was a sweetheart. I don't think I've seen her since, but she treated me nice, which was interesting, because everybody knew the power out there was Deborah. If you had to please anybody, you better please Deborah; Bryce, not so much. Neither of them were script divas.

DEBORAH JOY LEVINE: Dean is one of the greatest guys ever. He had no problem in our myriad of a thousand fittings, getting the suit to look right on him and making it part of the story and being comfortable in the suit. He never complained about it. He knew the part he was playing. In fact, early on in the season, I had written something — I forget what it was — and he turned to me and said, "Superman wouldn't say that." My first thought was, "How do *you* know what Superman would say?" But then I realized he really had become that character while he was obviously doing the part, and that he was invested in it and everything that came out of his mouth was so sincere. I mean, he may not have been the most polished of actors, but that didn't matter because he said everything with such truthfulness and sincerity that it just came out real. And that was the beauty of his acting.

BRYCE ZABEL: Dean had a real decency in essence and I never saw any politics from the guy at the time. I have since then of course, and I know that he's politically conservative. But you know what? Screw that. As long as he wasn't occupying the Capitol, he can be whatever he wants. He can have his own opinions and I always thought he was a decent guy. He treated me decently.

The next major role to be cast was that of Lex Luthor, who would be the show's regular villain in the first season. Eventually the part when to actor John Shea, born April 14, 1949 in North Conway, New Hampshire. Things kicked off for him as an actor in the mid-'70s when he starred in Yentl *on Broadway, taking home a Theatre World Award. TV and film roles followed, with the actor taking home a 1988 Emmy for his role in* Baby M. *Prior to* Lois & Clark, *he was in a total of 19 films, yet it was the series that brought him the most attention.*

DEBORAH JOY LEVINE: When it comes to villains, the way I envisioned it, and the way I told my writer to envision it, is more like the villains of 007. In other words, they are larger-than-life like Goldfinger — you know, cover people with gold and they perish. We tried to come up with really innovative and interesting villainy that was not necessarily someone who is from another planet. Luthor, of course, was going to be ever-present. I mean, here's Metropolis, a bright and shiny city, but the evil underneath usually leads to Lex Luthor.

ROBERT BUTLER: John Shea seemed a little different for Lex Luthor, but very credible. And that I thought was nice, because in some of the Superman movies, some of the villains got a little wild and that robs credibility in my mind. So when John brought credibility, I thought that was a good thing for him to have done. Ultimately all the political angles fell the right way, and by political angles I mean the network, the studio, ourselves, him — all of that stuff has to kind of be in sync and it was.

JOHN SHEA (actor, "Lex Luthor," *Lois & Clark: The New Adventures of Superman*)**:** In those days I was living in Los Angeles with my wife and kid, and one day my manager called me up and said, "Would you be interested in reading a script? They're doing a Superman show at Warner Bros. and they're looking for somebody to play Lex Luthor." Well I read that script and it was like love at first sight. It's like driving into a town and saying, "I want to live there." I knew Lex Luthor as a kid, I had grown up with him, reading the comic books, watching the original television show — I'm a big fan of the Superman franchise. And as I read this pilot script for *Lois & Clark*, I saw in my mind how Lex Luthor should be. It seemed to be that he should be a combination of Cary Grant or, in those days, Donald Trump — *in those days*. Also that he should wear cool suits and really feel like a ladies' man, but at the time you should think of Richard III; a total sociopath. So I worked on this audition at my home and drove to Warner Bros. I went into the office of the president of Warner Bros. and he said, "What do you want to do?"

In the 1990s, Dean Cain and Teri Hatcher nailed the romantic relationship between Clark Kent and Lois Lane (© and TM DC Comics/Warner Bros. Discovery)

I wanted to do this one speech that he gives and a couple of scenes. The way I thought of him is that he would be absolutely charming and *Metro* and there should be nothing overtly villain about him.

Even though I love Lex Luthor, he is our sociopath. He's like a lot of Presidents of the United States and heads of foreign countries and heads of major corporations — these are guys with no conscience. They are only after one thing, and that's to satisfy their appetites. And whatever their appetites might be, just get out of their way.

DEBORAH JOY LEVINE: I never asked him to go bald, because I really wanted his evilness to come out just in terms of who he was and what he was capable of. I thought that if I made him bald, it would sort of almost be humorous. I really didn't want any of that, because my whole philosophy was that this is really a game of good versus evil. That was my thinking between Superman and Lex Luthor, and at one point, in one of my shows, I even have Luthor saying, "Well, you're never going to win, because evil is going to win. I'm willing to blow up a school bus full of children in order to get what I want. And you're not. You're too moral, so you're never going to win." So this whole thing of good versus evil was the background of where I wanted Lex Luthor to be. I just wanted him to be suave, because I really think that if there is such a thing as a devil, they're not going to have horns. They're going to look like a CEO. Whatever horns Lex Luthor was going to have, meaning his bald head or whatever, I thought that evil also looks like that. DC Comics had no problem with this.

JOHN SHEA: I used to joke about the fact that Superman inherited all of his stuff while Lex Luthor *earned* all of his. But the truth about Superman is that Clark has a great heart. He is a good person and that goodness will always triumph over badness, evil, greed, unconscious desires to dominate and hurt people.

ROBERT BUTLER: John came in, very much hat in hand, respectfully saying he would really love to do it and please consider him. He hadn't done this kind of thing before, but he was certainly up to it. I think he read a couple of times, certainly wonderfully and ultimately the choice went to him.

ALAN BURKE: Look at how good John Shea is as Lex Luthor. There's that scene in the pilot where he's explaining to everybody in his penthouse for a big launch of his satellite or his space station, and he explains to Clark and Lois how he loves that everybody in the city has to look up to him. And then Superman, at the end, gives the line right back to him: "If you ever need to find me, just look up." And you can see the seething in John Shea's face.

CRAIG BYRNE: Watching years later, he's more manic than I recalled the first time around, but I think he fit the show very well. I wish we had seen more of him after season one, and I still remember how shocked I was when Lex jumped from the rooftop at the end of the first season. John Shea's excuse for not being bald — that he's rich, so of course he can find a way to have hair — was amusing, and I never quite figured out why he was bald when he returned for season two but never again later.

JOHN SHEA: The three of us — Teri Hatcher, Dean Cain and I — show up at Warner Bros. for the very first reading of the script, and they had the other principal members of the cast come in. We sat around the table and read the script, and I can tell you, from that very first moment I knew we were going to be a hit, because the script was so well-written. Deborah Joy Levine was a huge Superman fan who knew how to write for men and she knew how to write for women. But what she brought to the *Lois & Clark* concept was a kind of romantic triangle where Lex Luthor was going to be a part of it. It was a very different take on the whole thing.

Walter Lane Smith III — professionally known as Lane Smith — was cast as Perry White, editor-in-chief of the Daily Planet. *Born April 29, 1936 in Memphis, Tennessee, he studied acting at the Actors Studio in the late 1950s and early 1960s. Steady work in the New York theater was followed by small roles in films like* Rooster Cogburn *(1975),* Network *(1976) and* Prince of the City *(1981). A breakout year for him was 1984 when he appeared in the films* Red Dawn *and* Places in the Heart, *the following year taking on the part of Nathan Bates in* V: The Series, *spun off of two enormously popular miniseries. His portrayal of Perry White is still considered one of the strongest ever. The actor would pass away of Lou Gehrig's disease on June 13, 2005 at the age of 69.*

DEBORAH JOY LEVINE: Instead of "Great Caesar's Ghost," we had Perry White say, "Great Shades of Elvis," and I guess the biggest compliment paid to me is that DC then had Perry White in the comics saying the same thing. How that came about had to do with Lane Smith, our Perry White, who is from the South and it just seemed very natural for him to be saying something about Elvis. Part of his character is that he is a true devoted Elvis fan, even in death.

BRYCE ZABEL: I met Lane Smith on my first show *Kay O'Brien* in 1986, so I knew him very well when he came to the show. He was a terrific Perry White with all his "Great Shades of Elvis." I was sorry to see him go early. Because I'm a journalist by training, I liked being able to write Perry in there. Even in "Strange Visitor," Lois and Clark know they've got the story of this Bureau 39 and they bring Perry down to show him the warehouse where all this stuff is kept — and of course it's empty. I just really liked writing that scene because Perry knows what it's like to be a young reporter and he knows that they'd seen the evidence even though it's not there. He has to be the guy that says, "I feel for you, but this isn't enough. You need to go home and take some time and get back on the horse." That means that in the first episode they did after the pilot, Lois and Clark fail at getting the story. And what does happen in that first episode is that there was some feeling of completion when Lois is given the story of Superman by Clark, because he pretty much knows that Lois is in pain over not getting the story that they worked on together. It's a very touching moment and something I was very happy about.

LANE SMITH (actor, "Perry White," *Lois & Clark: The New Adventures of Superman***):** I didn't know whether I wanted to do another television series. I was really on the fence about this. My movie career was moving along pretty well, but they sent over the script and I looked at this thing and came up with this idea of making Perry White just totally outrageous. I figured they weren't going to buy this in a million years, but I went over, read for them and they just loved what I did and we signed a contract that afternoon.

DEBORAH JOY LEVINE: Lane Smith and Bob Butler nearly came to blows during the pilot. They were arguing about something — I can't remember what it was — and they were both kind of adamant about it. I passed by Lane's trailer and I heard them yelling at each other. I was like, "What's going on in there?" and they're saying, "You don't want to know." I never found out what it was about, but I'll tell you right now: Bob won. He always won.

ROBERT BUTLER: Lane Smith was always a good actor that one considers for a mature man. Michael Landes, who played Jimmy Olsen in the first season, came in and did a knockout job in the audition and I don't think we ever swerved from him. Tracy Scoggins, of course, is a luscious animal who's been around a bit. Everyone knew about her and she was a good potential candidate for Cat Grant from the get-go. That's a capsule of how the casting went.

Two additional integral cast members were K Callan and Eddie Jones as Clark's adopted parents Martha and Jonathan Kent. They may have been back in Smallville, but the distance, for Clark, was easily transversed.

ALAN BURKE: There was the chemistry between Clark and his parents, Eddie Jones as Jonathan Kent and K Callan as Martha. The fact that Kal-El is a lone orphan jettisoned from a dying planet moments before its total destruction is enough tragedy for one character. Allowing the Kents to survive well into Clark's adulthood allows for a lovely dynamic in which he has loving parents to counsel him, to guide him and to care for him as he navigates the trials of adulthood. In this version of the story, Clark often returns to Smallville to seek the advice of his parents when he is unsure of what to do both as Clark and as Superman. K Callan and Eddie Jones play the parts of Martha and Jonathan Kent with so much heart, I doubt you would find a single viewer that would not believe that they were Clark Kent's real-life loving parents.

SAM RIZZO: I love the *Superboy* show and I really enjoyed *Lois & Clark*. The first two seasons I thought were fantastic. I met K Callan, who played Martha Kent, about three years ago in Hollywood, and I told her the scene where she and Clark are standing in front of the mirror and he takes the glasses off, combined with the music of that moment, still gives me goosebumps. One of the things I love about *Lois & Clark* was the fact that Martha and Jonathan were part of developing the Superman character, helping Clark all the way.

As with every other live-action version of Superman that had been produced, one of the greatest challenges came in the form of flying sequences as well as trying to present special effects on what was a limited budget.

DEBORAH JOY LEVINE: The flying process is a real art to get it looking different. Part of the reason I was watching all the *Superman* movies is that I wanted our Clark to fly differently. I wanted him to fly more like a guy out on a Sunday fly. We studied that for a long time to try and get the look of the flying to be different.

ALAN BURKE: In almost any scene where Dean Cain is Superman, you can laugh about the effects; they're *not* great effects. You can often see the wire work. At the same time, when *Lois & Clark* came on, I didn't really know about the books or anything else. I had the four Christopher Reeve movies, but then there was a weekly Superman TV movie — or that's how it felt to me — a different movie every week where I could see Superman doing Superman stuff, and I loved it.

TERI HATCHER: I didn't really think about the flying and all of that as something that would be really fun. I mean, I'm very athletic and I like that, but I didn't think about it until we got to shooting those things. Then you think, "Oh, this is going to be really great. How fun getting to fly and then you put on these miserable harnesses and wear them for six hours, and get bruises all over your body. But the greatest thing about that shot in the first episode where we fly into the *Daily Planet*, where Dean and I are hanging about 30 feet in the air, you're out there for about 10 minutes, waiting for the camera to roll and everything, and we're kind of *not* so comfortable, but then they say, "Okay, we're getting ready to roll." We get into position and Dean picks me up, which is really miserable, because he's like straining his biceps and I'm sucking in my stomach, but as soon as they say, "Action," you start moving. The doors open and everyone's busy milling around the *Daily Planet* and we fly in. After we shot it the first time, I came down and said to Deborah, "That is the most romantic thing a woman could ever, ever do." It was *amazing.*

DEAN CAIN: It can be *very* painful. God, we spent five days doing it and I also had to do some practice time, learning how to fly. It's really difficult because you have two wires coming out just at my hips and you have to straighten out and your whole body has to tense. I called this specific headache — I get a headache really badly — the "green screen headache." After three days in that, every time I'd tense my body up, my head felt like it was going to explode. It got easier for me. It's like anything else: The more you do, the more your body adjusts its balance and things.

JIM MICHAELS (producer, *Lois & Clark: The New Adventures of Super-man*): They'd shot a bunch of green screen of Dean flying in the pilot and they kept trying to reuse it. What we eventually did was set up a couple of days on the green screen so that we could shoot a big library of shots. The problem was always Dean's availability, because he was so heavily in the show and was always working. But we finally got to the point where we could dedicate a couple of days to capturing all sorts of green screen stuff and we'd just digitally remove the rigging. As a result, any time the editor wanted to use it, he had to go through the library of green screen footage to find something that would work. And with Dean, we made those days work by having a pair of masseuses waiting for him when he came down. He'd be up on wires for 10 minutes at a time, which is actually a lot, because it takes a lot of core strength to do it, and Dean was in amazing shape. Then he'd come down and they'd massage him, loosen him up and he'd keep going. That made all the difference in the world, allowing us to get many more shots than we otherwise would have been able to.

We would still have to go back and shoot background plates for individual episodes, but in the end this saved a lot of time and money. Another solve was for us to create our own visual effects department, so everything moved in house rather than having to depend on outside vendors.

DEBORAH JOY LEVINE: CGI and green screen and all of this was rather unheard of in television. I remember the first green screen we went to, I looked at Bob Butler and said, "Do you know what you're doing?" and he said, "Absolutely not. I've never done this before. How about you?" and I said, "Absolutely not, not a clue." And he's like, "We'll figure it out together. Roll film!" I thought the effects continued to get better, but I remember one episode where we had a billboard coming down on someone and Superman saved her, which was a good stunt. However, I would have preferred for him to save 500 people from a roller coaster that was going into the ocean. *That* could be frustrating on television.

DAN LEVINE: The budget forced us to be clever. We often talked about gags, a moment out of the story where Clark in his daily passage through life runs across a situation where he has to use his superpowers. These were fun for the audience and they were fun for us. One gag would be that a kid lets go of his balloon, is upset by it and Superman flies up, catches the balloon and brings it back to him. But to film this created a lot of problems. It's a lot of wire work, it takes a lot of time and it can mean, in our tight shooting schedule, that we don't have time for things which are more integral to the story. So we cheat. What we do is we see the kid is crying, the balloon is floating up to the sky, his mother says, "C'mon, Billy we've got to go," and she grabs him around the corner. Then around the corner is Clark Kent holding the balloon and he hands it back to him. So we kind of skip the middle part, which we would have difficulty doing, but still retain the flavor of what it would be like to be Superman. In some ways this could be perceived as a strength. If you overload the superpowers too much, it becomes less interesting. I think you wear it out. Not that I want to hold this up as a model, but the series *The Incredible Hulk* limited his transformations, because if you did it all the time it would get boring. So we wanted to save Superman in the suit for things that really required that level of participation, and occasionally have Clark do something superish just as an aside.

ROBERT BUTLER: I winced a little bit at the cheating myself, but it might be that the audience sees so much big production with movies that I think maybe they were relieved at our sketching and short-cutting, and I think they blessed us for it. As we say, that isn't what the tube is about. The tube is about sly.

By all reports, the producers of Lois & Clark *had a fairly easygoing relationship with DC Comics in regards to things they wanted to do on the show, with the comics company mostly taking a hands-off approach to the show. That wasn't necessarily the way it was.*

BRYCE ZABEL: DC didn't give us carte blanche to change things. I thought they did. In fact I sat there at lunches and dinner with the DC guys where they said, "We're the comic book, you're the show. You get to do your thing and we'll do our thing." But that never turned out to be right. We tried to do something that they've done many times now, where we tried to introduce black into the costume. We tried to take out red and put in black or something so we'd have a more traditional-looking Superman. Frankly, costume dynamics have changed so much for the better. If you look at the costume Tyler Hoechlin gets to wear on *Superman & Lois*, it actually looks sort of like if you were an alien and operating on Earth. It's a form of clothing one might wear on an alien planet. But the *Lois & Clark* costume doesn't look like anything anybody would wear, which is why I guess it had to be made by his mother — although I don't know how it could have been made by his mother and be impervious to everything.

DEBORAH JOY LEVINE: The big issue at that time was that I wanted to cast a black man as Perry White. I'd spoken to James Earl Jones and he was up for it, but that was a no-no. Even DC Comics said, "Perry White black? Not gonna happen."

BRYCE ZABEL: The other thing about adapting a comic book to television is that in the comics they've made tens if not hundreds or thousands of decisions about the character, the world and everything else. And no television show can live with those constraints, because every television show has to make thousands of its own decisions. Large decisions. Deborah, Dan and myself had stacks of Superman comics sent over from DC, and I remember the first few days where I'd come in and would be like, "Oh my God, I'm a kid in a candy store." But I came to loathe them after a while because there were *so* many. Even if I devoted my entire life to it, I could never be up to speed with the comics, and that was a problem. I actually stopped reading them because I had too many other things on my mind. I felt like the built-in safety valve for the show was that all of our material was getting turned over to DC. And if they had an issue, somebody would call up and say, as I mentioned with the costume, "You can't add black to the costume or you can't do this or, by the way, Clark is this or that." At some point though, I just said, "I've got to treat my job as more of a television series gig; I'm not the keeper of the Superman flame." I also didn't want to get fired in the political machinations that were going on. Sometimes it felt like Deborah was picking fights with people, sometimes it seemed like they were picking fights with her. I'm sure it was a little bit of both, because she was in a very difficult situation. People gave her the keys to the car, except they didn't actually want to release the key. Let's face it, why else would Bob Singer have been brought in to run it?

He's referring to the fact that in the midst of the first season of the series — about seven episodes in — future Supernatural *producer Robert Singer was brought in as an executive producer, and pretty quickly there became a creative push and pull between he and Deborah Joy Levine. Then as the first season segued into the second, Levine left the show and most of the staff was replaced by Singer's own people.*

JIM MICHAELS: Robert Singer brought a team of us in after Les Moonves, who was the head of Warner Bros., said, "I've got this new hit show. We're having some particular production problems on set and post-production is kind of behind. I don't want to blow this." So we came in and invaded the show pretty quickly. As far as the writing is concerned, Bob would have to address that because I wasn't part of those conversations. What I can speak to is that I know physical production was behind schedule and a bit over-budget. The post-production, which I hadn't known was a little behind, was something where they weren't aware of how over-budget they were. They were behind the eight ball fiscally; there were definitely some numbers to the negative and they had to be made up. We were on budget by the end of the year.

BRYCE ZABEL: So the season is over, Robert Singer comes in and cleans house in terms of the writing staff. Even though I wasn't there, there were two things that happened. Deborah may have begun the process and saying it's about Lois and Clark, but then that encountered the inevitable reality of the fact that Clark is Superman, and we need drama, so we're going to have to put that in. I think Robert Singer came in probably saying, "I'm going to do more Superman, but then inevitably found that the show *is* called *Lois & Clark* and those *are* your two main characters.

DEBORAH JOY LEVINE: I just had a whole different creative viewpoint of what I wanted to do with the show, and I wasn't willing to compromise. If I was doing that show today or even five years ago when I understand that maybe I can't be that adamant about everything in a collaborative art, maybe I would have been more willing to compromise. But at that point I just wasn't. You know, I put in the scenes where he was breaking through vaults and stuff like that, but the scenes I really wanted to write were the romantic ones or the ones with his parents. They were the ones where he was talking about life and what it was like being an alien on the planet and being in love with Lois. What I really wanted to do was not what the network wanted to do. And the constant battle was just too much for me. I felt at that point that I really needed to walk away, which is what I did.

DEAN CAIN: What happened with Deborah is that as a showrunner, she maybe wasn't as proficient at that time in running the big machine. When you have all those pieces put in place and all the companies and things, and all the special effects, all the scripts and all the departments, it's a *big* machine. When Bob Singer came in, he had been doing that very well and was very well versed in all of that. So he came in and, yes, of course the show did change. It did get sillier. There were some silly villains, but I liked some of it. There was more action and I thought that we could have stayed with a balance of that *Moonlighting* thing. I liked that and was always rooting for it to go into uncharted territory; meaning that I wanted them to get together, and I wanted them to get married, and I wanted them to start having kids and start having trouble with it. And I really wanted to see where that would go. I thought that would be great to be able to do.

JIM MICHAELS: Like I said, Deborah's pilot was brilliant and very much a love story. This is speculation on my part, but I think to sustain that romance it had to be spread out over time. If you introduce more action and make it more comic bookey, for lack of a better word — and I don't mean that in a derogatory way — you spend more time with him seeing through walls, putting out fires, stopping a runaway train, rescuing people from falling helicopters and so on. If *every* week is about their relationship, they should be married by the end of the season. The changes that were made were about thinking in terms of the long game. You know, how do you keep the show on the air for more than one or two seasons? How do you keep it interesting and entertaining to an audience and perhaps attract a bigger audience? People say, "We want more romance!" Okay, you're going to get it, but first we have to deal with some evil, like with Luthor in the form of John Shea… who, by the way, is someone I wish we had continued to use more instead of moving him to occasional guest star after the first season. He was *so* good.

Again, I wasn't part of the conversation on why he wasn't used more, but I *think* it had something to do with the fact that in a movie you can go for two hours with the same bad guy. You can even do multiple movies. But can you go 22 one-hour episodes? That's 11 movies basically, with the same bad guy every week. Superman's *got* to get him, otherwise he's an inept superhero. We had to make room for other menaces.

All of this would culminate with Levine departing the series at the end of season one, with Singer assuming full control starting with season two.

This resulted in the addition of a new writing staff as well as many crew members. It also marked the aforementioned gradual shift in focus, where the storylines became lighter, oftentimes sillier, and there were effects sequences written which time and budget oftentimes wouldn't allow production to be brought to life properly.

MIKE CARLIN: The weak villains were there from the start and the Luthor stuff was pretty good when it first started. I did think that they had the romance stuff down really well. For my money, if we never saw the Superman costume and we just saw the curtains blowing every time Clark left the room, that would have been enough for me.

CRAIG BYRNE: The first season of the show under Deborah Joy Levine was my preference. The show was sophisticated and had a certain look and atmosphere. It was a big shock when the series returned for season two and characters such as Cat, Jack and Michael Landes' Jimmy were all gone, and there was no good recurring villain in the vein of Lex Luthor. The plots got a little bit sillier, but fortunately there was a course correction around the middle of the second season. The stories still had silly elements — the Jeffersons are the villains, or there's a sarcastic time traveler from the future! — but those elements were mixed with good writing and plots and, of course, chemistry between the two series leads.

DEBORAH JOY LEVINE: As it went on, it basically wasn't the show I wanted to do, yet I still felt the show was great because the cast was great and the situation is classic and works. I was more interested in character than action and I felt like later on they sort of ignored Lois a lot while I was always trying to come up with things that would really highlight Teri's immense talents. She was a singer, she was a dancer and she had a lot of great abilities that I wanted to showcase. And I think they were more interested in Superman versus whoever.

MATTHEW TRUEX (host, *Lois & Clark'd: The New Podcasts of Superman*): This might sound obvious, but the series' whole execution hinges on the title. Everything that came before was Superman-centric, but with that title, the producers could never move the spotlight too far away from Lois. I think that's the gift that series creator Deborah Joy Levine gave to the fandom. Even when the network or whoever wanted to steer more towards superheroics, they had to incorporate Lois and the relationship story. That's what kept the show watchable. There are some *bad* episodes of *Lois & Clark*, but thanks to Deborah and that title, they all have at least one good, emotionally truthful scene between the leading duo.

MIKE CARLIN: After Deborah Joy Levine left the show, it definitely became more like what everybody does with superhero shows. I can't tell you what was on the mind of the people making the show, but I can tell you that a lot of the people who write comic books is where you get the Paul Dinis of the world, the Jeff Loebs of the world and Marc DeMatteis of the world. When they do this stuff, we are all clearly *not* embarrassed by the source material. No matter how silly comics can be, you have to suspend your disbelief and dive in and play it straight. You can have humor, the characters can provide jokes and crack wise if you're doing Spider-Man or whatever, but there's no wink to the audience. There's no, "We're above this." That kind of stuff is deadly to the superhero shows, whether it's a cartoon or live-action show or a movie. The things that the *Batman* show of the '60s did right was nobody had done it before. They decided on a real strong point of view, although it's one that the comic book business is still living down unfortunately.

JIM MICHAELS: I think we were trying to have more fun with the show, and there was definitely an intent to make it lighter and more comic book and have fun and serve the audience. The audience is loyal but also incredibly smart, so you have to make it for them as well and let them come along for the ride with us. If you're doing 22 episodes in a season, they can't all be heavy. You've got to break it up some. Even on *Supernatural*, we'd do these *way* out of the box episodes to keep it fresh.

MIKE CARLIN: When you talk about the old *Batman* show, you have to look at what was going on in the world and entertainment at the time. There was nothing as creative as *Batman*. It was genius. They set their goal, they hit their target and it was a great show. The problem is that everybody who comes after that thinks that's the way to do it. And that is *a* way to do it. But again, they set their tone and then they played it straight within their parameters. A lot of these other shows kind of flounder around because they don't really know what to do. I mean, I've found over the years, whether it's *Superboy* or a Superman movie, or whatever, the first thing that writers tend to want to do is to take away Superman's powers because it's hard to come up with a threat that works. That can be cheap if you're doing it because you can't afford to do the effects. That's a real problem. And writers write what they know and they don't know what it's like to fly. People trusting their imagination and then getting behind it is what makes any great fantasy literature. And it's not apologizing for what *Peter Pan* is or what *Alice in Wonderland* is or what the *Lord of the Rings* is, or what superheroes are. Sometimes it is more even just about people have a real stylistic limitation, and they just can't do anything different than what they do. I don't know why they're drawn to the projects or get hired for them. But you know, sometimes the wrong guy is on the wrong project. There's no way around it. And then when it really clicks, and when it's clear, you get Dick Donner's *Superman*. And *that's* a guy with a point of view. End of speech.

ALAN BURKE: I didn't notice any drop in quality as a kid, but now looking back at it you can see a serious drop in quality compared to season one. Deborah Joy Levine leaving after season one was a huge loss to the team. There are so many of these unexplained firings. Tracy Scoggins as Cat Grant just disappeared in season two; Michael Landes was replaced with Justin Whalin as Jimmy Olsen in season two — the theory I've heard on that one is that he looked too much like Dean Cain. But season two is where the quality starts to drop off, although you still have great episodes.

DEAN CAIN: The show definitely got sillier and the villains became sillier, there's no question about it. Deborah Joy Levine created it and she really created strong characters. The romance was there and it was wonderful. I'm not sure when the change came in, but I'm not going to put it all on Robert Singer. I know that Deborah was replaced, and *that's* what shocked me: I didn't realize that you could create a show and write it and do the whole thing being an executive producer, and then get fired in a sense; that they could just replace you. I didn't even realize that until I was pitching a show and they were going to make this show that I wrote and created, and part of my contract was that they could fire me. I was shocked and they were like, "Dude, this is in every contract. There's nothing you can do about it."

CRAIG BYRNE: *Star Trek* fans refer to the "growing the beard" as around the time *Star Trek: The Next Generation* got good, referring to Jonathan Frakes. If *Lois & Clark* had a moment where it started going downhill, it was when Teri Hatcher cut her hair at the start of season three, which coincided with another shuffling of executive producers. While the season three premiere "We Have a Lot To Talk About" was one of the series' best, the show started getting really rough. A good story like "Ultra Woman" could be sullied by campy guest stars and awful costume design. There are still some great season three highlights like "Tempus Anyone," but the magic of season one was mostly evaporated. The less said about most of season four, the better.

ALAN BURKE: You go into season three and *that's* where they really dropped the ball. They did a story arc where Lois and Clark were getting married and it was kind of toted as, "This is it, guys. They're getting married!" And it turned into this really stupid, drawn-out five-episode arc where Lex kidnaps Lois and replaces her with a clone, and then she got amnesia and couldn't remember. It just really pissed off the fans and that's when the fans turned off to the show. You can't acknowledge that this is what the fans have been waiting for, and then give them the middle finger and expect them to come back next week.

JIM MICHAELS: Yeah, I think we may have gone a little too far there. I think there was the idea that we had to try and get them together sooner rather than later, and somehow this was a kind of trial to test the waters… with the frogs and all… yeah, it wasn't my favorite arc. I'll leave it at that.

MATT TRUEX: The show went through fairly distinct phases that are as much aesthetic as they are story-based. Season one is the kind of Coke Classic of it all. All the characters are where they're supposed to be and acting the way we've seen them act, but now with a focus on the forgotten kisses and stolen glances as

the two fall in love. After season one, the aesthetics get progressively bright —
less illustrative and more cartoony. In turn the stories also get brighter and more
action-packed. Let's call this the Rum and Coke era. Everybody lets loose and
writers start taking bigger swings at the narrative. They introduce a few comic
villains, try out some tropes and occasionally swing for the fences with characters like H.G. Wells and the homicidal time traveler Tempus.

To balance all the story and visual madness, the emotional arc between Lois
and Clark tends to be more and more real. As the world erupts around them,
they suddenly get to tackle their feelings head-on and deal with every permutation of loss, doubt and fear imaginable in a relationship. The craziness bonds
them together and solidifies their love for one another, which is always the most
compelling part of the series. Unfortunately that kind of energy is hard to maintain, and by the time they got to the end of season four it was closing time.

CRAIG BYRNE: I felt sparks between Dean and Teri from the very beginning and, for a while, the show slowly but cleverly gave us those moments that
would hint at more. The only problem is that the show never really allowed the
audience to see a period of the two of them dating — they finally got together,
and by the end of the second season Clark was proposing! I am glad that Lois
was able to learn Clark's secret by the start of season three, but I think the series
missed huge opportunities because they seemed to stop having fun with the
secret identity around that point. It would have been a lot of fun to see Lois
making excuses to cover for Clark's disappearances, for example, and that's an
aspect that we hadn't seen before in Superman projects.

JOHN KENNETH MUIR: The series wore out everyone's patience, with
the Lois and Clark wedding which turned out to be a sham: Clark ended up
marrying a frog-eating clone of Lois instead of the real thing. The next season, a
story called "Swear to God, This Time We're Not Kidding" got the real nuptials
out of the way, but it felt like an anti-climax.

CRAIG BYRNE: Beyond the bait and switch, I think this arc had multiple
aspects that turned the audience off. For starters, by adding the amnesia plot to
the clone story, with repeats factored in, the story seemed to go on for about
two months before we saw the "real" Lois again. Once that was taken care of,
the season ended with Clark going off to "New Krypton," delaying things even
more, and when the two finally got married, it seemed about six months too
late. The audience lost their patience with the show, and I assume the general audience especially felt really jerked around. The whole fake wedding thing could

have easily been avoided by not dangling the notion of marriage so soon.

ALAN BURKE: Season four fell off a cliff ratings-wise. The ratings were good for the first two seasons, and even the third, but they ended that one with a New Krypton arc where some Kryptonians had survived and were part of this new society, but they needed Clark, because he was the heir to the throne basically, and he had to stop a civil war. Season three ended with the first part, season four kicked off with the next two, but once that story finished, the show just crashed and burned. They shouldn't have gotten Lois and Clark together as early as they did; it took the tension away, but I will say that I'll always remember watching the episode where Lois actually does find out he's Superman. It's a *great* episode.

Season four was when the show was at its lowest. Teri had checked out at that point; she didn't want to be involved anymore, she was pregnant around that time and she was done with it. For a couple of years afterwards, she was fairly dismissive of the show. She did this kind of infamous interview where she said the show was for four- or five-year-olds and that it was a stupid show. Then she seems to have kind of turned the corner. Now years later, she attended Comic-Con *as* her '90s Lois Lane and she went around interviewing people outside.

DEAN CAIN: I think there was still definitely life left in the show in many ways, but it had run its course because we had stopped breaking new ground. I was always pushing to move things forward, but a lot of people within the studio system operate out of fear. I heard from everybody who works for Netflix where you go to 13 episodes and they'll go, "We're going to make this show." "Great. It's going to cost $10." "Okay, $10 to make the season, here's your $10, give us a season." And they're done *and* Netflix leaves you alone. We had notes all the time. This one has to be this, this has to be that, we have to be more Lois and Clark here, they want this, etc. So there are a lot of cooks in the kitchen. We had a lot more story to tell, but at the same time we were exhausted.

People always go, "You're a movie star, a television star, and it's all wonderful." No, it isn't. It's not very glamorous to shoot. It's a lot of work and it literally sucks up all of your time. You have no freedom and it's a strange place to be, especially then for me. Now I understand it, so can put it all in perspective, but that's a hard thing to look at and just go, "Oh yeah, I can jump into it." At the same time, I was ready to leave. We were picked up for season five and I was excited, ready to go. And then when they told me it was canceled, I was very happy because I felt like I had just bought freedom.

ROB O'CONNOR: The series was far from perfect, suffering from repetitive, increasingly goofy villains of the week and a tone that seemed to flip-flop from scene to scene (let alone episode to episode) and its charms may be lost on modern fans for that reason. Nevertheless it's what brought me to Metropolis, and every time I go back it reminds me why I find it so timeless, why I might never outgrow it.

ALAN BURKE: I know the show doesn't get as much love now, but a lot of that probably has to do with Dean's politics and the way he's kind of gone. But what I liked is that I always got the impression that if Superman had lost his powers, this Clark Kent could *still* kick your ass. And he should be able to do that!

DEAN CAIN: When it was over I wasn't worried about typecasting. This was a whole different role than the Man of Steel in the past and since the Christopher Reeve nerdy character. There's none of that. And this particular character was not someone I thought *could* be typecast; I thought it was a very broad-ranged character, so I wasn't really too concerned about that. But if people see me and think, "There's Superman," I hoped they would. It meant that I was doing my job, I suppose. I *was* a little concerned when I first heard about the project because of that, but after reading the script and seeing what they were doing with the project and the character, I wasn't concerned at all. I was actually extremely excited.

ROB O'CONNOR: While it obviously doesn't come close to the cinematic visuals of the Donner movies and while no one is going to pretend that Dean Cain holds a candle to Christopher Reeve, in every other respect it accomplishes what no other Superman incarnation has done outside the comics: It makes his inner-life feel real. Both Lois and Clark (especially in the first two seasons) feel very much like real people who could meet at a major metropolitan newspaper and fall in love. Over the course of the series, we see the evolution of the Superman identity (created by Clark and his Earth parents as a convenient disguise to enable his heroic feats without endangering his normal life) as a fledgling super-vigilante who doesn't quite believe in himself (even if Lois Lane does) into a true champion of justice worthy of the legend that's been built around him by Lois, the *Daily Planet* and the world at large. Whether this was by coincidence or design (probably the former given the revolving door of showrunners the series had) is beside the point. In season two the series sets itself apart from previous versions by firmly stating out loud its interpretation of the dual identity: "Superman is what I do. Clark *is* who I am."

TERI HATCHER: I have had quite a few people come up to me and share some really emotionally strong meaning in their life of what our show or either Dean or I meant to them in some journey of their life. I feel great that we were able to be there for them in some way that was inspiring. It also reminds me that, celebrity aside, you just never know how you might be able to affect someone even with just a smile or opening a door at a grocery store or letting somebody cut in line in front of you. We all have the power to help each other every single day.

DEAN CAIN: Here's something I was thinking about regarding Superman. I met someone from the INS yesterday and they asked me to sign a picture. I wrote "Do not deport me" on a Superman photo. We are a nation built on immigrants. It makes us so diverse and so strong, and here, with Superman, you get a guy coming in from another planet who is raised in small-town America on small-town values. And what does he say? He fights for truth, justice and the American way. I think that's what he represents and it's about as wholesome as it gets. And that to me is the essence of Superman and the essence of America. Something that is never brought up is that I'm a quarter-Japanese. My given name was Tanaka, and the funny thing was that when I was first cast the Internet was in its infancy. That's how old I am. And we were starting to hear comments from people, with one literary genius out there who wrote, "Cain and Superman — we want Superman, *not* Sushi Man." My brother laughed so hard like it was the funniest thing in history. And I thought it was hysterical because I was raised here in America and never saw myself looking like an outsider.

I have always been perceived as an All-American type of person. I was Catholic, on a football team, I did very well in school. I have never thought of myself as anything other than completely American, which I think is a great connection to Superman — a Kryptonian who is nothing but an American fighting for, again, truth, justice and the American way.

Romance would grow between Lois and Clark throughout the run of the show, culminating in their marriage at the end of season four. As noted, ABC had intended to bring the show back for a fifth season, but abruptly changed its corporate mind (this despite the show ending on a cliffhanger with the arrival of a mysterious baby). Both Cain and Hatcher still believe that a revival, even after all this time, could be in order.

CRAIG BYRNE: The series finale was pretty awful. I like Harry Anderson but "Fat Head" was ridiculous. I did get amusement from Beverly Garland's Ellen

Lane. But most egregious is that this aired a month after the show was formally cancelled, and ABC could have and should have just removed the cliffhanger and given us some sort of conclusion… even if it had just been a montage of the four years of the show.

DEAN CAIN: I would love to do six episodes of *Lois & Clark* to see where they are 25 years later and explore what's going on. That would be a lot of fun, to have a rebirth of the show to a whole new generation that hasn't seen it. We didn't get to finish our story; we're both parents. Kids have been in our lives for 20 years and I think it would be really important for Lois and Clark to have had a kid. Do they have superpowers? Fully? Only sometimes? There are a lot of different fun things that could happen. And I'd like to keep it fun because I think it needs to be fun and light. I don't love the current incarnation of the Superman character. I think Zack Snyder is a very good filmmaker, but I don't like his vision at all. It's too dark and Superman is too much of a Christ-like figure. There's not a sense of fun to it.

TERI HATCHER: I think we both would be very passionate to see what that would be. We both actually have college-aged kids in real life, and I'm very curious to see what a marriage would be like, what a relationship would be like when it becomes an empty next again. So imagining that their kid is old enough to have just gone out of the house, I think it would be interesting to see what they're dealing with, but I also think it would be interesting to see what kind of powers that child got or didn't get, and what they're choosing to do with them.

DEAN CAIN: Or children. Could be more than one.

TERI HATCHER: That's true.

DEAN CAIN: They could have procreated *a lot*.

TERI HATCHER: Yeah, we would've done that.

CRAIG BYRNE: I feel like this is probably as likely as that *Smallville* animated series that Michael Rosenbaum and Tom Welling keep teasing. I once brought this subject up to some former L&C producers at an event and they just looked at each other and laughed. Despite my not agreeing with Dean Cain's politics at all, I personally would love to see these versions of the characters again someday… but with certain *Crisis*-like exceptions; once we've moved on from a franchise, we've moved on. Yes, *Lois & Clark* had a huge audience, but how much of that audience really would line up to see them again, especially seeing what the show devolved to in its later years? I do wish we had seen them in the CW's *Crisis on Infinite Earths*, and if there's ever a big multiverse type story they could possibly be in, I'd welcome it. I just don't see it happening.

DEBORAH JOY LEVINE: What I always say about television shows is that if you're at the top of the ratings or the bottom of the ratings, you're the luckiest person alive. If you are at the top of the ratings, the network leaves you alone, and if you're at the bottom of the ratings they don't care and they leave you alone. If you're somewhere in the middle, then your life is hell because there are a lot of people that feel like they know how to fix it. This is a true story: At one point we were called into ABC, and I can't even remember who our development executive was at that point, but their big idea was that maybe Clark Kent should be a detective instead of a reporter. I was going to kill somebody. I was basically like, "You cannot be serious," and they had this whole thing and were saying, "Yeah, it's great. We're gonna have police action," and I was like, "Uh, Clark Kent. Mild-mannered reporter. *Hello.*" It's funny because I was always fighting with someone about this show. Even before we premiered, we were going up against Spielberg's new show *SeaQuest DSV*. I was arguing with ABC and with Warner Bros. that they should not put us up against that. At the time Spielberg had a dinosaur running around in the form of *Jurassic Park* and I thought people are not going to tune in to see *my* show. They're going to tune in to see Spielberg's show. But nobody would listen to me. Warner Bros. got mad at me for writing a letter to ABC about it and said, "You're not programming. Do *your* job."

What's funny is that years later I actually got a letter from one of my ABC development people who apologized to me and said that on a lot of the things that went on, and the arguments we had, *I was right.*

Overlapping Lois & Clark: The New Adventures of Superman *was* Superman: The Animated Series *from the team that had crafted the Batman animated series, which in turn had been birthed in the shadow of Tim Burton's 1989 production of* Batman. *That version, introducing Michael Keaton in the role of the Dark Knight, allowed the character to impact pop culture to its greatest extent since the 1966 to 1968 camp Adam West television series. One example was the 1992 arrival of* Batman: The Animated Series, *produced by Bruce Timm and credited for revolutionizing children's animation.*

Running for 65 episodes from 1996 to 2000, Superman: The Animated Series *features* Wings *star Tim Daly as the voice of Clark Kent/Superman, Dana Delany (who had most recently starred in the Vietnam drama* China Beach*) as Lois Lane and Clancy*

Brown (who had really earned a reputation for himself as on-screen villains, particularly with the Kurgan in the feature film Highlander). *As was the case with* Batman, *voice director Andrea Romano scored a wide variety of talent for different roles, some recurring and some one-time only. Among them were* Michel Ironside (Darkseid), Ed Asner *(Granny Goodness), Malcolm McDowell (Metallo), Ron Perlman (Jax-Ur), David Warner (Ra's al Ghul), Sarah Douglas (Mala), Finola Hughes (Lara), Olivia Hussey (Talia al Ghul) and Gilbert Gottfried (Mr. Mxyzptlk).*

BRUCE TIMM: Tim Daly's a great voice. I think we had 55 guys come in to audition before we found him. And Dana Delany is a delight as well. In the back of our heads we always thought we'd like to use her for Lois and we had been auditioning a couple of people when we heard that she was interested. So that was that. And then there's Clancy Brown as Lex Luthor, which is a *terrific* voice.

Tim Daly brought the Man of Steel to vocal life in this show from the creators of Batman: The Animated Series *(© and TM DC Comics/Warner Bros. Discovery).*

James Timothy Daly was born March 1, 1956 in New York City and is the younger brother of Cagney & Lacey *star Tyne Daly. He made his stage debut at the age of seven in* Jenny Kissed Me. *Three years later he was on television in an* American Playhouse *adaptation of* An Enemy of the People. *In 1978, he went pro with a starring role in* Equus. *He would continually find himself drawn back to the stage, but he would certainly make a name for himself in film and television as well. He's appeared in 33 films between 1982's* Diner *and 2016's* Submerged. *Although he appeared in many TV movies and guest starred on numerous series, his regular or recurring cast roles were on* Almost Grown *(1988 to 1989),* Wings *(1990 to 1997),* From the Earth to the Moon *(1998),* The Fugitive *(2000 to 2001),* The Sopranos *(2004 to 2007),* Eyes *(2005),* The Nine *(2006 to 2007),* Private Practice *(2007 to 2012),* Madam Secretary *(2014 to 2019) and* The Game *(beginning in 2021 and still going).*

TIM DALY (voice actor, "Clark Kent/Superman," *Superman: The Animated Series*): When I was originally cast as Superman, I was kind of shocked. I didn't really know what I was getting into and I didn't know this show was going to be much more than kind of a fun thing to do for kids to watch on Saturday morning. I had no idea how important Superman was to the world culture.

ANDREA ROMANO (voice director, *Superman: The Animated Series*): Tim is absolutely accurate when he said that he came into this not taking voice-over acting for animation as seriously as on-camera work. A lot of actors had that issue at the beginning too, of different series and different projects that I worked on. But as I watched Tim, number one, learn the process, learn how this is done, watch the other actors working with him and the respect they had for the project, and then see the response from fans as they watched his work, I actually watched him evolve. And it happened during production, it happened within the first season. You could see him start to take it more seriously. Now I never let his performance sound like he had any disregard, but nobody knows what a series is going to be when you start. You *hope* it's going to be hugely successful and carry on, but you never know what's going to happen.

TIM DALY: As I've gotten some perspective on the whole thing, I look back and realize that Superman is probably better described by an anthropologist or psychologist, because we all dream about flying, we dream about having super-powers and we dream about being a hero and saving people. What's interesting is that starting about 20 or 25 years ago, entertainment started trending really heavily towards dark, edgy, dystopian stories. I think that following the 25th anniversary of the series, that maybe it's time for a comeback. It's funny that a lot of people are talking about *Ted Lasso*, because it's unabashedly kind, generous and funny, and it doesn't have that tortured element that some of the Batman stuff has had. I think we want someone that represents all the good in us. I think *that* version of Superman is the thing that keeps him alive and the thing that will ultimately keep him going for another 100 years or more. He does represent hope for humanity.

ANDREA ROMANO: When he could actually see some of the footage back and could actually see what the work was doing, he gained tremendous respect. And he was probably the biggest fan of the show. He had this wonderful Superman doll that he had gotten and would bring it along on his *Daly Show* that he did, this wonderful streaming thing that was so fantastic. It would show up in all different shots and he'd be so proud. It was lovely to see the actor really change his opinion about the entire form, about animation, what it was and what he was doing. And by the fact that he was personally having an effect on how fans were getting their first exposure to these characters. I think that made him feel proud and suddenly it became a much more respectful thing. So he didn't start with disrespect, but he gained so much respect through the process, and that was delightful to watch.

TIM DALY: I wasn't a comic book kid. I wasn't one of those kids that read and collected them, but I *was* a huge fan of the Christopher Reeve movie and I watched the George Reeves Superman series when I was a kid. I watched the Adam West *Batman* a little bit, but I was by no means a fanboy. So for me, it was kind of an education to learn how important these characters were. All of it has become more important now than it was way back then. I wish that I had been a little bit more thoughtful about it at the moment while I was doing it, but I'm hopeful that I might get another chance at some point to voice Superman because I think he's important to the world culture. I don't think that I was condescending about it, but I was just clueless as to the importance that Superman had for so many people in the United States and around the world. Now that I *am* more aware of it, I want to pay better attention to that if I get a chance to do it again.

PAUL DINI (producer, *Superman: The Animated Series*): The incredible Tim Daly did triple duty on the series. He brought warmth and empathy to Clark, strength and integrity to Superman and paired humor and tragedy with Bizarro.

CLANCY BROWN (voice actor, "Lex Luthor," *Superman: The Animated Series*): Tim is *such* a good actor. I don't know if anybody appreciates just how good he is. He works all the time and he's saddled with those Superman good looks. He's my Superman and I always think of him as the character. He and Dana are like my family.

Daly does note that if he actually donned Superman's red and blue uniform as opposed to just voicing him, that it wouldn't result in a different take on the character.

TIM DALY: The difference wouldn't be much, because in my imagination I *was* the Man of Steel. I had a cape, a mask and those tights and whatever the hell else he wears. At the same time, when you're just doing the voice, it almost frees you in a way because it's *all* in your imagination. You can imagine yourself however you want in terms of how you looked, and then of course there's the imagination. But like I said, I think it's a release in a weird way to *not* have to get dressed in the costume.

You know, a lot of people have asked me about being a part of the Superman legacy. It's a hard thing to feel. I guess the closest thing that made me realize that was when I went to the Superman 75th anniversary panel at Comic-Con. I actually went because my son voiced Superman in *The Flashpoint Paradox*. I was in the audience and there was this huge room with like 4,000 people in it. They introduced me and I thought I would stand and wave for a little bit, and they gave me a thunderous standing ovation. I was absolutely shocked. I just couldn't believe that all these people were that appreciative and that it was that important to them. I was really humbled by that. So if that's true about being part of the legacy, I'm happy. I hope that I can live up to people's expectations.

The show's Lois Lane was born Dana Welles Delany on March 13, 1956 in New York City. Her desire to start acting came from attending numerous Broadway shows and films with her parents, and in school she started appearing on stage for different shows. She graduated from Wesleyan University in 1978. By the early 1980s she found work on the soap opera Love of Life *and* As the World Turns, *as well as in television commercials, on Broadway in* A Life *and off-Broadway in the critically-acclaimed* Blood Moon. *Guest-starring roles on* Moonlighting, Magnum, P.I. *and* thirtysomething *followed, after which she was cast as Nurse Colleen McMurphy on the Vietnam drama* China Beach, *which aired between 1988 and 1991. She has 30 movies to her credit between 1981's* The Fan *and 2017's* Literally, Right Before Aaron. *Many TV movies followed, a few guest spots and then regular or recurring roles on* Sweet Surrender *(1987),* Wing Commander Academy *(1996 a voice role),* Pasadena *(2001 to 2002),* Presidio Med *(2002 to 2003),* Kidnapped *(2006),* Desperate Housewives *(2007 to 2010, 2012),* Body of Proof *(2011 to 2013),* Hand of God *(2014 to 2017) and* The Comedians *(2015).*

Romano had first cast Dana Delany in the role of Andrea Beaumont in the animated feature film spinoff of Batman: The Animated Series, Batman: Mask of the Phantasm. *This would lead the actress to being cast as Lois Lane.*

ANDREA ROMANO: When you get to a project that's probably going to be recording once a week for at least a year, with ADR for another year after that, some actors who are film actors can't commit to that. Dana could do *Mask of the Phantasm* as far as time was concerned, but we had to talk to her to see if she was willing to make herself available for what we would need for production. Dana was absolutely willing and always did make herself available in our production, and she's just so darn good.

DANA DELANY (voice actor, "Lois Lane," *Superman: The Animated Series*): When they asked me to audition for *Superman*, it *really* mattered to me. I grew up on Superman, I started watching the TV series from the 1950s when I was four years old, and then I read the comic every Sunday. I'd go to church and then go to the drugstore to get my *Lois Lane* comic for 10 cents — that's what they cost then. So this really was part of my DNA. I remember reading the script for the pilot and thinking, "This is so good; this is such good writing and character as written by Paul Dini and Alan Burnett reminding me of Rosalind Russell and *His Girl Friday*, which is kind of who I modeled it on. You know, the gal with moxie. She had snappy dialogue and she didn't suffer fools gladly. I remember when I had to step up to the mic and say, "This is Dana Delany auditioning for Lois Lane," I was just thinking, "Oh my God, at least I got to say that." That would have been fine. Then I got to say that great scene looking at him flying and she says, "He's the Nietzschean ideal… Nice ass." I remember trying to just get enough of the "a" and the "s." And when I got the part — I'd forgotten this — when we taped the first episode, I cried. Andrea Romano reminded me of that. It was such a thrill for me; it was my childhood and I got to realize it.

ANDREA ROMANO: I remember when she auditioned, I always walk actors up to the microphone and chat them up to make them feel comfortable in the room because an audition is a bit of a trial. You're being judged and you can get a bit intimidated. Really good actors can get intimidated by the audition process, so I try to make them feel really comfortable. I walked Dana up to the microphone, chatted her up and went back to the booth. I asked if she was ready and said, "Okay, this is Dana Delany as Lois Lane." There was dead silence. She doesn't speak and I ask if she was okay and she says, "I'm just letting those words wash over me. I've waited so long to hear somebody say I could be Lois Lane." It was so charming that this established actress had such a desire to play this character. Put all that together and you've got a brilliant Lois Lane.

PAUL DINI: Alan Burnett and I had worked with Dana Delany on *Batman: Mask of the Phantasm* and we knew that she would be perfect to play Lois Lane. We were thrilled to learn that Dana loved the character and that she was up for playing her. I can't imagine anyone better.

DANA DELANY: I think Lois Lane is so important as a character. She's the human being amongst all these superheroes, first of all. She's kind of our touchstone; the person that we as humans follow. She's a great female role model, considering she started in 1938 and I just love that, in today's context, she's this woman who, in today's world, has to keep the secret of her husband/boyfriend

— whatever you want to call it in today's version.

I had just come off of *China Beach*, and that just really taught me the lesson that every role you take has an impact. It affects people, it affects the culture and that you as an actor have to take responsibility for that. From then on I would only choose roles that I felt I would be proud to say that I'd done and that reflects something about women in particular; where we are in the world. And I have to say that ever since I have never played the victim once. Never.

Whether it's voicing Mr. Krabs on SpongeBob SquarePants *or Lex Luthor in the DC Animated Universe, Clancy Brown does villains, both animated and live-action, like nobody else — much to his own personal frustration. Born Clarence John "Clancy" Brown III on January 5, 1959 in Urbana, Ohio, he had done stage work early on, but quickly made the transition to film with memorable parts in* Bad Boys *(1983),* Highlander *(1986, as the Kurgan),* The Shawshank Redemption *(1994),* The Adventures of Buckaroo Banzai Across the 8th Dimension *(1984),* The Bride *(1985, as the Frankenstein monster),* Shoot to Kill *(1988) and he's gone on from there — a total of 65 movies between the aforementioned* Bad Boys *and 2023's* John Wick: Chapter 4. *On television, there were a wide variety of TV movies, some guest performances and starring or recurring roles on* Earth 2 *(1994 to 1995),* ER *(1997 to 1998),* Breaking News *(2002),* Carnivale *(2003 to 2005),* The Deep End *(2010),* Aim High *(2011),* Sleepy Hollow *(2013 to 2016),* The Flash *(2014 to 2015),* Billions *(2018 to 2019),* Schooled *(2019),* Emergence *(2019 to 2020) and* Dexter: New Blood *(2021 to 2022). He's provided voice work in many projects, starting in 1995's* Gargoyles the Movie: The Heroes Awaken *through 2020's* The SpongeBob Movie: Sponge on the Run.

CLANCY BROWN: I was familiar with Superman. I remember going to my little local newsstand where you got comics off the circular rack where the owner would bellow, "This ain't no library!" I would buy them and sneak them back home, because my folds didn't like the idea that I would read comic books. I got one that was "The Death of Superman" from the 1960s, and I just found it so upsetting. After he died I said, "I'm never reading this again." The betrayal and duplicitous of Luthor was a little much for a 10-year-old to take. Then I just moved on to *Sgt. Rock*, who was gonna kill some Nazis.

Auditioning for the show, the story is that they were kind of casting around out of the box for people who had other credits. I went in originally for Superman and *really* wanted to play a good guy. I'd been doing a lot of bad guys or at least ambiguous guys. I also wanted to get involved with voiceover more and this would be a great way to do it. So I went in, I did my best Superman, and Andrea

Romano, who was directing it, and I assume Bruce Timm, said, "Could you wait?"

ANDREA ROMERO: Clancy came in to audition for Superman. He opened his mouth and said three words, and I looked at Bruce Timm and said, "We have to read him for Lex Luthor." If we hired Clancy Brown for Superman, how would we ever cast Lex Luthor to be a tougher guy?

CLANCY BROWN: They then put me outside for a minute and asked me to wait around because they had a bunch of other people there — it was a long line; they saw everybody for Superman. They asked me to wait around, which is usually a good sign — no guarantee, but a good sign. And after they had read everybody, they came back out and said, "Would you read for Lex Luthor?" I rolled my eyes and heaved inside heavily, and I said, "Oh man, why do I always have to read the bad guy?" Andrea was like, "Well you don't have to read it. It's okay. Thank you very much," and I'm like, "Wait, wait, wait… I didn't say I wouldn't read, I was just wondering why my life always takes this turn. I'll absolutely read for it." And then as soon as I started reading for him, I'm like, "Oh, this guy is *good*. This is gonna be fun," and I gave it my best shot. And you know, that's history. She was very sweet.

PAUL DINI: Clancy Brown was the ultimate Lex Luthor; Clancy can play every tough guy and villain on TV as far as I'm concerned.

CLANCY BROWN: As popular as Luthor is from the show, that's because of Bruce Timm and the writing of all of those guys who wrote him. All I did was say the words.

In regards to Luthor's hatred for Superman, Brown points out that the rationale behind it has altered over the years.

CLANCY BROWN: It's a different answer from now than it was back then. You know, in the first episode, he tried to convince Superman to join him. I think there's something missing in Lex, something that drives him. Something has occurred that has caused him to make those compromises. I also think he thinks that he's the solution to all the problems somehow. This alien shows up from another planet, who just follows the straight and narrow path and doesn't have any time for any compromise or nuance. or anything about that is either good or bad. He does, but not the way Lex thinks about it. It's an interesting character, Lex Luthor — over the years he started out just as a crime boss, and now he becomes like Mark Zuckerberg: He's become CEO… this subtle manipulator of capitalism… the king of peak capitalism.

Insofar as the show's creative team was concerned, and given the success of Batman: The Animated Series, *it was more a question of what circumstances would result in them having the opportunity to bring the Man of Steel to life in animated form. There seemed to be little doubt that it would happen.*

BRUCE TIMM: We always expected a Superman show after *Batman*, and it was just a matter of *when* they were going to do this. At the time there was talk of a live-action movie in features and they were in the middle of another major revision on their thinking over there. We were sort of waiting and suddenly Jean MacCurdy, who was our boss, said, "You know, we're going to start on *Superman*." They wanted it for 1996, and that's essentially how it began.

PAUL DINI: After the success of *Batman: The Animated Series*, the interest was high in doing another DC-based series. The *BTAS* crew loved the DC characters and wanted to keep creating within that universe. Superman felt like a completely natural, almost required, second act toward establishing an animated DC Universe. There had also been a lot of desire to see Superman in the Batman world and we had been wondering how we were going to do that. Eventually it worked out that there was a lot of interest in getting a Superman movie in the works, even though that looked to be like two or three years down the road, but everybody agreed that it was a good idea to have a Superman series too. It was too soon to do anything that would have tied into a movie, but it was not a bad idea to have the character out there, getting some exposure. That way you have kids who are five or six watching the Superman TV cartoon and then at eight or nine there will be a Superman movie they'll want to see. And at the same time *Lois & Clark* was on TV and so the character was out there. Again, this just seemed to be a natural extension of everything that was going on at the time.

BRUCE TIMM: As it turned out, every single aspect of the show was tougher than doing *Batman*. At the very beginning of *Batman*, we knew exactly what we wanted to do. We wanted to make an action-adventure Film Noir. Having that '40s frame of reference made everything easy to design. If we had to design a fork, a spoon and a glass, we'd look it up in the old art deco book and find something. You'd never have to worry about what something would look like. But on *Superman*, we were making everything up and flying by the seat of our pants.

PAUL DINI: At the start of development, a lot of ideas were on the table.

I remember seeing some '40s–era character model sheets by Bruce Timm. I think it would have been interesting to have gone that way, to do our take on the Fleischer Superman world, but it would have had to have been in its own universe somewhere. I couldn't see it as part of the DCAU expansion that would eventually lead to *Justice League*.

There was also pressure from the studio (Warner Bros.) to make sure that Superman *was a lighter show than* Batman *had been. While* Batman *lent himself to a dark, realistic world,* Superman *had to be lighter.*

PAUL DINI: Even younger viewers responded to the danger and darkness of Batman's world in an extremely positive way. When they saw Batman and the villains, the audience knew exactly what they were getting and they were on board for it. Superman is a more optimistic, inspiring character. The trick was imbuing both Superman and Clark Kent with attributes that the audience would recognize as engaging and not staid or boring. I think for the most part we did right by him.

BRUCE TIMM: Having us go more for the light was probably out of the feeling that it might be a little bit too spooky for the kids. What's a little surprising to me is that as successful a show as *Batman* was, there was kind of a backlash against it on the corporate level saying that it was really good, but if it wasn't quite so dark, it might have been even better. It's the strangest thing. At the same time I didn't want it to seem like we were some sort of one-trick-pony, even though my first inclination when we started developing the show was to basically bring it back as much as possible to the Fleischer cartoons and make it '40s style with that whole *Citizen Kane* kind of movie look. But once we got that edict, I said, "Okay fine, I'll throw that out the window."

PAUL DINI: When you sit down on a show like this, you think about what it was that originally attracted you to these characters, what made them cool and what do we absolutely *not* want to do with them. In most cases everybody was remarkably in sync with the dramatics of the show and the characters. Now if somebody had come to us and said, "Well, *Superman* really needs a couple of more kids and a dog to hang out with" — like it was on *Super Friends* — the crew would have quit. And I wouldn't have blamed them. I think *Batman* proved more than anything that you could do more adult cartoons and kids will watch it.

BRUCE TIMM: Everybody was asking how we would make Superman different for the '90s. I can't say that we made him all that different. What we were doing was the same thing that we did on *Batman*, which was look at the entire legacy of the character and picked and chose aspects that we liked throughout the years and meshed them into a new franchise. That's essentially what we'd done with *Superman*. For instance, the show brought on the character of Steel from the comics, there's the Phantom Zone from the '50s and '60s, Bizarro makes an appearance, Mxyzptlk makes an appearance. Some of the new villains developed in the last couple of decades, like Lobo. Luthor was our main villain. That's essentially how we developed this.

STAN BERKOWITZ: One of the things that was incredibly helpful was that Paul Levitz from DC met with the writers of *Superman* very early in the show's development and said that everyone has the same problem with the character. He said, "Listen, one of the things that has helped us write stories is that if Clark has a problem in his life, then somehow that impacts on Superman." As soon as he said that, I thought, "What if Clark Kent is killed?" The result was the episode "The Late Mr. Kent," which was fun to write because the story placed limits on what Superman could do. As strong as he was, he still had a problem that strength couldn't solve.

PAUL DINI: We didn't want to do *Super Friends*, where everybody just gets together to save the world and they all get along so well. Back then they felt like you couldn't broaden the superheroes to make them interesting, so that's why they put in the Wonder Twins and a bunch of sideline comic support characters. When, if you really gave some thought to the heroes themselves, you could make them fully-rounded, interesting characters. In that way you don't feel like you're cheapening the process by adding a whole lot of baggage. Or you can set out to write a funny story and Superman has to react to it. Like, we did a script for Mr. Mxyzptlk and that turned out great. It's their first meeting and he is really put out by this little imp who just decides to show up one day and mess with him, because Superman's the baddest guy on the planet. Mxy is a good challenge.

STAN BERKOWITZ: One of the first things I read there was Paul Dini's Mr. Mxyzptlk script and I thought, "Wow, this is really elegant," and the reason it worked is because Paul had taken a really interesting character with great visuals, and had created a story where Superman's strength didn't do him much good. He had to depend on his wits. I think some, if not all, of the writers were working on ways to get around the unlimited nature of his strength and power.

PAUL DINI: The first third of the Mxy episode, it's kind of a nightmare.

Superman thinks he's losing his mind because he can't understand why reality seems to be warping around him, so he goes home to his folks and says, "Listen, I'm ready to give up being Superman because I'm going nuts." But when he discovers it's Mxy and that somebody is controlling the situation, he recognizes that he might be able to win against him. And when he discovers the name backwards thing, it turns into a comedy and then it's Mxy who's on the ropes, because Superman figures out his secret and uses it again and again and again. He tricks him into saying his name backwards over and over again. And the episode takes place over the course of about a year, because he keeps vanishing for 90 days at a time and then reappearing until Superman tricks him into saying his name backwards again.

STAN BERKOWITZ: When you're writing these shows, you're keeping in mind your own mindset from when you were three or four years old, which is your potential viewer. And in this case, what we were trying to do is something that a kid could watch and enjoy, but an adult could sit with that kid and not have his or her intelligence insulted. We never wrote down to children. Nobody did. We took the kids seriously and were trying to give them, the children, what *we* had been given, but in an updated and a little bit more sophisticated version.

ALAN BURNETT: One of the episodes I like is "Knight Time," which is the one where Superman assumes Batman's identity because Batman's missing. And so he's working with Robin to try and track him down while Gotham's going a little wild because everybody thinks Batman's gone. And so he reappears as Batman and pretends to be him. Bob Goodman wrote that, and there's a lot of humor in it. There's one great scene where he beats up Bane and it's a great scene.

BRUCE TIMM: I like seeing Superman doing his impression of Batman. He's talking to Commissioner Gordon and he's standing ramrod stiff with his chin in the air and being all aloof.

PAUL DINI: There were grimmer episodes, like one where Lois is catapulted into a parallel dimension world which is basically run by a fascist Superman working in partnership with Lex Luthor. That's a hard-edged episode, but it shows the different ways we were seeing the characters and broadening them a bit. And when we did a *World's Finest* team-up with Batman, we definitely didn't make them pals. Batman and Superman are polar opposites in a way. Superman does not like Batman or his methods, and Batman has very little use for Superman. Yet they're working two ends of a big crime that they have to solve. That brings out a lot of intensity between the characters.

BRUCE TIMM: We went with a tough professional reporter take on Clark Kent as opposed to the mild-mannered guy that everyone is used to. And Lois is tough, so they have a rivalry going. It's a friendly rivalry, but they're definitely wary of each other. That's a little bit different from the way the relationship has been shown in the past.

PAUL DINI: Not only did we figure out a little bit more who Superman and Clark were over the course of the show, but there are also some interpersonal dynamics between Jimmy and Lois and Perry and the Kents. And you can go back and revisit that stuff and broaden those characters a little more once you've established them and use those for potential story material. Same with the villains too: You go in and you tweak them and you work with them a little bit, or you bring in some new characters, you know, perhaps from the comics, and shake things up and then you find yourself having fun with it.

BRUCE TIMM: When you're talking about Superman and Lois, if there's anything that comes close to the approach we took, I'd say it was the first season of George Reeves' *Adventures of Superman* in terms of that competitive thing between Lois and Clark. The one thing we were trying to avoid with our Lois, and it's not easy, is that we didn't want her to be foolish. We didn't want her to get in hot water because she's going to a place she shouldn't have and Superman has to rescue her.

PAUL DINI: We stayed in the vein of *Batman* as far as some elements of the writing goes. We wanted to give the supporting players in Superman's world, and indeed Superman himself, some depth that the Batman characters had achieved through the animated series. It was a conscientious decision to make the two worlds radically different, which was the best way to play up the contrast between them. Gotham is dark and very shrouded and threatening, and Metropolis is the city of tomorrow. It's bright, it has wide-open vistas and Superman is an extension of the city as much as Batman is an extension of his. Metropolis is almost as if the World's Fair of 1939 had gone on and we actually had some of those brilliant achievements of mankind.

CLANCY BROWN: The writing staff came over pretty intact from *Batman*, so they already had a relationship and way of working with each other — just an amazing alchemy of talent. They were completely original, and at the same time they had such a command of the mythology, which was obvious from the way they wrote everybody. They really wrote Metallo and Toyman and these other characters — they just wrote the hell of it and made all of these characters make sense. And they brought each other's game up.

STAN BERKOWITZ: The way it worked was that we all kind of chipped into everybody else's work. There are certainly stories that someone else might have written that I had nothing to do with, but generally you read it, you comment on it, or sometimes you edit something that someone else wrote.

PAUL DINI: What was exciting was the way all the writers were using their imaginations to come up with new ideas to stretch the characters of Clark and Superman, Lois and all the others... as well as coming up with interesting situations and visually exciting set pieces that could be animated.

ALAN BURNETT: The way it worked was that Warner Bros. had a contract with me and nothing for me to do, so I ended up going to *Superman* where I began throwing ideas their way. At the start of it I always thought it would be a neat idea if Brainiac actually came from Krypton; I thought it would hook everything together better than the comic books do and indeed, as it developed, it became the Internet of Krypton, and the destroyer of Krypton, but he was an AI that could leave the planet.

PAUL DINI: We also added a lot more characters than we anticipated because it seemed that Superman is a character who fits more with team-ups than somebody like Batman. He seems to be much more of an open personality, so other characters gravitate towards him. We also found we could bring out more of Superman's personality and change him from the kind of rock-jaw, straight-ahead Boy Scout-type character that he's always been if we bring in a colorful guest star. So if you pair him up with Lobo, which we did, that really tends to tax him because he's irritated with this big dope. The Flash is another one. The Flash is very confident, even over-confident, in his abilities and Superman is much more methodical. He doesn't really have much in common with Flash, who's literally a hot shot and always tooting his own horn and carrying on. The Flash is much more of a braggart and Superman is much more pragmatic, which is a very interesting dynamic to play with.

BRUCE TIMM: In dealing with people's perception that he was the Big Boy Scout and all of that, we feel like at least in the beginning of the show, he was a little bit more alien; a little more standoffish. He was not the kind of guy who drops in on a dedication by the major; he's more remote than the

Superman you're used to. That eventually changed over the course of the series. When *Batman* began, he was considered a vigilante and hunted by the police, but as they became aware of his motives and the fact that they needed this guy, things changed. In the pilot, Superman progresses from a kid who doesn't know about and is afraid of his own powers to a hero who is afraid of not being accepted by the people. And in the end he realizes that he will be. That's how his journey began.

STAN BERKOWITZ: We always tried to have a theme with everything we did at Warner Bros. It should be about *something*. Often as a story editor, what happens is that people pitch an idea like, "Superman fights a mummy." "Okay, but what's it about?" There was one episode where it was just a bunch of stuff happening with no emotional aspect to it. It ended up with Mercy Graves, Lex Luthor's right-hand person, being really mistreated by Luthor… I argued vociferously to make it a story about Luthor and Mercy and how Mercy was completely mistreated all the time — just so there'd be some kind of emotional thread to it rather than just Luthor's plot to do this, and then whatever it was doesn't happen. I think we were pretty good as a group in doing stories that had some emotional weight to them as opposed to just being a plot.

PAUL DINI: It was always challenging to come up with Superman stories, but I wouldn't say difficult. One of the things that makes Batman, I guess you could say, easier to write as a character is that his supporting cast is so terrific. There are other heroes he works with, like Batgirl and Robin, Alfred and Commissioner Gordon, *and* there are also tremendous villains. You can explore other personalities like Poison Ivy or the Joker or the Scarecrow or Two-Face — each one of them is a brilliant character unto themselves. I think any of the Batman rogues gallery characters could carry perhaps not a whole series, but at least certain solo episodes unto themselves. Superman doesn't really have that. If you spend too much time with Mr. Mxyzptlk, he gets really stupid really fast. We did one good episode with him and one not so good episode with him. I'd say the danger with that character is that he's fun to write, and yet he's also very easy to lose control of and it can just take over and the silliness runs rampant. You put Superman up against him, and there's nothing really for him to do other than play policeman and make the little guy go away before he causes too much damage. A character like Bizarro is more of a tragic mirror image of Superman. You can play up the Frankenstein-like quality of him or, if you're not careful, he gets kind of silly too.

Lex Luthor and Superman: There's a classic rivalry there; a classic hero versus enemy scenario. And yet even that tends to get old really quick. So Superman does not really have the same villains that challenge him in the way that Batman does. That's part of the problem. He's never had that effective a rogues gallery. And he himself is kind of an upstanding hero, so you're looking at different ways to challenge him, to bring in other things that will test him.

Part of the solution came in the form of Jack Kirby's Fourth World comics (original-ly consisting of Forever People, New Gods, Mister Miracle *and* Superman's Pal Jimmy Olsen*), particularly Darkseid, the ruler of Apokalips who on* Superman: The Animated Series *and the subsequent* Justice League *and* Justice League: Unlimit-ed *was someone who Superman could go toe-to-toe with.*

PAUL DINI: The idea of Superman vs. Darkseid, and bringing in Jack Kirby's entire Fourth World, is a rich enough idea to have been its own series. I feel we could have done several seasons just focusing on that alone. In many ways Darkseid is a much more fitting adversary for Superman than Brainiac or Luthor.

Darkseid, who was featured in the Justice League Snyder Cut, *shows up in episode 12 of* Superman, *"Tools of the Trade;" episodes 38 and 39, the two-part "Apokalips… Now!," in which Darkseid vaporizes human cop Dan Turpin and Superman almost goes over the edge; episode 40, "Little Girl Lost;" and in episodes 53 and 54, the two-part series finale "Legacy," in which a brainwashed Superman leads an army from Apokalips to Earth where much damage is done. Lois Lane helps him escape from Darkseid's control, which leads to a titanic battle between Superman and Darkseid, with a shocking resolu-tion. On top of all of that, Superman is horrified to discover that he has lost the trust of the people of Metropolis.*

PAUL DINI: The intention was to make Superman distrusted now, because in those last two episodes Darkseid took him over and he was doing things that he wouldn't have done had he not been under Darkseid's control. We established early on that one of Superman's greatest fears is that he wouldn't be trusted, and this brought that to fruition.

BRUCE TIMM: That whole last season of *Superman*, which didn't happen, was going to be a little bit more about the world learning to trust Superman again, and Superman trying to regain their trust. But here's the thing about Superman and Darkseid: Superman is such a powerful character that we have always had a problem finding powerful villains to throw up against him. So Jack Kirby's Darkseid character is one of major heavyhitters of the DC universe, and we're all big Jack Kirby fans anyway and look for any opportunity to use his stuff. Also, when the Fourth World was first introduced into the comics, one of the first books that it was introduced in was *Superman's Pal Jimmy Olsen*. There was already a Superman connection, so it's not like we were just dragging the Fourth World into the Superman mythos willy-nilly. I mean, there was a precedent for it. It's just a real rich comic book mythology. It's also a super-involved backstory, which we simplified of course for animation, but there's just a lot of really rich story material.

PAUL DINI: I think Darkseid was a great character to bring in and set opposite Superman, because he is kind of what Superman *could* be. Superman could very easily take control of the planet, and at first the most benevolent of reasons is to make sure that crime does not proliferate, that no country attacks any other, that there is law and order and peace. Yet as time goes on, he would just as surely turn into Darkseid or a creature very much like him, so he has to stay removed from mankind as somebody who takes a hand in daily activities, but holds himself up as a good example. You can follow his example or not. That's up to you. However, if you take it upon yourself to make life miserable for other people, that's when he going to get involved. So Superman is there as an inspiration to mankind. Batman's just out every night looking for trouble. They're two very different types of stories. At the same time, you're doing something that's a little lighter in tone so it has to be a little more for kids.

BRUCE TIMM: The thing about the Fourth World stuff is that it's really pretty involved. I mean, originally in the comics it was four separate interlocking comics and even then it was still just this big sprawling epic. And so we kind of had to really condense it down to its bare essentials to be able to shoehorn it into the Superman story. It wasn't limiting so much as just that it was tricky just trying to figure out how to condense it down and have it still make sense.

PAUL DINI: Not every hero starts off with a great cast of villains and Superman's are just okay. But when you bring in a character like Darkseid and the whole planet of Apokalips, you've got all these great characters who can match him power for power. And the idea that Darkseid is a dictator and Superman represents freedom, you can't beat that.

BRUCE TIMM: Once you got into Darkseid, the stories didn't necessarily become darker, but they became deeper. Especially after "Apokalips… Now!," what Superman goes through is such a horrendous thing, and from that point on, at the end of the story, Darkseid is way up at the top of Superman's hate list. After that, every time he ran across Darkseid or his minions, Superman instantly gets grouchy. It was always a bad day for Superman when Darkseid and gang show up. It's interesting to us, because Superman is one of those characters that you don't necessarily want to play dark or gritty or angry all the time. At the same time, he's so inherently good that you need to kind of break that mold a little bit every now and then so he's not just namby-pamby. You've got to test him a little bit, and Darkseid was really good for that.

PAUL DINI: Not only does Darkseid capture Superman, but he brainwashes him to think he was raised on Apokalips, and that Darkseid was his father rather than Jonathan Kent, *and* that he has been groomed to take his place. And those were all implanted memories, creating a *Manchurian Candidate*-like situation. I personally like "Legacy" because it's all of the things we shouldn't do with the character, *and* here's why you don't want to have Superman fly off the handle. You don't want to have him confront Darkseid and try and kill him, and you don't want Darkseid really to fight back. Because the thing with Darkseid is that his power comes from his cruelty, from his intelligence, from his sheer imposing nature. He's a big buff guy and he looks like he could settle a lot of problems if he got into a fight. But one of the things that Jack Kirby originally put out in the comic books was that it was beneath him to mix it up and to get into a brawl. But with this one, we wanted to break the rules and show why the rules should and shouldn't be broken. Superman goes to him looking for a fight, Darkseid gives him one and they beat each other silly. And at the end Superman does the most un-Superman thing you could do. He takes a defeated enemy, throws him in the street and frees the people of the planet. And then what does he discover?

They don't want to be free. They're used to this, this is their life, and Darkseid, even as badly wounded as he is, basically laughs at Superman and hands him one of the worst defeats of his life. He says, "You've attacked me, and yet you've gained nothing. You're going to go back to Earth and they're going to treat you like a pariah. There's no happy ending for you." And there isn't. And the bitter lesson Superman learns is that he can't fight by the same rules as a hero like Batman. His power is an awesome responsibility — much more so than a character that uses that mantra, Spider-Man. With Superman, there are certain things that, even though he's physically capable of doing, for whatever moral reason he just can't do. With all of that in mind, he goes back to Earth and even though he winds up probably at the lowest point of his life, he does gain the love of Lois Lane… which is not a bad tradeoff; not a bad trade off at all.

BRUCE TIMM: The last episode of *Superman* was the second of a two-part Darkseid story and it's actually a pivotal moment for our Superman and Lois in that they kiss for the first time, so it represents a turning point for them. Too bad it was the last episode.

And yet the story wasn't over — not really as the DC Animated Universe would continue to expand, first in the form of Justice League, *which teamed the Man of Steel with Batman, Wonder Woman, the John Stewart Green Lantern, Flash, Martian Manhunter and Hawkgirl.* Then *there was* Justice League Unlimited *which, running from 2004 to 2006, took the approach that at least one of the big three — Superman, Batman or Wonder Woman — work with other DC heroes to deal with various situations.*

BRUCE TIMM: When we were developing *Superman*, we didn't quite know what to do with him the way we did with Batman. Even though, again, we were dealing with a big iconic hero. We all kind of got Superman, we knew what made him tick, but he didn't have the psychological underpinnings that Batman did, which is what made Batman instantly interesting to us. One of the things we toyed with at the time was doing a Superman show that was half-Superman and half the Justice League, where it was almost a Superman team-up show. At that point, when we talked about doing a back door Justice League show, some of the lineup we picked for the pitch were not the standard Justice League characters. But when Marvel did their Avengers show in the '90s, they made a radical mistake by not having the Avengers be Captain America, Thor and Iron Man, plus the other guys. Anybody who's a comic book fan, when they hear there's an Avengers show, you want to see the big three and you feel a little bit cheated when you don't see them. All of these things were going through our minds when we decided on the lineup for *Justice League.*

For the writers, Superman — who was now being voiced by George Newbern — was still proving himself to be a problem, which is why in the first season of the show they seemingly disposed of him as quickly as they could so that the focus could be elsewhere.

STAN BERKOWITZ: On *Justice League*, there was less of a personal story for Superman. He becomes more of a leader or a father figure; an organizer as opposed to a guy who has various traumas. We could do our little emotional stories with subsidiary characters. In fact, that was the plan with *Justice League* — rather than seeing Batman, Superman and Wonder Woman every single week, we would use at least one of those three; at least one of those three plus guests and guest heroes. And it was easy to write for the guest hero because you're doing an origin story and then they had some kind of character arc with it.

JAMES TUCKER: Superman got beat up and knocked on his ass all the time on his own show. The difference was that the camera stayed on Superman because it was his show. There was no one else to come in and pick up the slack or change the focus to. Because the focus was on Superman, you waited until he got up and came back. Well on *Justice League*, Superman takes a licking, goes off screen and we don't necessarily follow him. We stay at that point and Green Lantern or Wonder Woman comes in. The main mistake we made with that was having him get hit all the time and not showing him recovering and coming right back. We erred on the side of caution because Superman theoretically should be able to handle all of these problems by himself. I don't think we made him weaker, we just didn't cover our bases as far as showing him *be* Superman.

RICH FOGEL (producer, *Superman: The Animated Series*): A lot of thought went into approaching the character. One was that we needed to get situations where the other heroes had an opportunity to show what they could do because they hadn't been in series before. We had to devise ways to knock Superman out of the picture so the other guys could do things. The other thing — and I don't know how to put this delicately — is that there was a certain inattentiveness to the storyboarding in the first season. There were certain bits of business that had been successful in the past with Superman in his own series that tended to get repeated a lot. These were not written in the scripts, it was in fleshing out the action that this happened. It wasn't until we got the footage back that we saw Superman was getting kicked around a lot. In the second season, we tried to pay better attention to it so that we were not letting things like that slip through the cracks.

J.M. DEMATTEIS: I have to be honest, a lot of those guys on staff did a lot of the heavy lifting where the story would be worked out beforehand, and my job was to create the teleplay. But here's my philosophy in general with these things: If you can get into the character's head and do something interesting, that's the most important thing. The powers after a certain point are immaterial. But I do understand the problem, because on one level Superman *is* the Justice League; what do you need those other guys for? But it's also reflective of who he is as a person that he *wants* to be with this team. He *wants* to work with these people together to be the best they can be and inspire them. Basically, every Justice League story reaches a point where somebody turns around and says, "This is the guy we all look up to." In his heart of hearts, that's the guy Batman looks up to as well… of course he'd never admit it.

JAMES TUCKER: There's no way to easily change directions mid-stream. It's like a ship leaving a dock: You can't turn around right away. You just have to make the best of what you've got, and if you get a pick up for another season, address then. That's what we did with "Twilight."

"Twilight" was the season two premiere which pit the Justice League against Brainiac and, more importantly Darkseid. As to changes in approaching Superman, at one point he warns the ruler of Apokalips, "I'm not stopping until you're a grease smear on my fist."

BRUCE TIMM: We felt we needed to draw a line in the sand and say, "This is our mission statement for season two," which is, "Goodbye Superwimp." We may have overcompensated in that episode; some of his dialogue is a little out there. It's definitely in context of him dealing with Darkseid. He'd never say it to Luthor, but he could to Darkseid. In any case, it represented a major change from season one. We also wanted to, as our season two opener, do as big, expansive and epic a storyline as we could. Bringing Darkseid back was definitely something that people had wanted to see, so it certainly made for a good stunt for the season two premiere.

A highlight of the episode's climax was when Batman tries to stop Superman's vendetta against Darkseid and is thrown violently against a wall.

BRUCE TIMM: It was a good spin on their relationship. I particularly love Superman's line at the end where he tells Batman that he's not always right. That's another thing we got accused of quite often, that Batman is the one with all the answers, and if he can take down the entire Injustice Gang by himself, what does he need the Justice League for? That was a good bit: to have Batman eat a slice of humble pie at the end.

Another significant episode for Superman was "Hereafter," in which the League believes that he's been vaporized while saving them, but in reality he's been transported to Earth's far future... where he is powerless and comes up against the still-living Vandal Savage.

DWAYNE MCDUFFIE (producer, *Justice League Unlimited*): My marching orders were to create a story that combined the comic book story "Under a Red Sun" with "Death of Superman." The problem with "Death of Superman" is everybody's seen that story. We didn't want to have Doomsday come in and punch Superman until he was dead, which is what happened in the comic book. I wanted Superman to die in sacrifice and I really wanted to do a story about what Superman meant to the other characters. And moreover, when you've got a character like Superman versus Batman, you want to show that Superman is formidable, that he's a hero without his powers. Sending him off to this future world where he doesn't have superpowers, but he's still the master of everything he comes up against, underlines the fact that if he didn't have the powers, he'd still be a very formidable person. I mean, how tough is it to be a hero when nothing can hurt you?

Superman was very much at the center of things in the first season of Justice League Unlimited, *with "For the Man Who Has Everything," based on the Alan Moore story of the same name from 1985's* Superman Annual #11. *Wonder Woman and Batman arrive at the Fortress of Solitude for Superman's birthday, but quickly discern that he is being held captive by Mongul in the Fortress, and is under the effects of a wish-fulfilling parasitic plant known as the Black Mercy, which has left him prisoner in a dream where Krypton was never destroyed and he leads an idyllic life. Batman and Wonder Woman have to break him free, no matter the consequences.*

ALAN MOORE (writer, comic story "The the Man Who Has Everything"): The idea behind the story was to examine the concept of escapism and fantasy dream worlds, including happy times in the past that we look back on and idealize, and longed-for points in the imagined future when we will finally achieve whatever our goal happens to be. I wanted to have a look at how useful these ideas actually are and how wide the gap is between the fantasy and any sort of credible reality. It was a story, if you like, for the people I've encountered who are fixated upon some point in the past where things could have gone differently or who are equally obsessed with some hypothetical point in the future when certain circumstances will have come to pass and they can finally be "happy." People who say, "If only I hadn't married that man or that woman. If only I'd stayed in college, left college earlier, settled down, gone off to see the world, got that job I turned down…" or who say, "When the mortgage is paid off, then I can enjoy myself. When I'm promoted and I get more money, then I can have a good time. When the divorce comes through, when the kids are grown up, when I finally manage to get my novel published…" These people are so enslaved by their perception of the past and future that they are incapable of properly experiencing the present until it's vanished. (*Alan Moore's Writing for Comics*)

J.M. DEMATTEIS: If I had been aware of how revered that story was when I adapted it, I would've been scared to death. They said they were going to adapt it and sent it to me and I said, "Oh, I've never read it." And when I did, I said, "Oh, this is a cool story." We worked out the adaptation and off we went. And I love those kind of "what if?" stories. It manages to be a present-day Superman story and an Elseworlds story at the same time, which is what's so much fun about it. In a weird way it's like *It's a Wonderful Life*. Superman is George Bailey in that with this thing on his face, he's stepping into this other life that he could have lived. I don't have any profound thoughts about it necessarily, although what I appreciate is that what pulls him back out of this sort of idyllic dream is that he's needed here, so he has to come back. And there's that question of how much he sacrificed to be what he is. There's a part of him that would've been happy to stay on the farm and help his folks and live that life, being a farmer for the rest of his life. But that's not the hand that fate dealt him and he always rises to the occasion.

Flash forward to the end of the series, the final two episodes, and Darkseid has returned, more powerful than ever and ready to decimate Earth. The Justice League is the only thing that stands between him and his goal, and it's Superman who takes him on in a way that he never has before. The Man of Steel delivers a devastating punch to the ruler of Apokalips, and then a short — but oh-so-character-rich — speech in which he proclaims, "I feel like I live in a world made of **cardboard**, *always taking constant care not to break something, to break* someone. *Never allowing myself to lose control even for a moment, or someone could* die. *But you can take it, can't you, big man? What we have here is a rare opportunity for me to cut loose and show you just how powerful I really am."*

BRUCE TIMM: *That's Dwayne McDuffie. Completely Dwayne. He pulled that out of his ass and it's one of his best bits of writing. It's just such a great scene between the two of them, and I think it brought real power and a real sense of finality to the whole thing.*

J.M. DEMATTEIS: The trick with these iconic characters also is to find corners of their psyches that haven't been explored before. It's almost like they're in a cage and you can't move outward because the cage is there. But you can always dig *deeper*. I did a story in the early 2000s called "Superman, Where is Thy Sting?" which I thought was dealing with something nobody ever had before. Forgetting the 10,000 other Kryptonians they've thrown our way over the years, if you're the sole survivor of a planet where everyone else died, on some level in your psyche, there has to be survivor's guilt. I used that as a springboard to jump into this story and expand and expound on that. You always have to look for things in the characters that haven't been touched on before. It gets harder and harder when they've been around for 60, 70, 80 years, but *that's* the challenge. When you write these characters, you have to find a way to make them interesting. And you can bend them only so far because you can't break them. Otherwise, they're not the character anymore.

The Adventures of Superman *radio series holds the record for being the longest-running version of the Man of Steel, airing from 1940 to 1951 for a total of an impressive*

2,088 episodes. Flash forward 50 years from that show's demise, and Smallville, *its next closest runner-up in terms of longevity, hit the television airwaves for what would be a 10-year run from 2001 to 2010 with 217 hour-long episodes produced.*

Smallville, *which ushered the filmed legacy of Superman into the 21st century, focuses on a teenaged Clark Kent who's dealing not only with the normal issues of adolescence, but also the newly-revealed fact that he's an alien accompanied by a variety of dawning superpowers that are suddenly making themselves known. On top of that, there's a foreboding destiny as laid out by his Kryptonian father Jor-El. Other integral characters are Lana Lang, the one person aside from Lois Lane (unless you count someone like mermaid Lori Lemaris from the comics) for whom the destined-to-be Man of Steel ever had*

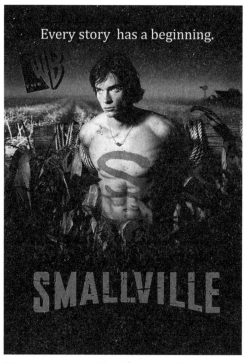

A Superman show without Superman? It sounded like a joke, but Smallville had the last laugh (© and TM DC Comics/Warner Bros. Discovery).

true feelings, and the twenty-something Lex Luthor, whose ruthless father Lionel has left him in Smallville to prove himself a proper heir to the family fortune.

Clark's best friends include Pete Ross and Chloe Sullivan, and there would be others, most notably Chloe's cousin, Lois Lane herself, a romance with Clark to gradually develop. On top of all of that, there's the arrival of a number of other DC characters, albeit altered for the world of Smallville, *including Oliver Queen/Green Arrow and Clark's Kryptonian cousin Kara Zor-El/Supergirl. Most integral to Clark's maturation process are his adopted Earth parents Jonathan and Martha Kent, who are his grounding force, particularly when he gets carried away with his powers.*

The set-up of the show has Clark's ship arriving on Earth in Smallville, Kansas, accompanied by huge amounts of Kryptonite meteorites, which not only have an impact on both Lana and Lex, but many of the denizens of the town who, as the years pass, develop uncanny abilities as a result. These latter facts fill Clark with guilt and a sense of responsibility to protect the people of the town with his newfound abilities.

AL GOUGH (co-creator/executive producer, *Smallville*): I think the metaphor of *Smallville* was definitely that this time of your life is one of change. Things in town are mutating, the town is mutating both literally and figuratively. The show was sort of crystallizing who you are.

ZACH MOORE (host, *Always Hold on to Smallville* podcast): Like any form or art or media, you bring yourself to it, so if you watch it at different points of your life, it means different things to you. When I was younger it was more about the fact that I was the same age as Clark and I'm growing up *with* him. When it started, it was *Dawson's Creek* with superpowers. That's what people said, and that was a pretty fair summary of what it was. Then it goes on so long that it becomes kind of a proto-Superman show. On that level you have to accept it like, "Hey, it's not a prequel to Superman anymore. This is the Superman story, just happening younger in a different interpretation."

JOHN KENNETH MUIR: I still remember the early days of *Smallville* when snarky geeks termed the program "Dawson's Cape" or "Kal-El's Creek." In truth, that comparison to another teen-centric WB hit series never exactly fit, and *Smallville* seemed to reinvent itself every couple of years anyway. *Smallville* began as a series that was part-*Buffy the Vampire Slayer* and part-*X-Files* since it focused on a team of adolescent "Scoobies" — Clark Kent, Lana, Pete Ross and high-school reporter Chloe Sullivan — investigating "Freaks of the Week" from Chloe's "Wall of Weird."

The irony is that Smallville *should not have worked at all given its "No tights, no flights" tagline, the translation of which is that we would not see Clark don his Superman outfit, nor would he be flying around (which didn't rule out tall leaps in a single bound). As things worked out though, it was probably that philosophical guideline which allowed the series to enjoy its duration as its appeal to a mainstream audience was greater than a straight Superman series likely would have been — which is precisely what co-creators Al Gough and Miles Millar were hoping for.*

AL GOUGH: Our idea was, "You know where the journey ends, this is where it begins." For us, the costume was never an issue. Batman's always been sort of cool and people can relate to him. One of the problems with Superman is how do you make him relatable? I think he's always been seen as the goody-two-shoes of superheroes. In truth, you never spent that much time in Smallville. It's a wonderful section of Richard Donner's movie, but it's only 15 minutes. There really hasn't been any set mythology in Smallville, which was really nice for us because that's why we were sort of able to go into it and be respectful of the Superman mythology without being slavish to it.

MILES MILLAR (co-creator/executive producer, *Smallville*): For us it was always a very compelling idea and in our minds we always knew it would succeed. We found it liberating to take him out of the suit and really see the reason Superman becomes the man he becomes; really get inside this kid's head and find out *why* he decides to do good for the world. Usually you see Superman as the character and Clark Kent as the foil, but here it's Clark Kent is the character and Superman will be the foil later on.

AL GOUGH: The series was done with the blessing and consultation of DC Comics, and the great thing about Superman is that it's always been reinterpreted for every generation throughout the decades. DC would be the first to tell you the mythology in *Smallville* was squishy at best. There is one version where Lex and Clark are friends, but then Superboy does something in his lab that causes him to lose his hair and hates him for the rest of his life, and a version years later where he's much older. When we came up with this new interpretation and pitched it to Jenette Kahn, she gave us her blessing.

MILES MILLAR: Early on we were criticized for our approach. You know, "He becomes Superman in Metropolis and not in Smallville." For us it was like, "You've seen *Lois & Clark*, you've seen the four Christopher Reeve movies, how do you do it differently? How do you take an area of his life you haven't seen before and do it in a way that's fresh and original?" We wanted to do something different and we thought the character was such a pop culture icon that people would still respond. We never wanted to have the massive comic book villains taking over the world kind of plots; we wanted to keep it real. When we were first introducing the series, someone suggested that we were doing the Marvel version of Superman, which we didn't understand at the time. Now that we've worked on *Spider-Man,* we understand it. We definitely see the emotional core of the character, which has always been a trademark of Marvel characters.

ZACH MOORE: You cannot get angry he's fighting Zod and Brainiac and all these things, or that Green Arrow was a main character. If it was a prequel to Superman, that would be very upsetting, but it's not breaking continuity because the show is its own continuity. And I think that's an important distinction when you look at something like *Smallville*. Then if you look at something like the *Star Wars* prequel trilogy or *Star Trek: Discovery*, or these other shows that are supposed to lead directly into other things, it causes a lot of fan frustration. When you love those things, you have this encyclopedic knowledge and you know how everything is supposed to look and where it ends up. It gets frustrating when you feel like everything has been ignored. With *Smallville* though, you can disconnect, because this isn't leading to *Superman: The Movie* or *Superman Returns* or *Lois & Clark*. It's its own thing.

MILES MILLAR: The interesting thing about the show is that from the outset you know how it's going to end. You know Lex and Clark are going to end up in Metropolis and be bitter enemies. For us, it was how interested and unexpected is the journey to Metropolis, because *that's* what the series was about.

CRAIG BYRNE (webmaster, kryptonsite.com): A big thing that worked for the series, especially in its basic concept, is that it wasn't just the story of Clark Kent's ascent into being Superman; it was also Lex Luthor's descent into evil. They went to great lengths to make sure that we had a Lex Luthor that everybody cared about, and it helped that they had an actor like Michael Rosenbaum's level of talent to do that.

Smallville's beginning can be traced back to the fact that the then WB — a network whose demographics skewered young and whose reputation was built on shows like Buffy the Vampire Slayer *and* Dawson's Creek *that would later become the CW — had begun developing a "Young Bruce Wayne" series that was designed to focus on the orphaned millionaire on his way to becoming* The Dark Knight. *The project ultimately fell apart, most likely due to the fact that the studio began to feel that it would interfere with their big-screen Batman franchise that they were hoping to reboot at the time. This is where Gough and Millar entered the scene.*

AL GOUGH: Miles and I got a call from Peter Roth, then president of Warner Bros. television. At Warners, the feature division controlled the Batman and Superman rights and they were developing two Batman movies at the time. As a result, they seemed more willing to let Superman go since their Superman movie was stuck in development hell. We got a call from Peter and he said, "I've gotten permission from the feature people to do a young Superman series." We said, "Well that sounds interesting, but we're not interested in doing Superboy." We told him our idea and he thought it was an interesting approach and we came up with our pitch, which was the idea of the meteor shower and that Clark's ship arrived with Kryptonite meteorites. *That*, I think, is the biggest change to the mythology. That gave us storytelling possibilities in that the place Clark lives is actually, in a way, home to his greatest weakness, which is Kryptonite. Then the Kryptonite itself allows you to do weird mutations. In the beginning we kept telling people that this show is *Dawson's Creek* on the surface and *Twin Peaks* underneath. It also allowed Clark to battle people who can have a superpower while at the same time discovering more about himself.

DAVID NUTTER (director of the *Smallville* pilot): Peter Roth had moved over to Warner Bros. and he wanted me to become a member of the Warner Bros. Television family. He brought me in, sat me down and talked to me about his dream of *Smallville*. In my early days as a director I was involved with *Superboy* for Viacom. Making Clark Kent accessible — someone people can relate to and understand and see that he is not indestructible — is what appealed to me. I wanted to make him a hero, not a superhero. My attitude was also let's not make this show what people would expect from Superman. Let's not do the things that will basically be things they expect. Let's make it new and different, and Al and Miles were on that path all the way.

CRAIG BYRNE: The series deserves credit for the things it added to the mythos, the meteor shower being possibly the largest, which just made sense. And then the notion that Kryptonite affected people in ways that usually were tied to the characters' personalities.

AL GOUGH: From a practical point of view, if a spaceship came to Earth in 1989, the rings of satellites around the world would allow someone to see it. For us, the meteor shower was sort of the cover for the spaceship. We're not in the '40s anymore. If anything comes into the atmosphere, somebody sees it instantly, so that's how the meteor shower came about.

DAVID NUTTER: The big thing for me on the pilot was that you were stepping on very hallowed ground, not only from the comic book perspective, but from the perspective of the Richard Donner film, which was so well made. My attitude was, and I thought the script was such, "If I get the teaser the right way I want to, the audience can watch color bars for the rest of the episode because I think I'll have them." I spent a lot of time on that teaser — in which Clark first arrives on Earth — and made it as cinematic as possible. I was very proud of how it turned out and thought it played really well. The show was a difficult one to do because it was setting the tone and the look of *everything*. I brought in a lot of people I'd worked with in the past; it was a group of people who set out to make something great and special, and we did just that. There was a lot of fear involved, but if you believe in what you're doing, you can't let the fear get in the way.

AL GOUGH: The other thing we did was tie Lana and Lex together in terms of the impact the meteors have on both their lives, killing her parents, making him lose his hair. And we came up with the idea of making Jonathan and Martha Kent younger. We went in, pitched it. Peter loved it, DC signed off on the change in the mythology — which was crucial — and then we pitched it to FOX and the WB and the WB really loved it. It just felt like a good fit for the network in terms of what they were trying to do. In truth, it's a lot of fun to reinvent iconic characters and see how they started. To us, Clark was like Anakin Skywalker, somebody whose future you know, but you get to see the journey, which is very interesting. Also, you get to see Lex's journey: How does he become Superman's arch-enemy when he and Clark start off as friends?

DARREN SWIMMER (co-executive producer, *Smallville*): The appeal of writing Clark and Lex was that they were characters who cared deeply for each other, yet ultimately can't be open with each other, which made for good drama. The same was true with Clark and Lana. It's also something we can all relate to, to some degree. The ultimate challenge in any relationship is accepting the other person for who they are, and what's appealing about these relationships is watching the characters navigate the labyrinths of secrecy.

KELLY SOUDERS (co-executive producer, *Smallville*): Clark and Lana reminded us every week how easy it is to let insecurities get in the way of love. It was great fun to write about the relationship between them because it seems impossible for them to find each other through the maze of their lives, but at the same time you have the overwhelming feeling of hope and a love that will prevail in the end.

BRIAN PETERSON (co-executive producer, *Smallville*): You know how in life sometimes you take a look at the people closest to you and ask yourself, "Why is this person my friend, we are so different?" Lex and Clark were trying to deal with the human condition from opposite ends of the spectrum and that's fascinating to me.

JOHN KENNETH MUIR: One key aspect of the program that elevated *Smallville* above mere ripoff of *Buffy* or *The X-Files* was the Clark/Lex Luthor relationship and dynamic. In this universe, Clark and Lex become best friends for a time, but friends with opposite — *and opposing* — destinies. The series often brilliantly played these two men as mirror images in terms of their choices and friendships, and even in terms of their family lives.

MICHAEL ROSENBAUM (actor, "Lex Luthor," *Smallville*): The Lex-Clark relationship was always great and, in fact, the writers made sure that no matter what, there was a Lex-Clark scene in every episode, even if it didn't make sense. They had to put one in there because of the chemistry. Tom and I loved it. We loved working together. People loved watching us. And it's fun! I think that you need a little Clark and Lex in every episode because ultimately that's the most important part of the show. It's the thing that everyone looks forward to, the yin and yang between them before they become enemies.

TOM WELLING (actor, "Clark Kent," *Smallville*): I loved working with Michael. He has great energy and holds a very high bar at work: "Let's get it right. Let's go. Let's keep it fresh. Let's do it again, because that was bullshit." He kept you on your toes. I enjoy acting with him, and the energy that he and I have seeped into the Clark and Lex relationship very well. I think because Michael and I are friends, we have an understanding of each other and are able to play these characters who have this intrinsic connection, but are still trying to figure each other out. For me, that makes their relationship the most interesting one on the show. When people are solely enemies, I don't believe you care very much. But when they have a relationship and a background, something can break and pit them against each other. Lex and Clark becoming friends sets them up for a good fall, and for them to eventually be enemies.

MARK VERHEIDEN (producer/writer, *Smallville*): The Clark/Lex relationship had something almost unique in television, in that viewers with even a cursory understanding of the Superman mythology know exactly where they're heading — to a very bad place. There's always a sense of destiny and foreboding when these two meet, despite their friendship. I have friends, big fans of the show, who begged me not to let Lex "go evil," so evidently we'd done a good job of humanizing a character who had a tendency to be over-the-top in previous incarnations. The Clark/Lana relationship was a whole other thing, and grounded more in a basic teenage reality, the incredible highs and lows that come with your first love. There's nothing more powerful or poignant than unrequited love.

Thomas "Tom" John Patrick Welling, born April 26, 1977 in Putnam Valley, New York, was cast as Clark Kent. He began working in construction when he elected to give modeling a shot in 1998 and proved successful at it. Prior to Smallville, *he had a recurring role on the legal drama* Judging Amy *and made guest appearances on the shows* Special Unit 2 *and* Undeclared.

AL GOUGH: We'd been looking at thousands of people for the Clark Kent role. It was a five-month casting process and we found Tom at the end.

DAVID NUTTER: In looking for Clark Kent, we needed to find the perfect person. I was actually in the L.A. casting person's office one frustrating afternoon, looking at pictures. I saw Tom Welling's picture and said, "What's his story?" She said, "Well, he's not going to come in because his manager says this could hurt his feature career." I called his manager, talked to him for 20 minutes and told him how in this environment in television, the WB *is* a platform to a feature career. With this project, Al and Miles' superb script as well as my track record, I said,

"You should at least come in and read the script and meet." He and Tom came in to read the script before Christmas. Right after Christmas, he came in and read for it. From that point on he was the guy.

AL GOUGH: Obviously he looked like Clark Kent, and that was one part of it — having someone who looked like Clark Kent/Superman in the comics was a contractual thing from DC. And because he never really acted before, he brought a certain naivete to it and a certain stilted quality, which kind of worked for the character because he was learning as Clark was learning. One of Tom's greatest strengths was that he knew what he didn't know, so he was always very open to learning and growing and getting better. There was an earnestness to him that I think really helped with the character. And then as you watch him over the seasons, you see him become a better actor, you see him grow in competence. To some degree his journey mirrored Clark's journey. Unlike a lot of actors, Tom has the ability to be still. If you watch a lot of scenes, he can still be in the scene, he can be listening and a lot of actors need business and things to do. Tom could do that, so he felt very much like Superman that way. There's a certain calmness to him.

MILES MILLAR: Tom was visually striking and such a great iteration of Superman and Clark Kent. Physically it was his height and breadth of his shoulders, and he also had this Midwestern charm, which was real. There was an innocence to him because he'd never done anything, and in the first season in particular it was a huge show and he was learning his chops every day. You see his progression as an actor and what happens in the first two seasons is he goes from not knowing anything and just being a complete novice who's been thrust into this position, and then proving himself to be someone who actually has incredible comedic and acting chops as he went on.

TOM WELLING: I actually made the choice when preparing for this role *not*

to do research on anything else that has been done with this character; really just take it from a fresh standpoint and create its own image. There's really no comparison; it was looking at these characters and showing them at an age you'd never seen them before.

PHIL MORRIS (actor, "John Jones/Martian Manhunter," *Smallville***):** Tom Welling at the time was not a big Superman guy. He didn't know anything about Superman when he got the job, but he learned and evolved. And every time I came up to Vancouver, he picked my brain about the DC universe. He couldn't get enough. And I was one of the few actors who knew a lot about it. He was just a sponge when I would get there and I really appreciated that.

TOM WELLING: What the show was about in the beginning is him finding out who he is and what he is here for. He's got these abilities that he doesn't necessarily understand and it alienates him in a lot of ways from just wanting to be a normal high school kid. What does that do to a person? It brings upon a sense of loneliness as well. Here you are, able to do all these things that no one else can do. He's a teenage kid, but he doesn't really have anyone to turn to and say, "Look at that. Look at how cool that is." He's not able to go out with his buddies and be like, "I can't hurt myself, let's see how far this goes. Let's go to the top of that building and jump off."

MILES MILLAR: We were really trying to mine those moments of what it would be like to be this kid growing up in Kansas with these superpowers. How would you react to that existence if you found you were an alien? That was always our touchstone: What's the emotion we're going to find in this episode? We had the idea that he was a closeted kid who told his parents his secret and they were protecting him from the world. That's changed a lot over the years, but for many gay kids it's not the same now. They are free to be who they are, but back then we did compare Clark to a closeted kid. We also talked about the idea of him being an illegal immigrant, so those are the two ideas that I think emotionally plant him in terms of archetypes.

BRIAN PETERSON: There's an innocence Tom brought to it and I'll just pinpoint it right away. There's an episode called "Hex," which is strangely one of my favorite episodes as far as his acting, because he forgets that he's Superman and that he has any powers — Zatanna has zapped him and he just forgets completely. And that episode kind of encapsulates to me the innocence that he brought to that character that I think helped as he evolved as a person and as an actor. As we all evolved as a show, he was able to grow with it in a way that felt really organic.

KELLY SOUDERS: There are in TV and film a lot of times people write to people's strengths or write around an actor's weaknesses. One of the things that was incredible about Tom is there is nothing that we threw his way that he didn't nail. And even when he played bad, corrupted by Red Kryptonite Clark, I remember everybody watching the dailies and thinking, "Oh my God… he's a really focused and dedicated actor who is so genuine in every moment on screen of *Smallville* that he deserves a lot of credit." And he's also incredibly hard-working. That's something that people don't realize, but we say as often as we can. I mean, who would come and sit in production meetings if he just was not shooting? And he'd sit in a concept meeting, just because he had a little break in acting and wanted to kind of learn more and be more involved. That speaks volumes of him as a dedicated actor.

CRAIG BYRNE: I also must give Tom credit for what a force he became behind the scenes. He knew every aspect of production and asked a lot of questions. The top of the call sheet always has to be the leader, and Tom Welling certainly accomplished that.

MILES MILLAR: The only person Clark could talk to was his parents and, for us, the parents are the guardians of the secret, unlike most shows where the kids have the secret in the clubhouse and the parents are in the dark. Clark actually *would* talk about his problems with his parents, and so for us that made a unique show in terms of a cross-generational discussion about events and problems. The relationship of Clark and his parents is a product of his environment. One thing John Schneider, who played Jonathan, said was, "What would happen if he was found by Lex's father? What kind of person would he turn out to be? At what point did he learn his values and morals?"

JOHN SCHNEIDER (actor, "Jonathan Kent," *Smallville*): We also have to put ourselves, as an audience, in a position of not knowing what this young man is going to become. We all know Superman, we know the legend, but it happens prior to that. There are no flights, no tights, no nothing. That has not happened yet. So from our perspective we were not dealing with Superman as a teenager, we were in effect dealing with a special needs child. I thought it was very important that we understood that the parents knew the secret before Clark did, so it's a conscious effort that keeps us from telling him about his special abilities or handicaps, if you will, whatever they are. And that it was a conscious decision to tell him when we did. For my money, having this kind of parental relationship with someone who is going to grow up to be Superman is something I thought was very beneficial to those who watched the show. I mean, young Clark Kent values and trusts and needs the advice and respect and counsel of his parents. That was important in the Schneider household, I don't know about yours, but I was very thankful to be part of something that was actually elevating the role of parents to where the show was taking it.

TOM WELLING: I talked to my father about the question of typecasting, and he said to me, "Look, it's as much of a career choice that you can really have, but you do your job, you do it well, and people will see that."

Portraying Lana Lang was Kristin Laura Kreuk, born December 30, 1982 in Vancouver, British Columbia. In 2001 she starred in the TV movie Snow White: The Fairest of Them All *and an episode of* The Weekenders. *From 2001 to 2005 she starred in 70 episodes of the Canadian teen drama* Edgemont, *shooting her episodes on Sundays during overlaps with* Smallville's *production schedule.*

KRISTEN KREUK (actor, "Lana Lang," *Smallville***):** When I first heard about it I was a little scared. What I got, first of all, was a breakdown, which basically said that this is a show about Clark Kent growing up, and then it listed the characters and talked about them. When I read it I didn't know if this would be a great show, but the scene they provided was this great scene from the pilot between Clark and Lana in the graveyard, and that kind of just pulls you in. It's good writing and it's a good character. It's not like my character didn't have any depth. So when I met David Nutter, who was directing the pilot, he was *so* enthusiastic about the show and he had so much faith in it, that *I* got excited about it. Peter Roth from Warner Bros. was so enthusiastic about it. Everyone was, so it kind of catches you. Then you read the script and you discover that there's so much in it and you realize that this is going to be a good show.

AL GOUGH: Our rule was if you're sitting in a room and you're watching these people audition and your mind starts to wander, you just have to move on to the next person. You want everybody who comes in the room to be good, but you have to remember how people watch TV. I know how *I* watch TV. If I'm bored, I click. But the first person whose tape we got was Kristen Kreuk. Before the whole script for the pilot was written, we'd written scenes for the actors to audition with. Kristen read the first draft of that scene, she was on video in Vancouver and she was absolutely stunning and captivating. We had casting directors all over the country and we all saw that tape and she was the only one we brought to the network.

MILES MILLAR: Kristen was just magnetic and had such gentle poise, and the beauty that we felt was perfect for Lana *and* the perfect soulmate for Clark in this new iteration. We'd always planned on casting Clark first, but when we saw her tape we all knew we had someone great. So we took her into the studio and everyone loved her there. We took her into the network and she got the role, which is really rare. Usually you take in three or four people from a cattle call kind of thing, but with Kristen we knew we had it. As the same time, I actually felt incredible guilt afterwards because she did not plan her life to be one as an actress. Speaking to her, she was incredibly shy to begin with and was only 18. I don't think she felt comfortable that this was her life's path. At the same time, from the cast of *Smallville,* she's probably done more than anyone and forged her own path as a producer as well. It's gratifying that she's been able to make such an incredible career.

KRISTEN KREUK: Her background and relationship with Clark Kent was very intriguing to me. Lana's parents died when she was three years old and she saw them die. That's something that still haunts her, as is it would anyone. It's a huge thing in her life and she's an orphan who grew up with her aunt. She's popular and a cheerleader and she's got this boyfriend who is the star quarterback. She has all these things that girls would look at and say, "Wow, she has a perfect life." But she doesn't. She's very lonely, and in the beginning I don't think she quite knows who she is yet. She's still discovering that, which I thought was very interesting.

And Lana and Clark have known each other since they were kids, though they've never had the opportunity to talk to each other and get to know each other, thanks to the fact that she wears a Kryptonite necklace and that they're in different social circles. Both of them are these people trying to find out who they are, and they're both on the same journey. They're both so lonely and I think they can see that in each other. That's kind of my take on the whole thing. I think their relationship is interesting. The truth is, there's a great connection there.

*The part of Lex Luthor fell to Michael Owen Rosenbaum, born July 11, 1972 in Oceanside, New York. Of the young cast, he had the most extensive pre-*Smallville *credits, including* The Devil & The Angel, The Day I Ran Into All My Ex-Boyfriends *and* Midnight in the Garden of Good and Evil *(all 1997),* 1999 *and* Urban Legend *(both 1998), the short* Eyeball Eddie *and voicing* "Ghoul" *in* Batman Beyond: Return of the Joker *(both 2000), and* Sweet November *and* Rave Macbeth *(both 2001). He was also a regular on the comedy* Zoe, Duncan, Jack and Jane *(1999 to 2000). In the same year* *that* Smallville *debuted, he voiced the character of The Flash on* Justice League *and then* Justice League Unlimited.

AL GOUGH: If the show was the trials of Clark Kent and the making of a hero, for Lex it was the making of an anti-hero. It was interesting just going into the casting, because people hear Lex Luthor and they would come in and give these very over-the-top Dr. Evil readings of the character. We always wanted somebody who was a comedian who, like a young Michael Keaton, had humor and charisma and a sense of danger to him. Michael came in and really gave us that in spades. Our thing was, you have to take the name Lex Luthor out of the equation. You see him traumatized in the pilot as a child where he loses his hair and that's led to him being kicked out of boarding schools across the world… and his father exiling him to basically run a shit factory in Smallville when he thought he was going to take his rightful place in LuthorCorp. in Metropolis. Throughout the series you see the relationship with Lex and his father and see how sort of twisted it is. Early on he sees in Clark somebody like himself who is alienated, and they become the best of friends because that's the only way you become mortal enemies is if you were the best of friends and then felt that betrayal. Lex is the friend that your parents don't like, but they don't really have a good reason to tell you not to hang out with him.

MICHAEL ROSENBAUM: It's absurd to think that someday you'll play somebody so legendary, and that someday you'll get the audition to play the role of Lex Luthor. Your attitude is, "Yeah, right. What's this going to be about? Some hokey TV show?" Then you read the script and you're enthralled by it. You're saying things like, "Wow, this isn't what I imagined." It's the story before the story. Everybody knows that Lex is evil, but they don't know how he got there. That's the most fun to play as an actor, working up to that.

I was always a Lex Luthor fan. From watching the *Superman* movies, you have to love Gene Hackman. You can't get around that. I was scared to think people were going to say, "He's not Gene Hackman." I was really doing a character before the character was developed. Everybody was seeing Lex Luthor as a villain, so for me I wanted to play it real and go with the writing that they were giving me and just trust it.

AL GOUGH: Michael brought energy and intensity and there was a vulnerability to him. I think comedians are people who want to be loved, so that's part of what Lex wanted. He wanted love and approval and Michael just brought that, and because he was a couple of years older than the other cast, there was a maturity that he had. And then when we put him with John Glover, it was just like, "Oh my God" — just fantastic.

MILES MILLAR: Michael was obviously much more of a seasoned pro. He'd done pilots, he was older than Tom and he had that experience from the get-go. He was incredible just in terms of commanding the screen. He knew what he was and we'd always wanted a comedian in that role, or someone who had comedic chops, because that was necessary for Lex Luthor. You also needed someone you could thrust into that relationship with Lionel Luthor, which is this toxic element in Lex's life that really made him who he is. So you have two extremes and contrast of personalities between Clark and Lex.

AL GOUGH: Also, the best villains don't believe they're villains. They believe they're totally in the right, and I think that's what Michael brought to it. He was basically a young man trying to find his way in the world with a father who is basically crushing him at every turn. The great thing about Lex is you always think, "Oh God, if there were moments that went another way, would he have turned out differently?" And I think Michael just brought a real subtlety to a role that could very easily have been over-the-top.

KELLY SOUDERS: The thing about Michael is that he really could fill the shoes of Lex Luther, but he also was able to constantly bring a vulnerability to his performance, which is what made him so great in the role: You were scared of him on one hand and just wanted to give him a big hug on the other. And it's how he was able to walk both sides of that line in every single scene. I don't know how he made Lex so human and so dangerous at the same time. He was always fascinating to watch on set. He really could bring such depth to a character that sometimes can be sort of two-dimensional… and he never took an easy route.

CRAIG BYRNE: Michael Rosenbaum is by far my favorite Lex Luthor, and I feel a big part of that is, oddly enough, Michael's background in comedy. I've read that comedians — Robin Williams, for instance — strive to be loved, and who on this show would strive for love more than the bald-headed son of Lionel Luthor? I did like the rare moments they let Lex be snarky. In retrospect it's a bit creepy that Lex would want to be friends with a teenager, but we accepted it at the time.

BRIAN PETERSON: There were a couple of seasons in, I can't remember if it was in season five or season six, and he was just sick of Clark's lying. And you were kind of on his side because he was like, "Are you kidding me?" And where I was like, "It's too bad sci-fi shows just never get nominated for Emmys" because there were a couple of scenes where I was like, "That is absolutely an Emmy-worthy performance. I mean that's phenomenal" — especially when he would go toe to toe with Glover. Those scenes were so fun to write; the way they played and the power of them…

And for Rosenbaum, one of the big dilemmas of the early days was whether or not he'd be willing to shave his head.

MICHAEL ROSENBAUM: I had a full head of hair at the time and it was really kind of an ultimatum: "You want to be Lex Luthor? Shave your head." None of us really knew what it was going to look like; they were scared out of their minds.

AL GOUGH: We were scared because people would come in to audition, and sometimes it was funny because they would be wearing these knit caps and you would be like, "What are they, a gangster or something?" And they were like, "No, we're trying to show what we would look like bald." That was a strange thing. We didn't want a bald cap because they just look fake, but to get Michael emotionally prepared, we brought him over to the studio so we could see how much time it took each day to put a bald cap on.

MICHAEL ROSENBAUM: I looked like a cone head so I said, "We're going to shave it. I'm not going to be dealing with putting this on every day." It takes you out of reality when you're watching a show and see some guy's bald cap with a crease in it. You've got to take some risks as an actor, and this was one of them. So I shaved it and had no big dents in my head, which was a good thing, and it grows back. They wanted to use chemicals and stuff on my head and I said, "No, we're not doing that. I've got to work later on in life," hopefully.

Clark's best friend Chloe Sullivan was played by Allison Christin Mack, born July 29, 1982 in Preetz, Schleswig-Holstein, West Germany. Her career began as a a model appearing in print ads and commercials for a German chocolate factory. Early film roles include Police Academy 6: City Under Siege *(1989),* Night Eyes 3 *(1993),* Camp Nowhere *(1994),* No Dessert, Dad, till You Mow the Lawn *(1995) and* Honey, We Shrunk Ourselves *(1997). On television she appeared in 12 TV movies between* I Know My Name is Steven *(1989) and* My Horrible Year! *(2001). As would be revealed much later, Mack was a part of the cult NXIVM and was sentenced to three years in jail beginning in 2021, having being found guilty of sex trafficking, sex trafficking conspiracy and forced labor conspiracy connected with the group.*

CRAIG BYRNE: I know talking about Allison Mack is a controversial thing

right about now, but Chloe was one of Al and Miles' best creations. At the start
— before they decided to make Chloe a meteor freak herself, which never really
worked for me — she was the outsider/Everyman-type character that a series
like this needed, and no one could deliver a quippy line better than Allison Mack.
Because Chloe wasn't the designated love interest for Clark, it allowed Allison and
Tom to have a great on-screen chemistry because they weren't trying to make it
awkward or tense. Clark and Lana would often have long pauses between times —
with these two, it was "bam, bam, bam." Despite what would later happen with her
in real life, Allison was a perfect addition.

*Pivotal in raising Clark into the morally centered man he becomes are his parents Jona-
than and Martha Kent. Jonathan is played by John Schneider, who at that point was most
famous for playing "Bo" Duke on the popular* Dukes of Hazzard *television series. Born
April 8, 1960 in Mount Kisco, New York, he began putting on magic shows when he was
eight years old. He was 18 when he was cast as Bo, the* Dukes *running from 1979 to 1985.
He appeared in many TV movies and miniseries prior to* Smallville, *and had recurring
or starring roles on* Grand Slam *(1990),* Heaven Help Us *(1994),* Second Chances
(1994), Dr. Quinn, Medicine Woman *(1997 to 1998),* Veronica's Closet *(1999 to
2000) and* Relic Hunter *(2000 to 2001).*

AL GOUGH: For Martha and Jonathan, we wanted to cast young. We were
like, "We're not casting grandma and grandpa here." Schneider came in and we
met him and he was very Jonathan. In all these shows, the parents are idiots or the
children are smarter than them. My kids don't give me advice and they don't pay
my bills, so he brought in good baggage. I believe Bo Duke would grow up to be
Jonathan Kent.

JOHN SCHNEIDER: We gave him a conscience or we fed the one he had,
or things could have gone horrifically wrong. The other thing that was so wonderful about *Smallville* — and Annette [O'Toole], Tom and I really have to take credit
for this — is we constantly reminded ourselves that there was no such thing as
Superman, so we had no idea where this was going. We hadn't read the books, we
hadn't seen the television show — Superman did not exist. This was our son Clark,
and in our minds we didn't know the end from the beginning, because otherwise
you take some of the import away from the moral dilemma.

On the surface, and this is a silly one, but the reason I wouldn't let him play
football for so long is because it wasn't fair — not because he was Superman, but
because he could kill somebody and he was also ridiculously impervious to pain.
He would get unfair lessons about sportsmanship, and that would damage him

later. As his powers would emerge, we would talk to one another on the set and say, "Okay, is this an ability or a disability? How are we going to treat X-ray vision or heat vision? We need to harness this, whatever it is, for good."

CRAIG BYRNE: Jonathan Kent was gruff but usually fair, and you could see that both he and Annette had affection for Tom Welling in the same way that Jonathan and Martha had for Clark. It was another of those aspects of the show that works.

Playing Jonathan's better half Martha is Annette O'Toole, born April 1, 1952 in Houston, Texas. She made her television debut at the age of 13 in a 1967 episode of The Danny Kaye Show, *followed by guest appearances on popular TV shows of the time, including* Gunsmoke *and* The Partridge Family. *It wasn't long before she started being cast in films, among them* Smile *(1975),* One on One *(1977),* Foolin' Around *(1980),* 48 Hrs. *and* Cat People *(both 1982). In 1983, she actually played Lana Lang opposite Christopher Reeve's Man of Steel in* Superman III, *and the film roles kept on coming, as did appearances in TV movies, miniseries and episodic series. She also had starring roles in* Nash Bridges *(1996 to 1998) and* The Huntress *(2000 to 2001).*

AL GOUGH: What Annette O'Toole conveyed is that she was the city girl who'd fallen in love with the country boy, and they moved to Smallville for love. And then there was the maternal aspect she brought to it. We just got incredibly lucky with that core cast.

CRAIG BYRNE: Annette O'Toole is one of the kindest people I've ever met, and I loved the heart that she brought to Martha Kent. I do feel sometimes that the series didn't do enough with her character, especially after Jonathan died. In my opinion, Jonathan Kent taught Clark about right and wrong, and Martha should have taught him about the heart and kindness that comes with humanity.

Bringing much in the way of gravitas to Smallville *was John Glover as Lex's father Lionel Luthor. He was born John Soursby Glover Jr. on August 7, 1944 in Kingston, New York and was initially drawn to the stage, but eventually made it to the big screen in Burt Reynolds' detective comedy-drama* Shamus *(1973), which would be followed by no less than 35 films between that and* On Edge *(2001), with many more to follow. In 1975 he guest starred on the Telly Savalas series* Kojak *and appeared on a variety of other shows and in TV movies. He starred on* Brimstone *(1998 to 1999) as the Devil.*

MILES MILLAR: The Lionel/Lex relationship was only meant to be in the pilot and maybe a few episodes after that, but as soon as we saw the connection between John and Michael, we realized we could be contrasting these parallel family units between the Luthors and Kents and the contrasting parenting styles. It felt like a no-brainer to keep John. That's what's great about television: When you see something like that, you can jump in and exploit it. It's really just something magical that happens between people and between the writing and the character, and when the magic does happen, it's incredible!

CRAIG BYRNE: *Smallville* hit the casting jackpot when they recruited John Glover for Lionel Luthor. The fans called Lionel a "magnificent bastard" and rightfully so. Every time he'd come on screen, especially in scenes with Lex, he'd turn things on their ear. John Glover is a man who clearly gives 120% to every part he plays, and Lionel was no exception.

In the first season, there was most definitely a formula for Smallville *that was born out of the fear that people might not be able to connect with the show. For this reason, there was a very clear decision made that the first batch of episodes would, while introducing the main characters, feature guest stars that were exposed to Kryptonite and would, in turn, have their DNA altered and find themselves endowed with bizarre abilities. The Kryptonite "freak of the week" may not have been the most sophisticated means of crafting stories, but they seemed to achieve the desired goal before those stories became decidedly more character-oriented.*

AL GOUGH: Truthfully, we did not approach the show with the attitude that everybody knew who Superman was and what Kryptonite was. When we were breaking the first five or six stories, we wanted to really make sure that the premise of the show — even if you had never seen Superman — was something you'd get. We did not want to go with the thought, "Oh, everybody's going to know what Kryptonite is." In truth, a lot of people — especially because we were on the WB and dealing with a younger audience of 12-25 — didn't grow up with the Richard Donner movie or *Lois & Clark*.

MILES MILLAR: We planned on five freaks of the week and did seven, which was too many. Basically we kept repeating the pilot. The general theory was that the avid viewer watches one in three weeks. For a new viewer, you wanted to establish that this is the show. At the time it was a really radical reinvention of Superman as Kryptonite had never done this stuff before. The concerns were understandable, though they underestimated the intelligence of the audience in a way. We didn't hit our stride until the first season episode "X-Ray." That's where we really thought we'd begun to find the balance between the three main characters of Lex, Lana and Clark. We found the fabric of the show.

Finding that fabric was very expensive. They were very generous with us in the first seven episodes. They said, "Go out and make it big," and we did. And we had a very big visual effects budget as well. The challenge was also in doing an action-adventure show of this scale in Vancouver. *The X-Files* began as a very small, under the radar show, and it evolved into this phenomenon — it didn't start that way, but we did. Finding a crew up there and finding the right production team was a challenge.

ZACH MOORE (host, *Always Hold on to Smallville* podcast): Some of the early seasons are a little bit cheesy, but I feel like the early seasons were the most true to the concept of the character of Clark Kent growing up in Smallville. And in those earlier episodes — not that it totally goes away — there was always some sort of through line that all that characters had, because they were going through a similar journey, particularly Lex, Clark and Lana. Yes, there was a freak of the week and a fun superpowered fight, or maybe Clark got a new superpower, but there was some kind of theme to it. They spent a lot of time and attention trying to do that.

JEPH LOEB (writer/producer, *Smallville*): Gough and Millar's inventiveness — the meteor shower creating Clark's ongoing guilt, giving you a compelling reason for him to be the hero and the entire Lex/Clark relationship with all its double meanings — was all very fertile ground that was new and unique to the character. Then, the Lana/Clark relationship was the heart of the show, and the relationship between Clark and Lex was the soul. Lex's future is decided so his youth is entirely up for grabs. Anything he does was second-guessed by the audience and in the show by Jonathan Kent, who happened to be the show's moral barometer. So the odds are stacked against him no matter what. The flip side is that there is a young, naïve Clark who so wants to be Lex's best friend that he can't see any flaws. And Lex was, at that point, sincerely interested in knowing Clark for the rest of his life. If you know what happens, then you have a resonance that all the money in the world can't buy you. It works and works, but it has to be done very carefully.

ZACH MOORE: When you get to the middle of *Smallville's* run, it starts to feel like we're spinning our wheels because the show in many ways was a victim of its own success in that it's supposed to be a prequel, but we can't end it now. So it's like three steps forward, 10 steps back. Analyzing it, you can nitpick it to death and it can be frustrating, but at the time you were just happy that the show was on and tackling things like the Lex/Clark relationship.

JEPH LOEB: I grew up with Lex living in Smallville and having lost his hair due to a mistake that Superboy made, so the concept of them being friends before enemies was there, but Al and Miles changed it entirely. Lex in the *Superboy* comic was just a junior version of his adult self. Since the stories were retrofitted to make it an "historical" relationship, Lex was just this evil kid who made bad robots to chase Superboy. It wasn't until John Byrne and Marv Wolfman (who is credited with the "new" Luthor) changed all that in 1986 that Lex didn't meet Superman or Clark until he came to Metropolis. This has some good things and some bad things, as any wrinkle in time will do. But in terms of how that dynamic worked in the first year of Superman, I spent an entire chapter of *Superman: For All Seasons* narrated by Lex, so you could hear *his* side of the story. As he said, it was a love story — between a man and a city, and the city betrayed him for another (i.e. Superman). He's very rational, he's brilliant. Hell, because of me and the rest of the gang in the Superman group at DC, he became President of the United States.

TOM WELLING: The Lex–Clark relationship is one of the most interesting of the show, just because we *know* where these people end up. Later on in these characters' lives — in the comics and in the movies — you don't hear so much about anyone *other* than Clark and Lex. So it makes sense that we spent a lot of time with them.

ZACH MOORE: As you were watching the show, it was fun to speculate on the how and when Clark and Lex were going to have a falling out, and how are they going to handle Lana leaving? Because clearly Clark doesn't end up with Lana, although I don't know if a lot of people watching the show then knew that. What I'm thinking is that if you watch the show when you're younger — not that this is the case with everyone — you maybe identify with Clark, and maybe when you're older and more mature and you're watching it, maybe you identify more with Lex. Or at least you can understand the more complicated themes of Lex and his dad; the Luthors and the Kents are really what the show's about — fathers and sons. And then, Michael Rosenbaum and John Glover are far and away the best actors on the show and anything they did is gold.

TOM WELLING: Season one was about getting to know Clark a little bit, introducing him to the viewing audience, letting you in on where he came from and what he's all about. Season one gave you the basis of who he *was*, and I think the rest of the series concentrates more and more on who he is *becoming*. We know that he becomes Superman, so the show is about what happens on the road to his becoming Superman — the things that shape who he is.

AL GOUGH: As we were coming out of season one, I was reminded of the notion that there are only three emotions in Hollywood: depression, surprise and relief. Well if you live in a "the glass is half-empty" world like I do, there's always that sort of gnawing concern in the back of your head when you're about to launch a second year. You start to think, "Is it a one-season wonder? Will people come back for season two? Not only that, but can you build your audience?" Network and studio executives always say, "Season two is when you're supposed to build your audience," and you kind of do wonder why more people are tuning in. The concern of course is that every year the network has to market new shows, and you wonder if you're going to get lost in the clutter of returning shows. I guess that *didn't* happen.

JOHN KENNETH MUIR: By the time of the second season, the freak-of-the-week paradigm became less repetitive, and the series focused on charting Clark's journey to manhood. Accordingly — and across a decade — *Smallville* became more confident of its identity as a more traditional re-assertion of the Superman legend, one featuring a variety of villains and heroes from DC comics, plus serialized storylines of remarkable complexity and maturity.

AL GOUGH: There was only about a quarter of the episodes in year two that had a freak-of-the-week, and even those were much stronger than they were in season one. I also think we got into more of the Superman mythology.

That came largely in the form of episodes that began to explore Clark's Kryptonian heritage, whether it be "Skinwalker," in which Indian cave walls reveal a legend that runs parallel to Clark's life; "Rosetta," which features Christopher Reeve as Dr. Virgil Swann, who tells Clark about Krypton and offers up even more background as well as a Kryptonian "key" that plays a significant role in several episodes; or the voice of Jor-El makes contact with Clark and demands that his time in Smallville is at an end and he must leave to embrace his destiny. Additionally, the season introduces the concept of Red Kryptonite, which in this incarnation of the mythos unleashes Clark's evil "bad boy" side, and explored Clark's heat vision for the first time.

AL GOUGH: We always wanted to introduce heat vision in a sex-ed class; the shows are fun when you can do the "puberty with superpowers" paradigm. We also finally got the heat vision the way that we wanted it; that was difficult.

MILES MILLAR: Back in the pilot, Al and I had written a scene where he has heat vision during sex education class; we kind of saved it from the pilot and put in season two's "Heat." It was cut due to budget and time, but we kept the idea that sex is the trigger. It's a light episode that gets dark toward the end.

MARK VERHEIDEN: Jonathan trying to give Clark heat vision lessons while Elvis Presley croons in the background cracks me up every time.

MAT BECK (visual effects supervisor, *Smallville*): The evolution of the look of the heat vision parallels one of Clark's own steps toward maturing, so we had to make his heat vision look different each time as he developed better control. Initially it's actually snaking around and flipping all over the place uncontrollably, but by the end of the episode he has really good control over it.

JEPH LOEB: Al and Miles wanted to do a "Red K" story and for the high school class ring to be the delivery device. It was a gift from them to me since I was pretty sure that getting to see Clark act out of character would be something unique for the show. Comic geek aside, "Red K" on Clark — particularly *our* Clark — would be a very cool thing. I also knew, and this is the one thing I was sure about, that the Clark-Lana kiss was the big moment of the show. It would slide earlier and later in the episode as the outline was worked on, but it was always *the* moment; it grew into Clark being able to act on his desires; the metaphor for drug use was pretty obvious, and the consequences of acting without conscience. The truth is that Clark and Superman so embody the best in us all, that to see him acting otherwise is a challenge — and I think we all did it well — Tom Welling in particular in his performance.

AL GOUGH: One friend of mine after seeing Red K Clark said, "There's something so '50s about *Smallville*. It felt like *Reefer Madness* with his idea of cutting loose being a leather jacket, sunglasses and talking back to his parents."

JEFF WOOLNOUGH (director, "Red"): As a director you come in and say, "What can I do to put my own spin on this?" One of the things you do is work with the director of photography and the production designer to come up with things that will be unique and specific to that particular episode. What we tried to do was put a lot of red in the episode while Clark is under the influence of the "Red K." If you look carefully, from the time Clark puts on the ring until the time his dad bashes it off with the sledgehammer, the tone of the show goes toward the red hue. You'll see red not only in camera filters, but in production design too. It just changes the look of the show ever so slightly.

AL GOUGH: Christopher Reeve appeared in "Rosetta," which was a big mythology episode and very much a quest. Miles and my approach to science-fiction is that you always want it to have a spiritual feel; spiritual in the way that *Close Encounters* had a very spiritual feel to its science-fiction. Richard Dreyfuss and all the characters are on a journey. That's what we wanted to do here with Clark by setting up that journey. What's interesting is that his home planet being Krypton and blowing up is news to no one *but* Clark. What we really tried to do in that scene was not make it just informational, but have him say, "When you find out all of this information, what are you going to do with it? How is this going to shape the person you will ultimately become?" This is a precursor to where we are at the end of the season and where we were going in season three. So he was laying the foundation for that and it's a great passing of the torch from one Superman to the next. It ended on sort of a dark twist, which is what *is* Clark's ultimate mission? What *did* his biological parents have in mind for him?

MILES MILLAR: This was the great payoff for the cave, the ship, Christopher Reeve — it all came together very well. And it was a big production challenge to get Christopher and shoot his sequence in New York. It was shot in the production design department of the show *Third Watch* on the same day we did the press conference and the public service announcement for Christopher's charity. James Marshall did a fantastic job of directing the show. What really makes it is the final scene with Jonathan and Clark and the realization that maybe Clark's destiny is not a good thing — that it could be that he must conquer this planet. After Jonathan tells Clark he can change his destiny, there's a great reveal of Jonathan's face that suggests he doesn't believe his own words. I loved the scenario of it and he did such a great job. It was definitely a career highlight for both Al and I.

KELLY SOUDERS: You can't be working on a Superman show and not feel the enormity of a legend. We grew up with Christopher Reeve as our Superman. So for us… I don't want to say it was like having God walk in the door, but it was the closest I've come to that.

BRIAN PETERSON: An interesting point on Christopher Reeve is… I hope I'm not pulling the curtain back too far, but it was this thing where Kelly and I were these baby writers. And he was supposed to show up in, I believe it was "Gone," and we had this metal guy who was slicing people, which was just supposed to be the B story. We wrote the script and we shot the script and we turned in the cut and the studio was like, "What's going on? Why isn't this complete?" We're like, "Oh, well it's missing all the scenes with Christopher Reeve." And they said, "Oh by the way, you don't get Christopher." What's there wasn't supposed to carry the episode. It was supposed to be this B story to this Christopher Reeve story.

KELLY SOUDERS: And it was supposed to set his journey up for the season. So the first cut of it didn't make any sense and everyone kept forgetting that the main scenes in it were all taken out after the fact... or not taken out, but never shot after the fact. It was a pretty big hole to fill.

GREG BEEMAN: James Marshall directed most of "Rosetta," but I directed the Reeve-Welling scene. I flew out to New York and was on the phone with the executives and publicity people from Warner Bros. They said, "We have this fantastic timetable. At 9 Christopher Reeve is going to arrive, at 10 the press conference will take place, then he needs to rest." And I'm like, "You just laid out a 10-hour day in which I get two hours to shoot a five-page scene." They said, "But we have all this amazing press." I was told that he had a lot of limitations — that Chris was going to get tired shooting this scene, a very important scene in the history of the show, and I was only going to have three or four hours to shoot it. When I first blocked it, I did it very simplistically. Then Christopher called Tom and I over and said, "You've got to move Tom around." We had a little discussion and he suggested this other blocking, which was much more complicated. I said, "That's better, but it's going to take a long time." He said, "It doesn't matter. This scene has to be great." And he was fantastic. It took a long time to shoot the scene, and he was great. He had two solid pages of dialogue, but he nailed it time after time.

CHRISTOPHER REEVE (actor, "Dr. Virgil Swann"): I thought the scene was well-written and the shooting went very smoothly. I was just glad it worked out. It was very nice of them to arrange it so that Tom could come to New York and do it. Tom is a very nice kid. He has a genuine warmth openness and simplicity that is just right for the part. I have to remind people that I *didn't* play young Clark in the movie. At that point in the story, Jeff East plays Clark. And don't forget that's the *real* Clark, the one on the farm with Glenn Ford, the one who is more like the Clark that Tom plays on the show. In the film, when Clark comes to Metropolis he puts on — as far as I'm concerned — the persona of this bumbling guy with glasses. So that's a *character*, the Clark at the *Daily Planet*, but the real Clark is the one Jeff played and especially the one that Tom was playing. That's the Clark Kent before he knows who he is. (*Ian Spelling*)

GREG BEEMAN: It was a very emotional scene for Tom and it was significant for him to meet Christopher. The mythic significance of us being there with him at that moment was real, we all felt it. We took our time and at that moment when he comes forward to the screen and Christopher calls him Kal-El for the first time — it was just *so* cool. I wanted to make sure that Tom was in the right emotional space at each of those moments. It's a great scene.

AL GOUGH: We wanted to incorporate the John Williams Superman themes, but do something different with them; use them and turn them a bit. Our composer Mark Snow not only tracked down the rights and figured out how we could do it, but then he actually did it. Honestly, this entire episode was the high point of that season.

JEPH LOEB: Al and Miles took things very carefully and used the mythology in very small doses. The thing to remember is that not everyone knows the legend. They've heard of it, but their relationship with these characters comes from the show *Smallville*. So sometimes a line like Lex's — "Our friendship will be the stuff of legend" — can go right over the head of the audience. It has to work totally at face value.

AL GOUGH: Mythology is good and bad. It can be like a crack pipe — you don't want to do too much because you don't want the show to be insular. You want new viewers to tune in, follow the show and be able to understand it. It was a line we rode well, I think, en route to exploring all of the characters. What Miles and I were happiest about is that all of the characters seemed to have an inner life of their own. I was joking and said, "I don't explore my own life in this much detail."

MILES MILLAR: It takes time for an audience to become invested in the characters, which is why it was a gradual process for the freak-of-the-week to give way to more character-oriented material. You can't immediately set off doing characters until you know who they are. To me, Lex is always the most fascinating character as is his father Lionel Luthor. John Glover is someone who was cast for the pilot, but he was so good that we kept bringing him back until he became a part of the fabric of the show, and Lionel has really helped parallel Clark and Lex and how their parents really form who they are. If Clark had been raised by Lionel, he'd be a very different person. Lana is a person who started off as somewhat of a cliché on the surface, but underneath she was something else. With episode three she resigned as a cheerleader and ever since became much more of an individual. The character really evolved.

AL GOUGH: We spent the first season laying a lot of foundation, a lot of groundwork. Certainly they first part of the first season was spent establishing the world and the Kryptonite villains. In the second half we started to delve more into the relationships and got more of the mythology — particularly with Clark's ship and leading up to the season finale. I think what we were able to do in season two was expand the family dynamics with both the Kents and the Luthors. And we gave the Clark/Lana relationship a new dimension, with the main thing standing between them — which always seems to be the case with superheroes — being his secret. With Lex and Clark we delved more into Clark's mythology and, in a way, got Lex onto his search for the truth. For instance, in "Skinwalkers" there are those caves in which there are paintings that describe Clark's journey. They've been there for hundreds of years and explore the notion that the Kryptonians were ancient astronauts.

ZACH MOORE: Even by the second season they brought in overarching plots. Did I love all the stories, like the Kawachi Caves? Not really, because it went nowhere ultimately. If you look at season one, it's probably 85% freak-of-the -eek episodes, and that's why those aren't the ones that really stick out. The season finale of season one is one of my favorite episodes and that's basically Superman fighting nature. It's tornadoes and a guy with superpowers. But there would also be themes, some deeper level going on.

The show also had some great guest stars, Amy Adams for instance. Now "Craving" is not a good episode, but just the fact that Amy Adams was a freak-of-the-week is pretty cool. And later on you had Jensen Ackles as a main character for a season. People totally forget, but he started on *Smallville* and then the next year he won *Supernatural* and never looked back. And good for him! That's the thing about *Smallville* — if you're going to have an entire TV show about young Superman, you have to have obstacles and villains to fight, and at least in the early years you're not going to bring in Brainiac or General Zod. You need villains, but not necessarily comic villains. And they were good about that, holding off on using them in the early years. As an alternative you've got to come up with characters, obstacles and even human antagonists for him to fight.

Season two ended with no less than five cliffhangers, among them Chloe going off the deep end for Clark not being honest with her about his relationship with Lana, which leads her to take Lionel up on his offer to investigate Clark; the voice of Jor-El and the ship get more proactive with Clark, warning him that if he does not embrace his destiny, those closest to him will be harmed; Clark, refusing to be dictated to or torn away from those he loves, uses a Kryptonite key stolen from Lionel to infect the ship, thus destroying it and, unfortunately, creating a shock wave that devastates a portion of the farm and strikes the truck that Jonathan and Martha are driving.

MILES MILLAR: Here you feel the tragedy in the Kent family and the guilt Clark feels, even though it's not really his fault. He's trying to do the right thing and these things happen as a result of that. But you understand why he's doing it and that there are forces at work that he can't control. There's the notion that the more he resists his destiny, the more he actually fulfills it. By destroying the ship he actually fulfills the prophecy that he would hurt people who are close to him. He hurts his parents and he hurts Lana.

Somehow Gough and Millar successfully navigated the cliffhangers as they brought their characters from the proverbial fire and used such dire situations to launch into the third season while deepening the character arcs. Also occurring that year, Clark, to escape his pain, uses Red Kryptonite again, stripping away his inhibitions and moral code; Jonathan makes a deal with Jor-El to be given the ability to stop Clark and return him to normal; and Lex is getting married to his fiancé Helen Bryce, but passes out on a flight they're on, awakening on a desert island and left for dead by her (spoiler alert: he doesn't die), and has to cope with the psychological impact of that.

AL GOUGH: I think Clark's arc brought him from running away from his destiny to, at the end of season three, starting to accept it as he realizes the consequences of his actions. He went from trying to deny his destiny and escape Jor-El, to ultimately knowing what he had to do and making a very heroic decision to save Jonathan's life. His relationship with Lex was illuminated and he realized that he couldn't tell Lana his secret if he wanted to be safe. Clark also spent the first third of the season trying to put the relationships in his life back together. He also had to come to terms with Chloe's betrayal and needed to know the deal that Jonathan made with Jor-El, which resulted in Jonathan's weakened heart.

MILES MILLAR: A significant highlight of the third season was the ongoing dynamic between Lex and Lionel Luthor — a Shakespearean tragedy in the making — and then there was the development of the Clark and Lana characters. The Lex-Lionel dynamic in year three was very cool. It was set up at the beginning and we carried it through to the very end. The results were a very powerful story.

AL GOUGH: Much of year three was spent with Lex being victimized by Lionel, which offers sufficient explanation as to why Lex moves down a darker path. Clark said it: "The more you battle your father, the more you become him." But Lex *needs* that thing in his life to rage against. He has that line in season three when he says, "Maybe I'm the hero of the story." That was a good moment and I think a very interesting one. Supervillains never see themselves as villains, they see themselves as heroes that just go about things in a different way. I think that's the way Lex sees himself, as a hero, not a villain. Our plan for season four was not for him to become entirely evil, but to find him in that Michael Corleone position of compromising himself. That's all Michael Corleone did: He compromised himself until he had no soul left. It's what Lex is doing and Lionel is out there giving him a big push.

MILES MILLAR: Lana in the first half of the third season was good, but we lost our way a little bit in the second half. It became repetitive. We introduced the character of Adam Knight, played by Ian Somerhalder, to be more of a romantic interest and part of a triangle, but the role was played differently than we wanted. When we saw them on screen together, we realized it wasn't going to work as a romance, but it *could* work if he was a psycho. We always knew he was there as a sort of plant from Lionel, but we made the character darker than we first intended.

GREG BEEMAN: At the same time, I think we all sort of collectively agreed that the Lana-Clark storyline ran out of steam. It began very well, but after eight or nine episodes it sort of stalled, and by the time we caught it and realized that it was stalling, it was even later. What happens in television is that by the time you see there's a problem, you're already four or five episodes past where you caught the problem. Both their performances were great and they clearly had a lot of interaction that's very valuable, but we sort of spun out the whole idea of, "I love you/Go away"-type stuff. We worked every single permutation of it, but I think we came up with some exciting ideas of where to take Lana that was planted at the end of season three. She goes away in the finale, and when she comes back I think there were some very interesting new dynamics.

CRAIG BYRNE: I most enjoyed Kristin Kreuk's Lana in the early episodes, when she'd do things like helping out at nursing homes or doing things for the community. I wasn't such a fan of the "you're keeping secrets from me" era. However, I do feel a bit of a protectiveness of her on the show and I'll never really care for the way she was written out of the show, literally being "toxic" to Clark. I'm sure the producers thought it was a clever call back to the beginning, but I think it was poorly done and it made it seem that Lois was a second choice because there was no way Clark would be with her. I do also wish Kristin had been in the series finale, even if it was a quick shot of her watching the arrival of Superman on TV.

AL GOUGH: If you look at the middle part of the season, there aren't that many Clark-Lana scenes at all in that run of episodes. But there's a magic with Clark and Lana that takes something away from the show when they're not there. What's interesting is that the online comic book fans didn't like her, but everyone else did. They *never* liked her online. She's too beautiful, basically. Chloe can betray Clark to Lionel Luthor and they'll forgive her. Lana looks at him wrong and she's damned.

As the show moved into its fourth season, Gough and Millar continued to prove themselves to be creative masochists. To wit: Lana has left Smallville for a new life in Paris, Clark has declared to Lex that their friendship is over, Pete Ross has moved out of town, Chloe appears to be the victim of an explosion, Lex has been poisoned, Lionel seems to be orchestrating much of what's happening from prison, and Clark, in a bid to save Jonathan from the fury of Jor-El, has seemingly given himself over to his destiny, allowing Jor-El to "take" him to another dimensional plane. While all of that was being dealt with, the show introduced the idea of a global search for three crystals of power which, when combined, would ultimately lead Clark to discover the Fortress of Solitude; Eric Durance joined the cast as Lois Lane — Chloe's cousin — with an instant love-hate chemistry struck with Tom Welling's Clark; and then there's Lex seeming to truly embrace his dark side.

Add to this, Clark's first self-propelled launch into the stratosphere and an encounter with the — or a — future Flash in the form of Bart Allen. At the same time, some were put off by other elements of the show. Chief among them was Lana's relationship with Jason Teague (Supernatural's Jensen Ackles) as her too-good-to-be-true boyfriend turned out to be just that as he was revealed to be a part of the machinations of his mother Genevieve (Jane Seymour), who wanted the mysterious crystals connected to Clark's Kryptonian heritage for herself. Additionally, there were, some would argue, too many personality switch episodes, with Lionel Luthor inexplicably bouncing back and forth from evil to good and back again; and a far too pervasive obsession with sex and suggested nudity that felt incongruous to the series.

MILES MILLAR: The fourth season premiere episode "Crusade" felt like the launch of a new series. It was actually very difficult to write because we were inventing the show in a way. We had Clark take flight for the first time — which was really cool — plus we had to introduce the crystal story and we made the scope more international by having Lex in Egypt, pursuing the crystal.

AL GOUGH: Every scene represented a new relationship or dynamic on the show, which is why the episode was really good, but there were no familiar

Smallville scenes; nothing to fall back on. I remember saying to Miles that it was like writing a new pilot because you're in the fourth year of a show and you have to shake things up. The hardest thing to do when you have a character-driven action-adventure show is to keep constantly changing the dynamics to keep it fresh. It's not like *CSI* or *Law & Order* where you just have a case to deal with. The problem with season three is that it didn't change things up enough at the beginning of the season. It started in a dark place and got darker. But I think with season four we really tried to shake it up and say that we were changing the dynamic of the show.

TOM WELLING: As the show went on, Clark found himself surrounded by father figures in the form of Jonathan, Dr. Swann, Jor-El and Lionel, pulling him in different directions. It was interesting for me because it's character development. Clark is trying to figure out who he is, and I find that fascinating because *I* want to know who Clark is. So it's intriguing in that those father figures give Clark a better understanding of himself. And Clark can learn from Lionel, just as Lex is learning from Jonathan.

MILES MILLAR: The characters were getting older, and in season four Clark lost his innocence in a way — thematically. He's getting older, he's a jock, he's really good-looking, he's interested in the subject of sex and somehow we have to deal with this. Otherwise you watch the show and feel like you're in the '50s. So the sex themes of some of it was keeping the show contemporary and making sure that it felt current. That for us was very important.

AL GOUGH: Season four fulfilled the goals we'd set for ourselves at the beginning of the year. We wanted to lighten the tone of the show and get back to the more sort of human stories that I think we told in the first two seasons and away from secret labs and sort of heavy dark mythology we got into in season three. We wanted to really exploit the fact that it was our last year in high school and this was the last time we were going to be able to do some of these stories. And it was fun to set up the crystal hunt, which in the season five opener leads to the Fortress of Solitude.

MILES MILLAR: We had a little bit of a down tick towards the very beginning, but then upped it by the time we actually did get to the end. For us, we always try to have the show make sense in terms of the character arcs and whether or not there are enough stories to sustain a season. Does everyone move forward? Do the relationships change? We had Lois in year four, Jason Teague, the Teague story, the crystal story, and to me it all crescendoed in a really good way. But one of the biggest strengths had to be Lois. It's always good to introduce a new person to a series, let alone an icon. We just really lucked out with Erica Durance. The character was a really cool interpretation of Lois and she brought humor to the show that we really hadn't had. She also sparked with Clark, which is nice.

ERICA DURANCE (actor, "Lois Lane," *Smallville*): I love how aggressive she is as a character. I love that she goes gangbusters and gets herself into all sorts of trouble, but doesn't feel sorry for herself and doesn't implode. I like that they've created a situation where I can find moments where I can keep going no matter what. I think the reason I like that as well is that's what women are to me. They're not just one thing that sits and pines for a man, they take their hits, they get up, they keep going, they're well-rounded, and I like that she's always doing something different. During a couple-of-week period I woke up and did a fight scene for two days straight, then I got up and I did some intensive interrogative scene and then I was making out. Everything was different and they always had something new and exciting for me to do.

AL GOUGH: We were not allowed to have Lois Lane, but then Peter Roth went and got her for basically 13 episodes. And then we kind of wore them down and were like, "We're keeping her." And she really brought something out in Tom. Like I was indicating, the stuff between Clark and Lana got a little tired for me after a while, but with Lois, she just brought out a fun and lightness in him. They just had great chemistry.

MILES MILLAR: Lois was supposed to be used for limited episodes, but we just kept putting her in. And Erica got the part because she was the opposite of Lana; a very ballsy character who says her piece and has a strength to her. I think she was a breath of fresh air. And obviously people love the idea of Lois and Clark, so it was showing the series evolve. And Erica brought her own energy to it as well.

AL GOUGH: Lois was the only person there who didn't feel as though Clark walked on water. I think in terms of the Lana/Clark relationship, Lana had a new boyfriend, but by the end of the season she was obviously getting closer to Clark and they professed their love for each other, which felt good. I also think that Lex and Clark spiraled away from each other as well. Lex had dark sides to him and Clark was having the realization that this is what Lex is starting to become. I think that's really the thing. There's still sides; Lex is not going to become mustache-twirling and he's still sort of fighting his demons, but he nonetheless gave in to them a little bit more as well that season. I think that was interesting, and it obviously got heated up in the last parts where he, clearly, thought Clark was totally lying to him and Lana didn't trust him. And in terms of the Genevieve/Jason storyline, it helped the Clark/Lana relationship. It got her away from Clark for a time, but then we got to play Lana and Clark in an actual relationship and not just for one episode. We earned that back.

MILES MILLAR: Erica, by the way, was sort of found at the last moment. She had her final network audition on a Friday and we were shooting Monday; it was really down to the wire. We needed to find the right Lois and we were very happy that we did. There were no close seconds. Some fans complained that Clark never met Lois in Smallville, but we just ignored that stuff. There was no meteor shower accompanying Clark's ship in the comic either, but that didn't stop us. We were very respectful of the mythology of the comic, but we were doing a TV show here and the interesting thing for the TV show is how these people *could* have met.

CRAIG BYRNE: I still remember the first time I was shown a photo of Erica Durance. She was beautiful! Her initial arc was a breath of fresh air in season four. I do think it was a disservice to the show that the producers were kind of forced to delay her character development due to other restrictions with the Superman franchise. As the show got to its later years, you could see that she was among the most still invested in the show and we could see it in her performance. I loved how she would rib Clark, and I enjoyed seeing that banter again in *Crisis on Infinite Earths*. It felt like 2009 all over again!

ERICA DURANCE: Obviously Lois has something for costumed heroes. She sees something in them that she would like to be or something that's part of herself that she hasn't embraced yet, and that's going after what's right and sticking with it, even if you have to do it by yourself and even if you've hurt yourself. One thing I liked about what the writers had done is ask, "Why does Clark fall for Lois? Of all the people in the world, why does he stick with her? Let's give people a reason; let's explore that." I think it comes from the fact that even though she's human, frail, can get hurt, she will throw herself into the exact same situation as him and go after and help people if she has to. In a strange way there's a little parallel thing going on. Even in an episode like "Stiletto," I dive in through the roof. Why? Because my friends are down there. If I get hurt, I get hurt — so there's that kind of dual heroism.

One weakness of the season that's often pointed to is the storyline involving Jason and Genevieve Teague.

AL GOUGH: Jane Seymour was fantastic. She just jumped right into the role and played it with a lot of gusto. I think her storyline started off really strong, but in the middle part of the season, episodes 14 through 17, it became more of a placeholder. She and Jensen were terrific together. I thought the story worked well and plugged Lana into the mythology of the season and gave her a purpose as well, *and* got her away from Clark for a time.

Noted above is the fact that the future Flash — Bart Allen — appeared in the episode "Run," marking the first DC Comics hero to do so besides Clark.

MILES MILLAR: Every year we had an idea we were never able to crack, and this is one we had since season one — how do we get the Flash on the show? Eventually we figured out a way to do it. In season four we wanted to bring in more DC characters, and it seemed like the right time. We really lucked out with Kyle Gallner, who played Bart Allen — just a great episode and one of the highlights of the season; the effects were fantastic and Clark and Kyle had a great rapport.

AL GOUGH: Steven DeKnight wrote a terrific script and really brought the character to life in an interesting way. It was a kid with superpowers who had a different point of view from Clark, which was, "Why is this such a curse? Let's have some fun."

And then there was the opening of the season, where Clark returns from his encounter with Jor-El, but as Kal-El, ready to fulfill his Kryptonian destiny and actually taking to the sky to pursue the jet Luthor is on and take the crystal he has obtained, before reverting back to Clark and "forgetting" how to fly again. As such, this was probably one of the most important sequences in the show's history.

AL GOUGH: Now that we had the visual effects to do the powers differently than they could in 1978, we'd always been striving to make them look cooler, distinct and modern. I think the flying was fantastic. Mat Beck and the guys at Entity FX really outdid themselves. So did Tom, because there was acting involved in that. That's the thing that people don't realize — the actor plays a role. It's not just stick him on a board and put him in front of a green screen. He's got to sell it and I think Tom did a great job.

MILES MILLAR: If we were going to break the "no flights, no tights" rule, we wanted it to be a significant moment in Clark's life, and I think we came up with a way to do so while setting in motion the events of season four in a really cool way.

MAT BECK: In terms of the actual flying, part of what we went for was not just Tom hanging there in front of a green screen. We were trying to give him the opportunity to do a little bit of performing, and Tom was better than fabulous. He was constantly looking for ways to look serious and motivated and intense, but at the same time doing slight movements that would motivate movements in flight. He gave us an enormous amount to work with.

From a technical standpoint, a new harness had been designed that would give Welling a great comfort level than most actors have had when they've been forced to go up on wires.

MAT BECK: We also had a belly pan that was sculpted to his body, but we ended up not using that just because in designing the sequence we determined that there would be a lot of shots where we would want to fly right under his stomach and the pan got in the way. Most of the flying sequences were done with either him on a harness or standing on a small green platform with the camera flying past him. That allowed him to be comfortable and give a lot of performance in terms of turning his body this way or that way.

The sequence begins with Clark crouching down and knocking his mother Martha aside. Initially she's frozen in space as the scene shifts into "Clark time." According to Beck, producer Ken Horton wanted there to be a kind of energy effect gathering around Clark before takeoff — which would be similar to Henry Cavill first taking flight years later in Man of Steel. *A great deal of experimentation was done with a variety of effects in an effort to get the proper angle and distortion so that the moment had a certain amount of energy, but didn't hide the entire scene at the same time.*

MAT BECK: In essence, he draws the energy to him, it compacts around him and launches him into the air. It's the kind of thing whereas in Clark time we have the opportunity to see it, normally you don't. In that scene you see his feet kind of descend a little into the ground. That was a practical effect, but we put a lot of stuff over it to kind of smooth it out and make it look like it was a global energy effect. We tweaked that a couple of times just to get it right. When he launches he's got these nice little energy waves coming off of him as he flies past camera — that's the shot looking down, where we've returned to real time and we see Martha fall away; she'd been frozen in mid-fall. He launches past camera and he's streaming these energy waves, which we added some color to, which kind of helps separate him and makes the shot look cool. Then we look over Martha's shoulder to see him disappearing into the distance. We gave him a bit of a contrail there, the remains of those energy waves come off him, which made him read better. Helping in that area were some clouds we put in there too.

The desire was to have Clark close to the camera some of the time, but at other moments within the sequence they wanted him to be little more than a dot. There is a bit where the camera just shows clouds, when you suddenly see a "bullet" shoot through the clouds so that the impact is one of surprise, not one of closeness to the camera. That, says Beck, was a completely synthetic shot.

MAT BECK: What was really cool is that we were able to pre-vis things extensively, and then when we were on the set I was able to say, "Okay, we're going to fly it this way and that way," and we got all the stuff that we needed. Because Tom was willing to keep exploring, we did additional shots — like we'll have him fly underneath camera, and over the top of camera, and then there was one great big shot where we wanted him to fly over and then go away. That was in the sequence early on, but one of the things that I thought would be really cool would be to have him so high that there are stars behind him. We wanted to add that in — I *really* wanted that shot. I had him on this harness where, when you're looking at him, he's against green; when you're looking away from him, he's against green; and when you're looking overhead, he's just against the roof of the stage. I said, "I don't care, we'll *make* that work." What's cool about that too is that in some of these shots it's Tom for part of the shot and then it's a CG Tom for the other part of the shot.

The overhead flying shot was accomplished with the addition of a number of 3D clouds that were created in front of a background of clouds that were painted in. The camera focuses on the seriousness of Welling's face, and then he arcs away toward a painting of the Earth, and then disappears.

MAT BECK: What's also really cool is that we just wanted some shots of him zooming along. What's ironic is we had some footage that was shot a long time ago for the Clint Eastwood movie *Firefox*, so they're in these backgrounds of clouds that are zooming away from us that we dropped in there. We steadied them, cleaned them up and made them usable for our purposes. And when he'd go through clouds, we'd just have him trailing a touch of CG mist to try and tie him in. The other irony is that *I* was the one who shot those clouds for *Firefox*. A long time ago I was a camera guy. There were a couple of shots where he comes right up to camera and kind of turns off and left. There's another one where he turns toward camera, goes through a couple of clouds, then drops underneath camera and then he's descending to see the plane. For that shot, that was a real cloud plate that we tracked in and did a lot of work on to stabilize, and we dropped the plane in at just the right spot, which you can see if you just look for it. He kind of drops and arcs toward that plane. Again, Ken Horton wanted it to be swoopy and acrobatic, and we were definitely on board with that.

For the shot when Clark approaches the plane, Beck says that he was trying to tell a story in a shot. To this end, the camera is looking up at the clouds and there's a dot approaching.

MAT BECK: And then we cross in underneath the plane, we're sliding left to right and the plane is sliding right to left over our heads. It took a lot of work to get that just right, but it was worth it because rather than just a stage shot of, "Okay, here he is just pulling up to the plane," we wanted to make it a series of surprises. So first we see him coming out of the clouds, then the plane crosses very close to camera and the camera slides underneath the plane so it's all plane. And then here he comes. He zooms down under the tail stabilizer, just missing the engine and zooms up to the door. In earlier versions he was coming up a little too slowly and Ken wanted to do a little bit more hot rodding, so we hot rodded him in. When we shot Tom for that particular shot, we had a curved green board that he grabbed on to. The way that he did it, you can actually see his legs kick out from the effort of doing it. It's an organic kind of thing because we had a real object for him to grab on to; it helped him with his action and he did it perfectly.

AL GOUGH: We thought Clark's flight came out great. We said "no flights, no tights," but then we did it because we're television producers and you want to have a big kickoff for your season. Part of the issue at the time with "no flights, no tights" was that the flying was so expensive, so we didn't want to do it creatively, but on top of that the visual effects were so expensive. Then the industry evolved so quickly, that even a couple of years later it wasn't as bad. We were able to do things in the later seasons that in seasons one or two just couldn't be done.

In season five, there were highs and lows of the Clark/Lana romance taking place, with Lana gradually finding herself pushed towards Lex, largely due to Clark's seeming lack of honesty. Sadly, Jonathan Kent died of a heart attack in the aftermath of the deal he made with Jor-El to save Clark; the show saw the arrival of DC characters Arthur Curry and Victor Stone (respectively Aquaman and Cyborg) as well as the computer conscious Brainiac, which takes human form and manipulates Clark before stranding him in the Phantom Zone while the spirit of the Kryptonian Zod takes over Lex. The year ends with Clark combining the three crystals everyone has been pursuing, which leads him to the Arctic and ultimately the construction of the Fortress of Solitude, which took its influence from Richard Donner's Superman: The Movie *and Bryan Singer's* Superman Returns, *which was released in*

2006.

Taken as a whole, it seemed that the Clark Kent of Smallville *was racing at super-speed towards his destiny as Superman given the events of the show's fifth season (which was, of course, before anyone knew that the series would last another five years).*

JOHN SCHNEIDER: I didn't want to go, but it was perhaps the best episode of the entire series. That was our 100th episode and it aired during our fifth season. Very few shows get past the fifth season, so they felt they had to do something to really get people's attention on the 100th episode, and killing Jonathan was it. I understand that; there's no animosity. Now had they known they were going to go 10 years, I honestly don't think they would have done that that soon, but you don't know.

AL GOUGH: Year five was a big growing-up-year for Clark. With his dad dying, he now had to step up and really take on his mantel, which I think you saw him starting to do. In year six, when he gets back from the Phantom Zone, which is the ultimate incarceration, he discovers the path of the hero is a difficult one. But in this case, he and Lex are enemies. He's unleashed this evil force on the world in the form of Zod, and so it's sort of where does he stand in his journey? Lex has embraced his darker elements and now has Lana, so I think a lot of the year is about the corruption of good as well with people sort of wandering around the paths they've chosen. Lex has obviously committed to his, and Clark will come back committed to his, but changed.

MILES MILLAR: Without question this was the best season we ever had. It was consistent, it had continuity, it had momentous change with the death of Jonathan, it had Clark maturing, it had him out of high school, the Daily Planet, the Fortress of Solitude, it had Lex and Lana, Lex going bad — just a bunch of really important, life-changing moments for Clark and the other characters.

AL GOUGH: And then there's Brainiac. He takes human form, like in *Terminator,* and he's a being of artificial intelligence who takes up the guise of Dr. Milton Fein, a college professor who ends up teaching Clark. We called this the grand seduction of Clark Kent, where Brainiac is trying to turn him against humanity in general and Lex Luthor in particular. He basically wants Clark to see that Krypton was better than Earth and that he's got the making here for a new society. Basically Brainiac was saying, "Here's a guy who you trusted that is getting darker, and this is basically what humans are like." Lex was the example of a larger problem that Kal-El would face, which is that humans would never accept him, so why should he be an outcast? And why would he want to be an outcast in an inferior race when he could rule this planet?

JAMES MARSTERS (actor, "Brainiac," *Smallville*): Al Gough took me out to dinner to talk about coming on *Smallville* and I said, "Al, I've got to be honest with you, man. I'm a Batman fan." And he asks, "Why is that?" I said, "Well when Batman goes to work, you don't know if he's coming home, because if you shoot that character, he's dead. And the most exciting part of the hero's journey is when he puts his life on the line to help others. That's the heroic thing. So if you're doing a movie about Superman, you can pull out the Kryptonite and it's fine. You get that big ending. But on a television show, you can't bring out Kryptonite every week or it becomes repetitive, right? So what are you going to do?" And he said, "Oh James, I got you covered. He's a teenager. He's going to to be vulnerable to everything; to his parents, to his girlfriend, to himself, everything. We'll have Kryptonite sometimes for fun, but we'll deal with those other vulnerabilities." At that point I just went, "You solved the most difficult character in all of drama." They solved it and were able to go for 10 years without getting repetitive, which is like a magic trick.

In the comic, the thing that freaked me out about Brainiac is that he was a robot, but he was sadistic. He had that maniacal smile when he was being mean to people, and as a kid that just freaked me out. The twist of the character on *Smallville* was that Clark didn't even know he was bad; Clark thought they were going to be friends, so it was all about being subtle. Later, when I'm throttling Tom Welling in the Fortress when he discovers the truth, I realized it was the moment where I could do *my* maniacal smile. So without being told I just went for the weirdest kind of smile I could, because I wanted to try to get back to those comics a little bit.

New to the mix was, as noted, the addition of other guest DC heroes, with a focus on how they impact each other and their ultimate destinies. These would take the form of Cyborg/Victor Stone, as played by the late Lee Thompson Young, and Arthur Curry, a.k.a. Aquaman, portrayed by Alan Ritchson, who would go on to play "Hawk" on the TV show Titans.

AL GOUGH: Victor Stone is a high school football star who has a full ride to USC, but then he's in a terrible car accident. In our version LuthorCorp takes him on as a project and sort of builds the limbs and the artificial intelligence that goes into that. It's really a question, just like in the Teen Titans show, of, "How much humanity do I have? How much machine am I?" Clark teaches him how to control his abilities. And he realizes his life isn't what he thought it was going to be, but he can still have a fulfilling life, and Clark helps put him on that road.

With Arthur Curry, we played him more of a Green Peace activist. He's determined to save the ocean and Lex is doing something nefarious involving a defense contract. In a weird way Arthur is probably two feet from being an eco-terrorist and Clark has to sort of reel him back in in terms of what he's willing to do. Aquaman learns that he has to use better judgment and can't just destroy things because he has the ability to do so. I think what he brings to Clark is that if Clark is going to use his powers, he has to think globally. Obviously Arthur's passion is the sea and protecting all of the inhabitants of the sea, which sort of really resonates with Clark because he has all of these abilities and, again, at some point he's going to become Earth's protector. His mind is currently Smallville and, to some degree, Metropolis, so that's what Aquaman brings to the table in the same way that the Flash got him to see that he could have some fun with his powers.

ALAN RITCHSON (actor, "Arthur Curry," *Smallville*): My career has sort of been bookended by *Smallville* and *Titans*. *Smallville* was one of the very first things I ever did. Stepping on that set I was so wide-eyed and asking, "What is happening?" But I think tonally things have changed, you know? I mean, we went from this kind of glowy soap opera on *Smallville* to a rather adult, gritty, kind of R-rated comic book-based show where everything's very heightened and realistic in a gory kind of sense. And it's interesting to see these superhero worlds portrayed in that way. So I like where things have gone. But you know, it's a heightened sense of realism and I think that bodes well for superhero comic book-based stories.

ZACH MOORE: When you talk about mythology, season three is where they really started to get deeper into stuff like the Kawachi Caves and that kind of thing, and the stones of power, which I wasn't the biggest fan of, but at least they were charting their own course. I also think *Superman Returns* coming out really influenced them. You never understood the way Warner Bros. thinks, but it was like you've got to have these things be the same. So by the time season five comes around, it's crystals, it's the Fortress of Solitude and all the stuff you see in the movies. Did you *need* to do that? No, but they did and it was really cool. So I would say season five is when they really go into the true Superman mythology. You have other Kryptonians showing up, you have Brainiac coming out of the Phantom Zone. Season five was like *Superman II* because Clark gives up his powers to be in a relationship and then he has to get them back, Zod shows up and all these things happen. It's also the full-on transition moving from high school, which is great since none of the cast were in high school anymore either. And truthfully you don't want to see these 27-year-olds running around in high school anyway.

AL GOUGH: The deal with Warners at the time, even though the show was on the air and was a big hit, was that whatever the movie division was doing, they were kind of the tail wagging the dog — even though they couldn't get a Superman movie going. I remember we had issues when J.J. Abrams' *Superman: Flyby* was going to be directed by McG, and in that script Krypton *didn't* blow up, which was *so* weird. I remember we were doing the season three episode "Memoria," which Miles directed, and we wanted Clark to have a flashback to see his parents putting him in the ship; just the hands putting him in. Paul Levitz, who was a huge supporter by the way, but was always saddled with kind of keeping everybody happy, I remember we got into that with him and I said, "What's the problem?" And he goes, "Well in the new movie the planet doesn't blow up?" I go, "Why am I arguing with you about this? There's 75 years of canon where the planet *did* blow up. How do you think the rocket got to Smallville?" I mean, I get that they're doing the movie, but it can exist in its own world. Anyway, we got past that, and then when Bryan Singer, who was a fan of the show, made *Superman Returns*, at a certain point we got together with him. They flew us down to Sydney (to the set of *Superman Returns*) because the Fortress of Solitude played a big part in it, and it was the end of season four when we had Clark throw the crystal. Season five was going to start airing right before that movie — the season was in 2005 and the movie came out in 2006 — and Bryan was great. He was like, "I think it's terrific that you're introducing the Fortress of Solitude so that when people come to the movie they know what it is."

We wanted to put Diana Prince and Bruce Wayne on the show, but we couldn't because at the time obviously Chris Nolan was doing his Batman movies and they were always trying to develop Wonder Woman. Even when we put the Flash in, we had to call him Impulse. Part of me was like, "Everybody's gonna know it's the Flash… but whatever." That was before you had the Flash in the Zack Snyder movies and a whole Flash television series and, guess what, nobody cared. People were happy to have it. I don't think the attitude is prevalent anymore, but at the time their thinking was that if they can watch it on TV, why are they going to go see the movies?

In season six, Clark's escape from the Phantom Zone (where Brainiac had imprisoned him) leads to several other criminals who have escaped as well, which he now has to round up; Lex deals with the ramifications of having been possessed by Zod; Lionel becomes the emissary of Jor-El, which obviously changes the relationship between he and Clark; Lana and Clark break up, she marries Lex (for reasons too complicated to explain here), but that dissolves as well when she realizes he's been lying to her about everything — including a seeming pregnancy; Martha becomes a senator and moves to Washington D.C.; and there was the introduction of Oliver Queen/Green Arrow (Justin Hartley) and Martian Manhunter (Phil Morris), while the episode "Justice" brought together Victor Stone, Arthur Curry and Bart Allen — along with Oliver Queen and Clark — as an embryonic version of the Justice League to take down Lex's 33.1 experiments.

MILES MILLAR: We took everything slow, which is why the show ran for years. We didn't start introducing additional superheroes too soon, and we kept them in high school for four years rather than two years. I think we made smart choices in terms of the longevity of the show.

AL GOUGH: It was definitely challenging. We started early in the season and booked all of the actors so that we had them lined up. We were building towards "Justice" with Green Arrow. Halfway through the season we decided there was going to be an event to bring all the superhero people that Clark's met before back together. We felt by season six we kind of earned it, and we liked the idea of presenting the first superhero team that we know Clark's going to have more of in the future. It was the first time we did that and it was a lot of fun. Overall we were very disciplined; we didn't really reach into the DC toy box until season four.

Those actors he's referring to are all people who had appeared on Smallville in the past, notably Kyle Gallner as Bart Allen (a.k.a. the Flash), Lee Thompson Young as Victor Stone ("Cyborg") and Alan Ritchson as Arthur Curry ("Aquaman" — before Hartley, who played Green Arrow here, was cast in the role in the spinoff pilot that was widely expected to go to series, but didn't).

AL GOUGH: Then it was a matter of crafting a story that was sort of containable; that had one sequence that showed off all of the Justice Leaguers' abilities. It's an important milestone for us, and thank God the episode turned out well. The worst would be to get all of these people together and end up with a crummy episode.

DARREN SWIMMER: The use of comic book lore was important, not only due to the fact that they oftentimes resulted in higher ratings, but as bonuses for the fans as well. DC elements were often gifts to the deep geek fans.

Even for viewers who don't get the references, I think it added some dimension
to the show and allowed us to get away from the Krypto-freaks. Any superhero
characters that did appear on *Smallville* from the comics went through some form
of "tweaking" prior to their appearance. First there's the look. In keeping with
the "no tights" credo of *Smallville*, most of the DC characters got a makeover. In
addition, we often pared down the complicated mythos of the visiting characters.
Many of these DC characters existed in dozens of incarnations and there are often
several different flavors of them. We'd usually go with what is most appropriate for
the show, and almost always pare down their complicated powers and traits. For
example, we avoided the use of Martian Manhunter's shape-shifting skills for the
sake of streamlining and clarity.

BRIAN PETERSON: We've always had to add our own spin to each new
DC character or piece of mythology. When that character falls into place, it's
a matter of making sure that we are consistent with what is happening in the
graphic novel world and the feature film world. Sometimes we have to totally
re-envision the look and attitude of something like a different color of Kryptonite
or a character, but our new version is always born from the same inspiration as any
previous versions.

*As noted, season six saw the introduction of actor Phil Morris in the role of John Jones,
better known as the Martian Manhunter, one of the few survivors from his home world.
Formerly an intergalactic bounty hunter, he knew Jor-El and promised him he would look
out for his son in Smallville.*

PHIL MORRIS: When I was first cast, I asked Al if making John Jones black
was a conscious decision, because, to me, it's a fricking brilliant solution for him.
He is displaced on this planet, he is an alien among aliens, even. He's just separate.
What ethnic group feels separated in their very own country? African Americans.
As much as any culture and race on the planet, African Americans feel as though
we built this country, but we don't feel a part of it. So I thought it was genius that
they cast an African American, because it falls into line with who he is. So, again,
when I asked Al whether it was conscious, he goes, "What? No. But every interview I do from now on I'm saying it was."

ZACH MOORE: When you look at *Smallville* incorporating comic book
characters, they probably thought, "Well, we are never going to go anywhere with
this, so we'll have him meet Perry White or the Flash. Then we'll change Flash to
Impulse, because WB has weird rights issues about who can be on TV and who
can be in movies." The fifth episode of the fourth season is where we meet Kyle,

and he was originally promoted as the Flash. So don't tell me he wasn't the Flash, because there's evidence. And then of course they were going to make that Ryan Reynolds Flash movie in the early 2000s, so they couldn't use the character. In any case, it's cool to see young Superman interact with young Flash and young Aquaman. I felt like these are really strong episodes because they told a good story. It's like the Flash was a street kid just stealing stuff, and Clark's like, "No, don't do this. This is not the way." So Superman is having a good influence on him and then Aquaman is being an eco-terrorist, which is strong. So these were really well-done.

KELLY SOUDERS: The thing is, we knew the fans would flip out. And anytime we knew the fans were going to flip out, it was just like a jolt of caffeine and excitement for the whole staff. Those actually were really monumental episodes inside the show, as well as outside the show. A lot of our excitement came from how we thought the fans would react.

BRIAN PETERSON: And I think it demonstrated a shift in kind of our audience at that point, because we realized our audience was different. At first we were very much a high school relationship show where he just happened to have superpowers. You didn't have to know a thing about Superman. It was a very accessible show that families watched together. And over time those viewers move on to other shows like that, whereas the Superman people stay. They stay and grow stronger and grow more intense. And so at first we really shied away from very clear comic booky things, which was part of Al and Miles' idea behind the show. And at that point, honestly, I was a little like, "Who are we getting? Are we getting two superheroes?" This is just me personally; I was wondering if we were jumping there fast. But after the reaction to "Justice," we were like, "All right, this is our future. We're here now."

Surprisingly it was Green Arrow/Oliver Queen that had the most impact, bringing Smallville *as close to a Superman-Batman dynamic as it got. As reimagined by the writers, Oliver Queen is a twenty-something multi-millionaire who attended the same prep school as Lex. He's come to Smallville in an effort to shut down Lex's operations, and en route romances Lois Lane, learns Clark's secret and encourages him to join him and other heroes that Clark has previously encountered to create a pseudo Justice League.*

Joining the show as a recurring character and eventually a regular was Justin Hartley, best-known these days for his role as Kevin Pearson on the critically-acclaimed drama This is Us.

DARREN SWIMMER: Justin Hartley was fantastic. He played against our cast with aplomb. Facing off with Lex and Lionel Luthor is no easy task for any actor, and Justin pulled it off with a style all his own.

ZACH MOORE: Green Arrow was the show's Batman proxy, which never bothered me because Green Arrow himself is a Batman ripoff. Everybody knows this. In early Green Arrow, he has an Arrow Cave and an Arrow Symbol, and Speedy is Robin — like it's copy and paste, but that's okay. I really like the dynamic between Clark and Oliver Queen and it's what I enjoy most about Superman and Batman where they're friends but they have different approaches. That's where their conflict should come from, not beating each other up.

KELLY SOUDERS: Al and Miles wanted to bring the Green Arrow into the show for various reasons. They knew that Clark meeting up with a fellow Justice hero would be the next step in his journey to Superman. The addition of Green Arrow revealed a lot about Clark, especially his tentative nature of using his powers for the greater good. But Green Arrow also brought a great deal of energy to the show.

STEVE S. DEKNIGHT (writer/director, "Justice"): At one point we were talking about bringing on either Green Arrow or Green Lantern. Green Lantern was a cool idea, but his power ring would have required massive CGI work so ultimately he just wasn't feasible. Once we decided on Green Arrow, the jitters set in. Bringing the character to life could have veered into a bad *Men in Tights* place, but our costume designer put together a brilliant interpretation of his comic book outfit, and I thought it turned out fantastic. As for his character, Oliver Queen/Green Arrow added a much-needed counterpoint to Clark's nascent heroics. Green Arrow continually pushed Clark to see the bigger picture, to look beyond his own backyard, and by the end of the season the two heroes came to respect each other's point of view. Clark saw his future through the eyes of Green Arrow, and even accepted the idea of being part of a larger hero community.

TODD SLAVKIN: The integration of Green Arrow provided a great way to humanize the show and depict a hero who is a human being as opposed to someone with powers, thus inspiring Clark in a way that no other character has done so before on this show. What it did was make Clark an active participant rather than reactive, which he had been throughout this series — and we all know Superman is an active hero. So Oliver Queen brought in a whole sense of justice, that it's every citizen's responsibility to kind of go in and tackle injustice in the world. I think that shook Clark up and propelled him toward his future destiny.

STEVEN S. DEKNIGHT: Their chemistry was truly amazing, on and off the screen. And yes, we were definitely going for that Batman vibe with Green Arrow… which, if memory serves, was how Green Arrow was originally conceived, as a Batman-esque type of hero.

ZACH MOORE: It brought a different style of heroism into the show, and "Justice" was such a seminal episode bringing together Cyborg, Aquaman, the Flash, Green Arrow and Superman. And then of course there was that great trope of having the cool guys who don't look back at the explosions as they walk away. And those characters all interplayed together very well. It's almost like you should establish each of these characters in their own way before putting them all together in one thing, but that's it's own conversation. The downside is that once they did that, they just couldn't go any further with it. The next thing you really got was in season nine with "Absolute Justice," and that brought in legacy heroes like Hawkman and Dr. Fate. Just thinking about the landscape of live-action superheroes back then, we take it for granted these days when there's been *Arrow, Flash, Supergirl, Legends of Tomorrow, Black Lightning* — all these shows. But back at the time of *Smallville*, it was just *Smallville*. And the show also gave us Blue Beetle, Booster Gold and Zantana live-action; all these characters that you had never seen before in live-action were brought awareness to.

STEVEN S. DEKNIGHT: The idea for "Justice" had its humble roots in "Run," the first *Smallville* episode I ever wrote when I came on board in season four. That's where we introduced Bart Allen, a.k.a. The Flash (or Impulse, as we were forced to refer to him later due to a DC request). We all loved the irreverence the character brought to the show and wanted to bring him back at some point down the road. We had a vague concept of Lex capturing him and putting him in a huge jar. "Flash in a Jar" became our shorthand for the episode, but it was two-and-a-half seasons later before it all came together with the introduction of Green Arrow. Once he was established, our world felt like it had moved closer to the comic book mythos of costumed heroes. From there it was a short leap to not only bringing Bart Allen back, but also Victor Stone and Arthur Curry. And hey, why not do it all at once and whip up a proto-Justice League?

Once we knew we were going to tackle the early formation of the Justice League, I dove in and started trying to come up with a story that would be entertaining, give each hero his moment and be cost-effective. That last requirement proved to be the toughest. One hero is expensive — five all in the same episode would be astronomical if not handled carefully. My angle was to concentrate on Bart, who I believe Clark had the strongest emotional attachment to based on their interaction in "Run." My pitch to Al and Miles was pretty simple: Bart returns, Bart gets captured by Lex, then Clark, Green Arrow, Cyborg and Aquaman have to rescue him in Act Four. That way we can save all the big money for the assault on LuthorCorp. As for changes, there were a lot of little tweaks but nothing major. We briefly considered Clark going up against a 33.1 Krypto freak while trying to rescue Bart, but quickly realized there was just no way to squeeze it in — or afford it. There was also a brief underwater sequence where we saw Aquaman bust into the facility, but we had to cut it late in production due to budget and time constraints. But the script held up surprisingly well all throughout the process.

ZACH MOORE: Whenever they could get away with Lex being a pure villain, it was *so* good. That's why Lex is so successful on the show, because you can only show Clark as Superman so much, depending on all the factors, but Lex — he's doing bad stuff, like having the Flash captured in a container and making him run, which is *such* a supervillain trap. That was *so* good and he was a good foil for them. Then the *Smallville* mythology had Lex and Green Arrow having their own kind of rivalry because of Oliver and Lex when they were kids. *Smallville* was at the time of the Christopher Nolan Batman movies, so they couldn't use that character.

STEVEN S. DEKNIGHT: Directing this one was definitely a pressure situation. Not only did I have the awesome responsibility of bringing the beloved Justice League to the small screen, but I was also still smarting from my last directorial effort which I thought, quite honestly, I had done substandard work on. So I really threw my back into "Justice," knowing I had something to prove (mostly to myself — I'm by far my biggest critic). Every part of directing "Justice" was a massive, daunting process. The budget was big, the action was big and the mythos was gigantic. From the start I knew I wanted to try some out-of-the-ordinary camera work, like the pull back from Aquaman in the mainframe room, or Clark's rescue of Bart. And much to the credit of Al, Miles and Ken Horton (our amazing executive producer in charge of post-production), everyone was willing to give me the latitude to go for it — not that everyone was convinced I could pull it off after that exploding baby fiasco ("Ageless").

I'll never forget the email Al sent me right before I headed up to Vancouver to start prep. Short, sweet and to the point: "Don't f$&k it up!" But once I got on the set I could feel something special was happening. The air was charged with excitement over what we were attempting to do. And that excitement continued on through the entire grueling shoot, even when halfway through I caught the mother of all colds and actually lost my voice for the first time in my life. I had to yell "action" and "cut" through a bullhorn so the cast could hear me. But I was still having the time of my life. Hell, it's the *Justice League*. They could have wheeled me out on a gurney and I would still have had a smile on my face.

BRIAN PETERSON: "Justice" really drove home to Clark the value of teamwork. Trust has always been a huge issue with Clark, and "Justice" demonstrated the dangers of refusing to admit your limits and put your faith in others.

Highlights of the seventh season included Lex growing ever closer to learning Clark's secret, Lana pulling away from the people she knows and loves from Smallville, and the appearance of Clark's biological cousin Kara Zor-El, who he tries to educate while dealing with Lex's attempts to find out what she is. The appearance of Kara (Laura Vandervoort) was significant for both the show and Clark's evolution into the man he's supposed to become. One of the jokes (actually more an annoyance to many) was the fact that Kara could fly and at the time Clark couldn't.

On top of that, Clark had to deal with the dual threat of the return of Brainiac and Lex's discovery that his father is involved with a secret society that might have the means of controlling Clark. It all ends in a showdown between Lex and Clark at the Fortress of Solitude, where the Fortress is brought down, setting things up for season eight.

ZACH MOORE: When they announced that Supergirl was coming to *Smallvile*, I was like, *what?* — because he can't have Supergirl when he's not even Superman yet, so I was skeptical. Now rewatching the show, I really did like the approach they took with her, because she is fresh from Krypton. She's been in suspended animation and she grew up there and has a very different mindset and alien worldview than Clark does on Earth. That's what makes Supergirl interesting as a character. And then her and Clark's dynamic is interesting together because they have different points of view on how to go about things, because they were raised differently and she's not attached to Earth the way Superman is.

AL GOUGH: Laura Vandervoort was the perfect combination of intelligence, naïveté, warmth and beauty. She was just a seamless addition into the fabric of the show.

LAURA VANDERVOORT (actor, "Kara Zor-El/Supergirl,"

Smallville): There has been no TV version of Supergirl before that. I mean, Helen Slater was great in the film version, but *Smallville* was a different kind of situation. The show already had a fan following and they really welcomed me, and Kara was a *great* character. I know there's a comic book mythology behind who she is and who she's supposed to be, but I think I kind of made her my own. They had written her as this rebellious teenager who didn't care about people, but we slowly developed her into a likable, *almost* human being who had faults of her own.

AL GOUGH: Here's somebody who's a flesh-and-blood family member who needs Clark's guidance, so it puts him into a little bit more of a parental-mentor role rather than being a child going to a parent. For us it felt very natural, and the next step in his evolution that he would have to sort of mentor not only a Kryptonian, but a cousin who's a girl, who's 19, who can fly and who doesn't have 18 years of living with the Kents as a moral background. So it makes for dramatic as well as comedic situations, which we wanted to take advantage of. But why can't he fly? That's the reason we wanted her to give him flying lessons. It's like, "I can jump really great!" "Wonderful, if we have a problem 1/4 mile away, we'll give you a call."

ZACH MOORE: Some of my favorite things with Supergirl on *Smallville* is Clark being in the mentor role, teaching her how to use the powers… and that's fun. Laura Vandervoort gave a great performance as Supergirl, and unfortunately the show just didn't know what to do with her. They made such a big deal out of introducing her as a main character in season seven, with the advertising and promotion, and then about halfway through the season they constantly found ways to remove her from the show, take away her powers, take away her memory, put her in the Phantom Zone and send her to the future. I was like, "Why did you introduce this character in the first place if you're going to remove her at every opportunity?"

LAURA VANDERVOORT: They actually had a spinoff in mind when I got the role. I was supposed to be a guest star for a few episodes and then it turned into the whole season and there was talk of a spinoff. Then the whole thing just fizzled out. But the impact of playing her was amazing, especially on little girls. I became aware of that at conventions where little girls would attend with their fathers in the hope of meeting me. There were also letters and tweets from mothers saying that I gave their daughters a role model to look up to. That's why I always want to make sure that I portray myself properly, and I'm true to who I am and don't give in to the L.A. industry and nightlife. I've never been interested in that and have always wanted to be a role model to little girls. Kara definitely played into that.

Smallville's real drama at the end of season seven was the cast and crew shakeup that took place. The contracts for both Kristin Kreuk and Michael Rosenbaum were up, and neither one of them wanted to continue in their respective roles of Lana and Lex. And then with the season having followed a hundred-day writers' strike — coupled with a budget cut from the network — Gough and Millar decided to leave the show. Replacing them would be their four co-executive producers, Brian Peterson, Kelly Souders, Darren Swimmer and Todd Slavkin.

AL GOUGH: When we got to the end of season seven, we had the strike that year and it had been tough. Tom's contract was up and we said to him, "Look, if you want to end it, we're happy to wrap it up, because it feels like we could do that at this point. But if you want to stay on, that's fine. Your answer will determine how we build an ending." Then there were a lot of other things that came into it and that's when we decided it was time to step away. Warners didn't want to end the show, and I get it and the plan is to just keep going. Did we ever think it would get to 10 seasons? No. Never.

The budget was definitely getting tight and it was going to get tighter into season eight. That happens on a long-running television show. They don't give you more money to make the show, but they increase the actor salaries because you're trying to keep them. And Michael was always like, "I don't want to be there if you guys aren't there," so for him seven years of Lex and shaving his head and Vancouver were enough. So we knew he wasn't coming back. But kudos to them, because guess what? They proved the show could exist without Lex. And that was the other thing: It wasn't interesting to us to write a show that didn't have Lex in it. We knew we had people who were qualified to carry on the torch without us, so we said, "Let's step away."

MILES MILLAR: At a certain point, when you've done seven years of a show, it's about making sausages. You've really squeezed that orange for all it's worth. We could have stayed and made a lot of money, but I thought I wanted to do lots of other things. There were other movies we wanted to write, so it was really about time management. I felt we'd run our creative course. We did a bunch of movies and created three more shows after that, so I have zero regrets about leaving and zero knowledge of what happened afterwards. *Smallville* is great, but we're literally always looking forward.

BRIAN PETERSON: When we inherited the showrunning responsibilities, they were like, "All right, here's the deal. You're losing Lex. You're losing Lana. You're not shooting on film anymore. You're losing a day of shooting. We're slashing your budget. Now, go." That was season eight. And we were like, "Oh, oh great. Great." But…

AL GOUGH: I think Kelly Souders and Brian Peterson found a gear for that show that obviously propelled it for three more seasons. When I dropped in on it, it certainly wasn't our show anymore, but it was fine, and there's a core fan base that certainly loved it. My theory is that if you loved the last three seasons, I'm glad I had nothing to do with it. And if you didn't, I had nothing to do with it. It simply wasn't our show, but by the way, when a show lasts 10 years, it's never the show it once was. It can't be. It has to evolve and find a different way to go and they found a gear that, quite frankly, we weren't willing to find.

BRIAN PETERSON: Season eight definitely had some criticism, especially toward the end, but what was funny — and I don't know that people remember this — is season eight kind of came out of the gate with a bang. I mean, the Comic-Con reaction was huge and our viewership went up because we brought in Black Canary and Aquaman, and obviously Green Arrow, and it was a team-up in a way we hadn't really done much since "Justice." And so that was an intent kind of going forward once Todd and Darren, and Kelly and I were in charge of the show. And then in season nine we were off to the races. We knew he had to become Superman. The clock was ticking from that point on.

KELLY SOUDERS: Saving people in *Smallville* was one thing, where Clark kind of had to run to the factory to save Chloe or the roads weren't very crowded. But being alive in Metropolis as Superman is a very different experience and he found out very quickly that it's not so easy when you're running through crowded streets or you have to run into a crowded crisis situation.

BRIAN PETERSON: Or you're accountable to Lois back at the *Daily Planet*. Up until that point we hadn't done a lot with Clark trying to balance the double identity of Clark Kent and his Superman figure, so season eight was very much about double identity and him learning the balance of that, because that's a long journey in itself that we hadn't even touched on until then.

TODD SLAVKIN: One criticism of Clark Kent was that he was always reactive in our show. His decision to go to the *Daily Planet* is his way of saying, "I've got to use my powers to help people."

DARREN SWIMMER: During it all, Green Arrow played a role in helping to solidify Clark's decision. There's an interesting dynamic between the Green Arrow and him, because Green Arrow was always the person nudging him and kind of giving him a little kick in the butt to go out and be more proactive and accept his destiny more. So while Clark, in season eight, is really accepting his destiny more, the Green Arrow starts questioning what his own destiny really is and what kind of superhero he really wants to be. That was an interesting dynamic.

All of which raises the question of the show now being run by the four executive producers, consisting of writing teams Peterson and Souders and Slavkin and Swimmer.

KELLY SOUDERS: Shockingly it was pretty easy. For one thing, Todd and Darren are like the brothers I've never had; Brian has a brother. We were always really close. They're fantastic human beings and just also very creative. And we'd been working so closely together forever that that part of it wasn't difficult at all. And I think the other thing is that Al and Miles really prepared us, and they'd been preparing us since like season two. They were constantly throwing us into situations that were teaching us the skill set we were going to need eventually one day. I can't say it was *all* smooth. Showrunners' jobs are insanely different than even high-level writer jobs. In fact, it's almost like a completely different job. So I think on some level you're always going to be swimming as fast as you can, trying to learn everything, but between Al and Miles giving us increased responsibilities every year, and just putting so much faith in us over those years, we had a lot of training before day one of that. Yes, four people running the show sounds like a nightmare, but it was a blast. That year was really special, I think, to the four of us.

BRIAN PETERSON: We started with Todd and Darren the same day on *Smallville*, so the group grew together and we all had mutual respect. And we knew there was a lot of work to do because those shows are very hard to break. And especially when you get the budget involved, a lot of production time is spent trying to figure out how to redo the show for what we can afford, given what we had envisioned. We just broke it up like, "Kelly, you do one, I do two, Todd and Darren do three, or Todd does three and Darren does four." And that's where we really just kind of became a little bit more autonomous. We weighed in, we helped each other, but we took rooms and we would just go and try to create the coolest shows we could, which I think worked really well out of the gate.

But as that went on, having so many people, it's almost impossible to have as cohesive an overall umbrella idea as maybe it is when Kelly and I or Todd and Darren take over. The fewer people that have to make those final decisions, it just starts to feel a little bit more cohesive. But we had a great time. It was really fun. It really was a good season though to want to work on the show. And we had a little rebound because fans were happy that we had started to bring in so many other superheroes.

ZACH MOORE: I am continuing to be surprised at how many people started watching the show and had no idea that it was connected to Superman or anything. And if you just watched the show, you would think that Clark and Lana were destined to be together because they just hammer that relationship home. And I often wonder if Kristen Kreuk had not left to do the *Streets of Fire* movie, would they have changed the mythology? You look at a show like *Arrow*, where Oliver Queen is supposed to be with Laurel Lance, the Black Canary. But then they see the fan reaction to Felicity Smoak, and I loved Felicity back in the day, but they just changed the mythology and had Oliver with Felicity. To be fair, *Smallville* did that first with Oliver Queen and Chloe Sullivan, so it's hard to complain about what *Arrow* did when *Smallville* did the same thing.

With Lex buried in the Fortress and presumed dead at the end of Season seven, and Lana leaving Clark and Smallville after the emotional and physical pain she'd endured, it paved the way in season eight for the arrival of Tess Mercer (Cassidy Freeman) to take over LuthorCorp and become the show's new semi-villain, and for some sparks to begin to fly between Clark and Lois. Additionally, the choice was made to go in a decidedly more Superman direction, with much of the action taking place in Metropolis as Clark began working with Lois at the Daily Planet, *and is also starting to come to grips with his dual identities. Added into the mix was Davis Bloome (Sam Witwer), an EMT revealed to be a* Smallville *take on Doomsday (the creature that killed Superman in the comics), and such DC luminaries as the Legion of Superheroes and Zatanna. It all culminated with the real Zod inadvertently being released on Earth by Tess.*

SAM WITWER (actor, "Davis Bloome/Doomsday," *Smallville*): *Smallville* was interesting. It was definitely a little bit stressful because people looked at my picture and said, "He doesn't look anything like a six-foot wide, eight-foot tall creature with bones coming out of his head." The fan reaction was quite negative, so I was walking into a situation where everything I read on the Internet was, "Who is this guy and why is he coming into our beloved franchise?" The good news is that once we started airing episodes, the opinion changed and that was really heartening. You work on it for a while and you don't know if people are going to like it, but you have some notion that maybe it should go in a certain way and it's really rewarding when people respond to it. We worked really hard to not just do our own thing, but also honor the source material. The important thing is that we weren't negating what the comic book said, we were just adding a piece of mythology to it that might be interesting. I had seen the animated film *Superman: Doomsday* about two weeks earlier, and my response was, "You want to play *that* guy?" I didn't think I was right for it, but *they* did.

ZACH MOORE: I give them a lot of credit for finding a way to continue after Michael Rosenbaum and Kristin Kreuk left, and it's very true to the comic books too, with the use of clones of Lex and things like that. That didn't really bother me honestly. I loved him on the show, but I felt like they took the character of Lex as far as they could without just going into the Superman world. It was almost a shot in the arm with a soft reboot of the show in season eight, which was great the first half. And with the use of Doomsday, to be fair, for a *Smallville* interpretation where you're a CW budget, what do you do? You do like a Wolfman Doomsday, and I think that really works the first half of the season and culminates in "Bride," which is the midseason finale.

A character like Doomsday served as proof positive that a show with as limited a budget as Smallville's *became, probably shouldn't tackle a character like that one. Generally speaking, you'd expect him to be created via CGI, but the show went the old-fashioned route by using makeup and a costume — which would have been fine had there been a truly climactic battle between he and Clark, but said battle essentially consisted of several powerful blows.*

SAM WITWER: You know what's funny? I said in one interview that I didn't necessarily agree with the ending, and the next day I was quoted all over the Internet with, "Sam Witwer hates the ending." I want to say this respectfully, because as an actor it's not my job to do anything but what I'm given. Having said that, I hope that when people watch the show, they see I'm kind of going for it with what it was they wanted me to do. But my personal take was, I thought it would end differently for that character. I'm going to be completely honest with you — yes, there are many valid ways you could end that character. I wasn't sure that the way we ended the character was something we'd earned. I think you could have done a few different things that would have made more sense, considering that he was sacrificing himself. He even tried to kill himself at one point.

He did some bad things, but he was mostly trying to do the right thing. Even when he would murder criminals, he was doing that to protect whole city blocks, realizing that he couldn't die. He was completely aware of the fact that he was impervious, so what do you do? The bad things he did, he really had no choice. The lying, the dishonesty, were really preferable to giving in and killing everyone in the entire city. My take on it was that until the very end, this is an honorable man put in a terrible situation, and I think the audience responded to that — at least I hope they did. I think we needed to stick with what was established. I'm not saying we couldn't deviate, but if we're going to turn him into a maniac at the end, we should set that up a little bit. But it's not my place. Please emphasize that point: It's not my place to fight it. Did I raise concerns when the script came out? Yes I did, but my job is to do what they've given me as well as I possibly can and bring it to life in a way that creates, hopefully, a dramatically satisfying moment.

BRIAN PETERSON: We had the best production crew ever that loved to do stunts and they loved to do things. But on that particular episode we were like, we don't have very much money. We've hidden the Doomsday thing. He was beautifully hidden by the cinematography, and so it worked. We were really anxious about the costume as well as the effects. And we were like, "Clark gets one great hit." He punches him and for the first time ever Clark goes into the stratosphere. We got one moment and the moment had to be epic. And every cent of the show had to be spent on that. And then somehow there's motorcycles and there's things happening, and we're like, "No, no, no, no, no, everyone that... No, it's not... It's supposed to be one gigantic epic moment." And to be honest, I don't think that would have even satisfied fans. Sadly, that's where our lack of money showed. It showed we scraped together all the episodes the best we could to save money for finales. And that one, we just couldn't deliver. It was so heartbreaking because production put so much work into it, everybody did. I feel bad because I wish people knew how much work went into even what went on screen; everybody bent over backwards to do what they could.

KELLY SOUDERS: It's interesting because when you get toward the end of a series, they start slashing the budget. At the same time, every year that goes by, people get little bumps and everything costs more. I honestly don't think those last few years of the show would've existed had we not had such a dedicated crew. The stories of different departments and the people in them literally spending their weekends, spending some of their own money... I mean, it says a lot. They were a very close-knit family, that crew, and they really, really outdid themselves in every area that they could.

BRIAN PETERSON: One time we didn't even have money for a birthday cake, so the props person came in and was like, "Hi, I baked the birthday cake." It was shoestring. It was ridiculous. But again, like Kelly said, everybody rallied and it sometimes made for better product. Sometimes we just kept going back to character.

ZACH MOORE: As the season is unfolding and you're building to Doomsday and you're thinking, "I guess Doomsday is not going to be his last battle. It'll be his first battle and what makes him become Superman or something." So the feeling was, "Give us *something*," and it was *nothing*. And it was infuriating. I actually like the Doomsday suit; I think he actually looked pretty cool, so it's not like it was a big CGI thing they couldn't afford. But they have Clark grappling with him and they're banging into walls, but it was nothing. Clark Kent just walks off into a *Field of Dreams* for some reason, and it's very strange.

Season nine begins in the aftermath of Clark's battle with Doomsday, determined to protect Metropolis as "The Blur" while wearing a long black trenchcoat and black T-shirt emblazoned with the Superman "S." As he fights crime, he leaves behind his symbol as a sign to the people. Along the way Lois becomes fascinated with The Blur at the same time that she and Clark begin to realize that there is something between them. Simultaneously, from Krypton's past comes Major Zod and his followers, who have arrived on Earth with a desire for conquest and a need to obtain the superpowers they mysteriously don't have; an alliance of sorts between Tess Mercer and Zod; and there's the arrival of such DC heroes as the Justice Society of America and the villains Metallo, Amanda Waller and Checkmate.

Behind the scenes there was a continuing shakeup with Darren Swimmer and Todd Slavkin departing, leaving Brian Peterson and Kelly Souders as showrunners, and they were determined to really move Clark towards his destiny as Superman.

KELLY SOUDERS: For us, this was a step closer to the actual Superman costume. Clark isn't a guy at that point who was probably going to put on the tights and the boots and get something made. He hadn't gone quite as far as Green Arrow; he was still on the path to becoming that man, but he was definitely recognizing that there is this second identity. As much as he knew what Clark Kent looked like, he needed to figure out what the Superman part of him looks like. Even though it wasn't quite the costume everybody was used to seeing, it was one step closer to getting there.

BRIAN PETERSON: What the writers and the cast were having fun with was that up until that point Clark had seen himself as human and saw his

Kryptonian identity as something he had to hide. In year nine he embraced his Kryptonian identity and saw himself solely as a hero, almost to the detriment of living as a human. It's really the pendulum swinging too much in the other direction as he found his ground in balancing the two identities and how he was kind of pulled back into being Clark Kent by his realization that he's in love with Lois Lane.

What we were trying to explore was the last stages Clark goes through in his decision to put on the cape and tights. It's kind of based on a couple of pieces of mythology from when he died in his Doomsday fight in the comics and the costume he wore after that, and that's kind of the basis of what we did with his look in year nine. The thrust of the year was twofold: one is Clark training with Jor-El and for the first time really embracing what it means to be a hero, trying to give up his human identity but finding how hard that is when you're in love with somebody. So that was kind of the thread, between Lois and Clark and The Blur, and his training with Jor-El.

ZACH MOORE: I think season nine is one of the best, start to finish. They had an arc and you could tell that they planned what they were doing, as opposed to some other seasons where they clearly had their ambitions set too high and couldn't deliver. But season nine is one of the strongest and to me almost justifies the show running as long as it did. I never stopped watching *Smallville*, but I was so dejected after the season eight finale that I didn't watch the first half of season nine, but I recorded them all. Then I watched it over the course of a couple of days and was like, "This is great. *Smallville's* back!"

CRAIG BYRNE: I know the final seasons were well-loved by a good portion of fans of the show, and I think Brian, Kelly, Todd and Darren were good successors for Al and Miles. I'm glad we got those seasons, and episodes like "Homecoming" really stand out to me as among the series' best. Personally I prefer the early years in Smallville and never expected to see a series like what Smallville had become, but that's okay. TV series evolve and there were quite a few gems in those later seasons. It wasn't the same show that Al and Miles created, but ultimately it didn't have to be. What I'd give for Al and Miles to do another DC show.

The big question facing the producers was whether Clark, who was coming ever closer to the Superman costume, would actually begin flying in year nine.

BRIAN PETERSON: We wouldn't be seeing him fly until he embraces being Superman. That's what Al and Miles started with and we were trying to carry that. That was always designed to be the final stage — him deciding who he wants to be.

KELLY SOUDERS: And the show was really the journey to that moment.

In the show's 10th and final season, following Zod's defeat, Lois comes to realize that Clark and The Blur are one and the same, and their romance begins to grow. In the meantime, public sentiment is turning against costumed heroes, encouraged by the minions of Darkseid from the planet Apokalips, who is manipulating humanity and threatening Earth. The season also offers spiritual guidance to Clark from Jonathan; Lionel Luthor from a parallel world tries to garner a power base for himself; Supergirl returns; the Chloe/Oliver Queen romance grows; Lex Luthor (very) briefly returns in the finale (with Michael Rosenbaum playing the role), though Tess wipes his memory; and at last Clark Kent becomes Superman by pushing Apokalips away and freeing humanity from his control (somehow).

LAURA VANDERVOORT: Returning as Kara was a little strange; I hadn't played her for almost two years. I had returned in season eight for an episode, but it was so brief, so it felt a little strange getting back into Kara, but once you get there it's not too difficult. I was excited — and she's almost a different character in season ten than she was in seven or eight: She's more mature, and she sort of figures out who she is, and the tables have kind of turned with her and Clark. In the past she would mess up and Clark would give her a lecture and teach her about her powers, and when she returns the tables are reversed: She's come back with more knowledge, and she's teaching him things and giving him ideas about who he could be in the future. She definitely plays a huge role in his becoming Superman.

BRIAN PETERSON: In season nine we really put Clark through the ringer as far as making some decisions that were maybe on the edge. We roughed up Tess a little bit, we burned down some buildings and we made some creative decisions to see what the boundaries were when you are God, and how far you can go. In year 10 we wanted to take a more positive spin and watch him as he's taking those lessons from the previous year and applying them.

KELLY SOUDERS: In season nine Clark sort of delved into his darkest hour, and I thought that was really interesting and something we needed to do that in order to go through a pretty rigorous test for him to make it to the Superman moment. But what was interesting about it was that by the end of the season he really *wasn't* Superman. He *wasn't* that bright, shiny inspiration. He kind of was a loner who wasn't trusting of the people around him, who hid on rooftops and in shadows, and that's a very different guy than Superman is. So it kind of made us look at the 22 episodes of season 10 as a way of getting him to that moment.

BRIAN PETERSON: The important thing is that we didn't want to just do an ending, we wanted to do a *beginning*. What we were aiming for was giving people the emotion of what's to come since the end of the show lines up with every movie and a lot of other things. Unlike other shows, we know where the story goes, so it's a handoff to those other pieces of mythology rather than just an ending.

CRAIG BYRNE: Honestly I was let down by a lot of what the series finale had to offer. The ending to the Darkseid story made no sense — if "inspiration from Superman" could stop him, why didn't they do that months ago?

ANTHONY DESIATO: The thing with Darkseid that was so weird to me was their approach with the characters seemed to be less that he was this alien being and more that he was this embodiment of evil. And we see him in a smoke form and all that — not entirely dissimilar from the first evil from the final *Buffy* season. You understand the limitations in terms of budget and technology that the show had. It's like, okay, if that's the way we're going to go with Darkseid, so be it. But then there was also the planet approaching Earth that Superman just pushes away. So I was really like, "What are we doing here?"

One point the audience is split on is the fact that Tom Welling never appears in the Superman uniform. It's suggested through CGI shots of the character and close-ups of the actor's face, but never a full-bodied shot of him truly revealing himself. The best we get is a final moment, accompanied by the John Williams Superman theme, where he rips open his shirt to reveal the iconic "S."

ZACH MOORE: I'll never understand the whole costume thing. Tom didn't want to be typecast, but it doesn't matter if you wear the costume or not: If you play a character for 10 years on a fairly successful television show, people are going to know and associate you with that character regardless of what you wear or not. I have very mixed feelings about the end of the show; they dropped the ball.

AL GOUGH: Tom not wearing the costume wasn't in any of the contracts that I'm aware of. At least in the beginning we were like, "You're not going to be in the costume." We didn't foresee a world where he was in the costume, though we did say, "Maybe in the last episode of the series he puts on the suit and flies off," but that was it. I just don't think he wanted to do it. I think Tom was always resistant to that aspect of it as we were getting closer to him taking on the mantle.

PHIL MORRIS: You know, there *is* that thing about the Superman curse and the question of how do you break it? Do you believe in it or not? Maybe Tom believed it. Maybe he needed to separate himself in a way that hadn't been done prior. I honestly don't know, but I just respect that he stuck it out for 10 years.

ANTHONY DESIATO: The thing with the *Smallville* finale is that I can't stress how excited I was going into it. I watched religiously every week for 10 years and I could not have been more excited. I was definitely mixed coming out of it. There was enough that I felt was a fitting payoff such that I wasn't totally turned off, but there were things that really frustrated me. The CGI costume was one.

CRAIG BYRNE: *Smallville* fandom had "shipper wars" of who Clark should be with, to the point of people doing mental gymnastics to suggest that Chloe Sullivan was the real Lois Lane. My choice for who Clark should be with was "Superman's cape." I wanted to see the costume at the end. After we had characters like Booster Gold telling us only a few episodes earlier what a big deal Superman's arrival would be, this was a huge letdown because I didn't get what I wanted. I *did* like that so many actors returned for the finale, and despite the lack of Superman, those final moments starting with the score of Superman: The Movie can be watched over and over again. But yeah, I was a bit disappointed overall.

MILES MILLAR: For us, the last moment of the show was always going to be Tom in the suit, flying — always! You'd see the red and blue and it would be, like, "Oh my God," as he's coming through the clouds — a beautiful, incredibly triumphant moment. There's a spirituality to Superman as well, which I think you need to capture in the final moment that would be deeply fulfilling for the audience who waited for that moment. *That* is his journey from this boy into a man and the man is called Superman. To not have that moment is a travesty, and I'd like to think it would've been there. We could have persuaded him to do that, I think. I don't know what happened, but that is definitely a flaw.

KELLY SOUDERS: I think ending 10 seasons of a show in 44 minutes or whatever, you're never going to make everybody happy. It's an impossible feat. I think it's why you end up with finales like *Seinfeld*'s, because it's like, why even bother? It's just too hard, so I think there's that. Al and Miles also always had some visions for that final episode, so we tried to honor those. I remember we did a studio screening for everybody who was in L.A., like the writers and the editors. I do remember people feeling really happy about how a lot of it turned out and people were emotional and I had a really nice feeling about it.

BRIAN PETERSON: I don' think people quite realize there's just stuff you can't do. At the end of the day it wasn't our choice. We had zero to do with that, and we felt so good because it was so much further than we thought we were going to be able to do. We thought we're going to be completely disappointed and not even see that. That CGI shot... you have no idea. And the very final rip getting the Superman emblem in there that very final moment, those were conversations 10 years in the making. And everybody had strong opinions, and the reason we feel so good is we knew that was never an option. We couldn't put a disclaimer on the episode saying, "By the way..."; we have to own it, and we felt so good with that moment where he crouches down and he goes up through the Fortress and you see the costume and the cape. For me, I felt like we didn't cheat people because they got that, and then they got the moment when we pull out and he's hovering in space. That connects to the comic book fan. To me, I felt like we did everything humanly possible to deliver what people wanted. On top of that, getting Jonathan and Lex back for the finale... it's just one of those things where I think people have an idealized view sometimes of how the industry works.

KELLY SOUDERS: One of the other things that was a bit last-minute was Michael Rosenbaum coming back, who we had been trying desperately to get back into the show and finally he agreed, and we were thrilled. And it was happening as we were writing the last episode, so it really was late. We were thrilled and wanted to make sure that we got to bring him in; he was such a huge part of that series and to see him and Clark again was so important to us.

BRIAN PETERSON: Tom ripping the shirt open was purely practical. That's where we were so thrilled, that he and everybody rallied. That was for real. Even though the other shots were CGI, *that* was real. That was Tom with the Superman shirt and, for us, that delivered.

ANTHONY DESIATO: The thing that really got me even more than the costume was the Lex mind-wipe. That was such a baffling choice to me because for 10 years the show did some things better than others, but I always enjoyed their handling of Lex, and his arc over the course of his seven seasons was very strong. And that scene between Clark and Lex in the mansion in the finale, one of my favorite scenes in the entire show, sets up what could be a really great dynamic for them in the future, even though we won't see it: this idea that they're going to be opposed, but there's still this bedrock of friendship between them. I can't stress how much I love that. Even as they're destined to be enemies, Lex is still encouraging Clark to save the day in that moment. Look, it's been so many years, but it's still right there for me. To erase his memory of Clark's secret is one thing, but to literally erase *all* of his memories just flies in the face of what I feel like the show was about.

CRAIG BYRNE: I loved seeing Lex again, though I was disappointed that they were only able to get Michael for a brief moment of shooting. It would have forever disappointed me if we had never seen Lex again. What I didn't like though is that the show took away Lex's memories. As mentioned before, the show is about Clark's ascent and Lex's descent, and what point is there for that with Lex if he doesn't remember anything?

ANTHONY DESIATO: The CGI costume was like, "All right, the guy didn't want to put it on, though I think it's ridiculous." But there was still enough that I enjoyed, like seeing Clark reunited with the ghost of Jonathan. I loved Jor-El showing Clark his trials, all the saves that he made over the course of the series. So again, there was enough of that that I enjoyed. The thing that in the end made me okay with all of it was — and it took me a little bit to come to this — I realized watching the show for 10 years, there were frustrations. And so the finale, to me, felt in keeping with the rest of the show. There was some great stuff and some frustrating things.

KELLY SOUDERS: It's an insane business and I think Brian and I probably are maybe the only people who had quite the same courtside seats to all the insanity that was going around that final episode, because we saw every single part of it and we were trying to put it all together. Given the restrictions, we're thrilled with what it was because it really did go further than we ever anticipated it being able to go.

Throughout its 10-year run, Smallville *hit many highs and lows, alternatively thrilling and exasperating viewers (to be fair, doing more of the former than the latter), but in the end its cast and crew created an important part of the Superman legacy that continues to resonate over a decade after wrapping production.*

KELLY SOUDERS: Al and Miles really had a very clear idea that they wanted the show to run for a long time, and they had really plotted it out in a way that it provided very long legs. They gradually dropped Easter eggs that would pay off down the line. The show was really well- designed from the beginning.

JOHN KENNETH MUIR: Another great thing about *Smallville's* long run is that it allowed a full exploration of Superman's youth without racing through any particular stage. The first few seasons of *Smallville* involve Clark's (Tom Welling) discovery of his extra-terrestrial origin and the development of such powers as his heat ray ("Heat") and X-ray vision ("X-Ray"), but as time goes on we get the creation of the Fortress of Solitude, the death of Clark's adopted father Jonathan, the introduction of Supergirl and, then, Lois; seasons eight to 10 move Clark and Lois to Metropolis and the *Daily Planet* for the traditional Superman story we have come to expect. Although fans complained about Clark's slow progress from adolescent to superhero, it's also fair to state that there's an arc and direction to *Smallville,* and that by going chapter-by-chapter, stage-by-stage, the series pays off in its high-flying 2011 conclusion, which features an inspiring, emotional reprise of John Williams' "Superman March."

AL GOUGH: I'm so glad it's the longest-running comic book-based show. I'm really grateful for that on so many levels.

ROB O'CONNOR: I love *Smallville's* early years when it really seemed to be building to an epic modern Superman origin, but as early as season three it became clear how it was designed to run for as long as possible, with no clear road map to the end game. I dropped away from the series by season five, hoping against hope that they would announce a final season, allowing them to finish what they'd started. I did eventually return to the show for season nine, and while there were glimmers of promise in those final two seasons, there was also quite a lot of junk (including an agonizingly subpar finale) that left me wondering what could have been. All of that being said, in an era where people keep complaining that there's no place for Superman and that origin stories are boring, it's quite wonderful that these showrunners saw Superman and specifically his origins as so mythic and so crucial to the landscape of American storytelling that they saw fit to draw it out for 10 years.

KELLY SOUDERS: One of the strengths of the show is that it touched a lot of people, which is the whole point of this business. You get into storytelling because you want to have people share an experience together that makes them think and makes them feel, and I think that absolutely is timeless about the show. We have people all the time talk to us about what the show meant to them and they've watched it with their family. I can't tell you how many people have told me, "Oh, I was estranged from my mom or my dad or my sister or whatever, but we would sit down every week and watch the show together." That's the part that still makes you choke up.

BRIAN PETERSON: I teach a class, and I show them the pilot as an example, because we both felt Al and Miles did such a brilliant job at writing the pilot. There were so many little Easter eggs in that pilot that we kept paying off in season eight, in season nine, in season 10. But most importantly it was a show that I think a lot of people that may not have tuned into a superhero show, tuned in for to watch him trying to get through high school, dealing with the family and life in middle America. He just happened to be a superhero. It was a very different take, a very different way in to the genre, which I think we really responded to. And we loved that we got to do a 10-year slow burn. It brought so many people together that were hardcore superhero fans and so many others. Everybody got to come together and watch him grow up in a way that we all could relate to. I absolutely credit Al and Miles for that.

KELLY SOUDERS: What was so amazing is that Al and Miles always had the heart of the show as the number-one priority, and that really showed. It's why it still has meaning today. And they did such a great job of fleshing out all the characters — the villains were as equally fleshed out as the heroes, and that made it insanely rich and allowed us to do 10 seasons of 22 episodes, not 10 seasons of eight episodes.

BRIAN PETERSON: And it allowed us to explore the idea of identity. There are so many people and so many issues in the world right now that are about identity and how you identify and how you label yourself and how people label you. I don't know if that was ever intended at the start, but it was one of the benefits of the show that allowed us to explore that in so many different ways.

AL GOUGH: When Miles and I started this, we were burned in effigy online. You know, "Who are these two? What are they doing with Superman?" Just a very vocal, fanboy reaction, and now what's interesting is that because the show had gone a decade, I think it very much is how that generation will know Superman. To the fanboys of the future, this is their Superman. It isn't a movie, it's certainly not *Superman Returns,* it's not another television show. It's *Smallville.* Like it or not, it's now ingrained in the Superman mythology, and in future incarnations will have to be dealt with one way or the other — which I think is great, and *that* is what television can do that movies can't. Movies do very well in terms of scope and size, but in the DC universe it accomplished a lot. With the exception of what Chris Nolan has done with Batman, which is extraordinary, I think what *Smallville* set out to do was to take something that had been something of a given, and explored it a little bit and tried to give the glasses, the spaceship and so on, a context in the modern world. It was literally trying to ground the mythology in a modern sensibility that people could relate to.

JEPH LOEB: The show's strength is its metaphor: You want to fit in, but you can't. You don't want to be who you are, but you can't change. Whether you're a five-year-old or 50, you know what that feels like. Clark makes us feel like it is going to be all right, that someday our lives will change for the better. *We* could be Superman. That's something else no one has ever done before Al and Miles. In the past, we always flew with Superman. Clark, as he is portrayed in the show, allows us to be him and learn as if we were him.

AL GOUGH: One of the things that *Smallville* did, which Miles and I are most proud of, was you took the most unrelatable superhero — an alien with all the powers in the world — and then tried to make him a person you could identify with. There's something about Superman where he's translated for the time he is in, whether it's World War II, the '50s, the '70s, the '90s and on. There's something about him and that story that always manages to stay relevant, which is a testament to that character. Whereas Batman is dark and cool, I don't think Superman has ever been cool. I don't think *Smallville* made him cool, I think it made him *relevant*. I think that's what it is — he's a guy who grew up on a farm, who has a good relationship with his parents, who is trying to do the right thing. That is not cool as defined by the word itself, but it works for that character and probably always will. We were at the dawn of the superhero era because Marvel hadn't really come on yet, beyond *X-Men*, which had been released the previous summer. The last iteration of Superman was *Lois & Clark* and the last iteration of Batman was *Batman and Robin*, so *nobody* was interested. Then it was us, and nine months later it was *Spider-Man*, so it was *Smallville* and *Spider-Man* that kind of really kicked it into high gear.

MILES MILLAR: I still think that *Smallville* definitely laid a foundation along with *X-Men* to allow what's happened to happen in terms of the embracing of superheroes' dominance in pop culture and grounding the characters in real human emotion, which hadn't really been done. Now, ironically, we're heading in the opposite direction with things like *Thor: Love and Thunder*, which to me is just a complete throwback to a total cheese-fest with cartoon figures and no emotion.

AL GOUGH: We were very fortunate in the respect that Jenette Kahn at DC, frankly, gave us the freedom to make the show. Ten years later we would've *never* been able to make that show because of corporate control and in some ways a slavish devotion to the comics. It's funny how these shows evolve, because my kids watched *The Flash* and *Arrow* and the shows in that era. Suddenly, the things that would take us a season to do, they'll do in an episode. By episode three everybody's in costume and you're like, "Whoa!" — which, by the way, I also understand. When we were doing it, you had to get people invested; they had to understand in a weird way that you're hiding Superman and trying to make this teen drama that happens to have a superhero element. You weren't leading with it, but now you can because you've had 20 years of people going, "Yeah, yeah, I know, it's an origin story."

BRIAN PETERSON: It's always been an overwhelming feeling since the first day I walked into this office, because Superman is so much bigger than any one person on the crew or cast. The fact that we got to flesh out a part of the mythology that was a little bit vacant is so exciting. And the fact that we were in a place where we could take what Al and Miles started and merge it into the world that is DC Comics and will be Superman is, sadly, probably the most exciting part of my career even as I look ahead to the next 20 years. It will always probably be the most exciting part of my career. It doesn't get any better than this.

MILES MILLAR: These stories have this sort of religious element to it as well, but are like Bible stories being handed down with different scholars and scribes making their interpretations of the same story, adding and adjusting and modifying for their era and for their time and their taste. I love that. The thing we brought to it was we didn't have a deep knowledge of it, but we had a deep respect for it and a deep respect for the legacy of Superman and what he stood for. Something that's very true to Superman is very true of the show: It was never cynical. It had an earnestness, a seriousness and deep respect for the legacy of Superman and for the legacy of what it's like to be an American hero. Those things we took to heart and I think that resonated.

AL GOUGH: Selfishly, as the co-creator, I would say it's an important part of the legacy, because it was the only time, certainly in live-action Superman, where you really get to see the humanity of Clark Kent. You get to live with the character for so long and it helps people understand why Superman is the person he is. He was an alien, he had all of these powers and you couldn't hurt him. There was something remote about Superman. Batman, people always understood as, "Oh, his parents were murdered in front of him and he is out for vengeance." People always flock to that. So how do you take this god-like figure and humanize him? That's really what *Smallville* did, and it allowed people to empathize with Clark Kent and Superman and not just admire him.

CHAPTER X
You'll Believe a Man Can Fly... Again... Eventually

"It doesn't matter if it's TV or if it's features, Warner Bros. seems determined to micro-manage every property to death. They have no faith whatsoever in the people they hire, and it seems to be a problem at the executive level company-wide... The feature division has been an endless Escher-style square dance, looping in and swallowing itself, endlessly developing variations on the characters."

This comment was written back on September 23, 2002 by "Moriarty," whose real name is Drew McWeeny, a reporter at the time for the Ain't It Cool News website in relation to the J.J. Abrams screenplay Superman: Flyby, *but in many ways it could very well have been written today rather than over 20 years ago. From the outside looking in, when it comes to Warner Bros. and DC, seemingly little has changed with projects continually being announced and canceled. A different path could evolve under the guidance of James Gunn and Peter Safaran, but at the moment it is too soon to tell.*

DREW MCWEENY (film critic, author): So many people assume that the 1978 *Superman* was a Warner Bros. movie, and you have to explain to them, "No, that was an independent production that Warner Bros. distributed. They did *not* make it... and frankly, wouldn't have if they had been left to their own devices. To me, it sums up how the entire history of DC superheroes has gone. It has always been an afterthought at that studio. They own it, but it seems like they're almost embarrassed to have to do anything with it. And they still feel like they're being shamed into trying the Marvel model; it's not like it's something they organically would want to do.

PAUL LEVITZ (writer, former DC Publisher): The movie business is just nuts by its nature, whether it's for good or for ill. When I'm teaching, I use this example: Director walks into the room, about 12 people around the table representing the different divisions of Warners that have to make money on something. "So for my next movie, I want to make a movie about a battle we didn't win. By the way, there aren't any Americans in this. And there's no hero in the story. There's a lot of people who do individual heroic things, but there's no central hero to the story. And nobody in America remembers this battle. Can I have $60-million please?" And the answer is, "Why yes, Christopher Nolan, you may have your $60-million, because you've made us so much money that we will trust you to do whatever the hell you want. Here's your check. Please make us a nice movie." And *Dunkirk* is, in fact, a nice movie and Warners does make its money back because Chris is brilliant. But how can you define that

Nicolas Cage, the man who came this close to playing Superman, but never did
(art © and courtesy D.C. Stuelpner; Superman © and TM DC Comics/Warner Bros. Discovery).

as a rational process?

DAN DIDIO (former co-publisher, DC Comics): When it comes to movies and TV shows based on DC characters, I completely ignored them. My opinion was that the comics are just a small fraction of the movie or TV audience, so I never wanted to follow the direction of a film; never wanted to follow a direction of a TV show, primarily because if they're setting the tone, if they're choosing the direction for the characters and *not* DC editorial or not DC writers, then we are just licensing our own characters from them. And that was unacceptable.

If you were to look up the phrase development hell, it's likely that Superman would come up as it took 15 years and numerous starts and stops before the Man of Steel finally did return to the big screen in 2006's Superman Returns, *which followed by 19 years the release of* Superman IV: The Quest for Peace.

SUPERVOID CINEMA (film historian): Following on from *Superman 5* — the Christopher Reeve sequel that never was — Hollywood producer Jon Peters obtained the rights from the Salkinds to produce a new Superman movie in 1994 in association with Warner Bros. Warner Bros. had somehow let the option to Superman slip away; Peters would pounce and obtain the rights to the franchise and tie them up in an ironclad contract, written by his former producing partner Peter Guber.

JON PETERS (producer, unfilmed *Superman Reborn* and *Superman Lives*): Superman was something that I had seen with Dick Donner and I loved and I was mesmerized by it. That was the granddaddy of all the superheroes. I made over 100 movies, movies that I did with PolyGram Pictures and all the movies that we produced and everything. I was the chairman of Sony and I was leaving. Peter [Guber] and I were splitting up. And they said to me, "You're not going to believe this, but we think Superman is available." So I got into negotiation with the Salkinds and their lawyers because Warner Bros. had not picked up the option. They didn't know that; it was before computers.

They would have had someone in the back room going through all these things, and if it was in the computer, it would normally be red-flagged. I got a call from Terry Semel, who was the head of Warner Bros., and he said, "We want you to come back to the studio." And I said, "I'm working on something now, which is really what I want to do. I think I bought the rights to Superman." He said, "You idiot. Warner Bros. owns it. I own it." I said, "No, you don't. Check." He came back and he said, "You're right. You do." (*courtesy Holly Payne*)

SUPERVOID CINEMA: Peters then struck another deal that would turn some rights back to Warner Bros. on the condition that Peters had the legal option to produce Superman movies for the rest of his life. Another contract was drawn up and it was made official. Peters would find himself in the company of producer Joel Silver and new Warners executive Lorenzo di Bonaventura at Silver's plantation in South Carolina for an informal meeting. Peters is told that this title is a top priority for the studio. The producer would agree to orchestrate the production and the first thing Peters decided was that he wanted to do away with the good-guy persona that had been Superman's defining characteristic for over 50 years and remold the Man of Steel to appeal to the so-called MTV Generation. As a favorite of Warner Bros. bosses, Peters was given the blessing to take the property in any direction he saw fit. Peters' first choice to write the script was the studio's in-house screenwriter Jonathan Lemkin.

JONATHAN LEMKIN (writer, unfilmed *Superman Reborn*): I was a studio writer with a two-year contract; there were, I guess, no more than a dozen of us in town. It was a throwback to the '40s. I had worked on *Showdown in Little Tokyo, Demolition Man, Under Siege 2: Dark Territory, The Devil's Advocate* and *Lethal Weapon* 4. I think, based on the action of *Lethal Weapon 4,* some of the more supernatural elements of *Devil's* Advocate and the fantasy elements of *Demolition* Man, everyone felt comfortable about going forward with me as the writer of the then-titled *Superman Reborn*. The storyline we came up with had to be presented to the CEOs of Warner Bros. Let's face it, I had been entrusted with this corporate asset and it's a very different process than any other script I've ever done. Superman is a *huge* corporate asset, and if you look at the marketing that can come from this, it's phenomenal.

I was comparing what we were doing to *Batman* and *Batman Returns* rather than *Superman: The Movie*. The Donner Superman film was from a different kind of joyful view of the world that I didn't think, at the moment, we were at. If anything, we were trying to remove ourselves from the legacy of the Donner film by changing the colors, changing the feeling and making it a whole new world. You have to remember what a big success the 1989 *Batman* film was in terms of reinventing Batman, because before that it had been the Adam West television series. And they turned it into a very dark, weird, Jack Nicholson-dancing-Prince-music-playing movie. And that's what I was directed to look at. You get into bed with madmen, hoping that they'll create bits of genius again.

The attempt was to update the character for the 1990s, though the hope was to hold on to the fact that Superman is not considered to be a conflicted hero and, as a result, he faces the film's adversary Doomsday without hesitation.

JONATHAN LEMKIN: There's something about Superman that's great in terms of his attitude of stepping into the breach, come what may. The timing for this movie just felt right. You have to remember that the biggest difference between Batman and Superman is that Batman is human. He's mortal. Superman came from another planet and demands fantasy elements that the others don't. I think that's much more exciting, and I feel that it's almost the result of what happens if you cross Batman with *Star Wars*. Superman versus human elements is not an interesting match. That's like me versus a slug. Who cares?

Lemkin's assignment was to shake things up, which he delivered on by focusing the first part of the story on the relationship between Clark and Lois, including Superman's inability to give his alien heart over to a human woman. It's only after the battle with Doomsday, when he lies dying in her arms, that he comes to grips with his feelings for her.

JONATHAN LEMKIN: He literally dies as he professes his love to her and his life force jumps between them. Superman dies and Lois later finds out that she's pregnant — immaculately. She gives birth to a child who grows 21 years in three weeks and is, essentially, the resurrected Superman. I thought it would be funny to piss off the Far Right. I think most people would have enjoyed the tongue-in-cheek quality of it. Look, Batman had nipples and a codpiece around that time for crying out loud.

In any good Superman movie, the fate of the whole planet should be at stake. The truth of the matter is that you've got to treat the legend with respect and at the same time put enough of a spin on it so that it's not something that people have seen before. It's really easy to get arch and coy, which is the last thing you want to do. Taking Superman seriously is sometimes hard, but that's what you have to do. You've got to have a villain whose powers and abilities demand Superman be the one that stops them. Their powers have to tax Superman to the limit. That's exciting and a challenge as well. All of the big myths are really about small truths and human moments. If you go out to slay a dragon, it's because your own hearth and home have been threatened. If there were any movies we kept looking to over and over again in relationship to this, it's *Star Wars* and *The Lion King*. They're the most mythological films we looked at. We were trying desperately to make something that taps into deep mythological stories, rather than just bad men come to town, cause trouble and we kick their ass. We wanted something with a little more resonance.

SUPERVOID CINEMA: Sadly for Lemkin, the studio didn't agree. The concept of having Superman's bloodline successor in the film, as opposed to Superman himself, seemed a little too off-track and Lemkin was dismissed from any further participation in the project. Officially, the writer was told that his script contained plot-beats that were deemed too thematically similar to then in-production *Batman Forever*. Peters was said to have been furious, but either way Lemkin was to be replaced, and so the next call was to Gregory Poirer, the writer of the Peters-produced historical drama *Rosewood*. Under commission from Peters, Poirer would write three different drafts across December '95 to March '96. Peters was happy with the new version, as by the time the third draft was handed in, all of the producer's notes and suggestions had been incorporated into the story, including the implicit suggestion to make Superman more of a Batman-like figure, motivated by vengeance and melancholy brooding.

Peters would tell bosses that this is the script the film would be based on. Warners, however, sent word back that since they were investing heavily in a chain of retail stores and merchandising outlets, a Superman suffering from an existential anxiety wasn't the easiest sell. It was decided that parents wouldn't exactly be lining up around the block to buy action figures of "Superman's Therapist" for these kids at Christmas, and so Poirer was paid up and dismissed from the project. Peters, who wasn't pleased with the second strike against his choice of writer, was told to go another way instead. It's at this point that writer-director Kevin Smith enters the story, and so begins the chapter of one of the most chronicled movie-development hells in the history of cinema. It's a song that by now we all know the words to and, of course, was the subject of a fan-funded documentary researched, written and directed as a personal passion project of the late, great Jon Schnepp.

HOLLY PAYNE (producer, *The Death of Superman Lives: What Happened?*): This project was a hundred percent Jon's obsession. For years he had been collecting whatever he could find on the Internet and putting images of concept art into a folder on his desktop. Any time an alert came up, he would just file it away. For him it wasn't a project in the beginning, it was more like a curiosity, wondering what different things would have been. Later it was suggested to him that he should do a documentary, but he said he didn't do them. He said, "I'm a director, I do videos, I do live-action, I do animation, I'm not a documentary director," which is when I came in. I said, "Why *don't* we do documentaries? You have more knowledge on this subject than probably anybody. It's a subject that hits on all kinds of levels: It's moviemaking, it's Superman, it's cult favorite Nicolas Cage, it's Tim Burton — it's all of these things kind of coming together that you can't imagine what it was going to be. Why not explore that for people and explore it for ourselves?" So we went on that journey and then we started crowd-funding the project, which is when we realized, "Oh my God, there's hundreds of thousands of people out there who want to know what happened." We started the process of doing interviews, and when Tim Burton came on board and we got his interview, all the other people started to say yes. That definitely opened the floodgates for sure.

A mind-blowing experience for both Payne and Schnepp was when they traveled to England to interview Burton and were given a USB drive containing 45 minutes of footage of Burton and Nicolas Cage engaged in conversation about the Superman Lives *project.*

HOLLY PAYNE: We watched it in our little London Airbnb with our jaws on the floor, because it was Tim and Nick, who are both fringe in their own right, talking about this beloved character — not just Superman, but really going into it about Clark Kent. And the two of them are spitballing what their ideas are about the characters. A lot of it is in the film of course, but it was an opportunity to watch their process.

JON SCHNEPP (writer/director, *The Death of Superman Lives: What Happened?*): I thought the concept designs for the *Superman Lives* project were really pushing the boundaries of what had been acceptable in the filmed versions of Superman or even the comic books, because he was like an electrical being at the time. Before that, he died and came back with a weird silver outfit and he had long hair. So Superman's always changed and in comic books characters die and they come back constantly. Ever since Marv Wolfman exploded the universe with *Crisis on Infinite Earths,* they realized rebooting the characters in general was probably a pretty good idea. At first it was every 25 years, then every 10 years and now it's every six years. It makes sense because you've got to refresh the genre. I grew up reading comics and I've gotten all these different versions of the Superman character in comic books. People who don't read comics, which is the masses in general, and just watch TV or go to movies, they know *Smallville* or *Superman Returns* or *Man of Steel.* So they come back to it and say, "Hey, where's *my* Superman," so I kind of get the idea of keeping something the same, but you also have to refresh the genre.

I look at movies and television as an Elseworld where you can take risks and try something different. If it fails, you try again. It doesn't have to hit it out of the park, but of course you want it to because it's a business. I think that's where *Superman*

Lives comes into play. For myself, it was something very different. They had original characters as in real-life people like Tim Burton, Nicolas Cage and Kevin Smith — all of these different talented people attached to this property that they're trying to reboot. Since *Superman IV: The Quest for Peace*, the property was dead and they were trying to reboot it. So of course Jon Peters got the rights; he'd already rebooted Batman where you had Jack Nicholson playing the Joker. You look at it now and it seems a little bit more comical, but back then that was cutting edge. Moviemaking is taking risks, and the people involved with *Superman Lives* were taking risks. When you go outside of the bubble, then you're in the business world where taking risks is scary and Warner Bros. was losing money with a lot of their other films at the time. Taking risks with Tim Burton and Nicolas Cage and a big $300-million budget was something that made them nervous.

MARK MILLAR (writer, *Superman: Red Son*): Don't laugh, but I thought Nic Cage was an interesting idea. I hated Dean Cain so much and thought he looked, acted and sounded more unlike Superman than Teri Hatcher. Compared to Cain, Cage actually *is* Superman, and the fact that he's an Oscar-winning actor would, I think, bring some much-needed dignity after the TV show. He doesn't look like Superman, granted, but *anyone* can look like a superhero with the right wig, make-up, special effects, etc. If I could choose anyone, I think I'd opt for Daniel Day-Lewis. Being Irish shouldn't prevent him from tackling such an all-American role. I mean, Superman's from Krypton, isn't he?

ROB O'CONNOR: I am a foremost *Superman Lives* apologist! While many fans thank goodness that film never saw the light of day, Jon Schnepp's wonderful documentary turned me around on the idea and I can't help wondering if it might have been fun to have had a curious '90s-tastic Tim Burton Kryptonian toybox with Nicolas Cage still in his Hollywood Heavyweight prime. The assumption has always been that Burton would just make Superman into Batman, but the documentary paints a very different portrait of the story he wanted to tell — that of an outsider trying to discover his origins and his place in the world while also trying to save it! Even if it had been disastrous (a la *Batman & Robin*), I feel like it might have forced Warners to reassess how they approach the character in mainstream movies and perhaps we might have had a more focused, truer modern Superman trilogy by now (a la Nolan's *Dark Knight* films following *Batman & Robin*) instead of the disappointing half-measures and false starts we keep getting. I am one of those weirdos who actually thinks the *Superman Lives* costume (the traditional blue, red and yellow one in photos that surfaced relatively recently) looks quite a bit better than the eventual *Superman Returns* one, and I would love to see Cage finally appear in some sort of multiverse shenanigans at some point in the future.

HOLLY PAYNE: I don't think Jon or I had any sort of preconceived negative feeling about the idea of *Superman Lives* being a disaster or a bullet that was dodged, which seems to be the consensus. Coming at it from *that* perspective, we weren't going at it with a negative bent, we just wanted to explore it.

JON SCHNEPP: *Superman Lives* was basically written by three different screenwriters, Kevin Smith, Wesley Strick and Dan Gilroy. All three scripts revolved around the same story basically taken from the comic book series *The Death of Superman*, where Superman fought the villains Lex Luthor, Brainiac and the killing machine Doomsday. Doomsday killed Superman in the comic books and then he came back to life using Kryptonian technology. This revitalized the comic book series. Warner Bros. took their cue from the comic books to revitalize their movie franchise.

Sometimes the interest in the "what if" is stronger than the actual final product because it fills your mind with the possibilities of what could have been. That's something that interested me when I saw the concept art for *Superman Lives* — amazing, strange designs, cosmic ideas, creatures, aliens, Superman with a strange metal "S." All these things interested me and I wanted to find out why it never got made.

KEVIN SMITH (writer, unfilmed *Superman Lives*): There was an exec at Warner Bros. named Basil Iwanyk. He'd heard some stuff about *Chasing Amy*, which hadn't been released yet, but he'd read the script and dug on it. So he called me in for a meeting about a few different Warner Bros. projects that were up for grabs. One of them was Superman, but we always assumed that was a long shot. There was a *Beetlejuice* sequel and *Architects of Fear*, based on an old *Outer Limits* episode. I read it and felt there was nothing I could do with it, and with *Beetlejuice* I figured leave well enough alone. But Superman was one I was kind of intrigued by because of comic books, and because I read the script they were working on at that time and hated it. The writer knew nothing about the character, nothing about comic books. It was just kind of cheese.

We had this big lunch where we sat down and talked about the script and I said, "Look, the script is really, really bad. It's a disservice and injustice to people who have been fans of the character for years, and just a disservice to the character himself to go forward and make this movie. What you're really looking at is if you make a Superman movie, people will show up. You're bound to make a hundred-million regardless. Why not make a good one? Don't throw it away on this.

It's embarrassing, it's everything that's wrong with comic book movies. There's just no understanding of Superman or the characters. It's just too campy. I'm not lobbying for the job here. Hire me or don't hire me, just don't make this script." I was thanked for my input and that was that. I figured if nothing else maybe I threw down some words that would maybe make them think twice before they went forward. It was an atrocity. This character was 60 years old. Don't make a movie where nobody's going to care that he's 60 years old because obviously Hollywood can't do anything with him had they made that movie. I thought that was it; I had blown my chance but at least I was honest with them.

Smith received a callback for a meeting with more Warner Bros. executives and was asked to present his views again. This led him to meeting with Jon Peters and Lorenzo Di Bonaventura.

KEVIN SMITH: Lorenzo is a great guy, a smart guy. And Jon Peters isn't really a great guy or smart guy. But I was fascinated by meeting with Jon Peters because this was the guy who produced *Batman,* and to hear him tell the story, you wouldn't think that Tim Burton meant anything to *Batman*. He says stuff like, "You know the reason that *Batman* worked? You know that alleyway scene where he's fighting those sword-bearing guys and they're attacking him? Those guys were real swordsmen; *that's* why that movie made like $300-million." I was like, "Oh really? All you need is real swordsmen to make a film such a hit?" But both of them dug on me, I guess. Jon's take was more from the gut than anything else, and way off-base too. He said, "You know why you and me are going to get this project right and make a great movie? Because you and me understand Superman; we're from the streets." I was like, "You were a hairdresser once, I'm from the suburbs. Neither of us are from the streets."

JON PETERS: I don't think people got over the fact that I started as a hairdresser.

LORENZO DI BONAVENTURA (executive in charge of unfilmed *Superman Lives***):** Jon Peters came to Warners and said, "Listen, I think we can put all these rights together." We put the rights together. Kevin Smith came in with a really great take. (*courtesy Holly Payne*)

KEVIN SMITH: Lorenzo took the more intellectual approach with it; doesn't claim to know everything about comics, but does know a few things and asked the right questions. When I was talking about the history and Superman being jettisoned from Krypton by his parents in a rocket, he said, "Well, why didn't Jor-El just build a rocket big enough for his whole family?" I was like, "Well... I don't know." He said that these were the kind of things that you want to address, as well as some fundamental questions that you want to attack. He forced me to work a little harder and not to just fall back on all the comics knowledge I had collected over the years. He got it too; he understood where I was going with it. We got along well. I even got along with Peters most of the time. He had kooky ideas and sometimes you had to reign him in and say, "You don't want to do that," but sometimes you have to succumb to the stupidity, like having Brainiac fight polar bears in the Antarctic when he goes to the Fortress of Solitude. It's embarrassing.

JON PETERS: Kevin came in. I felt free with him. He was an interesting character. We talked about a lot of different things. He was such a nut. And he was so animated. And he talks such a great game that I trusted him.

KEVIN SMITH: And he goes, "Okay, three things I want with this picture and I'll send you on your way. Number one: I don't want to see him fly." I said, "Okay. Ever?" He goes, "No, I think it looks fake. I hate all that flying shit, so I don't want to see him fly." I said, "Okay." Number two: I don't want to see him in that suit." I was like, "Which suit?" And he goes, "The suit he's always wearing." I was like, "Superman suit with the cape and a blue and a red and the yellow?" He goes, "Yeah, I don't like it." His words, not mine. "Too faggy." I said, "All right."

JON PETERS: None of that's true. Of course he has to fly. He always flew. He's Superman. Of course he's in the costume. None of those are true.

KEVIN SMITH: Number three: He has to fight a giant spider in the third act. I said, "Uh, okay. Really?"

JON PETERS: Well, that was a thing called a Thanagarian snare beast.

KEVIN SMITH: "What is this based on?" He goes, "Well, do you know anything about spiders? Spiders are the fiercest killers in the animal kingdom. You've got to be careful around spiders. So if you have a big one, imagine how deadly they are. I'm looking for my moment in this movie; like *King Kong* when I was a boy. And they opened up the gates and you saw the giant monkey. I want that. I want to open up the gates. And then you see this gigantic spider coming out and Superman's got to fight the spider. It's a vision I had." I was like, "Okay man, I'll spider it up for you and stuff."

He was also always saying that Brainiac should give Luthor a space dog; something from that menagerie of his. He gives Luthor a dog, Luthor is afraid of the dog and the dog hates him. I'm like, "It doesn't really lend to the story, why do you want that?" "Because I need a Chewie." This was during the time of *Star Wars'* re-release and he said, "Chewie's cuddly, man, you could make a toy out of him, so you've got to give me a dog.' It's something I fought the whole time, and finally I guess I won him over with, "Look, Jon, you don't need a Chewie." He's forever influenced by the things he's seen.

JON PETERS: If I remember correctly, I acted as the director for a while by bringing in people and starting to come up with my concepts on paper, so that ultimately when I brought in Tim Burgard or whoever we brought in, I would sit down and say, "Okay, this is where we are, this is what we've done."

TIM BURGARD (art department, unfilmed *Superman Lives*): Jon Peters wanted to convince the higher-ups to invest in a movie that is going to have something other than another guy in spandex fighting Superman. My initial job was to come up with this big scary freaking thing with a body kind of based on a black widow, but a face more like a tarantula. And I throw in maybe a little crab and stuff in there too. One of the illustrations was a digressed kind of thing. And it's what is called the opening of the Yanni and all these little face-hugger mini-spiders are coming down and covering Superman. He's not going up against a super-villain — he's going up against the Alien or the Predator or something that will try and kill him and maybe eat him or lay eggs in his eyeballs. That to me is super-cool because it takes it to a different level that we haven't seen before. (*courtesy Holly Payne*)

JON PETERS: This was all out of my mind. The Thanagarian snare beasts, I stole it from Jules Verne's *20,000 Leagues Under the Sea*; this giant squid, who tries to swallow up the submarine, so Superman would fight every tentacle, getting closer and closer and closer to his beak till he killed it, would have made an amazing sequence.

KEVIN SMITH: I appeased Warner Bros. by not calling it a spider. I call it Thanagarian snare beast; a Hawkman reference for the planet Thanagar or something; just little things that I threw in. And the Warner Bros. execs were like, "As long as it doesn't say spider, we don't give a shit. We know it's a spider."

JON PETERS: I wanted to do *The Death of Superman* because I love dramatic structures. So the idea is chaos rules, really, and I knew that could be amazing. I just felt it in my bones.

KEVIN SMITH: They wanted to do *The Death of Superman* storyline that had been done very successfully in the comics a few years before; the death and return storyline. It was one of those jobs where I was just like, "Fuck it, write your dream movie." You know what I'm saying? It's the dream job, go crazy, because whoever is going to direct is going to change anything they don't like anyway. I had the Eradicator in there, I had Cyborg Superman, Lex Luthor was in there, Doomsday was in there, Brainiac was a villain. It was packed.

JON SCHNEPP: One of the things that the script actually brought in, that now everyone's doing, is the crossover. Not only were a lot of different villains, like Deadshot, in it, but it also had Batman.

KEVIN SMITH: There was a sequence where it was during Superman's funeral, very dramatic — and it's clearly written by a Batman fan — it was almost the whole reason I took the job. It's kind of like Times Square, TVs everywhere, whatever. And then they all just go shoot, they're just taken over and there's a big bat symbol and then he comes on and he gives them this message of encouragement... like real whack stuff if you're a huge comic book nerd. And Lorenzo's like, "I like this." And Jon has people like Tracy Barone, who was running his company at that point, and Tracy goes, "You're going to come over tomorrow to have a meeting with Jon, right?" I said, "Talk about the script?" She goes, "To read the script." I go, "What do you mean, read the script?" And she says, "He likes to have the script read to him out loud." And I was like, "Get out of here, man. Do you want me to tuck him in after I'm done?" She's going, "I'm serious."

JON PETERS: I'm not a good reader, number one. Number two, everyone sometimes reads things differently. But you see it, it's pretty much what you see.

KEVIN SMITH: I said, "I understand I'm going to read you a script," and he says, "Totally. Let's do this, man." He lays down on his couch in tennis shorts and stuff and he's looking at the ceiling, and he was making director hands as he was laying there and this was the "movie screen" that he was placing onto his ceiling, so that while I was reading, he was seeing it on a canvas.

JON PETERS: I'm a visual guy so most things I do by visualization. Every script I ever get, I have someone read it to me and I just lay back and listen and I run it on my screen in my brain.

KEVIN SMITH: At one point he stops and goes, "Oh, nothing's happening. You got Brainiac come into the Fortress of Solitude. There's no fight. Where's the fight? Have Brainiac fighting Superman's guards." And I go, "Well, it's called the Fortress of Solitude — like *nobody's* up there, dude. He's alone. Plus, why would Superman need guards? He's Superman, dude. Think about it." And he goes, "Well, what about polar bears?" And I go, "Polar bears?" He goes, "Polar bears are the fiercest killers in the animal kingdom."

JON PETERS: I'm sure there were 50 other ideas we could have come up with, but at the time we created something that he could fight and there's nothing more ferocious than a 3,000-pound, giant 12-foot, 15-foot polar bear.

It was around this point that first thoughts were being bandied about regarding a possible director; the first name mentioned was Batman '89's *Tim Burton.*

KEVIN SMITH: Early on in the process I was talking to one exec about who would possibly direct and I suggested Tim Burton. They said, "Nah, Tim doesn't have the right kind of sensibility for this movie," and I said, "Yeah, I guess you're right, Tim's kind of dark and this movie's not about darkness, although the movie is set in darkness." Lo and behold, right before I turned in my second draft, all of a sudden Tim Burton comes to Warner Bros. where he's made *Mars Attacks!* which went right in the shitter and he wanted to do a sure thing. At one point he was thinking about doing *Scooby-Doo*, but they handed him the script for *Superman*, the one I'd done, and he dug on it. It was great for the studio because they had a script they liked and had worked on for a while, and they had a director who had made them over half-a-billion-dollars previously on a superhero franchise. Everything was looking rosy.

JON PETERS: Tim Burton was my number-one choice and obviously I didn't want to make a Superman that anybody else had made. I really wanted to run Superman through his brain.

KEVIN SMITH: As soon as Tim Burton signed his deal, the script became fair game. Tim Burton turned around and told the studio, "I want to do my own version of Superman, I want to go another way and I only work with these four writers, so I want Wesley Strick to redraft it." Now I'm on the phone with Warner Bros., I'm done at this point. I've done my two drafts but all through the process all the studio kept saying, and all Jon Peters kept saying, was that I would be on for the run of the show. They said I would be set writer, which would have been fun. The multiple drafts we would go through I would be doing.

Documentary filmmaker Jon Schnepp and director Tim Burton in a moment from **The Death of Superman Lives: What Happened?** *(photo © and courtesy Holly Payne).*

Suddenly that's it. At one point I said to Jon Peters, "Big studio movies usually have multiple writers," and he said, "Not this one. The director is going to be one of these MTV guys who's real in line with our vision. "Our" vision — like he had anything to do with it. He said, "He's going to listen to us, we're not going to let him get out of line because we control the script." As soon as Tim Burton was hired, all of that went right out the window.

JON PETERS: Kevin handed in his script and I call him and it just was no good, wasn't funny, it had no structure to it. It was just unimaginative. It was like it was an amateur writer who wasn't a crafted writer.

KEVIN SMITH: I didn't even talk to Jon once Tim Burton came on board — which is ironic because Jon had said early in the process that Tim wouldn't be right. So I said, "I should at least meet with Tim Burton; at least give me the benefit of the doubt to go in there and hear his kooky ideas, and if I can do them, I'll do them. If not, he can go off and get his other writer." But Tim Burton wouldn't do it; Tim Burton is too important, I guess, to meet with me. I don't know if I would have gone much differently, but faced with the choice of, "Well, we've got this director who's made us a bunch of dough and has a great history with a superhero on film, or we've got the *Clerks* guy whose script we love, who do we go with?" So… they backed Tim Burton.

While the script was being dealt with, Burton was actually approached and he was certainly open to the idea of being a part of the comic book movie genre again.

TIM BURTON (director, unfilmed *Superman Lives*): Growing up, I was a fan of horror movies, Ray Harryhausen and things like that. Obviously my favorite comic character was Batman. Just getting into the psychology of the superhero, that was at that time new territory. And so, when I got involved with Superman, it was just a different exploration of that kind of feeling of being different, feeling like somebody from another planet. Those kinds of themes were always quite strong in old monster movies, and then some of the comic books. The graphic novel came into play to explore the sort of psychology of the characters, so obviously a lot of the comic book characters fit into that kind of mythology. If somebody doesn't fit in and somebody doesn't belong, that's our exploration of feeling like an alien on a planet and being different and having to survive, hide yourself in some ways and suppress certain sides of yourself... and the sort of secretive internal nature of a character. So that, I think, was the thing at the root of it that was most interesting. (*courtesy Holly Payne*)

LORENZO DI BONAVENTURA: Hearing Tim's inspiration for the character was a great moment, where you were like, "Oh, God!' In a way it's so obvious, but of course the best ideas are not that easy to get to.

JON PETERS: When you give the Thanagarian snare beasts with all these characters, Tim Burton goes to work. He was such a visualist that he makes things happen through his mind that sometimes are not even on the page.

COLLEEN ATWOOD (costume designer, unfilmed *Superman Lives*): I met Tim on *Edward Scissorhands*, which was my first collaboration with him. We just hit it off and we had a good run after that. And then when *Superman* came up, it was a different kind of movie for me at the time to do. I hadn't ever done any big kind of superhero sort of things at all. With Tim you always start with who he thinks the people are, his sort of take on it, which is always unique and what makes Tim special. And his take on Superman was a new kind of version of it. He didn't want to go with a sort of Mr. Clean version, he wanted to go with kind of this unnoticed kind of person. (*courtesy Holly Payne*)

RICK HEINRICHS (production designer, unfilmed *Superman Lives*): But with Tim, you see this recurring theme of the outsider in a lot of his films. He's interested in characters who carry this extraordinary capability or gift of some kind. You'll see this in a lot of his films... and how that character interacts with the outside world; they don't often connect well; part of them needs to stay hidden because if you were to reveal their real self, it would be calamitous for that character. (*courtesy Holly Payne*)

JON SCHNEPP: Batman had a secondary role. He was Bruce Wayne, and then he was Batman. With the Superman character, there was Clark Kent.

TIM BURTON: The two are slightly similar, but this is on a global scale, in a way, in the sense of having to hide and you always try to put your personal feelings into it. And I felt like I was an alien. And I think a lot of people do, a lot of kids do. That was probably the core thing in a way. That was the main thing that interested me.

JON PETERS: All of us feel like aliens. Nobody is comfortable in their own skin all of the time. And we all feel that darkness. I wanted him to be able to talk about that darkness in a way that would be interesting for the audience.

LORENZO DI BONAVENTURA: I think the humanizing of Superman was what I would look at as sort of Tim's approach to him that made me really get excited, made Warners get excited.

WESLEY STRICK (writer, unfilmed *Superman Lives*): I got involved because I had worked with Tim on *Batman Returns* about six years earlier. I ended up staying for the whole shoot because he felt like he needed a writer at his side through the process. I remember him complaining about making superhero movies. He compared it to Chinese water torture. I asked him, "If you hate it so much, why are you doing the sequel?" And he said, "Because I think I learned a lot during the first Batman movie and I want a second movie in which I can put to use everything I learned," and undo the mistakes that he felt he had made in the first one.

I knew that there was a Kevin Smith script. I read it without any preconceived idea about it. But as I read it, there was a lot about it that wasn't sort of clicking with me because I'm not a Superman fanboy. I hadn't read any of *The Death of Superman* graphic novels. I wasn't up to speed with all that stuff. I was just sort of curious on what Tim's take on it was. I remember we met at the Chateau Marmont, in the lobby there. And I said, "So Tim, I read the Kevin Smith script." Before I was finished with my sentence he said, "I don't want to talk about that script." I was like, "Okay, so what do you want to do?" And he wasn't sure. We also were told by Warners aspects of Kevin's plot, if not his script, per se, that they wanted to keep intact. Obviously it was still based on *The Death of Superman* to some extent. Jon Peters was very much involved, right from the get-go. And Tim was, I think, really ambivalent about that too. He already had a sort of bad experience with Peters on *Batman* and told me that the reason he went to London to film it was to get away from Peters. And now he was making this Superman movie in L.A., in the same city as Jon, and he was already uptight about it. I think he kind of could see the future. (*courtesy Holly Payne*)

TIM BURTON: Jon is a force of nature and he's passionate about things. And I think where that sometimes becomes a problem is that he's trying to control the weather. You know, he can't really do it.

JON PETERS: Even though you're the producer, people get mad at me, saying I'm controlling, overbearing, a force of nature — all these crazy things, only because it takes tremendous energy to move most people who say it can't be done. And most people don't have the energy to be able to see the same vision and then get the money to do it.

WESLEY STRICK: Tim and I always discussed this as Superman versus Batman in that Superman takes place in daylight, in sunlight, and Batman would come out at night. I mean, that was sort of the real yin and yang of the two characters. And Tim was excited about doing that because I think he felt that a lot of his movies were sort of movies made in the shadows and darkness, and all of that. I think he wanted to challenge himself to see if he could make a movie that was brighter, sunny or maybe a little more optimistic than what he was accustomed to doing.

JON SCHNEPP: He basically changed Batman. He was the one who came in and said, "We're going to get Batman a brand-new look." We didn't really have the Internet back in 1988 when Burton was shooting this, so the grumbling, whiners and complainers didn't get a chance to attack as hard as they do nowadays. With the idea of Nicolas Cage as Superman, they complained that it was a weird choice, but the same could be said for Michael Keaton.

JON PETERS: Michael Keaton had done a movie called *Clean and Sober*, which I saw, and I thought this guy is a genius actor.

KEVIN SMITH: The shouting about Michael Keaton as Batman was so loud and proliferate in 1988-'89. Even though the Internet didn't exist, the Internet was still mad. People were like, "What, *Mr. Mom?*"

TIM BURTON: The reason he worked for me is because he looked like somebody who needed to dress like a bat to intimidate people.

JON PETERS: I knew, being a street fighter my whole life, that you can gauge the toughness of your opponent by the look in their eyes. And Michael Keaton had that look.

JON SCHNEPP: I just read Frank Miller's *The Dark Knight Returns*. I was like, "I want a darker Batman." I grew up as a little kid watching the Adam West Batman and *this* Batman was exactly what I wanted.

JON PETERS: And it did almost a billion dollars in those days. We had a line when he comes up and says, "I'm Batman." The line from the movie was originally, "I'm Batman, motherf-----," and Warners made me take it out. I wanted to do that because I knew the kids in the audience would go, "Yeah, *right!*"

TIM BURTON: There were lots of reasons why we chose Michael. And so, I knew in my heart that we weren't making a jump, but if the Internet had been around, then we would have had heard about it. It's like sure you can handle it, but it's tough out there.

SUPERVOID CINEMA: Warners was approached by Nicolas Cage's people with word that the actor was willing to offer his services as Lex Luthor or the Man of Steel himself. Cage was said to have been enamored with Smith's first draft, particularly the fan service and the fact that Smith was a comic book reader who wasn't ignorant to Superman's previous 60-year history and didn't act like the material was beneath him.

JON PETERS: Nic Cage reminded me of Michael Keaton. They both weren't the handsome guys, but both had this tremendous gift as an actor.

NICOLAS CAGE (actor, "Clark Kent/Superman," unfilmed *Superman Lives*): I'd never worked with Tim Burton. I've been a fan of his movies though. I liked *Ed Wood* immensely. He's also written some very tender stories that are unique and usually deal with feeling like the outside, so I knew that he was the perfect choice for the human aspects of the Superman story… which are really the only reasons why I wanted to make this movie.

KEVIN SMITH: Now when you think about if somebody was like, "Would you like to see a Nic Cage Superman movie?" I'd be like, "Yes, take all my money because I'm going to see what that looks like."

NICOLAS CAGE: I came on board the Superman project because I wanted to say something to children. And I know Superman appeals to all age groups, but it comes from the child's universe. I remember what I felt like as a child in school being teased. And if there's one kid out there who's being called a weirdo, or a freak, or something, and he goes home, and he's just not having a good day in his life, and his life at school is hell — if he sees Superman and he says, "Well, Superman is a weirdo. He's considered different. Maybe I'm Superman," that's enough for me to feel good about making the movie. That was the vision I got from it. And I think Tim Burton is the perfect director to do that.

TIM BURTON: The great thing about Nic was that he was a fan of the comics, but he also was a fan of the underpinnings and the psychology of it all. So that's, again, what's exciting. He understood both sides of it.

NICOLAS CAGE: Superman is a great story. It's one of those phenomena that operates on so many different levels that still haven't been explored. One of the things I like about Superman is the notion of nurture versus nature. Is he more Kryptonian, or is he more the Kents, his adopted parents? These are big issues that we were thinking about, like genetics and scientific things of that nature. So Superman is a remarkable achievement. These two guys [Jerry Siegel and Joe Shuster] were considered nerds, who were from Canada, they wore glasses, which back in the '30s was a big deal. These two guys who were oppressed invented the alter ego concept of being a super man. And everybody said, "Oh, don't do it, it's ridiculous." They knew they had gold, and they held on to it for four years. And then as soon as it came out, it was an overnight sensation. So there's something there. And I saw it for me as an opportunity to reach a lot of kids around the world and say something positive.

LORENZO DI BONAVENTURA: I think Tim looks at these things slightly off center. I mean, if you think about Michael Keaton, it's not the guy you would have thought of casting as Batman. And yet when you saw it, it was great. And I think when we first heard the Nic Cage idea, we were both intrigued and also going, "Well, that wasn't really the way we were thinking of it exactly."

WESLEY STRICK: I thought it was exciting that Warners was sort of pushing him up and not looking for a pretty boy like Christopher Reeve.

JON PETERS: It was my call, my idea. He could create a character that was an alien from another planet, so why couldn't he be a dark alien and light? I didn't want to make someone who was just pink. I wanted something for the street.

RICK HEINRICHS: Because he's such an eloquent actor, he's got a very powerful presence. He can convey doubt and torment. He can convey joy and happiness and humor. *And* he's an actor.

LORENZO DI BONAVENTURA: When you match that with this idea of making him a guy who has some insecurities, and Nic has that ability to play so vulnerable, it was actually a very natural fit to his take.

RICK HEINRICHS: A lot of the guts of the story is about an evolution that happens to our main character, and we wanted really to show that visually with the suits.

STEVE JOHNSON (special effects, unfilmed *Superman Lives*): Tim always talked about it almost as though it was an alien that was cradling him and bringing him back to life after he dies. But it was kind of a living organism.

JON SCHNEPP: I think what happened with the Kal-El character is that he had some kind of robotic assistant, that when Superman lost his powers, or actually when he got killed by Doomsday, he had this Kryptonian regeneration suit.

STEVE JOHNSON: I made it and I don't know what the hell I'm talking about.

COLLEEN ATWOOD: That was like the beginning of the regeneration suit, as the layers went on in the beginning when he was in the tank. So it's kind of the idea of replacing neural and circulatory things in your body that were under the fluid that could be laser-driven and stuff without the kind of ecto layer that you saw later on.

STEVE JOHNSON: So the first thing we did is we sculpted a suit and we cast it in silicone, but we did it into our Nic Cage light cast, kind of a biomechanical, much more standard-looking suit. We did this test on Nic with this basic solid silicone suit in New York and it was a complete disaster. He hated it. I hated it. Tim hated it. Colleen hated it. Surprised that he didn't fire me right there. The biggest problem with it: It's not clear enough, It's not alive enough, it's not iridescent enough and it doesn't really move very well. So how do we fix that? Vacuum forming is when you take plastic heated up and then take suction and suck it around a hard plastic mold that we previously laminated with an iridescent material. Once that's set up, we can then vacuform it. Something interesting happens. The iridescent qualities become amazing, like an oil slick, and we've done this on *The Abyss* and it looked really cool. So we thought, "Okay, that's step one." We tied them together on Tim's recommendation because he wanted to go a little *Edward Scissorhands* and make it haphazardly. So we had this weird tubing that was tying it together in a very asymmetrical fashion. We ran fiber optics and all kinds of patterns, sequenced them, laid into the Superman suit. You got to know that number one optic comes out at number one port, number two through hundreds of them, so that you can then pattern the shapes just like a Las Vegas sign.

COLLEEN ATWOOD: That was a layered costume, so it was a sculpt of musculature with a clear, almost like a plexi layer over it with etching in the plexi where it passed through it and it would have a glowing quality.

RICK HEINRICHS: It looked great. Tim was not a comic geek. His thing was film and television, and he was able to synthesize a lot of what he saw into a Tim Burton look and feel. I've always admired the fact that he doesn't approach things with the same kind of reverence that somebody who loves comics does.

COLLEEN ATWOOD: Within this story, Superman almost dies. He has a healing bath. He has a new suit at the end. So it was a big deal with costumes and all that. This would be the new, darker Superman. It feels like a little more organic suit. It feels a little more exposed in a way.

JON SCHNEPP: The "S" kind of broke apart almost like a boomerang.

COLLEEN ATWOOD: Like weaponry. And the logo was really important; that logo had to break up into elements. We knew what the material was and the shapes and all that, but as far as mechanically making all that stuff work, we weren't there yet. But this was going to have a super-polished feeling to just show all the different definitions of the muscles when you moved and when you flew. It would look really cool, but black is hard to film, so this kicked back enough light that you could see the body and feel the movement a little bit more. We were into a new discovery. We were looking for something that wasn't a leotard. We were looking for the definition of muscle, which was more different than the original Superman. That was more of that period where people didn't work out

RICK HEINRICHS: What she was doing was also using sculptors; they were sculpting this fantastic suit.

NICOLAS CAGE: I think the Superman costume would still be the classic costume — which I think is important, because I, like many people, am a fan of Americana and pop culture. I like the shape of the Coca-Cola bottle. I think they should stay true to the Superman costume. But I just want to try to use my acting to convey what it means to be an alien living on Earth. And all these heroic deeds — might they not be a compulsion to do good, so that I will be loved? Will you love me now, if I do this? That's sort of like what kids do with their parents: "If I could save my parents' lives, they'll love me." So that's sort of what I want to convey with the character.

LORENZO DI BONAVENTURA: I always looked at Superman and wanted to quickly get the diapers off of him.

COLLEEN ATWOOD: The red underwear on the outside — we tried all different ways to avoid that actually because people kind of tend to make fun of that element on Superman; like the old tighty whitey kind of vibe. With superhero costumes, it's always about the crotch. There was a suggestion that Superman wear basketball shorts, like the Lakers.

TIM BURTON: I don't even know where this came up; if I'm dreaming this or they started mentioning like Shaquille O'Neal, Kobe Bryant Laker outfits so it looks like a basketball Laker... I don't know.

COLLEEN ATWOOD: And you're just like, "Really?"

JON SCHNEPP: That's a horrible suggestion. I'm glad that they didn't go with that.

COLLEEN ATWOOD: It went away. We had capes and all different surfaces and colors as the costume changed and evolved, and the cape could also go from light to dark. And for different purposes.

JON PETERS: One of the things that I tried to get Tim to do at the time, and we may have done it, was to create a character out of the cape. So that in situations that he was in, he could take that cape and he could throw it and bring somebody to him, cut their head off or whatever it is, as a weapon that lived and came back on him.

TIM BURTON: The thing we were going to do, and obviously we just had the initial thing, was to give it whatever that vibe was, but to make it *him*. Usually it takes a while to sort of organically find what that image is in terms of the texture, the costume. All of that was just really initial stuff.

WESLEY STRICK: I remember that Jon, at the time, had like three separate houses up Benedict Canyon that he was renovating. Tim and I were always driving up there getting sort of uptight because you can never quite predict what it was going to be this time. It was always something. And then Tim and I got into a conflict with Lorenzo de Bonaventura. I'd been told that Terry Semel had never read the script. And he finally did. And he said, "What is this? I hate this." I was also told that Warners was changing its strategy in terms of the slate and they didn't want to swing for the fences anymore. They had gotten burned, I guess, on *Batman and Robin*. And Tim has always been upset about the fact that the Superman project was doomed by Joel Schumacher, who screwed up Tim's own franchise, and then screwed up Tim's Superman movies. And one day Tim said, "Could you come over?" This is like three or four months into the process. And I said, "What's going on?" And he started in this sheepish way to say, "Well Warner Bros. and Lorenzo and Terry Semel…" And I interrupted him, I saw where it was going. I said, "Tim, you're firing me." And he said, "Well, they told me to."

TIM BURTON: This is where it gets into that gray area of studio, the black hole development. That's the hardest thing to describe. But you go through it almost every time. Why? I don't know. It's just that I've been involved in so many scripts, where you're fixing it, but you're basically just smothering the life out of it. And you go down that track. It's not a good one, but it happens a lot of the time.

WESLEY STRICK: He told me that they were going to hire somebody else, which was Dan Gilroy, I think.

DAN GILROY (writer, unfilmed *Superman Lives*): I think the first meeting was at Jon Peters' house up in Bel Air. We started talking about the current script. And it was the idea of going deep with the characters and working on the action. And it became sort of a sense that the script wasn't where they wanted it. And the next day I was at Warner Bros., going to meet with Tim at the production office, and it just became a daily for the next year, became a seven-day-a-week job. And I think what was brilliant about what Tim did and what he wanted to explore is to take a classic superhero character who is beyond emotional turmoil. What Tim latched on to was, wait a minute, he's an outsider, because Superman is unique. He's not of the world. Batman's of the world, Spider-Man's of the world. All of the X-Men are of the world. They're mutants of the world. It was the emotional angst of somebody realizing that they are not one of us. I think people are drawn to fantasy because it's literally an escape from the bullshit nightmare societal damage that gets created by growing up.

Starts off Clark Kent is a guy who works at the newspaper, but he had an apartment, and inside his apartment he had a separate place where it was his changing room and a little man cave. And I remember around the wall he had a tremendous number of newspaper articles. And you could tell it's been a lot of research that he'd done trying to figure out what might have caused this condition that maybe this was some sort of medical condition that he had. So early on when Lex through LexCorp uncovers the fragment of spaceship near the Kent family farm the second that Clark Kent realizes that he's an alien, it is utterly devastating emotionally to him. And these are the things that dominated the conversations that I would have with Tim. (*courtesy Holly Payne*)

JON SCHNEPP: Both Tim and Nick had this idea that Clark Kent was going to be a bigger freak than Superman; almost like Clark Kent would be the alien.

COLLEEN ATWOOD: I guess the equivalent of Clark Kent now would be those guys, in Silicon Valley, those kinds of brainy guys. Who knows what their secret life is?

JON PETERS: It's a love story between Superman and Lois… and we tried to make it as simple as that. But he did have a dark side like many men do. On the other hand, he was extremely vulnerable because he didn't really have anybody and he was alone. She gave him the strength of feeling, like that he was who he was. And that she loved him anyhow.

DAN GILROY: The relationship we established early on was stalled. He had this deep concern. What if we have a baby? What if this baby punches its way out of you like *Alien*? What if the baby kills you? It's a judgment, but you can tell this is the dilemma.

LORENZO DI BONAVENTURA: He was going to get engaged to Lois. And he was sitting in a restaurant. He was literally pumping his leg like this, and the water and everybody's table was shaking. He's so anxiety-ridden that he leaves the restaurant. And I think it was a top of a building. And then he just flew around the building like 30 times trying to burn off steam.

MICHAEL ANTHONY JACKSON (art department, unfilmed *Superman Lives*): He doesn't change his suit; he doesn't look for a phone booth or anything. He just burns out of his suit; he takes off and that in itself is enough to just shred the clothes. Tim wanted more of a visceral physical punch that you saw in those Max Fleischer cartoons, which is an adaptation of what Siegel and Schuster's the original Superman was. That was our Kal-El, that was our Superman. He's not somebody who can fly. Tim said that he didn't like the idea of magical flying or just floating in space, so he said to everyone to ground it and tie it to physics. If he jumps three miles in the air, he comes right back down like a bullet. The first thing I'd done for that was almost a Superman parkour sequence on a grand scale. So it shows Superman leaping across the city; might take him five or six leaps, but he makes each leap being the equivalent of two miles or three miles. (*courtesy Holly Payne*)

TIM BURTON: I'm much more interested in somebody flying through the clouds and feeling the texture of that on their face. For me, very important was the idea of whatever's going on, the feeling of what it would feel like to be that kind of a character. So I was trying to get more into that visceral feel of it.

LORENZO DI BONAVENTURA: How do you make flying cool and also affordable?

RONALD G. SMITH: ILM got involved, they were going to do the visuals on the movie. So they ended up coming together, we did some tests of just shooting this stuff and then figuring out how Cage was going to fly.

COLLEEN ATWOOD: We did a lot of testing with that. And I think for the time the guys came up with some really great stuff. It was pretty exciting.

LORENZO DI BONAVENTURA: It was still early in the process. And we had some evolution we'd done to the techniques that Tim was going for, but we were going to get there. Then watching Nic Cage in an outfit I was like, "Whoa! There's Superman, the Nic Cage version!" That moment I remember really acutely because it was really like, "Whoa! We really are doing this."

Although it certainly seemed that way, with Superman Lives *apparently firing on all cylinders and every indication that it would be going into full production, the bottom fell out of the project.*

LORENZO DI BONAVENTURA: I don't think there's any one reason. There are always usually a combination of reasons and everybody will have a slightly different perspective. As somebody inside, Superman got caught in an unfortunate moment in time at Warner Bros.

DAN GILROY: So when you're working on this script, people are checking in with you on almost a daily basis. It was a studio movie with a huge budget. Before we handed in our first draft, nobody was talking about money in terms of the budget. It was just like, "We're going to be busy with a big movie, we're going to write this big." Then I got a phone call that Warner Bros. had run a budget and it was through the roof.

JON PETERS: It would have been 200 for the movie, another 100 for advertising, would have been a $300-million investment.

LORENZO DI BONAVENTURA: The budget was not an insignificant budget, it was a really large budget.

DAN GILROY: There was a period of four weeks where we got to retool this again and make this smaller; it's too expensive. We have to start cutting things. And these big huge action sequences that before had a blank check attached to them, suddenly were disappearing.

LORENZO DI BONAVENTURA: We had several films fail right around it, or underperform right around it. So suddenly the economic pressure on all of us was very significant.

DAN GILROY: In the conference room at Warner Bros., there's a big board, and it's literally the size of a wall. And it has their entire release dates for the year, including all the other films that are coming out that weekend. So it's broken up by weekend. Warner Bros. got on one of the all-time terrible rolls. Bob Daly and Terry Semel were in charge of the studio and they had a tremendous run. These are very talented people, but at this point, for some reason, things were misfiring. And you could just see it was just like every week the horse race was happening and their horse was coming in last. So as we're coming in to discuss at the conference table our incredibly large-budget film, with a Tim Burton take, which is deconstructionist and unusual and unique, what's going on around us is, you're looking at the board and you can just see the bombs as they're going up. Every time I come in the conference room, another executive had been fired. And as money starts getting tight and people have to make big decisions, safety becomes the big thing.

LORENZO DI BONAVENTURA: The risk that you can take when you're feeling confident is very different than when you're feeling a little bit on your heels. And we were on our heels at that moment. We were all interested in getting the script better, the filmmakers were too, and it was still in process.

DAN GILROY: Lorenzo is utterly right. It's like we needed to work on it. We needed to hone it. We needed to make it better all the time. But it was enough there that you could see what it was going to be.

JON PETERS: Dan Gilroy gave it some real shape and I kind of liked what he did. The studio didn't like it.

DAN GILROY: You never felt like you were on solid ground when you were going to talk about the script, because there was always the sense that it wasn't even a blinking green light. It was a green light. They were moving ahead.

STEVE JOHNSON: We built this test suit just for one of the people that worked in my studio. And by that time we got so excited that we were ready to spontaneously combust, because I thought we'd come up with exactly what Tim wanted…. and something pretty damn unique. Then we got the call that the show was off.

COLLEEN ATWOOD: Everything had finally come together and we were ready to go to the next step. Actually, the day of the camera test was the day that they came and told us the movie was off. So we only had elements of that costume to camera test to make sure it was all visually strong. We never got to make the whole thing. It's the one costume I've never gotten to really make that I've always thought would have been amazing.

JON PETERS: We were literally three weeks before production. We were ready to go. We were fully amped and ready to roll. It was like getting run over by a car.

DAN GILROY: That afternoon, they call us all in and I remember Tim and I and Jon went in. And we sat with Bob and Terry and Lorenzo. And it was the look; we're talking about this and we're talking about that. And the studio cannot sustain this film at this point. And they pulled the plug.

JON PETERS: Terry Semel came up. We did a show and tell, showed him everything that we had, the script, the storyboards — all the stuff. He was my closest friend and he took me in the room with Tim and he said, "We're going to cancel the movie, we're going to shut it down."

LORENZO DI BONAVENTURA: We were being asked to spend a lot of money at a moment in time where we were a bit ahead of where the script was, and then we had this overall pressure going on within the corporation. A financial reality when you're inside a company: When they're worried about their results, they look at the risk factor in a different way.

JON PETERS: I was angry, frustrated. I felt betrayed. But it was their call — budget, Nicolas Cage and Tim Burton. I think they didn't totally believe that Tim could make a Superman that would be commercial. People were scared of this movie, just like they were scared of Batman.

TIM BURTON: They were still freaked out about my *Batman Returns* or whatever the dynamic was. I've had this happen from the beginning where they're like, "Okay, yeah, do it." But then they're always slightly worried about you in some way.

LORENZO DI BONAVENTURA: When you have a transplanted organ, the body either rejects the organ or not. You have to have somebody in the body that says, no, I want that liver. And usually with these dangerous movies, people are kind of going, I don't know.

DAN GILROY: And Jon is a tremendous, passionate believer and proponent of the franchise. He fought like hell for this movie.

JON PETERS: I went in to Terry Semel and I threatened him with throwing him out of a window. I was like, "You can't do this to me. I've worked on this for too many years. We're ready to go. We've cast. We have one of the great directors who just made a billion-dollar franchise for you. Roll the dice, man." Nope. Tim was completely devastated. He ran out. He wouldn't talk to me or anybody for a month.

TIM BURTON: I have to say that it is painful to work so long on something.

JON PETERS: Once that was over with, I couldn't even get Tim on the phone to try to figure out a way to get it going again, because I wasn't going to give up until I got to made. Will Smith said yes to *Wild Wild West* and we went off and began shooting that movie.

DAN GILROY: They actually mentioned in the room while they were pulling the plug that the funds were going to be going over to *Wild Wild West*. And that's its own story.

KEVIN SMITH: I went to a movie theater years later to see a movie called *Wild Wild West*. All of a sudden the Kenneth Branagh character shows up in this gigantic metal walking spider, this monster spider.

(© and courtesy Super Skull Ship)

JON PETERS: I was so caught up with this spider, this Thanagarian snare beast, that we did a comedic version with *Wild Wild West*. And that's where the spider came in.

KEVIN SMITH: And I remember Jon Peters' name in the credits. I said, "Goddammit. That mother------- finally got his f---ing spider."

JON PETERS: Superman is such a bulls-eye that you have to hit. He's one of the most precious icons of our country and the fact is that Tim and I were pretty far down the road designing it. And I know where Tim and I were going to go, we would have done something really special. At least it's out there in the ether that could have happened. We don't have to make the movie. It's still interesting to people.

WESLEY STRICK: From that perspective it was a bit disappointing, because I think he would have really stretched in a way that he hadn't yet... And maybe hasn't since, I don't know. He hasn't really made that movie.

COLLEEN ATWOOD: It's just amazing to me to look back that way and look at what's going on now with these kinds of movies and wonder what that would have been then and what it could have become.

RICK HEINRICHS: It's just something where I think people should know that they're looking at a process, not a product. The ultimate product would have been an amazing film.

KEVIN SMITH: That was a big part of who I am today. That was the moment like going out there and telling that story over and over again. Because of *Superman Lives*, I realized my true talent, I think. Obviously it wasn't writing Superman. It was *talking* about writing Superman. That was where the real money was, I guess.

LORENZO DI BONAVENTURA: I think it would have definitely established the fact that you can make a tough guy have a great deal of insecurity.

MICHAEL ANTHONY: It might not have been a comic book Superman, the television Superman or Dick Donner Superman, but Tim Burton's Superman and it would have been something quite unique. And probably something we would still be talking about. We *are* talking about it anyway… didn't even get made and we're talking about it.

DAN GILROY: I've got to be honest, I think Tim Burton is one of the only people who could really do it justice, because he understands it. He's lived it. And man, he would have knocked it out of the park.

HOLLY PAYNE: What's really cool is that during the evolution of the project is the sea change that's gradually happening, and people realize that it's not at all what they thought it was going to be. They see that Polaroid of Nicolas Cage and are like, "Oh God, that would have been horrible!" But they don't realize the context and they don't realize what was happening in that photo, which was taken during costumes test when Nicolas Cage was tired, and it's actually a moment when a flash went off and his eyes were half-closed. That's in our film. That's just one example of people having misconceived ideas of what this would have been.

JON SCHNEPP: That photo Holly mentioned was one of the first costume tests of many and that was the 1997 costume test. There's a 1998 costume test in the film and then there's a latter 1998 final costume test three weeks before they were actually going to do the movie and it is a deal changer. You're like, "Wow, not only did Nic Cage emulate and feel like he's actually Superman in the film, but in the documentary you get the take that he and Tim Burton were coming at with the character fighting as an alien in the guise of playing Clark Kent, who's constantly hiding the fact that he's an alien; as Superman, hiding the fact that he's Clark Kent and he's an alien. You start to understand this character constantly feeling like he doesn't fit it, and that's what most comic book readers have always felt, that they're outcasts, bullied. This Superman is not a god floating around in the sky, invulnerable; he's actually more human, and anybody who's read the comic books would feel an empathy with that characterization. That was the strength of people like Tim Burton, Nicolas Cage and the writers.

HOLLY PAYNE: This may be one of the more interesting stories of a film that never got made because of all the elements involved, the people involved and the creative forces involved. I've been in and around this industry since I was little. My grandparents were movie stars, my great grandparents starred in the silent film era with Charlie Chaplin, so there's this whole history that I have that kind of precedes me. My knowledge base of the industry is such that this is a special case in that it's one we all really wish we could have seen, but nobody would've known about it if we hadn't made a documentary about it. And that's the case for hundreds of thousands of movies that get shelved and never seen after lots of money has been put into them. I wish there was more focus put onto those kinds of projects because of the amount of work put into them.

SUPERVOID CINEMA: A small fortune had already been spent, and seemingly squandered, on the doomed pre-production of *Superman Lives*. This meant that the investment had to be returned no matter what it took. There was no Tim Burton, no Nicolas Cage, no crew, no art department, no production office and no real idea as to how to move forward. The public and spectacular collapse of *Superman Lives*, not to mention the critical and commercial failure of its replacement *Wild Wild West*, didn't go unnoticed on the calculators, and in July 1999, co-chairmen Bob Daly and Terry Semel would announce their intention to quit and were to be replaced by incoming chairmen Alan Horn and Barry Meyer. One of that duo's first ports of call was to kick start the Superman project. It was decided that *The Death of Superman* story arc wasn't really work-ing and the studio was now open to suggestions.

Jon Peters, however, had become a big fan of the recently released *Charlie's Angels* big-screen reboot and was eager to meet with its director Joseph McGinty Nicol, known professionally as McG. Rather than adapt *The Death of*

Superman, the director would prefer to do something that fell more in line with his own frenetic, colorful, in-your-face style of cinematography and the director would suggest the up-and-coming talent J.J. Abrams. Abrams was approached about doing the movie and took a meeting. Abrams was a self-confessed fan of the property and would tell how his young son went to bed each night in Superman pajamas and that the opportunity was too great to turn down.

J.J. ABRAMS (writer, unfilmed *Superman: Flyby*): They approached me about doing the movie and I took a meeting. What was wonderful about working on Superman is that as a kid I was the biggest fan. My son used to go to bed every night wearing a Superman shirt. I couldn't pass it up. What was nice is that after a lot of years of trying to get this going and not succeeding, everyone was coming at it with a very fresh, open mind. What was exciting for me is that we had some incredible, really big ideas that go beyond just one story we were telling. *Alias* [at the time] was actually an amazing training ground for me. In this Superman we were talking a lot about where he's come from and where he's going. It was Superman for everyone and not just for people who already knew the character. It was for the uninitiated.

In Abrams' Superman: Flyby, *Superman is sent to Earth to help mankind, but has a much loftier destiny ahead of him: to return to Krypton in an effort to save his people. Along the way, audiences relive his origin, his life in Smallville and arrival in Metropolis, as well as experience a number of kick-ass battles. In all, it's an ambitious work that — not surprisingly, given the success of* Lord of the Rings *at the time — was being heralded as the first chapter in a trilogy. Part of the difficulty — beyond a first draft cliffhanger in which Lex Luthor is revealed to be a Kryptonian — was relaunching the Man of Steel on the big screen after so many years and telling the audience it was only act one.*

J.J. ABRAMS: The difficulty would be doing it in such a way that it *wasn't* the beginning of something larger. The way you do it so many years after the first film is that you stay true to the spirit of what people love, but you come at it from a fresh perspective, so you're not rehashing stuff that audiences have such familiarity with, that they're asking, "Why should I pay to see it again? Because of better special effects?" That's no reason to make the movie. That's what made it exciting: come from the point of view of this is the beginning of a new story, and making it a great story not only because it's Superman, but simultaneously *despite* it being Superman.

Being different, he noted, was part of the reason for doing a new Superman film, and not merely echoing what had come previously.

J.J. ABRAMS: What's interesting is realizing just how many different permutations of Superman exist already; how many different alterations and adjustments have been made to his origin story, notions of what has motivated certain characters and the relationships they've had. There have been so many versions, and the reason why is because you don't want to tell exactly the same story all over again with slightly different words and angles — in the comics or in a film. They are telling a story that is familiar and true to the characters people know and love, but also exciting. You want to find the twists that make it worthy of being retold.

GLEN OLIVER (pop culture historian): Abrams' *Superman* brings in a number of elements familiar from the Christopher Reeve era. Its central characters read and feel very much like the interpretations of Reeve, Margot Kidder, Jackie Cooper and Marc McClure, for example. Multiple Kryptonians here on Earth vs. Superman evokes *Superman II*, as does Luthor seeking allegiance with them. Superman addressing the United Nations to rally the nations together for a cause feels like *Superman IV*, etc. In this regard, J.J.'s *Superman* feels very much like the *Star Trek* interpretation he'd eventually bring to bear: a hodgepodge amalgam of inspirations and interpretations, some slavishly literal, some amplifying implicit themes and concepts and some rejiggering. If one liked J.J.'s Kelvin-verse *Trek* films, one would probably find a lot to love about his *Superman*. If one *didn't* like how he approached *Trek*...

Amplifying and expanding upon ingredients that were already there was often a smart and ingenious move on Abrams' part. For example, much value, some of it rather artistic, is attained from his interpretation of Clark's X-ray vision, including a scene in which young Clark uses it to see what's inside of wrapped Christmas presents. Other decisions feel more like pissing on material just to mark one's territory, and such choices aren't always seamless. Does the Superman character *really* need to be prophesized? Does Lex Luthor secretly being a Kryptonian soldier *really* add any needed flavoring to the mix? Do the Kents having been targeted directly by Jor-El as potential surrogate parents bring any necessary weight to the proceedings, or does this largely undercut the inherent "immigrant saga" nature of the Superman character?

DREW MCWEENY: I'm not so rigid that a Superman film has to be exactly one version, and with *Flyby* I was willing to go with it to a certain degree when it came to not blowing up Krypton. It's the weirdest reinvention of Superman that you could possibly do, except for making Lex Luthor a Kryptonian.

GLEN OLIVER: The first 75% of the script was propulsive, often clever and showed great promise, but the final 25% or so of the screenplay are *exhausting* — filled with too many finales, a few too many twists and turns, and its final moments don't feel entirely satisfying given that the script transitions pointedly into a sequel rather than being a satisfying closure in and of itself. If I had to guess, this over-wrought back quarter, combined with the imminently evident tremendous scale and cost of the — at least as presented — production, likely raised some eyebrows and potentially contributed to the project's demise. It's an interesting effort and exercise to be sure, filled with many exciting and wonderful moments; a script that was "well on its way," but far from reaching the finish line. I suspect the only way even a semblance of this story could be produced was by stripping away the same hugely costly element which made it interesting and provocative to begin with. Perhaps its failure to launch was, to some degree, a self-fulfilling paradox and prophecy?

DREW MCWEENY: For one movie to do both of those things — not having Krypton blowing up *and* revealing Lex Luthor to be a *Kryptonian* — that was where I think the level of bat-shittery went off the chart. "I have to write about this. You people are insane. And if you spent $150-million doing this, I won't be the last person to tell you that you're crazy. I just wanna be the *first* person to tell you you're crazy."

And McWeeney, under the pen name "Moriarty" at aintitcoolnews, was indeed the first one to proclaim the inmates had, in essence, taken over the asylum with his review of Abrams' first-draft screenplay, which posted on September 23, 2002. And which he concluded with this particular plea: "Don't do this. J.J. Abrams, you're better than this. I know Jon Peters is involved, and I know he's determined that any DC superhero film made has to be incredibly shitty and stupid, but don't *listen to him!! Please, Alan Horn, call Avi Arad. Ask him what the secret is. Learn from him. Hire someone who really loves this property and let them make a damn good Superman adventure film. I'm begging you. I put all this detail into this column because I want you to read the reactions of the Talk Backers below. I want you to pay attention to the reaction across the entire 'Net. Listen to the fans. They'll tell you if this is what they want." Well, that's exactly what happened.*

SUPERVOID CINEMA: Abrams' storyline would leak onto the Internet and receive a critical smashing that would alert studios to the power of the Internet to potentially make or break a film on word of mouth before a single frame of film had even been shot. The plot to Abrams' rough draft has since been recited on the web a million times over and much was made of Abrams' deviations from the source material and the fundamentals of Superman's origins. The fact that

Krypton doesn't explode at the start and that Lex Luthor is secretly a Krypto-nian super-villain were particular plot points that were savaged as the story of McG and Abrams' sacrilege travelled far and wide. Supposedly the whole project was now in doubt as Warners tried to deal with the fact that the script was leaked to the public, and that the script received such negative reviews. Once the story had gone public — to be discussed in chat rooms and fan communities, on message boards and blogs — the backlash and mockery didn't go unnoticed. The petitions and protests were one thing, but the death threats in particular had unnerved Abrams.

DREW MCWEENY: Was it fair to write that review? No. Would I do it now? No. I think it's because of my experience in the business since then, and because of my own experience with creators I've written about over time and talking to them about the long-term impact of what I've seen fandom in general metastasize into, which I am largely responsible for and take responsibility for. My cohort at that site will not own up to the fact that we helped create the Snyder Cult and this world of "Give me what I want, exactly the way I want it, and if you don't, I will harass you and torment you, even though you are making entertainment to be consumed. I will treat it as if you are my opponent and I must destroy you." At the same time, we weren't the extreme that you see now.

J.J. ABRAMS: I wasn't surprised that a first draft of the script, knowing how the Internet works, and people's rabid fascination with movies, especially something as beloved as Superman, would get out there. If you've looked online, you'll see that there have been positive reviews as well as negative. Either way, you can't really take it to heart. If you're open-minded and collaborative and you also know what it is you want, anyone's point of view — irrespective of their position in the industry or their experience — should be welcome. All this proved is that people have opinions. To deny that or be reactive is evident that you don't have any vision of what you want. You can't let anyone's criticism of what you're doing control what you're doing. You have to find your rhythm, your process, and hopefully it's one that invites commentary.

DREW MCWEENY: I worked in the business before there ever was an Aint It Cool News as a working writer. I had already had things purchased and produced, but I think anybody in their twenties who works in this feels like you know everything. I was in my twenties when Aint It Cool began and I felt like I knew everything, and even though I was working in the business I felt like I knew more than other people. So I got this platform where I could say, "Oh, these are the things I think." And when the platform is building, you don't quite realize you're the frog in the boiling pot or the ripple effect it will cause. We *were* the Internet. We were bratty kids and it was a place to talk freely and a platform that I could use and *Flyby* is the first time I saw it derail something. Something I wrote, though there were other factors at play, derailed a production that was getting ready to happen. I do believe that the hubbub that happened scared the shit out of McG, and I've talked to him about that since then, and after I did this to him a second time with his *Terminator* film. There was no malice intended, but looking at it from his perspective I did damage to that man twice, and both times they came out of places of reading something and saying, "You can't possibly be serious. This *can't* be what you're doing." More than anything, that's where it comes from.

Ultimately Superman: Flyby *collapsed under the weight of the criticism, though there was further development before it went away completely, including the fact that Matt Bomer (later to voice the character in the animated* Superman Unbound *and currently starring on* Doom Patrol) *and* The Mummy *star Brendan Fraser were up for the role.*

BRENDAN FRASER (actor, "Clark Kent/Superman," unfilmed *Superman: Flyby*): J.J. Abrams had a vision that was larger; it spanned galaxies. It was *Lord of the Rings*. It was *that* huge. It was a situation where very bad things were happening. It was like a third World War on Earth involving different planets and universes and sibling rivalry and the collision of enormous superpowers.

PAUL LEVITZ: I have infinite respect for J.J. Abrams, but I have a vivid memory of a meeting with about 12 of us from DC and Warner Bros. around a conference table with J.J. Abrams and Brent Ratner, who at that point was going to direct, on a speakerphone — just discussing what should be done in that script, and that script was *not* going to be a good thing. J.J. is a brilliant writer, so I'm not blaming him specifically, but whatever had transpired in that process, that's a movie that I'm very happy never started shooting.

CHAPTER XI
First Comes Love, Then Comes Marriage,
Then Comes... One Comic Reboot After Another!

The creation of the television series Lois & Clark: The New Adventures of Superman *in 1993, which was decidedly focused on the evolving romance between the two title characters, necessitated DC Comics Superman editor Mike Carlin and the creative teams on the various Man of Steel titles to shift gears. Their own plans to marry Lois Lane and Clark Kent were postponed to give the show room to breathe, and as a means of biding time,* The Death of Superman *came into being.*

In the comics, the couple began dating and fell in love in issues published in 1990, with Clark revealing his alter ego the following year. In 1993 he died fighting Doomsday and eventually returned to life.

PETER SANDERSON (comic historian and author): The true Man of Steel reappears in *Superman* #82 from October 1993, a full 10 months after his apparent demise. The resurrection story seemed rushed, perhaps because DC had to bring Superman back to life in time for the debut of *Lois & Clark* that fall, and Mike Carlin still had to hold off on the wedding until Lois and Clark got around to doing it on the TV show a few years later. He and his team had to come up with yet more "events" every so often in order to get the readers' attention and boost sales. And so there was "The Death of Clark Kent," in which Superman temporarily had to "kill off" his secret identity in order to contend against an enemy who threatened to reveal it to the world. Then for a time, Superman lost his powers. But like the "death" of Superman, most of these "events" had no real lasting impact, even though they allowed the writers to take the series in interesting new directions for a while.

Flash forward to October 1996, Lois and Clark got married on television and DC had the characters do the same in that year's December special comic Superman: The Wedding Album.

MIKE CARLIN (editor, DC Comics): The show turned out to be an okay-ish hit and it lasted for four seasons. They did ultimately get to the wedding and the reality was that the show worked. But one of the problems was, they didn't tell us until it was really close to happening. We had all of our notes from the original plan for the wedding, but some people originally there were really not around on the books anymore. Jerry Ordway was not around, but he came back to play on a few pages and scenes.

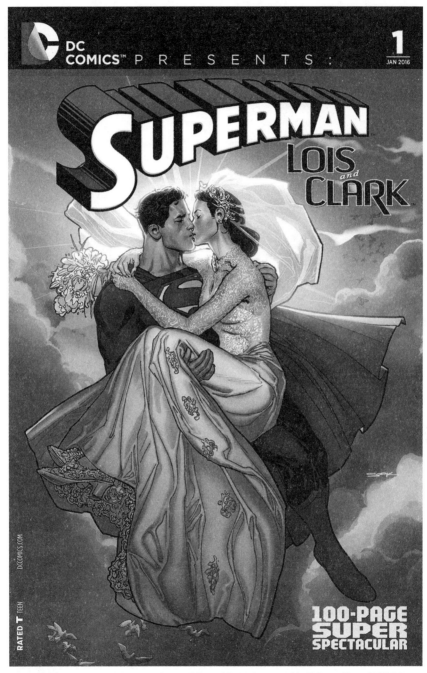

A special issue commemorating the wedding of Superman and Lois Lane (© and TM DC Comics/Warner Bros. Discovery).

PETER SANDERSON: Many past and present Superman writers and artists collaborated on the special issue, and Jerry Siegel himself, who had only recently passed away, was drawn into the story as the minister who pronounces Lois and Clark to be man and wife. Joe Shuster, who had died several years before, appeared in the story as a wedding guest.

MIKE CARLIN: We got as many people who've ever worked on Superman that were still around to work on this wedding issue. Curt Swan had passed away, but we had inventory stories that we took some pages out of and put in as flashbacks of the story, so we got Curt to be involved. In my estimation, for whatever reason, whether it was marketing, or editorial, it seemed like the right idea at the time and we got to do everything we wanted to.

PETER SANDERSON: This turn of events may seem to many to overturn a basic element of the whole series, but isn't a lot of the appeal of Superman the idea that the world at large, represented especially by Lois, underestimates "mild-mannered" Clark Kent, not realizing that beneath that ordinary façade exists a Superman? Isn't this something everyone can identity with? If you reveal to Lois that Superman and Clark are one and the same, don't you do away with the dramatic tension in their relationship?

On the other hand, Superman was not the loner he once was. Or to put it unkindly, he was not an emotional cripple like Batman. With the de-emphasis on his Kryptonian past and the undoing of his foster parents' deaths, Superman was no longer a semi-tragic figure doomed not to find happiness outside of "imaginary stories." And as the embodiment of traditional American ideals, it seemed appropriate that he should stand for marital love and devotion too. Perhaps most importantly, Superman was no longer being written for an audience almost entirely composed of male children uninterested in marriage. Now much, perhaps most, of the audience were teenagers and adults, and the editors and writers were former comics fans who were married themselves.

STEVE YOUNIS (webmaster, supermanhomepage.com): If someone told you back in the '60s or '70s that Superman was going to get married and have kids, they would've gone, "No way." But we accepted the marriage and now we've accepted him having a kid. I guess he grows with his audience, because let's face it, comic books are no longer for kids. They're for the audience that grew up with them as kids. And as we've matured, they've matured, so they become relevant to the generation that's reading them.

DAN JURGENS (Superman writer): I like that they got married, and the reason I do is because I've always said that Superman is very much defined by Lois Lane in that they both debuted in *Action Comics* #1 in 1938. Almost from page one, Superman and Lois were connected. And I view Lois, just like the Kents, as a human that helps to define who Superman is for us and how he functions within the DC Universe. That's one reason I'm not a fan of Superman and Wonder Woman, which would happen later, as a couple at all. Because as soon as you do that, Superman becomes more alien and more Kryptonian. The whole point of Superman is that he's human. He is supposed to be the most human of all the heroes, I think. So again, I liked them as a married couple.

PAUL LEVITZ (writer, former publisher, DC Comics): It's a story that Jerry Siegel had played with at one point way back in the '40s, but was rejected. We've done thousands of imaginary stories along that line, but it probably wasn't my idea of a wonderful direction to take the strip in. If you look at most cases where you've got romance going in popular culture, whether it's *Moonlighting* or *Cheers*, there's a scientifically-proven difference between how human beings react to anticipation and achievement. We react more powerfully to anticipation. It's more exciting to be going to the newsstand to get the new comics than it is to actually have gotten the new comics. Maybe that's because our heads are wired wrong, but that *is* how we're wired and I think that flows through to how we deal with fiction.

DAN JURGENS: In more recent years, we brought Clark and Lois' son Jon Kent into the world and said Superman and Lois are now parents. In that same vein of seeing Clark's relationship with his parents, seeing Clark's relationship with his child, and with Lois, adds to the tapestry of who he is as a character. By watching him as as a father, and by the way he interacts with Jon, adds to our informational basis on Clark Kent as a character, which of course leads to our interpretation of who Superman is as a character. It helps to explain why Superman represents humanity as well as he does. And this is where so many writers struggle with Superman. This is why almost every writer out there, the first thing it feels like so many of them want to do is, "Oh, here's my Superman-goes-evil story." No. The way you really build the character and explore the character is by showing us what makes him human.

PETER SANDERSON: Surely in large degree thanks to his success with the Superman books, Mike Carlin became executive editor of DC's entire superhero line. But the need to come up with new attention-getting event stories remained.

And what do you do after you've killed, resurrected and married off Superman? Children? Well, not at that point anyway.

DAN JURGENS: Once we had done *The Death of Superman*, and we found every time we crossed over among the books that we got more sales, what we got was more pressure from above to keep generating Superman-type events where all the books would crossover. We started to do more of that… and from a creative standpoint that's harder to do. I mean, it's much easier to sit here and write my own Superman stories, where maybe there's three pages of subplot with Bibbo and Jimmy that go from my book into the next book, than it is to constantly coordinate massive storytelling efforts. At the same time, the reality was, every time we connected the four books, the sales would go up. And they might only be that 25, 30, 40 percent, but they would still go up. So the pressure got to be more and more frequent of, "Oh, we know you can't sell 5-million, 6-million copies with another *Death of Superman*, but you can at least do another epic crossover." And that's where we started to do two to three of those a year. And they got a little bit longer because people print comics to make money. And Superman is there to be profitable. It became a little bit more of a job description at that point.

EDDIE BERGANZA (former Superman editor): In the past, way back from when the *The Death of Superman* and *The Return of Superman* happened, there had been a status quo established on the books where basically it had become a weekly. You could follow them weekly with each title connected to the other. Basically you had a serial where every issue ended on a cliffhanger and you had to pick up the next issue week after week. Mike Carlin, the editor at the time, established that; then he had two other editors follow who tried to keep up with what he had done. A lot of things were done to try and recapture *The Death* and *Return of Superman*.

DAN JURGENS: *The Death of Superman* was '92. And then he goes through '95 and '96 and I don't think we ever settled back down where it was before we did the death. It was still there. I think we kept it above those numbers. But all of comics are like this; it isn't just Superman. Its even truer now. It's sort of like there's this steady erosive effect across the board on all ongoing titles, and then the only way to goose those sales is a major story change or writer change or artist change or change the costume, change the powers, do this, do that, break it back, lose a job, get married, get divorced… I don't know, it's all that stuff. But on all titles, sales tend to erode a little bit each and every month, and you always have to give it a shot.

EDDIE BERGANZA: But as the crossovers kept happening, they kept getting farther away from Superman. The cast around Superman kept growing and growing until it came to the point that he was almost a guest star in his own book. There were people from the bottled city of Kandor, Lois Lane's sister had her own plotline going. You had guys on the books who had been there for 10 years. They had done everything they could with the main character so they began branching out. Unfortunately in doing that, again you were getting farther away from the basics of Superman. You got to the point where you had the Blue Superman and the Red Superman, and the *Daily Planet* had been closed down.

PETER SANDERSON: In 1997 Superman's powers abruptly mutated, turning him into a being of pure energy. However, he could will himself to take corporeal form as Clark Kent, but had no superpowers as long as he stayed that way. Along with his new powers, Superman acquired a new costume, described disparagingly by some as making him look like a figure skater. Even his skin was blue in his energy form. Once again, much of the public at large assumed that this was a permanent change in the character, and there was yet another *New York Times* editorial on the subject. By this time though, probably most of the comics' readership knew that this was yet another provocative stunt to generate a year's worth of unusual stories.

But probably what nobody expected is that as a being of pure energy, Superman was able to divide into two separate beings, and thus became the 1990s version of "Superman Red and Superman Blue" of Weisinger-era fame. But now it was the 1990s, and Weisinger's utopian fantasies were out of style. Instead, Superman Red and Superman Blue were more like a dysfunctional pair of twins squabbling over who was the "real" one (much to Lois' dismay) and learning how to cooperate with each other. Ultimately, the two Supermen sacrificed their separate existences in defeating the fin de siècle menaces called the Millennium Giants. They merged once more into a single being, with the classic powers and costume of the Man of Steel.

EDDIE BERGANZA: Nothing against the creators of those stories, but if you're on a gig for 10 years, you're going to try and spin it as many possible ways that you can just to keep it interesting. When I came on board, I was new to the book. The strange thing is that I wasn't the biggest Superman fan. I liked the character, but mostly from TV and the movies. I didn't feel like I had to do the umpteenth Krypto story or something like that. My attitude was that he was a cool character, and I also didn't have the marching orders to follow what these guys had done.

MICHAEL BAILEY (host, *Superman: From Crisis to Crisis* podcast): In 1995 or 1996, the general good will from *The Death of Superman* started to fade. The story model was individual stories that are all connected, leading to a big story. And then that ends and you do the little stories. After *The Death of Superman* there was "The Battle of Metropolis," where Luthor goes crazy and literally destroys the entire city, which led into the "Dead Again" storyline where Superman's body shows up and everyone's like, "Who's the real Superman?" And then "The Death of Clark Kent," after which you had the wedding of Superman and Lois, and then Electric Blue/Electric Red. If you were on the ride, the ride was pretty good, but I think some people started to get off the ride at that time.

EDDIE BERGANZA: The first thing I asked myself was, "What makes Superman, Superman?" I wanted to get back to the basics of that, because it had been a long time since that had been explored. The first issue was "reopen the *Daily Planet*." Then it was the idea of getting Luthor back to being a bad guy — not that he had become a good guy, but he became more of a business-man bad guy. While we couldn't go back to the old continuity where he used to wear a purple suit and fight Superman hand to hand, we figured he could start throwing more stuff at Superman and become a little more active. And for my thinking, he had also become overweight, so I got him on a diet. He also gained two female bodyguards whose origins are kind of a mystery. They may be Amazons; they may not be. They've got him working out. My role model for Luthor was John Malkovich. Malkovich with a shaved head is really scary, yet the power of the guy makes him really attractive. Again, going back to what Superman was about. I also really wanted to separate the four books and give them four distinct identities.

Helping to accomplish this was a shakeup of the books' creative teams, with Superman *written by Jeph Loeb and drawn by Ed McGuinness and Cam Smith;* Adventures of Superman *written by J.M. Dematteis with art by Mike Miller and Jose Marazan;* Man of Steel *written by Mark Schultz (the only holdover from a previous regime) and drawn by Doug Mahnke and Tom Nguyen; and* Action Comics *written by Joe Kelly and drawn by Kano and Marlo Alquiza.*

EDDIE BERGANZA: There were still continuing stories as we planned our first year and we ended up connecting them a lot more than we thought we would, but I tried to give each book a different identity. For instance, *Superman* would be the book where if you just wanted to pick up a Superman book, it would have all the classic elements. There would be Perry White at the *Daily Planet*, Lois Lane and Jimmy Olsen, Lex Luthor would do something nasty, we'd see the classic villains like Metallo, Brainiac and people like that. With *Adventures of Superman*, I wanted more of a human angle through the whole thing, with a focus on the people of Metropolis. *Man of Steel* would try to go into Superman's Kryptonian roots and the dangers that brings with it. And in *Action* he would be teaming up with the rest of the heroes from the DC universe, and it would pretty much be just that: action.

Jeph Loeb, the writer behind Superman *at the time, has one rule when he commences an interview: He won't comment on the creative teams that came before the current regime because, as he puts it, "I have a lot of respect for those guys."*

JEPH LOEB (writer, *Superman*): I had finished *Superman for All Seasons*, which people seemed to like, and I got approached by Eddie Berganza, the Superman editor-in-chief, and he asked whether or not I would come on board *Superman*, which in many people's minds is a lead title. I had to think about it. I wanted to make sure I could do both my best work and that we could do something different than what had been done before — not because there was anything wrong with what had been done before, but because we wanted to be able to separate ourselves, and be able to succeed or fail on our own terms.

MICHAEL BAILEY: Jeph Loeb first came onto Superman with *Superman for All Seasons*, which was just a one-shot story, but from the jump you saw that he not only understands Superman, he understood the *world* of Superman because the narration of *For All Seasons,* which was an after-thought, was Lois Lane, Lex Luthor and Lana Lane. He really got into all those characters' heads. His was the Superman title when he was on the books for those couple of years that I looked forward to the most, because he seemed to be able to have flashes of the pre-*Crisis* Superman and flashes of *Superman: The Movie*, while still being very much in the moment as far as how the stories were told.

JEPH LOEB: The first change I wanted to make was to bring aboard artist Ed McGuinness, who I'd worked with in the past. The second, and this is again not a criticism, is that my feeling was that in an effort to make Superman current or more interesting or hipper or for whatever reason, they'd come up with a lot of new characters and stories that didn't focus on the core group. What I like to tell people is that Superman, to me, is like an apple tree: It's solid, it's American and it's a beautiful thing to look at. Through the years, as each team came along, they sort of added little bells and trinkets and sparkles and all kinds of things until it didn't look like an apple tree anymore, it looked like a Christmas tree. I'm all in favor of Christmas trees! But when people said to me, "Wow, your approach to the book is so different,' I think all I really did was just pare it down to what it had originally been so people could see the apple tree once more. In an odd way, that became new again because people hadn't seen it. It was certainly my experience on *Superman for All Seasons* that this is the Superman we know. I was much more interested in the core cast, meaning that in Metropolis there was Lex Luthor, Perry White, Jimmy Olsen, Lois Lane, Clark Kent and Superman. Those are the people that live in Metropolis; anybody else exists because any of those people are interacting with them. In Smallville there are Ma and Pa Kent, Pete Ross and Lana Lang. Those are the only people that live in Smallville.

Neither myself or Joe Kelly, who started writing *Action* at the time, agreed with the arguments against Lois and Clark's marriage as being too challenging or not interesting enough. What we wanted to build was more of a *Thin Man* meets *Moonlighting* meets *West Wing* situation, where you can mix humor and drama together and have situations where two people who love each other very much can also be very angry with each other, can behave badly and still at the end of the day work it out and care about each other. I don't know if that's cool, I just know that it's an attempt to make the book more real from an emotional point of view, which is how I approach material.

Creatively, it would at first seem more fulfilling to keep all of the various Superman books separate from each other. Loeb refers to this as the "linkage debate," which asks whether or not the books should be read "horizontally" (weekly) or "vertically" (monthly).

JEPH LOEB: What we tried to do at the beginning was both. There were little subplots that got resolved in other books. But if you read only one title, you'd have a pretty good idea as to what was going on in the same kind of way that if you watch a television series where you understand who the characters are, if you miss an episode or two... and even if one of the characters died in the episode you missed, you're at least aware of it because of the way the characters are acting. So that was the first step. There were stories that we wound up coming up with that just seemed to work much better on a weekly basis because it enabled us to tell a bigger story over a shorter period of time. It worked both ways.

MICHAEL BAILEY: Jeph Loeb is very much on record that he didn't like the idea of the triangle numbering of the Superman titles and was very much against it. So you have this line of demarcation in 1999 where it was the same Superman, but it wasn't the same in terms of storytelling. There wasn't the connected universe with what was basically a weekly Superman book as there had been for the bulk of the '90s.

JEPH LOEB: What's funny is that when we went to our first Superman summit, Eddie asked us to write down how we saw Superman and what we wanted to accomplish in our individual books. We all saw Superman exactly the same way, but none of us wanted to approach the book in the same way, and that was terrific. What it meant was there would be a different voice on every single book, but the character himself would be treated with the same respect, the same tone and the same tenor, just with different angles to it.

Both Loeb and McGuinness also launched the Superman/Batman *monthly comic in August 2003, where they presented some really big ideas (adaptations of which would show up as the animated movies* Superman/Batman: Public Enemies *and* Superman/Batman: Apokalips*).*

MICHAEL BAILEY: Coming from Hollywood, Loeb understood that *Superman/Batman* was the big-budget movie comic. The design of the series was to tell huge stories about Superman and Batman with really good artists. And it's not just them teaming up randomly; there's a point to all the stories and I think the book lost that thread when he left.

One other point regarding Loeb's run on both Superman *and* Superman/Batman *is that in the former he set things up so that Lex Luthor could become President of the United States, and during the latter he had Superman and Batman being the ones responsible for taking him down and reminding the world about the true nature of the man. At the time a Luthor presidency seemed like a ridiculous notion at best, but now, given recent history, it seems downright prescient.*

JEPH LOEB: Joe Kelly was the one who pitched the idea. We were all sitting around a table in San Diego and he pitched the story. I said, "My God, you *have* to write that story." Everyone was so shocked at how stunned I was. But it really came out of one of those things where we were sitting around saying, "What are we going to do with Lex?" I always wanted to get him back in a power suit and give him some Kryptonite wings so he could beat the crap out of Superman, but that's not a plot; that's just sort of an idea. I do remember saying to Eddie Berganza, "If we do it, we have to make sure that everybody's okay with it." He came back the next day and said, "They're okay with it, as long as you can figure out how to get him out of the Oval Office." See, that was always the trick. You could kill anybody, you could splinter Superman and Batman, but you had to know how to put them back together again.

MICHAEL BAILEY: President Lex was something that could have failed, but it exceeded all expectations and worked spectacularly because it put Superman in the position that his arch-enemy is now President of the United States.

JEPH LOEB: It started off as a fun idea, but then it became remarkably believable. That was the part that was amazing. And we knew how and when we would be taking him down as President, so it worked out great.

DAN JURGENS: It's really weird, because at the time we wondered if it was *too* outlandish, but we decided, "That's what a bad guy would go for, right? Appear to be the *good* guy and become President." We thought it would work within the realm of "comic book reality" and actually had a lot of fun with it.

MARK WAID (writer, *Batman/Superman: World's Finest*): I don't know that it's ever explicitly said in the comics, but Jeph Loeb told me that the reason Superman didn't try to interfere in Lex's election was because he had faith that the American people wouldn't fall for electing such an obvious criminal to the highest office in the land. The Superman of 2016 would like to have a word with that Superman.

While the regular comics spun their tales, the continuing success of graphic novel compilations like The Dark Knight Returns *and* Watchmen *created a growing interest in more standalone stories or events apart from regularly-published comics. One of the early huge ones was* Kingdom Come, *a four-issue miniseries published in 1996 that was written by Mark Waid and Alex Ross, with art painted by Ross. Set in the near future of the DC Universe, it focuses on a new generation of heroes who have lost the morality of those who had preceded them, using violence in equal doses as their opponents. The Justice League comes out of retirement — though it takes a lot to convince Superman to do so — to restore the status quo and people's faith in real heroes.*

ALEX ROSS (co-writer/artist, *Kingdom Come*): *Kingdom Come* came about initially because I wanted to do a project with my dad co-starring with the DC heroes. I had a similar human-to-superhuman storyline with my work on *Marvels*, and I worked up a pitch to repeat some of the same approach. While working for Marvel on that series, I crafted a superhero civil war storyline in a lengthy outline along with extensive character redesigns that would make their way into the final project. I worked through contacts I made with DC in 1993

A possible future for the DC Universe as postulated by Mark Waid and Alex Ross
(© and TM DC Comics/Warner Bros. Discovery)

up until spring of 1994, where I finally got an editorial office that would take the proposal on, and through them be paired with Mark Waid. Mark and I worked together to plot the series and refine the concept.

MARK WAID: It was Alex's basic idea; he'd worked up a bunch of sketches and a few pages of notes here or there — not really about the story so much as about who the characters would be and so forth. I came to DC and at that point it was Archie Goodwin and his assistant Dan Raspler who were on the book and who had taken on the project. They had brought me out to lunch with Alex. We had a great conversation and they basically gave me the job based not so much on any of my writing work so much as the fact that I was the expert on DC Comics history. Then from that point it was Alex and me just batting back and forth. He had ideas and I had ideas and it was a good working relationship. I've never tried to undercut his role in terms of what he contributed to the story, which was a great deal.

MARK MILLAR (writer, *Superman: Red Son*): Mark and Alex pinned Superman down perfectly in *Kingdom Come*. This, to me, is the best DC Comics has ever been and should be suspended above the keyboard and drawing board of every freelancer. I'm also a massive fan of the mid-'70s Maggin/Bates/Swan stuff. *Kingdom Come* appealed to me because it evoked this period which inspired me so much.

ALEX ROSS: Ultimately I found myself more bonded to the character of Superman than I felt before doing the book. Once I put the time in with doing my impression of this key iconic hero, I only wanted to do more with him. I believed that I offered a return to form for the character, where he had a certain weight that he carried, both physically and metaphorically.

MICHAEL BAILEY: *Kingdom Come* represents a lot of things, and one of them is it pulled DC out of the early '90s. If you look at DC's covers from '94 to '95, it seemed that between *Kingdom Come* and [Grant] Morrison's *JLA*, they stopped trying to do the Image/Marvel aesthetic and said, "We're going to focus on something else." So in *Kingdom Come*, Superman quits. *Not* because Lois died — though that was part of it — but because society told him that they preferred the new hero Magrog; they preferred that type of hero and that was his failing. There's a line in the novel by Elliot S! Maggin or in the comic itself (they blur for me) where basically Superman failed to see his own importance in the world, which led to the events of *Kingdom Come*.

ALEX ROSS: Aside from the sense of responsibility that Superman feels toward a humanity he feels betrayed by, there is a more meta storyline being told about how the superhero legacy of countless characters came from his example, and the comics market of the 1990s was building to a collapse. Self-imposed destruction of the art form and genre we loved was informing the writing of this tale.

MICHAEL BAILEY: That story is all about Superman realizing that leaving was a mistake, but also trying to impose his will on everybody was a mistake. It's all about Superman being wrong and him finally realizing, through an even greater tragedy, that superheroes can't live above humanity; that they have to work *with* them. And really, *Kingdom Come* is all about the end of the idea of superheroes stuck in the second act. It's like, "No, we're going to move forward," so he writes a Superman that is very much the Bronze Age Superman, very much the Elliot S! Maggin version. In fact, he quoted from the novel *Miracle Monday* that there's a right and wrong in the universe and that distinction is not hard to make.

MARK WAID: What *Kingdom Come* says about Superman is that his values are a constant and they are a *good* constant. It reinforced his role as the moral compass of the DC universe and of superheroes in general.

ALEX ROSS: It was key to Mark Waid's belief about Superman that he wouldn't make the kind of mistakes that would lead to such a calamitous end in our story unless something essential had changed. This led to the thought that once Superman had forgone his "Clark" identity and life with Lois' passing, he had lost a part of himself and needed that perspective to guide him. I knew I wanted him to wind up in the role of sole superhuman survivor who comes close to killing those responsible for the act of genocide, for a scene inspired by Samson in the temple of the Philistines. The epiphany he is given, to see his own lost humanity as a core crisis he needs to face, is the idea we arrived at to serve competing concerns in making the story.

Superman: Red Son, *published in 2003 as three individual issues under the Elseworlds imprint, was written by Mark Millar and drawn by Dave Johnson. It explores what would have happened had Kal-El's rocket from Krypton landed on a Ukrainian collective farm instead of in Smallville, Kansas. He grows up to become Superman, only in this case as a defender for "Stalin, socialism and the international expansion of the Warsaw Pact." It eventually brings in different versions of Wonder Woman, Batman and Lex Luthor, their relationship with Superman quite altered from what we would expect.*

MARK MILLAR: *Red Son* is based on a thought that flitted through my head when I read *Superman #300* as a six-year-old. It was an imaginary story where Superman's rocket landed in neutral waters between the USA and the USSR and both sides were rushing to claim the baby. As a kid growing up in the shadow of the Cold War, the notion of what might have happened if the Soviets had reached him first just seemed fascinating to me. As I got older I started putting everything together and I first pitched something to DC when I was 13, I think, although it was in much cruder form of course, and my drawings weren't quite up to scratch.

MICHAEL BAILEY: *Red Son* is an evergreen story now, but I don't like Miller's tendency to write smart people as being so obnoxious, and the Lex Luthor in *Red Sun* is just the worst. He's the smartest guy in the room and he is going to tell you every chance he gets. But what he *did* do with that story, which is so essential to Superman as a character, is that he showed no matter where he lands in rural

America or rural USSR, he is going to end up being Superman. Even if for a very brief time he is a part of a totalitarian regime, he's going to be the one to make a difference because that is just who he is as a character. And because of that, I can't dislike his work on Superman.

J.M. DEMATTEIS (screenplay writer, *Superman: Red Son*): I did *Speeding Bullets* years ago where, instead of being found in Kansas by the Kents, Kal-El is found by the Waynes. He experiences the trauma of his parents' death and he grows up to be Batman. It's a story I'm very fond of, but the point in the end is that you can just bend Superman so far before he springs back. I don't believe in a vision of Superman where he is corruptible — I just don't! That's very innocent and naïve, but Superman is an innocent, naïve character in some ways and we need that sometimes. Now more than ever the world feels so dark that we need a character like that. I also did the movie adaptation of *Red Son* where, again, no matter how you bend or twist him, that inherent decency is going to spring back in the end. *That's* the nature of who he is, period. Being in Kansas only strengthened that decency.

MARK MILLAR: Superman, to me, was always a representation of everything great about America. He's up there with the Statue of Liberty because he's the flag-colored embodiment of the immigrant who came to America and made a success of himself. To take truth, justice and the American way and turning this on its head was fascinating. The trick, of course, was avoiding the clichés of Superman being raised as a Stalinesque tyrant or an overtly evil character. What I decided upon very early in this project was to have an idealistic young farm boy being raised in the Ukraine and believing with all his heart in the goodness of communism. Just as our own Superman isn't tarnished by the Americans dropping bombs in Vietnam or Iraq, this Soviet Superman isn't responsible for the Gulags or the mass killings. This Superman represents "The Dream" as much as the traditional Superman does, but watching him reluctantly take control of the USSR when the people beg him to and make communism an international success is quite fascinating. What we have as the story progresses is a world where this super-communism has been embraced by most of the planet and capitalism has completely fragmented… again, a reversal of what happened in the real world. The moral implications of one man or one country policing the entire world then becomes the big question. Superman finds himself wondering if total control is the best thing for the safety of the people he really wants to protect.

Published between 2003 and 2004 was Superman: Birthright, *a 12-issue limited series written by Mark Waid and drawn by Leinil Francis Yu and Gerry Alanguilan. In*

essence it was intended to be a 21st century view of the original Superman, though
it was never really allowed to take root
as canon.

Originally designed as a retcon origin story, Mark
Waid's Superman: Birthright *is, instead, pretty much
standalone (© and TM DC Comics/Warner Bros.
Discovery).*

MARK WAID: The goal was
to bring Superman kicking and
screaming into the 21st century
without losing any of the optimism,
without losing any of the hope,
without losing the brightness of the
character, which was very tough to
do given that we were in the raw,
post-9/11 period, which I really
had to account for. I mean, I *really*
had to account for the fact that
you couldn't just go in and destroy
office buildings with impunity. And
the fear of people seeing things fly
around in the sky — those are things
I had to deal with. So my primary
goal was to modernize the origin
without losing anything, and the
second goal was to show people why
I think Superman is cool and why
he's not a dull character. I wanted to
give him as much depth as I possibly
could. Probably no one, not even Jerry Siegel, has spent as much time in his life
thinking about Superman as I have, so I had all of that stuff I had to put down on
paper.

ROB O'CONNOR: *Superman: Birthright* to me is the best modern retelling
of Superman's origin. Where others (*Secret Origin*) opt to simply play the hits or
others (*Earth One*) go for cheap, lowest common denominator exploitation and
edginess, this story earnestly examines how the character could be real, why the
disguise could make sense and why journalism is the career he would embark on.
The first few issues showcasing Clark's journey around the world are so special to
me — a young man forging a destiny for himself rather than having it thrust upon
him (a la the movie versions).

ANTHONY DESIATO: *Birthright* remains my favorite telling of the origin story, and it's frustrating that it was set up as being the new definitive origin of Superman, yet DC never really seemed to comment on it. And it was just a few years later that we got *Superman: Secret Origin* from Geoff Johns. At the same time, do I think it was worthwhile? Absolutely, because that story exists unto itself. Even though it didn't take hold in continuity, it's still a great story and a great introduction to the character.

MICHAEL BAILEY: I remember Mark Waid doing an interview where Dan DiDio asks, "Why does Superman do what he does?" and Mark's just like, "Well, he does the right thing because it's the right thing to do." And DiDio said, "C'mon, we're paying you better than that." So with *Birthright* he gets the chance to be the guy that reinvents the legend for another generation. And he *doesn't*, which is key, reset everything back to the Silver or Bronze Age, which is the thing about Mark Waid that people misunderstand. While he loves that era and probably wanted to tell similar stories, he always understood that he was in a particular time and place and that you can't go back. He crafted a Superman origin that kept some of the best parts of post-*Crisis* and took in some of *Superman: The Movie*, some of the Bronze Age and the Silver Age and put that in a blender and came out with a Superman for that era. I think what got lost in all of that is that, once again, fanboys weren't really into wanting a new Superman origin. They thought the old one was just fine, which has a familiar ring to it. But it works so well as an origin for the character: He really set up a reason for everything to happen. Why does Clark Kent wear glasses? Why does that work as a disguise? Why does he wear his costume? Who is Lois? What is their relationship?

He didn't go out of his way to make Superman edgy or cool; he just wrote him as the character *should* be written, and it was good. One of my big take-aways was, "Oh my God, this is the blueprint for everything that should have come later. But the company itself went into dark mode." The ironic thing is that the main theme of *Infinite Crisis* was that we have to work together to get out of this darkness we're in, and then they completely forgot that.

MARK WAID: The reaction from DC was not good. In fact, it was a terrible reaction. Dan DiDio was the publisher and Dan didn't like it, even though he's the one who gave me the mission. He didn't like what I came up with, and I don't know why. Maybe it wasn't violent enough, dark, grim and gritty enough, but he took out a shovel with issue three or four and just buried it before we even finished. And it wasn't helped by the Jim Lee/Brian Azzarello Superman launch right around the same time. They're the ones that got the most attention, so the reaction within DC is that it was an Elseworlds or something, so who cares? Outside of DC, the reaction at the time was okay, but what grew out of that was an evergreen for DC. That's a book they still have in print and they continue to republish in new editions.

Another event and permutation was Grant Morrison's 2005 to 2008 12-issue maxi-series All-Star Superman. *In it, Lex Luthor realizes that he is aging and will someday die, so killing Superman becomes a priority. He orchestrates an event that oversaturates Superman's cells with solar radiation and the Man of Steel discovers that he is slowly dying. As a result, he goes about getting his affairs in order and dealing with his friends and the woman he loves. Luthor's gambit heads into checkmate when he finds a way to give himself superpowers, and a being known as Solaris turns the sun blue. Superman shows*

In All-Star Superman, writer Grant Morrison offers a loving tribute to the history of the Man of Steel (© and TM DC Comics/Warner Bros. Discovery).

Lex what he sees when he looks at the Earth, which causes him to weep before Superman knocks him out. Superman says goodbye to Lois and turns into a solar-consciousness, flying into the sun and repairing it. And that's where Superman stays as the Earth moves on with him.

GRANT MORRISON (writer, *All-Star Superman*): I immersed myself in Superman and I tried to find in all of these very diverse approaches the essential "Superman-ness" that powered the engine. I then extracted, purified and refined that essence and reined it into *All-Star*'s tank, recreating characters as my own dream versions without the baggage of strict continuity. In the end I saw Superman not as a superhero or even a science-fiction character, but as a story of Everyman. We're all Superman in our own adventures. We have our own Fortress of Solitude we retreat to, with our own special collections of valued stuff, our own super-pets, our own "bottle cities" that we feel guilty for neglecting. We have our own peers and rivals and bizarre emotional or moral tangles to deal with. I felt I'd really grasped the concept when I saw him as Everyman, or rather as the dreamed-of Everyman. The "S" is the radiant emblem of divinity we reveal when we rip off our stuffy shirts, our social masks, our neurosis, our constructed selves, and become who we truly are. (*Newsarama*)

MICHAEL BAILEY: *All-Star Superman* is one of the most beautiful Superman stories ever written and this is a story that stands on its own. At the end he dies, but he doesn't really. Grant Morrison understood the idea of Superman being a character that can do anything and he crafted a story where he brought all of these fun concepts back. One of my favorite things is at the Fortress of Solitude, instead of having a giant key that Superman flies into the lock, it's a key made of white dwarf matter that only Superman can pick up and it's under the mat. Then there's his relationship with Lois… just everything pops. He said everything he wanted to say about Superman, so when you get to *The New 52*, I really love the early part of his run because he was playing with the Superman "champion of the oppressed" idea, but they had to get away from that quickly because you had another Superman title that was taking place in the present where he is in the costume.

DWAYNE MCDUFFIE (screenwriter, *All-Star Superman*): The general take on the book is that it's episodic and that it's a bunch of great, great stories, not one story. It seemed very clear to me that it was primarily one single story, and approaching it from that angle, what should stay and what should go, and what we should focus on and what we focus off of just became crystal clear. It's Superman dealing with his morality. That's really the clear central piece of it. Secondarily, it's the final confrontation between Superman and Luthor, which is the conflict that has defined Superman's life.

J.M. DEMATTEIS: Talk about getting to the essence of Superman. It got to the root of those stories that I read as a kid; those classic, magical Silver Age stories, yet told in a modern way and told in a very sweet and moving way as well.

MICHAEL BAILEY: Grant Morrison has a view of Superman that I don't 100% agree with, but I 100% respect, because he is coming from such an honest place with his vision of who the character is. I personally like a more grounded Superman, where Superman's the most fantastic element in the story. It's why I love the George Reeves series so much, especially the first season, because you've got all these kind of normal guys and Superman is the most fantastic element.

DWAYNE MCDUFFIE: The conflict between Superman and Luthor in this is very faithful to the core of their relationship, going back to the old comics where it was two people who were very close friends who have a break and then spend the rest of their lives battling while knowing they should have been friends. In this case, Superman is such a redemptive force. One of the things that's wonderful about this book is everybody who he comes in contact with, he makes their lives better, and then he leaves and their lives are *still* better. It's not like he keeps them from getting killed in a bank robbery and goes away and they just have a good cocktail story. Instead, he transforms them in a fundamental way, and as he prepares for his death, he transforms the world in a fundamental way, which I think is really nice.

With Luthor, we decided to put more focus on his change than was in the comic. This is the part I was afraid of, because it's what I really changed. At the end of the comic he punches Luthor out and says, "You should have made the world better." And Luthor goes to his grave still being Luthor. I thought, "This is the last Superman story. He beats Luthor every week and then Luthor comes back. He's already escaped from jail like 900 times. Just because he's about to go to the chair, we don't believe it. And we don't believe that Luthor's really going to be punished and we don't believe Superman won. So the thing we changed is that at the last moment, Superman redeems Luthor.

GRANT MORRISON: I felt we had to live up to the big ideas behind Superman. I don't take my job lightly. It's all I've got. As the project got going, I wasn't thinking about Silver Ages or Dark Ages or anything about the comics I'd read, so much as the big shared idea of "Superman" and that "S" logo I see on T-shirts everywhere I go, on girls and boys — *that* communal Superman. I wanted us to get the precise energy of Platonic Superman down on the page. The "S" hieroglyph, the super-sigil, stands for the very best kind of man we can imagine, so the subject dictated the methodical, perfectionist approach. In honor of the character's primal position in the development of the superhero narrative, I hoped we could create an "ultimate" hero story, starring the ultimate superhero. Basically, I suppose I felt Superman deserved the utmost application of our craft and intelligence in order to truly do him justice… otherwise I couldn't have written this book if I hadn't watched my big, brilliant dad decline into incoherence and death. I couldn't have written it if I'd never had my heart broken or mended. I couldn't have written it if I hadn't known what it felt like to be idolized, misunderstood, hated for no clear reason, loved for all my faults, forgotten, remembered. Writing *All-Star Superman* was, in retrospect, also a way of keeping my mind in the clean sunshine while plumbing the murkiest depths of the imagination. (*Newsarama*)

DAN DIDIO (DC co–publisher, 2010 to 2020): *Superman: Birthright* was set up to be a relaunch originally and then ultimately we didn't get approval to do a relaunch, so we moved it aside and just did the story itself. It was felt that the story was strong enough to stand on its own. Same thing with *All-Star Superman*. Just before I got there, there was going to be a talent shift and I believe that Grant Morrison, Mark Waid, Mark Millar and Tom Peyer had put a whole outline together called *Superman 2000*, and they did a pitch on what they wanted Superman to be. It was up and running and then ultimately had to stop and be discarded because of internal politics.

MARK WAID: What happened is that I was talking to the Superman editor back then and he said, "I'm looking for a new angle; do you have a pitch?" I didn't, but I said that I would go home and think about it. I sat down with Grant, Mark and Tom and we started talking about it, and what we came up with was treating it like a writers' room situation where each of us would be responsible for one of those books, but all of us would be responsible for plotting and coming up with ideas. So I went back with the same pitch, but the editor had changed and the new editor Eddie Berganza was really excited and we were given the gig. I remember specifically the lunch at which Eddie was talking about his plans and what we should do and how we should do it and how we should set it up structurally. And then a few days later, his bosses learned that he had made these deals without their consent and lost their minds. They wrote us back in the kind of letter you would send to a six-year-old who sent you a crayon drawing of Superman, saying, "Thanks for your interest, but we're not really having this." The complaint was that we had somehow tried to poach the books from existing creators. That was *not* the case. We were asked specifically for a proposal. The problem was that we were asked by one editor and delivered to another one, and the former editor didn't ever come forth and say anything because he didn't want to get involved.

We were told at that point that we would *never* be handed the main Superman books, and of course years later Grant *was* when management had changed. But it was this ridiculously over-the-top rejection to what we had pitched. I'm still upset about it because it was a misunderstanding that could have easily been clarified if the right people had spoken up.

DAN DIDIO: I knew Grant's interest in Superman and Mark Waid's interest in Superman. Those are the two I really dealt with the most, and their energy and love of the character ultimately gives you *All-Star Superman* and *Superman: Birthright*. And they work on their own. This goes back to the differences between Batman and Superman — I always have to make those analogies — in that you could go into a bookstore and find a dozen books to pull off the shelf worth reading about Batman. You're hard-pressed to find a dozen seminal bodies of work on Superman. So that's one of the reasons we did *All-Star Superman* and things like *Birthright*, to create seminal bodies of work for Superman. It's the same way we had *Superman for All Seasons* early on, you had Alan Moore's *Whatever Happened to the Man of Tomorrow?*, which is a great story. But because monthly comics was a machine that churned out very similar product without progression, you never got that collection to put on the shelf. It's why we also did *Superman: Secret Identity* with Kirk Busiek. *All-Star Superman* is still the high-water mark, and then you have *Birthright*, we did *Earth One* with Joe Stracynski, which was something with a different sensibility. Those were the ideas on those books, to have something you can point to and ask, "What is the definitive Superman story? How do I learn the most about the character? What can I read?" You need to have books to point people to in order to answer those questions.

And when people ask about reader confusion over these different versions, you basically have to admit the dirty little secret that the level of new readers coming in was not appreciable. So as you're really selling to the same fan base on the periodical side, where the *real* growth was taking place was in the bookstore market. At one point, 55% of our sales were graphic novels, not periodicals — therefore reading order is not as much of a priority for people picking up individual things on a character or specific talent. *That* was what you were selling, so the desire for that clarity in interpretation isn't as deep, because more than half your readership is people with books on a shelf with no sense of when these things were created.

Bailey points out that there was very clearly a line in the sand that ushered in what would become many years of reboots, retcons, time shifts and a desire or need to continually create events across the DC line.

MICHAEL BAILEY: In 2001 they had a storyline where a hologram of Jor-El comes to Earth and tells Clark that everything he knew about his origin was a lie and that it really was the Silver Age, and he traveled to *that* Krypton. But the very next year they revealed, "Nah, we were kidding, this was actually an offshoot of the Phantom Zone and it wasn't really Krypton"… which kind of created the rift that eventually led to something like *Birthright*. And the problem is that because DC Comics, like all other comic book companies in the 2000s, was struggling to survive, it wasn't like the old days where you have a new origin and, boom, that's the origin for 20 years. They did *Birthright* in 2003 to 2004 and then jettisoned it two years later. But once you get into like 2004 to the present, there are like 15 origins with lots of starts and stops. From the outside, it looks crazy. From the inside, it looks crazy.

DAN DIDIO: It's hard to have a team built around the most powerful character in the universe and then find relevance for every other character to be helpful without diminishing Superman in the process. That was one of the shortfalls of the character: the need to diminish him in order to move a story forward. They made him so strong, that everybody spends so much time trying to take away things from him or make him behave in almost a slightly irrational manner in order for the story to work — which is a very long way of saying that he's a very hard character to write. There are some writers who hear that and get very annoyed because they feel he's *not* that hard to write; that you just have to tap into his vulnerabilities. What is his vulnerability? His heart and things like that? Maybe that's not dynamic enough a story? I don't know.

The way I used to describe it is that Batman used to be the policeman of the DC universe, Superman the fireman… meaning that he was always there to help people; didn't question who they were or what they were about, he was just there to help. Which is an interesting thing. The other thing I used to say is if Batman walks into a bar, everybody runs and hides, because they're afraid he's after them for something they might have done at some point in their life. Superman walks into the bar and everybody wants to pat him on the back and buy him a drink. Think about it: People were more comfortable with the most powerful character in the world and they were more uncomfortable with somebody who had no powers. *That* was the dichotomy between the two characters, so when you have a character that likable and natural, it's easy to do story snippets, but on an ongoing basis it gets repetitive because the challenges always seem false or external, never internal.

It's a point that many believe have led to the numerous events taking place in the world of Superman and the greater DC universe, which have had dramatic impact on the character himself.

DAN DIDIO: More recently it's more frequent, but if you think about it, Superman was Superman for the longest time and sometimes it changes with editors, sometimes it changes because of sales. If the numbers drop, they institute a change. When things are working, you don't touch it. If you see a change occurring, it probably has to do with something external driving that choice. If you look at Superman's history over any character that ever existed, you have Siegel and Shuster, you have Wayne Boring in the '50s and Curt Swan defining the look of Superman for over 30 years. So there was a lot of consistency and it was a very settled, smooth-running ship for a long period of time. But again, Superman is a character created in the late '30s/early '40s with a very clear sensibility reflective of the world around him. As the world changes, that's probably when you see Superman change.

When you look at DC Comics from the '40s to the '50s, everybody's coming home post-war, the world is changing, science-fiction themes become more prevalent and Superman takes those on. But the first crack in some of the Superman storytelling is that there is so much product being created for Superman because he's so popular that they have to really start to push him in different directions just not to repeat themselves. You suddenly have all of these different plots, which is why you have Superman here, you have Jimmy Olsen over here, Lois Lane has her own book over here, and *then* there's Superboy over here, and Superboy in the future over there — all of that happening, theoretically, to the same character who's at the center of it all. It's not until you get to the late '60s/early '70s when Julie Schwartz takes over and tries to depower him… but it doesn't stick, which is just the strength and weakness of the character. He was so ingrained in the minds and sensibilities of people that no matter how hard they made a physical effort to change it, they couldn't even stick to it themselves, the people who changed it. Because who he is, is so highly defined that they stayed within the parameters of that definition rather than where they were trying to push him.

It was, he feels, interesting to see and something that has been attempted numerous times when creators with fresh new ideas come in, but as DiDio puts it, they "almost freeze" because it dawns on them that they're about to take on an icon.

DAN DIDIO: And something that was so precious to them when they were younger, that the kid in them kicks in and it results in sort of a half-baked version of what they were trying to accomplish. They don't go all in with their changes and sort of hold themselves back, so it becomes neither fish nor fowl. And when it goes that way, the default setting is always back to what it was. And then you're back there again when the next person comes in and tries to reinvent the wheel, so to speak. Like I said, during my tenure at DC I saw that happen several times. Ironically, when Brian Bendis came on board, he had a whole storyline where he was creating another love interest for Superman that was creating some friction within there, but as soon as he came in, he didn't want to upset the Lois/Superman dynamic and sort of backed away from that story right away, which was interesting. There are even cases where writers created new powers for Superman that didn't stick. It's because ultimately there's so much product out there, again, that there is a default setting for a lot of these characters that people refer to. And especially with talent coming on board, what motivated them to do that character was something from their childhood and they immediately go back to the version that they remember more so than the version that's existing product at that time.

Once you make a choice you've got to go all in, which is why I think the John Byrne relaunch works. Ultimately it was an all-in bet, it had full support and they had the full control, so they made sure that it wasn't undermined in any way, shape or form; that this was the direction going forward no matter how it affected other products. They just stayed true to what they were redoing and that's why it made a lasting impression.

With major company-wide events taking place which transform many of the heroes in their wake, most notably Superman, the confusion that arises is an attempt to reverse faltering sales, or if the Man of Steel, for instance, is part of a big Hollywood movie, where he still seems to be big business.

DAN DIDIO: But the comic book business is built on the illusion that it's selling the same numbers as a movie and TV show, but it's far from that. Those aren't comparable. The reality is that if you're going to have a major venue, you want one of the major characters in there. The goal is to see how disruptive it is for the other stories taking place, and if you've got multiple titles taking place with the same character, you want at least one or two of those titled tied into the events and everybody else is tied in by association. So that's how you do it; you can't have a major event without Superman, Batman or Wonder Woman or it's not a major event.

When it comes to the comic events, boosting sales is mostly what it's about, unfortunately. When they did *Crisis on Infinite Earths*, it was a hail Mary pass for the most part. The DC lineup was in the toilet and they had to get it out of there. The only way they could do that is to do something dramatic, definitely shaking the lineup, and they did. And it helped for a period of time. And then what happens is that you get some crossovers here and there, but then you see the crossover becomes a main driver for sales events and elevates marginal titles that you need to feed the beast. But once you start doing too many events, the problem is that what makes an event valuable is the ramifications that follow the event, how it changes the world and how it affects things. *That's* what makes it valuable. The most successful events are the ones that have long-lasting effects. When you start to create events just for the sake of events, and then you have a world-changing moment followed by the next world-changing moment, followed by the next world-changing moment, none of these things are going to stick. Therefore they boost value along the way and they just have that initial impact when they were launched, but that's not going to have that long-lasting effect that makes them memorable years from now.

Crisis on Infinite Earths lasted because all the worlds were gone. All the multiverse was gone for so long, characters died and it mattered. And they held for a long time, so that gave the event value. That's what was important. And the more you can do things following an event that has lasting changes, the greater the strength of the event. I tell the story of *52*, the weekly series. When we finished that, we had to do another weekly series because they don't want to lose all the sales of the first one. And then we had some diminishing returns, but we still had big numbers on the second one. So we had to do a third one, and each one sold less than the one before that. But the other material that we would create didn't have the same potential, which is why you see so many sequels in the mix, because there's a predetermined value for the material, therefore people would rather take a bet on the predetermined value than risk things on something new. They've got their algorithms figured out. I remember people saying, "You get 80% return on a sequel," but the trick is not to overspend — of course they do, which is why you get the diminishing returns.

The bottom line is the bottom line. Nothing's greater than a critical success or fan enjoyment while making our numbers, but sometimes they're exclusive of each other and you have to find a way to keep it going. The problem is that everybody's always looking for definitive endings to definitive stories, but the truth is we've got to tell another story the very next month. You can put a nice bow on it, but the next person is going to have to untie that bow.

In 2005, DC launched the event Infinite Crisis, *in which Alexander Luthor, Superboy of Earth Prime and the Lois and Superman from Earth-2 had survived the original* Crisis on Infinite Earths. *They found refuge outside of reality, but between Lois' health failing and the world that replaced theirs growing darker by the moment, Alex and Superboy take action. Meanwhile, the heroes of the DC Universe are at their lowest after revelations of mind-wiping on the part of the Justice League tears the team apart. Batman, feeling betrayed, creates a satellite named Brother Eye to keep track of his fellow heroes, but that is usurped, first by Maxwell Lord and Checkmate, and then by Alexander Luthor. The heroes finally come together to defeat Alex and his forces, including an unhinged Superboy Prime and, in the end, reality remakes itself and the Superman of Earth-2 gives his life fighting Super-boy Prime.*

In 2006 to 2008's Last Son, *a young Kryptonian boy crash lands in Metropolis and is found by Superman. Clark and Lois take the boy in as their adoptive son, who they name Christopher. It is soon revealed that Christopher is actually the son of General Zod and Ursa, and was the prelude to an invasion of Earth by the villains of the Phantom Zone. Superman is temporarily trapped within the zone, but escapes with the help of the heroes of Earth and a handful of his enemies, including Lex Luthor, and the Zone villains are sent back. Unfortunately, so is Christopher as Clark and Lois deal with the loss of their adoptive son.*

Final Crisis in 2008 is a bit of an off-kilter one. On one level you have Darkseid taking over the world via the Anti-Life Equation. Superman deals head-on with this after teaming up with a bunch of Supermen from various worlds of the Multiverse. Superman is crucial to freeing the world of the Equation's effects, but Batman is seemingly killed. On another level, it's a battle between the different Monitors of the multiverse and it all gets very cosmic.

Also in 2008, writer Geoff Johns teamed up with Superman: The Movie *director Richard Donner for a Brainiac storyline, in which the android's probe attacks Metropolis while Superman flies into space to confront the villain. He learns that the various versions of Brainiac that he faced over the years were nothing more than advance probes. Superman is shrunk and stuck in the Bottle City of Kandor, but he escapes and manages to defeat Brainiac before it can capture the city of Metropolis. At the end of the story, Superman enlarges Kandor in the Arctic and suddenly the Earth's population is increased by 100,000 Kryptonians.*

MICHAEL BAILEY: It's different creators coming on and wanting to have their vision. Geoff Johns was coming onto *Action Comics* with Richard Donner post-*Infinite Crisis*. If you take the thousand-foot view, DC was doing this in general: They were trying to make everything count. Grant Morrison was trying to do that with Batman at the time. Like all those wacky stories from the '50s actually happened, but they were hallucinations that Batman had. So Geoff Johns and Kurt Busiek came on to *Action* and *Superman* respectively after *Infinite Crisis* and right away they kind of had differing views on it. But because Geoff Johns was the bigger muckity-muck at DC, his vision won out and his vision was *Superman: The Movie*, but all of the different versions of Krypton existed as different castes within Krypton. So you had the Military Guild, the Science Guild, the Art Guild and they all had outfits that reflected the entire history of Krypton up until that point. You had people in Silver Age outfits, people in the John Byrne Krypton outfits, and the overall theme of it was the Krypton from *Superman: The Movie*, because Geoff Johns loves that movie.

DAN DIDIO: When John Byrne relaunched Superman, he kept Jonathan and Martha Kent alive, but when Geoff Johns took over *Action*, he killed Jonathan Kent and that's because he wanted to get the setting of *Superman: The Movie*. He had worked with Richard Donner to craft that story, so they were being true to the movie in the same way that, years earlier, people were being true to the TV show. When *Superman: The Movie* becomes the iconography or the standard of the character and the character's behaviors, then it starts to reinvent itself along the way.

The Brainiac story leads directly to 2009's Superman: New Krypton, *which is more of a saga than a single story.* New Krypton *deals with the Earth not wanting the Kryptonians on their planet, leading to the creation of a planet in the same orbit as the Earth, just on the other "side." Forces within both humanity and New Krypton do not want any sort of peace, but it is the appearance of Brainiac that really brings the story to a head. New Krypton is destroyed and an army of survivors, led by General Zod, try to take over the Earth. Again, Superman stops them, but has to deal with the second loss of his people and a loss of trust from the people of Earth.*

MICHAEL BAILEY: There was an interesting evolution over the 2000s that started slow, but really gained momentum like a rock rolling down a hill, of people mistrusting Superman; people looking at Superman and saying, "He can do all these things. What if he turns against us?" They did the *New Krypton* storyline, which really played with that, where you've got 100,000 Kryptonians on the other side of the Sun and you have this contingent of the military led by a jerk version of Sam Lane, and you had it where humanity was *really* mistrusting Superman.

Grounded, *from writer J. Michael Straczynski and published between 2010 and 2011, begins with Superman getting slapped in the face by a woman whose husband died during the Kryptonian invasion (not because of the invasion, but of a brain tumor, and the woman believes Superman could have somehow saved her husband); Superman begins to walk across the United States in an effort to reconnect with humanity. He encounters literal aliens, abusive fathers and other normal problems that humanity has to deal with. Along the way he has to deal with a woman that gets possessed by one of the sunstones that fell to Earth after the destruction of New Krypton. In the end, Superman feels that he has reconnected with humanity and helps a woman who became possessed. There's also a bunch of high-end concepts, like the Fortress of Solidarity and descendants of Superman from the future coming to the present, but the sunstone-possessed woman was the main "villain" of the piece.*

The 2011 Flashpoint *event is really a Flash story where Barry Allen goes back in time and saves his mother from being killed by the Reverse Flash, which results in a new reality that is very different from the standard DCU. In the Flashpoint world, Kal-El is found by the military and kept hidden until Barry and the Batman of the Flashpoint universe team up to undo the damage that Barry doesn't realize he has caused at first. The Superman of this world eventually aids the heroes after the death of Lois and then it all gets wiped out, leading to the next event.*

Superman's backstory is changed once again in 2011's The New 52. *He's a baby when he leaves Krypton. He's found by the Kents, who instill in him a sense of social justice, but they die on the night of his prom and Clark has to make his way in the world alone. He starts out being a hero by wearing a T-shirt, jeans and the blanket he was sent to Earth in as a cape. Eventually he gets a more traditional Superman costume while facing off with a new version of Brainiac. This Superman was different. He was younger, moodier and more prone to anger. At one point his powers were diminished and he fought injustice wearing a T-shirt and jeans again. He eventually gets his powers back, but that eventually leads to his death.*

MICHAEL BAILEY: If you look at *Secret Origin*, that's where Geoff Johns was going through the origin process, so at first people don't know what to make of Superman and might be kind of scared — which touches on that whole idea of people being mistrustful of him — but then he does earn their trust. Afterwards, *The New 52* happened and there was this whole part of society that doesn't know what to make of Superman. It's basically taking Marvel concepts from the '60s and '70s and applying them to then modern DC. There was a show called *Fantasticast* that was covering the Fantastic Four. They had a running joke of "fear of the Thing," because in the early issues of *Fantastic Four*, everyone was afraid of the Thing. And that's what they did with Superman, and that is what the people from the movies glommed. If you look at *Man of Steel* or *Batman v. Superman*, we are told the public loves him. We see a statue of him. But from the jump in that movie, it's all about why Superman is a danger and they're even holding Senate Hearings about him.

Convergence is a 2015 two-month event that DC published as it moved its headquarters from New York City to California. The main story involves Brainiac learning of the dead universes of the past and collecting cities from those various realities. He leaves them in the charge of a being known as Telos, who pits the champions of those cities against each other to find which city will remain. Various versions of Superman show up during this event, including the Red Son *Superman, the Superman of Earth-2, the*

Pre-Crisis Superman and the Pre-Flashpoint Superman as well. The Convergence: Superman *two-issue series leads into* Superman: Lois and Clark, *an eight-issue miniseries telling the story of the Pre-Flashpoint Superman and Lois living on the* New 52 *Earth in secret and raising their son Jonathan.*

DAN JURGENS: The miniseries *Superman: Lois & Clark* was a chance to dip back into the mythos… and part of it was because if we go back to *The New 52*, there were two Superman books. Grant Morrison was writing *Action* and George Perez was writing *Superman* and drawing, and he wasn't happy on that book. So they asked me and Keith Giffen to come in. After that I talked to George and he said, "Well they kept wanting me to do stories, that to me, wasn't my Superman." And he struggled with it. So I went in, I think from issues 7 to 12, and I had the same problems: "Well, you're not letting me do Superman as I see Superman, this isn't the fit, this isn't right." Then I just went on my way as well. But then, just a few years later, it got to the point where they said, "Okay, we know we blew it, so what can we do to repair this?" And I did the *Superman: Lois & Clark* thing. I had already pitched them on the idea for Clark and Lois' son Jon earlier, so this became a place where we could more fully explore that. It got Superman and Lois and Clark back together again, because in the *New 52* they had not been an item, which I think is part of who Superman is. There are people who liked that Superman was in a relationship with Wonder Woman, but I thought that was the wrong pairing for him. That's not who he is.

The following year, The Final Days of Superman *chronicles the death of the* New 52 *Superman. After the various power surges from the "Truth" storyline and the* Darkseid War, *the* New 52 *Superman learns he is going to die. Along the way, he says goodbyes to Lana Lang and Wonder Woman and even meets the pre-Flashpoint Superman. In the end, he dies, leaving the pre-Flashpoint Superman behind to pick up the mantle once again.*

Also in 2016 was DC Rebirth, *DC's course correction after* The New 52 *fizzled out. Line-wide it was an attempt to reclaim the history and legacy that they had given up during the* New 52. *The main special deals with Wally West re-entering reality and learning that there is some kind of force behind his disappearance and the way reality changed. This was supposed to lead into* Doomsday Clock, *but by the time that story finally ended it really didn't matter as much. The Pre-Flashpoint Superman and Lois reclaim their lives, but something dark is in the background.*

DAN JURGENS: *New 52* was all about getting in new readers with new stories, and new fields for the characters or a new feel for all the characters, A through Z across the board. Some of that went too far, which is where *Rebirth* came in. *Rebirth* was five years after *New 52*. We needed to move back, because some of the characters had been moved too far away from what they were, with Superman being a case in point. And so when I came in as part of *Rebirth*, and did the *Superman: Lois and Clark* series on that, it was really rebalancing things and taking Superman back to the core of who he is, and who that character is. That needed to be done.

Superman Reborn in 2017 is where we learn that the mysterious Mister Oz had been keeping Mr. Mxyzptlk captive, but Mxy escapes. Through the course of the story, the pre-Flashpoint Superman and the New 52 Superman merge and a new, streamlined timeline emerges. Basically, it's the Pre-Flashpoint Superman with some of the New 52 trappings sprinkled in.

MICHAEL BAILEY: For two years they didn't have an origin for Superman. We were asking for one and they kept saying, "Just wait, be patient." Then they finally do it with *Secret Origin*, but a year later they jettison that for *The New 52*. And on top of that, you had the *Superman: Earth One* graphic novel, that JMS wrote that is very much its own thing, but it's yet *another* origin. And then in 2017, with *Superman Reborn*, a year into *Rebirth*, it's like, "Yeah, it was all Mxyzptlk. He's the one who created the *New 52* version of Superman," and they folded everything together again. And that's kind of what they're operating from today, but DC is also at this point trying to move forward with new versions of their existing characters, so basically continuity just doesn't matter. There is no continuity for the DC universe because you have all these different DC titles that are kind of existing on their own. I joke about this, but the guy I feel bad for is the one in charge of Superman merchandise from 2011 to 2017 with all the changes that had to constantly be implemented.

Between 2017 and 2019 there was Doomsday Clock, where we learn that Doctor Manhattan left his reality at the end of Watchmen and entered the DC Universe. He discovers that the DCU isn't a multiverse, but a metaverse that changes over time with Superman being the key figure. When Superman's backstory changes, the entire DCU changes. Manhattan creates his own reality, which is the New 52, but learns of Superman's ultimate importance and brings back both the Legion of Super-Heroes and the Justice Society of America. He also brings Clark's parents back to life.

Super Sons of Tomorrow, published between 2017 and 2018, sees Tim Drake of the future coming back in time to kill Jon Kent for a future crime. The current Teen Titans choose sides and the grown-up Titans from the future also head back in time for the fight.

The next big shift for Superman came about when writer Brian Michael Bendis' contract at Marvel came to an end and he was wooed over to DC Comics by co-publishers Dan DiDio and Jim Lee. He expressed his desire to take over Superman and, fortuitously, his arrival was in time for Action Comics #1000 *in June 2018. This would be followed by* The Man of Steel *miniseries and Bendis essentially serving as writer of both* Superman *and* Action *for a little over two years.*

As happened back in the 1980s with the arrival of John Byrne, which saw Superman writers like Cary Bates and Elliot S! Maggin removed from the character, the same thing happened with Bendis coming aboard.

ARLEN SCHUMER: Bendis represents, again, a top Marvel writer coming over to DC and writing the flagship characters. That's been going on since the '80s. Frank Miller went from Marvel to DC and did *The Dark Knight Returns*. It's gotten to the point now where DC and Marvel Comics, for however many decades, are interchangeable, which is both a good and bad thing. They both have the same great artists and mixtures.

DAN JURGENS: I think overall, in comics, we have seen great comics come out of that. We've seen shitty comics come out of that. And it all depends on who it is and what the character is and what they do. So I don't think there's any pat answer to that. Some things stick, some things don't. And I think where it gets a little difficult is, and this gets into *New 52* stuff a little bit too, which is, what are the parameters of this character? And I would ask simple questions like, has this Superman ever fought Doomsday? And at first some would say yes, and someone would say no. And I'd say, "Well, if you're gonna tell five million people who bought that comic book that that story didn't happen, you've got a bit of a problem." That's not how the psyche of readers work. You can pretend it isn't like that, but that's still how it is. And that's not a continuity-heavy issue. It's an issue of when you do stories that resonate with readers, because they so define a character, you need to embrace those stories.

BRIAN MICHAEL BENDIS (writer, *Superman* and *Action Comics*): Since I had done *Daredevil* at Marvel everyone was like, "You should do Batman, when are you going to do Batman? You're definitely going to do Batman." The whole time I'm going, "I like Batman, I'm not anti-Batman, but boy, Superman looks like a much more difficult project in that here we are today and he's selling truth, justice and the American way, and what the hell does any of that mean anymore? I would like to dive into *that!*" The other thing people talked to me about was the idea that Superman wasn't relevant to the modern world, that he was out of step with the times. Marvel has a couple of characters like this too, where they get mistaken for vanilla or plain or ordinary, like Cyclops or Captain America. My feeling was between them and Superman, you're talking about the three most interesting people in all of comics. What you have to do is dig deep and ask, "What do they want? What don't they have? What's missing? What's driving them?" With Superman, sometimes people just lean into one aspect of it. I think because Superman is invulnerable and handsome and good, people can get lost in those aspects of it and not challenge it. What I've learned from the earliest days in my superhero career, I'm like, "Whatever the theme of the character is — for Spider-Man it's with great power comes great responsibility; for Daredevil it's law and order — the story needs to challenge it in the hardest way so the character can really look at themselves and look at the world, and figure out what they want out of this.

ANTHONY DESIATO: There was a point in time where Bendis was really one of my very favorite writers. And at that point in time, if you had said he was going to Superman, I would have thought that was great. But that time has passed for me. I went into his Superman run with a relatively open mind and I thought he captured the voice of the character. I felt there were ways where Clark felt a little bit younger, more relatable in some of the narration and interactions. And that's a big piece of it for me. But there are major fundamental problems with a lot of the choices in that run, though I admit I don't know where the line is between Bendis' decisions versus what was editorially mandated.

During his run, the writer introduced a variety of elements to the Superman mythos, some well received and others controversial, to say the least. For starters, there was Rogol Zaar, a being created by Jor-El who, it turns out, was responsible for the destruction of Krypton, along with Empress Gandelo of the Trilium Collective, and who comes to Earth to destroy remaining Kryptonians Superman and Supergirl.

BRIAN MICHAEL BENDIS: Rogol Zaar was a big one, throwing a wrench into what Superman saw as the truth of his life. And it wasn't that it changes the facts. What I pitched to Dan was *not* that Krypton didn't explode, but instead, that there was a lot going on behind that explosion. I said, "It's like when you're a kid, you hear one version of history, and when you get older, it's like, 'Oh, that's the *real* history.'" So I wanted a Krypton version of that where it's, "Your dad was a complicated man with complicated choices in front of him." I invented this new character whose existence just rattles Superman. And it's someone who just hates you and there's nothing you can do that will ever change their mind; no good deed you can do, there's no hug to be had. We all have that at work where there's someone that hates you and you're not doing anything. There are people online that hate my guts, and I'm a dude trying to tell you a story. That's all I'm doing.

His choices continued to be met with controversial reactions as he went on, notably the decision to have Clark and Lois' 11-year-old son Jonathan Samuel Kent disappear into a time asynchronously for several weeks, but when he returns he's actually aged to 17 years old and is even more powerful than he was before.

DAN JURGENS: Part of the problem is that Lois suffered a lot by virtue of that story, because if I'm talking about relationships, and as I was with Clark's relationship with his parents and what we see through Superman's relationship with Jon and Lois, all of a sudden you take away Lois' chance to raise a child. What have you done to Lois Lane? So I think readers got cheated out of a strong set of stories, Lois got cheated out of a strong sense of stories and that's unfortunate. As we were going to go forward, I was writing *Action,* Pete Tomasi and Pat Gleason were doing *Superman* and we had some plans as to how those would go forward, but then they made the change and we were no longer doing the books. What I think fans would have gotten to see were some very nice, fun, developing stories on how a child learns to live as the son of Superman. And how do they function as a family unit? People were still into that. And I think that when you lose that, it's sort of like, as I said, Lois who got kicked in the teeth. And I think that's too bad.

MICHAEL BAILEY: I was actually excited that Bendis was coming on, because as much as I find some of his interviews prickly, I also find him to be somebody that is very passionate about his work. He's not in any way somebody that's just doing it for the sake of doing it, and he did an interview with the *The New York Times* where he was talking about how much he came to love the character and all the research he was doing. He did other interviews where he talked about how being a reporter is more important than ever, so he was going to dig into Clark Kent, but slowly, as the year went on, it seemed like he was dismantling everything that had happened during *Rebirth*. Like, *Rebirth* happens in 2016 and all of a sudden Superman's married again, he has a son, the *Daily Planet's* back — it's like all of the things that make Superman, Superman, had been put back into place. But over Bendis' first year, Lois wasn't around because she had gone off with Jonathan to travel space with Jor-El, who is back and not stable. Then she comes back and Jon is like 17 years old.

BRIAN MICHAEL BENDIS: The idea was for something to happen to Jon that *wasn't* a devastating tragedy in that, "Oh my God, we lost him" way, but instead, "Oh, here's something that happens to Jon that just lets Superman know you're about at the end of what you can do for him other than just be there." But there's going to be adventures and there's going to be scary stuff, and so we allowed something really bad to happen to Jon, but it wasn't really bad because Jon survived it using the skills his parents gave him. I hate to discount it, because he was tortured and kidnapped by a really bad person, but it's like he went away for the summer and came back and had his own adventure, and now you see, "Oh, you're an adult now. Now you've kind of figured it out." But people focus on that because I took something away from the Superman family. I stole little Jon from them... but it' to create a Superman level effect of emotion, a parenting emotion. For a Superman to have that feeling — we're talking about being a parent — it has to be Superman level, right?

This is also something that lets Superman look in the eyes of his son and realize what he's lost, and Superman doesn't lose a lot of things. To actually have him feel like he lost something and realize the gravity of it seemed pretty big, but there's two sides to that coin. Yes, they lost something, but they also got the, "Oh, he survived and he's not a bad guy. He survived with the grace and style of his mother and father, that's amazing." And that set him up for what was next, which was becoming part of the Legion of Super-Heroes. Jon is the one; the one who ultimately inspires the Legion 1,000 years in the future... and they know it too. They're not here for Superman, they're here for Jon, and there's no greater moment in my heart and it's probably the best moment in Clark's life when he quietly realizes what's going on. And he whispers to Lois, "They know it," and Lois says, "It's him."

PETER SANDERSON: Bendis also believed that the secret identity trope had outlived its usefulness, and so he had Superman reveal to the world that he is Clark Kent. But Superman continued to live a dual life, continuing to work as a reporter under the name Clark Kent while also operating as Superman.

STEVE YOUNIS: Bendis opened a can of worms and then he walked away, leaving a massive mess with Clark revealing his secret identity to the world. It's an interesting story as an Elseworlds story that you can have a look back at. But for the main titles, how do you put those worms back in the can? It's difficult to move forward with Clark Kent and Lois Lane having a son, and the Kents have to go into hiding. That can't be the status quo moving forward; they need to do a rest somewhere along the line. And we've had enough resets.

MICHAEL BAILEY: That was the kicker, and what actually led me to go,

"I'm out of here for now," was getting rid of the secret identity, which they had done in 2015. You'd think they would have learned their lesson, but he not only revealed the identity but framed it that Clark was living his truth. The first story that did this in 2015 was called "Truth," and so was this one, but this time it's Clark being honest with himself. I thought that was such a fundamental misreading of Superman and what Clark Kent represents to Superman, that it was my time to leave. I was actually angry for months.

BRIAN MICHAEL BENDIS: What snuck up on me — and there's always something that sneaks up on me — was him not needing the stupid identity anymore. Even Seinfeld made jokes in the '90s about Superman being a liar, and you're like, "Well, how is he truth and justice and you're just lying all day?" And it's a hypocrisy that's cheeky and fun, but as we get more and more into the genre, and as even my children are growing up with a much more sophisticated superhero palette than what we grew up with, an eight-year-old will turn to you and go, "Why is he Clark Kent?" And some of it is ghosts of a pop culture that just doesn't really exist anymore.

Superman walked all the way through and survived and continues to be Superman, but all of these characters evolved and changed with the times. Peter Parker did and Bruce Wayne did. And looking at Superman, one constant criticism is that he's from a different era. And so I'm thinking about that, and I'm like, "This is a true thing, man." And so I brought it up, and said with Daredevil, I gave it a lot of thought. We outed Daredevil too, but literally he was outed by the press, which happens. It was taken away from him, but in this regard I said, "I think what I'd like to do is have him just decide to do so, not because there's any stress coming up because Lex is about to do it, but because it just hits him: "I don't want to do it anymore." And I thought with what happened with his father Jor-El, and the legacy that was building around him and with Jon and all of that, it just made me feel like, "Yeah, I don't need to hide this. I still want to be Clark Kent. I'm still Clark. It's still how I represent myself, but I don't need it to be a secret anymore." And even going through the logic of, well, wouldn't that put Jimmy Olsen in terrible jeopardy? Let me ask you this: Who *doesn't* know Superman's friends with Jimmy? If anything, it might keep you away from the *Daily Planet*. "Well, he's definitely in there, let's not hit that building." So I put it out there, and I must say with the Daredevil thing as well, you're like, "All right, well I'm sure we'll put the genie back in the bottle eventually."

There was, he emphasizes, a lot of story available as a result, with a lot of people and many villains reacting differently. This led to a villains' special which Bendis collaborated on with Matt Fraction and Greg Rucka.

BRIAN MICHAEL BENDIS: Toyman, for instance, doesn't know what to do with himself and feels that everything he knew was a lie. Watching the trickle effect hit them all was a lot of fun, and I'm delighted it's still part of the story; that all of the writers and editors see the value in this modern version and maybe eventually we'll put it back. But I'm thrilled it's still out there the way it is. I know with every death and reveal, sometimes there's like a, "Oh, let's put it back the way it was," but a lot of times these things aren't done lightly and it's always done for a better story. It's funny, because from my perspective I get hired to shake things up a little bit or try new things, and I get yelled at when I do it, and then five years later when it's in a movie, everyone goes, "Yay, thanks for doing that."

ANTHONY DESIATO: The artificial aging of Jon really bugged me. The continued usage of Jor-El as this Mr. Oz figure just did not work for me. And this business about Rogol Zaar being responsible for the destruction of Krypton, and Superman revealing his secret identity to the world — those four pieces ran counter to a lot of the way that I see the character. And virtually in all of those instances, they took away more than they gave. I just really had fundamental disagreements about the choices that were made; they were from the conception missteps. Ironically, I got the sense that he loves the character; it's not like he came on and was trying to make Superman into someone he wasn't or that he doesn't understand the character or he doesn't have the voice. None of that was the case.

MICHAEL BAILEY: I will say this about Bendis: He did bring a passion to the character and he brought a lot of character to the character; for the first time since maybe 2006, when the creative team that had been on before *Infinite Crisis* shifted to the creative team that was after, so you go from Greg Rucka and Gail Simone and Mark Verheiden to Geoff Johns and Richard Donner and Kurt Busiek. The Superman books were going from strength to strength, and *Rebirth* had been a very good shot in the arm for the character. But now they're going to Bendis who is not only a big name, but coming to DC to do all of this. The feeling was that Superman was finally in a good position heading into his 80th anniversary. He had *Action Comics* #1000, and I had lived my life thinking that I would be buying these books for the entirely of it, but I realized it was finally time for me to get off the ride.

DAN DIDIO: When you bring in somebody like Bendis, you're paying them for their direction and their sensibilities, so you sort of know what you're going in to at that point. I was also the publisher, and you've got an executive editor and executive team in there who were managing and coordinating the story and approving it. All I did was approve the general direction, the big story, and the issue-by-issue execution was managed by everybody else. My main goal when Bendis came in on Superman was a new Legion of Superheroes, so I was hoping for a Superman that leads directly to a new Legion.

BRIAN MICHAEL BENDIS: There was a day last year when someone was really giving me the business about how I ruined Superman. The Hawkeye TV show was on, and this character Ronin that I created with Joe Quesada showed up and everybody online was like, "Yay, Ronin's here." I'm like, "No, no, no. When Ronin debuted in the books, you guys yelled at me, you screamed at me. There was no other side." So I live in this constant state of yay, boo, yay, yay, boo, boo, and I don't know which one to react to, so I just go straight ahead and do my thing. I know going in I'm going to make some changes, but I know in my heart that my choices aren't being made to mess with anybody. I really think we have a story to tell that's interesting and respectful.

I thought my best add to the Superman mythos is to take all of these ideas and really lean them into the modern family dynamic, and really don't take away anything from Superman, but take it a step further. My friend Matt Fraction says these books, they're like a baton relay raise, and you hold a baton for as long as you can, and you run as fast as you can for as long as you can, and you're going to hand it over to somebody else. So while you're doing it, just run the best you can. In my time, that's the story I wanted to tell.

In March 2021, Bendis was succeeded on Action *by writer Philip Kennedy Johnson, chronicling the* Warworld Saga, *in which a slightly depowered Man of Steel travels to the realm of Mongul, who has a planetoid of beings battling each other to the death. Superman's objective is nothing less than freeing an enslaved people. Meanwhile, the* Superman *comic was written by Tom Taylor and followed the exploits of Jon Kent as he takes on the mantle of Superman while his father is away. Some of the seeds for this was developed in a line-wise plan titled 5G, which would have focused on the next generation of heroes.*

DAN DIDIO: I laid some of the groundwork for that before I was out of that world. The original plan was we were going to get new versions of the character. Jonathan was supposed to become the new Superman. Clark is like a battery and he's losing his charge and can't recharge anymore. Like a rechargeable battery, after a while it doesn't hold the charge. Superman finds he's not as powerful as he used to be, so ultimately he starts trying to find ways to be just as effective without he same level of power, which causes him to make some moral mistakes along the way. Ultimately Clark and Bruce Wayne are going through the same thing at the same time; the two of them basically have one more rush for the gold so to speak. They've dropped that now, but the idea is that during the Warworld story, Superman starts to realize his power isn't the way it was anymore and he doesn't understand why.

BRIAN MICHAEL BENDIS: Some of what happened with *Warworld* was us. I think my pitch was that Superman doesn't lose his powers, but there's a moment, and it's not unlike the moment you see in *Superman* 25 where Superman and Supergirl are saving a cruise ship from something and then he goes to put it down and his knee buckles a little; just a little wobble. Nothing like, "Oh my God, my knee!" The knee buckle doesn't mean his powers went away or that he's not Superman anymore, but then he responded, "Oh, okay… well let's get Jon ready." I don't know if it's 10 years from now, I don't know if it's 100 years from now, but it does change your perspective on yourself. *That's* where it was going to go.

DAN DIDIO: There were two reasons for the changes we were planning. The real reason for me is you don't want to change the original character so much that he's unrecognizable in order to have a contemporary tone. Then the question is, do you change the character or do you get a different character to push that story forward and fill that gap? There's so much of what DC was built on being this generational storytelling. We hear that all the time, about generational characters, but the truth is that Superman, Batman and Wonder Woman were the only three characters that were not generational characters.

MICHAEL BAILEY: It's an interesting experiment because Superman has largely *not* been a legacy character. He's not like Green Lantern and Flash and Hawkman and others that had different iterations over the decades. Superman has always been superman, so it's kind of ballsy what they're doing by trying to introduce a new generation instead of taking Superman and making him younger, like they did in *The New 52*, which didn't work. I can say from personal opinion and looking at the sales figures, the books did not click with the readership at large. There are other factors that went into it, whereas *now* DC really is kind of free; instead of trying to have the entire line connected by one central idea and having little offshoots of graphic novels and all that, it really seems like what they're doing is trying to create a line that'll please a wide variety of readers. Having a new Superman, it's really too soon to make any kind of firm judgment on it, because we haven't seen what happens five years from now.

DAN DIDIO: Every other character had been changed or replaced or moved forward, because they were aging. The joke I used to tell all the time is that Dick Grayson was going to be older than Bruce Wayne. Same thing with Superman, he wasn't aging. The world was aging around him and he has a personality. If you don't want to change, it's set in a very particular time period. And you want to at least still understand who he is — even if the world doesn't clearly accept who he is anymore, but understands why he is the character he is and why he won't change what he believes in. He always stays true to his beliefs and always *should* stay true to his beliefs. And the way they went with the *Warworld* story is he's trying to set a people free, ultimately. You see what they did? That's why the story works, because they took the sensibilities of the 1940s Superman trying to liberate the world from tyranny, which is taking place in World War I and World War II. You take that same sensibility, but you move into a new locale and as a result you get to act and behave in the same way that we most clearly recognize the character — in a different setting, but accomplishing the same goal.

Had we gone out as originally planned, it would have been a big story. Batman goes on trial for murder, Superman breaks him out and it's those guys versus the DC universe. Superman decides to power up one last time, basically absorbing as much energy as possible to stave off the events that were taking place. He was either going to get saved by Batman or blows up and restarts the universe… dependent on where we were in sales at the time. [*laughs*]

MICHAEL BAILEY: DC in a sense has been able to have it both ways. You had Phillip Kennedy Johnson writing an older Superman who is on Warworld, and all the usual trappings of Superman aren't there, but it's still a Superman story. You have Jonathan Kent coming into his own as the Superman of Earth, dealing with Lex Luthor, training with Nightwing, which I think is adorable. And then you have Mark Waid on *World's Finest* doing old-school Superman/Batman stories where he's back in the costume with the trunks and Batman's in the costume with the trunks. And it's just a completely different feel. It's like everybody gets to have their version.

STEVE YOUNIS: The fact that Superman got us away from that for the whole Warworld story allowed us to stop thinking about it. It also allowed his son Jon to then come into his own and have the limelight as the Superman on Earth and explore his powers and what he can do without having the shadow of his father hanging over him all the time. He could step into the light and explore his sexuality, his powers, what have you, and not knowing whether his dad will ever come back. So it allowed them both to have their separate stories without having to be intermeshed. Now that they've come back, it's going to be interesting to see how that progresses and what Jon will do as far as his name, because they can't have two people called Superman at the same time on Earth. It just gets bloody confusing.

The story on Warworld was really interesting and got into who this character is and what he stands for as far as violence and finding another way and being able to rescue people and not just his powers, because he was limited with his powers there. I thought it was an interesting story, but I'm ready for them to get back into Clark Kent, *Daily Planet* reporter, and that kind of thing, which we've missed.

MICHAEL BAILEY: DC has not known what to do with Superman for two decades now. They were constantly shifting what they wanted to do with the character because they were trying to stay relevant. Every once in a while you'd get a creator on there that really cared about it, but not for lengthy runs. It also has to do with how people consume comics now. My generation — I started reading when I was 11 in 1987 — was the generation to stick around. We were the ones that were going to keep with it and keep up with it. Nowadays the readership has shifted, because it seems the more current readers of comics don't view it as an investment for the long-term. They're reading it now, but they're probably going to move on to something else. That's not a judgment call, but if you look at a couple of years ago, they revamped Batgirl and made her more Gen Z Millennial. That did very well for about two years, but by the end of it, the people that had really gotten into it had moved either to another book property or onto something else entirely, because geek culture is so omnipresent in our society and people are more Renaissance with their approach to consuming geek culture. It's not just focusing on rereading comics, it's going to all the Marvel movies, it's watching Doctor Who, it's watching *Game of Thrones*, it's Harry Potter, etc. People find their tribes that way, but it doesn't seem to indicate that they're into any of it for the long haul.

That, he feels, is reflected in DC Comics not creating something for the long haul when it comes to the character of Superman; that the company was seemingly second-guessing itself repeatedly. Yet there are signs of hope.

MICHAEL BAILEY: When *The New 52* came along, he was edgier, he was a little younger, he was a little angrier and, over the 2000s, they kept stripping away from Superman the things that made him Superman. They started pulling the supporting cast away and then they started pulling away the trappings. During *The New 52*, he quit the *Daily Planet* and became a blogger with Cat Grant for five minutes. Then they got rid of the Clark Kent identity in *The New 52* altogether, and halved his powers, until the end of that storyline where all of his powers are restored. But it got to the point where they had done so much to him, that their solution at the end of that was to kill him, because they had broken the toys so many times, that all they were left with were a bunch of broken toys. When they came to *Rebirth*, they took him back to being married. They made him a father and they brought back all the trappings from before. And it seemed like people were responding to that, which is why I think it's fascinating that Bendis comes on, and over the course of his first year he slowly dismantles all of that. So it seems that all DC wants to do is just break this character down to an essence, but that's not what makes Superman, Superman.

That being said, I think 2023 has the potential to be a great year for Superman in the comics. I recently came back to the titles (I left back in 2019 when they revealed the identity) and both Phillip K. Johnson and Tom Taylor have been telling fantastic stories both with Clark and with Jon. I've only just become familiar with [Superman writer] Joshua Williamson through *Dark Crisis* and *Infinite Frontier*, but he has a great handle on how to tell epic stories and still keep things grounded. I've caught up on the last year-and-a-half of books, so I can't call this a reset, but between the creators involved and the fact that the secret identity has been reinstated, I think the future is looking pretty good.

MARK WAID: At DC, I do know from talking to the editors, the creators, the writers and so forth, that they realize that the handling of Superman's a problem and they're doubling down to try to shore him up and make it a flagship book again — you know, actually starring *Superman;* not starring his son, not starring other characters. I actually think the books were strong coming out of the gate in 2023. The people involved have some really good ideas to put things back on track.

CHAPTER XII
21ˢᵗ Century Supermen

The year 2002 saw the latest attempt to resurrect the Man of Steel on the big screen in the form of the J.J. Abrams-written Superman: Flyby. *After that, there would be Wolfgang Peterson's proposed* Batman vs. Superman *with a script by Andrew Kevin Walker. But instead, Warner Bros. would eventually turn its corporate eye towards X-Men director Bryan Singer, signing him in 2004 to develop and direct what would become* Superman Returns *two years later, a quasi-sequel to the first two Richard Donner films.*

It's a story that begins with Superman returning to Earth after being away for five years, having erroneously been led to believe that remnants of Krypton survived. He discovers that the world in general and Lois Lane in particular have moved on, and what his role is in the lives of both is at the core of Superman Returns. *It is also the most dramatic battle between the Man of Steel and Lex Luthor ever presented.*

BRYAN SINGER (director, *Superman Returns*): I've always been a fan of Superman and I've always had this particular idea to make a Superman film. I pitched it to Richard Donner and Lauren Shuler Donner in a hotel room in Austin, Texas three years earlier in 2003. This was something that has always interested me.

MICHAEL DAUGHERTY (writer, *Superman Returns*): What happened was, he got to read the J.J. Abrams script and Warner Bros. was kind of hinting, "Would you be interested in doing this?" I think it was somewhere in that weird transition where it went from McG to Brett Ratner and back to McG and I think Brett had just left the project. They were speaking to Bryan casually about it. He read the J.J. script and said that it had some really great moments, but if he were going to do a Superman film, he would want to do it in line with the Donner movie. It was just a "what if?" scenario and we tabled it; it didn't come up again for a year. But we had a very different take on the material and we weren't trying to do a remake.

DAN HARRIS (writer, *Superman Returns*): In a sense, all of that stuff coming before us made it a little bit easier for me and Mike to take the plunge. There were starts and stops over 15 years and obviously there was artistic trouble with the third and fourth movies; maybe some of the second movie. It had been kind of tattered and tainted for me, the idea of a new Superman movie, if it was even possible — *until* we talked to Bryan and the three of us started to hammer out a "what if?" scenario for a new concept. This new concept came from Bryan,

Brandon Routh, who portrayed the Last Son of Krypton in 2006's **Superman Returns**
(art © and courtesy D.C. Stuelpner; Superman © and TM DC Comics/Warner Bros. Discovery).

and it's the basic big idea, which is we don't want to remake *Superman: The Movie* because we love that film. It is the canon to us, it's the Bible to us, and we didn't want to make a sequel to that, because those people aren't around and to make a direct sequel to that movie would be a little odd. But there was a kind of third idea on the table, the idea of a return story. And the idea of since he's been gone from cinemas and from people's eyes for so long, let's take him out of Metropolis for a period of time too. Let's send him away somewhere and bring him back to a world that has changed and kind of moved on without him. All of a sudden, he's lost his place.

MICHAEL DOUGHERTY: There are only a handful of films that influenced me as a kid, that you kind of watched over and over again. As we headed into the days of HBO and home video rental, *Superman* was one of those movies. It's weird, because I have fuzzy memories of seeing certain movies in the theater with my dad, and that was one of them —that and *Star Wars*. I remember a clear moment in the credits for *Superman I* that said, "*Superman II* Coming Soon," and I remember that very specific moment when my dad said, "There's going to be another one." That was my introduction to the idea of a sequel and I was so excited by that.

DAN HARRIS: The idea was so exciting to us and so classic — something we hadn't seen before — that over three days in Hawaii we banged out what is 90% of the movie now, but at the time was a 25- or 30-page treatment we sent to Alan Horn and Jeff Robinov to get the job for Bryan. We all believed it would be great to make another Superman movie, but we didn't want to do an episodic thing where Superman fights the villain of the day and we didn't want to remake a movie that we thought was great. We were so pumped and jazzed about that, we didn't think about how daunting and giant the movie was. At the time you're onto an idea that works and it doesn't really matter all the baggage that's attached to it. I think when that was presented to the studios, they saw something that was really tasteful and classic and didn't step on their toes. There are a lot of Superman toes at Warner Bros. — didn't step on *Smallville*'s toes, didn't step on their rerelease toes of *Superman: The Movie* and old TV series. It allowed us to say that this was part of a continuing legacy and just a new chapter in the same character's life.

BRYAN SINGER: I've just always been a huge fan of the character, from the George Reeves television series to the Richard Donner film. I'm adopted, Superman's adopted. I'm an only child, he's an only child. In my practical life, I'm fairly awkward and Christopher Reeve crafted a very awkward Clark in his portrayal of that masquerade. Also, we've had a lot of cynical and angst-ridden superheroes that have emerged and I thought it was time for one that is imbued with a greater sense of virtue and goodness. It kind of affords audiences today — in a very cynical world — a light at the end of the tunnel. Yet for Superman in the movie, things aren't as clear-cut as they might have been when he first arrived on Earth.

People in their inner-thinking like to believe they have a moral compass; a sense of what's right and wrong, so they view things from that perspective. Now they're returning to Earth with Superman, seeing the world change with Superman and seeing a rather cynical dilemma unfold through the eyes of Superman and through the eyes, ultimately, of their own moral compass. I think it's okay, because although Superman has remained the same, the world has changed. Where X-Men are cynical superheroes, here we have a virtuous superhero in a cynical world.

BRANDON ROUTH (actor, "Clark Kent/Superman," *Superman Returns***):** I think what's interesting about this film, and the script, is when Clark returns from his journey, he's learned that things about the world have changed. He's not found what he went after by going to the remains of Krypton. And he feels alone. He's not even sure if he wants to use his powers. It's at that point that he really tries to connect with the world, with humanity, with *his* humanity. I mean he's an alien, but he's human. He lives here. He wants to be part of that world. He uses shovels, he uses human instruments/tools instead of doing things he could do easily on his own, to feel that connection with the world.

The whole movie's about his humanity. He's only alien because he came from a different planet. I don't know the science behind that, but he can still be pretty much be like us, except he has these other powers of course. But I think the love story is very relatable to everyone. You lose love. You get it back. It's the journey you take to get the person you love back. Giving up things. Finding the positives in the negatives. All of these are human things. I trust that's evident in the film, in my portrayal… that even though he exudes this confidence, that it doesn't seem too far away as a possibility for all humanity to be like Superman. I think we are able to obtain close to that level of clarity of mind. He's very clear in almost all his thoughts. That's why it's easy for him to do things. He doesn't worry over saving things. The one worry that he has is his love of Lois because it's something that he doesn't understand, and it's hard for him because that's a very strong emotion, and it's the first person — the *only* person — he's ever truly loved in that way.

Given the connection that Superman Returns *makes with the previous films from*

Richard Donner — which turned out to be quite strong in the end — the real question was how it would appeal to viewers who were not as immersed in those movies.

BRYAN SINGER: There's enough going on in it that you don't need to have seen the Donner film as a compendium, but Superman has to look and sound and feel as though he stepped out of your collective conscious of who the character is. In most people's conscious and subconscious, the character shines most brightly from the Richard Donner film. When I see a film I deem a classic, I know I have to make something new, I know I have to depart, but it doesn't make sense for me to depart all the way. It would be great to have Christopher Reeve, but we don't have that option. At the same time, Brandon, for all of the moments that he channels Christopher Reeve, is a very different character; a very different Superman.

MICHAEL DOUGHERTY: As much as I love Christopher Reeve, I hear the theme as Superman music, *not* Christopher Reeve music. To me, it evokes the character and not the actor. In our movie, when you do hear the music over our footage, it doesn't jar you in a bad way. If anything, it gives you the chills in a good way. I think that music has become as synonymous with the character of Superman as the red cape and blue tights.

BRYAN SINGER: I never understood filmmakers and executives who wanted to avoid previous versions. How do you avoid the past? I didn't create these characters. The only reason I changed the costumes so drastically in *X-Men* is because the ones from the comics would just look silly in a movie. But I never understood people who take other people's characters, often created before they were born, and sort of change them that drastically.

MICHAEL DOUGHERTY: The approach we took was just so different than everything else that had come before it, in that it didn't try to reboot the franchise. It wasn't a remake and it wasn't entirely a sequel. I believe a lot of the previous efforts were flat-out remakes. You know, "Let's restart with his origin. Let's show him on Krypton. Let's show him being raised by the Kents." There are millions of different reasons a movie doesn't get made, but I think the reason that ours resonated maybe a little bit more is that we really approached it from an emotional point of view. There's all the obvious Superman action that comes when you're telling a story about the Man of Steel — you have bullets bouncing off chests, you have him saving planes, you have him doing all of these fantastic feats — so the real challenge becomes, how do you challenge the character and take him to a place that you haven't seen him before? Bryan felt that any new

Superman film should pay respect to the Donner film by continuing the storyline that it started; treat the Donner film like it's the origin. The other thing was, what if he disappeared and came back to a world that was different? There was something so mythic about that idea and so relevant to our ideas of messiahs and saviors and gods, and we hadn't seen that done in a superhero film before. We've seen origins, we've seen Superman's origin done so well, but we haven't seen that. It just felt right. He actually pitched us those two ideas while we were doing post on *X-Men 2*, just as, "Wouldn't it be cool if you could do a movie that continued the Donner legacy?"

DAN HARRIS: We looked at it as though we're making a story about this character, and this character we recognize has been everywhere. He was married to Lois Lane in *Lois & Clark*. People don't forget that; you can't ignore these things. You have to understand that this guy has been killed and resurrected, and through heaven and hell and all of these things. Nothing's precious. At the same time, things *are* precious. There are certain base things about Superman you don't change. Krypton was destroyed. That is what Superman is about. This idea was so big and everyone was so excited about it, that when it was presented, a lot of people let out a sigh of relief, because we'd come in with a different idea that was simplifying it and taking away a lot of their fears. A lot of fights and stories that have come out of the last few incarnations — the starting and stopping of the movie — have come from uncertainty in what big story was being told. For us to not be able to do one of those big changes and something that worked and not have to rewrite somebody else, was a big deal to us; everybody was in agreement.

MICHAEL DOUGHERTY: Everyone has dealt with Superman in a different way. With Lois, you obviously have the romantic angle; with Ma Kent, it's the maternal factor; and with Lex, they're mortal enemies. They all view each other in different ways and have different experiences with him, so what the film is about is now that he has come back after a five-year absence, how does it change all of their lives? They've kind of gotten used to the idea of *not* having him around. They're all either happy or completely heartbroken about that. It's how he's dealing with the changes he's facing when he comes home, played off how the people in his life are reacting to him. What he comes to find is that while everyone in the world is glad that he's back, the one person he cares about the most, Lois Lane, could care less. And that completely throws him for a loop. It's like if any one of us went to the hometown we all grew up in, and that one high school sweetheart doesn't want to have anything to do with you. How crushing can that be?

If he came back and he found Lois with a fiancé, which he does, and it was just a fiance, it's kind of all bets are off. They're not married; if she falls in love with me again, so be it. But the kid is a complete roadblock. What he is essentially facing when he comes home is a family. He's also looking at what he could have had, had he stayed. Especially when Clark Kent is sitting at his desk and he's looking across the bullpen at the *Daily Planet*, he sees Lois, her fiancé Richard; and the kid, he looks at what could have been him if he hadn't taken off.

Portraying Superman is a lot more than just putting on a pair of tights and a cape. For the actor doing so, it represents an opportunity to become a permanent fixture in pop culture history and assume the responsibility of a legacy that has spanned so many years. It's a fact that Brandon Routh discovered as he became the first actor since the late Christopher Reeve to play the character on the big screen.

Born on October 9, 1979 in Des Moines, Iowa and raised in nearby Norwalk, Brandon was a high school athlete who swam and played soccer as well as starred in several theatrical productions. He attended the University of Iowa for a year before deciding that the time had come for him to head out to Hollywood.

BRANDON ROUTH: I've always been a performer; I'm actually from a family of performers. My dad's a drummer. My mom's a singer. They met in a Des Moines big band, jazz band back in the '70s. I was in choir, swing choir, band, jazz band, marching band, solos, all kinds of theater, musical theater in high school. But as a small-town kid from Iowa, I didn't think that was really an option to go out to Hollywood and be an actual actor, so I never really invested a lot of time thinking about it. It wasn't until I was going to the University of Iowa and one thing led to another that I found myself at a modeling agency called Avant at the time in Des Moines. They were putting a good sell on my parents and me and talked me into going to New York to this big thing to find representation as a model and an actor. I did that, had some success and found people who were interested in representing me. I had family outside of Los Angeles, in Downey; my great aunt and uncle, and stayed with them for six months. I ended up booking my second audition, just kind of because I looked like the guy that they needed to say a few words in this sitcom *Odd Man Out*. It was an ABC family show on Friday nights, and Markie Post was the mom. I said four words, but to be there on tape night and to hear the laughter from the audience, I was like, ""Whoa, whoa, whoa. This is it."

My favorite of all my performances back in high school was when we did a silly comedy called *Hide and Shriek*, and I played a not very smart guy wearing bib overalls and was just kind of being a doofus, and I loved it. Making the audience laugh then was great. So it was in that moment, the laughter of the audience, even if they weren't laughing at me, I was like, "This is it. I love it." That's when I knew that it was something that I could really do and that I wanted to do, so that was the true moment when I thought I could do it. But before then, it was just that doors opened. I guess I could have been afraid to walk through them, but I was too naïve, thankfully, and ignorant of all the challenges, so I just said, "Yes. Okay, let's do that. That sounds cool."

He was there for six months, but returned to Iowa to make some money when his aunt and uncle sold their house and he needed somewhere else to stay. After accumulating some savings, he moved back out and got a new roommate before he started auditioning. In the fall of 2000, he auditioned for the role of Clark Kent, the future Superman, on Smallville.

BRANDON ROUTH: I thought I had it, because my first manager, who I met in New York, said, "Has anybody ever told you that you look like Superman? I'm a big fan of Christopher Reeve, and if there's ever a TV show or a movie, we're definitely going to get you in on that audition." Then when *Smallville* came around, I figured, "This is it!" You couldn't write the story any better. So I did an audition, got a callback… and didn't get the job. Obviously. A few months later I auditioned for a soap opera, which is something early on I said I didn't want to do. But they flew me to New York, I did a screentest and didn't get that role. But they had me do another scene and basically ended up writing a character for me, and I was on the show. However, they wrote a character that was nothing like me. It was supposed to be this edgy kid from the wrong side of the tracks, and I was nothing close to that, nor did I have the acting ability to really do that. I did my best, but the point in telling you this story is that when I lived in New York, *everywhere* — bus stop benches, buses, Times Square — there were images of Tom Welling shirtless. It's like, "Curse you, Tom Welling!" Many years later I apologized to Tom for cursing him all those years ago. We actually had a lot of fun; we've been to a couple of conventions together.

Routh was fired a year into the job, which led him back to Los Angeles where he didn't work for a year, losing his agent and manager in the process. Bartending and working for an online warehouse followed. Then he was contacted by a former assistant of his previous agent, who was working at a new agency and asked if he wanted to come in for possible represen-tation. He ultimately agreed to and that led him to his current manager. He quickly booked three guest appearances on Oliver Beene, Cold Case *and* Will & Grace.

BRANDON ROUTH: At the same time, I went to a karaoke birthday party, and there was this woman there I was sitting across the table from, just staring.

She said, "I'm sorry, but you look like Clark Kent or Superman. Has anybody ever told you that?" I was like, "Yeah, I've heard that from time to time," and she said, "My boss is writing the new Superman movie." I asked if it was the one with Nic Cage and she said, "No, they're not doing that anymore. They're looking for a new, younger Superman." I did *not* know that. She said if I gave her my headshot, maybe she'd give it to her boss. The next week I drive over to ABC Studios in Burbank, go through the gate and then I go to the *Alias* office to give her my headshot, because her boss is J.J. Abrams and he was writing *Superman: Flyby*.

So I left thinking, "Who knows if anything's going to happen?" But that inspired me then to dress up as Clark Kent during the Halloween party at Lucky Strike, where I was working. A photo was taken by my friend and that picture was circulated widely once news started breaking about me as Superman, which is funny. The year ended and we go into pilot season, and there was a pilot audition for a CW show called *The Mountain*, being produced by McG, who at the time was going to direct the new Superman movie. I did the audition, got a callback, but McG was not there. I kept calling my manager to see if he'd heard anything, then one day I get a call from him as I'm driving and he says, "Pull over." I did and he says, "I have some bad news and I have some good news." I said, "Okay, give me the bad news first." He said, "The bad news is, it's not going to work out on the show. They need somebody more edgy. And the good news is Stephanie Savage, McG's producing partner, thinks you should meet with McG about Superman." Three weeks later I met him, talking for about 20 minutes, but not much about Superman, and I left.

The first meeting with McG was in March 2003. A second followed in June, as did a screentest. They had a month to inform him of their decision, but then news breaks that the project is once again falling apart and McG is no longer attached. Then came word that Bryan Singer — who had, genre-wise, scored with the first two X-Men films — was coming aboard as director. At the last minute prior to Singer flying to Australia for location scouting, they met.

BRANDON ROUTH: I went to the Coffee Bean on Sunset, which is no longer there, and sat down with Bryan for this two-hour conversation, in the middle of which Kevin Spacey's agent or manager called. Bryan's not talking to me, he's talking on the phone, but *about* me as I'm sitting in front of him. He says, "I don't know, this might be the guy. I'm meeting with him right now." Then at the end, he basically said, "I have to go to Australia. I'll be gone for a couple of weeks. Would you come in and read with Roger Mussenden, our casting director?" I said, "Of course I'll come in and read." So I went and read with him. Then Bryan was back in town and I went and read for all of them, and then shortly thereafter I was doing a screentest again in late August. There were a couple of other things taking place around then that were quirky and weird and it was like, "What is happening there?" Then I see there are pictures of me at the production office — they had me come in and took pictures of my face with my hair swept back. Little did I know until later that they'd made mockups of me in the suit. They put my face on their prototype suit, all over the production office.

Then I did the screentest. I think I was the only one that screentested. If somebody else did, it was only one other person. Then I had to wait another week for Alan Horn to sign off. I had to have a meeting with Alan the next week. Meanwhile, news started breaking that it might be me, and I was freaked out and I hid in my apartment because I didn't want to talk to anybody because I didn't have an answer. So I just laid low until I had the meeting with Alan. Then I think later that day or the next day, I got a call from business affairs or something that I had the job. In total it was a seven- or eight-month process. Say what you will about destiny and all of those things, paths that people are meant to be on or whatever, but it seems like I was being shown sign posts to maintain my sanity and continue on the path believing in myself. I was feeling naïvely or ignorantly confident because of these compounding events that were happening in my life that seemed to be supporting me toward this journey.

One of my most sacred places was sitting in the church pew at the Norwalk Methodist Church when I was between the ages of 8 and 13. It's a non-typical-looking church, but it had huge ceilings and skylights and was just filled with light and joy and love; just a wonderful place for me. I loved the ambience, I guess, of all of it. Anyway, I sat there thinking, "I don't know what I'm going to do with my life, but whatever it is, it feels big and I want to make a difference. I want to help people." It was just a feeling. I had never thought at that time it would be this or that it would be as an actor, but I *did* want to be a role model and all of these things kind of clicked into place and made sense as my journey went on. The thing is, I never thought, "This is never going to happen." It was always, "Oh no, this is a real possibility. All signs are pointing to yes."

BRYAN SINGER: Brandon Routh brought a vulnerability to the character that this particular story required. Lois Lane has moved on, she has a fiancé, she has a child. Superman hasn't been around for five years and he has to face this, and Brandon brings a kind of vulnerability. Whereas Christopher Reeve played the character with a greater sense of confidence and at times was flirtatious, this Superman finds himself more lost and ultimately more vulnerable as he tries to redefine his place in the world.

The big moment for Routh — as it has been for those who have preceded and followed him in the part — was when he first donned the character's iconic red and blue uniform and cape.

BRANDON ROUTH: The first time I was on set in the suit was *that* moment, not during the costume fittings and all that, but stepping on to the set with people who hadn't seen me at all in any iteration. That was profound, to see grown men and women with stars in their eyes and sometimes crying. Guests came to the set and watching them turn into their child selves was really awesome and powerful. I mean, the costume absolutely makes a huge difference as far as moving gracefully and feeling powerful.

KATE BOSWORTH (actor, "Lois Lane," *Superman Returns*): The first time I saw Brandon in his Superman suit was the first pictures that we had taken of him in the suit. It was outside at Fox Studios on the lawn area. I remember it was a *very* big deal. It was like you would imagine it to be this sting operation or something. No photos had been released of him in the suit. So he had the suit on, but he had this black cape on over it. And he was sort of walking around. [laughs] And it was like the unveiling of the Mona Lisa or something. It was just amazing. And Bryan had called me down and said, "We want to take a shot of you. This will be the first time we take a picture and show the suit." I ran down and they took it off for a really quick second and I went "Oh, wow!" I felt so overwhelmed. It's amazing when you see such an important character for the first time in the flesh. It's an amazing feeling. You get chills. So we quickly took a picture and then the back cape was on immediately after.

LOUISE MIGENBACH (costume designer, *Superman Returns*): I must have had a hundred fittings with Brandon, even through production. Brandon's body was changing, of course, because he was continuing to work out and was on a specific diet. But Superman has such a legacy and history and is so ingrained in Americana that I think Bryan wanted to respect the story, which he clearly did, and the costume as well. He wanted it to look old school. The first day I went in to say hi to him and he said, "Hi, nice to see you. I don't want a big 'S', I want old school, I want the real thing, I want who Superman is. See you later, Louise." He very much knew from the beginning that he didn't want to depart from who Superman is. He wanted it updated, he wanted the "S" smaller, because Christopher Reeve's "S" was practically wrapping around his underarm. I think that everyone felt that looked dated and Bryan wanted the "S" to go back to the "S" in the '30s and '40s, which was much smaller. We changed the red and made it more burgundy, we changed the yellow and made it more gold.

BRANDON ROUTH: I was okay with everything; certainly at the time, I was all gung-ho. In retrospect, the one thing I would've changed was to make the "S" a little bit bigger. For me, the briefs were fine with me. I think Superman should have shorts of some sort; I don't like the non-shorts look, so I was fine with those.

LOUISE MIGENBACH: The cape was burgundy purely as an aesthetic decision on Bryan and my part. When you look at that primary red and primary yellow and primary blue all next to each other, it looks incredibly unsophisticated now, to me. It's very children's play toy. We fooled with the colors where it's still a red, but it's a moodier red. For filming it, it was more beautiful. You could create shadow with it, it could turn to black in certain lights. There was much more mystery to the red than bright red. And the blue… what we did was decide what color was going to be the really vibrant color. We wanted those colors to sing together better than they had in the past. We wanted the blue to be dominant and the other colors to support it.

BRANDON ROUTH: Actually, the biggest thing about the suit was the damage it was doing to my body because of the muscle suit underneath. The way it was constructed, it was earlier technology. I was one of the first people wearing that type of suit and it was incredibly restrictive. Even if it's not a muscle suit, it's there to build definition, because you can't flex all day, but at the same time you have to look good, so they all have something underneath. In any case, there are these little pads that were like a foam and the lycra didn't slide over the foam; it would catch. So every time I'd lift my arms, it was like a rubber band and I was fighting all of the weight of the stretches. I *still* have some back and shoulder challenges from that. The hours wouldn't have been troubling, the workouts were not troubling, all of the press would not have been as challenging for me if I had just been able to get in and out of the Superman suit more easily.

LOUISE MIGENBACH: The suit was a type of a spandex called a milliskin, a new product with an incredible amount of stretch and a flatness to it. When you say spandex, people think of Disco '70s, but it's come a long way since then. The stuff that Nike uses and Adidas uses for the swimsuits for the Olympics was fundamentally what we used. It's a highly developed and refined spandex. The cape was made of rubber, but the underside was rubber that laid in to a wool that we had milled in France on these looms that were a hundred years old, because nobody makes wool that wide anymore. It took six months just to get the wool lining manufactured. Why wool? We chose it because we had a wind test. We had all sorts of tests with Brandon and before Brandon was cast. We had a stand-in model and stand-in Superman just so we could develop the costume while they were trying to pick Superman. We did these wind tests where we did different strengths of wind to see how the cape would react. What we discovered was that the most beautiful cape, for Superman in his glory just standing there and with slight movement, with a nice swish behind him as he turned, was to back the rubber with wool.

What we discovered was that the wool was too heavy for flying. Those capes were best for when he was standing or fighting with Lex Luthor or when he's planted on the ground. The wool cape was most beautiful because it had a heaviness and integrity to it. What we were trying to desperately avoid was the '70s Superman where it kind of looked like a limp towel down his back; it had no body. So that's what the wool cape gave us, a body and a movement. We started doing a whole other set of experiments in Australia and made a couple of lightweight capes with a silk and we used polyester on some. So there was wool, a medium-weight silk and a very light polyester to give it different flutters. At supersonic speed, we used the polyester light cape because it gave us the fre quency of flutter that would simulate, we felt, high-speed flying. Then we need-ed a cape for softer flying. For takeoffs and landings, when we really got into the wire work, we had these three capes, and it was kind of on a case-by-case basis what cape would be necessary for what shot.

Despite popular belief, Superman's greatest weakness is not Kryptonite. It is, instead, Daily Planet reporter Lois Lane, the only woman to have completely captured his heart. It is for this reason that the casting of the character is of equal importance to the casting of Superman, for without that core relationship, any story involving the Man of Steel is devoid of its emotional center.

Singer filled that emotional center by casting actress Kate Bosworth, who has very quickly molded the character into her own while retaining key elements of past portrayals. Born on January 2, 1983, Bosworth achieved her first role at the age of 14 in the 1998 film The Horse Whisperer. *This was followed in 2000 by her being cast in* Remember the Titans. *In 2001 she moved to Los Angeles in the hope that it would result in better parts — a theory that worked. She was cast as one of the leads in 2001's* Blue Crush, *which was followed by 2002's* The Rules of Attraction, *2003's* Wonderland, *2004's* Win a Date with Tad Hamilton, Beyond the Sea *(which saw her acting with*

Kevin Spacey who, of course, plays Lex Luthor in Superman Returns*), and 2005's* Bee Season.

KATE BOSWORTH: It was very close to Christmas when I auditioned for the role, it was probably around December 15, and I was going to Brazil for Christmas and the New Year, and I was literally in the car on the way to the airport. I got a call and it was my manager. She knew I was going to Brazil and she knew my flight was in another hour, and she said, "Kate." And I just knew from the tone of her voice. I just knew. I just gasped and said, "Yes." And she said, "You're going to be Lois Lane." And I just screamed! [laughs] Probably freaked out the person who was driving me. And it was just amazing. I remember it was just overwhelming. Every emotion was running through my body, and it was just otherworldly. And I just thought, "Oh my God, I'm going to be Lois Lane!" And then immediately I went to, "Oh my God, I'm going to be Lois Lane." It was all these different ranges of emotion flying through in utter seconds. It was incredible. Definitely one I'll never forget.

I'd say having previously worked with Kevin Spacey was a huge part of my being cast. I'd done *Beyond the Sea* with Kevin, and Bryan came to see the film, and I guess he said to Kevin, "I'm trying to cast Lois Lane." And Kevin said, "Well you should come and take a look at this girl, you should come and take a look at the film." So I feel that a huge part of why I'm sitting here talking to you is because of Kevin. Bryan went and saw *Beyond the Sea* a few times, and then I auditioned for the role with Brandon. We did a screentest which was fantastic. We did a scene where he plays Clark Kent and then a scene where he was Superman. It was so amazing because I was very curious as well to see how he was. You know, because everyone says, "How's Superman? How's Brandon Routh?" And he was just so amazing. I remember standing in a white room, a white audition room, with just a little tripod camera. We first did the scene with Clark Kent and he was fantastic, perfectly clumsy and fumbling, and then we went to the Superman scene and his whole demeanor just changed. But it wasn't this huge, grand Superman stature. He just shifted his balance and stood up a bit straighter and held himself more confidently. I just remember getting totally lost in the scene with him, and I remember leaving the room and saying, "No matter what happens, it was a real pleasure to have had this moment with you." — because it *was* fantastic.

BRYAN SINGER: Kate Bosworth made a concerted effort *not* to watch the original film so she wouldn't be affected by Margot Kidder's performance. She is very young and had to play a mother, but I like the fact that she's young because I think she's a very young spirit, and Kate is really an actor mature far beyond her years. So I got the best of both worlds. I got her youthful impetuousness, which is classic Lois Lane, and at the same time a motherly sense, a protective sense regarding her child, who plays a significant role in the picture.

KATE BOSWORTH: Obviously I, Kate, don't have child, but I would imagine that your world completely changes in terms of having a child of your own come into the world and suddenly everything's not just about you. It's all about your child because that is, I think, the main difference in terms of Lois Lane. She's not as crazy and zany and all over the place, because she's had to focus her attention on this little being and grow up. And that's not just in terms of age; it's in terms of herself and how she carries herself, and maturity. I mean, she's still got that fire and spunk and craziness, but she does have a child to think of first and foremost.

BRYAN SINGER: There is very little with the exception of Kryptonite that Superman can't defeat. This dilemma is undefeatable. You can't turn back the clock for five years and erase a child. You may be able to woo her away from her fiancé, but it's a little more complicated than that. And it was the greatest obstacle I could come up with for Superman. Honestly, I was trying to come up with all kinds of obstacles and I thought, "What would be something that he cannot overcome?" Even in the original Superman, Lois Lane died and he overcame that by turning back time. Here, this child has been around for nearly five years and there's nothing he can do about it.

I think the world moves on either way, and the saddest part is that people tend to forget. In the case of any celebrity when they return, they're easy to accept, but it's not as easy for Lois Lane to accept him. Its really a story about what happens when old boyfriends come back into your life. That's at the very center of the story.

While it would seem that playing Superman's nemesis Lex Luthor in a $200-million production of Superman Returns *would be incentive enough for any actor, for Kevin Spacey there was more appeal in reuniting with director Bryan Singer — understandable considering that he won the Academy Award for Best Supporting Actor for Singer's* The Usual Suspects *(1995).*

Born on July 26, 1959, he attended New York's Julliard School, studying drama between 1979 and 1981. His first professional appearance on stage was as a messenger in a 1991 New York Shakespeare Festival performance of Henry VI, Part 1. *A year later he was on Broadway in Henrik Ibsen's* Ghosts. *Television beckoned next with the actor making a number of guest appearances, though his greatest claim to fame on the small screen was undoubtedly as Mel Profitt, a fairly insane arms and drugs dealer in the cult TV series* Wiseguy. *The big screen was next and such films as 1992's* Glengarry Glen Ross, *1995's* Se7en, *1997's* L.A. Confidential, *1999's* American Beauty *(for which he won the Best Actor Academy Award), 2000's* Pay It Forward, *2003's* The Life of David Gale *and 2005's* Beyond the Sea, *the Bobby Darin biopic he co-wrote and directed as well.*

When asked by Wizard *magazine about the adversarial relationship between villain and hero, Spacey noted, "For Lex and Superman, I think it's always been — from the comics to the films — about mind over muscle. That's what we have in this film — with some twists."*

BRYAN SINGER: When we were crafting the script, Kevin Spacey was very much in the forefront of our minds because I have a relationship with him and there are very few actors who can play that fine line between comedy and sinister, and he can do that better than anyone. Those are the primary aspects he brings to the character. You like watching him talk. In these movies where villains tend to be verbose, especially Lex Luthor who's always patting himself on the back for his own ingenuity, you want an actor that you just savor everything that comes out of his mouth, and Kevin is that kind of actor. For me, we hadn't worked together in 10 years, but it felt like it was yesterday. This Lex is much his own interpretation. There are moments where he's a bit funny and moments when he's very mean, very sadistic.

KEVIN SPACEY (actor, "Lex Luthor," *Superman Returns***):** When you have a relationship like Bryan and I have, the way we work together and the fact that we've been looking for something to do together for the past 10 years, I do what I did last time and just put myself in his hands. He guides me.

DAN HARRIS: They're both complicated this time around. They both have history. We're acknowledging that time has passed and people have moved on and things have happened in people's lives. With Lois, she's got a fiancé and a child with that man, and Superman comes back to that relationship. And the fiancé is a good guy. He's not a jerk or an asshole or somebody who can be taken away and Superman becomes the hero. If Superman comes back to the woman he loves and breaks up a relationship, that's a very bad thing. So that makes that relationship complicated, and more complicated by the kid. He would never step foot over that boundary, and yet that is a bit of what the movie is about. There are big things within those ideas, and I guess his relationship with Lex Luthor is the same. Lex has been in prison for the five years that Superman has been gone and it's changed him quite a bit. Lex is still witty and funny and can be fun at times, but Lex to me in this movie is a sadist. He's gotten very, very angry in prison and he's out for blood this time around. I think we see a whole other darker side of Lex Luthor this time around. I love Kevin in *Swimming with Sharks,* but Lex is scarier. That guy blows up all the time, but Lex saves it for when he needs it and he's very scary when he does. One thing I'm certain of is that people's fears of a campy Lex Luthor coming back would be totally gone. He's a scary motherf------!

KEVIN SPACEY: Bryan knows what the fan base really wants, but he also brings a new direction to the character and how people deal with each other. This film is a much darker Lex Luthor than the Gene Hackman character. This is a bitter Lex. This is a Lex after a long time in prison. But there's also still a lot of humor to it. Lex's argument is Superman is god-like so he saves people, but he doesn't give people what they need to save themselves. I think Lex has a slightly more capitalistic view, which is, give people what they want and Lex wants his share of it. And for him it's always been about land. All the movies and the character is about him wanting land. There's a lot of that. He doesn't just want to destroy Superman. That's too simple. That's something he knows he has to take care of and has spent a lot of years in prison coming up with exactly how to do it. But his bigger plan is to be the world's greatest real estate mogul.

MICHAEL DOUGHERTY: Lex is much more a sadist. We definitely wanted Lex to have a sense of humor; not as over the top as they did in Dick Donner's movie. Gene Hackman's performance was brilliant and I love Ned Beatty, and there are certain traces of that in him and in his relationship with the people around him, but we wanted to paint him much darker and much more angry for having been locked up in prison for five years. The way I view Lex is that he's mortal enemies with Superman, but in a lot of ways he almost just views Superman as a nuisance. He's like a land developer who's got these massive plans for something amazing he's working on, and this dog just keeps getting in the way and interfering with him. It's not like he's always out to get Superman and his only goal in life is to get Superman, but he has a bigger goal than that and Superman just keeps getting in the way. In a sick, perverse way he's not so much anti-Superman as he is pro-human. In a weird way he's xenophobic in that sense. He has such admiration and respect for real human beings — the Alexander the Greats, the Caesars — these men who built themselves up, and this alien drops to our planet and is just granted these superpowers and abilities, I think he almost views that as cheating in a way… and as a greater threat to mankind. Something we deal with is that when you have someone like that around, a savior who is constantly rescuing you and other people from certain scenarios, are you becoming dependent on them? Has the human race forgotten how to survive on its own? That's a viewpoint that Lex takes, that this false god is flying around claiming to be the end-all, be-all, when human beings really need to survive on their own. It's not just, "I'm bad, here's my evil plan." You sense a longer and deeper resentment underneath all of that.

DAN HARRIS: It's pretty classic in a slow build with a hero and a villain and how they face off at one crucial point. There is a final moment between the two of them that is a shocker and a chilling moment. For us, who wrote it and watched it be performed, and to see it, *is* powerful. It's certainly *not* putting a Kryptonite necklace around his neck.

BRYAN SINGER: There is a villain, the villain has a plan, he's taking precautions against Superman, there are those physical obstacles that Lex Luthor unleashes. There is that mind over muscle that Lex Luthor is so clever at employing, but you know that Superman is going to find a way. *This* is something that you don't really know how he's going to deal with. This becomes the genuine obstacle of the movie. There is heroism and things to overcome, but this is at the core of Superman's ultimate dilemma. The moments that you love, the ones that pump you up the most from any of your favorite action/adventure films, are generally character-motivated. The reason we love *Star Wars* so much is because there are five emotional epiphanies that occur in the span of five seconds at the end of that movie. The villain is thwarted off for a sequel, the Empire's weapon is destroyed, the rebellion is saved, Luke uses the Force and Han Solo conquers his greed. And even though it happens with a torpedo blast and an explosion, those are the things that make you go "Yeah!" and jump out of your seat, and it's not necessarily because something big has exploded.

Obviously, a lot in moviemaking had changed between 1978's Superman: The Movie *and 2006's* Superman Returns, *not the least of which was in terms of visual effects and, more specifically, giving Superman the ability to fly.*

R.A. RONDELL (stunt coordinator, *Superman Returns*): Visual effects help us do things we cannot do, and the audience believes that it's really the actors by putting the actors in difficult situations. When it's somebody else flying through the air, or say it's a reaction shot of somebody getting hit, thrown, tossed or falling, it's a little bit easier to do because it's a little more organic in how he falls and is more acceptable. But when he is supposed to fly like a plane or a missile, in that perfect form, it becomes quite a bit more difficult to do — not only in his body postures, but how his face reacts, his hair and of course the cape.

The entrances and exits we did real time, because that's our bread and butter. It's very hard for that to be CG or synthetic. Those are the moments that the audience will see him land or take off, and once he gets into the air, they believe you a little more and you can shift over to CG. Flying Superman is something that everybody has had to deal with, but the bar raises every year. With the era of Spider-Man and everything else, the audience has become very sophisticated, so it's a real challenge. And you get all of those geeks who are out there picking apart everything that you do, which is what keeps us honest. They're very hard to fool.

MARK STETSON (visual effects supervisor, *Superman Returns*): There's a lot of going back and forth between green screen, wire work and CG. Even the wire work alone has advanced a lot since those days. They did some very aggressive and adventurous stunts when they were making that movie, and some of those stunts would not be attempted nowadays for safety reasons. Some of the real aggressive flying outside exteriors with Christopher Reeve on wires, we just wouldn't do today, because we can do it more safely and can composite the results with the background and actually make it better. And with the CG Superman, a lot of time is spent finding a better camera angle and finding the emotion in the performance of a digital character. It's kind of cool we can do that.

BRANDON ROUTH: Flying is quite an experience. It's painful sometimes, long and arduous many times, and there is fun in it — sometimes. The fun stuff is when I'm actually interacting, lifting something or saving something, because then I've actually got my hands on something and I can see without having to visualize so much. Of course I still have to visualize the rest of the object because we can only use so much of a piece of a set before they CG the rest of it.

KATE BOSWORTH: Being able to fly with Superman… although we're on wires, I just sat there with Brandon across from me in this flowing cape and the "S" symbol and think, "I'm flying with Superman!" I mean, people get to say that?

BRANDON ROUTH: It's gone through many modifications, from flying in a body pan to the X-Y-Z rig, as they call it, to standing on a box, to being on a machine that spins you around, to wire work where I'm actually moving and flying vertical. *That's* the most fun stuff because I'm actually doing something and there's that exhilaration of when you reach the top and that sense of weightlessness that accompanies it. I was really psyched because it was nice to be moving, to not be standing still. To be *flying*.

A genuine highlight of Superman Returns *for the audience, and as it turns out, for Routh himself, was the character's first public appearance in the film, saving a planeload of passengers from what seems like a doomed flight.*

BRANDON ROUTH: When I saw the finished sequence, I thought it was magnificent. That holds up above anything else in the movie. It's a gripping, triumphant Superman moment. I think the issue was for a long time with the edit of the movie was how to get to that faster? How do we get to Superman's first appearance faster? It was an amazing cinematic moment and a real breakthrough. I'd never seen a Superman moment like that before. But the filming of it was the bane of my existence for a good three months.

The actor's filming schedule had been pretty intense through the months of March, April and May, but upon looking at the production schedule, he saw that his name was not on the board for June and July. For the briefest of moments, he fantasized about having the opportunity to really enjoy his time in Australia — until it was brought to his attention that he had been looking at the main production schedule, not *the second unit's work. As it turned out, his name was plastered all over that two-month period.*

BRANDON ROUTH: So began two months of me getting in and out of the suit three or four times a day; getting into various harnesses, depending on the rig that was set up. And that was just physically and emotionally the most taxing aspect of the shoot for me. I know that sounds odd, but it's not really, because the way the suit fit and the way it was made, it was very challenging to get in and out of that many times a day after I've already been hanging around on wires. So day after day, week after week, after working out every morning, that was challenging to say the least — but also amazing because of all of the flying. There were definitely highlights in those moments. The coolest part for me was flying down onto the wing; that was great because it kind of felt like I was really doing some of that stuff. I certainly owe a lot to Mike Massa, my stunt double, who did so much of the legwork of working with the stunt team and rigging team to see what was going to look good before I got in there. That meant they weren't testing things on me. It was all worth it.

Superman Returns, *some 15 years in the making if you were to include all aborted attempts at a relaunch of the franchise, was released on June 30, 2006 and had a global gross of nearly $392-million which, when compared with the $15-million gross of* Superman IV: The Quest for Peace, *is pretty impressive. However, what hurt the film was its budget of*

636

$270-million (including tens of millions of costs spent on those previous attempts).

BRAD RICCA (author, *Super Boys: The Amazing Adventures of Jerry Siegel and Joe Shuster — The Creators of Superman*): I liked *Superman Returns.* I liked that they weren't afraid to make changes to it. Making him a dad was really cool. Some of it was just insane, but I thought that was new.

ROB O'CONNOR (co-host, *All Star Superfan* podcast): It feels like every fan goes on a journey with this film — for me the hype is my most treasured memory surrounding *Superman Returns*: the feverish anticipation, the constant clickety clack of speculation on Superman Homepage message boards and the hunt for Mattel's action figures. When the film came out, I think I quietly convinced myself that it was brilliant and became one of its ardent defenders as it faced some very deserved criticism.

JOHN KENNETH MUIR (film historian; author, *Science Fiction and Fantasy Films of the 1970s*): Although it lacks the lyrical romanticism and visualizations of *Superman: The Movie* and *Superman II, Superman Returns* is nonetheless a cinematic restoration of dignity for the beloved superhero. The film also develops the religious symbolism of the Superman mythos about as far as it can be taken without becoming The Church of Superman. Superman (Brandon Routh, this time) is referred to throughout the film as a "savior" and Lois Lane has won a Pulitzer Prize for an article "*Why the World Doesn't Need Superman.*" It could have been titled "*Why the World Doesn't Need Christ.*" And then, of course, Superman is stabbed in the side by Lex Luthor (Kevin Spacey), reflecting the Gospel of John, which reports how a Roman soldier stabbed Jesus Christ in his side. More immediately obvious as a Christ parallel is Superman's tell-tale pose after saving the world from the emerging Kryptonian continent. He hovers in space, his arms outstretched horizontally, as if pinned to a cross.

ELLIOT S! MAGGIN (author, *Last Son of Krypton* and *Miracle Monday*): I liked *Superman Returns.* They did two things really deftly: (1) they dealt effectively with Superman's absence the day the World Trade Center fell, much better than we ever did justifying his apparent absence during World War II, and (2) the disposition of the relationship with Lois was, I thought, just perfect and appropriately bittersweet.

ROB O'CONNOR: Reflecting on it now, the film is a mess of unfinished ideas and half-baked attempts to tie into what Donner created, but with none of the charm or the all-important verisimilitude. Both Lois Lane and Superman himself are rendered accidentally unlikable by the film's misguided script — a Superman film should never have you wishing for the Man of Steel to break up a happy family. Kate Bosworth was far too young to be playing a Pulitzer Prize-winning mother of one, and to be honest, while Brandon Routh does his best Christopher Reeve impression, he was far too young to carry the weight of what was supposed to be a seasoned Man of Steel. Ironically, the little boy playing Superman's son is as cold and expressionless as Damien from Donners other classic *The Omen*.

JOHN KENNETH MUIR: The film is overlong and perhaps too rooted in nostalgia for the Reeve Era, but it is also a welcome return to form, especially for longtime fans. This film takes Superman seriously, continues the religious leitmotif of the better Reeve films, and seems like a solid platform for a new series of movies that… didn't happen.

ROB O'CONNOR: I'm not even a fan of Singer's retro World's Fair production design or his eternally-twilight skyscapes. Metropolis is supposed to be the world of tomorrow — a place of impossible industry, of beaming blue skies, sunshine and excitement, not contemplative sunsets and melancholy starlight.

PAUL LEVITZ: After a while you get used to the fact that it's your job to try to do what you can to make these things successful, and because it's a job that involves something that you love, there are moments that are magic. *And* there are moments that suck. When Bryan Singer was shooting *Superman Returns*, he decided that the week he wanted me out for the shooting — not particularly because he wanted my advice, but because he had to do the courtesy of having DC at least show up for the shooting — was a specific week in April, May or June, whatever it was. And my daughter was coming home from her term abroad in England that Monday; I hadn't seen her for six months. *And* there was an annual meeting of Time Warner that Friday that was going to unveil the new DC logo. So I flew to Australia to only be there for 36 hours. I was a senior executive, so I won't claim this as torture. It's *not* how I recommend doing a trip to Australia. And it was a rough day of shooting for Bryan, so I think it was close to midnight by the time he surfaced for 15 minutes of joining me and the producers. On the other hand, it was the day that he was shooting the scene with Jack Larson, so I got to see Jack again, who I'd become friendly with. And I got to see him in performance, so to my inner 10-year-old who grew up watching Jack going, "Jeepers, Mr. Kent," that was special.

ROB O'CONNOR: The film is interesting as a standalone curio, but the fact that it was ever supposed to spin off into a franchise is baffling. Where would they have gone? Nearly every fanboy speculation invariably ended up with either Jason or Richard White (harmless innocents in this film) descending into scum and villainy so that Lois could fall back into Superman's arms and the status quo could be restored as morbidly as possible. It remains a huge missed opportunity and the worst thing about it is that it unwittingly convinced Holly-wood executives that a film about the traditional character of Superman would never work, when in fact there's never been anything wrong with the character, people just insist on making mediocre films about him.

For a number of years there was talk of a more action-oriented follow-up, but those became moot when Warner Bros. announced that Zack Snyder would be directing Henry Cavill in a 2013 production that would be known as Man of Steel.

BRANDON ROUTH: The lack of knowing what was going on for so long was definitely a challenge, because I felt the need to uphold an image. No one asked me to uphold one, but that's how much I cared about the character. I felt certain things might be off-limits, certain roles… at least for the first couple of years when I thought we'd be coming back. As it got further away, that be-came less and less of an issue.

BRYAN SINGER: I think that *Superman Returns* was a bit nostalgic and romantic, and I don't think that was what people were expecting, especially in the summer. What I had noticed is that there weren't a lot of women lining up to see a comic book movie, but they *were* lining up to see *The Devil Wears Prada*, which may have been something I wanted to address. When I was in the middle of making it, there wasn't always a clarity of thought about that sort of thing — instead you're thinking, "Wow, I want to make a romantic movie that harkens back to the Richard Donner movie that I love so much." And that's what I did.

Quentin Tarantino and I had a big conversation about it. He has a fascination with this film, but the Lois Lane part of it has always been a stickler with him. This is me extrapolating, but the relationship in the Donner film was so black and white and here it was complex. Then there was the child. Again, I really do think I was making it for that *Devil Wears Prada* audience of women who wouldn't normally come to a superhero film.

BRANDON ROUTH: I really like the movie, though I agree that Su-perman should have thrown a few more punches. I also would have preferred more practical effects than CG, but I had no influence on that. Those are small, personal things. But I think it was a very nice movie; it may not have been the Superman movie everyone wanted and I completely understand that — it's hard to please everybody — but I'm very proud of it still… and proud of Bryan and everyone who worked so hard to make it.

I think its greatest strengths is transitioning audiences from Chris to a new Superman. It was an unenviable task in some regards for both filmmaker and actor to do that, because the most beloved Superman ever is Christopher Reeve. *That's* Superman. So how do you do that without alienating audiences? If you go fully the other way, are people going to like that or are they going to be like, "You're just totally being disrespectful to what's come before you?" I think honoring Chris, Richard Donner, John Williams, Margot Kidder — everybody — in energy and tonally, is the strength. Given an opportunity to do the second film, we would've further delineated ourselves and made distinctions from what had become before, once we'd established, "Okay, this is the new thing. It's not too much different from the old thing, but it's something you can be okay with," and then we could move on from that a little bit.

BRYAN SINGER: The biggest differences I could see in making the movie now would be to have tightened up the first act and maybe open with the exciting plane rescue sequence that occurs later on. And maybe there *was* too much my being a fan of Donner's take. But what's interesting is that people know I'm a big Trekkie and they're always saying, "Why don't you do a *Star Trek*?" and I say, "I think I'm too big a fan of *Star Trek*. You'd feel like you were watching *Wrath of Khan* again." With Superman, I guess it was a similar thing. On the X-Men films, I tried to shed all the comic-ness and tried to make it real. Here, though, I embraced the comic-ness and made this alternate, bucolic Metropolis. But I *am* very much in love with the Donner picture. For me, the journey was exciting because I got the chance to reprise those images and explore it. When you're fascinated by something and you love it, part of making the movie is trying to please everyone and make a successful movie, but part of it is an experimental kind of thing.

BRANDON ROUTH: I think the weaknesses of the film would be that the relationship between Lois and Superman could have been handled in a different way so that people who have complaints about Superman being a stalker or breaking up a relationship or all those things, could have eased those tensions and concerns. I think there certainly could have been more fighting and more action, which would have helped. And I think I would have liked to have seen Superman have more charming moments. The only opportunity that I really got to do that was with Kitty Kowalski, which is one of my favorite scenes in the movie, working with Parker Posey. In that moment he gets to be a charming, happy Superman instead of sad, trying to get Lois back Superman, which is what's going on for a lot of the film other than when he's Clark. The Clark and Jimmy moments are great; it could've always used more of that. More Sam Huntington, always!

Following Superman Returns, *Routh has appeared in 18 films, from 2008's* Fling and Zack and Miri Make a Porno *to 2020's* Anastasia: Once Upon a Time. *On television, he had recurring roles on* Chuck, Chosen *and* The Rookie, *while being in the main cast of* Partners *and DC's* Legends of Tomorrow, *portraying Ray Palmer/ The Atom on that show as well as 21 episodes of* Arrow *(where he originated the role) and five episodes of* The Flash.

Although there never was a sequel to Superman Returns, *Routh actually did get a sense of closure when he reprised the role of Superman on the* Crisis on Infinite Earths *crossover event that aired on the CW, that actually saw him encounter Tyler Hoechlin's Man of Steel from the* Supergirl *and* Superman & Lois *television series. For his part, Routh's appearance was met with excitement and acclaim from both critics and fans... and tremendous personal joy as well.*

MARC GUGGENHEIM (creative consultant, *DC's Legends of Tomorrow*): Brandon was still working on *Legends of Tomorrow* when we were doing *Crisis on Infinite Earths*, so it wasn't a question of getting Brandon back so much as it was a question of getting Brandon back in the Superman suit. I would say Brandon was very deliberate in making the decision to say yes, which I absolutely respect. An additional factor was the fact that we couldn't use the original *Superman Returns* outfit for a variety of reasons, so I pitched to Brandon using the *Kingdom Come* outfit and making that a part of his story. Again, Brandon was very deliberate in his decision-making and we spent a lot of time talking out the story and the pros and cons. For me, the best part was Brandon recreating the "Christopher Reeve Flyby" at the end of *Crisis*. It's the single moment in the whole thing that brings the biggest smile to my face. I pitched Brandon the idea because he already had to do green screen work for the Superman-on-Superman fight, and was already rigged up there. Also, having the two Supermen fight was, quite frankly, a no-brainer for us. You have two Supermen on screen, they've got to take punches at each other — it's a comic book rule; at least that was *my* thinking. Brandon and I talked a lot about the Superman fighting himself sequence in *Superman III*.

BRANDON ROUTH: The whole experience was life-changing for me. I was often asked in years leading up to that if I ever thought I'd be Superman again or was there a chance, or would they use me somewhere in the Arrowverse as Superman. But after Tyler, who's done an amazing job, was cast, that pretty much sealed that. So that's not going to happen. For positivity, I don't totally shut the door, but I really didn't think it was in the realm of possibility. When Marc Guggenheim called me and said, "Hey, I'd like to have you be a big part of *Crisis*, and would you be interested in wearing a different colored suit as well?" I was like, "Hold on, wait. What are you asking?" I was always very honored that he would ask, that DC would sign off and Warner Bros. signed off, that everybody was okay with me returning, and that was incredibly validating. That was the beginning of — I'm using the term closing the book; the book is still open, but at least the monkey was off my back, because I did it.

The reprisal was also gratifying due to the fact that Superman Returns *did not get a sequel, and was, he feels, unnecessarily dumped on in an effort to pave the way for a new story.*

BRANDON ROUTH: I don't like that then makes fans who are true fans of the movie feel weird for liking it. By and large it was well-reviewed and made almost $400-million in box office. It was a good movie, it did well, just not as well as they would have liked. There were many other reasons why there was no sequel. To have the opportunity to come back was incredibly validating to me, and then to hear the fan response — I'm just *so* grateful for everyone who was supportive. It really did mean a lot to me. They always were a part of the journey, but they became an even bigger part of the journey of Superman in that moment for me.

All of this has obviously had a massive impact on my life and continues to. Once you play Superman on the level that I did, it's with me the rest of my life. I am effectively carrying the light of Superman in a way, because for some people I will forever be their *first* Superman. I will be the Superman that got them into comics. *Or* I will be the Superman that they don't like. *Or* all of the above. Of course I've done other things, but by and large, most of the time it's Superman and Clark that people respond to. And it's great. Even showing up at the grocery store or unexpectedly somewhere, people are like, "Oh, hey, it's Superman!" And it puts a smile on people's faces. Even that simple thing is great and I absolutely embrace that. As I've gotten older and better able to deal with the attention, I've embraced it more, which is cool.

My journey and my deep dive into what it would be like to be the most powerful being on Earth, has impacted my life in positive ways. I learn from thinking about Superman, from answering questions like these to all kinds of things about the possibilities of humanity. That is something that is eternally interesting to me:

how we can can become better versions of ourselves all the time.

Although the idea of a sequel to Superman Returns *was eventually dropped, it didn't mean that the Man of Steel's filmed adventures at the time were over. In fact, in 2007 Warner Bros. began an initiative to create original animated movies featuring original stories, adaptations of classic comics and more. It kicked off with that year's* Superman: Doomsday, *a not-very-faithful take on the* Death of Superman *storyline, but extremely successful. In fact, there have been 48 of these films featuring a wide variety of characters. Superman has starred in several solo adventures, teamed up with Batman on two and was part of the Justice League on many more.*

Rather than have one actor voice a particular character through them all, attempts were made to get some star power in there, each, when it comes to Superman, of whom have their own views on him.

ADAM BALDWIN (*Superman: Doomsday,* 2007): I remember watching George Reeves as a kid, and I thought that was cool. I'm not a purist, but that was my introduction. Later I remember seeing Christopher Reeve brilliantly portray him on film. That's the depth of my knowledge. But those didn't influence my performance. This didn't really allow me to go to some of those stylings, especially the comedy. This is really a story with a lot of "more' — more intense, more emotion, more action, more investigation into relationships, and ultimately we're dealing with the death of Superman and the effect that event has on our primary characters and the world itself. It's arguably the darkest of all Superman films.

KYLE MACLACHLAN (*Justice League: The New Frontier,* 2008): There's a sort of moral imperative that Superman has, and I think the language he uses is a little more proper — he's just not a guy who uses his words casually. So maybe, unconsciously, that 1950s tone just creeps in there for me. The physical performance is fun — you have to use your imagination a lot more. It's a lot of grunts and oomphs and ughs, which you just can't help but act out physically. I'm sure it looks funny from the other side of the glass [of the recording booth]. Like in one scene, it was about getting hit with a pterodactyl wing versus getting punched by a super-villain. There's apparently a difference in that sound, so you have to shade it a bit and use the imagination.

TIM DALY (*Superman/Batman: Public Enemies,* 2009): The most surprising thing about voicing Superman for this film was that I realized how much I missed it. I found that I really had missed doing Superman. I thought that this particular script was really good and, for those of us who are interested and aware of certain things in our world and our country, I think that it presents a very kind of subtle social commentary. I think that makes it cool and relatively bold for something that's an animated Superman film.

MARK HARMON (*Justice League: Crisis on Two Earths*, 2010): I'm actually a little uncomfortable playing Superman. I mean, he's the guy, but I actually look at this much more as being a part of this amazing team of actors. That's one of the things that really attracted me to the film. And I'm more comfortable with being included than I am trying to stand out in any way. I wouldn't have done this just to say I played Superman — that's not important to me. To me, growing up watching Superman on black-and-white television or reading it in the comic books, all the superhuman things he did were cool. But the things that attracted me are really the human part of the character, or at least the part that was more real. Hopefully that's what I brought to that. He's a leader. He's a quarterback. He can be tough when he needs to be. He can certainly be direct. No matter who he's talking to, he tries to speak honestly. I understand those values.

JAMES DENTON (*All-Star Superman*, 2011): While Superman is not monotone, he's also not very emotional. In voice work you tend to go a little further than you would if people were watching you in a camera, so it's a little bit melodramatic, but with Superman you can't do that. You can't go to these emotional places because that's not what Superman does. And then you have fun with Clark Kent, which is the challenge — not to be the bumbling idiot. So the fun thing was making Clark Kent human while taking much more of the emotion out of Superman to make him more controlled. I remember [writer] Grant Morrison saying one time that there were kind of three people there: Superman and Clark Kent are the masks, and the real guy is the Clark Kent who was very secure, very strong, knew how to drive a tractor and was raised by Ma and Pa Kent. That really struck me and made it more interesting. In the end I wasn't that worried about flattening him out emotionally because I kind of heard Grant's voice in my head saying, "That's what the real Clark Kent is sort of putting on — he's putting on Superman as well."

GEORGE NEWBERN (*Superman vs. The Elite*, 2012): I think you watch an actor like Jimmy Stewart in *Mr. Smith Goes to Washington* or *It's a Wonderful Life* and you try to find the humanity of an Everyman like that. When I think of an all-American hero, I think of an actor in a role like that. And that's what Superman really is — an American hero. Superpowers are just ancillary. It's that character, with all those principles and understanding, that's who he is right there. I think I tried to portray a sense of trust and power and charisma for Superman. I think that's what we believe Superman is.

MARK VALLEY (*The Dark Knight Returns, Part 2*, 2013): It's fun to play a hero, but I love to be able to put a little bit of irreverence into it, or a little bit of humanity as well as sarcasm or irony. It's kind of fun to see who these people are with these immense abilities and huge responsibilities but still have time to kind of have fun with it.

MATT BOMER (*Superman Unbound*, 2013): I think I was five or six. My mom made me a homemade cape for Halloween. First, I was a Superboy to my brother's Superman, because whatever superhero he was, I was either the lesser version of it or the sidekick. So when he was Batman, I was Robin. When he was Superman, I was Superboy. But like any four-year-old, it played very heavily into my psychology. And I think that's what makes the character resonate for so long, with so many people. He's who we hope we could be, in the most dire of circumstances. But my mom made me a homemade cape, and I wore that thing out for two years. I didn't even care. I had no shame about it. I would strap it on. It had a snap. I'd get on my bike and just let it trail behind me. People would laugh. I didn't give a damn. I was Superman! Now, I'm the voice of Superman.

I tried to keep up some of the consistencies of the characters that are maintained throughout every incarnation of the story, and then just deal with the script that we were given. In this particular story, it's a very mature Superman that we're seeing. He's always dealing with weighty issues, but he's very paternal towards Supergirl, he's very protective of Lois and he's also having to deal with Brainiac, who is a very intense adversary. So I tried to balance the heavier, more mature version of him with a lighter, fun, more charming sense of playfulness with Lois in our scenes.

SAM DALY (Justice League: *The Flashpoint Paradox*, 2013): To be honest, at first I was like, "Wow, he's really weak and soft. Thanks, Andrea." [*laughs*] Reading it, what's so great about the Superman character in this one is that he has an interesting — even though he may not have many words of dialogue — arc in the movie. He starts off and he's classic Superman. He's *huge* in the first scene; he's the extra-bulky Superman. But then in this alternate world to have this sort of weaker, frail Superman is such a different side that we're not used to seeing him as. And through it all to overcome the obstacles and rise up again and become the Man of Steel and save the day again in some way, was really something that I could tap into as an actor to bring my voice to that and try to give him a little bit of an arc. Through it all at the end he comes back as hero and friend and preserving truth, justice and the American way. Superman seems to always instinctually do the right thing, and I think that's something his character has always stood for and always will. He's always on the right side of things. I really saw it as a challenge and saw it as something that, luckily, Andrea was able to help direct me through. I also learned that I could grunt in many different ways. [*laughs*] That's what you learn quickly doing the voices of superheroes.

ALAN TUDYK (*Justice League: War***, 2014):** Let me tell you about Superman. I was really looking forward to being Superman and being that good-guy Super-man who's pure and awesome, but instead I was voicing this young Superman who's really not sure of himself. You want him to say, "Taste my justice," or what-ever. But they were like, "He's not really that sure of himself, he's a little uncertain, he's not quite that strong." So they must have been like, "Get me somebody who's not quite sure of himself to voice Superman."

JERRY O'CONNELL (*Justice League: Throne of Atlantis***, 2015):** My psychi-atrist tells me not to do this, but I read pretty much all the tweets and comments and you do get compared to not only everyone who portrayed Superman, but pretty much anyone who's acted or voiced any superheroes. Thank God I'm just a part of this team, because *The Death of Superman* is the highest-rated film I've been a part of according to Rotten Tomatoes… and I was in *Jerry Maguire Stand by Me, Scream 2*. But *Death of Superman* is my crown jewel. Superman is an ideal. Not to get too hokey, but we're in a pretty tumultuous, fragile time right now in society. Superman really just represents that international ideal of safety and of being a guardian.

BENJAMIN BRATT (*Justice League: Gods and Monsters***, 2015):** We live in different times, and what I appreciate about this film is that it's sort of built for a more plugged-in audience: one that's aware of world politics and social upheaval and things that seem to be on everyone's minds these days. It's not about lifting the car off the tracks, we're talking about the actual saving of humanity. I would say this Superman has a lot more edge than any Superman I've ever encountered. He retains a sort of goodness from the original, but this Superman's got more balls.

JASON ISAACS (*Superman: Red Son***, 2020):** The thing about Superman is whilst he's raised in Russia and he is unlike regular Superman, he has a view to how the country is being run. He's interested in equality and fairness and he's en-gaged in politics in the way that the Western Superman never is. He's actually the same guy. He has a very firm, ethical, moral universe and he's only about truth and justice and doing the right thing. He just has landed in a place where he thinks that's happening under a different system.

DARREN CRISS (*Superman: Man of Tomorrow*, 2020): This was an honor. Superman is bigger than all of us just as an ubiquitous cultural symbol, and anything I can do to bring to him is a privilege, and I hope that I didn't screw it up too much for all the fans who are far more discerning than I am.

JUSTIN HARTLEY (*Injustice*, 2021): I loved the arc of the character. I love the way it started and how you get behind him. You go, "This is very cool to see him at home and resting and having a good time." And then all hell breaks out and I loved the idea that they wrote this guy flawed and this idea of Superman not having all of the answers… and sometimes, the answers that he has are outrageous. You don't typically see that, and then when he is unleashed, how the hell do you deal with that? We did a couple of those storylines on *Smallville,* but how *do* you stop Superman? In this state of mind, he's an unstoppable thing.

TRAVIS WILLINGHAM (*Batman and Superman: Battle of the Super Sons*, 2022): When I grew up, Superman was my idol and he's always been my favorite comic book character. A lot of people will jump on that and say that's not a very interesting choice, but they're wrong. And hearing that would just destroy me, because the most amazing quality that Superman has is that he has the ability to change the world. He can do all of these things, but he uses it for good instead of wrong or evil. I remember being a kid and having all these books that were explaining who Clark Kent was, that he had powers on a farm in Smallville. And I remember Lex Luthor had the purple and green suit with the rocket boosters ankles that he would hop into, and it just sent my imagination soaring. So I've always felt a great sense of debt to Superman and a great deal of closeness with the character. And to be able to come around and finally play him as an adult is just beyond my wildest expectations.

By the time you get to the 2010s, there was a strange transition happening in the world of the Man of Steel. In the comics, growing with popularity was the imagery of a grimacing Superman, eyes glowing red as though he is about to unleash his heat vision and occasionally dipping into his darker impulses. On the video game front, there was 2013's Injustice: Gods Among Us, *which is set off after the Joker manipulates Superman's mind into believing he's fighting Doomsday, but in truth he is murdering Lois Lane and their unborn child. In response, once he comes to his senses, Superman murders the Joker in vengeance and proclaims himself as peacekeeper of the world, which gradually evolves into a brutal and violent reign, the death of many heroes and villains and Batman determined to stop him. Just a video game, right? Not when it inspires years of comic book prequels, adaptations and spinoffs, a follow-up game and an animated film.*

DAN DIDIO (former co-publisher, DC Comics): People have an easier time writing an evil Superman than a good Superman. There's a clever button that people press when they do these things. I'm on record saying I never liked Elseworlds and never liked the Multiverse; I felt that by creating these universes and alternate takes on the same characters, they were short cuts to tell stories with characters that they had a hard time writing; meaning they didn't know how to write a character, so therefore they had to change aspects of the character and had to change the character itself to make it work for them. We used to say we were changing them with the times to contemporize them, but sometimes they changed them so much because they just couldn't get into the head space of how those characters work to be able to write them properly. That's why you'll hear a bit of outrage from some people who understand the character, and know how to make it work, like Grant Morrison. He understands it, others didn't.

CASE AIKEN (host, *Men of Steel* podcast): It's frustrating how much in vogue the idea of "Dark Superman" is right now, isn't it? The first time I saw a story doing something like that, it felt really cool. The idea of an evil version of Superman goes back a really long time, like to Ultraman on a DC alternate Earth. That character has its place, but he's also not on our Earth, so the consequences of his actions might break through to Earth sometimes, but we've got our own super-heroes to protect us. So those are cool stories to do just a story, but as a status quo, we have Superman, *not* Ultraman. There's a reason why the "evil" Superman of the main world was Bizarro, who was more just broken, not bad. He would try to do right, and what's fun is Bizarro allows you to talk about the morality of Superman, where he's not infallible and you can see there are consequences of his actions. But it's not mean-spirited. Then there are things like Homelander on *The Boys* and Omniman on *Invincible*, although they bounce back and forth between, "Are we doing a good Superman or an evil Superman story?" But I don't want Superman to fundamentally be perceived as a bad guy.

DAN DIDIO: When I first got to DC, I used to go to talent and ask them, "What do you work on? What do you *want* to work on? What characters do you want to work on?" The majority of the talent inside the United States said, "Batman," the majority of talent outside of the United States said, "Superman." I asked why that was, and it came back to me that a lot of people outside of the United States identified Superman with America 100% — the benevolent, powerful character, always trying to help, but somehow not getting it right all the time. They saw Superman as the physical representation of America. With Batman, they had much more of the sense of vigilantism and cleaning the world up from the inside. It took people from the U.K. and other countries to explain that to me.

ANTHONY DESIATO (host, *Digging for Kryptonite* podcast): I'm not really a fan of these alt takes on Superman where it's like, "What if he were evil?" He's interesting to me because he's not, because he could do whatever he wants and he chooses not to. And so these stories where it's like, "What if he were raised by Darkseid? What if he were raised by communists?" Okay, he would be different, though I don't always know how much it reveals about him.

DAN DIDIO: The frustration of working on Superman is that the writers see people doing these imitations and getting free reign on how the characters behave, so they want to bring that same sensibility and same level of freedom. But you can't; it's in a box. I used to tell people the best books are the ones where you're in a box, and what I mean by that is that if you're in a box, there are rules of the character that can't change. So you're going to push and you're going to pull and you're going to punch on the sides; you're going to try to change it any way you possibly can. But you can't change the heart of the character. And that's when you get your best story, when you're struggling against the trappings.

TOM TAYLOR (writer, *Injustice* prequel comic): I thought the game's story was pretty horrific. It was a really great story, but it was in a really, really hard place. And to realize that I had to get these beloved characters to this place was a challenge. But it was a challenge I relished, particularly working with Superman, who's my favorite superhero. Getting to write him for the first time in my life and realizing that that's what I had to turn him into, was not the greatest. I think that's possibly why the comic books work so well, because people could feel my pain. I did try to capture the classic version of the character when there were flashbacks or dream sequences; you need those moments of hope to drive the moments of despair. You need those moments of levity and humor so that the drama balances. And as much as I didn't like doing what I had to do to a character that I love, I know that it was really effective and people were hanging on… and giving them a cliffhanger every week, there were people clamoring to get back to it.

BRIAN BUCCELETTO (writer, *Injustice* comic): It seems that ever since the '80s and Frank Miller, and the dawn of the anti-hero, people have looked at Superman in kind of a negative light as being too goody-goody, not haunted or edgy and that sort of thing. My personal feeling is that Superman as played by Christopher Reeve is good, he's the hero. He's the first superhero and creatively that creates a challenge as writers, because he *is* so powerful. In my first issue of *Injustice*, there's a bit where young Clark can't sleep so he sits guard in the house in case anything should happen — flash forward, and because he went through this horrendous trauma of losing his wife and unborn child, he's dealing with the fact that he's the most powerful man in the universe and he couldn't save them. That *has* to have an effect on him.

TOM TAYLOR: I knew that Lois Lane and Superman's unborn child had to die, which I hated, and it was the first thing I had to do. But I wanted to establish just how much they loved each other, just what this child meant to the two of them and how it was going to change their lives. And then show Batman, who is going to be this wonderful godfather, and then really tear all of that apart. I looked at the first year of *Injustice* in particular as the breakup of the World's Finest friendship. To me it was to get to the point where Batman and Superman, who *are* the World's Finest, see their friendship irreparably broken.

ERNIE ALTBAKER (writer, *Injustice* animated film): He loses the love of his life and his unborn child, *and* his city, and he snaps for one second. And what does he do? He says, "I'm going to keep everybody safe from this horrible thing." His first reaction is to go, "I don't want anybody else to go through this," and then it's the classic slippery slope where he is like, "No, I need to take away all that stuff and I'm going to make sure that nobody else has an army. Then I'm going to provide security for everyone, and then we're going to be judge and jury, because those people could be compromised. And because we only had 72 minutes, it goes downhill shockingly fast, though it's all earned.

TOM TAYLOR: I think the overall strength of *Injustice* is that we are seeing characters that people know and love put in a position they've never been put in before, and constantly adapting to that position. We're seeing real relationships torn apart, we're seeing real love torn apart and death that really strikes and then you're allowed to have a reaction to it. Often in comics you'll see deaths happen and everyone kind of knows that they'll be back in a few months or a year — whereas in *Injustice*, once they're gone, they're gone. And two years later the characters are still feeling the impact of that. At the same time, *Injustice* has a lot of humor, which we really emphasize when we can. The idea was to have levity so that it wouldn't be grim story every week with another death and more violence.

In essence, Injustice *shows one road Superman could have taken following such a devastating loss, but the 1996 comic* Kingdom Come, *as well as elements of it that appeared on the* Crisis on Infinite Earths *television event, show another.*

BRANDON ROUTH (actor, "Clark Kent/Superman," *Crisis on Infinite Earth***):** I think if we were to see that backstory that we didn't see, having just heard about it as taken from the events of *Kingdom Come* and inserted into *Crisis on Infinite Earths* when the Joker gassed the *Daily Planet*, obviously Superman would've been incredibly devastated and didn't make healthy choices right away, but I think the power with Superman is to show that struggle and challenge, but not allow himself to completely lose it. Or even if he does completely lose it, you *have* to show the other side. He has to come back to understanding that isn't the way ultimately to deal with loss. The other way is just letting your anger out; it's not emotional resilience. It's not building emotional control. So I disagree with the way *Injustice* went with it.

Falling into the darker underbelly of the DC Universe — though not as dark as Injustice — *is the Snyderverse, films based on DC characters as directed by Zack Snyder (300, Sucker Punch). It started off Superman-centric with 2013's* Man of Steel *and rapidly expanded to include other characters, most notably the Dark Knight and Wonder Woman in 2016's* Batman v. Superman: Dawn of Justice, *and the addition of the Flash, Aquaman and Cyborg in 2021's "Snydercut" of* Justice League, *which aired on HBO Max.*

Keeping the focus on Superman, as played by British actor Henry Cavill, his origin (including his love story with Amy Adams' Lois Lane) is recounted in Man of Steel. *As is his battle with Kryptonian antagonist General Zod and his soldiers, which results in the near destruction of Metropolis with the planet to follow, culminating with Superman having no choice but to snap Zod's neck to save a family in danger. In* Batman v. Superman, *Ben Affleck's Batman becomes obsessed with destroying Superman for fear of what he could do to humanity if he should turn against it, leading to the two of them fighting close to the death, though the revelation that the name of both characters' mothers is Martha, which suddenly makes Batman recognize his opponent's humanity, stops their fight in its tracks.*

Thanks to the machinations of Jesse Eisenberg's Lex Luthor, a version of the Doomsday creature arises, which Superman has to sacrifice himself to destroy. The film ends in the aftermath of the Man of Steel's death. Then in Justice League, *Steppenwolf (voiced by Ciaran Hinds) attempts to unite a trio of Mother Boxes (from Jack Kirby's Fourth World comics) to pave the way for Darkseid (voiced by Ray Porter) to come to Earth and dominate the planet. Eventually the heroes come to realize that they're just not powerful*

*enough, so they engage in a process that resurrects Superman, who returns violent and con-
fused, but eventually becomes the hero he is known to be.*

*When producer/director Christopher Nolan and his producing wife Emma Thomas
pitched the concept of* Man of Steel *to Zack Snyder and his producing wife Deborah, they
were instantly intrigued. The question, of course, was whether or not the script by David S.
Goyer would live up to that pitch. Flash forward a couple of days and someone arrived at the
Snyder household at 7 a.m., handed the duo the script and sat in the driveway while they
read it.*

ZACK SNYDER (director, *Man of Steel*): I'm a big fan of the character, but
at first I was really skeptical. Even before meeting Chris Nolan and talking about
this version of the movie and what we could do, there was a time a few years earlier, before *Watchmen*, where we talked about whether or not there was a Superman
movie we could do. I was in a different sort of mindset. *Watchmen* and the Doctor
Manhattan character is as close to Superman as I felt like I was going to get. But
in doing that movie, the why of superheroes, which is so carefully dissected in that
film, made me, in a weird way, love the mythology and wanted me to support the
mythology rather than dissect it. I loved dissecting it in *Watchmen* because that's
what it was about, but when we came to Superman, it was almost like you've got
to know the rules before you can break them. I had broken the rules, and suddenly
we had this character and I wanted to get to the why of this mythology and
respect it and understand it. All of my films have been slightly ironic, from *Dawn
of the Dead* to *300*. There's a visual irony or irony in every story. The biggest irony
of Superman is that it's *not* ironic at all. It's the most realistic movie I've made; the
most emotionally and physically realistic movie I've made, which I think is fun.

DEBORAH SNYDER (producer, *Man of Steel*): No pressure there, but
it was really awesome and they really figured out how to make him relatable to a
modern audience; to make you care about him as a character. That's what's really
difficult. We will never know what it's like to have these incredible powers, be able
to fly and do all of these things. But I think in the past his human side as Clark has
been portrayed as this really ultra-good Boy Scout; so perfect in a way that isn't
relatable. The thing we strived to do was make you feel like you could relate to
certain aspects of his life.

DAVID S. GOYER (writer, *Man of Steel*): In the case of Superman, many
people have possessory feelings about him, but then there have been a lot of different iterations. It's no small thing to say you're going to do Superman… but which
Superman? Which era are you going to adhere to? Which elements are you going

to adhere to? We were in the same place we were at with *Batman Begins*. If you think about *Batman Begins*, there had been these previous iterations of Batman, the TV show, the Burton films, and we were trying to do something that's different. We were going against the tide. The public perception of Superman comes largely from the Donner films. Superman's been preserved in amber since then, and for the general public he hasn't really shifted since. Any time you do something different, shake up the orthodoxy, you risk offending people. Superman has been reinterpreted many times over the decades, and if he is going to remain a vibrant myth, he needs to continue to be reinterpreted.

ZACK SNYDER: You have to think about what makes any movie relevant. It's not necessarily that it's topical like, "Oooh, it's about the economy" or "It's about North Korea." I don't think people really care about that. But what they *do* care about is the difference between being topical and being timeless, or a movie that is done with heart and respect for a character. Our big thing when we made the movie was, "Can we make Superman into a character that you can relate to?" Whether that makes him topical or not, I don't know, but that was what we really went after and that was the big work of the movie. It was making you go, "Hey, if I were Superman, that's what *I* would do!" That was a thing that I thought no one had really gotten to. He was always the "other" that you could look to; this god whose adventures you could appreciate, but really didn't allow you to say, "That touches a part of who I am." I feel the original *intent* of the character — this immigrant orphan story — was the mythology of Superman, and that's what we went after in a lot of ways.

CHARLES ROVEN (producer, *Batman v. Superman: Dawn of Justice*): We don't think that Superman is irrelevant. We actually think that he, in a number of ways, is both inspirational and aspirational. The reason we wanted to do the movie and our take on the film is that we wanted to make him a much more relevant character for today — which means that he's a much more complex character. The Superman of the past was pretty much the guy with the white hat with superpowers; didn't have any significantly big emotional decisions or hard decisions to make, because he saw the world as black and white. But the world isn't that way any longer. We've created a character that we think is relevant and relatable because he's got issues. He grows into who he becomes, like we all do.

DEBORAH SNYDER: He's on this journey of self-discovery. He's feeling a little lost in the film when we find him, and I feel like that's a place that we all have maybe been in our lives. Or as a kid you don't feel like you fit in, you feel different; you're in a job and you don't know if you're on the right job. You're asking, "What is my purpose in life?" I think those aspects of him, his human aspects, if you can relate to him, you care about him as a character. And if you care about him as a character, then you care about all of these other things that you might not otherwise be able to imagine or relate to.

ZACK SNYDER: It's not so much looking up to see a god among us, but more like what if one of us was elevated above just being a human being. And then you still have all of the same emotional pitfalls and problems; you still don't know where you belong in the world. All of those things are still real and those are things we are all asking ourselves when we look in the mirror. What am I? Who am I? What is my purpose? What is my point? *That's* what Superman is doing, too, every day.

The perception of Man of Steel *right from the outset was that, given Nolan's name attached as producer, it would mirror the grittiness of the Batman films.*

DEBORAH SNYDER: That's an easy thing to grab on to. This is such a different story. It *is* about good and evil and making choices for the good. I feel like our film has a hopefulness to it. It is so much of what Superman is, but it's also what this movie and the story we're telling is. Listen, it has amazing sci-fi and really great action, but at its heart it has a lot to do with family and who you are and what defines you as a person.

ZACK SNYDER: There's real emotional depth and problems that this guy faces. It's not as slick, let's say, as the Marvel approach, but there's so much heart in it. And the character is so big. People asked me how I compared to the Marvel films and I said, "It's Superman. What do you want me to say?" Iron Man is cool, but this is Superman. In the mythological realm, pop culture is pop culture and it takes what it wants and rejects what it wants, so those characters are as giant as pop culture will allow them to be. But in the pantheon, in historical terms, Superman is a *big* deal.

CHARLES ROVEN: Superman is very much a hopeful character, and a very different character from Bruce Wayne. Bruce Wayne is a very dark character with a lot of complexity, a lot of emotional and psychological issues. He's damaged in every way. What was so great about the *Dark Knight* trilogy is that that character sees some light at the end of the tunnel. But he shares only one thing with Kal-El/Clark: They were both orphans. In every other way, Kal-El is a very different character — not just because he's an alien, but because of how he was brought up and where he was from. I don't think the movie feels anything at all like the *Dark Knight* trilogy. Certainly it wasn't Chris or David's intention to go in that direction. We wanted the film to be true to what it needed to be.

DARYN KIRSCHT (author, *The Snyderverse Saga: The Culture-Shattering Phenomena Behind Zack Snyder's DC Film Universe*): When Zack Snyder cast Henry Cavill in the role of Clark Kent/Superman, the big talking point for casting a relatively unknown actor in such a big role was that Cavill looked the part. He didn't look silly. There was a believability to him when he walked in the room. He literally became and embodied Superman. He had the exact look of what a modern-day Superman would look like, particularly his physique. Plus, when people got to know Cavill the person through interviews and social media, many have stated that he is a humble, kind and caring person. He literally is Superman in real life. When you also factor in how much he truly cares about how people perceive the role of Superman and the responsibility that goes along with that, you couldn't ask for a better actor to take on the Man of Steel.

Born May 5, 1983 on the island of Jersey in Britain's Channel Islands, Henry Cavill is the fourth of five boys, the rest of which have careers in the military, with him being the only one choosing a career in acting. Prior to being cast as Superman in Man of Steel, *his biggest claim to fame up to this point has been a a number of British TV roles, a co-starring role in Showtime's* The Tudors *as well as the Greek hero drama* Immortals *and 2012's* The Cold Light of Day. *There's no question that his life has changed (likely forever) as he suddenly finds himself an "A" star, his every move captured on the Internet by paparazzi and fans.*

HENRY CAVILL (actor, "Superman," *Man of Steel*): Is it hard to deal with attention? Not really. If I were to take everyone's comments to heart, then of course I think it would be very hurtful. There's also wonderful stuff out there too, so I'd be somewhere between having an enormous ego and a very small, crushed one. [*laughs*] It's all part of the entertainment. It's going to happen and people are going to talk, which is great. If they're talking, it means they're being entertained one way or the other, so carry on! At the same time, it *is* a microscope and you've just got to remember that the people who are really important to you in your life, when *they're* inspecting you under a microscope and finding flaws, *that's* a really bad thing. But for everyone else, they're fully entitled to their opinions and they can fly away, they can troll on the Internet forums and do whatever they want, and good for them!

In his youth, Cavill had a vision for his future career, and according to him those expectations actually weren't that far removed from what's happened in some ways.

HENRY CAVILL: Everything that's happened has been enormously reward-ing and very gratifying and a real boost to my self-belief and trust in myself and my abilities. As a young lad you think, "I'd love to be an actor and play these won-derful roles and these big characters and entertain." It took 11 years and I was very fortunate that I had all the right opportunities, and it's a wonderful feeling to have things work out as I really hoped they would. I had a very bold imagination and still do. I have never set limits on myself, although obviously with these particular roles there was no one thing where I said, "I want to play that, I want to play this." I just wanted to go for the very big things. From the very beginning I didn't want to settle for small stuff; I wanted to aim high and go down in a blaze of glory if I didn't make it and try something else. But it's paid off so far and I'm enjoying it. Everything's an experience and a journey and an adventure, and if you're not enjoying it, what's the point? So far it's been great. Sure, it's been terrible at points as well, but I've tried to take everything I could from those terrible, difficult mo-ments I've had and it's all part of the journey.

In the years prior to Man of Steel, *Cavill actually came close to being cast as James Bond, Batman and Superman (in* Superman: Flyby, *written by J.J. Abrams and scheduled to be directed by McG.) Even though he didn't make the final cut, coming close brought its own level of satisfaction.*

HENRY CAVILL: My feeling was that if these people who had been doing this for years noticed something in me and said, "Okay, we're willing to put him and another guy up for the role and that's it," then there's got to be something there they're seeing. That was certainly a real confidence booster. Although it wasn't any-thing of material value and acting is a very intangible skill, you never know when it's going to happen or *if* it's going to happen. It's not like doing many repetitions of an exercise where once you've done it, you know you can do it. Acting is differ-ent. It's not like that; you don't know if it's going to happen as well or as power-fully or as strongly as it's happened in the past. When you hear people like that say, "Yes, you've got something which is very special" — they may not necessarily say it directly, but in their actions in putting you up next to the last two guys — that in itself is the medal. It's a Silver Medal, it's not the Gold, which is getting the role, but it's still a medal that makes you want to work that much harder and go for the gold.

Cavill comes from a family with a great number of military personnel in it, who seemed to have no problem in referring to him as a "soft" actor in those days, though one would

Henry Cavill, the most recent big-screen Superman, playing the part in the "Snyderverse"
(art © and courtesy D.C. Stuelpner; Superman © and TM DC Comics/Warner Bros. Discovery).

imagine their views may have changed since then. Also changing has been his physical appearance, which could have brought with it some emotional or psychological differences when he walks in a room.

HENRY CAVILL: The mindset when you change your body physically, and your ability physically, there's more of a self-belief. There is more of a security in yourself. It's quite a unique feeling when you have a moment and you're rested, and you're not exhausted and everything else, you think, "I can do this stuff; I'm probably in the top 10 of physically fit people in this room," and that's a very good feeling. Of course someone like me, I always keep myself in check because it means I'm going to continue to push hard. I never allow myself to spread into an arrogance, because that, I believe, and there are people who say otherwise, will hold me back as opposed to help me advance. When it comes to playing a role like Superman, it does help an awful lot because the environment around you behaves differently. The people perceive you differently, and that helps you be the character which you're trying to be. We are indeed a product of those around us because we often behave in response to the way we're treated. When people are looking at you in that sort of way and going, "Whoa! He looks kind of dangerous" or "That guy looks like he can protect me," it gives you that extra bit of something that helps you play a character in a more realistic, effective way.

There's more than just the physicality to a role like Supes. There's something far deeper. Anyone who is willing to put the work in and have that willpower can be in that kind of physical shape, but the question is, "Do they give off that something else that makes them different or special?" That's up to a performer to work out how to give people that impression. That's something different. Physicality helps, but there's something else; there's a way that you make people feel that physicality can enhance but not necessarily be the cause of.

Given the roles he's chosen or been cast in — Theseus in Immortals, *Napoleon Solo in* The Man from U.N.C.L.E., *August Walker in* Mission Impossible: Fallout, *Geralt of Rivia in* The Witcher — *there would seem to be something of an appeal to Cavill for Greek mythology and comic book lore.*

HENRY CAVILL: I've always loved reading historical fiction. I remember a book when I was a very young boy, which was all about Greek mythology — it was a collection of short stories. I loved reading those and looking at the pictures. That sort of world — Ancient Greece, Ancient Egypt, Ancient Rome, the tales of warriors and battles and warlords and conquerors and empires… all of that, I loved it! Although there was no dedicated study in any one direction, I loved the worlds and those stories, and to play them now is incredibly exciting. It's the kind of thing that I've always wanted to do, so I'm a very happy camper right now.

ZACK SNYDER: This shows the power of the character and Henry playing him: When we did Henry's screentest, we had the Christopher Reeve costume. We had the whole crew — it was like a film screen shooting this screentest — and Henry comes out in that costume. It's the difference between someone dressing up as Superman and *being* Superman. The Christopher Reeve costume is a spandex costume. It is *not* cool, other than it being a Superman costume. It is literally a really high-end Halloween costume. But he comes out in it and *nobody* laughed. Nobody said anything except, "Wow, that's awesome." You realized the power of the icon; it's just a bunch of fabric sewn together, but that "S" is something. It was really impressive to me to see the reverence for it among these grown men, who are pretty gruff men. The suit was *respected*, and it was cool. You would think that it would be that way, but you have nothing to prepare yourself for it. Henry comes out of the trailer in that costume, with that hair and his frickin' chiseled face, and in that costume he just looks like a million bucks. All of a sudden, everybody there has forgotten that we're doing the whole Hollywood casting process thing, and instead they're saying, "Look, it's Superman." It's a child-like response, which is very cool. He's in the Christopher Reeve suit, but he's projecting this timeless quality — and *that's* the thing that you need. If that happens, then it's up to me to screw up.

In regards to how he and Snyder approached the character of Superman to make him more appealing to audiences of 2013, he expresses that it felt like what they were doing was a "modernization" of the character and a realistic view of an extraordinary person.

HENRY CAVILL: It's an unreal situation, but it's approached from a very practical viewpoint. We wanted to make the character easier to identify with. It's important to do the role justice. There are a lot of people relying on me to do this well. I gladly accept that responsibility, and it's a great one to have because it's a wonderful opportunity. I don't let the pressure get to me because that would have hindered my performance and therefore let people down. So I chose to ignore the pressure side of it and focus on doing justice to Superman. To research in the beginning, I went after anything I could get my hands on as far as comic books were concerned. My favorites that I went to were *The Death of Superman* and *The Return of Superman*, because they really clarified what Superman is, what lengths he's willing to go to, the fact that there are different aspects of the character and the perceptions people have about him. All of that was incredibly helpful.

ZACK SNYDER: We did a scene and he did a great acting job, but I also feel like just talking to him and being around him, he is an earnest guy — not in a super-square way, but in a real way. The decisions that Superman makes — he doesn't have to really stretch his acting abilities, which are vast by the way. But I think it allows him a stronger performance within the part, because all of it is within his real-life persona. Other than being able to fly, bend steel in his bare hands and all of that stuff, he's just a good guy and you want to just fill the canvas with that; the rest you can build on top of it. That's what really struck me: He was just being honest. And by the way, he never took the job for granted. He works super-hard, he trained super-hard. We had that suit and he said, "I don't want everyone to think they built me a rubber suit with muscles." I said, "Okay, I know how to do that."

We said, "How do we get this thing to look like all of the things that I love about Superman?" And I'm not a rookie at the physical iconography of what is heroic proportions and physical form and all of that stuff. It's a thing that I've made a little bit of a career out of by accident. My wife is like, "Oh great, more nude male icons. I'm a little worried about you." I'm like, "It is what it is. I can't help it." It's probably why I made *Sucker Punch*, because I needed to get my girl on. Also, with this I really wanted there to be a nod to the comic book and let the comics live through him in a lot of ways; all of those pages, all of those thousands of stories that Superman has inhabited over the years. You can't just put him in a leather jacket with an "S" on it and say, "The kids will love this." *No!*

HENRY CAVILL: It's a wonderful feeling being a part of Superman's history, and there's certainly an aspect of it that could be an enormous amount of pressure, which could end up affecting me, but I try and focus more on the honor of it and the excitement of being the person who was chosen to take up the mantle. It's a wonderful opportunity, it's exciting, and it's *so much fun.*

ZACK SNYDER: I think the film's real strength is heart. You have this character who's forced to make these big choices — like most superheroes. But you really understand the *why* of those choices in the sense that he's raised by Jonathan and Martha Kent, and they gave him something that is the real emotional heart at his core. That's what will be its power in the end. Yes, it's a visual effects extravaganza like nothing you've ever seen, but what will make you feel that Superman is awesome is that heart.

It's an enormous responsibility as an artist, filmmaker and fan combined. It's a character that keeps on giving, so for me it's an honor. I'm just lucky it all worked out. Every day I was working on it, I just tried to make it as good s I could. We all worked really hard to make him something special. I'd heard that the Superman "S" glyph is the second most recognized symbol on the planet Earth other than the Christian cross. You hear that and it's scary and awesome at the same time. In the end, that responsibility to make him great was just magnified by those things. I wasn't scared as much as I was excited to make him awesome — because he deserves it.

DARYN KIRSCHT: I think many people unfairly judged the way Clark Kent and Superman were portrayed in *Man of Steel*. He was on the Joseph Campbellian hero's journey throughout not just *Man of Steel*, but all three films he appeared in. The take that Zack Snyder, Christopher Nolan and David S. Goyer were going for in *Man of Steel* was to showcase what would happen if an alien like Superman showed up in the real world. How would people react if someone with his abilities were here on Earth? It would not be all sunshine and rainbows. People would either fear him or view him as a God-like figure.

MICHAEL BAILEY (host, *Superman: From Crisis to Crisis* podcast): When *Superman Returns* happened, it kind of gave all the Christopher Reeve fans something to surround themselves with, except for the fact that it felt like a movie from decades before. You had some in-fighting among Superman fans, but it was all really localized because there wasn't social media as it exists today. These people were arguing on comment sections on websites and message boards where you had to sign in and create an account, and where you had moderators who were kind of the dictators of the board. But I remember in 2013 when *Man of Steel* came out, and I was looking at my phone on that first Friday and Saturday, watching friendships end, because they disagreed about the movie. There was this visceral reaction on the part of more old-school Superman fans who were against the film versus the new people that were coming in and liked it and saw something in it. And I'm gong to fully admit the old-school guys went too far, too often. I joke that at some point I'm going to do a parody of Ken Burns' *Civil War*, with violin music playing in the background, do letters home to my wife from being on the front lines, "They've once again deployed the panel from *Whatever Happened to the Man of Tomorrow?* where he talks about killing as their weapon."

DARYN KIRSCHT: Clark is in a fish-out-of-water story early on with his quest to figure out why he is so different from everyone else. When he eventually does become Superman, he is still very new to the concept. Now imagine

General Zod arriving on Earth and threatening to terraform the Earth to Krypton, effectively killing every human on the planet. Kal-El is not the Superman that we have seen in the comics or even the Christopher Reeve Superman films just yet. People also say the character never smiles in the movie, yet it happens on numerous occasions. It isn't all dark, gloomy and serious. The take on the character and the film as whole was simply more serious and complex than in previous iterations to provide the realism and relatability necessary for a modern take on the character.

Throughout the film, Clark tries and fails numerous times to find his place in society. Cavill stated in an interview for the film that the character feels isolated and lonely. In the real world it would not be easy to stay under the radar and attempt to try and live a normal life. But the more he learns about his heritage and abilities, the more confident he becomes. You can especially see growth in terms of his upbringing usually via Jonathan and Martha Kent.

JOHN KENNETH MUIR (film historian, author, *Science Fiction and Fantasy Films of the 1970s*): *Man of Steel* is an endless and numbing paean to falling skyscrapers, vehicles tossed into the sky and super-powered people throwing each other into the air at near warp velocities. The rampant destruction continues for such a long time in the film — *and is so colossal in scope* —that in the end not a single action scene packs a psychic punch or has the tiniest emotional impact. The makers of this film never heard that less can be more, apparently. And their choice to make the third act of *Man of Steel* all-action-all-the-time consumes precious moments that would have been better spent establishing the characters and their lives.

DARYN KIRSCHT: One of the major talking points about the film was the third act. The damage to Smallville and Metropolis was extensive, and the battle concludes with Superman making the choice to snap Zod's neck to save the life of a human family caught in the crossfire. Goyer stated after the film's release that avoiding catastrophic damage in an alien invasion would be impossible. What prison was going to hold Zod? He was not going to stop. I really enjoyed how Snyder put Superman in that position. In taking the life of the only remaining member of Krypton, he saved the entire planet. It was a tremendous learning experience, as you can see by Superman's reaction after the fact. Life is not always easy, but he made the most of a bad situation and saved the planet. All in all, I thoroughly enjoyed the new iteration of the character.

ROB O'CONNOR (co-host, *All Star Superfan Podcast*): Like *Superman*

Returns before it, *Man of Steel* represents a great missed opportunity. Marred by yet another undercooked script and an overzealous, shallow director, it fancies itself as this grand, biblical rise to heroism with beautiful post-*Crisis* comic book wallpaper, when throughout it feels like little more than a cheap exploitation movie remake of Donner's first two films — once again Clark is robbed of any agency by simply being told by space Dad to become Superman. Once again Zod swears revenge, only this time Superman doesn't draw him away from the populated area, instead opting to assist Zod in punching the city to bits.

JOHN KENNETH MUIR: In fact, *Man of Steel's* climax eventually becomes unintentionally funny. The whole of Metropolis — *literally entire city blocks* — are destroyed and aflame, but Superman rescues Lois Lane in the nick of time from a singularity that has been intentionally opened up over the city. Superman lands her on the street… er rubble, safely and a *Daily Planet* intern soon shouts triumphantly: "*He saved us!*" This is an optimistic opinion, for there are precisely *four* people left standing and visible in the frame: Perry White, the intern, another *Daily Planet* reporter and Lois. Meanwhile, the city smolders, and the landscape appears post-apocalyptic. The "*He saved us!*" line actually elicited laughs in the theater from other patrons because the staging — *and the overt, monumental destruction* — suggests that Superman hasn't really "saved" much at all.

MICHAEL EURY (editor, *The Krypton Companion*): They did not learn a single lesson from *Superman II* because, if you remember, there's the great battle scene in Metropolis which now looks primitive, but it's still the ultimate superhero fight scene ever in the movies because it was really the first one — even if the special effects were using a manhole as a Frisbee and hitting Superman in the solar plexus. But Superman takes a quick diversion to rescue people on the street from falling building debris, while Zod says he's figured out his weakness: He cares. They just don't get it. They're ruthless, but it shows the power of Superman. He *does* care because he's not one of us, but he is.

JOHN KENNETH MUIR: Despite the fact of rampant destruction, the screenplay does not provide a single line — *not one word* — about the herculean task of rebuilding the city, which now looms. Indeed, the film ends with Clark Kent merrily taking his place at the Daily Planet, which looks clean and orderly… as if nothing ever happened. The entirety of *Man of Steel's* last act is filled with oversights of this dramatic and clumsy nature. As noted above, the plan to get rid of General Zod involves creating a singularity — *a black hole, essentially* — just a couple of hundred feet over downtown Metropolis. Once more, the film never includes even a single line of dialogue to suggest how the singularity is to be closed. Finally, it is spectacularly lacking in creativity and imagination that *Man of Steel* ends with Superman breaking Zod's neck, rather than finding a way to neuter him, banish him or otherwise defeat him. I can't fathom how Superman can be said — *in this film* — to be a figure of "hope" when he pulverizes half of Metropolis (and Smallville too), and then, for his last act, commits murder. People wouldn't be inspired by this Superman. *They'd be terrified of him*. The merits of Zod's murder can be debated of course. There was a human family to rescue, and Zod clearly wasn't going to stop fighting, no matter what. Yet virtually by definition, being "Superman" means finding good, creative, *meaningful* alternatives to murder in times of crisis, pain and suffering. On top of all the excessive carnage highlighted in the film, the murder of Zod simply confirms the film's misunderstanding of a great American icon.

MICHAEL BAILEY: The "no killing" thing is one of my constant fascinations with Superman fandom, because there are people out there who are *so* anti-it that while I get where they're coming from, it's all about context. In 1988, Byrne had Superman execute three Phantom Zone villains from an alternate reality, because we can't make this complicated enough apparently. But instead of just ignoring that which, honestly, Mike Carlin, Jerry Ordway and Roger Stern could have done and just begun a whole new era, they chose to explore the ramifications of what Superman did and what that does to Superman. And that led to the "Exile" storyline. And if you don't have "Exile," you never get "Death of Superman," because there is a direct line between those two stories, and if one doesn't happen, the other doesn't exist in the form that it came out in. When he kills at the end of *Man of Steel*, I disagreed with it. I'm kind of in the Mark Waid camp of, "Wow, you put him in this position, but never explored it in the next film." They went right into Batman not liking Superman, but they decide to get along at the end.

JOHN KENNETH MUIR: What *Man of Steel* profoundly misses is that Superman is designed to be a symbol of all that is good in America, and all that is right, and is supposed to be a role model for children and adults alike. To have him in his first rebooted adventure pulp a city, a small town, and mete out death to his enemy with his bare hands, suggests the kind of "reboot" of a beloved character one can't really get behind. Oh, the shadow of the Dark Knight is a considerable one indeed, and these days all superheroes must be tortured... dark ones apparently, even beacons of hope like Superman.

Snyder admits that if things hadn't evolved the way that they did — starting with Man of Steel *— there was no way that he would have tackled the idea of bringing Superman* *and Batman together out of sheer intimidation.*

ZACK SNYDER: If, for instance, someone came up to me and said, "Hey, do you want to do a movie where Batman fights Superman," I would have been like, "Okay. Ease back a little bit." But because it kind of evolved over time, by the time we were shooting, it was the first time I realized 100%, "Oh shit! That's going to happen;" it was at the camera test when I was actually looking at Batman and Superman in their costumes. It was amazing and fun and an honor to deal with these icons.

HENRY CAVILL: The appeal of this idea for me, as I always say, was going to the source material. There's a lot of psychology in Superman. It's the one way you can find a crack in the shell. When it comes to playing the character, especially in this movie, we still see the growth of Superman before seeing the finished product of what we know and love from the character in the comic books. It was just delving in the psychology and weaknesses they're in and playing with the relationship between him and Lois and him and Martha; and then of course the conflict he has when facing the likes of Batman.

DARYN KIRSCHT: In *Man of Steel*, Clark is on the journey of self-discovery, which in turn means he is on the journey to becoming Superman much like Bruce Wayne was on the journey to becoming Batman in *Batman Begins*. Even after Clark dons the suit and learns how to fly, that doesn't automatically mean he is the traditional Superman. He has to go through the threshold from the monomyth. He has to learn on the fly, no pun intended, how to utilize his unique skill set to accomplish an insurmountable task. It is through the act of doing so that he learns what it means to truly be a hero and thus become Superman.

In *Batman v Superman*, Clark is on the next step of that journey. Now that he has become Superman and works at the Daily Planet as Clark Kent, he is confronted with the harsh reality of how the world reacts to having a God-like being here among mortals. When you consider what happened in *Man of Steel*, General Zod gave a pretty bad reputation for outsiders with nearly invincible abilities. Even though Superman helped save them, people are afraid of what they cannot understand or control. That concept only becomes heightened. Superman gets framed by powerful people, like Lex Luthor, for their own selfish gain. Batman blames Superman for what happened in *Man of Steel*. The media debate his existence and what it means for humanity. In a way, it is one big story arc that involves Clark truly becoming a member of Earth.

BEN AFFLECK (actor, "Batman," *Batman v Superman: Dawn of Justice*)**:** For me, there was enough material in the screenplay that Chris Terrio wrote, and with Zack's direction, there was plenty for me to grab on to and use my imagination to try to build this character. It's certainly daunting because of the people who have played this character before and the great filmmakers. More recently Christian Bale and Chris Nolan did three brilliant movies and all the guys who went before them. There's that element of healthy respect you have for the project and for the characters and their history and it raises the bar certainly. I felt it was in really good hands with the script and with Zack, and that is where I focused my attention.

ZACK SNYDER: Only once we committed to the ridiculous idea of this movie did we see the implication of a whole universe where Batman and Superman exist together. I know it seems obvious in the comic book world, but it had not existed really in the movies. But once that idea took root and existed as reality, it was only then that I was obsessed. I am and have been obsessed with the trinity and have wanted to see the trinity — that being Batman, Superman and Wonder Woman — in a single moment. That's a thing that I was really interested in trying to get in this movie, not that I didn't have enough to deal with already but I thought that would be a cool scene. And those conversations are really what led to this *Dawn of Justice* subheading for the film. We could now and begin to talk about or have conversations about the Justice League, and the DC universe could evolve from this. It's a difficult notion especially with a studio like this that's really filmmaker-driven and project to project. It's a difficult notion to say, "Oh, you're making a movie," but it's actually connected to that guy's movie and connected to that guy's movie and it's all going to be a big, great fun sandbox and we're all going to play nice in it. It's a great thing but it's a difficult thing to make appear. That's what the luck and serendipitous nature of this movie that's allowed the worlds now to coalesce. It became a plan and it's becoming a thing, but it was only in this infancy that we realized, "Yeah, oh my gosh," this can be a thing.

DEBORAH SNYDER: At the same time, I think we wanted to set up and introduce these characters, but we also had a really rich story to tell. It was a careful balance about telling the Batman and Superman story and giving a little hint and a tease to this story of Justice League that was yet to come.

ZACK SNYDER: A controversial aspect of the film was the whole "Martha" thing, but it's from the comic book. When we were talking about that aspect of the movie and what is the thing that humanizes Superman or Batman, it seemed really interesting that he's basically now looking at someone else with a mother.

BEN AFFLECK: There's a duality to both Batman and Superman. Zack often said that Bruce Wayne was a mask that he put on as much as Batman's was. Putting on a mask and presenting this alter ego to Bruce Wayne to the world was interesting. I liked the idea that both Bruce Wayne and Batman were screwed-up, unhealthy people who were engaging in unhealthy behavior at night as a result of psychological scars they bore from childhood, and that duality was really interesting to explore.

HENRY CAVILL: For me this felt like the development of Superman the character we love and know in the comic books. We're still not there. We are looking at the guy growing up. He's become this Superman after discovering that he was Kal-El in the first movie and now he's facing off the second guy. It's a tough outing for him because it's against a psychological enemy as opposed to a physical enemy like Zod was. We see him make mistakes and we see him grow from those mistakes and learn from them.

MICHAEL BAILEY: What happened in my mind is that between *Man of Steel* and *Batman v Superman: Dawn of Justice*, the Snyder fans took that vitriol and turned around and became bullies themselves. So you had a very dedicated group of people that loved *Man of Steel* which, as a film, holds up better than *Superman Returns*, because it was establishing something new instead of trying to establish something new with the backdrop of something from 1978. It was a weird needle to thread.

CASE AIKEN: The internal response to *Man of Steel* was more like, "Let's make Superman bad. Let's set up a nightmare of a future where he's bad and his eyes are red all the time." It just felt like they rushed into all of the things that used to work as a subversion. Like *The Dark Knight Returns* worked as a subversion, with Superman being a tool of the government trying his best not to be that, but still has to take Batman in. That worked because we had 50 years at that point of Superman and Batman being best friends and playing baseball and things like that. It just would've been more interesting if Batman was established in a second *Man of Steel* movie as being out there, and then they collide in the movie after that. But instead it was, "Let's just run into Batman and have them be instant enemies."

DAN JURGENS (Superman writer): In a perfect world I would love to see a movie that was *The Death of Superman*, kind of as we did it. We do not live in a perfect world. So much of Doomsday, the way they did it, was right; there was a lot that I liked about it. And I even understood why they had to adjust the origin and come up with their version of the origin as opposed to the one that I did in *Superman/Doomsday: Hunter/Prey*. For me, it's funny because I think for a writer artist, a movie exists on a couple of different levels. One is the idea in general, and you're using your characters, and it's fun to see them realized in live-action. The other one is, artistically, if they stay pretty close to your design, there's something about that that is cool. And they did that with Doomsday. I mean, 90% of it was what we had done in the books.

And the other part of it is, because this is more rare, when the director goes out of his way to recapture scenes that you drew as the artist up there on screen. So here's Superman being cradled by Lois, which is right out of the books. And we were all sitting there watching the movie. And I could see where they had done some of the same stuff with Frank's work. Frank Miller's work as far as Batman goes, and they did it with mine. It's just this tremendous surge that you get inside, when you see them try and interpret what you drew and recreate it in live action. So, when you sit there, as the creator, I have a reaction that exists on different levels. One is as the writer, one is as the artistic creator, and another one just as the guy who drew it. And it's overall quite a charge.

MICHAEL BAILEY: I believe in my heart of hearts that they did not earn the ending to *BvS* that they did, and unfortunately they took a live-action Doomsday off the table for a while as well — because Zack Snyder didn't make a film so much as he took a bunch of graphic novels and took the really cool images from them and created a story around it. I mean, there are so many *Dark Knight Returns* flashes in that film, it's not even funny. But I don't think they got to the point where you felt enough for Superman that his death was going to be meaningful for you. It turns out that they're really good at establishing Superman and they're really good at killing him, but only on television can you have the middle part and it works. Maybe that has to do with more people emotionally invested in a television series, because you're getting it on a weekly basis. As in the case of *Superman and Lois*, you get to know these characters because you're watching them over 15 to 22 episodes, whereas with a movie you have two-and-a-half to four hours long and it comes out every few years. So there isn't as much of an emotional response to it… unlike the Marvel films, where they release three films a year and they're different characters, but it's all connected. It feels like you're continuing the story that way.

DARYN KIRSCHT: The obvious difference between the theatrical cut and ultimate edition of the film is the half-hour of footage that helps flesh out the story and has it make more sense. The pacing is much improved and allows an opportunity to live in and get a feel for that world. We get to see Clark going to Gotham to investigate Batman and Lois as she tracks down who was behind the incident in Africa (and what actually happened) as well as the incident on Capitol Hill. The ending with the death of Superman also features more material… whereas before the audience had to put the pieces together in their head.

Plus, you have the artistic master class that is the ultimate edition which is what Zack Snyder originally intended. You cannot cut 30 minutes out of a movie meant to be a longer story and still have it make sense. He went through the same thing with *Watchmen*. It was meant to be a longer movie (which was necessary when you consider the source material), and when you cut out that much footage, it takes away from the story and characters. Warner Bros. can deem it necessary to cut the run time to gain more screenings (in theory, making more money), but if you taint the quality of your product in doing so, nobody will want to go back to watch it a second time (or even a first time). It also drives some of the audience away from watching the ultimate edition when it comes out on home video.

RAY FISHER (actor, "Cyborg," *Justice League*): These days, the idea of Superman being universal hope, while it's a very enticing idea, looking at the world, that doesn't necessarily seem to be represented anywhere. When Superman was created in the 1930s, things were presented in such a way where it was, "This is right, this is wrong. These are the good guys, these are the bad guys" — giving the character a little bit more, or in some cases a lot more, reason to doubt himself and doubt the world around them, and *still* having that character at the end of the day make the ultimate sacrifice and do what's right; even for certain people who may not like him, but may not despise him, it has to mean something.

One of the big themes for me in watching *BvS* specifically is that you look at Lex Luthor and Bruce Wayne: They're a perfect study as to what's going on in the world around us. And you think about Superman, who is basically a penniless, orphaned immigrant who simply wants to do good and nobody will let him. And you have two of the most powerful and intelligent men on the planet who have had their places in our world basically upended. They're basically told, "You were at the top of the food chain, but here's this person who could literally do more than you ever could and doesn't want a single thing. He doesn't want to take advantage of anybody, he's not after money, he's not after anything except to do the right thing." And that *would* make people nervous. For Superman, hope in and of itself may not be optimistic all the time, but as long as hope stays alive, as long as there's that glimmer… Even at the end of *BvS*, you see that little bit of dirt rising off the coffin, you see that little bit of hope.

BEN AFFLECK: In *BvS*, Bruce was a man obsessed with the past and the wrongs he perceived had been done by Superman's hand. What he went through in that film gave him a totally different understanding of those events and of who Superman really was. In *Justice League*, he realizes the hope that Superman gave to the world and that, without him, the hope is gone as well. In *Justice League* he started from a place of looking forward; he knows there is extreme danger coming and he now sees the value of including others in his fight.

MICHAEL EURY: I think Cavill is a perfect screen Superman, and it's just that the material they've given him is questionable. I'm about to violate a personal dictum: I normally don't like to talk too much about contemporary material because I also realize that I'm not the demo, right? But I still would pay my $10 to go see a movie, but technically I know they're not being made for me. But you know, Zack Snyder just didn't get it, with all due respect. You do *not* bring Superman down to our level to make him relatable, you bring us up to Superman's level. *That's* what Christopher Reeve did so darn well. Just a couple of years after Watergate, we had a President resign in disgrace in 1974, but four years later, all we needed was Reeve's Superman to just smile at Lois Lane and say, "Lois, I never lie." I'm sure some people chuckled at that in the theaters back then, but he was someone to look up to; not a creepy Superman or a morose Superman who is going to sit there as a kid and let his dad die. Superman's smart. He can figure out how to do things and *still* not reveal himself, but it's just that Snyder didn't get it.

MICHAEL BAILEY: Whereas Marvel is like, "We're getting 'em in the costume within the first movie and establishing all of this," DC's like, "No, we're going to take an entire film to set everything up, so that with the *next one* we can do, *this*." But there is no next one. Look at *Justice League*. To be fair, Warner Bros. screwed the pooch on *Justice League* every which way they could. The fact that those people aren't in charge anymore doesn't surprise me in the least, because if you're going to pull somebody off a film and put somebody else in, make sure it's going to work instead of having this mess of a film that has three different tones and none of them work together. It's these executives sitting in these meetings who are the ones that ultimately decide the fate of these characters that just don't get the idea of somebody that just does the right thing, simply because it's the right thing to do. Like they have to bring him down to their level. Yeah, it's not an easy thing to do. He is not a tough character to write, it's just tough to find a person that can write him.

You talk to creators who understand the character, and they get it. It's almost like faith — you either have it or you don't. You either buy into this character or you don't. But if you *don't*, then you can't change the character to fit your world view and have Martha Kent say, which is a motherly thing to say, to her son, "Be their hero or don't. You don't owe them anything." Now that's *a* Martha Kent raising Clark Kent, but it's not *the* Martha Kent who raised him. We're in this perfect storm of fandom that hasn't decided what it wants from Superman, and the people that give us Superman can't decide on what they want to give us, so it's a giant mess.

ANTHONY DESIATO: I know people are very divided when it comes to the Snyderverse. It's really intense. I like where I am because watching *Man of Steel* and *Batman v Superman* in theaters, I came away from both viewing experiences a little mixed, they didn't line up with the expectations that I had of what they would be. But I always felt that they were better than what a lot of people said about them. And that was sort of always my defense. I'm like, "Well, they're not that bad."

CASE AIKEN: My biggest problem with the Snyder movies was they rushed into, "We can't trust Superman, so let's get Batman to fight him, and then suddenly the world news *loves* Superman after he's dead." It's like, "Wait a minute... *what?*" I think we missed a *Man of Steel 2* where he's actually the good hero there. The movie didn't do quite as well as they wanted, so they course-corrected by trying to appeal too much to iconography that people responded to, like putting Batman in there, because Batman movies sell. As a result, it felt like a rushed project whereas it could've spent a little more time with Superman proving that he *is* Superman. It would've felt better to the folks who reacted negatively to it. The Snyder fandom online is frustrating because you can't have mixed feelings about these properties. As a result, you either love it or you hate it. And I'm like, "I like *Man of Steel* fine. I thought it was a fine movie. I thought Cavill was a good Superman. I think the Smallville fight in act two is better than the third act fight in Metropolis." If you had a strong sequel immediately coming after that, people would look back on it and be like, "It was a good movie."

RAY MORTON: Another 1986 book that did damage to Superman was Frank Miller's *The Dark Knight Returns*. Miller's unique take on an aging Batman also presented a new spin on Superman, turning him into an establishment figure — a willing agent of a right wing government, a bit of a fascist and a self-righteous prig who was willing to sell out Batman (with whom he had previously been friends). This negative interpretation of the Man of Steel worked perfectly for Miller's dystopian tale. Unfortunately, because this seems to be the only comic book a lot of Hollywood executives have ever read, it is in large part responsible for the rather dreary take on the character we have seen on screen ever since, as well as the common complaint that Superman is a bore who you can't do anything with (the "Big Blue Boy Scout" put down). Folks who hold this opinion clearly haven't read the early years of the comic or the '70s stuff, because it would be impossible for them to hold this opinion if they did.

BRAD RICCA: I really liked *The Snyder Cut* because I think it captured the idea of what a world without Superman would be like. What that says to me is that here is somebody — Zack Snyder — capable of telling a really good Superman story, but then in that final scene it's the exact opposite of what you were setting up.

MICHAEL BAILEY: Superman dies at the end of *Batman v Superman*, and then you get into Zack Snyder's *Justice League,* where he comes back and you're like, "Okay, cool. He's back and he's okay." Snyder wanted him in the black outfit, but whatever… that's an aesthetic choice. You know, apparently Zack Snyder is a Rolling Stones fan, which is fine. But *then,* you hear that the very next step — and you see it in the epilogue where the next time we see Superman, he's flying around carrying Batman's head — was to make Superman evil. And that's *another* thing we've been fighting for like 10 years. There is the contingent of people where the only thing they can really think of to do with Superman is have him turn against humanity.

ANTHONY DESIATO: In more recent years though, with some time and perspective and rewatching, and watching the ultimate edition of *Batman v Superman* — which really made a difference, really helped fill in a lot — I really just came to understand what Snyder was going for, and the world that he was creating, the lens that he was looking at these characters through, and I think through the lens of a modern, realistic world that would probably not view an alien being with that power favorably, the way they do in the Donner movie. I think that inner conflict and that angst that you see in Henry Cavill's portrayal, I think that's very appropriate in terms of this lens that we're reviewing the world and the character through.

Now someone might say, "Well, I don't want to see the more realistic take," or whatever you want to call it, and that's fine. I think that the choices that are made in those movies make sense, for me at least, and it's definitely a different take. It really works for me. I found a lot of meaning in those movies. I'm definitely a fan.

MICHAEL BAILEY: And *then*, the angry eyes of anger… I blame that on Jim Lee. I know that the cliché is to blame everything on a hot artist, who I think is still a publisher on some level, though you don't really hear much from him as you used to. But when he started doing covers, and other artists started doing the same thing, their way to make Superman edgy was to get his heat vision going. The first time you really saw the heat vision as a scary weapon was Alan Moore's "For the Man Who Has Everything," where he uses his heat vision to burn Mongol after he's been put through the hell he put him through. And the post-*Crisis* guys would use heat vision, and there were like one or two images where the eyes were smoldering, but it was always something that was kept in reserve. Like if he's doing that, it's *really* bad. Where now it's Tuesday, so we have to make him look cool or like a badass. It's just such a narrative crutch that, again, shows you that they don't know what to do with this character.

And it's very obvious from the way the character was handled that the powers-that-be at DC Comics either didn't get him or didn't like him. I got the sense that Dan DiDio and Lee did not care for Superman all that much. They would pay lip service when it was important and there was a time around 2014 that Dan said in an interview, "It's weird, when Superman does bad, the whole line does bad, so we've got to get him back to where he needs to be." But then they would always make the wrong decisions.

The Justice League Snyder Cut *is likely the last film within the DC universe to come from Zack Snyder, and it was presumed, as time has dragged on, that the situation would be the same with Henry Cavill's portrayal of Superman. And yet the new regime at Warner Bros., encouraged by Dwayne Johnson, seemed to have had a change of heart given the tag sequence of the actor's* Black Adam, *which features Henry Cavill's Superman lowering into frame, accompanied by the John Williams theme, stating that the two of them need to talk. That brief moment — music and all — suggested the return of a more classic version of the character, or one that has come out of* Justice League *as a genuine beacon of hope.*

DARYN KIRSCHT: I think it was awesome that Henry Cavill got to return to the role. It was a shame that he was not able to do so literally since filming *Zack Snyder's Justice League* in 2016. Cavill deserves it. Even critics of Snyder's films still believe Cavill could excel as Superman. Not often do you have people on both sides of the aisle saying he should be Superman, as well as having that particular actor care so deeply about the character.

HENRY CAVILL: There is such a bright future ahead for the character, and I'm so excited to tell a story with an enormously joyful Superman. As an actor, you have to learn that there are things out of your control, no matter what you may think, no matter how your performance was, no matter what factors were not in your control in the first place, no matter how the audience feels. Superman was something which I had to very gently hold onto in my heart, because I didn't know whether I would have the opportunity to play it again. But the opportunity was very important to get again.

DARYN KIRSCHT: At that time, many people questioned what kind of Superman we would be getting with Cavill. Would it be a restoration and contin-uation of the Snyderverse? Would it be more in line with "Josstice League?" Or would it be a completely new thing with no strings attached to either previous incarnation? To me, the Snyderverse will not be restored unless Zack Snyder is involved in some creative fashion, whether that be director, writer, producer, etc. In *Black Adam*, seeing Superman in the *Man of Steel* suit might give some Snyder fans hope, but it is clearly edited to be much brighter and entails the iconic John Williams theme from the Christopher Reeve Superman films instead of the Hans Zimmer theme from Snyder's films. I might not appreciate it as much as others will, but I was happy for Cavill to be able to have a say in how he wanted Super-man to be portrayed moving forward like Christopher Reeve did. He deserved to have more opportunities to portray the character, especially in another Superman movie.

HENRY CAVILL: There is something so true and honest and hopeful, which is the best of all of us, and I love that. I think it's the thing which we all truly yearn for deep, deep down, which is goodness and everyone else being good and good to one another and helping one another. Even at our most cynical, I think that, deep down, that's what we want.

As it turns out, Cavill's return as Superman was short-lived indeed. No sooner had Black Adam *been released and the actor made his statement about it, than James Gunn and Peter Safaran were appointed as the head of DC Films and TV by Warner Bros., and their plans are obviously very different.* Superman Legacy, *with a new actor in the role of the Man of Steel and focusing on his early days, is going to be released July 11, 2025.*

JAMES GUNN (co-head of DC Films; writer, *Superman Legacy*): Peter and I have a DC slate ready to go, which we couldn't be more over the moon about. Among those on the slate is Superman. In the initial stages, our story will be focusing on an earlier part of Superman's life, so the character will not be played by Henry Cavill. But we had a great meeting with Henry and we're big fans and we talked about a number of exciting possibilities to work together in the future.

PETER SAFRAN (co-head of DC Films): *Superman Legacy* is not an origins story. It focuses on Superman's balancing his Kryptonian heritage with his human upbringing. He's the embodiment of of truth, justice and the American way. He's kindness in a world that thinks of kindness as old fashioned.

DARYN KIRSCHT: To think that Cavill had just come back to film a cameo for *Black Adam* and was so excited to do so and now will not be able to see that through in such a short amount of time is quite bizarre and hard to wrap my head around. Now that he had finally become the traditionally-portrayed Superman after his return in *Zack Snyder's Justice League*, many people were hoping he would receive another opportunity to continue in the role. On the other hand, I understand the desire to wipe the slate clean so that James Gunn can have complete creative freedom to craft the universe he envisions. Obviously, we have no idea yet as to what kind of Superman story he will tell, but I guess we will all have to move forward knowing it will not involve Cavill — and I feel awful for him. Just thinking of all the troubled productions and lack of movement on solo Superman projects he has been through only strengthens those feelings.

ANTHONY DESIATO: Needless to say, it has not been an easy few years for fans of Superman on the big screen, going from the nebulous post-Justice League years to the promising *Black Adam* cameo to, ultimately, the news of Cavill's ouster from the role. As much as I enjoyed Cavill's performance and felt he had more to do, I do believe that a clean break is the best way for the DCEU to move forward. I'm hard-pressed to see how mixing and matching the Snyderverse and the "Gunnverse" would serve anyone well. Also, as exciting as it was to see Cavill in that *Black Adam* post-credits scene, I'm somewhat wary about what a non-Snyder Cavill film would have looked like. I'm well aware that plenty of people love that notion; however, based on Cavill's comments, I can't shake the feeling that the movie would have tried too hard to move away from the prior films. Hopefully it still would have honored the journey Clark went on from *Man of Steel* through Zack Snyder's *Justice League* (and, in fairness, the *Black Adam* appearance struck a fair balance), but it's hard to say.

DARYN KIRSCHT: I would rather not taint the work he has done with mismanagement or soft reboots that don't do Cavill or the character proper justice. Henry Cavill will always be the Superman of my generation, no matter what happens. And I would never trade that for the world.

BRANDON ROUTH: I'm certainly very optimistic about James Gunn, with whom I'm socially friendly. Peter Safaran I've not met, but I am a fan of James and what he's done with *Guardians of the Galaxy* and *Peacemaker. Peacemaker* is very raunchy and out there — a lot of his stuff is — but he cares about the characters, he cares about the relationships between the characters and he creates families. And *that* is what's missing in so much of the DC content that is in the Marvel content, especially in *Guardians*. And that's what people respond to. There's hope, there's joy and there's love for the characters, so I'm very excited for the future of DC and all of its many branches.

ANTHONY DESIATO: As for Gunn's planned "young Superman" movie, my main hope is that it plays up Clark as a reporter and the idea that he actually enjoys journalism, rather than it merely being a convenient cover. Casting-wise, I've learned enough by now to know that there's always someone out there, so I look forward to seeing the next incarnation.

MICHAEL BAILEY: I'm torn on the whole Henry Cavill thing because, on one hand, I'd love to see more of him in the role. He was never the problem and, frankly, the whole roll-out of the DC cinematic universe was bungled on a number of levels. On the other hand, I'm excited that Superman as a character is getting another movie. Starting in his early career as opposed to retelling the origin from scratch is the way to go. I know I'm too plugged into these things, so take this with that in mind, but I think the origin doesn't need to be retold in a dramatic way. People know who Superman is and it's my gut feeling that the general audience just wants to see him doing his thing. The popularity of *Superman and Lois* points to this.

MARK WAID: I feel very good about this development. Gunn's sensibilities are more in line with who Superman is than Snyder's were, and I very much look forward to seeing a joyous, hopeful Superman on the silver screen once more.

Amidst all of this, in 2015 the "El" family got a shot of optimism with the arrival of

Supergirl — *starring Melissa Benoist* — *the television series that first aired on CBS before moving to the CW with shows like* Arrow *and* The Flash, *later to be joined by* DC's Legends of Tomorrow, Black Lightning *and* Batwoman. *Particularly in its early days, the show projected a similar sensibility to Richard Donner's* Superman: The Movie *in the idea of the hope that Superman brought with it.*

SARAH SECHTER (executive producer, *Supergirl*): We absolutely invoked Richard Donner's name so many times in talking about his work and we were trying to honor that and make it real for the time; making this woman be a powerful woman, but ultimately, who cares if she's a woman? We just wanted to see a hero. That was really our challenge.

ANDREW KREISBERG (executive producer, *Supergirl*): I say this with zero disrespect to any iteration of Superman that came after the Donner film, but for us, that was the one that really touched us as children. There is just something about it that's in your DNA and was the star that we were guided by, because there was a truth to the Donner version and a reality and, ironically, a groundedness that we felt very strongly that we wanted to capture. And truthfully, that wasn't really what was out there at the time in the comic book world: that sort of unabashed hope and brightness and light. What's funny is that Peter Roth, who ran Warner Bros. television, after he saw the pilot said of Melissa, "That's the closest feeling connection to Superman I've seen since Christopher Reeve," and we feel that way too.

MELISSA BENOIST (actress, "Kara Zor-El/Supergirl," *Supergirl*): I definitely think Supergirl, or Kara, has that too. That's one of the key words that came to mind when we were shooting the pilot, that I had to feel that almost internally. I always had to feel hopeful and believe that she doesn't quit. So I definitely think she is a beacon of hope for her friends and family.

In the show's second season the decision was made to introduce Kara's cousin Superman on the show in the form of actor Tyler Hoechlin.

MELISSA BENOIST: I'd wanted Superman to be on the show from the beginning. During the first season, whenever Kara interacted with Clark through Instant Messaging, I always felt like there was something missing.

SARAH SCHECTER: What was important to us was that Supergirl not be in the shadow of Superman. At the same time, what we liked to do on the show, besides delivering action and comedy and drama, was to make it a family story.

For us it was really interesting to get deeper into Kara's family, and that includes Clark. Clark is the only surviving member of her family, so at a certain point it's strange *not* to have that be part of her story.

MELISSA BENOIST: I always wanted them to interact because it's such an important relationship, and they have learned so much from each other. She has things he doesn't have, he has things she doesn't have, but they've learned from each other, so I think it's perfect.

CHYLER LEIGH (actor, "Alex Danvers," *Supergirl*): I was so surprised when I heard they were adding Superman, because everybody had been saying, "Oh, it's not going to happen." And then script number one of season two comes in and you're like, "Oh, there he is! Well that's cool." And you kind of get to see a little bit of Alex and Superman's relationship, because he's been part of the family so there's a dynamic that's always been there. As a result, it delivers some pretty funny little moments.

JEREMY JORDAN (actor, "Winn Schott," *Supergirl*): I was surprised too, but I think it's a testament to the show and to how solidly we had established the Supergirl character that they feel like they can bring in Superman and it won't detract from her. As far as Winn's concerned, he's all about Superman. If there was one man that Winn would turn for, it would probably be Superman… not that I'm teasing *anything*, because I'm not.

MEHCAD BROOKS (actor, "James Olsen," *Supergirl*): Character-wise, it's great for the show because the conversation that everybody's been waiting for is, "Yo, bro, you're dating my cousin." That is happening and it's a great conversation to have — especially since it doesn't end up in any punching or choking. Thank God, because he's a big guy. He gives me some good advice about dating her, and I give him some good advice about who she's become.

SARAH SCHECHTER: The difficult part was finding the person to play Superman. And then we met Tyler Hoechlin. I'd actually had the privilege of seeing him in the suit, and when people see him they'll realize, "Oh, *that's* why they chose him." As soon as he put it on, we were slack-jawed and like, "Oh my God, we're with Superman."

TYLER HOECHLIN (actor, "Superman," *Supergirl*): Honestly, it was a little bit surreal, but I liked that because it is a little bit easier to really just look at the character for who he is. Seeing the suit as a symbol, it takes care of itself;

realizing that this is just like any other person putting on a suit in the morning, going out to do what they do. That's kind of made it a little bit easier to approach it. I'm just excited about finding out who Clark is and who Superman is as his human self outside of being able to do everything he does.

SARAH SCHECHTER: Tyler has the charisma and the kindness, as well as the strength, and I think what people see is how fun it is to have Superman. It certainly does not overshadow Kara and Supergirl. The dynamic between them — that you'll see in the first two episodes — is just a lot of fun.

DAVID HAREWOOD (actor, "Martian Manhunter, *Supergirl*): I have to say that I kind of geeked out when I saw Melissa wearing the "S," so to see Tyler as well… that's just going to be crazy. Crazy good. He looks the part, so that's going to be awesome.

TYLER HOECHLIN: This show is so hopeful and optimistic and Superman fits right in there. It's the "truth, justice and the American way" element that I love. *That's* the person you hope would exist and do what he does with the powers that he has. They're just trying to embody that, and there are obviously struggles that go along with being someone who has that much responsibility. But in the end, I think he's incredibly happy to be able to do what he can do.

MELISSA BENOIST: Hope remained a key ingredient of the show. One of the things that I admired most about Kara is her sheer will and the fact that she never, ever gives up, even when things are at there most grim. It's a quality that runs in the family.

TYLER HOECHLIN: Not to just sit on that word, but I do think Superman's role is one of hope: the belief that things can be better and people with powers will do good things. I know it's one of the issues right now in the world in that there are a lot of people in power who, if you look at it on the surface, you just assume are either self-serving or 'evil,' but here you have someone who is capable of really taking over, yet he *chooses* not to use his powers selfishly. Instead he helps other people. That is *such* a symbol and statement of who he truly is. That's something I would really want to focus on; to make it a top priority of who he is.

From 2016 to 2018, Cartoon Network aired the animated series Justice League Action, *geared for a younger audience as DC's heroes go up against an assortment of villains.*

The cast featured the late Kevin Conroy reprising Batman/Bruce Wayne, James Woods as Lex Luthor and Jason J. Lewis as Superman.

JASON J. LEWIS (Superman voice actor, *Justice League Action*): As iconic as Superman is, for me the key was trying to find a way into him that would be a bit different than we've recently seen. I wanted to bring back aspects of him where he didn't take himself very seriously, though he took the job seriously. I also want- ed to play up the Midwestern Clark Kent aspect of him, yet have him be a little bit more on the naïve side, yet still have that sincerity. When I was kind of building his character with my voice, I realized that what they were asking for was not that different from who I am, so that was the key to helping him sound so sincere, not create some kind of silly voice and make it as real as possible.

Superman was given the prequel treatment in the 2018 to 2019 live-action television series Krypton. *The focus is on Kal-El's grandfather Seg-El (Cameron Cuffe) some 200 years before the planet's destruction. In it, the House of El has been ostracized and shamed, which leads to Seg struggling to reclaim the family's honor. The show also stars Shaun Sipos as Adam Strange, a human from the future who is there to warn Seg-El about the computer intelligence Brainiac, but also to prevent the past from being altered, resulting in Superman never being born. But this is no* Back to the Future-*like approach with easy solutions; there are genuine consequences to every action.*

DAVID S. GOYER (creator, *Krypton*): By design I'd always intended *Man of Steel* to be a deeper dive into Krypton than we've ever seen in a movie before. I'd done a lot of thinking about Kryptonian society and culture; even things that didn't ultimately wind up in the movie, but certainly the production designer and I talked about a lot. It really forced me to consider Krypton and what that world was like. As a result I started generating a lot more ideas. Although Warner Bros. didn't express interest in a show based on Krypton, I laid out the basic idea of the Kryptonian guilds and how by birth it was pre-determined who you would be, your vocation and who you mate with, coupled with the idea of young people rising up against all of that.

CAMERON CUFFE (actor, "Seg-El," *Krypton*): I found this to be a really deep, high-concept science-fiction with fantastically complicated characters; char- acters who aren't necessarily heroes or villains, and characters who aren't emotion- ally or morally fully formed yet, and what their ideals are. I saw an opportunity to make a show that had really complex shades of gray in terms of the choices that the characters make, which was the main thing as an actor that drew me to the role and made me feel that I have to be a part of this… on top of it being a show about my favorite character of all time.

DAVID S. GOYER: Then there was the idea of flipping the "El" symbol — the "S" — on its head where it is actually the Scarlet letter in that our hero Seg-El has to earn that back. As we talked about it, they started to see the possibilities. Then when we folded in the concept of time travel — or as we call it, the "re-determinator" element — that got them even more excited because it meant that there's the possibility of rewriting history. I mean, maybe in our show Krypton *doesn't* explode. That makes it different than a classic prequel like *Gotham,* because no one knows the fate of any of these characters. With *Gotham,* you know young Bruce Wayne will become Batman. Taking nothing away from that show, it's hard to build in a lot of surprises. So that's how it began.

CAMERON CUFFE (actor, "Seg-El," *Krypton*): Someone comes along, and that someone is Adam Strange, and says, "One day, your grandson will be the greatest superhero the universe has ever known, and I need your help to save him." None of this makes any sense to Seg, but he's gonna have to confront his past, which is very painful for him, as well as look to a future that he never possibly imagined. He's going to have to go from a Rankless street hustler to someone who is capable of saving the multiverse. That's a heck of a journey. That really is what the show is about. How does that symbol come to become the symbol we know and love today? How does it come to stand for hope for millions across the universe?

When Jerry Siegel and Joe Shuster created this character, they grounded it very much in the world of science-fiction. The first panel in *Action Comics* number one is the planet Krypton. That's the origin of superheroes. That's where it all comes from. It has all of the fun and all of the wonder of everything about the great genre that are superhero comic books. It also has those wonderful shades of gray, and hopefully the allegories to the real world that great science-fiction like Blade Runner has. That's the show we were trying to make.

Tyler Hoechlin was back in the superhero news again, first when he appeared on the CW's Arrowverse crossover event Crisis on Infinite Earths, *where he would briefly battle Brandon Routh's version of the Man of Steel, but then in 2021, the decision was made to spin him off into his own show,* Superman & Lois, *which sees him playing Clark Kent/Superman with Elizabeth Tulloch as his wife Lois Lane, Jordan Elsass (in the first two seasons) and Michael Bishop (in season three) as their son Jonathan and Alex Garfin as his brother Jordan. What needs to be emphasized is that this take on the Man of Steel is a more hopeful one, with darkness kept to a minimum as the show deftly balances superheroics and family drama.*

Tyler Hoechlin was introduced as the character on Supergirl, *but was spun off into the series* Superman & Lois *(art © and courtesy D.C. Stuelpner; Superman © and TM DC Comics/Warner Bros. Discovery).*

ROB O'CONNOR: Tyler Hoechlin may not be the greatest Superman of them all, but what he is is a charming, solid lead who you want to root for and who you could envision wanting to hang out with. Despite being a man not even in his mid 30s, he carries a charisma and an elder authority that makes him completely convincing as the father of teenage boys, not to mention a seasoned Man of Steel. I think more attention could be paid to making a delineation between the "public Clark Kent persona" and the "public Superman persona" however, especially visually — even Dean Cain changed his hairstyle and wore glasses that seemed to change the entire shape of his eyes! Nonetheless, his work has been utterly charming and I look forward to following the evolution of the *Superman & Lois* series — I do secretly hope that the series gets a short and sweet five seasons however, rather than falling into the familiar trap of outstaying its welcome, as nearly every Superman show (*Superboy* being the exception) has done.

DAN JURGENS: That show would not exist if not for the *Superman: Lois & Clark* comic I did with Lee Weeks. I think embryonic material from what we did in the books is all there in the show, whether it's the farm house, the stuff out in

Smallville living remotely, and them still being a couple that has tangible interactions with the world around them. So yeah, I think that a lot of that is there.

CASE AIKEN: There's always going to be episodes that aren't your favorite, but I really like the show as a whole. The dynamic of Superman as dad works so well here and it really sells several things. The biggest thing was Clark Kent as dad works great; one of my favorite scenes in the show is when Clark becomes the assistant coach for the football team and he is purposely doing all the Clark Kent-schtick of klutzy and embarrassing things just to mess with his kids. He's goofy, but is also a good dad. I think that the dynamic of the show really touched on that, and something that the character had skirted around for a long time, but the idea of Superman as dad is a really good one. Having to be Superman and taking him away from his kids is a really good dramatic device, and I think that should be explored more. I'm a little bummed that the comics introduced Jonathan as a son of Superman and then raced him up to adulthood. As a result, we really lost out on the opportunity to really do stories of Superman having all of these huge responsibilities that no one can really understand, and at the same time having very understandable responsibilities in the form of being a father.

ALAN BURKE (cohost, *All Star Super Fan Podcast*): Tyler Hoechlin has been a real breath of fresh air to the role and world of Superman. From his first appearance in *Supergirl*, it was clear to anyone watching that this man wanted to be Superman and, even more importantly, that he enjoyed playing the part. His portrayal has been a back-to-basics return to the roots of the character, and watching him has been fun. Though the *Supergirl* series often appeared to want to undermine the Man of Steel, to take away from him in order to build their heroine up, the likability of Hoechlin made this almost impossible, resulting in the inevitable creation of *Superman & Lois*, which has been a thoroughly enjoyable watch thus far.

TYLER HOECHLIN: When we did Superman on *Supergirl* and the crossovers, it was a Superman who's been himself for a while and he's been doing very well. He's won every battle he's ever fought. There really hasn't been a streak of letdowns, whereas now, with this story we're telling that has he and Lois as parents, it's a completely new challenge for him, and one that he hasn't necessarily risen to the occasion on. What I love about him is that no matter what he's facing, he remains persistent. He's always hopeful and always working towards making "it" happen. But at this point it's been a few years of not necessarily seeing the results that he would hope for and not being enough for these two children that are his. You're seeing Clark Kent at a place in his life where he's *not* just winning all the time. It's a genuine struggle that he's having to work through.

Despite the fact that he'd been acting for well over 20 years and played a variety of roles, there's no question that Hoechlin has gained the greatest amount of attention for his portrayal of Superman. As such, it's a long way from the kid who dreamt of being a baseball player. Born September 11, 1987 in Corona, California, he spent a good portion of his youth focused on the double-track of baseball and acting, both of which he felt passionately about.

TYLER HOECHLIN: Basically I played literally from the time I can remember. My dad had played, my older brother played, so I always wanted to be like my older brother. That just kind of was a natural thing that I fell into. I was one of those kids that started playing year-round when I was probably, God, seven years old. I was never one of those kids that felt like I *had* to go to practice or that I was being made to go to practice or forced to play the game. Baseball was a natural fit for me. Then acting was a really random situation. I was at home and my mom for some reason had brought up that I had been in commercials when I was a baby. I had no recollection of this. At the time I was like seven or eight years old, and I brought up, "Oh, that'd be kind of cool to go and make my own money so I could buy my own video games."

That was my thing, I was trying to be an entrepreneur at seven years old. So that was a thought that had come across my mind, but nothing really came out of it. Then ironically, maybe a few months later, we got a letter in the mail for some more of those acting schools that were popping up around Southern California at the time. This one was called Beverly Hills Studios, and we got a random letter in the mail for an audition at a convention center. We were driving up to Moreno Valley for a baseball game, and my coach called and said, "Hey, turn around, game's been cancelled. It's got a rain-out" — which we had never had in Moreno Valley. I played in Moreno Valley through high school, so in the time span of ten, eleven years I played there, I think I might have had two games rained out.

One could argue — depending on your belief — that this situation was akin to a form of divine intervention.

TYLER HOECHLIN: This *is* that fate moment. We had nothing else to do that day, and we were like, "What are we going to do?" "Oh, let's go to that audition for that acting class." We did, and we got into this acting school, and from there we got an agent about six months later. On my fifth audition I got my first job and just kind of went from there. That was really the beginning of it. I think I was about nine years old when I got my first job; had a blast doing it, just kind of finished that school curriculum, whatever it was, and then went on and found another acting school, acting class, tried out a few different things. I was thirteen years old when I got *Road to Perdition*. That was kind of the moment where I knew I really enjoyed acting, and that if and when baseball is done, this is what I will do. That was really where both of those things started and when it became an official tandem thing for me.

I still saw baseball as a possible future. That was always my first goal, my first passion. In high school I played in every Scout Showcase tournament. I played in the Area Code Games, which is roughly the top 250 high school students in the country that compete. It's for college coaches and professional scouts to see them play against each other for about a week. I played in that going into my sopho-more year, I played in it going into my junior year. Then I got a scholarship to Arizona State, and I played there for a year, and then transferred out to UC-Ir-vine, played there for two years. The team I was on at Arizona State, we went to Omaha. The team I was on at UC-Irvine, we were an out away from going back to Omaha. It is always a sad, sad story, but yeah, that was my intention. I loved playing baseball, and the only reason I played was to play professional baseball. I wanted that to be my career for a long time. I turned down multiple jobs and meetings because of it.

There did come a moment — when Hoechlin was playing collegiate summer leave in Michigan in the North Woods League — where things changed, pushing him more towards acting.

TYLER HOECHLIN: I remember I was playing collegiate summer league out in Michigan in the North Woods League, and I got a call from my agent. He's like, "Oh man, you're going to love me, you're going to love me. I need you to get back to L.A. I've got you a meeting with Francis Ford Coppola." I went, "Chris, I can't, I'm sorry, man." He's like, "You can't?" "No, I can't. I'm in the middle of nowhere in Michigan. The team bus is only going from the field to the hotel, and the nearest airport is five hours away. I can't get a cab and go to the airport." "So you can't make the meeting with Coppola?" "No, tell him I'm sorry." I love my agent for this, because he stuck with me for all these years, but those were the things that I would say no to. I had to say no to a meeting with Coppola, I turned down a role in *Twilight* because it was two weeks before a season was starting, and I would have missed the first four weeks of the year. I was the starting second baseman, and we were ranked pre-season Top Ten and supposed to go back to the College World Series. I couldn't leave my teammates;

it was just something I wouldn't do. So that was from day one always my Plan A. When I did finally decide to stop, it was one of those moments where I had always said that I would never stop until someone literally looked me in the face and said, "Stop playing. Go do acting." I imagined that being someday in pro ball I would have been Kevin Costner in *Bull Durham*. If I had never discovered acting, I literally would have been *that* guy. Even though you make twelve hundred bucks a month, if I was making twelve hundred bucks a month to play baseball, I would have done it. I would have stayed.

In his junior year, he pulled his hamstring during the summer and he simply wasn't at a hundred percent and couldn't play on the same level that he had been.

TYLER HOECHLIN: It was one of those things where I had, the year before, turned down meetings left and right and auditions all the time for practice, because it's college baseball. You can't miss a practice. It's not like you're twelve years old anymore and it's an extracurricular. This is now a career and something that people are committed to. I would turn down meetings, and this year I was hurt, I wasn't starting, I wasn't playing. I'd go to the coach a little more often to say, "Hey, I've got an audition, would it be okay if I missed?" He was always really great about it. I didn't do it too often, but he was good when I did ask. But there was one time where I was testing for a pilot, and I went to him, and I asked, "Hey, would this be okay?" He was like, "Yeah, I think after this one though, maybe you and I need to have a conversation." I said, "Okay, yeah, that's fair." I had the audition, I didn't get the job, and I came to him and said, "Hey, just so you know, I didn't get the job." He goes, "Okay, well, I just want to have a conversation about moving forward, because right now I feel like you are hurting yourself by trying to balance these two things. I feel like you have great potential in both, but at this point I really think you're only going to be able to move forward in either by picking one."

I knew that day was going to come, I always knew it would eventually present itself, but I just didn't know *when*. This kind of conversation came up, and you know, I'm there on scholarship, he has nothing to gain by me leaving. He's like, "Look, I've been around this for a long time. You're a good player. If you stay and finish, will you get drafted? Probably, you'll probably play in pro ball. Who knows how far you'll go? But I think you have a very unique opportunity that a lot of people don't get, over in L.A." And that was fair. It was exactly what I've always asked for, to know that it was time, because I literally would have been the guy that would have played pro ball until they came to me and said, "Go home, you don't work here anymore." That was going to be my life. We had that conversation on a Friday and it became another one of those weird destiny things. The new quarter of school was starting that Monday. I said, "Can I finish the weekend, play these three games? Then we'll just move on after Monday?" He said, "Yeah, that's great." In a weird way I knew my last three games were my last three games. It was the most amazing feeling, because for the last, God, ten years, baseball had been like, "I have to do well today, I have to do well today, I have to do well today." Because it was all part of the process of moving forward and onward.

This was the first time since I was probably twelve, thirteen years old, that baseball was just purely fun, because I had no tomorrow. Stretching was the best thing ever, warming up was the best thing ever, guys just bullshitting and telling stories in the dugout was the best time ever. I had three days to really just remember what I loved about the game, loved about the locker room and about being on a team, that a lot of guys don't get. Because a lot of times, it's just after a game, "Hey, sorry, you're done." I got to know that my last 72 hours were my last 72, and I got to *really* enjoy those. I still cried like a baby after that last game; spent an extra hour-and-a-half in the locker room that I probably didn't need to, but yeah, it was a good close.

His focus shifted to acting, where he got to work with Tom Hanks and Paul Newman in the aforementioned Road to Perdition *when he was 13. He became a part of the television series* 7th Heaven *followed by the TV version of* Teen Wolf.

TYLER HOECHLIN: The audition was at the end of 2009, and this was right when *Twilight* was really out and popular. People were kind of jumping off of that and coat-tailing that so badly, that everything you read was vampire and werewolf. Going in to read the script for *Teen Wolf*, I was expecting it to be that. But I read the pilot, and it was great. It was such a well-written script, the characters were so great. I loved the Romeo and Juliet of the whole thing; this forbidden love between these two characters. I really enjoyed the pilot, and so I went in and read for it. I eventually was offered it, and coming out of not having been fully into the acting thing for quite a while, and being fully committed to baseball, that was a chance for me to jump back into something and dive into a character and work really consistently for a while. That was the hope. I had a conversation with [series creator] Jeff Davis when we were shooting the pilot about where he saw everything going, and I just thought it was a great vision for it. God, who knew that it would really turn out to be what it was? It kind of just took off.

Not long afterwards would come the opportunity to play Clark Kent/Superman on

Supergirl, *the interest of which could have been overwhelming to most people.*

TYLER HOECHLIN: I've been fortunate to be around this business for a long time and so I've seen things that should get a lot of attention get no attention. I've seen things that were not supposed to be a big deal become the biggest thing in the world. When it comes to how much attention something gets or how much attention it draws, I really kind of just try to expect nothing at this point. Whatever it turns into, it turns into. I think any time those larger-than-life characters are going to be presented in a new setting, it just garners attention no matter what. It's something that so many people follow and so many people are passionate about that, inevitably, there's going to be a lot of chatter about it.

Attending Comic-Con after the announcement was interesting, because people were like, "Oh, you're Superman now." I was like, "No, I'm not, I haven't done it yet. Let me go play it." Even then it didn't feel real until I think the morning of the first episode. I remember talking to my dad and being like, "Oh, it's kind of weird, after today there will always be some footage that exists of me playing this character." It didn't feel real until then. Going into it, I think I should have really felt nervous about the whole situation. For whatever reason, I had such a great meeting with [executive producers] Greg Berlanti and Andrew Kreisberg when I first got the job, that I just felt really confident in them and I felt they were really confident in me; that we knew what we were going for. I felt really comfortable the whole time.

Melissa Benoist and the rest of the cast were so great and so welcoming from day one, so it kind of felt like home. They made it a really seamless transition for me to be there. I would say it was just the most pure fun that I've had playing a character and shooting something. I had this great experience on set where a P.A. pulled over four kids, two of them were like seven or eight years old, two boys, two girls. I had the suit on, and they come over, and their eyes just light up. For ten minutes I was like, "Oh my God, to these kids, I *am* Superman. They don't know my name, they don't know who I am, they don't know what I've done. They have no idea." I couldn't love that more. This is so great. I could make these kids' day, and it has nothing to do with me. It's just I'm the guy wearing the "S." And that's it. That was such a cool experience to be able to do that for them, and then I always say that, selfishly, as an actor, it was really informative, because I went, "You know what? That's who this guy is. He's there to make kids feel like they can do anything, they can be anyone, that good can triumph over evil" and all these things.

It also kind of reminds us to be a kid again and have that kind of incredibly hopeful, optimistic outlook before we turn cynical when we get older. That's what

I kind of started falling towards as a character, wanting kids to think that that optimistic view that you have when you're a kid of what the world can be, that we can still make it that, regardless of how many times the world tells us we can't.

In an early appearance on the show, there's a moment where Superman saves a father and his kids from a drone. Afterwards, he smiles, winks at the kids and takes off — a moment that genuinely encapsulated Superman.

TYLER HOECHLIN: It was in the script, and we had a lot of fun with that. I remember reading that for the first time and I loved it. That's such a great moment. I do think it's that little nod of, "I gotcha, kid, and you know what? You can do this too." For me, it captures everything about Superman in this whole thing. I really tried to lean on that, especially it being a big character coming into a world where the title character is *not* him. It's not *his* origin story; it's not about him.

Everything for me in this was support. He's there to support Supergirl, he's there to help her, if and when she needs it. And to impart wisdom where he can, but at this point of this story, I don't think anything is about him. You know what I mean? When he's Clark, yeah, it can be about Clark, and it's about his work and it's about his relationship with Lois and stuff. We're not really there for that. You can see a little bit of Clark, and we'll see more of it again, but when he's there as Superman especially, he's there to help, he's there to support, he's there to encourage and make it about other people. I do compare it to that experience of being in a locker room. There's the veteran guys and there's the rookies. The veteran guys have been around enough, the coaches don't really need to come to the veteran guys anymore. They know what they're doing, they're comfortable in their own skin, they know how it works, they know how it goes. The veteran guys are now there to help the younger guys come up. They're there to encourage them to become the next veterans. That's kind of what it is. So that's something that I had been able to relate it to as well. Superman's only hope and idea at that point is to encourage others to reach their potential as well, and that's all he wants to do.

This is captured in a moment when he thanks a group of soldiers for their hard work, despite their being awe-struck in his presence.

TYLER HOECHLIN: I remember telling Melissa, after a couple of takes of that, I went up to her and I was like, "This is the hardest scene." "Oh really? Why?" "Well because I don't like attention. It's so many eyeballs, which is crazy."

She was like, "You know what's great though? I don't think he would either." I'm like, "No, I don't think he does." So that was something that in that moment I connected to as well, which is that he understands the symbol that he is and what he means to a lot of people, and so he has to live up to that. Whether that's a part of his personality or not, I think something fun about the character was that really you're kind of playing three or four, sometimes five characters in that guy. Because you have Clark when he's just very much Clark, you have Clark when he's around the people who know that he's Superman, then you have Superman, and then you have Clark around people that don't know that he's Superman and can't know that he's Superman.

There's just so many different layers of his personality to where, I think for me, the true Clark/Superman/Kal-El is really when he's being Clark around people that know he's Superman. *That* is the truest him, that's him not putting on any kind of extra show, playing anything up, playing anything down. For me, he enjoys the moment with the little kids and being able to encourage, but the idea of being looked at and revered? I'm not really sure he loves that. It's something he understands and he'll take it on as that's part of his role, but I don't think it's necessarily something where he walks around going, "Oh yeah, man, people think I'm great."

Something not many people may realize is the fact that Hoechlin actually auditioned for director Zack Snyder's Man of Steel, *though obviously he didn't get the role.*

TYLER HOECHLIN: That was when I was much younger, but there were things about the character that kind of hit me for the first time when I was going in for that. It is funny, because again, I haven't seen them, but I know the tones are different. And I get it, because going in for that audition, it was very much different. I read those scenes completely differently than the way that I played the character in this. That's because you have to know the story that you're telling, and you have to know the tone in which the story is being told. Those ideas stayed with me of who I thought he was. The way that they're played out is just different, because it's a different story that you're telling.

The story of Superman & Lois — *which is decidedly* not *set in the Arrowverse, and therefore takes on a completely different approach in terms of storytelling and look — has the Kent family relocating from Metropolis to Smallville in the aftermath of the death of Clark's adopted mother Martha Kent. And this is not the Smallville from the show of the same name, but rather a more modern interpretation of a small town that has fallen on hard times. Naturally things escalate from that premise in terms of Superman and what he's facing.*

LEE TOLAND KRIEGER (director, *Superman & Lois* pilot): Todd Helbing and I did talk about this, but as far as we were concerned, other than Tyler and Bitsie [Elizabeth Tulloch] being in the show, this is completely hitting the reset button. It's tricky because there's a lot out there between the crossovers and *Supergirl* that I'm sure fans are aware of, but in trying to create a new palette for the show and a new playing field, we didn't necessarily want to try and pick up in any way where those left off and to just basically start anew.

TODD HELBING (showrunner/executive producer, *Superman & Lois*): We really just wanted to make our mark and have it feel different and the tone feel different. When I first sat down with our director Lee, we were talking about Terrence Malick and *Days of Heaven*, and *Man of Steel* obviously came up quite a bit. On top of that, Greg Berlanti and I talked about *Everwood* a lot, a family show, and *Friday Night Lights* — personally one of my favorites. If you want to call this show a teenage drama family show, grounding it in every way that we could was the idea, and in that we were hoping that it would all stand out.

LEE TOLAND KRIEGER: I watched the trailer for Zack Snyder's *Man of Steel* a gazillion times and I *still* tear up every time I watch it. That has largely to do with the fact that the hopeful aspect of Superman is what drives that trailer. We talked about the idea of making a show that felt like that trailer felt, as odd as that is to say. Obviously there's more woven in there, and I'm sure Todd has spoken about the idea of taking *Friday Night Lights* and dropping Superman into a show like that. But the feeling of the trailer captivated us both as fathers and Superman lovers.

TODD HELBING: There are so many small towns in the country that are drying up, and there's a line in the show that says, "It used to be that people would come back to the communities that nurtured them. I'm a classic example of somebody who *didn't* do that. I grew up in a small town in the Midwest where it was a great childhood. I loved it and still do, but I came out to L.A. and I've never gone back. In a lot of ways, because of those scenarios and people like me that leave, the towns are struggling and we felt that was a really good story to tell with Superman. What would it be like for the guy that created the greatest hero of all time to find out that his town is struggling? That was one of the story points that Greg and I talked about from the beginning.

ELIZABETH TULLOCH (actor, "Lois Lane," *Superman & Lois*):

Honestly, part of why Tyler and I even agreed to do a series, and potentially devote years of our lives to it, is that when Todd Helbing was developing it with Greg Berlanti, they were very clear that nobody wanted to do another Arrowverse show like the rest of them, no matter how good they are. They really wanted this to be different and edgier and darker, more cinematic and grounded and real. What Todd had said was, "I want it to be like *Friday Night Lights* tonally, with a dash of Superman and Lois. Of course we'll have set pieces and all of this, but that's not what the show is really about. It's about a family." And I feel like we've achieved that.

TYLER HOECHLIN: When we spoke to Greg Berlanti, the idea was for this to stand on its own; to be its own thing. And as much as you hear that and we talked about that beforehand, you never *really* know until you're on set and actually creating it and shooting it. But on our first day, I remember seeing our incredible director Lee Tolland Krieger set up the shot and it hit me: "We *are* doing this and it's got to be its own thing." From that moment on, I had an idea of how I would feel differently with the character, so as familiar as I am with him, it's been a fresh start for me with the whole thing — and that makes it exciting.

ELIZABETH TULLOCH: Part of our hesitation is that there had been so many Arrowverse shows. At that point we were talking about it, *Arrow* was still on the air, this is *Supergirl*'s last season and *Black Lightning* is ending soon. Then there had been such a plethora of shows that Tyler and I were like, "Why do you want to make this one? Is it going to be different or is it just going to follow the same formula?" Not that we would have said no if it *had* followed the same formula, but especially as grownups and as actors, we were really interested in the idea of having it be more real. And I thought it was such a great pitch to do *Friday Night Lights* with Superman and Lois, but to have these superheroes who could be your next-door neighbors — *and* they're having the same struggles as anyone else.

Interestingly, while Hoechlin and Tulloch played off of each other well enough previously, somehow they've managed to achieve what feels like a much deeper connection on screen between them, conveying that they're a couple who have been through the highs and lows of life while raising two kids.

TODD HELBING: Both Tyler and Bitsie just possess the qualities of Clark Kent/Superman and Lois Lane. Bitsie is fearless. She's one of those people that's good at everything. Tyler played baseball in college, he's a natural athlete and a natural leader. He's also one of the nicest guys on the planet; there's no ego with him. And then, together, they have this chemistry as friends that is instant and they just spread this leadership throughout the crew. The main quality you need to have for these characters is relatability. And with both of them, there's an accessibility where they don't seem like they are not one of us. They seem like they're just great versions of us.

TYLER HOECHLIN: It's definitely a combination of things. Bitsie and I have gotten to know each other better over the years. We're such good friends and we have way too much fun working together, but there's definitely areas where we're in complete sync. And on top of that, because the tone of the show is so different, we're not necessarily just kind of hopping in and out of these scenes anymore. With the crossovers, there's so many superheroes to fit into it that you only get to see them and hear them say one or two things. Now it's been really getting to sit with each other and the characters have really been able to interact and connect on those deeper levels. It's allowing us to breathe in those scenes and have the nuances that speak for themselves.

ELIZABETH TULLOCH: Part of it is that prior to this we were essentially guest stars on other people's shows. So we never had as deep of a backstory when we were doing the crossover episodes. *Now* we have these really rich histories and these rich lives. And Tyler and I were very lucky, because we didn't do a chemistry read before we were cast, and I was really nervous the first day I was working on the *Elseworlds* crossover that the chemistry wasn't going to be great or I wasn't going to like working with him. But from the first day I felt like we had a great sort of romantic chemistry. And not just romantic chemistry, which is definitely there, but it also feels like they're partners — partners in their jobs and their careers, and they have a lot of respect for each other. They give each other space. And as parents, it really just feels like a partnership in that they really adore each other and it is definitely rooted in respect. I like, too, that there has been tension between the two of them. I do think they remain a very iconic couple just in the way that they communicate to each other and they love each other, but there are definitely sources of tension throughout the series, like there is with any couple.

CHAPTER XIII
The State of the "S"

Over 85 years after he was first conceived by Jerry Siegel and Joe Shuster, the adventures of Superman continue unabated, consistently — as has been the case almost since his introduction to the world — appearing in different mediums and new stories. Some delve into darker elements of the mythology, but most — in looking back at what has come before in its totality, and what may come in the form of Michael B. Jordan playing the Val-Zod version of the character and Ta-Nehisi Coates writing yet another take — embracing what the Man of Steel has more frequently come to represent: hope for the future, belief in humanity and — as they now say in the comics — truth, justice and a better tomorrow.

TIM DEFOREST (author, *Storytelling in the Pulps, Comics and Radio: How Technology Changed Popular Fiction in America*): He still represents hope because he represents the ability, no matter how bad things are, to do the right

During the 2018 Superman Celebration in Metropolis, IL, fans dressed as various versions of the character from over the years (photo © Ed Gross; Superman © and Trademark DC Comics/Warner Bros. Discovery).

thing to help people and to use the abilities you have to help others. That's part of the reason he's always been relevant and probably why the character will never completely disappear from pop culture. There have been dark times before and Superman was around for World War II and Vietnam and he was still a popular character — because, again, he represents the ability to make the decision to do the right thing no matter what the situation is around you.

DANA DELANY (voice actor, "Lois Lane," *Superman: The Animated Series*): He's about acceptance. I mean, Superman is an alien from another planet, and it's all about fitting in and not judging people and not being scared. Back in my day in the '50s, it was about nuclear war and the atomic bomb. That was the big fear. Now we have other fears, but we still have structural destruction, climate change and you still have to worry about bombs. I think it's all about inclusiveness right now. When Siegel and Shuster started, it was in reaction to what was going on in the world with anti-Semitism and World War II and Nazism and all that stuff. And people confuse it with truth, justice and the American way of doing well. It's not that. It's about standing up for what's right.

ROB O'CONNOR (co-host, *All-Star Superfan Podcast*): Superman couldn't be more in touch with the modern world — an immigrant who is illegally brought to the United States of America, brought in by a kindly well-meaning couple who embody everything that's great about that country and who becomes an investigative journalist, exposing the evils of megalomaniacal capitalists who think they have the right do whatever they want. If anything, he's decidedly more relevant than Batman — an intensely wealthy, mentally ill fascist who spends his evenings pummeling the lower class and throwing them into a poorly-funded insane asylum.

DEAN CAIN (actor, "Clark Kent/Superman," *Lois & Clark: The New Adventures of Superman*): There's all these complaints about diversity inclusion, and I'm so past that. The idea that Michael B. Jordan could play Superman makes perfect sense to me. I know Michael real well; he's one of the nicest men you'll ever meet. He has that kindness, the warmth, the vulnerability and everything that you'd want in that character and *need* in that character. I don't even think, "Oh gosh, he's a black Superman… I'm an Asian Superman." I don't think those things, because Superman's a Kryptonian. He could be anything. Michael would be a fantastic Superman.

RAY MORTON (film historian and author): Superman has always been and will always remain the greatest of all superheroes and there are several reasons for this. The first is that he is the original; the first character to be endowed with amazing powers and abilities, who uses those powers and abilities to serve the greater good, who wears what we have come to know as a classic superhero uniform (based on the trunks, tights and capes of circus athletes, acrobats and aerialists), and has a secret identity. All of the elements of the Superman character come from other sources: from myth, from literature, from the pulps and from other comics — but Superman is the first one to put all of those elements together in the same package. The second is that Superman's powers — super-strength, super-senses and especially the ability to fly — are the ones all humans aspire to have. Also, the Superman/Clark Kent concept connects directly with one of the most basic of human desires: to know that there is more to us than what appears to be on the surface — that beneath our seemingly ordinary exteriors lies something great and powerful and wonderful. No other superhero character addresses this dream more exactly or directly.

KEVIN SMITH (writer, unfilmed *Superman Lives*): What appealed to me about Superman, and what kept bringing me back over and over again, is I want to believe in my heart of hearts that at the worst possible moment in my life, somebody will be there to rescue me. That's what a superhero is. That's why we love Superman. He can hear anything. He's like Santa and Jesus — he grants wishes. He can hear you screaming from worlds away and get there in enough time to save you. He does it for Lois Lane, he does it for Jimmy Olsen, conceivably he can do it for you.

It's just the idea of somebody who has nothing to gain. He's not getting paid to do it. This isn't his job, it's just a passion — a passion for human life… life, like in the case of Superman, far inferior to his own. The same way we look at animals is conceivably the way Superman could look at us. Some people look at animals with compassion, and some are like, "You dumb dog!" and kick 'em and stuff like that. Superman looks at us with the compassion that we look at the animals we love, and he's always going out of his way to protect us in the same way we always go out of our way to protect things that are weaker than ourselves. *That*, to me, has always been the driving force of that character and every comic book character.

BEAU WEAVER (voice actor, "Clark Kent/Superman," *Superman*): Whether it will sell or not, I don't know, but the idea of Superman is more important now than ever. Men are in a confused, dangerous and toxic relationship with their own power. Superman fully owned his power, but it was connected to a greater cause than himself. You know, truth, justice and the American way; doing the right thing. Many of the men that I know and work with are super-ambivalent about power, because of what male power in this culture has done, so they run away from it. But there is a way in which men can come to own and cultivate their power in service of the Earth, in service of the divine, in service of the women and children. I've spent a bunch of years learning the culture of the Plains Indians, the Lakota people of South Dakota. And in that culture, men are taught they are expendable. As a man, your purpose is to make the camp circle safe; to keep the women, the children and the elders thriving. *That's* your purpose. And if you have to die in serving to that purpose, then bring it on, baby. To me, *that's* Superman — restoring men to a connection with their power in the service of something greater than themselves.

MICHAEL EURY (editor, *The Krypton Companion*): When I was a member of the Rotary Club, it was transformational for me, and I thought this is kind of something that the Christopher Reeve Superman would have said to himself in the mirror every day. It's the four questions created by Paul Harris, the guy who started Rotary as an international benefactor group: 1) Is is the truth? 2) Is it fair to all concerned? 3) Will is build good will and better friendships? 4) Is it beneficial to all concerned? I admit I fall short of that a lot, but I really try to remember it, and it changed me the first time I really said that and thought about it. As far as I'm concerned, I'm still living on Earth One and I still believe. Part of it is that Christopher Reeve is still an inspiration beating in my heart, and then there are just the values of classic Superman. Not the Superman who would knock a wife beater through the wall — even though he deserved it — but a Superman who makes us realize that we can be better than we are… and makes us ask, "Is it the truth?" I have really kind of cleaned up my act over the years thinking about that. Not that I was ever a liar or manipulator, but is it *the truth*? And I could easily hear Superman ask that question.

DAN JURGENS (Superman comics writer): When we get into that general realm of questioning, these are all variations on the same thing: Is Superman too much of a Boy Scout? Is Superman too much of a throwback? Is Superman too much of a goody-goody-two-shoes that we can't relate to him? And what I always say is, well, look, if that's the case, it isn't because Superman has changed. It's because *we've* changed. And if you're going to tell me that justice and truth and hope are not in vogue anymore … again, that's more on us, because this is our world, it's the one we've created. And, so, in general, my response is, if things are getting worse, I think that points out the need for Superman even more. And I would say that there are times when Superman gets to be, I think, a little more relevant that way and I think maybe we're looking at a time like that now. But no, I never see him as being out of step. I see us, culturally, being out of step. And what I've always said is, Batman is who we are. Superman is who we should aspire to be. Batman is all about kicking ass on the bad guys. I mean, I don't think Batman cares about the victims. Superman cares about the victims.

We always see Batman come down from the rooftop. If some of the bad guys are attacking someone in an alley, Batman takes them out and goes away. The victim? Who cares? Were they stabbed? Did they get robbed? He doesn't care, he just goes away. Superman takes that individual to the hospital, and he takes them home, does what they need to do. There's a lot of difference between the two characters that way, but yeah, Superman is, I think, when we're in our better moments, who we should and do aspire to be.

TOM DE HAVEN (author, *It's Superman*): Spider-Man started out conflict-ed, and we always knew that was the basis of the character. Batman was the same way. I mean, in the '40s he was working in the shadows and in the '50s he could be goofy. Superman, except for that brief period where he fought for social justice and was FDR's sidekick, was just an unconflicted, patriotic, upright guy. When you try to make him conflicted or put him with red eyes and angry, it doesn't quite work because it goes against what everyone knows is the fundamental Super-man. If Peter Parker had no problems whatsoever, I don't think we would accept that version of Spider-Man. Batman was always psychotic, but when you turn Superman psychotic, something's wrong and you feel funny about it, because that's not him. But then you see the Superman who is benevolent and someone who simply wants to do good and *that's* his reward. In the 21st century, and also the last couple of decades of the 20th century, that seems out of sync with how we see the world… and kind of childish.

ROB O'CONNOR: Superman represents all the wonders of what the Amer-ican Dream once meant and he will always be a symbol for standing up for the helpless and the oppressed. If he's out of touch in any way, it's only because I'm not entirely sure that level of symbolic selflessness is best represented by an able-bodied Caucasian man in today's more inclusive society. Despite all the hardship that Clark Kent may have gone through, there is always an element of "check your privilege" about a white guy telling people that they can be better, and perhaps that is why Warner Bros. has so consistently struggled to believe in the character on the big screen. The recent success of Black Panther and the Wonder Woman films suggest that perhaps what Superman stands for is better represented by other, similar char-acters, at least on the main stage.

ELIZABETH TULLOCH (actor, "Lois Lane," *Superman & Lois*): This is a character who has the power to destroy the world, but doesn't. He's not this maniacal figure who just wants to be powerful. He could use his powers for selfish pursuits and get away with it, but he doesn't because he believes in being a good person. He believes in decency. So, especially starting in 2021, we have a new President of the United States and there has been more push-back against some of the nationalist sentiment that we're seeing, not only in the States, but around the world. We have this Superman who's really embodying that you don't have to have power or be crazy strong to be good and decent and kind. And if he was just Clark Kent without the powers, he would be the same man.

BRAD RICCA (author, *Super Boys: The Amazing Adventures of Jerry Siegel and Joe Shuster — The Creators of Superman*): We live in cynical times, and who's the hero people say they turn to in cynical times? Superman. But that's *not* true. During cynical times, the number-one-selling superhero is actually Batman. When things are bad, it seems like people want to wallow in it a little bit and fight back. When things are real and physical and raw, it's Batman. When you look at sales and stuff when things are more stable and peaceful, there's Superman. Now there are a lot of problems with that theory, but I'm going to go with it anyway. That's how I see it.

ALEX ROSS (co-writer/artist, *Kingdom Come*): I'm afraid the role for Superman going forward will demand that he show his roots of fighting for the vulnerable and putting right injustices here and abroad. That way becomes complicated when his corporate owner would not want his image associated with a singular point of view, especially if it will be seen as divisive in our world and culture. There are clear issues of our day that the man who could do anything would not stay out of.

TODD HELLBING (showrunner/executive producer, *Superman & Lois*): His role is bringing people together. I feel like this is a perfect time to have a Superman show. Everybody is in their homes, people are losing their jobs, our country has never been as polarized. The world in a lot of ways is polarized, and you're telling a story about this guy that came from a different planet, and all he's trying to do is unite and help and be there for this community that welcomes him in; and then to sort of approach this show and Superman in a way that we can ground him and show everybody, "Look, this guy has troubles. He has troubles with his kids. He doesn't have all the answers. He's clumsy a lot of times as a parent, and that's okay." As long as you try and do your best, that's all you can ask for.

ROBERT GREENBERGER (writer, former DC editor): I can equate Superman to Captain America for Marvel in the same way they kept America the square-jawed hero from a different time period who stands for all of these ideals. And every now and then you need that figure; that person to remind you what we're fighting for and the American way of life coming together to face odds. You need that icon, that torchbearer, to show us the way. The best of the comics reminds us that's what he's there for.

GEORGE NEWBERN (voice actor, "Clark Kent/Superman," *Justice League Unlimited*): I'd hope that Superman could be symbolic of common sense being the right way, the non-spin way. That when something is obviously wrong, don't pretend that it's not — whatever side of the political spectrum you want to be on. I would think that the best takeaway from Superman would be, even in today's world, don't disengage, keep engaged.

LEE TOLAND KRIEGER (director, *Superman & Lois*): For me, he represents somebody who's sort of apolitical and agnostics in the best sort of way. It's not that he doesn't care, but he sees humanity *as* humanity and not as sections that have cordoned themselves off into this tribalism that we've sort of found ourselves in. He's a knight, an ideal to strive towards. There he is, especially now when the world, and maybe this country in particular, is so desperate for a great leader to look up to and represent the best of who we are. Superman does that better than any person in pop culture ever. I feel that right now, with the divisiveness and the people's clear desire to have a leader to point the way, *that's* what he represents. That's why I believe this show and this incarnation of Superman will be a welcome reprieve from a lot of the discord we're all seeing and feeling right now.

TOM DE HAVEN: Superman was a character for children, but he's obviously in these adult stories. The problem is that we really don't know how to view him. In the past, Superman was in *Action* and *Superman* comics and in *World's Finest*, and it was basically the same character. In fact, when you had the George Reeves series, he was different from the guy in the comic books and that was a little troubling for younger people. But now we have 50 different versions of our heroes. There are enough of us who like that idea, but the ordinary person thinks of Superman as a benevolent guy who has superpowers and helps people. For them, these other versions don't quite jive. But like I said in my book, in the end it doesn't bother me, because all of it can exist as long as you have these certain fundamentals of the character.

PHIL MORRIS (actor, "John Jones/Martian Manhunter," *Smallville*):

The modern day iterations of Superman have been very humanistic, so we have this alien visitor who deals with all these human emotions and bouts of compassion and we relate to it. I mean, when the most powerful of us is laid low and bends the knee, we respect it. Within is where we need to find it, but we all look for it outside of ourselves.

ROGER STERN (author, *The Death of Superman* novel): I still recall how, after the crew of the Challenger space shuttle was lost, there was a young boy that *Life* magazine quoted as saying, "I wish I had been Superman so I could have saved them." I can't think of a better way to explain Superman's appeal.

TYLER HOECHLIN (actor, "Clark Kent/Superman," *Superman & Lois*): What I've always really loved about the character is that, to me, it's never really been about his powers that are above and beyond what everybody else has. To me, Superman is the guy who just does the thing that everybody wishes the person next to them would do when someone needs help. You know what I mean? I just think that he's always represented hope and a better tomorrow. If you think about it, he could just leave. He doesn't have to do this, but for him to constantly make the effort to do right, to do good, and to help out, speaks to his belief that humanity will sort itself out, but we have these things that come up along the way. In no way do I say we've made enough progress — we never make enough progress — but we are moving forward. Change doesn't occur without resistance; you have to have it, otherwise you don't get change. For him, it's just this constant belief, "I will continue to do the small acts," because no matter what, he can't do everything. He can do *anything*, but he can't do everything.

J.M. DEMATTEIS (writer, *Superboy, Justice League*): He continues to reflect the best in us. I was just talking to somebody about the whole business of comic book characters and their psyches. When you write a great villain, you want to find the good in him to make him interesting. At the same time, you want to find the darkness in the hero to make them interesting. We're all so divided and polarized, and with extreme cases aside — the wiring in some people's brains is just wrong — most people have decency and goodness within them. Superman is the reflection of that. To me, he is the best in all of us. It has nothing to do with left wing or right wing or anything like that, because there is a shadow in all of us. And there's good in all of us. I am very idealistic and somewhat naïve, even after all these years, and I think most people go through life looking to be treated with kindness and respect, and to treat others with kindness and respect. His superpower is not that he can lift the world, his superpower is that he's the embodiment of the best of us. We always need something to look up to, and Superman gives people permission to be their best selves.

MARK WAID (writer, *Superman: Birthright*): Superman still stands for truth, which seems far too easy to deny and decry in this country in the here and now, but hopefully he can still be a beacon of inspiration for Americans of all beliefs.

MICHAEL EURY: Today I was at Planet Fitness and there's this woman who I see every day who has a beautiful smile. Today of all days, thinking about the fact that I'd be talking about Superman, I passed her and said, "I need to pay you a compliment: Every day I see you smiling and you have the most beautiful smile and it always brings a smile to my face. Thank you." And that smile got even bigger. These are little acts of kindness, really. That's all it takes. We carry the Superman brand with us, and every day, if we just do a little thing — if more people try to do that — it really wouldn't be as bleak a world as it seems to be now.

JOHN KENNETH MUIR (film historian and author): Superman is about gentleness as strength, not weakness, and about the idea of justice, not revenge, as a motivating factor. Instead of lowering himself to his opponents' level, Superman is about the idea that you succeed by being true to yourself, and your own sense of morality. He calls to the best angels of human nature. Some people do view Superman as being out of touch. Those same people probably tend to see violence, revenge, angst, darkness and vigilantism as somehow cool, but Superman doesn't need any of those crutches. He's just a person doing the best he can but carrying a tremendous burden. I don't think Superman is thus a beacon for us, to guide us through the corruption and short-sightedness of the current world. We need more heroes like Superman, not fewer. We need more heroes who forgive, less who hate. We need more heroes who stand above the ugliness, rather than wallowing in it.

TYLER HOECHLIN: I try to say that to people as well when they ask about how to help out. Today, there's such a huge thing about scale. If it's not viral, then it's not a real thing. If it's not helping a million people, it's not helpful. And that's so not true. This world works on one good deed at a time, like a dinner for one person who needs it. Whether it's a hundred people or a million people, they all add up. He is just a symbol of hope, a symbol of being there for someone who's in need. That, to me, is always the most important thing. Superman does everything he can. It's not everything, but it's all he's got. The inspiration is that anyone can be that person. If you're giving and you're helping to the greatest extent that you can, then you're being your own Superman or Superwoman.

BRANDON ROUTH (actor, "Clark Kent/Superman," *Superman Returns*): For me, Superman remains on the mission that Jor-El sent him on: "They lack the light to show them the way." To me, he is a light, a torch, and he wants to light the torch of others so they can continue to light up the world and literally bring them out of darkness. As I have lived with the character, thought about this and been asked about his place in the world, the evolution would be for him as much a teacher as a physical savior — a teacher helping to bring joy, togetherness and acceptance.

AFTERWORD
by Mark Waid

When I was first approached about being interviewed for this book, I threw down a challenge without realizing it. "C'mon, Ed. I'm the world's foremost authority on Superman," I said, like Icarus flying too close to the sun.

"I take it as a point of pride that I'm probably the only person alive who's read every Superman comic and newspaper strip and piece of prose and history, listened to every radio show, and seen every cartoon and live-action adventure," I added, oblivious to the wax starting to drip from my wings. "I own some of the rarest Superman ephemera on Earth, Ed. I know Clark Kent's Social Security Number.* Sure, I'll lend my voice, but with all respect, I'm not likely to learn anything new from my fellow interviewees."

I write to you now from the bottom of the Aegean Sea, banging out an afterword that is, in part, penitence for what I was forced to stop calling "youthful arrogance" about 40 years ago.

What an informational journey reading this book has been for me. Whether you realized this or not as you read it, what you're holding in your hands right now is an incredible and unique achievement. There have been entire encyclopedias chronicling the Man of Steel's comic book adventures, countless books and articles written about his radio programs, his films and his television appearances, but those are only individual facets of the lore, pieces of a whole. Ed Gross has — by reaching out to dozens of experts and key players — spared no effort in assembling all their vital knowledge in one volume using nothing but the voices of Those Who Were There Along The Way.

Even when we contradicted each other, even when we offered up not broad facts but the most personal of anecdotes, everything recorded here is illuminating in some way. That's the beauty of an oral history; not being filtered through an editorial lens leads to some spontaneous revelations and insights. Until Ed got me on a roll, I'm not sure even I had ever properly articulated exactly why being fat and/or bald was always presented as the Ultimate Curse in Superman stories of the '60s. You'll find that of many of the other Voices from Krypton herein, Ed's free-wheeling, extraordinarily patient style of interviewing allowed us all to ramble on freely and at length, dredging up long-buried recollections from many of us, delightfully surprising us as they coalesced into fresh takes. What came of these interviews, years in the making, is what I now consider the Definitive Book on

Superman, and I am grateful to be offered a seat at Ed's astoundingly diverse round table of chroniclers who helped him in some small part to produce a book that not only educates but celebrates. I tip my cape to you, sir.

---

*092-09-6616. You're welcome.

PREVIOUS BOOKS BY EDWARD GROSS

Chevrons Locked: The Unofficial, Unauthorized Oral History of Stargate SG-1 — The First 25 Years
(Nacelle Books)

They Shouldn't Have Shot His Dog: The Unofficial, Unauthorized Oral History of John Wick, Gun-Fu and the New Age of Action
(St. Martin's Press)

Secrets of the Force: The Unofficial, Unauthorized Oral History of Star Wars
(St. Martin's Press)

Nobody Does It Better: The Unofficial, Unauthorized Oral History of James Bond
(Forge Books)

So Say We All: The Unofficial, Unauthorized Oral History of Battlestar Galactica
(Tor Books)

Slayers & Vampires: The Unofficial, Unauthorized Oral History of Buffy the Vampire Slayer and Angel
(Tor Books)

The Fifty-Year Mission: The Next 25 Years — The Unofficial, Unauthorized Oral History of Star Trek
(Thomas Dunne Books)

The Fifty-Year Mission: The First 25 Years — The Unofficial, Unauthorized Oral History of Star Trek
(Thomas Dunne Books)

Rocky: The Complete Guide
(DK Books)

Spider-Man: Confidential
(Hyperion)

ABOUT THE AUTHOR

EDWARD GROSS is a veteran entertainment journalist who has covered film, television and comic book history for a wide variety of publications over his 40+ year career. He has served on the editorial staff of such magazines as *Starlog* (as New York correspondent), *Cinescape, Femme Fatales, Cinefantastique, Life Story, SFX, Movie Magic, Film Fantasy, Super Hero Spectacular* and *Geek*. Online, he has been Editor, US for empireonline.com, Film/TV Editor for closerweekly. com, intouchweekly.com, lifeandstylemag.com and j14.com, and Nostalgia Editor for doyouremember.com.